Brie Masters
Love in Submission
Submissive in Love

By
Red Phoenix

RedPhoenix69@live.com

Red Phoenix
12722 Jasmine St. Unit C
Thornton, CO 80602

Edited by Amy Parker, Proofed by Becki Wyer

Book cover design by Viola Estrella; Photo by Christina Gwin
Phoenix symbol by Nicole Delfs

Huge thanks to my lovely betas: Marla, Brandi, Jacque, and Christina.
They have been with me from the beginning.

Extra hug to Marilyn for her assistance in a crunch,
and her fabulous idea of making a wedding album for the happy couple.
So many cards being sent by fans!

I want to personally thank the talented and wonderful Kallypso Masters for collaborating on a scene with me in this book to introduce her characters Kristoffer and Pamela. I'm glad they could join Brie and Master Anderson in the infamous "Cat Scene". It was a fun adventure for both of us and something I know our mutual fans will enjoy.

Tons of love to my husband, affectionately known as MrRed.

Not only is he my everything, but he continues to be my biggest supporter.

You make my life beautiful!

~Red Phoenix

Get all three novels and enjoy the whole journey:

Brie Learns the Art of Submission

* Available in eBook, paperback, and audio book

Brie Embraces the Heart of Submission

* Available in eBook, paperback, and audio book

Brie Masters Love in Submission

* Available in eBook, paperback, and soon audio book

Table of Contents

Brie's Tokyo Tryst

The Dream

Tono was laughing as he bound her in rope, joyous laughter that made Brie smile. He ran his hands over her skin, checking his knots before lifting her in the air. Her stomach did a little flip, the way it always did when he hoisted her upwards. She threw back her head, purring in sweet pleasure—there was nothing like flying with Tono.

"Breathe with me, toriko."

She turned towards his voice but, as she matched her breath with his, she saw a change in him. The joy in his eyes was replaced with profound pain and sorrow.

"Tono…"

The air around them became dark and empty. She found it difficult to breathe and struggled in her bonds. Without speaking, he lowered her to the floor and began untying her. Once she was free, he took the jute and cast it away. Tono glanced at her once, then turned, walking into the darkness without another word.

"Tono, come back!"

He ignored her, disappearing into the smothering darkness, leaving Brie choking and gasping for air.

She woke up with a start and found herself still struggling to breathe.

"What's wrong, Brie?"

She couldn't shake the feeling of desperation. "Something's wrong with Tono Nosaka, Sir!"

At his urging, she called Tono's cell phone later that morning. She was surprised to hear a recording stating it was out of service, and her anxiety only increased.

"I'm sure everything is fine, Brie. I suggest you find out where his next stop is on the tour and mail a letter to the hotel where he's scheduled to stay."

Brie got the needed address and penned a quick note.

Dear Tono,

I've been wondering how you're doing. Is the tour a success and everything you envisioned it to be?

I sincerely hope things are well. I had an upsetting dream about you and just needed to check in.

Sending you thoughts of happiness and peace.

Sincerely,
~Brie

She folded the letter, slid it into an envelope and lovingly placed a stamp on it before handing it to Sir. "Would you like to read it before I lick the seal?"

"No, that is unnecessary. Although I will be interested in his reply."

She placed her letter on the pile of bills that were going out that day and gave it one last caress before returning to her desk. She missed the Asian Dom more than she would ever have imagined. It was one thing to know he was on the other side of town and there was a chance of running into him on occasion at The Haven or the Training Center. Knowing he was on the other side of the world was hard, but even more difficult was not knowing how Tono was faring.

In her heart, despite Sir's assurances, Brie felt he was suffering and it deeply troubled her.

Breathe with me, toriko…

Sir was struggling with legal disputes involving some of his oldest clients. Sadly, he was still dealing with the negative fallout to his business caused by Brie's controversial documentary. It didn't seem fair that he should suffer for her career now that it had finally taken off. However, Brie was thrilled that her film had been nominated for several prestigious awards, and she'd already been on several talk shows to discuss it, as well as her personal experiences at the Training Center. There seemed to be a real interest building among the public about the D/s lifestyle.

While the spotlight was still on her, Brie tried to use her newfound fame to secure support for her upcoming documentary about Sir's father, Alonzo Davis. Although there was public interest in Sir as a Dominant, producers in the film industry did not feel it would extend to his deceased father, even though the man had been a renowned musical talent. Brie strongly disagreed and remained steadfast in her vision for the project, despite the lack of interest.

However, with Sir busy concluding the last of the litigation, Brie was left sitting alone at home, twiddling her thumbs. To pass the time, she researched Alonzo Davis through old newspaper clippings, TV interviews and musical recordings, but she longed to go back to Italy with Sir and get the information from the source—his family.

All that extra time also gave Brie the chance to worry about Tono. After weeks of silence, she tried to track him down online. In her search, she was shocked to discover all his Kinbaku engagements had been postponed indefinitely. His last known location was the hotel she'd sent the letter to, but after he'd completed his final performance there, Tono had disappeared. No one knew where he'd gone after that.

Brie was beside herself, but Sir assured her, "When Nosaka wants to be found, he will contact you. Until then, you must respect his need for privacy."

It was nearly impossible not to obsess over Tono's silence, but thankfully Mr. Holloway provided a welcome distraction when he asked for a meeting.

"Miss Bennett, it appears your film has struck a chord with the American public. We've received numerous letters and emails from fans of the documentary who are curious to know what's become of Mary since the collaring ceremony, and whether Tono and Faelan have secured permanent subs."

Brie chuckled.

"Viewers are also demanding more footage of Marquis and a session with Ms. Clark. It seems they're curious about her and want to see the Domme in action."

"She *is* a commanding presence," Brie agreed.

"Is that a yes, then? You'll do a sequel?"

Brie hesitated. Although her documentary had thrown her into the spotlight, it had also succeeded in labeling her as a director of kink. It seemed that Hollywood proper did not take her seriously, and the only interest in her had been for soft porn gigs, which was so *not* the direction she wanted to go. Would doing a sequel only help cement that perception?

"Let me get back to you on that, Mr. Holloway."

Brie remained unsure about working on a sequel until she received a heartfelt email from a fan:

Dear Brianna Bennett,

I can't tell you how much you've inspired me. I've been curious about the D/s lifestyle for years, but had no idea what it was really like or even how to find out. I felt as if I were with you as you discovered your strengths and limitations at the Submissive Training Center.

To be honest, watching your film made me long to experience the lifestyle myself. The men I've been attracted to all my life were bossy but they were not respectful like the men in your documentary. I realize now I want more than a dominant male; I want a man who prides himself on being a Dominant. I want to share that journey of discovery with someone worthy, and "gift" my loyalty and submission only to him.

I would never have had that life-changing revelation if it hadn't been for your film. Thank you, Miss Bennett, a hundred times over.

Bless you for your courage in sharing your personal journey, as well as facing those who would attack you and your Master for it. I hope someday D/s couples will be as socially acceptable as vanilla couples. Trust me, your film has helped to move public opinion in the right direction.

I will try to be as brave as you as I embark on my own journey.

Thanks again,
Lucy

Her email was not the first Brie had received—she'd gotten numerous messages and letters from people who'd enjoyed the film—but Lucy's openness struck a chord with Brie. Despite the public discussions on the subject, there was still so much misinformation and prejudice concerning the BDSM community. Lucy's hope for the future set a fire under Brie, kindling her interest in the new project.

The challenge now that she'd graduated from the Submissive Training Center was to find a different focus for the storyline. The second film would certainly prove more difficult than the first since many of the major players had moved out of the LA area.

After careful consideration and much soul-searching, she submitted a proposal to Mr. Holloway with Sir's blessing. She anxiously awaited his approval; if Holloway liked the direction Brie wanted to take, she would have an exciting year ahead involving *lots* of travel.

She scoured the mail daily, hoping to see a contract from the producer. When that day finally arrived, she squealed with delight. "I have a good feeling about this, Sir!" she said, ripping open the manila envelope.

Brie started jumping in place as she read the contents.

"I take it he accepted your proposal," Sir replied with obvious amusement, getting up from his desk and walking over to her.

She grinned proudly as she presented the acceptance letter. "He did, Sir! In fact, he loves the idea."

"Well done, babygirl. You're well on your way." He kissed her on the forehead. The skin his lips had touched tingled in gratitude.

She looked up at Sir, basking in his praise. "Thank you."

He smiled, but his expression changed as he picked up another letter from the pile. "What's this?"

As important as the contract was to her, Sir was holding something of far more significance—her first contact from Tono since she'd written him. She knew it was from the Kinbaku Master because of the simple orchid sketched on the back of the envelope. It seemed that everything Tono touched was artistic and beautiful.

Instead of tearing it open, she carefully released the seal so she wouldn't ruin the painted flower. Brie pulled out the special rice paper and quickly unfolded it.

Dear Brie,

I was heartened to receive your letter. Your dream did not mislead you. I canceled my tour because my father is dying. I've kept quiet about it, as I do not want the public to know until he's passed. We are a private family and this is a private battle.

It has not been easy, as Otosama is in great pain.

Jute is my peace—my escape—but even that has been taken from me. Your letter, however, brought a smile. Thank you for it.

Give your Master my best.

Respectfully yours,
Ren Nosaka

Tears pricked Brie's eyes after reading his brief letter; the pain radiating from the printed words seemed to permeate the air around her.

"From Nosaka?"

She nodded, handing the letter to Sir. He looked it over, then slowly folded it before giving it back. "Your thoughts?"

"My heart breaks for him."

"Do you feel a visit is in order?"

Brie's heart leapt at the suggestion. "Really, Sir? Can we?"

"I'm almost finished here. Although I'd prefer to see it to the end, I'll talk with my lawyer to confirm he can handle the final details alone."

Sir beckoned her to sit with him as he moved to the couch. Brie glided over to her Master in only her collar, the skin of her naked young body tingling in anticipation of his masculine touch. She gladly curled up at his feet. With hands that soothed her soul, he began stroking her hair. "Nosaka has been there for us when we needed him. It's time we returned the favor."

She looked up at him, proud beyond words to be his submissive. "You are an honorable man, Sir. The best!"

He chuckled softly. "Maybe not quite as honorable as you presume. I plan to make a few calls and see if I can turn this into a business opportunity while we're there."

"You are as wise as you are honorable, Sir."

He raised his eyebrow before swiftly picking her up and placing her over his knee. He took hold of her wrists with one hand, holding them tight, and rubbed her naked ass.

"When will you learn, wayward sub?"

Brie yelped in pain when his hand made contact, but loved the warm feeling that dissipated from the area and radiated throughout her loins. She struggled in his arms as he took several more hard swats, the sounds of which echoed through the apartment.

He rubbed her ass tenderly, before slipping his fingers between her legs. "Wet with only a couple of smacks?" His fingers leisurely stroked her pussy, building her arousal. She stopped struggling, becoming still as she concentrated on the delicious feel of his sensual touch.

"I love my Master's hand," she purred.

"Do you, now?" He swatted her four more times, making her squeak in pleasurable pain.

"Very much, Sir."

His fingers returned to her pussy, slipping into her wet recesses. He knew the exact location of her G-spot and caressed it skillfully, causing her body to tense with an impending climax. "I wonder if I should reward your insolence with an orgasm."

She bit her lip, then replied playfully, "If it pleases you, Sir."

He chuckled softly. "It pleases me…"

Brie closed her eyes and let the orgasm roll over her. The rhythmic tightening of her inner muscles announced her climax, and he grunted with satisfaction. "I do love making you come, babygirl." He slapped her on the ass one more time, then commanded, "Present yourself to me." She immediately got down on all fours and opened herself to him, longing to be filled by her Master's shaft.

She trembled as he undressed and slowly knelt down behind her. He slid his manhood against her wet sex and caressed the folds of her pussy with the head of his cock, teasing her opening.

Brie pushed against his rigidity, wanting to be filled.

"No topping from the bottom, téa."

She whimpered in disappointment when he pulled away. It was hard not to be greedy for his shaft.

"Be still," he scolded lightly.

"Yes, Master."

Brie remained unmoving when his cock returned. Although she held her body in check, she expressed her pleasure in a purring moan. It still surprised her how much connecting with Sir in this way expanded her, making her joyously complete.

When he finally slipped his cock inside, Brie cried out in deep satisfaction. He slapped her ass. "You're a naughty girl, téa." He wrapped his hand in Brie's hair and pulled her head back. "So I will fuck you like a slut."

"Thank you, Master…" she moaned.

He grabbed her waist with his other hand, using it as leverage as he began to pound her hard, challenging her with his depth. Her body started humming with sexual electricity in response to his unrelenting assault. When Sir used her like this, she felt totally…completely…female. Her body became an instrument of gratification, his guttural growls of satisfaction her ultimate reward.

His fucking was selfish, rough and hard—everything she wanted at that moment. "More please," she begged.

Sir increased the tempo, making her cry out as her body began to ready itself for an orgasm.

"Do not come, téa," he commanded when her pussy began to quiver with needed release.

Brie knew Sir wanted her to concentrate solely on *his* climax. To add to his sensual pleasure, she began squeezing her inner muscles, caressing his shaft as he pounded into her.

"Fuck…" he groaned. Sir let go of her hair and grabbed her ass with both hands, having been taken to the edge. "Feel your Master's satisfaction."

Brie closed her eyes and focused on his shaft pulsing with each release of his come. She threw her head back and joined his vocalizations, the two of them united in their passion.

His Reality

Sir wasted no time arranging the trip to Japan after the arrival of Tono's letter. He'd admitted his concern to Brie. "His father's death will impact Ren in ways he does not foresee yet."

Brie loved that Sir genuinely cared about Tono's wellbeing. The two Doms had always respected each other, but it seemed that because of their close connection with Brie, they were becoming real friends.

The plane ride to Japan was uneventful. Sir spent the time calling potential clients to set up his agenda for the week-long trip, while she silently worried about Tono. Sir explained between phone calls, "These meetings will give you an opportunity to spend time alone with Nosaka. I do not think he'll be open with you if I'm present."

Brie wasn't entirely convinced Tono would be open with her even if they were alone. He'd disclosed so little in his letter, and it distressed her. She had to trust the spiritual connection they shared was powerful enough that her presence alone would prove comforting if he chose to keep distant.

"Sleep if you can, Brie," Sir suggested. "You'll need to be fully rested in order to face the challenges ahead."

"I'd rather stay up with you, Sir."

He caressed her cheek before putting his hand over her eyes. He leaned over her, whispering, "Your dedication to your Master is charming, but I would prefer one of us sleep." She kept her eyes closed when he took his hand away, but she pouted to show her protest.

Sir leaned forward and kissed her, biting her pouty lip lightly before pulling away.

Damn, the man is sexy...

She almost opened her eyes, but remained true to her Master's wishes.

Sighing with frustration, she curled up in a more comfortable position in the overly large airplane seat. Brie was lulled to sleep by the authoritative tones of Sir's business voice.

When they landed in Tokyo at midnight, Brie expected they'd head straight to the hotel, but Sir suggested they explore the city first and hailed a cab.

She found Tokyo fascinating. Driving on the left side of the road rather than the right brought its own unique, nervous thrill and she couldn't help whimpering every time they made a right-hand turn.

"I sure would hate to drive here," she told Sir.

He disagreed. "I'd find it invigorating. In fact, I should really get an international license, since I'm growing my international client base." Sir stared up at the tall high-rises surrounding them on both sides. "The culture here is definitely intriguing."

Brie was surprised to see a bright yellow version of what looked like the Eiffel Tower in the middle of the city. "What *is* that?"

"*That*, my dear, is Tokyo Tower."

"It sure looks like the Eiffel Tower, Sir."

"It's meant to. It's the most attractive antenna I've seen. I do like that about the Japanese culture. They take ordinary, practical things and make them appear beautiful, even artistic."

She snuggled against Sir, soaking in the excitement of the downtown area. The lights of Tokyo were far more colorful than in any city Brie had seen, even putting Vegas to shame. Every building was lit up with bright, vivid signs or animated screens. It appealed to her youthful nature, beckoning her to come and play.

"Can we take a walk, Sir?"

"Right now?"

"If it pleases you."

He had the cab driver pull over and told him to wait for them. Sir helped Brie out of the vehicle and placed his arm around her waist as he guided her through the streets.

Brie found herself subconsciously looking for Tono in the faces of all those they passed. Knowing they were in the same city made her feel as if Tono were close by, even though a chance meeting would be impossible in a place as crowded as this.

They walked up to an upscale bar and Sir ushered her inside. The walls were made of smoky glass with rich purple neon lighting up the bar area. Above, multicolored lanterns accented the ceiling, dotting the floor with their fun punch of color. She squeezed Sir's hand, charmed by the artistically modern yet playful decor.

Although the place was packed, Sir found two open seats at the bar. He ordered martinis for them both, then nodded his approval when he tasted the drink. "Damn fine martini. Drink up, téa."

As she was taking a sip, Sir discreetly slipped his hand up the inside of her thigh. She smiled as she opened her legs a little wider. There was an irresistible thrill knowing she was *his*, whenever and wherever he wanted.

Sir lightly brushed her sensitive clit, before removing his hand and dragging it slowly over his lips. It was his promise to her; later he would partake of her taste… She wiggled in her seat, her body tingling with sensual pleasure.

Brie glanced up at a large TV screen and was shocked to see an image of Tono's father. Although she could not understand what was being said, it was easy to follow the news story when they showed an outside shot of a hospital, then cut to an outdated shot of Tono and his mother.

Brie whispered hesitantly, "Is he dead?"

Sir shook his head. "No, but I believe the privacy Tono was trying to preserve has been compromised."

"Then we got here just in time," she breathed in relief.

The joy she'd felt just minutes ago was lost in a sea of new worry. Sir paid for the drinks and quickly escorted her back to the cab. "I hope you got the sleep you needed on the plane, babygirl. It doesn't appear you're going to get more anytime soon."

Sir spent several hours tracking Tono down. Despite some language barrier issues, he not only found the location of the hospital where Tono's father was staying, but also a phone number for Tono's mother. "Unfortunately, we won't be able to reach Nosaka until the morning to inform him we've arrived," he explained.

"Tono knows we're coming, doesn't he?"

He surprised her by shaking his head.

"Then why are we here, Sir?"

"Nosaka is drowning. You sensed it, and his unusual actions confirmed it. The man needs our support."

Sir's pronouncement gave Brie chills, but the fact he had come to assist Tono touched her deeply. She struggled to speak, her throat choked up with emotion. "I can't believe you would do that, Sir."

"Nosaka is a good man," Sir said, wrapping his arm around her. "He should not suffer alone."

While he got ready for bed, Sir instructed Brie to undress completely, pulling her close when she joined him in the bed. "Everything will be okay, babygirl."

She pressed against him and closed her eyes, trusting him.

The next morning Sir tried to call Tono at his mother's, but only got a busy signal. "Not surprising," he stated. "They probably took it off the hook once the media got wind of the story."

Brie felt butterflies when they pulled up to Tono's family home, knowing that he had no idea they were coming. She hadn't understood the love and devotion the people had towards the famous *bakushi* until she was forced to wade through a crowd of journalists and grieving fans of the elder Kinbaku Master.

The home was charmingly traditional, with a large, decorative roof, thin dark wood accents and paper walls. Sir knocked on the door and announced loudly, "Ren Nosaka, it's the Davises."

Brie blushed with unexpected joy. Although they were engaged, they hadn't set a date for the wedding yet. Sir hadn't had time with all the litigation, and Brie hadn't wanted to push. However, she had to admit that hearing his last name associated with her was absolutely heart-melting.

It took several minutes, with the scrutiny of every eye on them, as they waited for the door to finally slide open. A petite older woman who shared Tono's facial features stood before them. Unfortunately, she wore an unwelcoming expression on her face.

"Visitors another day…please!"

Brie understood that was her polite way of saying "Go away", but Sir wasn't going anywhere and called into the house, "Ren, we aren't leaving until we speak to you."

When there was no movement or sound from within, the woman began to slide the door shut.

Brie called out, "Please, Tono Nosaka, I *have* to see you."

The door shut with a little added force, leaving Sir and Brie staring at each other. She glanced at the crowd of photographers behind them, listening to the rapid clicking of their cameras. "What do we do now?"

"We wait," Sir said patiently.

Brie put her hands behind her back and straightened her stance to match her Master's. The two stared at the door, ignoring the numerous shutter clicks fluttering behind them. After a few more excruciating minutes, the door slid back open and the old women ushered them inside before quickly closing the door again.

It was easy to tell by her sour look that Mrs. Nosaka was not happy with their intrusion.

Sir bowed to her and asked, "Where is your son, Nosaka-*sama*?"

The woman frowned, but pointed to an open door down the hall on the right. Sir bowed again and smiled politely, choosing to ignore the woman's obvious displeasure as he placed his hand on Brie's back and guided her towards the room.

Sir cleared his throat at the threshold to get Tono's attention. The Asian Dom was bent over a small table, pouring three cups of hot tea.

Brie's heart fell when Tono looked up. His appearance was physically jarring—his face gaunt and hollow. He seemed a husk of the man he'd once been.

"Tono…" she whispered in distress.

He looked down at the teapot, choosing not to acknowledge her presence.

Sir quietly closed the door behind them and directed Brie to sit next to Tono. She sat beside her dear friend and tentatively reached out to touch his sleeve, but Tono deftly moved out of the way and addressed Sir.

"There was no reason for you to come, but please sit." He indicated that Sir should sit opposite him and placed a steaming cup in front of Sir. Without addressing Brie, he pushed the next cup towards her, then picked up the last one for himself, holding it up reverently to Sir. "Although I appreciate the gesture of your visit, it was unnecessary." He nodded before taking a sip.

Sir looked at Brie and indicated that she should join them. She had to choke back the tears of rejection as she took a sip of the soothing green tea.

Even though Tono was purposely ignoring Brie, she felt the pain he was suffering and assured him, "We've come to support you, Tono Nosaka."

He shrugged off her words with a roll of his shoulders and told Sir, "I didn't need you to come."

For the first time, he glanced in her direction, his eyes devoid of their inner light. Brie was struck dumb by the depth of pain those rich chocolate eyes revealed.

Sir replied smoothly, "I'm sorry to see the media has become involved."

Tono took another sip of tea before responding. "We would prefer to suffer this battle alone with dignity, but even that has been taken from us."

Brie wanted to wrap her arms around him, but knew it would only upset him further, based on his behavior towards her. She sat there feeling useless while Sir explained to him, "I believe I can help if your father's . doctors are willing to move him to another facility. Give me the go-ahead and I'll see what I can do."

"Although I doubt we can escape the paparazzi, you have my permission to try."

"How can I help?" Brie offered, determined to get past the emotional barrier between them.

Tono sighed, reluctantly meeting her gaze. "I do not need you here, Miss Bennett. Please go."

She couldn't hide her hurt and looked desperately at Sir.

He gave her a private smile, commanding, "Téa, you will stay here while I make the arrangements." Before Tono could protest, Sir stood up and exited the room.

Brie sat beside Tono in uncomfortable silence. As he continued to sip his tea, she listened to his breathing out of habit, and instinctively slowed her breath to match his unique rhythm. Once they were in sync, she noticed his muscles relax.

Finally, he broke the painful silence. "Why? Why have you come, Brie?"

The tone of his voice sounded reproachful, but she answered his question in earnest. "Tono, the dream I wrote to you about has haunted me. As much as you may not want me here, I felt just as strongly that I *had* to come."

He closed his eyes and groaned. "You can't know how much your presence both comforts and wounds me."

His words cut her like a knife, but rather than reply, she took a sip of her tea and wondered, *What changed so drastically between us?* The two of them had developed a comfortable friendship despite their romantic past, but now it seemed all that had changed…

He pushed back from the small table and lay down on the mat, not looking at her as he spoke. "I was doing well, enjoying the tour, until I got the phone call. I thought my world was falling apart when I heard my father was in the hospital, but at the time I had no idea how serious it really was."

"What's wrong with your father, Tono?"

He snorted in disgust. "He went in for simple back surgery, but complications arose and he left the operating table paralyzed from the waist down. I arrived in Japan a day after he received the devastating news."

Tono turned his head towards Brie. "My father is a strong man—strong not only physically, but mentally. Even that prognosis did not deter him. He was determined to walk again so he could return to the art he loved, but fate has not been kind. A week later, he contracted a virulent strain of pneumonia. Now he fights for every breath and his body is growing weaker by the minute."

"I can't imagine how difficult it must be watching your father suffer."

He let out a painful sigh. "There's no hope. He will die from this, but he can't willingly leave this Earth. It is not in his nature; he will fight this until the end."

"As difficult as it is for you, Tono, his warrior spirit is truly inspiring."

"I have always admired my father, Brie." She watched in sympathy as a lone tear fell down his handsome face. "I'm not the warrior he is. I can't handle watching him suffer day in and day out. It's killing me inside."

Brie moved away from the table and sat next to Tono, taking his hands in hers. "I'm so sorry, Tono. Just so deeply sorry…"

"I wish I could switch places with him. I could handle that better than standing by having to watch him suffer like this. Every breath is a fight." He laid his head back and covered his eyes with his forearm. "I can't face it, yet I will again today, forced to make my way through the wall of media as added punishment."

"I'll go with you and push them out of the way if I have to."

Relief flooded through her when she saw him smile slightly.

"How is your mother holding up?" she asked quietly.

Tono shook his head, lowering his voice when he answered. "She has become unbearable. She feels as helpless as I do, but reacts by attempting to control things that are not hers to control. I spend my days at the hospital putting out the fires she creates. Naturally, her disdain is not limited to the nursing staff. All of us are an affront to her control. If she were not my mother, I… Let's just say I am struggling to manage her."

"Is there any way I can help?"

"You? No, your presence has only increased her distress."

Brie opened her mouth, ready to offer to leave, but he reached over and placed his finger on her lips. "But she deserves the challenge."

She nodded slowly, and his finger fell from her lips. Instead of dwelling on his mother, she brought the conversation back to his father. "I can't imagine losing my own father, but he isn't my mentor and trainer as well."

Tono closed his eyes. "Only those who have had an *osensei* can truly understand. My father poured all that he was into my instruction. When we trained, we were no longer bound by blood, but it was because of those blood ties that it meant so much more to me. I was his prize pupil and I flourished under his focused tutelage."

"If you felt that way, why did you end up leaving Japan?"

He smiled sadly as he sat up and gracefully crossed his legs. "Two reasons. I was interested in spreading my wings and discovering what America had to offer. I'd grown tired of others seeing me as only my father's protégé, a toy to be tested and critiqued for their entertainment."

"What was the other?"

"I could not stomach the relationship between my father and mother. Her lack of respect for him transferred to me as well. Whereas he felt the need to acquiesce to her, I did not. The only way to preserve the familial ties was to leave."

"It must have been difficult leaving your father behind."

"While it wasn't easy, I don't regret leaving. However, I do regret the time lost with him. Time I will never get back."

She put her hand on his shoulder. "But you're with him now."

He frowned. "Yes, we've had a few opportunities to talk, between the coughing spasms and the excruciating pain. However, our conversations have only reminded me how much…I've lost."

Brie felt he was holding something back, but she didn't press him to explain, grateful he was being as open as he was. "I'm afraid anything I say will only come off as a sad platitude," she apologized, squeezing him tight—*needing* to be of comfort to him. "I've never been in your shoes, but my heart genuinely hurts for you, Tono."

He lifted his hand and tenderly caressed her cheek. "I did not ask you to share in this pain, little one."

She pressed her hand against his, closing her eyes. "We're connected. Your pain is my pain. Time and distance do not affect that."

Unresolved Demons

The door slipped open and Tono's mother stood before them, eyes glaring. She spat out a stream of words obviously meant as an insult. Brie just smiled at her, getting up and walking over to the woman. Brie knew she must be hurting underneath all that anger, so she gave her a hug.

The woman's muscles churned underneath Brie's touch and she let out another wave of insults. Brie remained undeterred, laying her head on the woman's shoulder and squeezing her tighter as the woman struggled. She did her best to infuse Tono's mother with peace before letting go.

The look on Mrs. Nosaka's face was one of horror and offense. Tono stood up to speak, but was interrupted by his mother's vicious protests. The way Tono remained calm in the midst of her fury was truly heroic, but it was easy to see the toll it was taking on him.

Brie regretted her spontaneous gesture and hated that Tono was paying for it. When he had finished placating his mother, he sat at the table and slowly poured hot tea into his own cup, offering it to his mother. He then filled the two other cups, giving Sir's cup to Brie. He took hers and lifted it to his lips, indicating that they should all drink.

Watching Tono sip from her cup created an intimate and private connection between them.

His mother gave Brie one more disparaging look before accepting the tea Tono offered. Mother and son sat across from each other, sipping in silence.

They looked like two warring parties, not close family members.

Brie was relieved to hear a knock on the front door. When Tono's mother started to get up, Brie bowed and announced she was going to answer it. She could barely suppress her joy when she saw Sir standing on the doorstep.

"I'm so glad you're back, Sir," she whispered, as she escorted him down the hallway.

"You'll have to fill me in later," he stated before entering the room and bowing to both mother and son. "Ren, you'll be happy to know that your father is ready to be transported as soon as you give the hospital admin your approval. If you don't mind leaving through the back, I have a car waiting so you can join him at the more secure facility."

Tono nodded. "My deepest gratitude, Sir Davis." He then turned to his mother and explained the new arrangement. The woman became livid and started berating Tono. Although Brie could not understand her words, the venom behind them was clear.

It was not the reaction Brie had expected at all.

Sir seemed unfazed, and gave Tono a subtle nod before leaving the room with Brie. "I think I understand now what you meant about Ren's mother. He has his hands full with that one."

"I'm shocked. I thought she would be happy about the new arrangements you made, Sir."

"The fact is I chose not to discuss it with her. I must take partial responsibility for her negative response."

"Poor Tono…our being here has only increased his burden, not lessened it."

"I beg to differ, Brie. His mother will eventually see the benefit of the move and I noticed a marked difference in Tono's demeanor after the short time you two were together. Your instincts about him were spot on."

Sir smiled sadly. "No one should have to face such difficult circumstances alone, but it is hard to ask for assistance—especially for a Dominant. Our mission is to help Tono to temporarily escape this hell, even if it's just for a few days."

With Tono's god-like patience, he was eventually able to convince his mother to join them in the car waiting in a nearby alley behind the house. Mrs. Nosaka refused to acknowledge Brie and Sir, sitting in the front with the driver to avoid all contact with them.

It gave Sir the chance to discuss the details of the transfer with Tono. "If you agree, call this number and they will transfer him to the new facility under the name Haru Satou. As far as the press is concerned, your father remains at the current hospital in intensive care."

"Thank you again, Sir Davis. Both my mother and I are grateful, even if it does not appear that way at the moment. Neither of us do well with the media."

"Think nothing of it, Ren. I owed you one."

After a long drive through the streets of Tokyo, they arrived at a small hospital surrounded by a forest of bamboo. It had a secluded, serene look to it, despite it being surrounded by the bustling city.

"This is perfect," Tono stated as he got out and helped his mother from the car. As soon as they entered the building, Mrs. Nosaka began to interrogate the staff.

Brie thought her heart was in the right place—it was natural for a wife to want to make everything suitable for her husband—but Mrs. Nosaka's methods only alienated the staff who would be caring for him. Tono was already putting out fires, and they hadn't been there five minutes.

Sir made a quick phone call and told him, "Your father is ten minutes out. Why don't you wait outside for him and I'll attempt to manage the tidal wave of resentment your mother just created."

"It is not your battle to fight," Tono objected.

Sir put his hand on the Asian Dom's shoulder. "We are only here for a short while, so take us up on our offers to assist you." When Tono did not appear convinced, Sir added, "Do not dishonor me by refusing my request to help."

Tono cracked a rare smile. "Very well."

He escorted his mother out, to her vehement protests. Sir instructed Brie to follow, telling her, "Tono needs your calming presence. He's been stretched too far for too long. That serene look on his face hides a tempest ready to be released."

Brie had sensed Tono's tension as well, and hurried outside to join him. As soon as she exited the building, Tono's mother stopped her vocal tirade on her son. The woman glared bitterly at Brie, but she just shrugged and smiled, choosing to stand on the *other* side of Tono.

The three stood in awkward silence, while birds chirped and crickets sweetly serenaded them. Brie matched her breath with Tono's and noticed the tension of his jaw muscle slowly relax.

He winked when he caught her staring. There was nothing about Tono that Brie didn't love. He was loyal to his family and he honored his responsibilities with complete integrity, even when it was at great cost to himself. Truly, the man deserved an exceptional woman by his side—one who would support and love him completely.

She looked up at the clouds drifting by. *To the powers that be, could you bring Tono his soulmate? I can think of no one else who deserves your intervention more.*

Mrs. Nosaka snapped something at Brie, then turned to Tono, expecting him to translate for her. He cleared his throat, prefacing her statement with, "Take this with a grain of salt, Brie. My mother would like you to wipe that foolish look off your face."

Brie grinned, wondering what her expression had been when she'd said her little prayer for Tono. She turned to his mother and looked her directly in the eye, saying with a pleasant smile, "Tell her I will cease, and I'm sorry to have upset her."

Tono seemed relieved by her response and repeated Brie's words in Japanese. Mrs. Nosaka glared at her. She spat something to Tono, raising her eyebrow while looking down her nose at Brie.

"My mother also wishes that you would refrain from looking her in the eye."

Brie pursed her lips. So…she had another Ms. Clark on her hands. *I've been trained well for this.*

Brie lowered her eyes and bowed before Mrs. Nosaka. Although she heard an angry huff, the woman said no more.

Tono lightly brushed against Brie's arm and she smiled to herself. She knew it was his way of thanking her for submitting to his mother. The simple fact was, Brie would do anything to help him.

A short time later, the ambulance pulled up. Brie stayed where she was as Tono and Mrs. Nosaka approached it. As soon as the driver opened the back of the ambulance, Mrs. Nosaka began her instructions and complaints. Brie tried not to laugh as she watched the ambulance workers maneuver around her as they tried to get Tono's father out.

It was shocking to see Master Nosaka. He looked so frail now, a ghost of the imposing man he used to be. Brie had to hold back the tears as they rolled him by her. She followed, and returned to Sir as they wheeled Tono's father to a private room.

Brie took Sir's hand and whispered, "I feel so bad for him."

"I feel sympathy for all three."

"Yes…"

Sir directed her to the waiting room while he made her a cup of tea. The warmth of the liquid was appreciated, but what Brie really craved was caffeine. She stifled a yawn as she took another sip, finding herself struggling to adjust to the jetlag. Yet Sir looked refreshed and alert. It seemed almost inhuman.

"Do you ever get tired?"

He gave her a little smirk. "I'm used to international travel. It doesn't affect me like it did when I was a boy."

She looked up at him and grinned. "I bet you were the cutest little boy, Sir."

He rolled his eyes, chuckling as he patted her knee.

"I really wish I could have known you in your gawky teen years." She stared at her Master more critically. "You probably didn't even have them, did you?"

He shook his head knowingly. "Something tells me your tiredness is playing into this conversation."

"But did you, Sir?"

"Did I what?"

"Did you have awkward teenage years?"

"If I answer, will you stop asking questions?"

She nodded, purring with inner satisfaction.

"When I was fourteen, I experienced a growth spurt that left me overly tall for my skinny frame. I was referred to as the Rod for years…and it wasn't meant as a compliment."

Brie batted her eyelids, saying teasingly, "If the girls gave you the nickname, I'm positive they meant it as a compliment, Sir."

He shook his head, but couldn't hide his smile.

Tono's mother exited Master Nosaka's room and went directly to the staff desk, making a new list of demands. Brie was surprised by how well the staff handled it.

"What did you say to them?" she asked Sir as she watched the encounter.

He leaned close and whispered, "I explained Mrs. Nosaka's unique requirements and how best to handle them."

"Well, whatever you said, it seems you've worked a miracle, Sir."

"Let's hope—"

Sir was interrupted when Tono came out and surprised them both by telling Brie, "My father would like to speak with you." The last time the two had met, Tono's father had called her '*dame*', claiming she was not good for Tono.

When she hesitated to respond, Tono assured her, "He asked specifically for you."

Brie wasn't prepared to be rejected again and glanced at Sir. "Can you come with me?"

Tono explained with regret, "Visitors are strictly limited. *Otosama's* condition is extremely compromised."

"Of course…" Brie looked back at Sir with trepidation before entering the room. He nodded confidently, giving her the extra shot of courage she needed, but she fully expected Tono's father would ask her to leave Japan.

Tono quietly shut the door and led Brie to the dying man, who was covered in tubes, wires and plastic hoses.

"*Otosama,*" Tono said softly.

The old man's eyes fluttered open. He glanced in Brie's direction, although it did not seem as if he could actually see her, then he mumbled something she couldn't understand.

Tono told her, "He would like you to come closer, Brie."

She bent down and smiled at him.

"*Sumimasen*" he whispered, before he began coughing violently.

Brie was absolutely stunned that his father had just apologized to her.

She stood back and watched as Tono comforted him through the coughing episode, her heart racing as she realized how very close Master Nosaka was to death. Brie had never been around someone dying before and it frightened her, especially knowing what a strong person he'd been only a few weeks ago.

Tono seemed uneasy when he explained, "My father wanted to apologize for upsetting you the night of graduation."

Brie smiled at the old man again and said respectfully said thank you, grateful for her exposure to Japanese anime when she was younger. "*Domo arigatou gozaimasu*, Nosaka-*sama.*"

For the first time, she saw the old man's eyes soften. It was very slight, but brought her great joy.

Although Tono was smiling as well, his eyes did not reflect it. Brie assumed he was too consumed with grief and instinctively gave him a hug. Tono stiffened in her embrace, shaking his head.

Brie realized she must have broken some unspoken social protocol and quickly broke away, apologizing to Tono under her breath.

Master Nosaka called out his son's name and Tono quickly returned to his father's side. The old man whispered something that caused Tono's eyes to water. It broke Brie's heart to see him in pain and she glanced away, but when she heard his chuckle, she braved a peek.

"*Hai,*" Tono answered his father with a definite blush on his cheeks.

What had the old man asked him?

Master Nosaka lifted his hand slightly and Tono grasped it, bowing until his forehead touched his father's hand. Brie admired the respect Tono had for him; it was deeply moving to witness firsthand.

Tono bowed formally one more time before escorting Brie out of the room. She bowed as well, then waved goodbye as she walked out the door—a chill running through her as she realized this might be the last time she'd ever see his father alive.

Tono led her to Sir and announced, "My father would like me to show you a favorite pastime of ours."

"Besides Kinbaku?" Brie asked, surprised.

That mysterious blush showed up again, coloring Tono's cheeks when he answered. "Yes."

"Well, now you have me intrigued, Nosaka," Sir replied. "When and where?"

Tono looked towards his father's room. "It would be best if we did it as soon as possible. I hate to leave my father in this condition, but he insists. Are you free tonight? I can pick you up at the hotel around eight."

Brie was equally curious, and hoped her question would shed some light on the night's festivities. "Formal or causal dress?"

Tono smiled when he answered her. "Casual." Then he turned to Sir, adding, "A few favorite toys would be advisable as well."

What the heck does Tono have planned tonight? she wondered with delight.

Whatever it was had the experienced Dom's cheeks turning a light shade of pink, so Brie knew it had to be something exceedingly wicked.

They left the hospital soon after to give Tono time with his father. In the car, Brie began to cry.

"Did Mr. Nosaka say something unkind, Brie?" Sir asked gently.

"No, Sir. He apologized to me."

Sir raised his eyebrow. "Now that *is* unexpected. He's not a man to take back an opinion once it's voiced."

"I'm in shock as well, Sir."

"So why are you crying, babygirl?"

"Being in that room, seeing Tono with his father... It was both touching and heartbreaking. I wish I could do something to change what's about to happen."

"Death is a struggle, but it's a journey all of us must travel, Brie. As much as you may wish to carry his burden, grief is a solitary endeavor. The most we can hope to do is act as a distraction from the pain and be there for Ren later, when everyone else has moved on."

Brie thought of Sir as a young man, having suffered the traumatic death of his father with no one supporting him other than his uncle, Mr. Reynolds. The ruthless curiosity of the press must have been excruciating to bear at such a young age.

She suspected that as hard as it was for her to see Tono's father dying, it must be churning up painful memories for Sir as well. However, when she tried to broach the subject, he immediately cut her off with a stern lecture.

"This is not about me, this is about Nosaka!"

She knew better than to press him, but now there was no doubt in her mind that Sir was struggling emotionally. When they arrived at the hotel, she squeezed his hand as he helped her out of the car. Brie needed him to know that she was there for him—in whatever capacity he wanted—and went on tiptoe to whisper, "I'm here, Sir, however you need me."

His eyes stared past her, as if he were being tormented by some agonizing memory he couldn't get past. It continued to eat at him, his face becoming stern and unyielding as they entered the hotel room.

In a distant voice he informed her, "I need to prepare for my meeting tomorrow and will most likely be on the phone for the next few hours. It would be better if you stayed out here and worked on your documentary while I retire to the bedroom."

Brie nodded, although the last thing she wanted to do was work on the film. She *needed* to be with Sir, to understand what was troubling him. She called out as she watched him walk away from her. "Please, Sir…"

He turned back, his voice almost cruel in its fierceness. "What is it, Brie?"

She lost her nerve and replied timidly, "I hope your meeting goes well tomorrow."

He narrowed his eyes, knowing that was not what she had wanted to say, but he did not question her on it. Instead, he entered the room and closed the door behind him, effectively shutting her out.

Brie swallowed back the tears. Even after all this time together, there were still moments when he cut himself off from her. It hurt deeply, more than she wanted to admit. He'd insisted that grieving was a solitary journey, and it appeared he still believed that to be true—but she didn't—so Brie gathered her courage and knocked on the door.

"What is it?" he asked in a harsh tone.

"May I come in?"

"No. I thought I'd made myself clear."

She was shocked by his denial of entrance, but would not be deterred by it. She laid her head against the door and pleaded, "Please tell me what's wrong, Sir." When he didn't answer, she reminded him, "We're condors."

The door was yanked open, leaving Brie teetering as she tried to keep from falling. His eyes shone with unveiled resentment. "As my sub, you are expected to follow my orders, téa. Do you need a lesson in obedience?"

She looked at the floor and answered meekly, "No, Master."

"Good. We both have jobs to do. I suggest you get to work."

She dutifully returned to the other room after he closed the door with unnecessary force. Brie got out her computer and stared at the screen, unable to think about the film.

Something had changed; she'd felt it in the car. Her frustration only grew knowing she had done nothing wrong, but she reminded herself that she was a condor. It was her honor and duty to see her Master through whatever was tearing at his soul, even when she was required to take the brunt of his misdirected anger.

Brie was certain Sir would cancel their outing with Tono, and was surprised when he emerged from the room thirty minutes before eight dressed in a dark shirt and jeans.

"Get dressed and meet me in the lobby."

Although his voice sounded warm, his expression was still distant and haunted. As she walked past him, however, Sir put his hand on her shoulder.

She stopped, her head bowed but her heart gladdened by the simple contact.

"It's not you, Brie."

She nodded with tears in her eyes. "I needed to hear that, Sir. Thank you."

"Tonight we concentrate our efforts on Nosaka, since that is the main reason we came to Japan." When Sir took his hand away, the comforting connection it created disappeared. He left her in the hotel room with things feeling just as distant as before.

It worried her.

With shaking hands, Brie dressed herself and went to join her Master in the lobby.

Tono's Secret

T ono entered the hotel looking stylish in his simple black kimono. Brie noticed a group of young women stare at him and then whisper amongst themselves excitedly.

"I see you brought the requested items," Tono commented, glancing at the backpack Sir had slung over his shoulder.

"Just a few essentials."

"Perfect." Tono glanced at Brie for a moment, then back at Sir. "Is anything wrong?"

Leave it to Tono to pick up on the tension between them.

"No," Sir assured him, "but I believe Brie is suffering from jetlag."

Tono asked Brie, "Would you rather skip tonight?"

"Absolutely not," Sir answered for her. "My sub is in need of a little adventure this evening."

Brie smiled, nodding her agreement.

With a glint in his eye, Tono said, "Good."

His countenance completely changed once they left the hotel. He became guarded, speaking in hushed tones. "What we do must remain a secret. You can tell no one where we've been tonight."

Brie's eyes widened, charmed by his mysterious behavior. Was there a Japanese BDSM underground? The way Tono was acting, she figured the club must be extremely taboo.

She remembered how stunned she'd been to learn that Rytsar was a sadist. Was she about to find out something equally shocking about Tono?

Brie shivered.

She took a long, hard look at Tono once they were in his car. She quickly came to the conclusion that he wasn't the type to indulge in extreme play. His spirit was far too gentle—other than his feisty bouts of spanking.

She was stumped by what secret Tono and his father could be hiding, but it pleased her heart that the elder Nosaka wanted her to know it.

If Sir was burning with the same curiosity, he sure didn't show it. He looked calm and collected, as if he knew exactly where they were headed, so Brie leaned over and asked, "Where are we going, Sir?"

"I haven't a clue," he answered, giving her a slight smile before staring out the window. She looked down at the backpack on his lap and decided that their destination was unimportant.

Sir was right in his assertion that the only thing that mattered tonight was helping Tono.

The Asian Dom's behavior remained aloof after he parked the car, leading them through a labyrinth of narrow alleyways deep within an older section of the city. The location seemed to hint at something illicit or even dangerous. Sir put his arm protectively around Brie as if he felt the same way.

The building Tono eventually led them to had a brightly lit sign and crowds of young people milling about. To Brie it looked like a dance club from the outside, but she was in for a surprise when they walked through the entrance and were greeted by a steep set of stairs leading to a dark basement below.

A young man met them at the bottom of the stairs and bowed to Tono before asking him a series of questions in Japanese. There was a quick exchange of funds, then Tono told them to follow as he walked down a dimly lit corridor with vividly painted red doors on either side.

He led them to the farthest room and opened it with a shy grin, motioning them to enter.

Brie had no idea what to expect as she walked in, but she was surprised to see connected couches lining three of the walls of the room, with a low-lying wooden table in the center, and a large white screen covering the farthest wall.

"Please take a seat," Tono told them.

Sir placed his pack on the table and sat on the couch, patting the area next to him. Brie sat by his side, although she would have preferred kneeling at his feet.

As she glanced around, Brie concluded it must be a private screening room for bondage videos. Tono picked up a remote lying on the table and the speakers popped into life as a list of titles in Japanese appeared on the screen. Her curiosity increased when he went to a shelf in the corner and took something from a box there.

He returned with an item that looked suspiciously like a smaller version of a Hitachi Magic Wand. Brie giggled as it dawned on her that he was holding a mic, which meant they must be in a private karaoke room.

"No way…" she giggled.

Sir looked at him with amusement, chuckling to himself.

Tono tilted his head charmingly and asked, "Do you sing?"

Brie shook her head violently. "No! I'm sorry, Tono. I can't sing, not even a note."

He answered her protest with an engaging smile. "Come on, Brie— come sing with me."

"I'm serious, Tono. I would only make your eardrums bleed if I did."

"Please…"

His earnest plea pulled at her heartstrings, but Brie couldn't hide her horror at the idea of singing in front of either Dom and stated firmly, "I can't."

Tono looked to Sir for assistance.

Sir shook his head as he lay back on the couch. "I must admit, Nosaka, you've surprised me with this one. I never suspected this would be where we ended up. However, if you are serious about wanting to proceed further, I suggest *sake* may be in order. We will need to loosen Brie up and heighten our own tolerance for pain."

She blushed. Sir had once heard her sing in the shower and requested afterwards that she refrain from doing so again.

"I'm sure she's not as bad as you claim," Tono insisted, but he heeded Sir's warning and put down his mic, picking up a phone on the wall instead. He ordered the *sake*, but after noticing Sir holding up two fingers, he amended the order.

Tono sat next to Brie while they waited. She couldn't help grinning when she asked, "So this is really what you and your father do in secret?"

Tono smirked. "*Hai.* Wasn't what were you expecting?"

"Well, when you suggested bringing our favorite toys, I naturally imagined something a little…um…kinkier."

Tono's smile spread across his face, lighting up his brown eyes. "I wanted to try something a little different tonight. Clients are only bothered if they choose to order drinks, so we will remain undisturbed for hours."

"Ah…" She glanced around the room again, noting the expansive couches as well as the sturdy wooden table in front of her. Sure, she agreed there was a world of possibilities for the creatively gifted, but still…*karaoke?*

"Did you and your father come here often?" Sir asked.

"As often as our schedules allowed when I lived in Japan. It was our…secret pleasure."

There was a knock on the door and a striking young Japanese woman entered the room. She gracefully placed two warmed *sake* containers and three cups on the table, and bowed to Tono before leaving.

Sir sat up and grabbed a flask. "Mind if I pour? Since I've had the dubious pleasure of hearing Brie sing before, I need to fortify myself."

Brie felt the need to confess to Tono before things went any further. "My singing is even worse than my cooking."

"I won't believe it until I hear it," Tono replied, taking the cup Sir offered him.

She giggled nervously as Sir handed over her *sake,* trying to quell the butterflies when she lifted the cup in reverence, then swallowed the warm liquid.

Brie noted with amusement how Sir reminded her of Rytsar in the way he quickly refilled the cups each time they drank. By the time her Master stopped pouring, both Doms had become unusually open and chatty.

"What an odd activity to share with your father, Ren," Sir stated. "I never pictured you as a singer."

He shrugged. "To me it's no different than going fishing or hunting like you Americans do with your fathers. It's simply a bonding experience between generations—one that only he and I shared." He smiled sadly, looking around the room. "Here my father was not my *otosama* and I was not his protégé. We were equals, sharing a mutual passion."

"I find it oddly fascinating…" Sir mused. "Do you consider yourself a good singer, Nosaka?"

"I'm fair. Not quite at the level of my father, but I've heard no complaints."

Sir snorted. "Is that because you normally tie and gag your audience?"

Tono burst out laughing. "Well, there's only one way to find out if I speak the truth." He retrieved another mic from the shelf and tried to hand it to Brie. "Your time has come, little one. Let me hear this infamous voice of yours."

She cringed and refused to take it, hesitant to ruin Tono's good impression of her.

He seemed surprised by her reaction, but took it in stride. "Very well. If I go first, you will join me for the next song."

Brie glanced at Sir, hoping for an out. "Only if it pleases my Master."

Sir raised his eyebrow, but said nothing.

"I will take that as a yes."

Tono started flipping through the sea of titles, explaining, "You may find it surprising that my father is a huge Elvis Presley fan. I'm singing this first one in honor of him."

Brie grinned when she recognized the song *Jailhouse Rock*. The foolish grin remained on her face, until she heard Tono's voice…

It was smooth, deep and warmly romantic.

She couldn't help staring at him, her jaw slack in admiration. Her whole perception of Tono changed and expanded as she listened to the rich tenor of his voice. He delighted her even more when he added a few thrusting Elvis moves at the end of his performance.

Brie clapped her hands enthusiastically, begging for more.

"I would definitely say you can sing, Nosaka," Sir complimented him.

Tono turned to Brie, twirling the mic. "Now to see if you are as poor a singer as you believe."

She groaned in protest. "Tono, I will only murder that beautiful sound of yours if I try to sing with you. Trust me."

He handed her the microphone. "Don't think, just follow my lead and sing."

Tono switched the subtitles to English while she waited. Brie stood beside him, dreading the moment her humiliation would be made complete. However, she found herself laughing when an old song from the movie *Dirty Dancing* began to play. The ballad, *I've Had the Time of My Life*, had been a favorite of hers when she was growing up.

Tono started, his voice low and alluring as he sang the male part of the popular love song. Having him sing such a silly, romantic tune took away some of her anxiety; enough that Brie smiled at Sir when her part came up on the screen. She opened her mouth, and… Brie chickened out at the last second, only whispering the words.

Tono shook his head and leaned in close, singing the female part with her. With the *sake* in her veins, bolstering her courage, Brie stared into his chocolate-brown eyes. It reminded her of the time they'd danced together the night of graduation, when she had trusted him to lead her on the dance floor. What came from her lips was a tragic sound, but Tono cheered her on with a smile.

Soon Brie was relaxed enough to let all her inhibitions down, and she fell into natural rhythm with Tono, her voice following his. Although she noticed that he cringed every time she sang off pitch, he never lost his smile—not once.

Sir clapped afterwards, and poured them another round of drinks. "I'm almost there," he teased, handing them each the *sake*. "Just a little more alcohol will deaden the last of these nerves." He wrapped his arm around Brie, kissing the top of her head. "Wow, babygirl, you really *can't* sing."

She looked up and giggled, taking no offense at his critique because it was true. She shot back playfully, "Now it's your turn, Sir."

"I don't sing, Brie, you know that," he admonished. Sir turned to Tono. "However, I think we would both like to hear you sing again—solo."

Brie nodded eagerly.

"I won't perform alone," Tono said, riffling through the box on the shelf and producing a tambourine for Brie. She jumped at the chance to accompany him without her voice.

Brie faced Sir as she practiced tapping the instrument against her hip, trying to entice him with her lusty moves. Sir sat back to admire her, but he stared at her with distant eyes, as if his mind kept wandering elsewhere.

Tono explained to Brie, "Although my father is a die-hard Elvis fan, I prefer something more current and a little more country."

Country? Brie couldn't believe Tono was a closet country fan.

Although she personally disliked country music, the moment Tono began to sing *The Dance* by Garth Brooks, all doubts about his choice of music were silenced.

Tono drew Brie in with his voice and broke her heart with the lyrics of the song. She forgot about the tambourine in her hand as she struggled to keep her emotions in check when he sang the words, "Our lives are better left to chance; I could have missed the pain, but I'd have had to miss the dance."

"That…that was beautiful, Tono," she muttered afterwards, not trusting herself to say more.

He looked at her tenderly and nodded, before holding out the microphone to Sir. "Your turn, Sir Davis."

"I already said that I don't sing."

Tono answered him in no uncertain terms, "No one leaves the room without singing."

"Not going to happen, Ren," Sir growled.

Brie was disappointed that he was refusing. She'd never heard her Master's singing voice and knew this might be her only chance. Racking her brain, she searched for a valid reason why he must. When it finally came to her, Brie smiled to herself.

"Sir, didn't you once tell me that you would never ask me to do something you weren't willing to do yourself?"

He shook his head slowly, rubbing the area over his heart. "I can't believe you're using your Master's words against him, téa."

She noted that he'd used her sub name and knelt down at his feet like a proper submissive. With head bowed, she held up the microphone beseechingly. "Please, Master."

He was slow to take it. "Understand, my willful sub, my song will come at a steep price."

She kept her eyes down, trying to hide her glee. "Since I've never heard you sing, Master, it will be worth any price I must pay."

Sir stood up, looking at the microphone as if it were a foreign instrument of BDSM he had yet to master. He announced to Tono, "This will be the only song I sing tonight."

The Asian Dom bowed slightly. "Understood, Sir Davis."

Sir stared at Brie for several moments before instructing Tono to find *Demons* by the band Imagine Dragons. While he waited for Tono to locate the song, Sir slowly rolled up his sleeves, one at a time.

Brie felt butterflies, knowing this opportunity wasn't likely to be repeated.

Once Tono had highlighted the song, he handed Sir the remote and sat next to Brie.

"Would you like me to play the tambourine, Master?" she asked playfully.

"No, téa. I want you to *listen.*"

Brie nodded, waiting with bated breath to hear Sir's voice. It was low and gravely, which perfectly matched the song he'd chosen. The lyrics to *Demons* were haunting and sad, unbearably sad…

Brie could not hold back the tears when she realized halfway through that his choice of song was meant as an apology to her. Sir refused to look in her direction as he sang of love and the darkness of inner demons that still haunted his soul. When it ended, the room was silent.

Sir put down the mic and turned to face her. She stood up and walked into his open arms.

"I don't mean to hurt you, Brie," he whispered, kissing her forehead. She let out a deep sigh of emotional release, grateful that their connection had been reestablished.

Tono watched their private scene play out before him, and said nothing as he collected the mics and tambourine, depositing them back in the box.

"Shall we go, then?"

Sir shook his head. "No, Ren. My sub has a debt that must be paid."

Paying her Debt

Brie trembled in Sir's arms, knowing that playtime was about begin, but having no idea what he had planned. Sir let go of her and picked up the backpack. "Did you bring anything, Nosaka?"

Tono nodded, producing a length of jute from inside his kimono.

"That will do nicely." Sir surprised Brie when he abruptly pulled off his T-shirt, exposing his manly chest. Then her Master sat down on the couch, and with an ominous grin, he slowly unbuttoned his pants.

Brie ached just watching Sir undress in front of her. When he commanded, "On your knees, téa. Right where you stand," she instantly dropped to a kneeling position.

"Take off your top."

Brie gracefully removed her blouse and folded it, laying it on the floor beside her. When she looked up, he nodded at her bra. "All of it."

She unfastened her bra next and laid it on top of the blouse, waiting anxiously for his next order.

"Hands behind your back."

She thrust her breasts forward proudly, her nipples hardening under the appreciative gaze of her Master. The fact that Tono was also in the room only added to her excitement.

"Nosaka, bind téa's chest so that her breasts present nicely and secure her hands behind her back."

Brie's heart rate increased as she felt Tono approach and heard the swish of silk as he separated his kimono to kneel behind her. In a voice both commanding and calm, he ordered, "Wrists together."

Brie looked at her Master while Tono began the slow and sensual process of binding her. Sir's eyes remained trained on her as she was lulled and seduced by the jute.

Tono knew just how to caress and tease her as he placed the rope under her breasts, adjusting it carefully with gentle hands. The jute slid over her skin flirtatiously, tugging against her with each pull and tie of the rope, constricting her movement further with each new pass…

Brie moaned with pleasure when he laced the rope around her forearms and tightened it, forcing her chest farther forward.

"That's perfect," Sir complimented.

Tono grunted his agreement. Brie swayed under the Kinbaku Master's fluid movements, the call of his jute beckoning her to give in to its seductive power. She awakened from the provocative trance he'd created when Sir stood up, his cock stiff and ready before her.

"Come to your Master and open those pretty lips."

Brie moved slowly to remain graceful and alluring, as she made her way over to him on her knees with her arms bound. Once she reached him, she looked up at her Master innocently and opened her lips wide.

He smiled down at her. "Do you remember the first time you sucked my cock, téa?"

She purred in response.

Sir eased his shaft into her mouth. "I want you to suck my cock exactly the way you did that first time."

Brie kept her eyes on him as she took his shaft deeply. Sir moved her hair to the side and held her head so he could watch her. She pulled back and took him deeper.

"That's it, téa…"

She swallowed, allowing the head of his cock to travel down her taut throat, forcing him deeper until her lips touched the very base of his shaft. Once there, she rocked gently back and forth, letting her throat caress his manhood with its tight constriction.

When Brie pulled back to catch her breath, she let him drop from her mouth and looked up, smiling at her Master.

"Again, babygirl."

Brie eagerly obliged, taking several deep breaths before opening her lips and taking him back in her mouth. This time Sir guided her using his hands, thrusting slowly. She stared up at him with love. Being taken like this took her to a different level of submission, one where she was purely female in the most primal form.

He pulled out and pushed her head back, running his fingers through her hair as he praised, "My good girl…"

Sir asked her to stand, then grasped her throat possessively. "I think it is time you attended to our host," he whispered, turning her around to face Tono. He undressed her completely, only leaving her collar.

"Kneel before him with your legs spread open."

Brie walked over to Tono, her heart beating faster with each step. The Asian Dom stared at her with an amorous gaze as she knelt down before him, spreading herself open as Sir had commanded.

"Please Nosaka with your lips, but do not open them, téa."

Tono loosened his sash and opened his kimono. Brie took in his toned body, then smiled to herself when she saw his arousal. She watched with admiration as he removed his underwear, exposing his erection.

Brie was grateful to be allowed the honor of ministering to his masculine need.

With lips that lightly teased, she kissed his cock, making her way from the base to the tip of his shaft. Brie looked up when she heard his intake of breath, and smiled when she saw the passionate look in his eye.

She used her soft lips to tease the frenulum and smooth head of his cock, then rubbed her cheek lovingly against his rigid shaft, like a feline. She bowed lower to give attention to his balls and to caress the perineum, the soft area underneath his scrotum, with feather-light kisses. She felt his whole body stiffen, his enjoyment of her attention obvious.

Brie saw a drop of his pre-come on the end of his shaft and rubbed her lips against it. She looked up at him, licking her lips seductively as she tasted his excitement. Tono groaned, his breath coming shallow and fast.

She turned her head and kept her lips closed as she rubbed them up and down the length of him, mimicking the motion and pace of slow thrusting. When he fisted her hair and pressed her lips harder against his cock, increasing the pace, her pussy tightened in pleasure, responding to his possessive grip.

That was when Sir knelt down behind her...

Brie moaned on Tono's shaft when Sir began to caress her clit, swirling her juices to slicken the sensitive flesh before briskly rubbing against it. Brie's breath quickly increased, meeting Tono's as they rode the tension building inside them both.

"Concentrate," Sir commanded.

Brie realized that she had stopped the motion on Tono's shaft, and resumed the pace she'd had before, looking up at him apologetically.

If Tono minded, his face didn't show it. He gazed down at her, the two in sync as their orgasms threatened to peak. Sir pulled his fingers away, allowing her to regain control of her body. Brie copied his actions by pulling away from Tono's cock.

Sir started up again, his touch slower and lighter. Brie shuddered, her libido now heightened and much easier to manipulate—just the way Sir liked it.

"Nosaka, reach into the bag there," he commanded.

Tono moved away from Brie, pulling out a large red candle.

"The lighter is in the front pocket," Sir informed him, as he returned to her clit and teased it relentlessly with his vigorous rubbing. "Place them on the table."

Brie held her breath, forcing her orgasm back as she watched Tono put down the beloved tools for wax play.

"Good girl," Sir growled in her ear, reaching forward and tugging on her nipples.

She groaned with pleasure and frustration, her pussy contracting in response to the manipulation, ruining her previous restraint. "Master…"

Sir chuckled, knowing that she was struggling to obey him. He added a bite on her neck to make things nearly impossible. Brie's whole body stiffened, so close to coming that tears formed in her eyes.

"Please."

Sir wrapped his hand around her throat, lifting her head so she looked him in the eyes. "Please what, téa?"

"Release…" she begged through gritted teeth, as he increased the pace and pressure on her clit.

"No."

She shuddered again. Sometimes her Master was a cruel man, but there was always purpose behind his actions—a method to his madness.

"Shall I test your resolve, téa?"

She shook her head, but answered dutifully, "If it pleases you, Master."

"I question your sincerity, little sub."

Brie took a deep breath, realizing he was not jesting. With renewed conviction, she responded, "It would be my honor to have my resolve tested, Master."

"Good." He swirled his finger against her clit, slowly and rhythmically, drawing her close to the edge again. Brie concentrated on a dark spot on the ceiling, putting all her energy into that black spot to get through his torturous teasing.

Sir released his hold on her and pulled out a Wartenberg wheel from the backpack. The smile on his face was dangerously wicked when he held it up for her to see. The spiked instrument was a challenging tool, and her skin tingled with fearful anticipation.

"Lay her on the couch, Nosaka, with her head near the end."

Tono cradled her in his arms as he picked her up gently and laid her per Sir's instruction, adjusting her bound arms to a more comfortable position before he lit the candle on the table. She trembled where she lay, her pussy aching with desire at the thought of enduring both Doms' 'tests'.

Sir seated himself between her thighs and lightly ran his fingers up her leg. "Such soft, delicate skin…"

Tono picked up the candle, which now had a pool of melted wax. He knelt beside her and lifted the candle over her chest. "Close your eyes, Brie."

She did so, anticipating the burning drip of the hot wax and the wicked prickling of the Wartenberg wheel, wondering which of the two she would feel first.

However, the Doms were in control, and they surprised her.

Tono's gentle lips descended on hers as Sir kissed her inner thigh, slowly moving upwards. Brie was unprepared for such tender contact, and her control melted under their attention. When Sir fingered her pussy again, she lifted her pelvis out of his reach to prevent a cascading orgasm.

"No, téa. You must remain still."

Brie slowly settled her ass back onto the couch, gasping softly when his fingers returned. When Tono slipped his tongue into her mouth, her pussy began its prelude to an orgasmic dance without her permission.

The sharp prick of the wheel ran across the top of her mound as hot wax dripped onto her left nipple, shocking her senses and helping her to regain power over her body. Brie moaned, the explicit combination of pleasure and pain teasing her. The hot liquid rolled down the side of her breast before cooling into hard wax.

Sir rolled the wicked wheel down her left thigh, pressing hard enough to make her skin break out in tingling goosebumps while Tono brushed his hand slightly over her right breast, adding to her chills.

When the Asian Dom covered her nipple with the hot liquid, Brie arched her back in pleasure, loving the momentary burn followed by the ticklish trails the wax created. Sir focused his attention on her clit as Tono began crafting a simple design of a large flower on her stomach. The fact that Tono could excite Brie with the wax while making her a beautiful piece of artwork in the process totally enchanted her. But she tensed when Sir resumed his sensual rubbing of her clit as he teasingly tortured the sensitive soles of her feet with the wheel.

Sir challenged her further when he rolled the spiky instrument over the outside of her thigh and the shapely swell of her ass, applying more pressure than before. Brie realized she could fight against the impending orgasm he was building, or transcend it. She forced herself to relax against her Master's insistent caress, letting the fire between her legs burn hotter.

Rather than focusing on resisting the orgasm, she concentrated on the burn of the wax, the needle points of the wheel, and allowed those sensations to carry her.

"That's my good girl, fly for me…" Sir said gruffly, kissing her inner thigh as he rolled the spiky instrument over the arch of her foot.

"Ahhh…" she gasped, welcoming the challenge of the Wartenberg wheel because it helped her to soar higher into subspace.

The smell of smoke from the candle signaled that Tono had finished his creation. His warm lips teased her, kissing her cheeks, forehead and the tip of her nose. "You are beautiful, *toriko*," he whispered, before kissing her passionately on the lips.

She opened her eyes and stared into his. The use of his chosen sub name for her surprised Brie and had an amorous effect, making her pussy respond with waves of undeniable desire.

"I think it's time to change this up, Nosaka."

Sir put the wheel down on the table and the two Doms switched places. Sir pulled her head farther off the edge and stroked her throat with his fingers. "I will fuck your face slowly, *téa*."

"Let me blindfold her first," Tono suggested, taking his silk sash and tying it securely over her eyes. It smelled of him.

Brie laid her head back down, now completely reliant on her other senses.

"You were successful in denying your desire," Sir complimented her. "Now it's time to embrace it—don't hold anything back."

She lay there, waiting. When nothing happened, she wondered if the two Doms were communicating silently.

OMG, what were they planning for her now? *Breathe, Brie, breathe…*

"Open," Sir commanded.

Brie parted her lips to take in his hard shaft. Her tongue met with the distinctive tang of Sir's pre-come—a taste she adored—then flickered against the underside of his cock. He pushed his shaft deeper into her throat and groaned, making her gush with wetness at hearing his need.

She was completely unprepared when she felt Tono's tongue press against her pussy. She moaned on Sir's manhood as her body violently released the pent-up orgasm she'd been so valiantly fighting. Her pussy lifted into the air of its own accord, bouncing up and down in rhythmic motion, in time with her pulsing orgasm.

Tono stayed with her, licking and sucking her clit as it quivered. She struggled against Sir's cock, her body unable to handle the intense stimulation.

"Be still," Sir commanded.

Brie froze, telling herself that to accept the intense stimulation, she had to transcend it. She forced her body to relax and embraced Tono's oral caress while Sir pressed his shaft deep into her throat.

A second orgasm rolled through Brie in a matter of seconds.

"Good girl," Sir praised her as he pulled out. "I want you to keep coming until I tell you to stop."

There was a time when she would have celebrated such a command, but experience had taught her how challenging it actually was. She understood that this was the very same test as earlier, just in reverse.

Sir eased his cock back into her mouth. "Suck."

Brie obediently began to suck, and found Tono matching her rhythm between her legs. The synergy of the act initiated another orgasm, and Brie desperately struggled not to move as her body was rocked by it.

Tono murmured his approval. "Her come is so sweet."

"Again," Sir commanded softly. He grabbed her throat with one hand, pressing down on it as he began to make slow love to her mouth.

The feeling of total possession, forced submission and tender love-making was a combination that completely undid her.

Brie moaned as Tono brought her to another orgasm, one that refused to end. Her thighs trembled uncontrollably as she rode each wave. Sir added to the intensity by holding her in his tight grasp, his cock thrust far down her throat.

Tears of pure bliss were soaked up by her blindfold as she gave in to the continuous orgasm and flew...

"Come back to me."

Brie heard those words several times before realizing they were meant for her. She had to concentrate on following them. She opened her eyes and found Sir looking down at her, the blindfold removed.

"Enjoy yourself, téa?"

"Yes, Master...thank you."

"Thank Nosaka as well."

Brie lifted her head groggily and smiled at Tono. "Thank you, Tono Nosaka."

Sir caressed her cheek. "Now we will reward your tenacity, my sub. Swallow my pleasure while Nosaka covers you in his."

Brie opened her mouth to take in Sir's shaft, while Tono positioned himself, kneeling between her legs. She heard the slippery sound as the Asian Dom stroked his own manhood, while Sir began gently thrusting in her mouth, increasing the pace until he threw back his head and cried out.

Her muffled cries of pure ecstasy filled the room. Brie swallowed her Master's seed as Tono's hot come covered her bare mound. Having both men orgasm at the same time was a glorious experience.

Brie kissed the tip of Sir's cock tenderly when he pulled out of her mouth, then focused her attention on Tono's gentle hands as he cleaned his essence from her skin. Every touch was meaningful, articulating his thoughts without voice, and what he was expressing tonight was appreciation—and love.

Brie was slow to dress and needed to lean on Sir as they made their way out of the karaoke club and through the narrow alleyways back to the car. She was still flying from the encounter, and giggled periodically as they walked.

"What's so funny, Brie?" Tono asked.

She tried to formulate an answer but her thoughts were scattered because of the pleasant, lingering haze of subspace.

Sir answered for her. "She sometimes gets like this after an intense session. It's been happening more often lately. Unsure why that is."

Brie giggled. "Because I'm a very happy sub, Sir. Very happy."

Sir patted her hand, which she had wrapped around his arm for support. The sweet gesture made Brie giggle again.

He raised his eyebrow, giving Tono an exasperated look. "See what I mean?"

Tono smiled. "It pleases me to see her so giddy. It is not an emotion I've encountered recently."

His statement reminded Brie of his tragic circumstances. The joy she felt fled her heart and tears started running down her face.

"What's wrong, Brie?" Sir questioned, stunned to suddenly find her crying.

She didn't want to ruin the evening, so she smiled up at him and stated, "I'm so happy, it makes me teary."

Sir gave her a private grin. "You are a mystery, Miss Bennett. One I believe it will take me a lifetime to solve."

A New Kind of Kinbaku

Brie was tickled that Sir had convinced Tono to perform part of his traveling Kinbaku act for them. Sir explained to her that getting Tono involved in his art again would help the jute Master to process the grief that was coming.

"There are times when you must be forced to do those things that are healthy for you. Nosaka will benefit greatly from the escape of Kinbaku in the months ahead."

Sir was always observing people and assessing their needs. Even though he was no longer part of the Training Center, that aspect of his nature could not be quelled. Brie admired that about him, but it also worried her. Sir was meant to train others; his natural talent, as well as his passion and experience, made him an exceedingly effective trainer. She hadn't felt guilt about his resignation from the Center in months, but now it returned with a vengeance.

Brie wondered if Sir still missed his position as headmaster. How could *her* personal training make up for all that he had given up? She shook off her doubts, reminding herself that Sir was an upfront man. If it was truly a problem, he would find a way to resolve it.

That second night, Brie and Sir visited Master Nosaka's studio. It was kind of eerie, knowing that Tono's father was fighting for his life just a few miles away, but it was obvious from Tono's countenance that for him the place brought peace.

Brie understood that this place was a tangible connection to his father, and wondered how many hours Tono had spent inside these walls, training and learning with the man. How young had he been when his training began? She'd never thought to ask him.

As she glanced around, Brie imagined Tono as a young boy, his long bangs hiding his lack of confidence as his father corrected him on a malformed knot. It made her smile to envision the scene.

Her thoughts were interrupted when a woman entered the large studio wearing a bright yellow kimono and dark red lipstick. She was young, like Brie, but with straight, waist-length hair and soft brown eyes. The girl bowed low to Tono, speaking words Brie did not understand.

He smiled, and told her to rise as he introduced her to his guests. "This is Chikako. She is one of my father's favorite partners to work with."

The girl turned to Brie and Sir and bowed again. In perfect English she said, "It is my pleasure to entertain you tonight."

Brie bowed to her as Sir answered, "We are honored to observe your scene."

Tono directed Chikako to sit on a jute mat in the middle of the room while he explained to them, "I'm going to show you a new routine I've been working on. Something that embraces the old traditions while adding a modern element to the mix. I hope to attract the younger generation to the ancient art."

"You have me intrigued yet again, Nosaka."

Brie felt a thrill of sensual excitement, knowing she was going to see Tono's mastery at work. "I can't wait!"

Tono directed them to sit on the floor as he pulled bundled strands of multicolored jute from his bag and placed them beside the girl. There was a psychological component to his placement. Brie knew the girl was already anticipating the caress of the rope as she watched him lay out the various colors of jute. Each new bundle meant another length of rope would sensually constrict her. It made Brie shiver just to think about it.

Tono turned down the lights and put on music to accompany the performance. Although it was his customary flute melody, this one had drum beats behind it, giving it an edgier sound. Brie smiled, liking the added element.

"What makes this performance unique," Tono informed them, "is the rope I am using. It has been specially treated to glow under black light." He switched on ultraviolet lights from above, and suddenly the rope on the ground glowed in a multitude of vibrant rainbow colors.

Brie clapped her hands. "Oh, I love it, Tono. I really love the bright colors!"

Tono smiled at her. "I thought it might appeal to you."

"Very clever, Nosaka," Sir complimented. "Please enlighten us further."

Tono bowed slightly, then sat behind Chikako. He whispered to her as he gathered her in his arms and closed his eyes. Brie knew they were matching their breaths, finding their connection.

The young woman began to sway slightly in time with the music, the look on her face one of peaceful expectation. Brie was envious; there was no way around it. Any time she saw Tono performing his craft, there was a touch of jealousy—she always longed to be the one under his skilled hands, feeling the rope's seductive caress.

Tono whispered a command, and Chikako took a kneeling position. He took a length of glowing blue rope and tied her long hair into a ponytail, binding it in a pattern of decorative knots. Then he took the end of her long rope of hair and secured it to a ring above her. Once she was immobilized, Tono began to tease the girl by sliding the rope against her skin as he pleased her with gentle caresses.

In time with the music, he raised her arms above her head and bound them into an attractive ballerina pose.

As the music built in tempo and sensuality, the anticipation in the room heightened. From behind the girl, Tono took hold of the front of her silk kimono and waited, ripping it open at the dramatic crescendo of the song. The aggressive movement caught Brie by surprise, and she found it quite exhilarating.

She held her breath as Tono readied the girl for flight, reliving that incredible feeling herself—the moment when the body leaves the ground for the first time. Brie moaned softly as she watched Chikako lifted into the air, bound in the glowing rope, the full beauty of the intricate bindings and her pose finally realized.

It was visually stunning!

Tono caressed his partner as he checked the knots, his movements in time with the melody. When the intensity and mood of the music changed, Tono's binding changed with it. He began to bind the sub roughly, slapping the jute hard on the floor, pulling and tugging on it as he tightly constricted her chest with his rope.

Brie trembled, imagining the feel of the forceful binding, and grabbed Sir's hand in response. He lightly trailed his finger over her skin, sexual energy flowing from him.

The feeling of eroticism between Tono and his partner definitely transferred to their audience, making it a shared experience for all. There was no doubt that Tono was on to something huge with this new kind of Kinbaku.

Brie's nipples ached as she watched the Asian Master possess the young woman with the jute. The act was raw in nature, but as always, Tono created beautiful art as he interwove the different colors, making simple designs that transformed into something unexpected and visually captivating.

He untied certain portions of rope as he went, turning the girl and binding her into new positions. Tono did it with such precision and speed that it became a slow dance as the young woman moved from graceful pose to graceful pose.

Brie was thoroughly entranced, admiring the strength of the sub as well as Tono's exceptional skill. It was easy to see how deeply she was under Tono's spell from the look of sensual bliss on her face. Brie could almost feel their connection—every touch, every slide of rope, every tug tingling on her own skin.

Tono gently touched his partner as he checked the knots again, his movements always in time with the song. Then he pushed her heel and the girl began to spin like a ballerina. Brie gasped, captivated by the pose.

"You like, *téa?*" Sir whispered.

"Yes, Master..."

His hand lightly brushed against her erect nipple, sending sensual shockwaves to her groin. "Feel my desire," he growled, biting her earlobe as he placed her hand on his hardening cock.

Brie moaned softly.

He placed her hand back in her lap and patted it, looking forward with a sexy smirk on his lips.

Such a wicked man.

Tono's light caresses and careful unbinding as he released the sub from the jute were every bit as arousing as when he was tying her up. When he was finished, he held the girl in his arms and spoke to her softly as he kissed her.

Brie always loved seeing aftercare between partners—it was so intimate and tender.

"Shall we leave Nosaka and tend to our own needs?" Sir suggested.

Brie purred in approval. "Please, Master."

Sir went over to the couple sitting on the mat and quietly thanked them both for the scene, not wanting to disturb their aftercare any more than necessary. As Brie walked out of the studio behind Sir, she turned back and stared at the pair, wondering if Chikako might be the one...

Sir paid the cab that had been waiting for them, and took Brie for a walk instead. They made their leisurely way down the quiet streets of the neighborhood. It was charming to hear the families gathered at their dinner tables, talking and laughing from open windows in the numerous apartments surrounding the studio.

The full moon was so bright that everything was visible, covered in its pale blue light. Brie tentatively took Sir's hand. He squeezed it and smiled down at her. "Who are you, téa?"

She looked deep into his eyes and stated proudly, "I'm a condor, Master."

He nodded, gently affirming, "Yes, we both are."

Sir took a detour when he saw a park set in the center of the apartment buildings. They walked down the wandering path, taking in the unique beauty of the foliage tinted by moonlight. The night had an almost fairyland quality to it.

Sir directed her to sit under a large cherry tree, the sweet scent of its blossoms drifting down from the branches. He told her to lie down in the grass, then his hands began their exploration of her, passing over her clothing first before seeking more intimate access underneath the thin material.

She smiled up at him, adoring how cute he looked framed by the blossoms of the tree above.

"You are more than a condor, téa," he said, leaning over her. Sir added in a whisper, "You're also my babygirl." Her heart melted when he bent down and kissed her in the silvery moonlight. Their hands sought each other out, rubbing, caressing and teasing each other. The sexual excitement left over from Tono's performance only added fuel to their raging fire.

When Sir covered her mouth and growled, "Come for me," Brie shuddered in orgasmic release, moaning into his hand.

Afterwards she begged, "Now let me please you, Master."

Sir lay down beside her and unzipped his pants, putting her hand onto his stiff cock. Brie rubbed it, then stuck her fingers underneath the material of his briefs. She stroked his shaft with a slow, tight grip, moving from base to tip, just the way he liked it. When his breath became ragged, she added a twist of her wrist to bring him over the edge.

Sir grabbed the back of her head, forcing her lips onto his cock. Brie gratefully swallowed his essence, but as she did so she heard voices in the distance.

Her lips released their hold on his shaft so Sir could zip his pants. Then they sat up and he gathered her into his arms, whispering sweet nothings in her ear as the old couple smiled at them while they slowly shuffled past.

Brie waved at them, sighing in contentment. It seemed like a dream, being here in Sir's arms—the man who was both lover and Master.

Could anything be more romantic?

The Kiss

Brie spent the morning giggling over Japanese television in their hotel room, while Sir met with potential clients. Her sides ached from laughing so hard at the practical jokes played on unsuspecting bystanders—it was pure silliness.

Suddenly, the screen changed as the local newscast broke in. Brie instantly recognized the private hospital and a cold chill ran down her spine when Master Nosaka's photo popped onto the screen with the dates of his birth—and death.

She picked up her cell and called Sir to inform him of the tragic news.

"Go to the hospital," Sir instructed. "Nosaka will need you now."

Brie jumped into a cab, handing the man extra money and begging him to hurry. The cabbie had to park far from the hospital as a barricade had already been set up. Brie pushed through the reporters, as well as Master Nosaka's many supporters, but she was stopped at the door by security.

She would not be denied and started screaming, "Tono! Tono Nosaka!" when she saw him through the glass doors. He turned at the sound of her voice, then nodded to a staff member beside him. The security guard did not open the door until he got verbal approval.

Tono looked at her with a sad smile when she walked up to him. "Brie…"

She buried her head in his chest as she wrapped her arms around him. He was stiff and unyielding, his whole body shaking with unreleased grief. She looked up into his sad, chocolate-brown eyes and whispered, "Breathe with me, Tono."

He let out a subtle but heartbreaking groan. Her cheeks became wet as she cried the tears he was unable to shed. Brie squeezed him tighter, making a point to breathe slowly and deeply. She sensed his initial resistance, but in time his breath slowed to match hers.

They stood in the middle of the bustling hospital, in tune with each other, but oblivious to everything else as his sorrow became hers and her strength became his.

Finally, Tono whispered, "He's gone."

Brie nodded, knowing how great his loss was. Not only had he just lost a parent, but his teacher and mentor. "I'm so sorry."

Tono shook his head, fighting to maintain composure. "I will not cry, not here."

She took his hand and squeezed it. "Let's go somewhere private."

He led her out of the hospital, trying to guide her through the crowd of reporters to get to his car. To Brie's surprise and gratitude, Master Nosaka's fans pushed back the journalists to make a safe path for his son.

Tono drove away in excruciating silence, his grief overwhelming her with its darkness and depth. Brie struggled to breathe slowly as she accepted the onslaught of his crushing emotions.

He took her to Shinjuku Gyoen, a beautiful city park filled with over a thousand blooming cherry trees and the soothing sound of moving water. He walked with long strides, oblivious to her desperate attempts to keep up with him. She followed as close as she could while he led her deep into the park. Tono stopped for a brief moment when he came to a bridge before crossing over it to a small island dominated by an ancient tree.

There he sat under its immense branches and began to sob as he stared at the water—a black hole of grief Brie could not hope to penetrate. She settled beside him and the two sat in collective sorrow.

Eventually, when the tears stopped, he spoke. "Thank you."

She looked at him questioningly. "For what?"

"For being here, for not asking questions or trying to comfort me with meaningless words."

"I can't begin to know your pain, but this garden," she said, looking around, "it is a good place to mourn, Tono."

He tilted his head back and rested it against the tree. "It doesn't seem real. A man of great strength and wisdom is gone, yet the day continues unaffected." He turned to look at her. "It is both tragic and reassuring to me."

Brie smiled sadly.

"To never hear his praise again, or his correction—I can't fathom it."

"Neither can I."

He looked at her with fresh tears in his eyes. "*Otosama* is dead."

The pain behind his statement crushed her. "But you're not alone,

Tono. I'm here with you."

His eyes reflected even deeper sorrow. "I wish that were true."

She squeezed his arm reassuringly. "It is! I'll always be here for you—both Sir and I will."

Tono looked deep into her eyes. It was the kind of gaze that was disconcerting because of its raw intensity.

"Brie, I…"

"What?" she urged when he stopped.

"I've kept something from you. Something I've been hesitant to share, even though it has been eating me alive."

"I *knew* you were hiding something. Please, Tono, I need to know."

He looked at her uncertainly, then nodded. "My father said something just before you arrived in Japan. Something that has tormented me ever since he mentioned it." He let out a long, drawn-out sigh, looking up towards the sky.

When Tono said nothing more, she encouraged him, "Whatever it is, I'm sure he never meant to hurt you. It's obvious that your father loved you very much."

He shook his head. "Brie, I've heard many words of criticism over the years, and have no problem receiving them from him."

"What is it, then?" she asked, suddenly concerned when she saw the look of agony in his eyes. What terrible secret had his father shared?

Tono groaned, hitting the back of his head against the tree and closing his eyes. "My father said he was sorry."

She was relieved to hear it, but couldn't fathom the reason for Tono's odd reaction. "Why would that make you upset? I don't understand."

He refused to look at her when he explained, "*Otosama* apologized for being wrong about you."

Brie's heart skipped a beat. She said nothing as the gravity of those words slowly sank in.

With eyes still closed, he told her, "As my father lay dying, he said it troubled him deeply knowing that he'd influenced your decision at the Collaring Ceremony."

The joy she felt that Tono's father had come to believe she was worthy of his son was tempered by the fact that it had changed the course of the evening—of both their lives.

Tono opened his eyes and turned his head towards her. "Thoughts spurred on by his confession have plagued me ever since, especially when my father admitted that you and I shared something he'd never known. He wished he hadn't taken that from me and begged for my forgiveness."

Brie stared ahead, reliving that night and his father's cold rejection of her. She asked quietly, "Did you give it to him, Tono? Your forgiveness?"

"Of course. It wasn't done maliciously."

Master Nosaka's rejection on graduation night had forced Brie to make a decision she hadn't been prepared to make. It had led her into the arms of Sir.

Tono stroked her cheek lightly. "If my father had said nothing, everything would be different, and that's what constantly haunts my thoughts now."

She closed her eyes, rocked by the revelation.

"Toriko…"

Brie opened her eyes when Tono's warm lips pressed against hers. She could feel his desperate need for connection—a connection that could release him from the pain and grief.

She instinctively pulled away and jumped to her feet. "No!" She ran from him, frightened by his emotional need as well as her desire to meet it.

"I'm sorry, Brie…" Tono called after her. "It was a mistake. There's no need to run from me."

She stumbled blindly out of the park, grabbing the first taxi she could find. Brie wrung her hands in the cab, wondering how she would explain it to Sir. Would he be understanding or angry, punishing Tono for this transgression?

In her heart, Brie understood the reason behind Tono's kiss. He was in agony and longed for the natural connection they shared to alleviate his suffering. The Asian Dom was a man of high principles, but in his raw grief he had given in to his human need.

She arrived at the hotel and anxiously waited for Sir's return. Rather than disturb him at his meeting, Brie undressed and knelt at the door. She contemplated how to break the news, praying she would be successful in swaying his reaction towards Tono.

Thankfully, all her worries were unfounded. When Sir opened the door and saw her, a slow smile spread across his face. "My beautiful pet."

He walked over and placed his hand on her head, stating quietly, "Stand and serve your Master."

She stood up gracefully, her eyes not leaving his. "Sir…"

He put his finger to her lips. "I know, Brie. Nosaka informed me what happened."

"It was an acci—"

He shook his head. "Although it was *not* an accident, I do believe it was a gut reaction to the death of his father." He brushed her cheek lightly. "I knew you would bring him comfort at this difficult time, but this was uncharacteristic of him. I noticed a similar breach of protocol when we scened together a few nights ago and he called you *toriko*. At the time, I had assumed it was a simple slip, him using his sub name for you, but now…" He rubbed his chin thoughtfully. "There is something else going on. I'm certain of it." Sir tilted her head up. "Did he tell you what that is?"

Brie met his gaze, although she was tempted to look away. She licked her lips nervously when she asked, "Did he share what his father said?"

"No."

"Master Nosaka told Tono that he regretted his influence during the Collaring Ceremony. He asked Tono to forgive him because he was wrong."

Sir took a deep intake of breath. "What a difficult confession for Nosaka to hear. No wonder he is reeling from it."

"You should also know that Tono apologized right after the kiss. He knew it was inappropriate, but I was so shocked by it that I just ran. My only thought was to come back to you and explain what had happened. I didn't want you to be angry with me—or with him."

"Brie," Sir said reassuringly, "there was no reason to worry. Nosaka is *not* Mr. Wallace." He played with a stray curl, smiling down at her. "Although we've been down this road before, you are not the same woman I first collared. You have learned much since then, and the truth is…I've grown as well."

She smiled as she laid her head against his chest. "I never want you to doubt my love, Sir. Never."

He answered her heartfelt declaration with a question. "I want an honest answer, Brie. Take time to think about it if you need before you speak."

She hugged him tighter. "Yes, Sir."

"How does this new admission make you feel towards Nosaka?"

She looked up at him shyly. "At first I was thrilled to know Tono's father had changed his opinion of me. His rejection hurt me deeply." She let out a long sigh. "But then I realized that if he *had* approved of me that night, I wouldn't be here with you now."

"And that makes you feel how?" Sir pressed.

Brie told him the simple truth. "The moment you put this collar around my neck," she lightly touched the silver collar, "my fate was sealed. I want no other, even though I still love Tono Nosaka."

Sir leaned down and brushed his lips against hers. "Good."

She smiled, crushing herself against his hard frame. He briefly returned her hug, but pulled away, stating, "Ren has lost his father today, and has compounded his suffering by embarrassing himself with us. I can't imagine his state of mind right now. Even though it will not be easy for him, I think it's best that we meet. In my eyes, what he's done is understandable, even though it broke protocol. I have no problem overlooking the incident, because he is not someone who will allow that to happen again."

Brie let out a sigh of relief. "I love being collared to such an exceptional man."

Sir chuckled lightly. "You make me nervous with the height of the pedestal you have me on, Brie."

She shook her head. "No, Sir, I have you set squarely on the ground. I realize you're human, but you are an incredible specimen of humanity—in many ways." She ran her hands over his chest and breathed in his masculine scent. "And I adore your modesty."

He lifted her chin, *tsking*. "Do not mock your Master, sub."

She grinned. "Never, Master."

He kissed her nose, stating, "Let's put Nosaka out of his misery."

The meeting with Tono at his mother's home was uncomfortable to begin with. It was obvious from his swollen eyes that Tono had been grieving, but one would never know it based on the serene expression on his face.

Sir held out his hand. "Ren, I want to express again our deepest sympathies for your loss."

Tono nodded stiffly as he shook it. "It was expected."

Sir put his other hand over Tono's and shook with more conviction. "Expected or not, it's still just as significant."

Tono grunted. "True. Knowing his death was imminent has not lessened the loss." He added sadly, "I'd hoped it would."

Brie noticed he was purposely avoiding looking in her direction.

Sir noticed it too. "Rather than dance around the elephant in the room, let me just say that I understand why you broke protocol. There is no reason for any tension between us."

"It was inexcusable," Tono replied, glancing briefly at Brie.

"No, Ren. It was unfortunate, but not inexcusable."

Tono turned to Brie, bowing before her formally. "I'm truly sorry, Miss Bennett."

"Such formality is unnecessary between friends," Sir said, patting Tono's back.

"Fine." Tono looked at her self-consciously and added, "I *am* sorry, Brie."

She smiled. "I accept your apology with a full heart, Tono Nosaka."

His mother interrupted their conversation, and refused to leave until

Tono excused himself to attend to her. Despite her husband's death, the woman seemed untouched, keeping the same tough exterior as before. However, Brie believed that under that shield of indifference, she must be secretly weeping. Mrs. Nosaka was alone now, and she still had plenty of years ahead.

When Tono returned, he told them, "I have many arrangements to make and must ask you to leave, but I have a favor to ask. Would you join me tonight? There will be a private wake. Before you agree, I must warn you that it will be an all-night affair."

"We would be honored," Sir answered.

"It will be a private ceremony. Later, my family will have an event for his many followers, but tonight my mother and I covet our privacy. Although she is uncomfortable with you being invited, she understands it is important to me and welcomes you to join us."

Brie bowed to him. "Thank you for including us, Tono. Please thank your mother as well."

"I'm grateful to have you with me." He looked at Sir and added, "Both of you."

Sir and Brie spent the day getting themselves prepared for the wake. First, Sir purchased the appropriate clothing, stating that black was the only acceptable attire. He purchased a suit of black, from his jacket and tie to his socks, as well as Brie's modest dress, simple hose and shoes.

Sir explained as he paid for them, "In a sense, we are acting as part of Tono's family. It is important that we fit in as seamlessly as possible."

"Agreed, Sir."

Next he took her to a tiny shop, and purchased a small white envelope with black-and-white ribbon as well as a box of colored pencils. She was curious and asked about the purchases, but Sir told her he would explain later.

When they arrived back at the hotel, he got the ice bucket and set it on the coffee table. Picking up a set of chopsticks, he commanded, "I want to you to practice picking up the pencils and putting them in the container."

She found the task odd, but carefully laid the set of pencils on the table and tried to pick them up with the chopsticks. It wasn't easy, and she dropped many of them in the process, but eventually she transferred all of them safely into the bucket.

He shook his head and stated, "Again."

She looked up at him, chagrined, but dutifully started the process again with only slightly better success.

"Brie, this is important. You must pick up each pencil and gently place it in the container. You cannot drop any of them. Continue with your practice until you are able to do so flawlessly, then summon me so that I may observe it."

He disappeared into the bedroom to use his laptop, leaving Brie to her odd assignment. She knew that this exercise had some bigger meaning, because Sir did not indulge in silly games. Everything he did had a purpose; *everything* he asked of her was important and must be mastered.

Sadly, it took hours before she was able to consistently get the pencils from the table to the bucket without mishap. She was bursting with pride when she finally went to him and announced, "I'm ready, Sir."

He looked up from his work and smiled. "Good. Impress me, baby-girl." He followed her out to the sitting room and watched with interest as she carefully picked up each pencil and deposited it in the container with care.

"Well done. Were the occasion less melancholy, I would reward you with a session. But given the circumstances, my words of praise must suffice, my dear."

She smiled shyly. "Your praise is always cherished, Sir. May I ask the reason for the task?"

"It will become evident should the need arise. I'm unsure how much we will be involved in the wake and funeral, but it is better to be fully prepared than woefully lacking." He looked at his watch. "It's time to dress. Put your hair up in a modest style, and only use minimal makeup."

They returned to the bedroom together in silence, the mood between them somber as they dressed for the wake. Brie wondered what it would be like and desperately hoped she could be a true comfort to Tono, rather than an unwanted distraction.

A Touching Farewell

They arrived at the Nosaka home just as the sun was setting. Before Brie exited the car, Sir handed her the white envelope, which he'd wrapped in black-and-white ribbon.

"What is this, Sir?"

"It's our *koden*, our condolence money. It's tradition at a wake. A tricky business, too, because giving too much signifies a closer relationship than you have with the deceased, but giving too little is seen as an insult."

"How did you know how much to give, Sir?"

He gave her a playful wink. "I googled it."

They stood behind a group of Tono's family members as they waited for the door to be answered. No one acknowledged them, making Brie extremely grateful when Tono was the one who opened the door. He greeted each person individually before inviting them inside. His calm demeanor and gentle voice belied the fact that his heart was breaking.

Tono's smile was genuine when he saw Brie, but he addressed his greeting to Sir. "Thank you both for joining me tonight."

"We owe you no less, Ren. It's a privilege to be included among your close relatives."

Tono led them to the room that held his father. The body had been packed in dry ice, and a white cloth covered his face. People were already seated on the floor, facing the body. Sir directed Brie to sit at the back, but Tono asked them to join him at the front. Brie knew it must be an unusual request, and was not surprised to hear a protest from his mother.

Tono answered his mother by pointing to Sir and stating simply, "*Ani*" and then gesturing to Brie and saying, "*Imouto*". His mother grunted under her breath, but nodded and put her hands together, bowing to them from where she sat.

"I told her you are like a brother and sister to me," Tono explained.

Brie smiled, and returned his mother's bow before sitting down beside Tono. Being so close to him, she was able to sync her breath to his, and the peace of that connection floated between them.

A Buddhist priest began chanting, and the smell of burning incense filled the room. Many of those in attendance were fingering prayer beads as he spoke. Eventually, the priest gave a signal and the family members closest to the body began to get up, one at a time, offering incense at an altar beside his father's body. When Tono's turn came, he stood up and nodded to Brie, indicating that he wanted her to do the same. Brie watched carefully as he knelt beside the altar, took a pinch of incense and brought it to his forehead before sprinkling it into the flaming bowl. He did this three times and bowed again before sitting back down beside her.

Brie got up and went to the altar, terrified of doing something wrong and offending his extended family in some way. She swallowed down that fear as she knelt gracefully and stared at the picture of Master Nosaka on the altar. While she remembered vividly how cold and hurtful those eyes could be, in this picture he was smiling slightly and his eyes shone with pride.

She took a pinch of the incense and sent a silent message to the man. *Thank you for raising Tono to be such an honorable person.* She sprinkled the incense into the flame and took another pinch. *Thank you for teaching him your skill of Kinbaku.* She let the incense burn and took a final pinch. *And thank you for finding me worthy of your son.* Tears pricked her eyes as she sprinkled the incense into the fire and watched it smoke. She stared at the still body beside her and said with silent conviction, *Although we cannot be together, I promise I will do everything in my power to support your son now and in the future.*

As she bowed one last time, Brie whispered, "Thank you for sharing your talent of singing, too. It is a charming side of you both I never suspected."

When she returned to Tono's side, Sir got up. She watched as he paid his respects. This quiet, reverent ceremony was beautiful in its simplicity. It allowed those who had known the deceased to reflect on memories of him in the safety and warmth of the place he'd called home.

When everyone had offered incense, the priest finished with more chanting. The ceremony ended once he was done, and most of the people in the room left at that time. Brie watched as Tono handed each person a small box before they walked out the door.

She whispered to Sir, "What's he doing?"

"He is giving a thank you gift to them."

An older woman touched Sir's sleeve and gestured that they should follow her. Sir guided Brie down the hallway and into a dining room with a low-lying table laden with food.

Just like in the States, food played a central part when people passed away. Those already seated at the table spoke in quiet tones as they waited for Tono to arrive. Brie discreetly took hold of Sir's hand under the table and squeezed it.

As soon as Tono entered, the level of conversation became livelier. Plates were passed out and people used chopsticks to help themselves to the feast. Brie looked dubiously at the food, realizing that most of what was on the table was seafood—something Brie could not stomach. How could she possibly navigate the meal without offending anyone?

Tono noticed her hesitation and offered several suggestions about what she would find appetizing. He winked, telling her, "As long as you do not put it on your plate, you are not expected to eat it."

She took a rice ball and a little of each food he'd suggested, and settled back to eat it, grateful for Sir's insistence that she practice her chopstick skills at the hotel. It allowed her to observe those at the table now without worrying about embarrassing herself.

Brie found it easy to pick out Master Nosaka's siblings. They all had similar features and the same stoic expression. Despite their serious demeanor, the discussions were animated and several times the entire table broke out in laughter. She desperately wished she knew Japanese so she could savor the stories they were sharing.

She glanced in Mrs. Nosaka's direction. The woman had a cross look on her face, but Brie noticed she was staring off into the distance, as if lost in old memories. If she would have welcomed it, Brie would have given her a hug.

Instead, Brie turned to Tono and asked, "How are you doing tonight?"

He gave a tired sigh. "Still in shock, unable to accept that he's really gone."

He looked thoroughly exhausted and emotionally beaten. "You should get some rest after the meal," she suggested.

Tono snorted, sounding insulted when he replied, "No, tonight we stay up and watch over my father."

Sir replied smoothly, "Of course, Nosaka. Brie was just expressing her concern for you."

Tono nodded in understanding and explained to her, "This is my last night with my father. I gladly give up rest."

After dinner, they went back into the room with his father. One woman was already there, standing beside the body, talking softly. The three of them sat down quietly, so as not to disturb her, with Brie and Sir sitting on either side of Tono.

The sound of the woman's voice was light, as if she was recalling happy memories, but near the end her voice became raw and anguished. Brie couldn't bear her pain and looked down as a tear fell into her lap. She glanced sideways at Tono.

He sat with a rigid back, his eyes focused on his father. Multiple people came to talk with Master Nosaka throughout the night, as if he were still alive, and Brie found it touching. However, Tono never moved; his gaze never wavered.

As dawn approached, the price of his vigilance made itself known when he tried to shake off the exhaustion. Brie got up and whispered to Sir, asking permission before she slipped her hand into Tono's, willing her energy to flow from her into him.

Tono closed his eyes, not outwardly acknowledging the contact, but he held on to her hand tightly. They remained that way until hours later, when his mother beckoned to him to speak with her outside the room.

His movements were stiff as he got up to leave. Tono returned a short time later with a small box in his hand. "Thank you for your company, Sir Davis, Miss Bennett. Please return to your hotel room and rest if you can. We'll meet again at noon. There are things I must take care of before the funeral." He handed Sir a card with directions and gave Brie the gift.

"Can I help in any way?" Sir asked.

"No. This is my honor and duty. Please rest." He bowed to them before leaving the room.

Brie was surprised when they arrived hours later and saw the funeral home swarmed by journalists. "Poor Tono! Why can't they leave his family alone?"

Sir said with a frustrated sigh, "It's unfortunate, but the intrusion must be endured." He opened the car door and held out his hand. "Come, Brie." They ignored the cameras and flurry of questions in English, as they sought to find Tono inside.

To Brie's relief, they found him with his father, whose body had been placed in a casket. She was surprised to see young children in the room. The smell of incense filled the air as the priest spoke and people paid their final respects, leaving flowers in the casket.

Afterwards, the casket was sealed and rolled away with silent reverence. "What's going on, Sir?" Brie whispered as people began filing out of the room.

"They're going to cremate Master Nosaka's body while we wait."

She glanced behind her, shuddering at the thought. It seemed so...final.

Tono joined them, smiling curtly at Brie. Was she the only one who saw the agony behind those chocolate-brown eyes?

"It's a shame the funeral was publicized," Sir told him.

"Yes, it has my mother in an unpleasant state. I reminded her that last night was undisturbed, but it seems to be of little comfort to her now."

The room he led them to was expansive, with plenty of seating and large amounts of food set out for the mourners, but eating was the last thing on Brie's mind. She thought she spotted Chikako across the room and asked Tono, "Is that your partner from the studio?"

"Yes," he answered. "Many people my father worked with are here to pay their respects today. They were like family to *Otosama*, so I invited them to attend the funeral despite my mother's objections. Funerals are meant for the living, not the dead."

"And who are the children?" Brie asked, as a tiny girl with pigtails walked past.

"Part of my father's side of the family."

"You have adorable relatives," Brie complimented, waving to the little girl, who giggled and waved back.

"Please partake of the food while I defuse the confrontation about to take place," Tono growled under his breath, heading towards his mother.

Brie wasn't interested in eating, so she watched the other people in the room, wondering what their stories were and what role they had played in Tono's life. One thing that struck her was the respect they all showed to Tono. It was gratifying to see.

After he'd neutralized the situation, Tono disappeared from the room.

"Brie, go after him," Sir commanded. "He's almost at his breaking point."

She hurried out to the hallway and followed it down until she found Tono leaning against a wall, his eyes closed—the pain he suffered rolling off him in tangible waves.

"Tono," she whispered as she approached.

He opened his eyes, shaking his head. "I'm not strong enough for this."

"Then you can lean on me today," she offered.

He laughed miserably. "Today I can handle. It's the countless days ahead I can't face."

Brie felt certain that once he was far from his mother, he would regain his peace. "How much longer do you plan on staying, Tono?"

"You don't understand, do you? As the only child, it is my duty to care for my mother."

"But you can't," Brie protested. "It will crush your spirit to remain here with her."

He closed his eyes again. "The moment I realized that my father was dying, I knew what lay ahead for me. This is *not* the life I wanted, but it is the one I must live out."

Tono smiled down at her sadly. "The only consolation I have is that by not collaring you, I did not make this your fate as well."

"Oh, Tono…"

He said with certainty, "It's better this way. I understand that now."

"But I don't want this for you!" Brie cried.

Tono took her forcefully by the shoulders. "What I *need* is your understanding and support."

Brie bit her lip and nodded. "You have my unwavering support, Tono. You always will."

"Good," he said, releasing his hold on her. "Then go back home and start on your new film. It would bring me joy to see your career grow. Make me proud, Brie."

Tears of love and gratitude ran down her cheeks as she hugged him. "I don't want to leave you."

"But you must."

He guided her back to the gathering in silence.

When they arrived, the attendant was directing people to a new room. Brie left Tono's side as he helped to escort his relatives out of the room. She made her way through the crowd to rejoin Sir.

"How did it go?" he asked.

She wiped away the remnants of her tears. "He's staying in Japan, Sir."

"I assumed he would." As they followed behind the large party, Sir told her, "Keep an open mind, Brie. The Japanese culture holds many meaningful rituals we're unfamiliar with in the West."

She thought he was talking about Tono's choice to stay, but realized he wasn't as soon as she entered the new room. She paused for a moment, taken aback.

Brie stared down at the white ashes of Tono's father, and tears came to her eyes.

"As acting members of Tono's family," Sir explained, "we will be helping to separate his bones from the ashes." A gold tray lay across the middle of the receptacle that held the ashes. On it sat a beautifully decorated urn, one Brie was certain Tono had painted himself.

As she watched, the family members began reverently picking up bone fragments with special chopsticks and placing them into the urn.

"Come, Brie," Sir commanded, handing her a set of the chopsticks. She steadied her hand as she stood beside Tono and helped in the ritual, silently thanking Sir for his earlier lesson.

Tono nodded his approval as she carefully deposited a piece of bone into the urn.

Everyone participated, even the children, as the family made sure Master Nosaka's remains were lovingly retrieved and put in the vessel. Afterwards, the lid was placed on the urn and handed to Tono.

His mother grabbed it from him and held it to her chest, her fingers turning white from her deathlike grip on it—the first outward sign of her grief.

Tono escorted his mother through the crush of reporters and took her to his car, but before he drove off he came back to Brie and Sir.

"I will never forget the honor you paid my father today."

"It was not only for him, Nosaka."

Tono bowed to Sir. "*Domo.*"

Brie was surprised when Tono suddenly embraced Sir. The two men hugged each other, both familiar with the grief of losing their fathers.

"May I?" Tono asked him afterwards, turning to Brie.

"Certainly, Ren."

Tono took Brie in his arms and held her tenderly for several moments before the obnoxious clicking of the cameras became too much. "Thank you," he whispered when he let her go.

Brie's eyes watered as Tono drove away. So much grief and hardship faced him in the weeks and months ahead.

"He'll be fine, Brie."

"I hope so, Sir."

"I guarantee it. In all my life, I've never met a stronger man."

Denver-Bound

Brie was emotionally and physically spent after the funeral, and collapsed on the hotel bed. But the gift Tono had given them at the wake caught her eye. She heeded its call and pulled herself off the bed to retrieve the white box.

Untying the jute binding, Brie smiled when she found a perfect white orchid inside. It had been painted in some kind of hard preserving material so that the flower remained looking as fresh as the day it'd been picked. The exquisite blossom was attached to a silver comb.

Sir took it from her and placed it in her hair. "It looks beautiful on you."

Brie lightly fingered the flower and smiled. "I'll wear it whenever I film."

"An excellent plan. Although I have a few more days left here, I think it would be best for you to return to the States to begin your documentary."

"But Sir…"

He shook his head. "You have done all you can for Nosaka. It's time to honor his request."

"But we didn't get to say goodbye," she whimpered.

"Yesterday was his farewell, Brie."

Her heart sank when she realized Sir was right.

"Return to the US and write him letters sharing details about your filming. *That* is how you will help to support Nosaka through this."

She understood, but her heart was breaking just the same.

Sir chuckled kindly, caressing her cheek. "Every emotion plays out on your face. I love that about you, téa." He kissed her on the lips slowly, tenderly.

Brie gave in to the magic of his touch as he carefully took out the comb and laid it on the table.

"Let me make love to you before we say goodbye," he said, pushing her gently onto the bed. "Death has a way of helping you to appreciate what you have."

She closed her eyes as he undid the buttons on her blouse and moved the material aside to stare at her chest. He kissed the round swell of her breast before returning to her lips.

"Right now, all that exists is you, me and this moment in time."

She opened her eyes and nodded, lifting her lips to meet his.

Sir's lovemaking was unusually gentle and sweet. Light, lingering kisses and soft, teasing caresses carried her to heavenly release...

Later that night, he printed out her plane tickets and handed them over to her. "In just a few hours, you'll be Denver-bound."

Denver? She looked down at her ticket to confirm she'd heard him correctly.

"I think a trip to Master Anderson's new Training Center will prove quite helpful for your new film."

"Oh, my gosh, I'll get to see Lea!"

Sir smiled. "I can just imagine the giggles now."

Brie threw her arms around him. "Thank you, Sir. This is exactly what I needed!"

He chuckled warmly, returning her embrace. "I'll join you when I'm done here. I'm curious myself to see how their new Center is faring." Brie wondered if Sir wanted to personally check up on Ms. Clark, as well.

"I'll get to see Baron, too! Maybe even do a little sightseeing while I'm there," she squealed.

"Take it all in, Brie," he encouraged, lightly grazing her lips with his finger.

"Does anyone know I'm coming?"

He said with a smirk, "Only Brad."

"Eek! I can't wait to see the look on Lea's face when I show up."

"Yes, I believe Anderson has a little something planned for your reunion with her. I look forward to hearing about it."

Brie grinned at her tickets, before attacking Sir with a flurry of kisses.

Ready or not, Denver, here I come...

Brie's Denver Desire

A Slave's Dream

She had been called to join Master Anderson in room eighteen. Although it was highly unusual to meet after school hours, Sir had assured her the lesson was essential if she wanted to graduate from the Center.

Brie had been working hard for nearly six weeks—*nothing* was going to stand in the way of her making it to Graduation Night. She hurried through the familiar hallways, awkwardly sprinting in her six-inch heels to make it to her class on time.

She opened the door and froze for a second. Master Anderson was tightly gripping the bullwhip in his hand. She'd already felt its bite at The Haven and didn't want to relive the experience.

"Come in, young Brie."

She walked hesitantly over the threshold and took off her blouse and bra with shaking fingers. She knelt down, putting her hands behind her back in the position Sir had instructed she take upon entering a room with a trainer.

Her heart rate shot up as she listened to his boots echoing in the large room as he approached. Master Anderson put his hand on her head and stated in a sultry voice, "Stand and serve me well, slave."

Her stomach did a flip-flop when he called her 'slave'. She gracefully rocked off her heels and stood before him. "It would be my honor, Master Anderson."

"You will call me only Master tonight."

She bowed her head in acknowledgement of his command, but her heart fluttered. Calling him Master had a completely different feel to it, especially since she was to be his slave for the session.

"Master, what is the focus of tonight's lesson?"

"We are going to test your willingness to please in the face of challenge."

Brie sucked in her breath. This did not sound as if it was going to be an easy lesson—a part of her wanted to bolt from the room, but she'd come too far to give up now.

"Challenge me, Master," she stated confidently.

"Stand on the X to receive my pleasure."

Brie shivered as she made her way to the brightly painted red X on the floor. The skin on her back tingled in anticipation, knowing the sensations she was about to experience.

"Hands up, slave."

She lifted her arms and he secured her trembling wrists in the leather cuffs attached to overhanging chains. The clinking sound of the metal announced that there was no escape for her.

Brie heard the door open as another set of footsteps announced someone else had entered the room. She felt a commanding presence behind her, then a familiar deep, baritone voice asked, "Is she ready for me?"

Her breath caught and that old feeling of fear mixed with expectation washed over her. *Was* she ready for Baron?

"Undress her," Master Anderson stated.

Brie felt the dark Dom's strong hands caress her small waist before he unzipped her skirt and let it fall to the floor. She held her breath when his lips landed on her neck as he slipped off her lace panties.

Once she was naked, he wrapped his strong hands around her hip bones and pressed his hardening cock against her. "You will be well used tonight, kitten."

Brie let out a ragged gasp when Baron bit down on her neck before releasing her.

She swayed in the chains, unsure whether she could handle the lesson the two Doms had planned for her. Baron moved her long hair forward so it swished against her erect nipples, while he whispered in her ear, "I must make the path clear...."

Brie shivered when he moved away, knowing her skin would soon feel the fiery bite of Master Anderson's bullwhip. Without meaning to, she whimpered.

"Are you scared, slave?" Master Anderson asked.

It would be foolish to lie to her trainer, so she answered clearly, "I am, Master."

She heard him warm up as he cracked the whip behind her. She unintentionally stiffened in response to the intimidating sound. "Relax..." he encouraged just as the whip flicked across her back, licking her skin with its light caress.

Brie had forgotten how sweet the bullwhip could be and purred in pleasure, closing her eyes to take in the gentle strokes applied by Master Anderson's skillful hand. After several minutes of light play he stopped, and Baron approached again, gliding his fingers over her womanly curves, concentrating his efforts on her sensitive breasts.

"Your body begs to be played with." Baron rolled her nipples between his fingers, causing her to moan as waves of heat traveled down to her loins. She squirmed on the red X, the chains clinking with every slight movement.

Baron shifted around to face her. He lifted Brie's chin and kissed her with those delicious full lips. She groaned this time, her pussy already wet, preparing itself for the impending coupling.

His sensual lips slowly traveled from her mouth to her chin, farther down her throat until they landed on her left nipple. He suckled it, sending ripples of pleasure through her.

Brie moaned when she felt Master Anderson come up behind, his need obvious as his cock settled between her butt cheeks. "Slave, you will take my challenging strokes, then you will service both your Doms."

"At the same time, Master?" she asked breathlessly as Baron continued to consume her with his hungry kisses.

"Naturally, slave."

Brie's knees buckled when she heard his answer for she knew how well-endowed Master Anderson was.

He chuckled as he slipped his hand between her legs and pressed his fingers against her mound as he lifted her back to her feet. "You can feign resistance, but this pussy tells me otherwise."

Swirling his fingers over her wet clit, Master Anderson then slowly pressed three of them against her opening. With his massive cock still wedged between the cheeks of her ass, he commanded, "Push against my fingers. Force them inside you."

Brie moaned with desire as she strove to obey his command. Baron switched to her other nipple as she leaned harder on Master Anderson's hand, the width of all three fingers stretching her inner lips.

"Good slave. Show your Master how desperate you are to be fucked by two men."

She started to grind against him, begging, "Your slave *needs* to be used for pleasure, Master."

He slowly thrust his fingers while Baron ravished her breasts with his talented mouth. The aggressive attention of both men was incredibly hot and had her pussy aching with need.

Without warning, the two pulled away. She cried out, desperate for their continued caresses.

"Ready yourself, slave," Master Anderson stated, snapping the bull-whip. "The next cry you make will come because of my lash."

Her burning need for them overcame her fear of the whip and she dutifully steeled herself for his onslaught. She shifted in the chains, forcing her muscles to relax.

"Isn't she beautiful like this?" Master Anderson asked Baron. "Totally helpless and afraid, yet completely willing."

"Yes—as stunning as she is bound, it's her enthusiasm for what is about to come that makes my cock ache for her."

Brie smiled, coveting the praise of both Doms.

"Open your legs wider," Master Anderson commanded.

Brie spread her legs farther, which forced her to tiptoe to keep that position. She could only imagine the erotic pose it presented to the men. Although it was challenging, it made her that much more focused and attentive.

"This will bite, slave," Master Anderson warned her as the first stroke exploded across her skin. Brie held her cry to a whimper as she swayed from the impact. The burning sensation radiated over her entire back. The second lash was just as intense, taking her breath away. She concentrated on the fire, not resisting its burn.

Master Anderson took his time, pausing between pairings. The third and fourth lashes challenged her, but by the fifth she'd started to fly.

She squeaked when she felt Baron's warm tongue licking her moist sex below. He shouldn't be there with Master Anderson still whipping her back, and she looked down in surprise, moaning when he grabbed her buttocks, burying his face in her mound.

Brie relaxed and allowed his tongue to possess her, assuming the bullwhip session had ended. She screamed out in unexpected ecstasy when another slash across her skin caused a fiery burst that rushed straight to her groin.

The next stroke of Master Anderson's whip brought on an orgasm that Baron rode with his tongue. Brie cried as reality blurred, mingling with the dual sensations. She was finally experiencing that elusive state she'd longed for—floating between the balance of passion and exquisite pain.

When they eventually stopped, Baron moved her legs together so she could stand comfortably, but she hung from the chains, her whole body weak from their intense play.

Master Anderson's rough hands caressed her sweaty shoulders, then he lightly traced the welts he had created on her back. Gently wiping the tears from Brie's face, he murmured his comfort and praise. When his lips landed firmly on hers, the demanding kiss awakened her inner animal. She growled, her tongue becoming aggressive as she explored Master Anderson's mouth.

He grabbed her head with both hands and kissed her harder, inciting a greater need to be satisfied. Brie's mind swirled with insatiable desire and she bit his bottom lip when he tried to pull away. Master Anderson slapped her ass hard, chuckling as he slowly unbuckled her wrists from the cuffs. She collapsed into Baron's waiting arms and was carried to a bed on the other side of the room.

Baron laid her down carefully, then proceeded to undress before her. His glistening dark skin, rigid shaft and masculine scent called to her and she reached out to him. "I need you."

His response was to flash a mischievous smile. "Not yet, kitten."

Brie glanced over and saw Master Anderson cleaning his whip. Her pussy contracted when he looked in her direction. The lust in those green eyes captivated her. She stared into them like a frightened deer that knew it was about to be devoured—and oh, how she wanted to be devoured by him.

As he walked towards her, Master Anderson stripped off his shirt then unlatched his belt, dropping it to the floor. By the time he reached the edge of the bed, he'd already unzipped his pants to reveal his massive shaft. "Now that we have you loosened up, we will show you no mercy, slave."

"No mercy," she agreed, licking her lips in anticipation.

Brie's breath came in quick gasps as she watched the men lubricate their cocks. Baron's shaft was dark, handsome and thick, while Master Anderson's was ruddy, and branchlike in its length and circumference—a challenging cock for any woman. To take both seemed impossible for her small frame.

Master Anderson wiped his hands before joining her on the bed. He lay on his back and commanded lustfully, "Force my cock inside you, slave."

Brie was slow to straddle him, still a bit shaky from her sub-high. She raised herself over his impressive shaft and, with his support, lowered herself onto it. Initially her body resisted his girth. She bit her lip as she pressed against the head of his enormous shaft, refusing to fail this lesson. Her pussy lips stretched out achingly as his manhood finally slid into her.

Brie gasped as Master Anderson's manhood filled her, but she smiled triumphantly at him once she'd settled fully onto it. He gripped her waist and lifted her up, letting her slowly descend back down. She continued the slow dance, enthralled by the fire it created between them.

"Are you ready for me?" Baron said in a slow drawl, stroking his shaft as he watched.

For the first time Brie felt a twinge of fear, but the thought of pushing her body to the ultimate limit was actually exciting for her. She moaned when she felt the bed shift as Baron made his way to her.

Caressing her ass, he commented, "I've never had the opportunity to enjoy this part of you." Baron gently coated her tight hole with extra lubricant and began to massage her rosette, slowly pushing his finger inside her. She closed her eyes, her whole body tingling at the thought of his thick shaft claiming her.

"Slave."

Brie opened her eyes and stared into Master Anderson's intense, jade-colored ones. His lustful need demanded she satiate it.

"Hold yourself open for him."

She obediently lay her torso on Master Anderson's broad chest and put her arms behind her, spreading herself open for Baron. It added an element of exposure and vulnerability.

"Kitten…" Baron growled as he pressed his cock against her resistant opening. She expected he would force himself in, but he seemed to be waiting.

Brie looked back questioningly.

"That's it, kitten, look at me."

Brie whimpered as the roundness of his thick head pressed hard against her. Taking his full circumference seemed unachievable, but after several minutes of gentle thrusts, her taut muscles relaxed enough to draw him inside.

Both men groaned.

She started to pant heavily as Baron rocked his shaft deeper into her. Master Anderson told her to prop herself up on his chest so he could play with her breasts. As soon as his hands began to tug and pull on her nipples, her body's resistance eased, allowing the manly invasion.

Master Anderson grabbed her buttocks while Baron wrapped his hands around her waist and both men began to thrust at the same time. Brie cried out, her whole body shuddering from the deep ache it caused. It took everything in her to accept the movement of both shafts, but she willingly gave herself to the sensation, begging them to take her deeper.

"Slave," Master Anderson called as she started to fly from their dual attention. She resisted his call, wanting to get lost in the feeling of complete surrender. "Slave," he insisted.

Brie reluctantly opened her eyes, looking at him in confusion when he instructed, "Return your seats to an upright position and keep your seatbelts fastened until we are parked safely at the gate."

Brie woke with a start, and found herself gazing into the questioning eyes of her seatmate on the plane.

"Good dream?" the middle-aged woman asked with obvious amusement.

Mistress Isa

Brie smiled self-consciously as she stared out the airplane window at the snow-capped mountains while the plane slowly pulled up to the gate. She'd always pictured Denver being closer to the Rocky Mountains, but that didn't seem to be the case at all. It was more like a sprawling city on the flat plains, with the mountains acting as a magnificent backdrop.

She would have been disappointed, but the fact that Lea lived here made Denver a magical place. Brie longed to see the look on her best friend's face when she surprised her. Sir had mentioned that Master Anderson had something special in mind for their initial meeting. Brie couldn't begin to guess what it might be, however she trusted it would prove entertaining.

Master Anderson was the kind of Dom who could make you laugh one instant and bring you to your knees the next.

When the plane came to a complete stop, Brie pulled her cell phone from her purse and texted him, a hint of a blush coloring her cheeks as she thought back on her dream.

I'm here!

She glanced nervously at her phone when she exited the airport train. Master Anderson had yet to respond to her text and Sir hadn't given her any instructions other than to meet the Dom once she landed. She had no idea where Master Anderson might be and wasn't allowed to call Lea to find out.

Brie headed up the escalator to the main terminal and looked around anxiously. There was a crowd of people waiting to greet loved ones coming off the train. Out of curiosity, she scanned the signs the limo drivers held up and was surprised to see the name "Young Brie". Her eyes trailed from the sign to the face of the man holding it. She grinned when she saw

Master Anderson, who happened to be looking damn sexy in the cowboy hat he was wearing.

She ran up to him, giggling when he lifted her into the air and twirled her around. When he set her back on the ground, he tipped his hat. "Good to see you again, young Brie."

Brie gazed at him bashfully, taken in by his leather boots, tight jeans and plaid shirt unbuttoned just enough to show off his muscular chest. "I never suspected you were a cowboy, Mast—Mr. Anderson."

He winked at her. "Grew up in Greely but outgrew my cowboy ways by college. Now I only dress this way to welcome friends to the Mile High City." He leaned down. "I've noticed it seems to fluster women, and if my eyes don't deceive me, I do believe there's a rosy blush on those cheeks."

Brie looked away, turning a deeper shade of red as images of her naughty dream resurfaced. Master Anderson had no idea…

"Come with me," he said, holding out his elbow. She smiled as she took his arm, quite aware of the slew of women openly ogling him as they made their way to the baggage claim area. She snuck a glance at him as they waited for her luggage to arrive. Yep, her old trainer looked quite devastating in that black cowboy hat.

To avoid further wicked thoughts, she asked him, "Did you learn your skills with the bullwhip as a little boy in Greely, then?"

When he grinned down at her, Brie heard a woman beside her murmur to herself, "Yum…" It made Brie giggle. Master Anderson was quite the charmer.

"Yes, I played around with it while my father was off herding cattle. Rather humorous and painful sessions, as I recall. I was small and couldn't handle the whip's length. Even then, however, it felt like an extension of myself—my calling, so to speak."

Brie blushed again, remembering her session with him at The Haven. "I agree that it's your calling, Mr. Anderson. You are very skil—"

"Pardon me," the woman behind her interrupted. She twirled her bleached blonde hair in a flirtatious manner when she asked, "Are you a famous bull rider or something?"

Master Anderson laughed. "I am not."

"So no chance I'll be seeing you at the State Fair this year?"

"No, my time is taken up wrangling young heifers with my whip."

"Oooh…" the young woman squealed. "I like the sound of that. Maybe I can watch you sometime?"

Master Anderson tipped his hat before grabbing Brie's luggage from the carousel. "I believe my style of wrangling would alarm you, miss. Better you chase those bull riders at the rodeo."

She pouted as Master Anderson guided Brie out of the airport.

Once they left the building and were safe from being overheard, Brie admitted, "I fully expected you to invite her to your new training center."

He raised his eyebrow. "That young woman? She's not submissive material."

"Really? How can you tell?"

"There's a gut feeling whenever I interact with women." Master Anderson threw her luggage into the back of his Chevy truck and opened the door for her. "Plus the fact she interrupted you to flirt with me. Submissives tend not to be overly aggressive—and most have much better manners."

It turned out the drive to his new training center was a long one, since the airport was east of the city and Master Anderson's training center was southwest of it, nestled against the foothills. While he navigated through heavy traffic, Master Anderson explained his elaborate plan to surprise Lea—but it wasn't just her best friend his little stunt would involve.

Brie protested after he'd finished explaining it to her, "Ms. Clark is going to hate me even more than she already does."

"For your information, Samantha is far less uptight these days."

Master Anderson added curtly, "Besides, your Master told you to obey me in this. Regardless of the consequences, I expect full cooperation from you."

The Dom had effectively put her in her place, and she bowed her head. "Yes, Master Anderson."

He chuckled to himself, "Oh, young Brie, the fun I have planned this week..." His obvious mirth delighted Brie. Truly, pleasing him would be worth the wrath of the infamous Ms. Clark.

Brie was excited as the magnificent peaks loomed ever closer on their drive, but he surprised her by not going straight to his training center. Instead Master Anderson took her to an upscale community in the mountainous valley just west of the city. It looked like an exclusive neighborhood—the kind that comprised the elite of Denver society.

He pulled into a long driveway that led up to a ranch-style home. The natural color of the house blended well with the environment around it. It was unique in its rustic style compared to the fancier homes in the area.

He sighed deeply as he stared at his house. "I had to give up my old Victorian in town. After purchasing the building for my Academy, I found the daily commute unbearable. Fortunately, by giving up the historical charm of my old place, I no longer have to fight traffic and I now get to enjoy this fantastic view."

Brie got out of the car and admired the scenic foothills surrounding them. He was right, the view was truly impressive. She took in a deep breath and swore the mountain air seemed lighter, more vibrant. "I can definitely see why you like it here."

"Glad you approve."

Master Anderson proudly escorted her into his home. It turned out to be equally impressive. The main room had tall ceilings and large windows showcasing his immaculate backyard. Before she had a chance to take it all in, he pointed to the first door on the right. "You'll find your outfit on the bed."

Brie was curious what he had picked out, and laughed out loud when she saw her costume. She called from the bedroom, "You can't be serious."

His deep voice answered, "I'm quite serious."

After donning the long-sleeved tunic with an oversized hood, she looked in the mirror and shook her head. "I look like Obi-Wan Kenobi."

Brie walked out of the room and sat down on a leather couch, waiting for Master Anderson to join her. To the left was a well-equipped kitchen, with even more gadgets and doodads than his home in California.

The great room sported a massive stone fireplace. Instead of family photos decorating his mantel, there was a kayak mounted high on the wall, complete with two wooden oars.

Her eyes were drawn to the greenery of the backyard just beyond. It had a large fence lined with young trees and bushes. Most notable, however, was the wooden pole in the center. Brie knew it was used for bullwhip practice and wondered what his new neighbors thought about the oddly placed post.

Master Anderson came out a short time later, looking refined and businesslike in a tailored gray suit.

"Why the change of dress?" Brie asked, standing as he entered the room.

"A very important person from the Orient is coming to the Academy of Denver today. Naturally I would dress up for such a prestigious individual."

"I can't believe you are making me do this," she groaned.

He grabbed her chin. "One hundred percent commitment, young Brie. When you walk in, I want them to feel your dominance. No...make it arrogance. You *are* Mistress Isa, highly respected Dominatrix from China."

In response to his command, she removed his hand from her wrist and lifted her chin defiantly. "Do not touch me—I am your equal."

He smiled but corrected her. "No, my dear, you are my superior. I cannot equal your expertise, which is why you have been invited to join us at the Academy."

She sighed nervously; this was so far out of her comfort zone.

"No more sighs, Mistress Isa."

"No more sighs," she agreed.

As Brie got up, she began to mentally embrace her role. She strode past Master Anderson with an air of supremacy as she left the house. She waited beside the truck, going over in her mind the persona she was taking on.

She was a Mistress from China, renowned for her use of acupuncture during BDSM play. Having an adventurous spirit and a natural curiosity about American culture, she'd come to Colorado at the invitation of Master Anderson. She was not intimidated by others because she knew her skills were unparalleled. Doms and subs alike showed her the respect she was due. Her odd tunic had a purpose. It hid her identity until she was ready to reveal it—it left her in control.

As Brie belted herself in, she noted how incongruous Master Anderson looked in a business suit, driving his huge truck. "Master Anderson, if you don't consider yourself a cowboy, why do you drive this vehicle?"

He smirked. "No matter how much I deny it, you can't take the cowboy out of the man."

He drove her fifteen minutes away, to a large building that looked like a giant warehouse. It was not at all what she had been expecting.

"This is your training center?"

"This is the Academy of Denver," he answered.

"It's so…huge."

"I will have you know a converted home improvement depot is *the* ideal training facility, especially for the practice of bullwhips. High ceilings and large open spaces make the optimal environment. The vast warehouse also leaves plenty of room for future expansion."

"I see, Master Anderson. I meant no offense."

"None taken, young Brie." His eyes sparkled with a mischievous glint. "Now let's have a little fun with my staff."

Brie's heart raced at the thought of seeing Lea again, but she needed to maintain an outer countenance of calm. Master Anderson leaned over and placed the hood over her head so her face was obscured by the ample amount of material. "They'll never see this coming…"

He walked her into the facility, where they were greeted by the receptionist, who struck Brie as both professional and assertive in her sharp business suit.

"Hello, Mistress Isa. It is an honor to meet you."

Brie just nodded in response, as Master Anderson had instructed her to.

"Is all the staff present, Lisa?" Master Anderson asked.

"Yes, Master Anderson. They are waiting for you in the conference room."

"Fine. Oh, and call Adam at the Masters at Arms Club. Let him know I'd like to talk to him about an upcoming charity event."

"Certainly, Master Anderson. What time works best for you to meet?"

"Better make it next week. I want to set time aside so I can introduce Mistress Isa to the many charms of Denver."

"Wonderful." Lisa addressed Brie again. "I hope you will find our city to your liking, Mistress Isa."

Brie gave the slightest of nods and turned from her. It grated on her nerves not to respond with a bow and a thank you, but she was determined to maintain the mystery and poise of Mistress Isa.

Master Anderson explained as they walked, "I want you to wait near the doorway until I come out to get you."

"Naturally I would not enter a room unescorted," she answered, with a coy smile he could not see.

"Nice," he complimented. "That's the attitude I was hoping for."

Master Anderson left her then, joining his staff. The first voice she heard was that of Ms. Clark.

"Is she here? Why didn't you show her in?"

"Calm yourself, Samantha. I wanted to talk to you all first."

"Pardon me," she answered curtly, "but I've been looking forward to meeting Mistress Isa and hate to think of her waiting unnecessarily." Ms. Clark added with just a hint of fangirling in her voice, "To add various stimuli only acupuncture can provide during a scene... I've never had that kind of power. The possibilities are endless."

"I expect her expertise will give our training facility an edge over others in the area. Therefore I've decided to make major changes to the current team."

"What kind of changes?" Ms. Clark asked, suddenly sounding alarmed.

"While some of you may struggle with my decision, keep in mind we are extremely fortunate that Mistress Isa has agreed to join the Academy."

Brie giggled softly to herself.

Baron's rich voice filled the room. "I'm sure I'll be fine with whatever you've decided."

"Agreed!" Lea piped up.

Brie had to hold in the squeal of joy that threatened to escape her lips when she heard Lea's voice.

"Because she has such extensive knowledge and expertise in many areas, I've asked her to lead the Academy. Think of me as more of an overseer for the training facility."

"You're making her Headmistress of the school?" Ms. Clark asked in disbelief.

"Precisely. She will run the program while I run the business side of things."

"But—"

Baron interrupted. "If Master Anderson is confident she will lead us well, I have no issue with the change in leadership."

"But..." Ms. Clark stammered, "We haven't even met her yet. Being Headmistress is so much more than being an expert at training submissives."

"I understand that, Samantha, and I'm telling you that she is the one I want running the Academy."

Lea spoke up. "Will she have authority over the submissive staff as well, Master Anderson?"

"Yes."

"Like Baron, I trust your judgment and look forward to serving under her," Lea replied amiably.

Ms. Clark was forthright in her response to Master Anderson's announcement. "While I'm humbled to have such a talented Dominatrix included in our organization, I'm a little stunned you're giving up your Headmaster position."

"Mistress Isa is *that* good," Master Anderson assured her.

"Having two Doms and two Dommes on the panel should prove interesting," Baron stated, sounding either intrigued or amused by the thought—Brie couldn't tell which.

"I do understand your concerns, Samantha," Master Anderson said, "so let me be equally frank. Do you think you can work under another woman?"

Ms. Clark took a moment to answer. "Although I do not care for the leadership of other women, Mistress Isa's unique talent and your confidence in her have weight with me. I will find a way to make it work."

"Very good, but a word to the wise—she will not speak or reveal herself unless she finds you worthy. First impressions matter greatly to her."

"I feel as if I'm about to meet royalty," Lea giggled.

Brie heard Master Anderson's footsteps heading towards the door. He stopped midway and stated, "Oh, and another thing—she cannot tolerate others staring her in the eye—especially women." Brie had to cover her mouth to keep from laughing.

A feeling of lightheadedness hit her when Master Anderson emerged from the room to retrieve her. What she was about to do was absolutely crazy!

"Are you ready, Mistress Isa?" he asked with a smirk.

Brie's eagerness to see Lea overcame her misgivings, and she nodded under the massive hood.

"Good." He leaned down and whispered, "Tease them a little before you reveal yourself."

Brie walked into the room, feeling their eyes on her as she glided across the floor to stand before them. *I am your Mistress*, she thought to herself.

"Mistress Isa, this is my staff. To the right is Baron. He is my right-hand man, so to speak."

"It is a pleasure to meet you, Mistress Isa," Baron replied, his voice drawing her in with its deep, rich tone. Brie nodded once.

"Ms. Clark is seated next to him. She was a part of the training staff at the Submissive Training Center in California for many years and has graciously agreed to act as such for my facility."

Brie peeked up to see whether Ms. Clark was looking at her. To her delight, the trainer held her gaze down when she spoke. "We are grateful to have you join us, Mistress Isa."

Brie took a longer time to nod—just to make Ms. Clark sweat a little.

"Lastly, I have Ms. Taylor. She is the leader of the submissives who will be helping to train Dominants. Our staff is small at this point, but we have plans to expand as the program grows."

Lea got up and moved over to Brie, giving her a proper bow. "Your reputation precedes you, Mistress Isa. Welcome."

Brie grinned as she placed her hand on Lea's head. There was no fear that Lea would look up and notice who really was under the hood, because her friend was a well-trained submissive. When Brie took her hand away, Lea kept her eyes to the floor as she gracefully returned to her seat.

Brie suddenly got a wild hair up her ass and pointed towards Ms. Clark.

It was clear by the silence that followed that the Domme had no idea what to say or do.

Master Anderson encouraged her, "Mistress Isa would like you to speak."

"Certainly…" Ms. Clark replied, pausing as she tried to figure out what Brie wanted. To have that kind of power over someone else was danger-ously exhilarating.

"Well, as Master Anderson mentioned, I was a trainer at the Submissive Training Center. I'd like to note that I was the first woman on the panel and my influence led the Dominant training team at the Center to add a woman to their staff as well."

Brie shrugged as if that meant nothing to her, but she knew she would pay a heavy price for putting Ms. Clark in this position despite the fact Master Anderson put her up to it.

Ms. Clark forged onward. "I enjoy working with both male and female submissives and have spent time under a Dominatrix to expand my knowledge."

Brie said nothing, but waved her hand, gesturing that she wanted to hear more.

It was obvious by the slight timbre of her voice that Ms. Clark was flustered. "I look forward to learning your expertise in acupuncture as well. The idea of using Eastern knowledge to enhance BDSM play fascinates me."

"As it should," Brie said in a deep, alluring voice.

"I trust you will impart the techniques you employ to the staff," Ms. Clark added hopefully.

"No."

Ms. Clark gasped softly but said nothing.

Brie was *so* going to pay for this little ruse, but she couldn't help herself. She prayed Master Anderson would protect her from Ms. Clark's justified wrath. She turned to face Baron, still keeping her voice low. "However, you I will teach."

Ms. Clark looked up, an expression of disbelief on her face. The room was uncomfortably silent but Brie could feel Master Anderson's amusement radiating from the man. Brie hoped he would earn Ms. Clark's caning—not she.

Baron replied, "Surely, Mistress Isa, it would be best if the entire staff were familiar with your skills."

"I agree," Master Anderson stated. "Mistress Isa, would you consider demonstrating them on our sub, Ms. Taylor, right now?"

Brie paused, pretending to ponder his request. She knew Lea didn't care for needles, and giggled to herself when she saw her friend twitch in her seat. Master Anderson was delightfully evil on so many levels, but she had something even better in mind.

"Come," she commanded, gesturing to Ms. Clark instead.

From under the hood she watched the trainer's stunned face. Ms. Clark looked to Master Anderson.

He walked over to her and Brie could hear him whisper in the trainer's ear, "This is a good sign, Samantha. She approves of you."

Ms. Clark didn't hesitate. She stood and walked over to Brie. "Please enlighten us, Mistress Isa."

Brie nodded. "As you wish…"

She threw back her hood and grinned at everyone.

Ms. Clark stared at her in shock, as Lea jumped up from her seat and ran over with her arms outstretched.

"It's my Brie!"

Bad Joke

The two girls hugged as Baron slowly clapped his hands. "Well played."
Lea squeezed Brie tight, smothering her with her large bosom.
"Oh, my gosh, I can't believe you're really here!"

Brie giggled, disengaging herself in order to catch her breath. "Here in the flesh, girlfriend!"

"Miss Bennett."

"Master Anderson made me do it," Brie blurted, fully expecting to face Ms. Clark's harsh glare, but instead she swore there was a twinkle in the Domme's eyes. It threw her off and she smiled tentatively at the trainer.

Ms. Clark turned to Master Anderson. "I need to stop trusting you. Naturally, I had my doubts when you said Mistress Isa was coming to join the Academy, so I researched her online and found a whole website devoted to the Dominatrix. Based on that, I had to assume she was an actual person."

Master Anderson grinned like a naughty schoolboy. "I did have fun setting that little baby up. Gratifying to know you actually visited the site."

"As did I," Baron replied. "What else would you expect from your training staff?"

Master Anderson threw back his head and laughed. "God, I love running this Academy!"

"If you weren't Headmaster, I would lock you in the stockades," Ms. Clark grumbled, but it was easy to tell she found his prank amusing. She turned her attention back to Brie and Lea. "It appears at least one person is happy to see you, Miss Bennett."

"Yes, it does." Brie gave Lea an extra-hard squeeze and smiled at Ms. Clark, shocked she'd gotten off so easily with the trainer. Would she be made to pay later?

Baron stood from the table and walked over to the group. "It is good to see you again, kitten."

Brie let go of Lea and gave him a hug, resting her head against his broad chest. There'd always been something comforting about the dark Dom—he was her safe place—and she inhaled deeply, taking in his spicy scent.

"How is Sir Davis?"

She broke the embrace and smiled up at him. "He is doing well. Finishing up some business in Japan then joining me here."

"And Tono Nosaka?"

Brie kept it positive, knowing it was what Tono wanted—*needed*—from her. "He's deeply saddened by the loss of his father, but Tono is determined to care for his mother and make the best of a difficult situation."

"That is good to hear," Baron replied in his low, soothing voice. "Tono Nosaka is someone I admire."

"Me too." Brie grinned and hugged him again. "It's just so good to see you again. I've missed you, Baron."

His thick lips curled up in a sexy smirk. "So you miss the old Baron, do you?"

"Of course! Not only did you help me through the first night at the Center, but you saved me from that creep at the Kinky Goat. You hold a special place in my heart, Baron. You always will." Old habits die hard, and she *almost* went up on her tiptoes to kiss those delicious lips. However, Brie fought the urge, concentrating instead on the reassuring weight of the collar around her neck.

"How long are you here, Brie?" Lea asked, spinning her around to face her.

Oh, how Brie had missed Lea's infectious enthusiasm. "Only a week, I think. Sir is a busy man and I don't think he'll have time to visit very long."

Master Anderson put his hand on her shoulder, his confident hold on her making Brie feel warm and tingly all over. "We'll take however much time we're given. Right now, however, Ms. Clark, Baron and I have some serious culling to do of the submissive entrants. Why don't you and Lea spend some time catching up while we make our determinations?"

"How many videos today?" Baron asked.

Master Anderson grinned. "Only seven, but we can only choose two more for this coming session."

Lea happily led her out of the conference room, but Brie glanced back and shivered involuntarily. To think that all the trainers at the Submissive Training Center had evaluated her own entrance video was a sobering thought.

It was a good thing she'd only imagined Sir watching it when she'd filmed her application or she would have lost her nerve. She looked briefly at Ms. Clark. What had the Domme thought when she'd viewed it? Had there been division among the trainers even then about her being part of the program?

Brie wondered if it was a blessing to be ignorant of the inner workings of a training center. Wise or not, she found herself hungry to know more and asked Lea, "Have you ever watched an entrance video?"

"Oh no—they're very strict about that. Only the trainers see them, then they're erased once the students have been chosen. They take the applicants' privacy very seriously."

"That's good to know..." As Lea led her down the hall to the Submissive Lounge, Brie asked a question that had been needling her. "Do they ever talk about what happens in those videos?"

"No, silly, I told you—they're very protective of the entries. It's serious business, girlfriend. Each applicant is treated with the same respect they give their students." She bumped Brie on the hip. "Why? Was there something in your submission video you're worried about? Come on, spill the beans!"

"Nothing too embarrassing, but you have to admit that thin little stick of a dildo was humorous to work with."

Lea giggled. "I bet they did that just to see if we could suck tiny dicks without laughing."

"Yeah, probably a requirement for submission to the Center. You know...just in case," Brie added with an exaggerated wink. "I wonder what other subs do to make themselves stand out in their videos."

Lea answered with a wicked twinkle in her eye. "I cracked a couple of my famous jokes and showed off my gorgeous boobs when I did mine. I'm positive that's why I was picked. What about you?"

Brie blushed. "I...umm...cried out a certain Headmaster's name. Of course, I didn't know who he was at the time, but he certainly inspired my performance."

"OMG, Brie!" Lea put her arm around Brie's shoulders. "Tell me more, girlfriend."

"Let's just say that Sir Thane Davis told me it was one of the finest entries he's ever seen."

"I bet!"

Brie nervously confessed, "I just can't help wondering what Coen, Marquis and Clark thought when they saw it."

"If you cried out Sir's name, I'm sure he had a lot of explaining to do."

Brie frowned. "You're probably right, but how can I find out for sure?"

"Hey, here's a novel thought. Why don't you ask Sir? You know what they say, girlfriend. Communication is the cornerstone of a healthy D/s relationship."

"Yeah, yeah…" Brie conceded.

Lea dragged her to a couch and sat her down. "So tell me what happened in Japan. I was devastated to hear about Tono's father."

Brie quickly caught her up, but she purposely left out the confession Tono's father had made, as well as her disappointment that Tono was staying in Japan to care for his mother.

"So Tono can really sing, huh?"

"Oh yeah, Lea, you wouldn't believe it. He could sing professionally if he wanted to."

"Who knew the man was multitalented?"

"I know! Can you just imagine him and his father belting it out in secret?"

Lea shook her head. "No, I can't. I really can't."

"Well, I couldn't have either until I visited his father this last time. I saw a whole new side to him."

"That's good…and kind of sad."

Brie sighed. "Yes, it is. I didn't come to understand the man until he was dying."

"I came across a joke recently that made me think of Tono."

Brie knew that was Lea's way of trying to add some lightheartedness to a tough situation, so she sacrificed for the team. "Okay…let me hear it."

Lea squealed. "Great! You can share it with Tono, if you want, the next time you see him."

"I will, but only if it's funny."

"Of course it is! Do you know why I didn't enjoy my time at the bondage club last night?"

"No, Lea. Why didn't you enjoy your time at the bondage club last night?"

"All I wanted was sex with no strings attached."

Brie groaned. "Boo!"

"Ooh, ooh, I've got another one!"

"I'm not sure I can handle another one."

"Bondage is brilliant!" Lea exclaimed, wrapping her arms tightly around herself. "Truss me."

Brie groaned as she shook her head. "Those were both terrible."

"But they made you smile," Lea insisted.

"Only because they were so bad."

"Exactly! That's the beauty of a good bad joke—you can't help but love them."

"The only thing I love is you. The jokes? Not so much."

"Aww, aren't you just the sweetest stinky cheese? Wait! I've got one more."

"No more, Lea. Please, no more."

"But this one's for you," she said, pouting.

Lea was hard to resist, so Brie relented against her better judgment. "Fine, but I'm only letting you because I love you."

"I love you too, Brie," she cooed, giving her a tight squeeze. "So...did you hear about the French cheese factory that exploded?"

"Nope."

"All that was left was de Brie."

This time Brie actually laughed.

"De Brie! Isn't that great?"

"It's stupid, but I love it," Brie admitted. "Thanks, Lea."

"Anytime, girlfriend. So what are your plans while you're here?"

"Well, I'm hoping to film a few scenes at the Academy. But mostly I just want to spend every minute I can hanging out with you."

"Me too! But...not tonight."

Brie was crushed. "Why not?"

"I already made plans with another friend."

"Can't I join you?"

Lea hesitated. "She's extremely shy, Brie. It's taken me weeks just to get her to agree to go out with me tonight."

Brie thought she understood and asked in a hushed tone, "Is she a new *girl*friend, by any chance?"

Lea rolled her eyes. "No, silly. She's a really cool person I want to know better but if I ask you to join us, she'll bail on me."

"But Lea," Brie whimpered, "I haven't seen you in like...forever. I'm only here for a week. *Please* don't leave me hanging tonight."

In answer, Lea gave Brie another squeeze. "I know this stinks, but if things go well tonight I'll ask if she'd like to meet you. I make no promises and you can't be offended if she says no."

Now it was Brie's turn to roll her eyes. "What, is this girl a mountain hermit or something?"

Lea hemmed and hawed before answering, "You could say that, I guess."

Her best friend was being so weird and secretive that it turned Brie off. Even if this mystery person agreed to meet, Brie wasn't sure she would like the girl. "I only have a week here," she reminded Lea.

"I know, I know! But remember, I had no idea you were coming until you threw off your hood today."

Brie giggled. "Oh, my goodness, wasn't that nuts?"

"Master Anderson is so bad!" Lea agreed. "It's another reason I love it here."

"Do you think Ms. Clark will forgive me? I was really surprised she handled it so well."

Lea suddenly became serious. "Although Mistress Clark still maintains her strict demeanor, around the staff she's been much more open and fun." Lea mused out loud, "It seems she's less tortured than before. I'm unsure if it's moving to Denver, Master Anderson's crazy antics or what, but whatever the reason, it's nice that others are getting to see the person I fell in love with."

Brie wondered if letting go of Rytsar Durov had been the biggest contributing factor for the change in the Domme's attitude. "Are the two of you finally an item now?"

Lea shrugged. "She's still trying to find her way. I don't think even *she* knows what she wants, but I'm willing to wait. In the meantime I'm having tons of fun getting to know the other Dominants and submissives in Denver. They're a friendly bunch, let me tell you."

Brie clasped her hand. "I'm happy to hear it. It sounds as if I'll have to be content with seeing you tomorrow, then." She stuck out her bottom lip and whimpered, "But I don't know how I'll survive."

Lea held out her little finger and grinned. "I promise to make it up to you—pinky swear." Brie wrapped her pinky around Lea's and they shook to seal the deal.

Baron peeked his head into the room. "Ms. Taylor, Master Anderson has requested that you return to the staff room."

Lea got up reluctantly. "I'm sorry I have to leave you, Brie."

"Don't concern yourself," Baron replied smoothly. "I'm taking Miss Bennett to the Rocky Mountain Brewery while you attend the meeting."

Brie loved the idea of getting to spend time alone with Baron, and waved goodbye to her best friend. "I'll be fine, woman. Go have fun with all that behind-the-scenes stuff you do."

"Later, 'gator," Lea called, throwing a kiss before traipsing out of the room.

"So, kitten, which do you prefer—dark or light beer?"

"I like it dark," she answered with a cheeky grin.

"Indeed."

He took her to the local brewery within walking distance of the training facility. It was lovely to stroll beside the handsome Dom under the blue skies of Denver. "Do you like it here, Baron?"

"It's different from LA. I'd say it's more laid back and more out-doorsy, but the people seem genuine. Yeah, I like it well enough."

"But your heart's still in Los Angeles?" Brie asked, detecting a hint of sadness in his voice.

"I miss the places and things that remind me of Adrianna."

It hurt Brie's heart to know that Baron was missing his submissive. She could only imagine how she would feel if she ever lost Sir. "Do you mind me asking how she died?"

"No, kitten, but let's get a beer and sit down first."

When they entered the Rocky Mountain Brewery he ordered two of their darkest brew at the bar, then settled beside Brie at a booth near the window, sliding a glass over to her.

Baron took a long drink and licked off the foam that rested on his upper lip. It was casually sexy, an unintended effect that made it all that much more charming.

"You were saying?" Brie prompted.

"Adrianna…" He said her name in a wistful, anguished tone. "She was my dream made flesh. Sir Davis invited me to her graduation party and introduced us personally. I knew then that she was the one. Our courtship was quick, her submission unconditional." He looked up from his beer. "I knew the love of a good woman, and it is because of that I survived the aftermath of her death."

Brie was gutted to see the love and pain expressed in his hazel eyes. "What happened to her?"

"Wrong place, wrong time… Adrianna and I had gone to a late-night movie at our neighborhood theater. It was raining, so I went to get the car. Three hoodlums walked past Adrianna while she was waiting. They attempted to mug her, but when she wouldn't give up her purse they beat my baby unconscious. I pulled up to find her on the pavement, bloody and unresponsive. Although I rushed her to the hospital…" He paused, looking away when he added gruffly, "My baby never woke up."

Brie grasped his hand. "I'm so sorry, Baron."

He smiled sadly at her. "As penance for not being there when she needed me, I've dedicated my life to protecting other women from the scum of the Earth."

"So that's why you were at the Kinky Goat…"

"Yes, but the last thing I wanted to see was you there."

Brie hung her head in shame. "It was a terrible mistake."

"You did nothing wrong, other than meet with your friends at a place you weren't familiar with. In some ways it was similar to what happened to my Adrianna—wrong place, wrong time."

"She must be so proud of you now. Proud of your strength to carry on, proud of the many women you've helped."

He furrowed his brow, his eyes dull with unresolved pain. "I hope she has forgiven me for not being there." He shook his head. "Every time I think of that night, I hear her crying out my name, trusting I would save her—but I never came."

Brie swallowed down the lump in her throat. "Adrianna wouldn't have blamed you. I only have to put myself in that situation to know how she felt. Although she would have been praying you'd come in time, she died knowing she'd see you again, and that would have brought her peace."

He blinked away the tears that welled up in his eyes, and took another draught of beer. "Thank you, kitten," he said hoarsely.

Brie nodded, picking up her glass. "Do you think you'll end up going back to LA?"

He shrugged his broad shoulders. "I'm uncertain at this point. Mentally I understand the benefits of moving on, but my heart does not. It's not an easy thing to do."

"Do you like being a trainer at the Denver Academy?"

He chuckled. "I do enjoy being in the trainer role. It's much less formal than the Submissive Training Center, but I appreciate Master Anderson's vision."

Brie grinned, nodding in agreement. "He's no Master Coen."

"No, he's not. However, they both have their place."

"Agreed."

"Whether it's fair or not, I will always compare the Headmasters I work under to Sir Davis."

"He was amazing in that role, wasn't he?" Brie agreed, squelching the guilt that threatened to rise.

"I was saddened to hear about his troubles."

Brie felt a chill run through her and she slowly put down her glass after taking a drink. "What do you mean?"

He stared at her for several moments before replying, "I'm talking about his mother, kitten."

She breathed an inward sigh of relief. "I'm telling you, that woman is insane! However, I admire how Sir handled the situation with her."

Baron's hazel eyes penetrated her with their intensity and she squirmed under his gaze. Had she said too much? Brie picked up her beer and sipped it nervously.

Thankfully, Master Anderson walked through the doors and straight over to their table. "Are you ready? It appears I'm to be your entertainment for the evening, young Brie."

Blast from the Past

"**D**on't feel you need to take me out, Master Anderson," Brie told him, as she jumped into his massive truck.

"It's the least I can do. After all, I was the one who wanted to keep your arrival under wraps. I'm responsible for the fact you have no friend to hang with tonight." He started up the vehicle then turned to her. "I'll show you some of my old haunts so you can get a native's feel for Denver."

Brie forced a smile. Although she was appreciative of his offer to entertain her, she would much rather have hung with Lea. However, she realized it was a rare chance to get to know the Dom on a more personal level, and readjusted her attitude. Even though Sir was good friends with Master Anderson, she knew practically nothing about the man other than the fact that he was a jokester, a skilled expert with the bullwhip and an excellent cook.

He drove her into Denver so she could admire, in passing, the tall buildings of the downtown area as well as the charm of horse-drawn carriages on the 16th Street mall, before taking her to an older neighborhood lined with tall trees.

He eventually parked in front of a magnificent Victorian home. Brie loved the inviting porch, the detailed trim, the lancet windows and the castle feel of its charming turret.

Master Anderson stared at it with a small grin playing across his lips. "I miss that house."

"So that's where you used to live?" she asked in surprise.

"Yes. I purchased it when it was in severe disrepair. I was young and had the energy and time to give it the care it deserved. After I'd finished restoring the extensive scrollwork and trim, I played with the inside. Still keeping to the Gothic style, I added a special room at the back for my…unique brand of entertainment." His eyes twinkled when he pointed to the left side of the residence. "Inside there is a secret door. How I enjoyed the surprised gasps from my submissives the first time I introduced them to what my friends affectionately called 'The Room'."

"Oh, I wish I could see it, Master Anderson. I can't help but wonder what the new owners think of your play room."

"They were told it was a private room I used as an office." He chuckled to himself. "I wonder if they can still hear the squeals of delight that regularly echoed in that room." Master Anderson's eyes drifted affectionately to the yard. "After the interior was complete, I started on the neglected garden."

Brie looked beyond the dark iron gate. He'd filled the front yard with bushes, each with its own unique pigment which made the garden colorful but definitely kept a masculine feel to it.

"Wow, your garden is actually as impressive as the house," she complimented.

"Thank you. I'm quite proud of my work."

"Do you regret giving this place up?"

He looked at Brie thoughtfully. "My new home has the space this one lacked. Although they appear to be polar opposites, both homes have a style that speaks to me."

"You are a complicated man, Master Anderson. A cowboy as a child, a carpenter as a young man and now Headmaster of a BDSM training school."

"You are missing an important part of the journey." He started up the truck and drove her back to visit the downtown area. He helped her out of his vehicle, then walked Brie through a thriving college campus. "Once the house was complete, I had time on my hands and an ambition to be my own boss, so I took classes at night to get my business degree."

She looked at him in amazement. "How did you find the time?"

He raised his eyebrow. "I was not tied down to a partner and only played with subs on an occasional basis. It left me with an abundance of time, and I am not a man to waste it." He pointed towards a large glass-and-brick building with the impressive Rockies as its backdrop.

"I took classes at night here. While it took longer to get my business degree, it has all led me to where I am now. I was able to redesign the warehouse into the Academy, and I have the business background necessary to ensure its success. Of course, it doesn't hurt that Thane let me see the inner workings of the Training Center."

Brie felt a pang of remorse. Why did the mention of Sir's prior status as Headmaster always hurt her heart?

Master Anderson walked her between the campus buildings, down a pleasant path of new trees and budding flowers. He shared memories of the professors he'd learned under and classes he'd taken. Although much of what he shared made no sense to her, Brie enjoyed hearing the tone of his voice change when he talked about business and how what he learned played into his endeavors now. "I want our school to adapt to the market, reacting to the needs of the local community as they change. I invite change, as long we never lose sight of our fundamental purpose."

He led her to a small Italian restaurant, opening the bright red door with a gentlemanly flourish. "A favorite place of mine back in the da—"

She looked up at him and was surprised to see his face lose all color as a cute redhead with a large baby bump made her way out the door.

"Pardon me," the young woman murmured with a smile. Then she stopped short and said in astonishment, "Brad?"

Master Anderson stiffened upon hearing his name. He froze temporarily, taking time before he replied, "Amy, I never expected to run into you here."

The redhead blushed. "Well, I love the food and seem to crave it more these days." She rubbed her belly lovingly. "Thank you for introducing me to this place. I visit a least once a week now."

He looked at her warily, as if she were a poison to him. Brie's heart went out to Master Anderson as the awkward silence stretched, so she stuck out her hand. "Hi, I'm Brie."

The girl glanced briefly at Brie's collar before taking her hand. "Hi, Brie. I'm Amy. I was good friends with Brad when we were taking night classes together."

Master Anderson seemed to snap out of his stupor and spoke, "Yes, Amy and I spent many stimulating nights at my house. How have you been?" He looked at her stomach. "I notice you have a bun in the oven."

Amy laughed sweetly. "Yes, we do. A little girl, if the ultrasound proves to be right. I sure hope so, because the nursery is all pink and my mother already bought a ton of lacy outfits for her."

Brie saw a flash of pain flit across Master Anderson's face before he hid it with a casual smile. "I take it you're still with Troy."

Amy looked at him sadly, letting Brie know there was so much between them that wasn't being said.

"Yes." There was another uncomfortably long pause as Amy played with the ring on her finger. "Troy and I got married last year."

"I see."

Brie slipped her hand into Master Anderson's and squeezed it, offering him moral support.

"Looks as if you two didn't waste any time," she teased Amy.

The redhead shrugged, caressing her stomach affectionately. "Who'd have guessed we'd be so compatible?"

Master Anderson tightened his hold on Brie's hand, almost hurting her with his grip. "Congratulations, Amy. Be sure to give your husband my best. I hope you'll excuse us, as Brie and I have a schedule to keep."

Amy's gaze drifted back to Brie's collar. "I'm sure the two of you have a wonderful evening planned." She gave Master Anderson a clumsy hug, her large stomach getting in the way. "It was wonderful to see you again, Brad. You look great, and it's such a joy to meet your girlfriend."

Master Anderson didn't correct Amy's mistake, so Brie made a bold move, saying as she kissed him on the cheek, "Mr. Anderson is in high demand these days. I'm a very lucky girl."

"Yes…I'm sure," Amy replied, turning a bright shade of red. She added as she hurried off, "Have a great evening, you two." She looked back briefly before disappearing around the corner.

Master Anderson watched her go with a look of regret on his face. "I don't feel hungry. Do you mind if we head back to my place?"

"Not at all, Master Anderson."

The drive back was unbearably silent. Brie had never seen the Dom unraveled before. Her heart ached for him, but it was not her place to ask about the girl, so she stared out of the window admiring the snowy peaks in the distance.

Sir texted her as they waited in traffic. *How's my sexy submissive?*

Brie smiled when she saw his message and told Master Anderson, "It's Sir. Do you mind if I text him back?"

"Please. I'm sure he misses you."

The sadness in his voice was not lost on her. "Thank you, Master Anderson."

She quickly typed, *I'm good, Sir. How are you?*

Doing well. In a couple of days I'll be better.

Why?

You'll be in my arms.

Brie squeaked, which caught Master Anderson's attention, so she explained, "Sir's coming here in a few days."

"That's good to hear. Tell him hello from me."

Brie dutifully typed, *Master Anderson says hi.*

I assumed you would be with Lea tonight, Brie.

She's busy, so Master Anderson took me on a tour of Denver.

Is he taking good care of my sub?

Of course, but do you have any idea who Amy is?

He took his time before texting back. *Why?*

Master Anderson met her today and seems extremely sad now.

I have an assignment for you, téa.

Yes, Master.

When you get off the phone, pull your skirt up and play with yourself.

It was Brie's turn to hesitate.
He continued to type. *Make yourself orgasm. Be vocal about it.*
??? She texted in surprise.

Trust your Master. Hang up now and do as I say.

Brie put the phone away and sighed, building up her courage. She hiked her skirt up, not daring to look in Master Anderson's direction.

With tentative fingers, she started to caress her pussy through her panties. It didn't take long for her body to react to the pleasurable sensation. She moaned a little, shifting to get a better angle. She could feel Master Anderson's eyes on her.

Brie slipped her hand under the wet material and swirled her finger over her clit. With a teasing motion she rubbed the sensitive area more rapidly and purred. Here they were in the middle of rush-hour traffic and she was playing with herself... Thankfully she was safe from the majority of prying eyes because of the height of his truck.

Master Anderson said nothing as he watched the road—and her.

Brie closed her eyes, arching her back, forcing her fingers inside as she imagined the head of Sir's cock penetrating her. He fucked her slowly, wanting her to feel and appreciate the full length of his shaft. Then she pulled her fingers out and rapidly rubbed her hungry clit.

The combination of penetration and clit play always brought on a delicious orgasm. She adjusted herself, putting a leg up on the dash for freer access. She needed deeper penetration, so she thrust her fingers more aggressively. The lace panties made it a little more difficult, but also added an element of naughtiness. With the angle he had, Master Anderson couldn't see what she was doing but he could certainly imagine it.

There finally came a point when the increasing fire between her legs transformed into pulses, letting her know an orgasm was near. She pressed her fingers hard against her clit and began to rub at a furious pace.

Her cries of passion filled the cabin of the truck as she gave in to the intensity of her self-made orgasm. "Oh, oh, ooohhh…" she moaned as it crashed over her. She felt her pussy contract in waves of pleasure. Afterwards she pressed her hand over her sex, enjoying those last little delicious pulses.

Without looking in Master Anderson's direction, she righted herself, pulling her skirt down and folding her hands in her lap.

"Your Master told you to do that?"

She looked at him shyly. "Yes, Master Anderson."

Brie was glad to see him smile for the first time since the unexpected meeting with Amy. "Leave it to Thane to know just what I needed. Well done, young Brie."

She smiled back. "I'm glad you approve, Master Anderson."

He raised his eyebrow. "You know I love watching a woman pleasure herself."

Brie blushed, thrilled that her little performance had been pleasing to him.

Maser Anderson drove high into the foothills, pulling off the road at a turnabout which gave them a spectacular view of Denver. He turned off the truck, staring at the sprawling city below. Without being asked, he shared, "I met Amy in a communications class. I knew the moment I laid eyes on her that I was meant to tame her."

"Tame her?" Brie asked, unfamiliar with the term.

He answered with a smirk. "Back then I loved the challenge of taking a strong woman unused to kink and showing her the excitement of submission. I affectionately refer to them as the 'wild ones', those women who don't realize their true nature—yet."

"So you liked educating totally vanilla girls?"

"Yes. However, Amy was different. That redheaded vixen intrigued me more than my previous conquests, and she proved far more resistant. Took me longer to tame her than any I'd had before, but when she finally submitted—*truly* submitted—I was lost."

"Lost how?" Brie asked, deeply honored that he was being so open with her.

"Amy broke my heart," Master Anderson stated with a sad half-smile. "Although I'd always enjoyed conquering wild ones, she was the first and only one to conquer me. I didn't realize how deeply I'd fallen until that ass came into the picture."

"Who?"

Master Anderson spat out the name disdainfully, "Troy Dawson."

"Is that her husband?"

Master Anderson snarled. "That selfish bastard doesn't deserve her. He was always making her cry, leaving her to chase his dreams then coming back, expecting her to welcome him with open arms. He didn't love her like I did. Damn it, I would have done anything for Amy. In fact…" His voice trailed off and he just stared at the horizon, lost in his painful memories.

Brie said nothing, instinctively putting her hand on his shoulder to express her empathy.

"I lost a part of myself the day she walked away from me. No explanation—she just walked into his arms and we were no more. But as hurt as I was, I never stopped loving the girl and willingly played the fool again when I saw an opportunity to win her back."

Brie couldn't imagine Master Anderson ever playing the fool and stated, "I don't believe it."

"I hate to admit it, but I ran to Amy's side when I heard she was seriously hurt. It was no surprise to me that Troy was nowhere to be found."

Master Anderson paused, a hint of regret in his voice when he added, "I did things I'm not proud of. Have you ever loved someone so desperately you compromised yourself to keep them?"

He looked critically at Brie for a moment, then answered his own question. "No, you haven't. That isn't your nature."

"What did you do?" Brie asked, intrigued that the Dom had found himself in such a position. "I can't imagine you ever compromising yourself."

"No one is immune to life's lessons, young Brie. Looking back on it now, I understand what a fool I was, but back then I justified my actions. She was mine—she'd freely given her submission to me. I also knew she needed to stay far away from that miserable excuse of a man. When fate saw fit to erase her memories, I took it as a sign. It was my second chance and I wasn't going to allow anything or *anyone* to fuck it up."

"What happened?" Brie prodded, now even more curious.

"I chose not to mention that she'd ever known Troy Dawson. Why would I? I wanted to protect her from that asshole."

"So you did it because you loved her?"

"Yes. If Amy hadn't returned my feelings, I never would've been so persistent, nor would I have asked her to marry me. I tell you, young Brie—the day she accepted my proposal, I'd never felt so happy, didn't know it was possible to feel that level of joy."

He snarled in frustration. "Naturally, that's when *he* showed up. Troy always returned just when she was getting her life back together. I tried to warn her that he was no good, but her heart was set."

Master Anderson stared out at the city, sighing deeply. "When she turned me down that second time, I was done." He added in a low, angry growl, "But to see her now. To see her heavy with child, with *his* child… It should have been mine."

Tears came to Brie's eyes as she realized how hurt he was. Although Master Anderson was a strong, confident Dom, he was still human. They sat in the truck, silently watching two black starlings swoop and twist in the orange sky as the sun set.

His next words were heartbreaking, and something Brie would never forget. "What I had failed to appreciate was that I had won her submission and love, but I never had her heart."

She wrapped her arms around his muscular shoulders. "I'm sorry your heart was broken by your first love."

He stated with conviction, "I will never be that weak again."

Brie replied with equal conviction, "Master Anderson, I believe true love makes you strong—not weak."

He stared at her for several seconds before giving her a hint of a smile. "Spoken like a sage. I suppose I still hold out hope of finding what you share with Thane. That's why his little stunt tonight was perfect. I needed to be reminded there are subs who love their Masters and remain completely devoted to them."

"Your sub is out there, Master Anderson," Brie declared. "She's just waiting to rock your world."

He chuckled. "You never knew this, but I was concerned for Thane when I first met you. His obsession reminded me of my own. I was certain my friend would suffer the same fate I had."

Brie proclaimed proudly, "We are condors, Sir and I."

Master Anderson appeared amused by her statement. "You *do* realize condors are vultures? They eat the meat of rotting animals."

Brie giggled. "They do, but they also mate for life."

"Lots of animals mate for life. You could have chosen swans, wolves or even turtle doves." He shook his head, chuckling under his breath. "Why condors, of all things?"

Brie was not offended by his teasing and happily enlightened him. "The condor is the perfect choice, Master Anderson. While the world concentrates on what they perceive as our flaws, we focus only on each other. They will never know the beauty we see every day."

The amusement on his face faded. "That's profound, young Brie."

Master Anderson started up the truck again. "I've suddenly had a change of heart. Let's go clubbing tonight, vanilla style."

Brie squealed as he peeled out of the turnabout and headed back down the mountain.

Wicked King

B rie woke up in a panic. She glanced around the unfamiliar bedroom, struggling to remember where she was. It took several moments before her heart stopped racing, once she realized she was at Master Anderson's.

The frightening dream which had awakened her was already disappearing into the murky recesses of her mind, but she felt certain that Sir's mother, Ruth, had been part of it.

She shook off the unpleasant aftereffects of the dream and hurried to the shower to begin her day. When she returned to her room, Brie was pleasantly surprised to find her fantasy journal lying on the bed. She picked it up, along with the note beside it.

Your Master wants to read a new fantasy, téa. ~ Sir

Brie flipped through the pages of her beloved journal, realizing that Sir must have had it shipped to Master Anderson's house from their apartment. It'd been a while since she'd written in its pages—far too long. There were so many wonderful memories wrapped up in that little book; from her very first fantasy, which Rytsar had made into delicious reality during her auction, to her Sun God fantasy that Boa managed to fulfill with his gargantuan cock. Then there was her Naughty King fantasy, which Sir had played out as Khan just before Graduation Day.

She pressed the book against her chest, thrilled to be holding it again, and whispered, "Thank you, Sir."

Brie curled up on the bed and began to write, grateful there was no time constraint this time as she began to pen her fantasy.

"*Stop. Step away from her.*"

The priest moves away from me. The relief on his face would be insulting, but I understand why. He's grateful that he will not have to break his vows to God to prove his loyalty to our King.

I am relieved as well, pleased to have my virginity still intact.

"*Girl.*"

The men holding me down release my wrists. I get up slowly, straightening my skirt with shaking hands.

"*Retire to my room,*" my King orders. "*I will partake of you later.*"

I bow to him, honored to have been granted such a privilege. I glance up to see the proud look on my father's face. I'm escorted from the great hall and led through the castle. All the splendor and wealth displayed on the walls gives me hope. Surely after tonight, the King will forgive our family's debt.

The guards lead me to a section of the castle that few are allowed to enter. The King's room is covered in large, intricate tapestries depicting his many battles over the years. I look around, flattered that my virginity will be given to such a great man.

The next few hours are spent with attendants as they ready me for the King. After a thorough bath and cleaning, I am covered in sweet-smelling perfume. My hair is curled and tied up into a traditional bun, which signifies my virginal status.

I'm then dressed in a white, gossamer gown. The thin material lightly brushes against my nipples as it slides down and settles into place. I feel like a princess, a beautiful princess about to be taken by her handsome King.

Two men enter the King's chamber. "*So this is the one?*" the younger of the two asks.

"*Yes.*"

"*A virgin?*"

"*That is what she claims,*" the other replies.

"*I'm required to check.*" When the young one approaches me, I freeze. "*I will not hurt you, child,*" he says reassuringly as his hand disappears under my gown. I stiffen when I feel his finger press against my mound. "*Open your legs, girl.*"

I look to the other man, who nods. I reluctantly move my feet apart and gasp as his finger presses against my tiny opening.

"*By God, she's tight*". He switches fingers, penetrating me with his pinky. It is the first time I have ever felt such an invasion and I whimper with discomfort.

"*You break that hymen and it'll be your head,*" the other man growls.

The first man removes his finger and looks hungrily at me. "*I would love to watch this one lose her virginity.*"

"*You can, for a price,*" the other states proudly.

"*How?*"

"*The risk is considerable, but it can be done.*"

The man looks me over again. "*I'll pay it, whatever the cost. I want to hear her scream."*

I ignore the two men, disgusted by their behavior. However, they have foolishly given me valuable information. Should the King prove ungenerous, I can blackmail them to guarantee my family's survival.

"It'll be worth the considerable price, my friend," the older man assures him. "The King has particular tastes when it comes to virgins."

Two other girls enter the room upon his words, followed by an imposing eunuch. The young maidens are dressed in identical white gowns.

The older male smiles lewdly as he explains to his partner, "Our Majesty likes to take them three at a time."

The eunuch holds rope in his hand. He takes the wrists of the girl closest to him and ties her hands together before guiding her to the giant bed. We all watch as he orders her to kneel on the edge of it. He makes quick work of binding her so her legs are spread and her arms secure.

He motions to the other girl. She glides over to the bed and willingly offers her hands to him. He grunts in satisfaction as he trusses the second girl beside the first. He looks up at me next, holding up the last of the rope.

My heart races as I approach; I know there is no escape from my fate once I am bound. I glance briefly at the door but know my choice is already made.

I hold up my wrists to him. My heart skips a beat as he wraps them in the rope, then directs me to kneel on the bed like the other two girls. With competent hands he spreads my legs and binds them, securing me to the frame of the bed. I struggle in my bonds, testing their strength.

"You aren't going anywhere," the eunuch informs me arrogantly.

All three men exit, leaving us young girls alone in the King's chamber. The other two are as silent as I am, probably contemplating what the night ahead holds for us.

I'm frightened. I will no longer be innocent after tonight, but there is another part of me that longs to become a woman in the arms of my King. Despite my eagerness, I jump like a scared rabbit when I hear his voice just outside the door. He enters and chuckles to himself when he sees the three of us. I hear the swish of fabric as he is undressed by his manservant.

"Leave me," he orders, and I hear the man make a quick exit.

We are now alone with our King...

I watch through veiled eyes as he ties a gag over the mouth of the virgin farthest away from me. The other girl and I tense as our King places his large hands on her buttocks. My view of his manhood is obstructed, but based on the girl's stifled moans, our King has an impressive cock.

Her muffled cry announces her entrance into womanhood.

Our King grunts as he thrusts into her, making me tremble with fearful excitement. I have guarded my maidenhead diligently to ensure my future as a bride, but now I will be giving it away to my King.

He pulls out and moves to the next girl. Another sash comes out and he gags her. This girl whimpers when he starts pressing into her. He slaps her ass hard, the sound of it echoing through the expansive chamber. "Quiet."

She closes her eyes and is completely silent when he begins to thrust. He growls with passion. "Move with me."

My King groans in satisfaction as he takes her more deeply. I cannot stop shaking, knowing my turn is approaching. In just a few moments I will be a woman in every sense of the word…

I gasp involuntarily when he pulls out of her and grabs my ass with both hands.

"Desperate for your King, are you?"

I nod, surprised when he does not gag me like the others.

"You have not been raised for this like the other girls. I shall savor your maidenhead that much more."

I look back at him, becoming entranced by his lustful stare. Being desired by a man is a new and intoxicating experience for me and I find I'm no longer resentful of my father—I desire my King to have my virginity for purely selfish reasons.

I purr in pleasure when he undoes my bun and lets my long hair fall over my back. Then he wraps his hand in my silky tresses and pulls my head back. I feel his hard shaft pressing against my tight opening, and whimper in fear and anticipation, knowing my moment is at hand.

"Remember this night, girl."

I start to pant as he forces himself inside me. My body is resistant even though I desperately want to feel the fullness of him. I push against his shaft, hoping to break through my virginal resistance, but he slaps my ass in protest.

"Stay still."

I do not move and my whole world expands as I relax, allowing his Kingly shaft to open me up. The pain is replaced with wonder when he begins to stroke me with his manhood. Nothing else exists but the two of us as I revel in this new connection.

Closing my eyes, I concentrate on the sensation of his shaft forcing itself deeper. Oh, this wondrous feeling of being utterly possessed!

I'm saddened when he pulls out, and cry, "More, my King."

He seems amused by my heartfelt plea. "Are you begging, girl?" Slapping my pink ass, he replies, "I have already taken your virginity—what else of value do you have for your King?"

"I would give you anything," I answer confidently as he bends down and bites my shoulder, his rigid shaft pressing against me.

"Anything?"

"Yes."

He takes his manhood in his hand and repositions it against my forbidden hole.

I can't breathe, taken by complete surprise by his demand.

"Are you still as willing?" he challenges.

I'm shocked by my own answer. "Yes, my King."

He covers my mouth with one hand, while grabbing my ass with the other. This possession will not be like the first.

"Give in to me, girl. Don't resist."

Although I am frightened, I imagine his shaft deep inside me and my body responds favorably. The round head of his cock breaches my entrance and I groan into his hand. My ass aches as I take his length.

My breath comes in gasps when he begins to move inside me. I feel dirty and yet delightfully wicked being taken this way by him.

My King's muscles tense as he forces himself farther into my darkness.

I am now completely and utterly His.

Brie put down the pen and sighed with unreleased need. She wondered what Sir would think when he read about the return of the King. She flipped through the pages again, noting that this fantasy was much longer than the others in her journal. Having been given unlimited time, she'd been able to fully detail her fantasy while still leaving her Master leeway to take it wherever he desired.

What will Sir do with this particular fantasy? Brie wondered. It had elements of Lea's birthday gift with the addition of other girls, while continuing the Khan fantasy he'd played out with her just before Graduation. This time, however, it included one of his favorite pastimes—her ass.

Brie kissed her beloved journal before slipping it into the overnight envelope. Although she was grateful for the connection that writing her fantasy had given her, it also made her miss Sir that much more.

She decided that must be the life of a condor—the continuous longing and need for the other. While some might see it as a weakness, she saw it as part of their strength. When they were separated, each of them was still strengthened by the knowledge that the other was thinking of them and impatient to reunite. Then when they finally came back together, the intensity of the union seemed that much more powerful.

Brie hugged the package one more time before dropping it into Master Anderson's mailbox. She felt a thrill of excitement, knowing her journal was headed off to her Master.

Fun with the Neighbors

S ince Brie had no idea what Master Anderson planned for the day, she'd dressed casually but with a stylish flair. She was still applying her makeup when she heard his call.

"Come out here, young Brie."

She hurried out of her room and found him in the kitchen, cooking breakfast. He looked up and smiled charmingly at her. "Sleep well?"

Brie frowned momentarily, thinking back on her dream. "I woke up from a bad dream this morning, but overall I had a restful sleep."

He directed her to a stool at the counter so she could watch while he cooked. His hands moved with grace and speed as he cut vegetables and added them to the omelet. At least Master Anderson understood and appreciated the beauty of a good omelet.

He moved around his kitchen with the skill and precision he brought to a session with the bullwhip. Brie would have bet that if she blindfolded him, he would have no problem navigating the kitchen as he cooked.

In no time, he slid a perfectly cooked omelet onto a plate and placed it in front of her. He handed Brie a fork, telling her, "Please eat while it's still hot."

She cut into his omelet of perfection and brought it to her lips, blowing lightly before taking a bite. Brie sighed in contentment. It was impossibly fluffy and light, a texture she'd never been able to achieve herself. "Wow, Master Anderson. Just, wow…"

He assembled his own omelet with finesse and sat next to her. "I like to start the day with eggs. Nature's perfect protein."

"Amen to that," she said, clinking forks with him. "I sure wish Sir liked eggs."

"It certainly makes you two an unfortunate pairing, doesn't it?"

She giggled. "Only if eating is important to him." She was about to take another bite when Master Anderson swept the plate from her. "Sorry, young Brie. I just noticed Ms. Courtney is out in her backyard."

"So?" Brie pouted, watching forlornly as he dumped their omelets in the trash.

"They won't be worth saving once they get cold," he assured her.

How Master Anderson could throw away a masterpiece like that was unfathomable to Brie, but the gleam in his eye had her more than a little curious—his mischievous nature was charming.

He explained to her, "I've wanted to teach my neighbor a lesson ever since I caught her snooping around my place uninvited. I insist on you joining me in the back, right now."

She nodded and asked, "What do you need me to do?"

"Simply follow my instructions. You may improvise where you deem appropriate." He escorted her out into the backyard and she could hear the neighbor talking loudly to a friend. The two seemed awfully chatty so early in the morning.

Brie scanned Master Anderson's yard. It backed up to a steep, mountainous hill and was landscaped with a wide variety of bushes and young trees with unusual cacti artfully placed throughout. For a splash of color, he'd added several types of columbine.

His well-manicured backyard maintained a manly feel that seemed to complement the solitary pole planted in the center. Brie knew *exactly* what that pole was used for, and understood the necessity of the privacy fence that separated it from his neighbors.

"Your yard is gorgeous, Master Anderson! Every bit as impressive as your other house, although the landscaping is different."

"Knowing your plants and the climate they thrive in is the key," he informed her. "The environment up here is completely different than in town. Most homeowners fail to appreciate that." He stroked the leaf of a flourishing bush nearby, looking every bit the proud papa.

Master Anderson walked back over to her and whispered, "I'm going to retrieve the necessary items. Do not stray from this spot."

He spoke loudly so the women on the other side of the fence could hear, "Let's finish breakfast before we begin." He disappeared into the house, leaving Brie to eavesdrop on the ladies conversing on the other side of the fence.

"I don't have a clue, Wendy. All I know is that he works odd hours and is drop-dead gorgeous—as well as single."

"It seems he already has a girlfriend, Courtney. How else do you explain that girl being here so early in the morning?"

Courtney tsked dismissively. "I've never seen her before. Probably his sister visiting or something."

"I can't believe I let you talk me into coming. I'm missing my Pilates class for this, and you know how I get whenever I miss Pilates."

"I'm telling you, once you see this guy you'll be on your knees kissing my feet."

Brie smirked to herself. It seemed his neighbor, Courtney, was determined to set Master Anderson up with the Pilates girl.

He came back out grinning as he held up a set of leather bindings and his tool bag. Brie had to remind herself to breathe. She hadn't counted on a session with him, especially with a vanilla audience listening nearby.

Master Anderson declared boisterously, "I forgot your name, so I'll just call you 'baby' to avoid confusion."

"My na—" Brie started.

"No, I really couldn't care less what it is."

Brie bit her lip, smiling at his devilish humor. What would those poor women think? Little did they suspect he was just getting started.

"Kneel and open that pretty little mouth."

Brie obediently sank to her knees with her mouth slightly open in a pleasing manner. She looked up innocently, enjoying her role.

He handed Brie the tool bag and commanded, "Unzip it slowly. I want to you admire what's inside." She did as he asked, knowing the sound could easily be mistaken for the unzipping of pants. "Do you like what you see, baby?" he asked huskily.

She smiled.

"Of course you do," he answered for her. "Now take it out. I want you to handle it properly before I use it on you."

Brie heard an audible gasp on the other side of the fence and had to bite her lip to keep back the laughter. She took the bullwhip out of the bag and touched its deceptively smooth, braided leather. For something so pleasant to the touch, it definitely had a wickedly painful side to it.

"I want you to kiss it."

Brie leaned over and pressed her lips against the fierce tool. Her heart skipped a beat, her body still remembering its bite.

"That's it, baby. Pucker those pink lips and kiss the length of that bad boy."

Brie left a trail of kisses down the handle of the bullwhip.

Master Anderson took it from her. "Take that thing off," he said, pointing to her top. "I want those tits to bounce when we do this."

A utensil clattered onto the patio concrete on the other side of the fence. There was no doubt they had a captive audience.

Brie unbuttoned her blouse, and was about to undo her bra but Master Anderson shook his head. She handed him her shirt, grateful not to be naked in case Courtney decided to peek over the fence.

He draped it across a patio chair, warning her, "I will not be gentle with you."

"I like it rough," Brie replied, wanting the women eavesdropping to know this was a consensual encounter, in case they were considering calling the police.

Pointing to the wooden pole, he commanded, "Stand and present yourself over there."

Brie's stomach fluttered as she willingly walked up to it, unsure if she was prepared to take the harsh onslaught of his whip so early in the morning.

"Hands up, baby," he said in a deceptively amiable voice. He bound her wrists in leather and secured them to a hook attached to the post. He swept her hair away so that her back was exposed to him. Brie's nipples hardened in anticipation of what was coming—fear seemed to have that effect on her.

"Spread those legs."

When she did, he growled sensually. "Wider…"

Brie couldn't imagine what the ladies were thinking. She heard the swish of the bullwhip cut through the air as Master Anderson warmed up, but he did not crack it. She closed her eyes, the anticipation of contact almost unraveling her.

"No tears this time."

She whimpered in answer.

There was an angry huff from the other side of the fence. Brie stifled her giggle. If he wasn't careful, Master Anderson might have a riot on his hands.

"My strokes will come hard and fast. Are you ready?"

Brie hesitated for dramatic effect before saying timidly, "Yes."

It was as silent as the grave on the other side of the fence.

When the first lash contacted her back, Brie was surprised to find it challengingly pleasant—a strike that was light but hard enough to stimulate the skin. She let out a passionate moan when the second lash found its way home.

"You like it hard, don't you?"

Brie enjoyed egging the women on with the naughty banter and purred, "The harder the better." She trusted Master Anderson understood she was only kidding.

He rained down a series of lashes, precise in his placement, with exactly the same intensity as the first. Truly, this man *was* a master of the whip.

Brie's cries were of pure, sexual bliss.

"Quiet, you'll wake the neighbors," he warned cheekily.

"You make it hurt so good..." she panted.

"It's true I know how to handle my tool," he replied in a playfully arrogant voice. "Hell, I've been stroking young heifers with it since I was a boy."

There was an audible gasp on the other side of the fence.

"But I'm becoming bored with this. Let's try something new—something I know you're not going to like."

He untied Brie from the pole and handed over her blouse. With her skin still tingling from the quick bullwhip session, she buttoned it up and waited for his next command.

"Move over to the fence and bend over with your ass in the air."

She walked over to the spot he'd indicated, just opposite of the two ladies, and did as he'd instructed.

As Master Anderson approached he explained, "This isn't about you. This is about what I want. Understand?"

"But—"

"Not another word."

He came up behind her and handed her a set of gardening gloves. Then he leaned over and grabbed her hands, guiding them to a spiky weed. "Grasp it with both hands and pull hard."

The needlelike thorns pressed through the glove material and pricked her sensitive palms. It was slightly uncomfortable, so she whimpered pathetically for the benefit of their audience.

"I don't care if it hurts, baby. Pull on it like you mean it."

Master Anderson aided her by gripping the offending weed below her hands. With his help, the stubborn plant came up without any problem.

"That wasn't so bad, now was it?"

"Yes, it was," she complained with a grin.

"I want you to do it again."

She whined pitifully, "But it hurt..."

"I don't care if it hurt. Bend over and yank harder this time."

"That's it!" Courtney roared from the other side of the fence, "For God's sake, leave that poor girl alone!"

Both women peeked over the fence in unison. If looks could kill, Master Anderson would have been struck dead on the spot.

He looked up at them innocently. "Howdy, ladies—sorry if we disturbed you. My girl here is wimpy when it comes to yard work."

Brie smiled up at them, her hands still clutching the plant.

The two women couldn't comprehend what they were seeing versus what they'd just heard. They stared at Brie, too flabbergasted to speak.

"I really hate weeding," Brie confessed with a shrug.

Courtney sputtered, "I…uh…we…uh…"

"We heard you doing things to this girl," Wendy insisted, looking accusingly at Master Anderson.

"Heard what, exactly?" he questioned, ignoring Wendy as he stared hard at his neighbor.

Master Anderson's gaze unnerved Courtney and she answered sheepishly, "Nothing. Come on, Wendy." The two slunk back down on their side of the fence and hurried into the house.

Once her sliding glass door slammed shut, Master Anderson threw back his head and gave a full-bellied laugh. When he was done he wiped away a pretend tear. "They make it too easy for me."

"Your devilish humor is going to get you in trouble someday, Master Anderson," Brie warned.

He pinched her cheeks, wiggling them gently from side to side. "You were brilliant, my little accomplice. That last little, 'But it hurt…' was the absolute kicker. How could they resist a peek, in the name of all that is holy?"

As she walked back into the house, she stated casually, "You know, Courtney was just trying to pair you off with her friend."

Master Anderson smirked, looking back at his neighbor's house. "Really?"

"I thought you'd enjoy knowing that little tidbit. To think that your evil ways have caused you to miss out on the future Mrs. Anderson. Such a shame."

He ruffled her hair. "Totally worth it. The look on their faces when they peeked over to find you weeding—priceless!"

Mysterious Autumn

Lea honked her horn three times to let Brie know she'd arrived to pick her up. Brie was actually nervous about meeting Lea's new friend. All the mystery surrounding the girl, along with her unwillingness to meet on that first night, made Brie uneasy. Despite Lea's assurances that she would adore the girl, Brie still had serious doubts.

She apologized to Sir, who was on the phone, having taken a moment out of his busy schedule to check on her. "I'm sorry, Sir, but Lea's here."

"Not a problem, Brie. I'm glad you're finally getting to spend time with her."

Brie smiled into the phone. "But I hate to say goodbye to you."

"We'll see each other soon enough. Go enjoy your time with Lea."

"I love you, Sir."

"I love you too, babygirl."

She pressed the end button and stuffed her phone in her purse, skipping out the door to meet her best friend.

"Lea!"

Lea jumped out of her car and ran to the passenger side to give Brie a hug. "I'm going to squeeze you as much as I can while you're here. I've missed my Stinky Cheese."

The two hugged several times before hopping into Lea's beat-up excuse of a ride. The poor car was so full of dents it reminded Brie of a golf ball.

Once they were on the road, Brie asked her, "So, girl, where are we headed this fine Colorado evening?"

"We're going to do something a little daring tonight."

"Oh no. Now you have me worried."

Lea laughed, patting her knee. "You're going to love it. Trust me."

After the Kinky Goat incident, Brie wasn't taking any chances. "Out with it, Lea. Where are we headed?"

"To a skating rink, silly."

"What, like roller-skating?"

"Oh heck, no, that's for children. We're going ice-skating."

"But I can't ice-skate."

"Neither can I," Lea stated enthusiastically.

"If neither of us can skate, why the heck are we going?"

"Don't be such a stick-in-the-mud, Brie. This is Autumn's favorite place."

Brie looked out the car window and grumbled, "My ass is going to be bruised by the end of the night."

"Then it's no different from a night at The Haven, now, is it?"

Brie turned to her and giggled. "I suppose you're right. So tell me, is this girl some kind of Olympic athlete or something? Is that the reason for all the secrecy?"

"Nah, Autumn is just like us." Lea bumped shoulders with Brie and in the process almost ran her car off the road.

Brie clutched the door handle and squealed, "Sir will kill you if we die tonight."

"How?" Lea joked. "Is he going to come up to Heaven and kill me just to prove a point?"

Brie burst out laughing. Dang, it was great being with Lea again. "I've missed you, woman! Sure wish you'd come back to LA."

"I miss you too, but I like it here. Like, seriously."

"Why? What does Denver have that LA doesn't?"

"The snowcapped mountains and changing seasons. I can't explain it, but I love it here. It's like the best of all worlds."

"Well, I know one thing this city doesn't have."

"What?"

"Me."

"Aww...Brie." Lea tried to give her a hug and almost ran them off the road again.

"Hands on the wheel, woman!"

Lea's infectious laughter filled the tiny car. "I promise no more hugs until we've made it safely to the rink. I don't need Sir going after my ghostly ass."

Brie giggled. "God, you're such a nut."

"And that's why you love me."

"Yeah, and the only reason I put up with all your lame-ass jokes."

"By the way, I've got another one for you."

Brie covered her ears. "Nope."

Lea pouted, her bottom lip quivering as she looked at Brie. Lea knew she couldn't resist that look.

"Fine," she sighed, "insult my sense of humor."

"Goodie! You know you're a kinky mom when…" Lea paused, waiting to make sure Brie was listening.

"When what?" Brie asked dryly.

"Your son's Boy Scout troop thinks you're the bomb because you helped them earn their merit badge for tying knots."

Brie chuckled despite herself. "That's barely funny."

She pointed to Brie's lips. "I heard you laugh. You know you love it."

"Well, only slightly…I think."

Lea grinned. "Oh, you'll be remembering that little joke and thinking of me when you're surrounded by your brood. Just you wait."

The idea of holding a tiny Sir in her arms made Brie's heart flutter. She couldn't really imagine it, yet the thought of having his child enchanted her.

Lea glanced over at her. "Hey, what's that adorable look on your face all about?"

Brie blushed. "It's nothing. Just glad to be with you again, girlfriend."

Once they'd pulled up to the ice-skating rink and parked, Lea got out her phone to text the girl they were meeting. Lea smiled when she read the response. "Autumn is already here and can't wait to meet you."

"Great," Brie said, with more enthusiasm than she felt. Making a fool of herself on the ice was not her idea of fun, and she still had reservations about Lea's new friend.

Lea grabbed Brie by the arm and squeezed her tight. "I can't believe it. I have my bestest friend meeting my new best friend. I feel so lucky!"

Autumn was waiting for them in the main lobby, hiding in the shadows in the corner. Lea released Brie and went straight for her, pulling her away from the wall.

Brie noticed two things right away. First, the girl wore a scarf that covered most of her face. Second, she moved stiffly when Lea pulled her away from the wall. Neither was off-putting, just odd. Brie held out her hand and smiled at Autumn. "Hello. I've heard a lot about you from Lea. Well, that's not true. I've heard very little about you, just that Lea thinks you're the best thing to happen since sliced bread."

The girl's eyes twinkled as she took the hand Brie offered. "I've heard all about you, Brie. Lea can't stop talking about her favorite Stinky Cheese."

Brie gave Lea a sideways glance. "Stinky Cheese? Really, Lea? The two of us haven't even met yet and she's already calling me Stinky Cheese."

Lea shrugged, grinning like the Cheshire Cat but Autumn took pity on Brie.

"You're right, I haven't introduced myself properly. It's unfair that I know so much about you but you know nothing of me." She moved away from the main entrance and into a darkened hallway. With a graceful movement, Autumn unwound the scarf around her head and revealed her face to Brie. She had a deep scar running from her ear to her lip, underneath her right cheekbone. Autumn smiled hesitantly at Brie.

"There's no reason to cover your face. You're beautiful," Brie assured her.

"You're very kind to say that." She caressed the scar self-consciously. "I prefer to get to know people before I show my face. Normally I wouldn't be so bold with someone I've just met, but based on everything Lea's shared, I feel as if I know you already. Plus I have this good feeling about you—it's as if we've been friends for a long time."

Brie was honored Autumn felt that way. "I'm not sure if it's because Lea loves you so much or you're just naturally awesome, but I feel the same way."

Autumn's smile was genuine and warm. It made the scar on her face invisible to Brie.

Lea giggled, hugging both girls at the same time. "Now that you two have met, my life is complete."

Brie rolled her eyes.

"Lea is a bit over-the-top, but I like that about her," Autumn said, glancing at Lea with affection.

"I like that about Lea the Lame too," Brie agreed, pinching Lea's cheeks as if she were a child.

"So would you two like to skate now?" Autumn asked, gesturing to the rink on the other side of the large double doors.

Brie grimaced. "Sorry, but I don't know how to skate."

"I'd be happy to teach you both," Autumn offered.

Lea and Brie looked at each other and shrugged, giggling as they made their way to the skate rental counter while Autumn headed into the rink. "Meet you on the ice," she called to them.

"Sure thing," Lea answered, waving to her. "Hey, Autumn, what did the doctor say to the girl who fell on her bum while ice-skating?"

"I don't know," Autumn shot back enthusiastically.

"Do you want some ice for that?"

Autumn's twittering laughter echoed down the hallway.

"I seriously can't believe she laughed at that," Brie teased.

"I'll have you know that Autumn laughs at all my jokes."

"I'll try not to hold that against her."

Once they had their skates in hand, the girls walked through the double doors into the rink area. There Brie saw Autumn in all her glory. She'd shed her heavy clothes and wore only a simple top and white skirt. Brie watched in amazement as the girl floated on the ice, turning in graceful circles on two legs, one of which happened to be made of metal.

"She's incredible," Brie whispered to Lea.

"She really is," Lea agreed, "in so many ways." She hugged Brie again. "I just *knew* you two would hit it off!"

Autumn spent the evening patiently instructing them on the fundamentals of skating. She also had a few lame jokes of her own to add as they practiced skating around the rink.

"How do you know you aren't making the Olympic skating team?"

Lea almost tripped when she looked up from her skates to ask, "I don't know, Autumn—how do I know I'm not making the Olympic team?"

"Your coach keeps screaming, 'Let go of the railing! Let go of the railing!'"

When Lea started laughing, she promptly fell on the ice.

Brie quickly grabbed onto the railing to prevent the same thing from happening to her. "Hey, is that supposed to be a commentary on our skating abilities?"

Autumn skated past them going backwards, holding up both thumbs. "You're doing *grrreat!*"

Brie looked over and saw Lea struggling to get up off the ice. "Lea, I think your friend is toying with us."

After several failed attempts to get back on her feet, Lea gave up and crawled to the wall. "I'm afraid you're right, Brie. I think it's time for some hot cocoa."

"I'm right behind ya, sister."

"But ladies, I have so much more to teach you," Autumn called from the ice, doing a beautiful spiral before them.

"Another day, Autumn. I don't want you to abuse Brie too much on her first day meeting you."

"Wimps!"

"A wimp and proud of it," Brie shot back, holding up both thumbs.

Once they'd settled in a booth with hot chocolate in hand, Brie decided to ask the obvious. "So, Autumn, do you mind me asking what happened?"

"No, not at all. I was in a car accident when I was a kid. After I lost my leg, my mom decided to sign me up for ice-skating to give me something to focus on and strive towards." Autumn looked back longingly at the rink. "It's only on the ice I'm as graceful and beautiful as I feel in my heart."

Brie was touched by her words. "You're a strong person."

The girl picked up her Styrofoam cup and smiled at Brie. "I'm lucky to be alive, and I keep that to the forefront of my mind any day I start feeling sorry for myself."

"Those are words we all should live by," Brie replied, admiring her even more.

Lea gave Autumn a hug. "I told you she was something special."

"You know what I like about you, Brie?" Autumn asked, still nestled against Lea's big boobs.

Brie felt heat rise to her cheeks. "I can't imagine."

"You're a famous director, and you didn't bring it up all evening. You were just genuine and fun."

"I'm not famous, Autumn. Lea's been exaggerating."

Autumn sat back up and smiled at her. "I know who you are, Brie Bennett. I've been following your story ever since the documentary came out. It's the reason I was brave enough to approach Lea. She was such a goof on screen; I just *had* to meet her in real life."

"Aww…" Lea pressed Autumn's face back against her chest one more time. "I can't believe I'm goofy enough for you, friend."

"You're even goofier than me, and I didn't think that was possible."

Brie enjoyed watching their friendly teasing. "So, Autumn, are you into the lifestyle yourself?"

"Oh no, I could never…"

"Too kinky for you?"

"No, it's just that I don't think I could handle being intimate with someone like that. I…I don't have the confidence. Besides, I'm much happier on the ice."

"Even though I've just met you, I can tell you're a beautiful person—and it's not just on the ice."

Autumn blushed a deep shade of crimson, then made a classic Lea move. "Why shouldn't you tell jokes while ice skating?"

Brie shook her head, knowing it was going to be bad. "No clue."

"Because the ice might crack up."

Lea and Brie started snickering, then broke out in giggles that wouldn't stop.

Autumn shook her head in amusement. "It wasn't that funny, but thanks."

The girls had another round of hot cocoa before heading home. Before they parted, Brie asked Autumn, "Do you mind if I give you a hug?"

"With kindred spirits, hugs are always welcome."

Brie wrapped her arms around the extraordinary woman. A sense of peace and wellbeing radiated from Autumn, surrounding Brie as she held her. "It was truly an honor to meet you tonight. Thanks for giving me a chance."

"Hey, I appreciate you putting up with me and my odd ways," Autumn said.

Brie turned to Lea. "And thank *you* for bringing us together, girlfriend."

"Actually, Brie, it was you and your film."

Brie paused to think about it. "I guess you're right. Amazing to think that everything we do has a ripple effect we're not aware of." She smiled at Lea and Autumn. "If you take it a step further, the three of us would never have met if Sir hadn't left his business card at the tobacco shop."

Brie smiled to herself. *Thank you, Sir!*

A Session with Clark

B rie was anxious about filming Ms. Clark again, and placed Tono's white orchid in her hair with trembling hands. *Help me to breathe, Tono,* she silently prayed.

She hadn't gotten a chance to talk privately with the Domme since Master Anderson's prank. Despite Lea's assurances, Brie was worried she might end up in the stockades during the session today. However, it was a risk worth taking since her producer, Mr. Holloway, had specifically requested she include a scene that featured the Dominatrix. The documentary was extremely important to Brie, and she was willing to do whatever was required to ensure Ms. Clark was part of it.

Brie took solace in the fact that the trainer herself had scheduled the session. Just like the first time, Ms. Clark surprised Brie with her willingness to help with the documentary, despite their many differences. She was unsure if it was because of the Domme's close relationship with Sir, or if there were other things in play she was unaware of. Regardless, Brie was determined to capture the beauty and allure of a skilled Domme on film. She owed the public no less.

Unfortunately for Brie, she arrived ten minutes late to the session through no fault of her own. Brie prided herself on being on time and fully expected to be reprimanded by the Domme, but Ms. Clark was the epitome of calm. She looked up when Brie entered the room.

"Good afternoon, Miss Bennett."

Her serene demeanor was startling, but it was not the only thing that struck Brie. The Domme had dressed in a sexy red corset and black hose, with dangerous-looking heels that ended in gold-tipped spikes. Her long blonde hair framed her flawless makeup, and her perfect lips sported the same vibrant red as the corset.

Ms. Clark was absolutely stunning, making it difficult for Brie to keep her eyes from straying back to the Domme as she set up her equipment.

"So, Miss Bennett, collared life treating you well?" Ms. Clark asked, a smile playing on her sensuous lips.

Brie stopped adjusting the camera to answer her. "Very well, Ms. Clark. I have grown tenfold under Sir's guidance."

"He seems to agree, and only has good things to say about you."

Brie cocked her head in surprise. "He talks about me to you?"

"Yes. We still keep in contact. Are you surprised by that?"

"I knew he called you on occasion, but I never suspected I was part of the conversation." Brie went back to work, hiding her smile.

Ms. Clark sighed in irritation. "I'm still not pleased you know as much as you do about my past, but I suppose it can't be helped. You are, after all, Sir's submissive. It's his choice what to share and to not share with you."

The way she said it put Brie on edge. Her words were true enough, but her tone of voice hinted that there were things Sir was *not* sharing with Brie. It upset her, but she refused to let her emotions muddy this opportunity to film the trainer.

"Ms. Clark, how will this scene play out today?"

"You will call me Mistress Clark during this session."

Brie nodded. "It will be my pleasure."

"I thought your audience would be interested in watching a Domme work with both a male and a female."

Brie's eyes lit up at the suggestion. She'd never seen Ms. Clark work with a man before, and she knew Mr. Holloway would approve. "If that's the case, where exactly in the room will both scenes take place? I want to make sure we have proper lighting."

Ms. Clark stood and walked slowly to the center of the room, turning around to face her. The Domme gestured to either side of her and gave Brie a beguiling smile.

It was unsettling—the allure of the woman was undeniable, and Brie found herself responding to it much the same as she would a confident Dom. She answered with a disinterested voice, not wanting her old trainer to pick up on her body's confusing reaction. "Perfect—that will make it easy for me."

Brie concentrated on the lighting while Ms. Clark set up her table of instruments. She glanced across the room and saw that the Domme had laid out a variety of canes of various lengths and widths, as well as a set of floggers. Brie remembered that the Dominatrix favored the cane, but she had never seen the woman wield it. She actually felt sorry for Lea.

When two unknown subs entered the room, Brie was taken aback. She'd naturally assumed that the Domme would be working with Lea for this scene.

The female submissive was stout, with a beautiful face, bleached hair and a boyish haircut, while the male was tall and lean with unusually long, brown hair. The two complemented each other well.

Brie watched them bow before Ms. Clark. They did not move or speak after bowing before their Mistress, and she did not acknowledge them as she finished setting up the table. Once she was done, she looked at Brie. "Ready?"

"Yes, Mistress Clark. I will simply film. I won't disturb the scene, but if at any point you wish me to stop, just signal to me."

"Good," she replied dismissively. Ms. Clark turned and addressed her subs. "Stand, Breeze and Leo. Thank Miss Bennett for the privilege of being filmed today."

They both stood gracefully and turned to Brie, bowing their heads slightly. "Thank you, Miss Bennett," they said in unison.

"My pleasure," Brie answered, smiling encouragingly at them. "There is no reason to be nervous about the camera or me. This is just a scene with your Mistress. Don't even think about it."

Ms. Clark walked around her submissives, tracing her long fingernail over their chests. Both were wearing black, Leo in form-fitting boxers and Breeze in a sports bra and thong. "My subs know to focus their attention only on me. Anything less would require swift and painful punishment."

Brie shivered, having experienced Ms. Clark's punishment in the past—she never thought of a paddle in the same way after that session.

Ms. Clark smiled alluringly at Brie. "Are you ready to begin, Miss Bennett?"

"Absolutely, Mistress Clark—just say the word."

The Domme instructed her subs where to stand. The two stood in exactly the same position, with their hands held at their sides in an open and pleasing manner, legs spread comfortably apart, heads lowered in a submissive stance. Their pose alone was artfully sensuous, inviting play.

"We begin," the Domme announced, picking up a thin rattan cane from the table and slapping it against her hand as she walked around her subs, openly admiring the two. "Leo, handsome and compliant. And then there's Breeze, striking and willful."

She caressed Leo's leg muscles with her cane, and Brie could see his physical arousal caused by the simple contact. Ms. Clark whacked him playfully on the ass as she passed, and he grunted in satisfaction.

When she came up to Breeze, she put the cane between her legs and tapped from side to side. The girl opened her legs into a wider stance.

"Better."

Ms. Clark moved around to face the sub and used the side of the thin cane to stroke the girl's breasts. She then caressed the sub's thighs with the instrument, using a gentle touch like that of a lover.

The Domme stepped back and lightly bounced the instrument up the front of the sub's thighs. Ms. Clark skipped over her mound and continued to tap up her stomach, stopping just below the crease of her breasts.

The Mistress then moved behind the sub and started to travel leisurely up her legs with the cane, tapping over the roundness of her ass and up the back. The strength of the contact was still playful.

"Watch as I play with my sub," the Domme commanded Leo. He dutifully lifted his head and turned to watch the seductress at work.

Ms. Clark rubbed the girl's ass with the side of the cane in lazy circles, letting the sub know which area would be first to feel its sting. Brie held her breath, waiting for the moment.

With lightning-quick speed, the Domme cracked the cane three times on Breeze's ass. The girl moaned in pleasure, obviously liking the sting the cane delivered. Ms. Clark came up behind her, almost but not quite touching. "Head up, Breeze." The sub stared at the ceiling as the Domme wrapped her arm around her, rubbing the cane over the front of her thighs just below her mound. The next area had been selected…

Brie watched expectantly as the Mistress delivered three quick strokes to the girl's groin. The sub moaned again.

Ms. Clark looked into the camera as she spoke. "I know what you want, Breeze."

Brie's breath caught. The way Ms. Clark pronounced the name…she could have sworn the trainer was speaking directly to her. Brie bit her lip to stop any unintended expression, knowing the Domme was staring at her.

"But I'm not going to give it to you," the Domme announced, breaking contact with the camera and whispering to her sub loud enough to be heard, "Yet."

Ms. Clark tapped the end of the cane on each nipple before moving over to the male sub and roughly grabbing his chin, planting a firm kiss on his lips. She ran her fingernails over his chest with one hand, still holding the cane with the other. The way she held it was like a promise—and a warning.

"Breeze, you may watch."

The girl lowered her gaze from the ceiling and turned to observe. Brie appreciated the sexual charm of being paired with another sub. She'd experienced it once with Lea. Seeing and hearing another person being played with was a total turn-on, especially when you knew you would be next.

"Do not move, sub," Ms. Clark said as she rubbed his torso with her cane before sliding it down over his groin. She struck the cane against his cock three times, causing it to swell underneath the fabric. The Domme looked down and smiled. "Yes, you enjoy the feel of the cane, don't you?"

"I do, Mistress," he agreed.

"But you like it harder," she purred, moving over to the table to pick up a thicker cane made of bamboo. "Hands behind your neck," she ordered.

He lifted his arms, showing off his chest and the large bulge in his boxers to the camera as Ms. Clark took her position beside him. It was a powerful scene, the virile male sub waiting to receive a caning from his stunning Mistress.

"Count out loud, Leo."

"Yes, Mistress."

Brie heard the satisfying thud as the bamboo made contact. Ms. Clark held it there for several seconds. Brie knew from experience that it allowed the sensation of the strike to dissipate throughout the body.

"One," Leo called out.

The Domme struck him again, harder the second time, and pressed the cane against his skin afterwards.

"Two," he said in a low, satisfied tone.

Each successive hit was slightly more intense than the last—she delivered them with impressive strength. The sub's shaft plainly showed what he thought of his Mistress' caning skills. She stopped at ten and rubbed the area with her palm as she kissed him deeply.

It was erotic and intimate.

She whispered something to Leo before breaking away and smiling at her other sub. "I have not forgotten you…"

Ms. Clark went back to the table and selected a cane braided in red leather. It was not as thin as the first, but similar in size. "Your Mistress knows your heart's desire, Breeze." She told the girl to hold out both hands.

The sub held them in front of her, palm side up.

"Good girl." The sensual way Ms. Clark said those simple words caused goose bumps to rise on Brie's skin. The Domme placed the cane in the sub's grasp, then began to run her hands over the girl's body, not aggressively or crudely. They were light, romantic caresses that traveled near the sensitive areas but never quite touched.

The amorous look on Breeze's face showed through the camera lens. Ms. Clark not only had her two subs captivated, but Brie knew her audience would be as well. This filming session was pure gold, she could feel it in her bones.

The Domme took the cane from the girl and commanded, "Bend over and grab your ankles."

The sub put her hands on her knees and slowly slid them down to her ankles in a sensual move. Mistress and sub were an erotic pair, bewitching the camera with every movement.

"Would you like to wear my marks, Breeze?"

"I would be honored, Mistress."

"Hold the position and make no sound."

Ms. Clark moved beside her and held the cane away from the girl's fleshy ass, making her wait—making everyone wait—for the Domme's pleasure.

Brilliant! Brie mused.

The strokes came in quick succession, one after the other down her ass to her thighs. When Ms. Clark finally stopped, Brie let out a breath. The girl had not made a peep.

Ms. Clark knelt down and lifted the sub's head. "Again?"

"Yes, if it pleases you, Mistress."

The Domme stood and glanced briefly at the camera with a confident look before she returned to her position. Again she made the sub wait to receive her attention. It was like riding a roller coaster and hanging at the top for those few seconds before falling.

The rain of rapping was as quick and thorough as the first set. The sub let out a moan at the end.

"I said no sound."

"Yes, Mistress."

Ms. Clark struck her swiftly, just a single stroke that had to hurt. The girl squirmed from the impact but remained silent. Another stroke landed seconds later.

"Stand. You took your punishment well, Breeze," the Domme complimented. The sub rolled gracefully up from her stance, a look of joy on her face despite the tears in her eyes.

Ms. Clark ran her hand over the girl's ass with a look of pride. "The marks look lovely on you, by the way. I knew they would."

"I love wearing your marks, Mistress," Breeze answered breathlessly.

Ms. Clark hovered achingly near the girl's mouth for a few seconds before kissing her. She broke the passionate kiss to put the cane down on the table, instructing the sub to join Leo.

Breeze moved beside Leo, the sides of their feet touching so they were connected physically as they stood before their Mistress.

Ms. Clark returned to the male sub, tracing her fingers over his jawbone. Brie could see a subtle shiver ripple through his body at her touch. He was on fire for her.

"I will end today's session with you together."

"Thank you, Mistress," he said gruffly.

She went back to the table and picked up the two floggers. "Relax and enjoy your reward."

The Domme started out caressing her subs by running the multiple tails of the floggers lightly over their skin at the same time. It was gentle and tender, a moment of connection between the three of them before she began.

Ms. Clark stepped away and began to swing the floggers in the air. She swung in large, lazy circles that landed on their skin with light thuds. Both submissives were smiling. Brie knew the pleasant feel of the flogger and felt a twinge of jealousy as she watched.

Soon the Domme switched the pattern, doing simultaneous figure eights. It took skill to deliver both strokes with equal strength while keeping a consistent rhythm between the two floggers. The pleasant sound of leather against skin filled the room as Ms. Clark increased the power of her strokes.

The visual effect of the dual floggers flying in the air was stunning to watch, but the graceful movement of the Domme wielding the tools was even more impressive. Brie could not take her eyes off her.

Ms. Clark changed things up again by swinging in tight circles while increasing the speed, so that the contact made was quick and intense. She moved her attention down to their asses, causing a rippling effect on their fleshy buttocks as the floggers made contact. It was sensual to watch, and hearing both subs groan with pleasure made it that much hotter.

Brie shifted in her chair, grateful she'd remembered to bring a towel this time. She knew Marquis Gray would have been proud of her forethought.

The Mistress ended her scene by slowing her swings and returning to figure eights. It was fascinating to watch the floggers hang in the air as they leisurely danced over the submissives' red skin.

Ms. Clark put the floggers down on the table and returned to her subs. She began to caress the backs of her submissives, whispering as she gently touched them. After several moments, she looked up at Brie and signaled her to stop filming.

While Brie was packing up her equipment, Ms. Clark walked over to her. "You and I should talk sometime, Miss Bennett. There are certain things we need to discuss."

"Yes, Ms. Clark." Brie wasn't sure what the Domme wanted to chat about, but before she ever set up a meeting with her old trainer, she would have to talk to Sir. "Thank you for today's session. It was truly exquisite to watch."

The Domme arched her eyebrow and asked, "You enjoyed yourself, did you? I'm curious, Miss Bennett, what appealed to you more? The play with the male sub or the play with the female?"

Certain it was a loaded question, Brie grabbed her last remaining items and hurriedly stuffed them into her bag. She decided to answer the question with a compliment. "You have delivered a beautiful example of both, Ms. Clark. It will be interesting to see how the public reacts. I don't think you could have done a better job representing both ends of the spectrum."

Unsure of Ms. Clark's motives, Brie rushed out of the room before the Domme could respond or ask a follow-up question.

Seeds of Doubt

Brie waited impatiently for Sir to call. He had yet to confirm a time or a date for his arrival in Denver and she was extremely unhappy about it. She *needed* to feel his strong arms around her, especially now, with all the nagging doubts swimming in her head.

Lea had casually mentioned the fundamental requirement of open communication between D/s partners, and the fact was that Brie had been hiding something from Sir for the last few days. Tonight she was not going to dishonor him or their relationship any longer by being a coward.

We're condors, she reminded herself when her phone finally rang.

"Good evening, Brie. I apologize for the lateness of the call."

"I don't mind, Sir. I'm just happy to hear your voice."

"How did filming go today?"

"Mistress Clark was amazing, Sir. Truly amazing! I'm still blown away by the scene and I've watched it five times."

"Mistress Clark? Why 'Mistress'?"

Brie giggled self-consciously. "She asked me to call her that while I was filming today. It slipped out just now." She immediately changed the subject, not willing to wait any longer and possibly lose her courage to confront him. "Any idea when you will be coming, Sir?"

"Actually, yes. I'll be boarding the plane tomorrow. Should be landing in Denver early Friday morning."

"Oh, I can't wait! I feel like it's been months, not days, since I've seen you."

"I agree, it does seem an unnaturally long time apart."

Before she lost her nerve, she asked, "Sir, this may seem silly, but I've been getting a weird vibe here and want to ask you something."

He chuckled. "A weird vibe, you say?"

She closed her eyes, forcing herself to say the thing she had been afraid to voice out loud to anyone. "Sir, are you keeping something important from me?"

The line was silent on the other end.

As the moments dragged on, Brie's fear increased.

"Sir?"

His next question did nothing to relieve her concerns. "Is there a reason you're asking, Brie?"

"There are several reasons, actually. First, Baron told me he was sorry to hear about your troubles with your mother, and this afternoon Ms. Clark seemed to imply that you're not being completely open with me. Then there was the dream I had the other night."

"A dream?" He laughed, but it sounded forced.

"I can't remember what happened, but I know your mother was part of it."

The dead silence on the other end was frightening to her.

"Sir, you *are* keeping something from me, aren't you?" When he didn't answer, she demanded, "I have a right to know! I remember when I had to kneel on rice because I kept something from you. What consequence is there if you do the same to me?"

"You don't know what's happened."

"Exactly! We're condors, Sir. Does that mean *nothing* to you? Why does everyone else seem to know, but the person closest to you is left in the dark?"

"Brie, I think it would be best if we both returned to LA, where we can discuss this in person, alone."

Her heart sank. The tone of his voice let her know it was far more serious than she'd imagined. When she hung up the phone, she felt completely numb. It wasn't until she had made it to the bed and was curled up in the blankets that she finally broke down and cried.

Brie's Christmas Pearls

Unfamiliar Territory

B rie woke up from a dream that involved Tono and a trail of orchids. She stretched out her arms above her head with a huge smile on her lips, the gentle presence of the Asian Dom still lingering. That smile died as soon as she remembered her phone call with Sir.

Rather than revisit those unwelcome feelings, she got up from her bed and walked to the desk in the corner. She opened the drawer, thrilled that Master Anderson had stocked it with stationary.

She pulled out several sheets of paper and a well-sharpened pencil. Brie stared at the writing instrument for a moment. How long had it been since she'd written with a pencil?

Inventory at the tobacco shop…

With that thought, a flood of memories came to mind: Mr. Reynolds' fatherly smile, that lazy ass Jeff, all those damn cigarettes—and Sir.

Brie shook off the feeling of sadness that threatened to smother her and began her letter.

Dear Tono,

I woke up this morning thinking of you and decided I should write you a letter.

I can't tell you how much I disliked leaving Japan, but I'm grateful for the time I got to spend with you, and for the chance to know your father before his passing. I will never forget honoring his memory with your family at his wake. It is something I'll always hold dear.

I'm beginning to understand why you chose to stay behind. There are times we must do what is right, even though it's hard and might tear us up inside. I respect you for remaining true to your values, especially when it comes at great cost.

I hope, with all my heart, you are able to find a balance where you can fulfill your duty to your mother and still honor your own needs. I think back on that night of glowing rope, the erotic beat of the music and the talent of your hands, and I know you have hit on something revolutionary. I hope you pursue it further, maybe even find your escape in it when you have need.

My time in Denver has been crazy. Lea is as full of bad jokes as ever, and wants me to share one with you. If you would like me to subject you to the torture, just say the word and I will include it in my next correspondence. Lea also introduced me to a new friend she met because of my documentary.

Autumn is truly amazing, Tono. Despite losing her leg as a child, she glides on the ice like an angel. I admire her strong spirit, and hope to hang out with her again soon. How cool that my film brought those two together. I just love that!

Although the training center in Denver is very different from the one in LA (practical jokes are the norm here), it seems to have a positive effect on the staff. Even Ms. Clark seems happy.

I think you should know I wear the beautiful comb you gave me whenever I film now. I can't tell you the number of times I hear your reassuring voice reminding me to breathe Thank you for the positive influence you are in my life.

Love, Brie

Writing to Tono Nosaka had a calming effect on her, as if she'd actually spent time in his presence. She sealed up the letter, saying aloud, "*Domo arigato*, Tono."

Brie spent her afternoon with Lea at a nearby park, under the colorful foliage of a stunning Colorado fall. They lay out on a large blanket, side by side, relaxing in the warmth of the autumn sun. The sky was a spectacular shade of blue, something Brie had never seen before.

"Is it extra blue because we're a mile above sea level?" she asked.

Lea shrugged, turning her head lazily towards Brie and smiled. "I don't know and don't care. I just love being here." She looked back up at the sky and took in a deep breath.

Brie did the same, breathing in the unique scent of fall. It reminded her of pumpkins, trick-or-treating and dressing in silly costumes as a child in the midwest. She'd missed that smell in California, but hadn't realized it until now.

"I wish I could stop time and just lie here in the sun forever."

"And look like a mummified piece of burnt bacon after a few weeks? No, thank you!" Lea replied, elbowing her.

"You know what I mean," Brie scolded gently.

"Yes. You don't want to face Sir."

Brie sighed in misery, vexed her friend knew her so well. "No, I don't. It makes it that much worse that everyone knows what's happened except me."

A tear fell down her cheek.

"I feel like a big joke, Lea."

Her friend rolled onto her side to face Brie, propping her head up with her hand. "No, girlfriend. No one feels that way about you. None of us would have known anything if the press hadn't gotten wind of it, and what we know is only what we've heard on TV."

"Why didn't you say anything to me?"

"Because Master Anderson asked me not to when he realized you didn't know. Seeing as we're besties, he figured it would come up in conversation, and he felt strongly that Sir should be the one to tell you."

"Well, I'm asking you now."

Lea groaned and lay back down, looking up at the sky. "I can't."

"Why?" Brie cried. "You're my best friend."

Lea turned towards her again, fidgeting with a stray thread on the blanket. "I know, and it's killing me not to say anything, but it wouldn't be fair to Sir."

"It's not fair to *me*," Brie complained.

Lea looked around apprehensively, then leaned close and whispered, "Okay, I'll only tell you that it was all over the news a few days before you showed up. It has to do with his mother and it's not good."

"Is Ruth coming after Sir again?"

Lea shook her head sadly. "No, nothing like that."

"What, then?" Brie pleaded.

"Look, sweetie, there has to be a reason he didn't tell you when you were in Japan. You'll have to give him the benefit of the doubt until you talk to him in person."

Brie put her hands to her face, covering her eyes to keep from crying. "I remember when Baron spoke about her; I sat there like a complete idiot complaining about how crazy she was. I should have known something was up when he acted so strangely. Then there was Ms. Clark. She mentioned that Sir was keeping things from me just before we started to film." Brie rolled away from Lea, staring at the mountains in the far distance. "All of which makes me feel like a fool."

Lea scooted over and hugged her, pressing her large boobs against Brie's back. "No one thinks you're a fool. We're just worried about you two."

Brie curled up into a ball. "I don't want to go home, Lea. I'm so angry with Sir for putting me in this situation, but I'm terrified that whatever he's hiding will tear us apart."

Lea squeezed her tighter. "Nothing can tear you two apart."

"I thought that once, but I'm not so sure now…"

Lea rolled Brie back over and said forcibly, "Don't think like that, not even for a second."

The tears started, and Brie was defenseless to stop them.

Lea wiped them away, stating in a serious tone, "A condor pair were nibbling on a dead clown. The male condor asked the female, 'Does this taste funny to you?'"

"Oh, Lea," Brie groaned, but as she mulled it over in her head it struck her as perfect. The joke not only referred to their condor love but hinted at her cooking skills. She smiled, but complained as she did so. "I hate that I love your bad jokes."

"I know, honey."

Master Anderson saw Brie off at the airport early the next morning, wearing his cowboy hat and tight-fitting blue jeans. He tipped the brim of his black hat as he said goodbye at the entrance of the security line. "Tell Thane I expect you two to return. He owes me."

Brie tried to sound more positive than she felt. "Sure."

Master Anderson lifted her chin, his intense green eyes boring into hers. "Young Brie, Thane is dedicated to you. Do not doubt that, even if current circumstances suggest otherwise."

She looked down at the floor, unable to look at him when she admitted, "It's humiliating to be the last to know."

"Look at me."

Brie gazed up, facing his penetrating gaze.

"Are the opinions of others more important than his?"

She shook her head slowly.

"Instead of worrying what others think, what you should be concerned with is the fact that he felt the need to protect you. Knowing Thane, only something extreme would evoke such a reaction from him."

"And you know what it is, don't you?"

"Although I know what's happened with his mother, I don't know Thane's reaction to it. He hasn't spoken to anyone—and that distresses me."

Brie suddenly felt ashamed. The whole time she'd been fuming about being shut out, not once had she considered Sir's emotional state. Something dreadful must have happened for him to isolate himself like that.

She told Master Anderson with renewed conviction, "Sir has called me home to talk. I trust we can work through it, whatever it is we have to face."

"You'd better, young Brie, or I will lose all hope that true love exists."

She smiled. "It does, Mr. Anderson, and your turn is coming."

Brie squealed when he lifted her off the floor in his strong arms. "What? Are you convinced that if you keep saying that, it'll make it come true?"

She met his gaze under the brim of his cowboy hat. "I only speak the truth, Mr. Anderson."

He chuckled as he put her back down, spanking her lightly on the bottom as if she were a child. "Run along, young lady, and bring comfort to your man."

She scooted towards the line but looked back at him, struck by how handsome he looked. "Thank you for this week…and for the candid talk."

He tipped his hat to her. "Anytime, little heifer."

She giggled, finding it humorous that he'd just called her a cow—and she liked it. "Be off with you, Mr. Cowboy. Go find yourself a new heifer to play with."

He nodded towards two girls at a magazine rack nearby, who'd been staring at him. "Actually, I've just spied my next conquest."

Brie waved one last time as she settled into line, smiling to herself as she watched him heading towards the girls. Her smile faded when he walked past the two and headed out the doors. She sighed with frustration but sent out a thought to him. *Don't lose hope, Master Anderson. Your day is coming.*

She got on the plane feeling more hopeful than she had before, because of her talk with Master Anderson. She truly believed that condor love was an impenetrable force, but she'd forgotten that in her shock. Unfortunately, when she landed in LA, Sir's text message rekindled her doubt.

I will meet you at home.

Brie frowned, disappointed that he would not be picking her up at the airport, but she took solace in the word 'home'. It spoke of warmth and comfort—a safe place to gather in the storm.

She felt a mixture of excitement and dread as she entered their apartment. Although she longed to see Sir again, she did not want to face the confrontation about to take place. Brie was disappointed to find the apartment dark and silent as she walked in.

She set her luggage down in the hallway, noting that the smell of Sir lingered in the air, which hinted to the fact that he'd been there recently. She glanced around their place and was startled to see her journal haphazardly thrown on the coffee table, along with other items from his recent trip. She walked over to her beloved journal and picked up the wrapped package. Sir had never even opened it.

What did that mean?

She walked into the bedroom and placed it in its normal resting place inside the drawer of her nightstand. Brie turned away, feeling profoundly hurt. A sense of foreboding gnawed at her heart knowing that whatever Sir was hiding truly *did* have the potential to tear them apart.

What had Ruth done this time? How was the witch planning to ruin their lives now?

She decided to do the only thing that would bring her peace. After unpacking her suitcase, she lit a fragrant candle and turned out the lights. Then she slowly undressed and knelt at the front door, waiting for Sir.

Brie closed her eyes and commanded herself not to dwell on the *what ifs*. Instead she thought back to the last time they'd been together, reliving it in her mind. The night before she'd left Japan—a precious memory of hers.

"Let me make love to you before we say goodbye," Sir told her, pushing her gently onto the bed. "Death has a way of helping you to appreciate what you have…"

She closed her eyes as he undressed her, desperate for the healing power of his touch.

"Right now all that exists is you, me and this moment in time." Her heart melted when he growled those words into her ear. She needed this cherished intimacy with Sir before she left his side, bound for Denver.

Things had been difficult with the passing of Tono's father—so many raw emotions exposed—but it was knowing that Tono Nosaka would not be returning to America that absolutely crushed her. It was tragic that the talented Dom would be staying in Japan to care for his ungrateful mother, giving up everything he loved and worked hard for.

Brie hadn't been able to shake off the feeling of grief until Sir had wrapped her in his loving embrace. "This is all I need," she confessed.

He kissed her tenderly. "I agree."

Brie mulled over those simple words, as she knelt waiting for him in the dark. They held more significance now that she understood. That night he'd kept his terrible secret inside as he made love to her, finding his escape in her embrace—and she had been oblivious. Instead of concentrating on his own pain, he had focused on relieving hers.

Time had seemed to stop when he began kissing her lightly, trailing a path from her neck down to her stomach, making a leisurely detour to kiss and suckle her breasts…

"You have gorgeous breasts, babygirl," Sir complimented as he kneaded and rolled them in his fingertips. He sucked and flicked his tongue against her erect nipples until her pussy ached with longing. Continuing lower, he licked and nibbled her stomach, causing her entire body to focus on his mouth as she anticipated his wicked attention to her clit.

That first, long, drawn-out lick made her shudder with desire. Sir tasting her wetness, seeming to savor it, made her feel sexually irresistible. She pressed her mound against his skilled tongue, begging for more of his attention.

Sir grabbed her ass cheeks and dived into her, lapping, sucking and teasing her pussy with his mouth. It was obvious that he took as much pleasure in eating her as she did in sucking him. She tilted her head back as she grasped his head, surrendering to his tongue.

"You will come many times tonight," he informed her. "Not because I command it, but because I plan to love your body well."

She moaned as the first orgasm began to build in intensity.

"Don't resist me tonight, babygirl. Let your body respond freely."

She closed her eyes, overwhelmed by the love flowing from him. She let her climax build until it reached a glorious level before letting go, needing him to feel how much he pleased her.

"That's my good girl…" he murmured between her legs. Sir rode out her orgasm with his tongue pressed against her pulsating clit, then he moved slowly down her legs, teasing her with sensual nibbles and licks. He stopped at her feet, tickling them with light kisses until she giggled and squirmed.

Sir paused, looking at her intently, the smile on his lips about doing her in. "Lie still and let me have my way with you."

Brie willingly opened her legs to him again and purred, "Have your way with me, Thane."

Using his given name had a definite effect on Sir. He hesitated for a second before crawling between her legs. He stopped to gaze down into her eyes before taking her. "I count on your love more than you know."

At the time, she'd thought he'd meant it as a sweet nothing, but now she understood he'd been speaking from a heart overwhelmed with pain.

Brie was brought back to reality by that revelation. She swallowed back tears, straightening her posture. One sobering thought echoed in her mind as she knelt on the floor waiting for him...

Sir needed me that night.

She'd been blind to his pain, greedily receiving the love he offered, ravenous for its healing power. All the tension and sadness caused by her week in Tokyo dissolved the moment he'd entered her. Afterwards she'd lain in his arms, exhausted but content, reflecting on his earlier statement that death had the ability to help a person appreciate what they have.

Brie distinctly remembered looking at his handsome face as she caressed his strong jaw, and being filled with a deep sense of gratitude.

In response, he'd taken her hand and placed it over the brand on his chest.

The Truth

When she heard the jingle of keys as the door was unlocked, her heart almost stopped. This moment before confrontation was excruciatingly cruel; the knowledge that it could either end well or in complete disaster.

Think before you speak, but don't hold back, she commanded herself.

The door swung open, but Sir stayed in the hallway for a moment before entering their apartment. He shut the door and walked over to her, placing his hand on her head. A flood of energy passed between them, even though neither had spoken. When he removed his hand, she looked up at him expectantly.

"Stand, Brie."

The use of her given name was significant in this situation. Although he had accepted her submission by placing his hand on her head, Sir wanted to speak to her as an equal.

Brie stood up gracefully, keeping her head bowed, suddenly aware how naked she felt standing before him—it was a new and unwelcome feeling.

In a move uncharacteristic of Sir, he took off his jacket and covered her with it. Rather than it being a tender gesture meant as comfort, it made her feel cold inside. Something was fundamentally wrong between them.

"Would you like a drink?" he asked.

It was only ten in the morning, but she realized he must still be on Japan time. "No thank you, Sir."

He gestured that she should take a seat on the couch while he fixed himself a martini. She listened to the ice clinking in the metal shaker. Normally the sound of his vigorous shaking brought a thrill, but today it only caused her concern.

Sir needs a drink to talk to me…

When he came out of the kitchen, he avoided looking at her as he walked to the window and gazed at the city below. Sir took several sips of his drink before speaking.

"I know this was unfair to you."

Brie let out a sigh of relief. At least he'd acknowledged it. "I want to know what happened, Sir."

He shook his head, taking another sip. She sensed his emotional walls go up with that simple request. Was he going to keep it from her even now?

"I deserve to know."

He glanced at her briefly, then looked back over the city. "How much do you know already?"

Brie got up from the couch and walked over, unhappy with the distance between them—both physical and emotional.

"Almost nothing, because no one would talk to me about it. However, I'm certain it involves your mother, because I was told it made the national news."

"I didn't anticipate that. Why the hell would it make the news?" he muttered, tilting his glass back to finish the rest of its contents.

Brie pulled at the long sleeves of Sir's jacket to expose her hands, then she drew near to him, touching him lightly on the arm. He lowered his head, a look of torment clouding his eyes.

"Tell me…please," she whispered, standing on tiptoes to kiss him on the mouth.

His lips were unresponsive, but she saw tears in his eyes. "I'm a mess, Brie."

"Condors, Sir."

He stared at her for a moment before nodding. Sir put down his glass and led her to the kitchen. He pulled out a chair for her at the table, then went into the pantry, bringing out the bag of rice. He plopped it on the kitchen table, sitting down on the chair opposite her. "When I'm done, if you deem it necessary, I will kneel on rice."

A smile tugged at her lips. "Fine. I'll make that determination after you explain your silence to me."

He stared at Brie, the tortured look in his eyes breaking her heart, but no words came forth. She met his gaze and waited patiently.

Sir finally cleared his throat, stating, "I received news of my mother while we were in Tokyo."

Brie nodded encouragingly.

"I didn't see the point of burdening you with it at the time."

"Bu—"

He shook his head. "You were already stretched emotionally trying to support Tono and truthfully…I could not process the news myself."

A chill ran down Brie's spine as she thought back on the trip. "I know exactly when you got the news. You were different in the car after I visited Tono's father."

Sir nodded. "I *did* receive the call at the hospital while you were talking to Master Nosaka." He looked at her suspiciously. "But how could you possibly know that?"

"You were different, Sir. I could sense it, but simply assumed that seeing Tono's father on the verge of dying had brought up bad memories for you."

He frowned. "I failed to realize how adept you are at reading people. It's a gift and a curse."

She took his hand in hers and squeezed it. "Not a curse, Sir. It's a characteristic condors share. Please tell me what's happened with your mother."

"You really don't know?" he asked in disbelief.

"No one would tell me, out of respect for you."

"I have good friends, I suppose," he said half-heartedly, staring past her.

"You do, Sir."

He let out a long sigh, putting his hands to his temples as he closed his eyes. "There was an earthquake in China."

"Oh, my God, is Ruth dead?"

Sir opened his eyes and shook his head slowly, his eyes clouded with pain. "My mother was providing relief in a remote area deep in the interior of China. She wasn't found for days after the quake. How ironic is that? She was there to provide medical relief, yet there was none to be had when she needed it."

He looked away, grimacing. "Doctors tell me if my mother had received immediate care, she would have survived the incident. Instead she lies in a coma, connected to feeding and breathing tubes to keep her alive."

Brie got up from her chair and moved over to him, settling on his lap when he offered it. She hugged him tightly, whispering, "I'm so sorry."

"How many times have I wished she would die? But damn it, not like this…" He pressed her against his chest. "This is my fault, Brie. I sent her there as penance, and now she is frozen between life and death."

Brie pulled away and looked him in the eye. "What's happened is not your fault. You gave her a second chance even though she didn't deserve it."

He growled fiercely. "As much as I hate the Beast, I never wanted this!"

Brie knew exactly what was needed. "We should go see her, Sir. Right now." She tried to get off his lap, but he held her tighter.

"That's where I just came from. As soon as you left, I flew to China to assess her condition and see if anything could be done."

"Oh…" Brie couldn't hide how much not being included hurt.

Sir lifted her chin, forcing her to look him in the eye. "Even though you are angry with me now, I do not regret keeping this from you. I was too full of rage and sorrow at the time." He gazed at her with tenderness. "Truthfully, Brie, I did it to protect you—from me."

"But I'm not afraid of you, Sir," she declared defiantly.

"You should be. Although I would never hurt you physically, I'm quite capable of tearing you apart."

"You should know that I can bear the brunt of your anger, as long as I understand its source."

He groaned as he released his hold on her. "When I shared that I have my demons, it was not simply idle talk, Brie. I *am* my mother's son. I know you admire my ability to assess people and deliver what they need, but what you don't understand is that it can also be used to harm them. There are times I have to fight against the urge to destroy."

She cradled his face in her hands. "You are a good man, Thane Davis. You would not harm me."

He sighed, shaking his head. "That day, when I got the news…it festered inside me like poison, growing in intensity with each passing second. If I had not retired into the bedroom, I guarantee you would have been hurt."

"It's not healthy to hide things from each other," Brie insisted.

"You were having a hard enough time dealing with Tono. Remember?"

"But I could have handled it, Sir. Being left in the dark is far, far worse."

"Don't you understand, Brie? I needed time to process and compartmentalize my feelings before they controlled my actions and I did something I would regret."

"While I believe you felt that you were protecting me, I'm still resentful you let me fly off to Denver like a clueless idiot, believing things were okay, while you faced your mother's situation alone."

He closed his eyes and nodded, taking in her words. "Yes, it was unfair to send you away unaware, but it brought me comfort to know you were happy and safe."

She pressed her forehead against his. "I love that you want to protect me, Sir, but I'm not fragile. I won't break."

He brushed her cheek tenderly. "You must allow me the space I need, Brie."

"I can't be the last to know. We're partners, Sir."

He huffed in frustration. "How could I know the media would cover it here in the States? I didn't intend to put you in that situation, and there is no way in hell I could have foreseen that."

"Fine," she conceded, "as long as it doesn't happen again."

He leaned forward, his mouth centimeters from her lips. "Rice or no rice?"

As tempting as those lips were, Brie avoided the kiss and reached for the bag. She looked at it thoughtfully before stating, "You deserve to be punished, regardless of your good intentions. However, I'm a reasonable submissive and won't punish you—this time. As long as it never happens again."

"Rest assured I shall come to you first, but I still need my space. Forcing the issue will only be met with resistance."

"I respect your need for space, but don't take too long to include me. It hurts."

He kissed her on the lips, murmuring, "Forgive me, Brie."

His tone was light, but she saw the tortured look in his eyes when he lifted her off him and picked up the bag of rice to return it to the pantry.

Sir hadn't spoken about his feelings after seeing his mother—he'd purposely avoided the issue—but Brie was willing to give him more time, grateful they had successfully navigated this first crisis.

She smiled when he came back to the table, saying as she sank to the kitchen floor, "Let my lips show you just how much you've been missed, Sir."

Coen's Lesson on Spanking

It didn't take long for Brie to realize they hadn't navigated anything at all. She could see Sir was struggling under the weight of his emotions, but he still was unwilling to speak of them. Instead, he became uncharacteristically moody and withdrawn as he devoted his time and focus to work in an attempt to escape the pain that threatened to consume him.

Brie felt his torment and longed to share the burden he was carrying. Since he was unwilling to confront it, she broached the subject one morning while sipping coffee.

"Sir, can we talk?"

He looked at her warily but answered, "Certainly, Brie."

She took his hand, hoping the contact would ease his building anxiety. "You haven't really told me how you feel about what's happened to your mother."

Brie could feel the walls instantly rise as he tried to pull away from her, but she'd been prepared for that. "I can see it's eating you up inside, Sir."

His nostrils flared. "Why bring up unpleasant emotions? Talking about it will only drag out memories of a past I have no interest in revisiting."

She smiled at him sympathetically. "But keeping those feeling buried is killing you. I see it in your eyes; I feel it in your touch."

His response was curt and dismissive. "I don't want to discuss it with you."

Brie squeezed his hand, maintaining their connection. "You told me to give you space and I've done as you've asked. However, things are not getting better. It's only getting worse."

"Brie," he snarled menacingly, "don't force me down this path with you. You will regret it." He stood up and broke away from her, grabbing his car keys. "I'll be out all day. Don't bother calling."

Brie swallowed the feelings of rejection as the door slammed shut. Every time she thought they were moving forward as a couple, she found herself in the same place, excluded and alone.

She understood that Sir had been reluctant to take her as his submissive for this very reason—she *knew* that—but it didn't make his rejection any easier.

Brie was scheduled to meet with Master Coen that day to film a scene for the new documentary. Although she was sorely tempted to cancel, she didn't want to disrespect the Headmaster's time.

God, how she wished Lea was around—hell, even Mary would have been a comfort to her right now.

Brie got up and dutifully went to the bathroom to apply her makeup, putting her hair in a ponytail to avoid having to style it. She added Tono's white orchid to give herself a more finished look. Out of respect for Master Coen, she dressed in a business suit and high heels, when all she really wanted was to slip on a pair of comfortable sweats.

Pulling into the parking lot of the Submissive Training Center brought back memories of more carefree days, when life had seemed full of promise and laughter. She got out of her car and walked to the entrance, smiling when a young man graciously opened the door for her. She thanked him—images of Faelan dancing in her head.

She hadn't thought of Todd Wallace in ages, and hoped Faelan and Mary were doing well together. No one had heard from the couple since they'd joined the commune. Cell phones were not allowed there, and Mary hadn't made any effort to contact Brie since she'd left.

You'd better be having the time of your life, bitch, Brie thought with a grin.

"Hello, Miss Bennett, would you like me to inform Headmaster Coen that you are here?" the receptionist asked pleasantly.

"Please."

Brie stood beside the welcome center, lowering her gaze to avoid eye contact when she noticed some of the male students approaching on their way to business classes. She'd been trained well, but she jumped like a newbie when the receptionist announced, "Good morning, Marquis Gray."

Brie held her breath, drumming up courage before turning around and greeting him with a bright smile.

"Miss Bennett, what brings you here?" the ghostlike Dom asked.

"I'm filming a scene with Headmaster Coen today."

"Ah, for the new documentary, I take it."

"Yes, I'm hoping to film a few scenes here for the second one."

He took the mail the receptionist handed him and looked it over before nodding to Brie. "I trust the filming will go well. Please see me after you're done."

Brie's smile faltered for a moment, but she responded appropriately, "It would be my pleasure, Marquis Gray."

The elevators opened and Master Coen walked out, as impressive-looking as the first time she'd met him—all muscle, but with a sophisticated air about him.

"You've returned, Miss Bennett."

"I can't seem to stay away, Headmaster Coen."

He chuckled good-naturedly as he guided her into the elevator. Master Coen led her to his office—Sir's old office. Again, memories assailed her as she glanced around the room. "Is this year's class performing well?" she asked, needing the distraction of idle conversation.

"As well as can be expected this early on. At least we aren't distracted by unnecessary drama."

She smiled knowingly, certain the Headmaster was referring to her fraternization with Sir during her training. Master Coen added with a charming smile, "Best thing that ever happened was you settling down so the world could continue."

"And yet I always find myself back here."

"Troublemaker to the core."

She laughed, but was unsure if he partially meant it. "How are your submissives doing?"

"We've added a third to the mix—seems to be the perfect combination of personalities."

"Three?" she asked in surprise. "I guess you're well on your way to a harem."

He sat back in his chair. "I would have no complaints about that, as long as my girls all get along. The real skill is recognizing who would be an asset and who would just bring chaos to our home."

"I suppose you would never have considered me a good fit, then."

"No," he agreed. "You invite chaos to the most stable of institutions."

She ignored his cheeky insult. "I assume we are still filming a spanking scene today."

He nodded, with a glint in his eye. "Yes. I noticed you were lacking a spanking scene in your first documentary."

"That I was."

"Well, today I plan to educate the American public on the pleasures of spanking." He got up from Sir's desk and held the door open for her. "My newest submissive will be joining us on the stage in a few minutes."

So it was to be in the auditorium? Brie felt honored that Master Coen was giving the world a glimpse into the heart of the Center itself.

While Brie readied her camera, she watched the Headmaster set a scene reminiscent of the one he'd done with her during training. With arms of muscular steel, Master Coen lifted the teacher's desk and set it on the stage. He returned with a chalk board and props, including a ruler, a container of pencils and an apple. He placed them carefully on the desk, taking obvious pride in setting up the scene.

"Do you have enough light, Miss Bennett?"

She shook her head. "If we could turn them up a bit, that would be optimal."

He went to the back of the auditorium and turned them up until the stage was bathed in bright light. "Enough?"

She looked through her viewfinder and gave him a thumbs-up. "Perfect."

He pulled out his cell phone to call his sub. "Meet me at the auditorium doors." While they waited, he explained to Brie, "I want you to capture the expressions on her face."

"I was thinking the same thing," she agreed. "I've set up the camera at this angle so it will center on her face and the swing of your hand. It will also allow you to strip her ass bare if you need to without exposing her nakedness."

He took a peek through the viewfinder. "Excellent, Miss Bennett."

There was a soft knock. Master Coen smiled as he walked to the door to greet his sub. A middle-aged woman entered the auditorium, dressed in a school uniform complete with knee-high socks, pigtails and a tiny little skirt. He cupped his sub's chin and kissed her before introducing her to Brie.

"Miss Bennett, I would like you to meet the newest member of my family. Her official name is raven, but we all call her rae at home. You may call her rae as well if you wish."

Brie held out her hand, admiring the woman's thick black hair. "It's a pleasure to meet you, rae. Thanks for agreeing to film with me today."

The woman shook her hand enthusiastically. "I can't believe I'm getting to be part of your film!" She turned to Master Coen. "I'm such a lucky sub."

"Yes, you are," he replied, sounding amused by her obvious excitement. His pride in her was touching to witness, but Brie had to swallow down feelings of sadness knowing Sir used to look at her the same way.

Breathe…

She played with the flower in her hair as she explained, "Just as I did in the first film, I'll stay behind the camera. Don't pay attention to it or to me. If at any time you need to stop filming, just give me the signal."

Master Coen grabbed his sub's ass with his beefy hands, pressing her against him. "Are you ready to make film history, rae?"

"Ready and willing, Master."

"Then stand next to the chalkboard and write *I will not talk when the teacher is speaking* fifty times."

Rae bowed to him before skipping up to the stage and going to the chalkboard to begin her assigned task.

"You may begin filming," Master Coen stated as he headed onto the stage to join her.

Brie followed him with the lens as Master Coen ascended the steps. She couldn't keep from smiling when he picked up the ruler from the desk and questioned, "What happens to willful students?"

Rae answered timidly, "They get punished, Headmaster."

"Yes, they do. In your case, since this is the second offense, I believe a harsher punishment is in order."

Rae stopped writing and turned to him. "Please, Headmaster, I promise to be good."

"You promised me that the last time." He hit the ruler against the desk. "Put the chalk down and lean against the desk, legs together, palms flat on the wood."

She put down the chalk hesitantly and approached the desk with a shy smile directed at him.

"Don't move," he instructed, pushing her head down on the desk so she faced the camera.

Brie felt her body respond to his forcefulness, remembering their own scene together. She hadn't really known Master Coen at that point in her training. When Brie scened with him that first time, she'd been frightened that he planned to hurt her as punishment for her involvement with Sir. Instead, the muscular trainer introduced her to the sensuality of a good spanking. It had been a surprising lesson she'd never forgotten.

Brie felt tingling sensations course down her spine as he positioned himself behind his willing sub. The Headmaster reached over and grabbed a pencil from the desk. "Open," he commanded, putting the wooden pencil near her lips. "Bite down on it. I want to be certain the other classes aren't disturbed while you take your punishment."

He took off his jacket and hung it on the chair, then unbuttoned his cuffs before slowly rolling up each sleeve to expose his impressive arms. Brie wondered how many women in America would be daydreaming of being punished by his bare hand after seeing this film.

"Ten swats to start off with." He lifted her tiny skirt and caressed her ass through the thin material of her white cotton underwear. "Young women need to learn to respect their superiors."

Rae nodded.

Brie held her breath as he swung his hand back, readying for the first swat. The distance let her know it was going to be a hard one. His hand came down on rae's right ass cheek, the sound of it echoing in the auditorium. Rae whimpered as she bit on the pencil. He delivered the second with the same force on her left ass cheek.

Rae cried out between her clenched teeth.

"Shh…" he said soothingly, rubbing her buttocks with his large hand.

Rae wiggled her ass, apparently begging for more.

He took his time, teasing her with light caresses before he finished the remaining swats. He didn't stop until all had been delivered. Rae's whimpers filled the large room, her eyes tearing up by the end.

Master Coen took the pencil from her mouth and set it on the desk. He caressed her ass gently and asked, "Why are you being punished?"

She answered sweetly, "Because I was talking in class."

"And why is that a problem?"

"You were lecturing, Headmaster."

"Yes, and I was in the middle of a very important lecture. How dare you compromise the success of other students by interrupting my lesson like that. As this is your second infraction, I can't let you off lightly."

Rea smiled, her cheek still resting on the desk. "I understand, Headmaster."

"Don't cry out."

She nodded, her eyes half-closed and glazed over with lust.

He looked at her ass and shook his head disapprovingly. "I cannot punish you properly with these on." The angle of the camera let Brie barely see the swell of her naked ass as he stripped off her panties.

"Open those legs," he commanded.

Rae adjusted her posture, keeping her cheek pressed against the wood.

"Good girl. Now let's make that ass a little pinker." He picked up the ruler and got into position. "I think another ten will do."

Rae took her punishment, moaning and gasping through it but never once crying out. The sound of wood slapping against skin was erotic, but watching rae squirm and wiggle as he applied the ruler was even sexier to Brie.

When he finally put the ruler down, both Brie and rae let out sighs. He caressed the woman's sore buttocks. "Now that's a nice shade of pink. I think you're ready for a proper spanking."

Master Coen rubbed his hands together vigorously, making them warm with friction. "I want you to count out your punishment in your prettiest voice."

Rae answered in a low, flirtatious tone, "Yes, Headmaster."

He swatted her hard, moving repeatedly from one ass cheek to the other. Rae called each one out as she had been instructed, keeping her voice light and inviting.

He stopped after twelve and leaned forward, whispering something in her ear. Then his hand disappeared under rae's skirt as he nibbled on her earlobe. The soft moans she made let Brie know she was very much enjoying what Master Coen's hand.

He kissed her cheek chastely before positioning himself for another round of spanking. Although rae whimpered on several occasions, she counted out each swat in the same flirtatious tone; it would allow the audience to enjoy their play. However, it was the mystery of not seeing what Master Coen's hand was doing under the skirt whenever he stopped spanking that had Brie worked up.

This was an extremely naughty scene that kept an air of innocence because of the props, rae's cute little outfit and the modest camera angle. Brie hoped it would meet with Mr. Holloway's approval, even though she swore rae came at least four times during the filming.

After the scene was over, Master Coen handed his sub the apple from the desk. "To replenish your energy. I plan to ravish you in a few minutes."

Brie hurried to put her equipment away so the couple could enjoy the high they'd created together. While she was finishing up, Master Coen came over and asked, "Did you find the scene satisfactory, Miss Bennett?"

"Yes, it was...an invigorating scene."

"Rae has a fetish for spanking. Easiest way to get her off is with the bare hand," he said, looking proudly at his palm.

Brie stared at his hand, knowing its feel and allure. "You did a fine job showcasing a spanking scene, Headmaster. I especially appreciated the role-playing. I think it will read well on screen."

Rae skipped up to them. "I love playing the naughty student. Could you tell?" she asked with a grin, just before she took a big bite of her apple.

"Yes, it was quite obvious that you enjoyed it. Maybe a little *too* obvious," Brie replied with a wink.

"Spanking can get you in all kinds of delicious trouble," rae said, giving Master Coen a flirtatious bow.

That seemed to be Brie's cue to leave, so she picked up her camera bag and started towards the door. On her way out, Master Coen mentioned to her, "I suggest a visit to Nosh, the head trainer for the Dominants."

Brie turned to face him. "You think he might be interested in filming a scene?"

"It's possible."

She remembered the commanding presence of the Native American trainer during her critique of Faelan. His long hair and brown skin had been attractive to Brie, but it was his stern gaze she remembered the most.

"Nosh doesn't tolerate foolishness," Master Coen informed her.

Brie felt a pit in her stomach at the thought of meeting with him. "Is he expecting me?"

"No, but he knows of the project. I'm uncertain whether he's interested."

"Ah..."

Brie thanked Master Coen and made her way to the Dominant Training side of the school, despite her misgivings. The halls of the Training Center were empty during the day, although the business college above bustled with activity. It made for a lonely walk to the head trainer's office.

She refused to let her fear get the better of her, so she screwed up her courage, straightening her posture and throwing back her shoulders before knocking on Nosh's office door. When she heard no invitation to come in, she knocked again with a little more force. Brie was actually thrilled when she got no response. The fact was, she felt ill-prepared to face such an intimidating presence in her current emotional state.

As Brie walked to the elevator, a sense of pride washed over her. In spite of wanting to curl up and die, she had just filmed another winning scene for her documentary. Proof that she was meant to succeed in the industry, no matter what life threw at her. Still, she was anxious to get out of the Center before Nosh showed up.

She hit the elevator button several times, willing it to hurry. Naturally, that was when she heard her name being called from the commons area.

"Miss Bennett."

Confrontation

Brie closed her eyes and steeled herself before walking over to Marquis Gray. The man read her far too easily.

"You seemed in a hurry just now. Did you forget you were meeting with me?"

She avoided his eyes as she sat down, not wanting him to know she *had* forgotten his request. "I was told by the Headmaster to meet with Master Nosh. Since he isn't in his office, I had hoped the receptionist might know his whereabouts."

"Master Nosh is out for the day, so I'm afraid you will have to schedule a meeting with him later."

"Good to know." She finally met Marquis' gaze and smiled. "Then I guess we can talk if you're free now."

"Actually, I've been waiting for you. I'm growing concerned, Miss Bennett. I've invited Sir Davis to join me for dinner on several occasions, but he has yet to respond. It's not like him. Can you shed some light on the matter?"

Brie was careful with her answer, not wanting Marquis to know of their recent struggles. "Sir has been preoccupied with work lately. I'm sure it is simply an oversight."

"I thought so too, until I saw you today."

Brie groaned inwardly.

Raising an eyebrow he asked, "Are things going well?"

"As I said, Sir has been working long hours. His overseas business is beginning to take off, but it requires an inordinate amount of time."

Not a man to mince words, Marquis Gray demanded, "What's wrong? I only ask because I was your trainer and am invested in your success."

"I appreciate your concern, but it's unnecessary." Brie cursed herself when her lip trembled slightly, but was grateful that Marquis Gray didn't seem to notice.

"Why don't you invite Sir Davis for me personally, then? Saturday night. Tell him I won't accept no for an answer. You will join us as well. I know Celestia has missed your youthful presence."

Brie silently congratulated herself for successfully thwarting Marquis' intuitive powers. "I'll be happy to relay the message, Marquis Gray."

"Good. I expect to see you both at six. It appears we have much to discuss."

It was obvious that Sir was *not* anxious to meet with Marquis for dinner, although he agreed to go. As retribution, Sir made her cook an egg custard to take for dessert. She groaned as she fished out a piece of shell from the bowl of cracked eggs. The smell of vanilla, nutmeg and cinnamon was tantalizing, but she knew Marquis would never eat the dessert. She held out hope that Celestia might give her first attempt at custard a try.

Brie sprayed air deodorizer in the kitchen and down the hallway to the bedroom as the custard finished baking, just in case the smell of eggs had settled there. She knew having her make an egg dish was as much a punishment for Sir as it was for Marquis.

She was surprised Sir was uncharacteristically late picking her up that night. He did not provide her with any explanation, nor did he attempt to make up for lost time on the road.

They did not arrive at Marquis Gray's home until well after six. The door opened before they even set foot on the porch.

"I wasn't sure you were coming," Marquis told Sir, ushering Brie in with a slight smile.

"Yet here I am," Sir answered curtly, following Brie inside.

The conversation between the two Doms remained terse and formal the entire evening, a far cry from the last time they'd visited together. Luckily, Celestia was her gentle and calming self, bringing a needed sense of ease to the gathering as she took Brie's offering of dessert and directed them to seat themselves at the table.

Humorously, the first course was a Caprese salad. Brie had to stifle a giggle. Evidently both Doms thought alike. Marquis was well aware that Sir disliked tomatoes, leaving Sir to set them aside, eating only the mozzarella and basil left on his salad plate.

Marquis kept the conversation going throughout the dinner with questions about Sir's business, his trip to Japan and his future plans for his consulting business. Sir responded by peppering him with a number of questions as well. Through their discussions, Brie discovered that after her documentary released, Marquis had begun crafting custom floggers.

It seemed that a flogger handmade by the now-famous Marquis Gray was quite the 'it' item.

When the time for dessert finally came, Brie started wringing her hands under the table. Celestia brought out the covered dish and lifted the lid with a flourish.

Marquis Gray stared at the custard without any expression on his face. "Did you make this, Miss Bennett?"

"I did, Marquis Gray."

"I find myself too full to eat dessert," he announced.

"I understand."

"But I can't wait to try it," Celestia exclaimed.

Brie cut the custard pie, noting the light texture. She handed a piece to Celestia, confident it was going to be good. She then cut a small piece for herself and watched in eager anticipation as Celestia brought the dessert to her lips.

Ruby lips encased Brie's creation, but the expression on Celestia's face was not one of pleasure but of shock as she quickly swallowed and put her fork down.

Brie didn't understand and took her own bite, spitting it out immediately.

Marquis Gray picked up Celestia's plate and sniffed it, then looked it over carefully, appearing amused. "Perfectly cooked, correct consistency… Let me guess, someone mistook salt for sugar."

Brie let out a little whimper.

"Is that true?" Sir asked her.

Brie's bottom lip quivered when she answered him, "I'm afraid so, Sir. It's inedible."

"No, it's not that bad," Celestia insisted, picking up her fork and cutting another piece. Marquis grabbed her wrist before she could put it in her mouth, forcibly taking the utensil from her.

"I will not let you poison yourself." He addressed Brie sternly. "Did I not stress numerous times during the cooking session that you must always taste your food? No one, I repeat, *no one* should ever have to eat your mistakes."

Brie looked down in shame, then turned to Sir when he said her name. She barely had enough courage to look him in the eyes.

Sir's hard stare was chilling, but then she saw a glimmer of a smile creep across his face before he began chuckling loudly. "As if eggs weren't bad enough."

As soon as Marquis and Celestia joined in his laughter, Brie let out a sigh of relief, knowing she'd been forgiven. "I apologize for the custard. I will not make that mistake again."

"No, Miss Bennett, you will *not*," Marquis asserted.

Sir held out his arms and Brie gratefully settled into them, resting her head on his chest. "Take it easy on her, Gray. She was doing me a favor."

Sir took her chin and shook it gently back and forth. "I knew I was getting a non-cook when I collared you, but I failed to realize how deep your ineptitude goes—incredible, simply incredible."

Brie was grateful when he kissed her on the lips. At least Sir wasn't holding her honest mistake against her.

"Now that you've had your bit of fun, Sir Davis," Marquis said, "why don't we retire to the other room and let our subs clean up? There are certain things we need to discuss."

"If you feel it is necessary," Sir replied with disdain.

"Critical."

Sir kissed Brie one more time before getting up. "Thank you for the custard, my dear. It was *exactly* what the doctor ordered."

Brie watched with concern as Sir followed Marquis into the living room.

"They'll be fine," Celestia assured her.

I'm not so certain, Brie thought as she gathered the plates.

Her worries were confirmed when she returned from the kitchen to hear Sir growl angrily, "What the hell did Brie tell you?"

She cringed at the venomous tone behind the accusation. Celestia came up beside her and wrapped an arm around her waist in support as they listened to the heated exchange.

"She said nothing, Sir Davis," Marquis Gray answered. "I only had to look at her face to know that things are not well between you."

"And how is this any of your business?"

"I was her trainer, your colleague and, I thought, your friend. I consider you a rational man, but your current actions dispute that. I understand that you are weighed down by your mother's situation, but that should not dictate how you relate to the rest of the world."

"You know nothing about it."

"Let me be frank here. You are not the person I used to know."

Sir roared defiantly, "And you're not my father, Gray!"

"Damn it, man. You promised to care for and nurture that girl in there. Have you forgotten the vows you made in front of the entire community?"

Sir's voice had become low and ominous. "I *repeat*, this is none of your business."

"You're mistaken to think so. We are a community, Sir Davis. We look out for one another, and I see you starting to spiral out of control. I *must* do something, for both your sakes."

"You're overstepping the line, here."

Marquis' answer was confident and sure. "No, I am not. You must deal head-on with the situation concerning your mother, and include Miss Bennett in the process, or you will lose her."

"You're being over-dramatic, Gray."

"And you're a blind fool if you believe that."

"Don't throw those words around so casually with me," Sir warned. "I'm not your sub."

Marquis Gray went for the jugular. "I only suspected you were a fool when you took Miss Bennett during training, but now you're proving I was correct."

Sir spat angrily, "And you've held that single indiscretion over my head ever since."

"Your impulsive nature showed a lack of control and common sense." Marquis added in a tone of disbelief, "To think that as Headmaster you risked the Center's reputation and your position to *play* with a trainee? It was inconceivable to me."

Sir's voice dripped with acid. "Cease with the lecture, old man. I repeat, you're not my father."

"Well, someone needs to be, since you're acting like a child."

"You're sorely mistaken if you think a past indiscretion gives you the right to pry into my personal life. I won't stand for this."

"Running away, Sir Davis?" Marquis taunted. "I know that has been your *modus operandi* since you were a boy, but it doesn't work for adults. Demons don't disappear on their own. They must be faced and dealt with."

The timbre of Sir's voice was frightening when he replied, "Stop pushing me, Gray, or I will be forced to push back—and I know you better than you think."

Marquis was unmoved by the threat. "Your response highlights the depths of your spiral. As I stated before, you are not the man I once knew. No wonder Miss Bennett is floundering under your care. The answer is simple. Confront the issue with your mother, or you will destroy everything you have built, including your relationship with Miss Bennett."

"I will never forget this, Gray," Sir growled, heading back to the dining room.

Marquis' sarcastic laugh followed him. "No, I'm sure you won't, but let's hope you're man enough to take heed."

"Brie!" Sir barked.

She let out the breath she'd been holding and looked apologetically at Celestia before moving to Sir's side.

"We're leaving. Gather our things and meet me in the car." Without looking back, he marched to the front door, slamming it behind him. Brie scurried to pick up her purse and coat, while Celestia covered the custard dish and handed it to her.

Brie took it with shaking hands, a tangled mess of emotions. She froze when she felt Marquis Gray's firm grip on her shoulder.

"This was unfortunate but necessary, Miss Bennett."

She nodded, unable to speak.

"Don't run outside wildly, reflecting your Master's irrational outburst. Walk to the car with confidence. It is important that you support him through this, but do not become his emotional punching bag. You do not deserve it, and it is not what he needs from you."

She glanced up at Marquis, the lump in her throat making it difficult to speak. "Thank you, Marquis Gray."

His encouraging smile calmed her frayed emotions. "We're all forced to face our demons at some point, Miss Bennett. I believe it is part of God's plan. Whether we meet them with courage or fearful avoidance is up to the individual, but the consequences of those decisions determine the course of our lives."

She clutched the custard dish to her chest, admitting quietly, "I'm afraid for Sir."

"I trust he will come through this. He is not a weak individual."

"No, he is not," she agreed vehemently.

The car horn blared from outside.

She jumped, but took a deep breath and nodded to Marquis Gray before walking to the door and opening it. Sir required her strength. She would give it to him on her terms, because that was what he needed from her.

A Gift of Flogging

The ride home was quiet. Not filled with the raging anger she'd expected, but a brooding silence—which was worse.

Rather than disturb him, Brie sat up straight and stared ahead. *I am téa, sub and lover of Sir Thane Davis. I am his condor. I will always stand beside him, I will always love him, and I will be his strength when he falters. It is my joy to do so.*

"What did Gray tell you?" Sir snarled, breaking the silence.

She turned to him, not allowing herself to react to his hostility. "He told me to stand beside you."

"Really?" It sounded as if Sir didn't believe her, but he turned his eyes back to the road. "I can't tolerate people prying into our lives."

"I understand, Sir."

He added, "I appreciate that you did not run to him with our problems."

"We are partners. What happens between us is private."

"At least *you* understand that," he spat venomously.

"Marquis only meant well."

He growled under his breath, "As if his opinion matters to me."

Despite his protests, Brie knew very well that it *did* matter to him. Everyone respected Marquis Gray—including Sir.

Over the course of several minutes, she watched his expression change from anger to pain. Sir suddenly made a U-turn and headed for the foothills, ending up at the same place they'd gone to when he'd broken down after the initial confrontation with his mother.

It was high above the city, with an impressive view of LA. Sir got out of his Lotus and walked around to the other side, opening the door and taking her hand to help her out.

Brie took it as a positive sign.

They stood in the dark, watching the vibrant city below. Even as far up as they were, the sounds of sirens, horns blaring and dogs barking floated from below, while cars constantly moved through the congested streets as airplanes flew above their heads. The city was alive—a living, breathing entity.

Brie had grown up in a small town, but she loved LA for its diversity and promise. Great things could happen here; she still believed it.

"Seeing the Beast was unnerving, Brie. That unnaturally preserved face with its expression of superiority, still beautiful even with all the tubes. Although I've been told she's braindead, looking at her, I felt she might open her eyes at any moment."

"How did seeing her like that make you feel?"

"I wasn't prepared for the opposing emotions. I thought I was, had spent two days in Japan bracing myself for it, but seeing her..."

Brie could almost imagine the love and loss he must have felt, despite the fact that his mother had been so cruel to him. Sadly, Ruth *was* his mother, and that bond was so deep it couldn't be severed no matter what she'd done to him.

"I fully expected to be overwhelmed with emotion, but not by the one emotion that consumed me."

"What was that, Sir?"

He shocked her with his answer. "I wanted to punch that smug look off her face. A grown man shouldn't feel that way." He looked up at the night sky and sighed with frustration. "Even in that state, she has power over me. Every cruel deed, every unkind word still resonates within me.

Sir shook his head with a disgusted look on his face. "That was when I realized that all the issues in my past I'd thought I'd conquered, all the growth I'd assumed I'd made were just an illusion. I'm still that boy, standing in the doorway, helpless to stop what is about to happen as she watches my father lift the gun and end my world."

Brie wrapped her arms around Sir, laying her head against his shoulder, wishing desperately that she could take away the painful memories.

"I looked at her lying in that hospital bed, Brie, and had to fight the urge to physically choke the life out of her." He brushed his hair back, a look of resignation on his face. "And yet..."

"You still love her."

"Love is an ugly word when it's associated with that woman. My feelings are tangled in a hatred so dark it scares me." He groaned, looking up at the stars again. "I counted on having resolution with her someday—it didn't matter whether it ended well, I needed that final confrontation with her. I never realized how much I depended on it. To have it stolen from me is a loss I cannot bear. I'm left floundering like a drowning man."

"It's completely understandable," she assured him, hugging Sir tighter.

His voice broke when he admitted, "I know this should be a simple decision, Brie. She needs to die, but I find myself…struggling."

Brie took his strong hand in hers. "I stand beside you, whatever you decide."

"Being next to me is a dangerous place in my current state."

"I will not fail you."

He disengaged from her embrace. "But I will fail you."

She tried to protest, but he hushed her with his finger.

"Marquis is right. I had no business collaring you. My past makes me unfit to be your Master. I knew that, but for a moment you had me believing differently."

She refused to listen. "You followed your heart. You've always insisted that if I trust my instincts, they won't steer me wrong. It's sound advice, Sir."

He disagreed, shaking his head slowly. "Instincts and the heart are two different animals. The heart cannot be trusted."

Brie smiled, taking his hand and pressing it against her cheek. "But it led me to you, Sir."

"You could have done so much better, my dear."

She could hear the pain behind his sarcastic tone, but she shook her head in defiance of his words, still smiling at him.

"Brie, I will hurt you. Hell, I already have. I'm broken, and no amount of wishful thinking can change that. I'm not what you need."

"Sir, you have chosen a path of integrity and followed it relentlessly. I admire you, and am honored to be collared by you. I'm willing to suffer alongside you now because I see a future ahead full of promise. It will be glorious."

He cupped her chin. "You are naïve and sweet, but naivety is fragile and sweetness can quickly turn to bitterness."

"I am enhanced by you, not diminished."

He gave an amused smile, shaking her chin from side to side. "Stubborn."

"Like a condor."

He laughed out loud.

Brie wanted to follow Marquis' advice and be the strength Sir needed. With trepidation, she told him, "I have a humble suggestion concerning your mother."

He raised one eyebrow, the expression on his face turning suspicious. "Speak."

Brie forged ahead, despite her sudden misgivings. "Nothing needs to be decided now. Your mother owes you for the wrongs she's done. She can wait until you're ready."

Rather than the gratitude she'd expected, his eyes blazed with renewed anger. "I do not care for the suggestion. It was not wanted, nor is it appreciated."

It seemed all the progress she'd made had been swept away in an instant, and they walked back to the car in silence.

While Brie was sipping her morning coffee the next day, Sir's cell phone rang. She picked it up off the counter and walked over to where he was working. He took it from her without a word.

"Hello?" he said into the phone. That was the first word she'd heard since their discussion the night before.

"Why are you calling?" Sir growled, obviously not pleased with the caller's identity.

He stared at Brie briefly before replying, "It's not your right."

Sir listened intently, then flared his nostrils in anger. "Fine, I'll be joining her, then." He hung up and tossed the phone onto the table in an angry huff.

"Who was that, Sir?"

"That was the infamous Gray. He's asked to film a session with you as his partner."

"With me? But why?"

"That was exactly my question. However, his explanation has merit and I won't be the one to hinder your filming career. You should know, however, that I insisted on attending the session."

Brie shook her head, knowing how badly he wanted to avoid Marquis. "You don't need to, Sir. I'll talk to him and respectfully decline his offer."

"No, Brie, I've already agreed to watch."

She gave him a troubled look. "When is the filming supposed to take place?"

"Today, before training classes begin at the Center. He asked that you call him to go over the particulars of the scene."

"I'm sorry, Sir."

"This is not your doing. I've only agreed because I believe the opportunity is a good one for your career."

She accepted his answer, but left Sir's side feeling a little light-headed.

A scene with Marquis Gray? She hadn't been under his hand since Graduation Night…

When she called Marquis, he informed her that it would be a flogging scene—an instrument he knew she enjoyed. He also shared that he was planning to use a new flogger he'd been practicing with recently, one she might find a little intimidating.

Because of her unwavering trust in Marquis, Brie agreed to the scene, but began to have second thoughts when she entered the Training Center a few hours later with Sir.

Sir picked up on her unease and stopped her in the hallway. "If at any time you wish to end it, you have my full support."

She was grateful for his sensitivity and encouragement. "I'm sure it will go well, but I appreciate you telling me that, Sir." He nodded, resting his hand against the small of her back as he escorted her into the room.

Marquis Gray seemed pleased to see them both, but directed his attention to Sir. "We'll keep this short, Sir Davis, since time is limited for both of us."

"It's best we don't speak, then," Sir replied. "Let's waste no more time than necessary."

"Agreed." Marquis turned from Sir to ask Brie, "You understand the dynamics of the scene, yes?"

"I do, Marquis Gray, but may I see your new flogger before we begin?"

"Certainly." Marquis pulled the biggest flogger she had ever seen from out of his bag. Brie couldn't even count the number of tails on the two-handed instrument. She touched the strips of leather, feeling a sense of trepidation.

"How many tails does it have?" she asked.

"Eighty."

Brie cringed. "That many?"

"It has a real thud to it," he replied, with a glint in his eye.

She backed away from the flogger. "To be honest, I'm…a little frightened of it."

"I appreciate that you are fearful, Miss Bennett. However, trust that I will warm you up to receive its unique…sensation."

She looked over at Sir, unable to hide her concern.

"You'll be fine, Brie," Sir assured her, handing her the camera.

His assertion bolstered her resolve to continue with the filming. "It may take me a few minutes to set up, Marquis Gray."

"Not an issue, Miss Bennett. I need to set out my instruments and warm up."

She worked in silence, intent on the job at hand. It wasn't until Brie caught Marquis in motion through the camera's lens that she was hit by the fact she was really about to scene with the Master.

Although it was true she'd scened with Marquis while Sir had observed her during training, it felt completely different now that she was collared. She found herself glancing apprehensively at her Master.

"Come here," Sir ordered.

Brie walked over to him, staring hard at the floor. He took her face in both hands and gazed into her eyes.

"I want to see you enjoy this scene today. This is not just about your film. This is an opportunity to let your father see what we do and why it suits you so well. He could never watch if I were your partner, but you and I both know he has respect for Marquis Gray."

She looked at him with new understanding, agreeing with his assessment.

Sir leaned down and whispered in her ear. "I don't want you looking back at me during the scene. This is about you, Gray and the flogger."

"I understand, Sir."

Brie still felt apprehensive, but there was already a positive to doing this scene with Marquis Gray. Sir was talking to her again, and for that Brie was eternally grateful.

She checked her equipment one last time, stating regretfully, "This will have to be a static shot."

"Of course it will," Marquis answered. "It helps with the documentary's authenticity. If the girl behind the camera is in the scene being filmed, it stands to reason there is no one else working the camera. As long as the area I blocked out is in the shot, it should be fine."

She looked through the viewfinder one more time to double check before answering. "It is, Marquis Gray."

"Then undress, and come to me."

Brie felt butterflies as she slowly removed her clothes. For the shoot, Brie and Sir had decided on a two-piece set of activewear made of a thin red material. It would allow the unhindered sensation of impact play while maintaining her modesty on camera. She folded her clothes neatly and set them on the floor, just as she had during her training sessions.

Once undressed, she turned on the camera and held up her fingers, counting down silently from three to one before walking towards Marquis. She suddenly felt shy before the ghostly white Dom with eyes that penetrated her soul. It reminded her of those first days of submissive training.

Brie fingered the white orchid in her hair nervously as she approached. Marquis nodded to her as he held out his hand, murmuring, "Remember who you are."

A sense of self-confidence flooded through her hearing his words. Yes, she did know who she was and why she was here today. Brie held her head up a little higher, her eyes brimming with renewed conviction.

"Very good," he stated, directing her to stand facing the St. Andrew's cross. He knelt down at her feet to buckle her ankles first. "On your toes," Marquis ordered.

Brie stood on tiptoes for him, taking a deep breath as he restrained her ankles. Then the ghostly Dom stood and bound her wrists. Once she was secure, he gently moved her long curls out of the way before tying a strip of lace over her eyes.

"Like old times…" he whispered.

She smiled, knowing the audience would wonder what he'd just said to her. It was an exhilarating feeling, this private dance between them being played out before the camera.

She heard Marquis Gray move away, then Mozart filled the room. Brie sighed with contentment, loving that unique element of Marquis Gray's scenes. The next sound was of a flogger cutting the air, alerting her to the fact that he was about to begin. Instead of fear, she felt only excitement and longing. She hadn't forgotten his skill with the instrument, and neither had her body.

Brie knew the moment the tails slapped across her skin that it was the same flogger he'd used in their first scene together during training—the one that had helped her to fly for the very first time.

"Color?"

"Green, Marquis Gray."

He continued lightly stimulating her skin with the flogger, using slow, fluid movements that matched the tempo of the music. It left her back warm and her muscles relaxed when he was done.

Marquis put down the instrument and returned to her, caressing her skin with a rough material she knew well.

"Lace," Brie sighed.

"Red lace."

"I'd forgotten how good it felt."

His chuckle was low and irresistible as he moved away again. After picking up the next flogger, he informed her, "This next one will demand a little more of you."

If it had been Rytsar, Brie would have tensed. However, she knew Marquis well. There was no reason to fear him, only to anticipate…

The song changed and a more lively melody started up. It made her want to move to the music, but her restraints prevented it. Instead Brie stood on her toes, her calf muscles burning, but she relished the challenge of the pose. It kept her focused on Marquis, the position showing off the beauty of her submission in physical form.

When the new flogger made contact, Brie let out a soft moan.

"Color, Miss Bennett?"

"A lovely shade of green," she answered.

The strokes were perfectly timed to match the energetic rhythm of the classical piece. It took the sensations of the physical and transformed them into a spiritual experience, connecting the stimulation with the timeless melody, etching it in her mind.

Brie felt the first hint of subspace tugging at her, demanding that she let go.

Marquis stopped at the end of the song and returned to her side. Soft fur glided over her skin, causing a cascade of pleasant shivers.

"That feels incredible," she purred.

"Nothing like opposing stimuli to heighten sensation."

"You're a true Master."

He chuckled warmly as he continued to rub the soft fur over her arms, back and neck, drawing her into connection with him—readying her mind and body for the final experience.

"It's time to fly," he announced.

Brie's heart fluttered when he left her side. The thought of that intimidating flogger stroking her back was daunting, but Marquis' skillful guidance during the scene had Brie wanting to know its character—longing to experience its unknown touch.

The music became more dramatic, matching the mood of the finale of his scene. She heard the massive flogger cutting the air before it even made contact. The impact covered her entire back, eighty tails striking at once. It was like nothing she'd experienced before.

He stroked her again, the thud of the giant flogger taking her breath away.

"Color?"

"A brilliant shade of green."

"So you enjoy the thud of this one?"

She nodded, smiling in the direction of the camera so there would be no doubt in the minds of the audience.

"Then you have my permission to fly."

Brie's loins contracted in pleasure as Marquis began stroking her with the two-handed flogger. The large area, along with the strength of the impact, meant every lash was perfect and all-encompassing.

As the strokes he applied became harder and faster, her body began to tingle, starting at the area of impact and traveling outward to her fingers and toes. Brie lost herself in the feeling, anticipating each stroke as it came and reveling in the warm sensation that coursed through her from its impact.

Eventually everything blurred, even her connection to Marquis, as she became one with the flogger. When he paused to ask her color, Brie fought to answer, knowing he was asking for the benefit of the audience that would be watching.

She stilled herself enough to answer clearly, "Green", in case her father ever watched.

"Excellent."

The thud of the flogger began again. This time she let go and allowed herself to fly…

Brie felt hands on her and heard Marquis' deep voice, but she couldn't understand what he was saying, nor did she care. She just smiled as he released her wrists, lightly rubbing them both before releasing her ankles and doing the same.

Marquis picked her up, cradling her in his arms as he whispered intimately, "Well done, Miss Bennett."

She smiled at him drunkenly. "I like your new flogger, Marquis."

"I was confident you would."

He carried Brie over to Sir and she heard her Master say begrudgingly, "That was an impressive scene, Gray."

"Thank you, Sir Davis. I've grown quite fond of the new flogger." He handed Brie over to Sir, stating abruptly, "I'm sure you understand that due to tonight's training, I have no time for aftercare."

Marquis walked over and turned off the camera before returning to Brie. "It was a pleasure to work with you again."

She was still flying on the high he'd created and grinned. "Thank you, Marquis of the Master Flogger."

Sir said nothing as he watched Marquis leave, but once the door had shut he looked down tenderly at her and said, "Well, someone needs to look after my little flier."

He carried Brie to a large lounge chair and sat down with her still in his arms. Sir gently stroked her hair with his fingertips, creating tiny trails of tickling sensation.

"You were beautiful to watch," he said softly.

She looked up at Sir, feeling a profound sense of love. "What was it like? Watching?"

"Marquis' motion reminded me of swordplay; the way he wielded that two-handed flogger was both graceful and intense." Sir gazed down at her and asked, "Did you enjoy it as much as it appeared?"

She nodded unashamedly.

Sir muttered, almost as an afterthought, "Sometimes I forget how extraordinary you are." He crushed her against his chest, rocking her gently in his protective arms for a long time before he added, "I will consider what you said about my mother."

Marquis Gray is a cunning man, Brie thought. Somehow, by having Sir watch the scene and then forcing him to take care of her afterwards, Marquis had broken down the wall between them.

It was sobering to realize what a formidable force Marquis Gray truly was.

His Virgin

S ir surprised Brie when they arrived home that night, after filming with Marquis. "Being back in my old stomping grounds and watching your scene today has brought back many pleasant memories. I have a mind to recreate one right now. Are you game, Brie?"

Brie was quick to answer. "Always, Sir."

He picked her up amid a peal of laughter and squeals, marching her straight to the bedroom. He threw her onto the bed, staring down at her hungrily. "We will relive the taking of your virginal ass, but change it up a little."

She trembled at the thought. "Change it how, Sir?"

"I'm not your trainer and you are not my student."

"Go on," she encouraged, now *very* intrigued.

"We've just met at a party with mutual friends. I'm infatuated by that perfectly shaped ass, and after much persuading you have agreed to let me take your anal virginity. I can tell you're nervous, but you invite me to your bed anyway."

Brie bit her lip, her whole body responding to his suggestion. "That sounds delicious, Sir."

"No names tonight. We don't want to ruin the illusion."

She nodded her agreement. "No names."

"Get into character, my dear," he commanded gently.

Brie closed her eyes, imagining the thrill and excitement of bringing a stranger to her bed. The girl she was imagining had been without a partner for so long that she was nervous about being intimate with such a handsome and captivating man. Naturally, she was hesitant to give away such a private part of herself, but his confidence and interest in her was intoxicating. She might give him *anything* if he asked...

Brie opened her eyes and crossed her legs, nonchalantly covering her breasts with her arm so that she appeared less exposed, more modest. Gazing up at Sir, she swore he looked different—as if he were younger, less sure of himself. However, the hunger in his eyes remained, drawing her to him. It seemed Sir was every bit as good at getting into character as she was, and it thrilled her to the core.

She patted the area beside her on the bed, beseeching him to join her.

He smiled down at Brie as he meticulously unbuttoned his shirt and casually cast it to the floor. She held her breath when he lay next to her, suddenly feeling unsure of herself.

He cupped her chin gently and kissed her—and all uncertainty melted away. His kiss was demanding, yet tender at the same time. When he pulled away, she sighed with contentment. Without asking, he took her wrist and moved her arm to her side so he could stare unimpeded at her breasts. Her nipples hardened under the material of her blouse because of his intense scrutiny.

She held her breath when his finger lightly grazed her erect nipple, sending wavelets of energy down to her groin. She moaned into her pillow, wondering what kind of power he possessed.

"How long has it been?"

Brie laughed in disbelief. "You don't ask a girl a question like that. It's considered rude."

He continued to lightly play with her nipples as he replied, "I only asked to gauge how I should proceed with you."

She pursed her lips, embarrassed to admit the truth. "A year and three months…and five days."

He gave her a charming half-grin. "Such an exact answer."

"Yeah, so it's been a while," she replied, in a voice that didn't invite any more questions or comments on the subject.

He circled her nipple lazily with his finger, looking rather amused. "Then I suppose I should take it slow with you."

"As opposed to?"

"As opposed to turning you over right now, holding you down, ripping your clothes off and fucking that sweet little ass."

Her pussy contracted with pleasure as she imagined him on top of her, pumping his cock into her, but she definitely wasn't ready to be ravished like that—at least not yet.

"Slow is nice," she agreed.

He took her hand and moved it down so she could feel his growing erection. She swallowed nervously, shocked that she was really going let a stranger fuck her but excited by the prospect.

She bit her lip in concentration as she caressed and squeezed his hard cock, while his hand traveled to her ass and cupped her butt cheek. "I think we need you out of these clothes."

She quickly ripped off her shirt and removed her bra, tossing them onto the nightstand. He pushed her down gently and unbuttoned her jeans, slowly pulling them off along with her panties. Then he stared at her.

She shivered under his admiring gaze, unused to such attention. When she tried to cover herself, he slowly shook his head. She couldn't help smiling as she relaxed her arms and let him stare freely at her body.

This perfect man lay with her again, nibbling her ear as he grabbed her ass. "There's something about untouched territory that is so damn sexy to me."

She stiffened in his arms when she felt him lightly rim her anus with his finger. Brie vividly remembered when Sir had taken her that first time. She'd been fearful but too turned on to deny him. That moment when his cock had breached her virginal ass was something she'd never forgotten. And now she was getting to relive it again with Sir.

"Don't be afraid," he whispered.

Just him saying that made her heart race.

He slowly turned her over onto her stomach and proceeded to caress her bare bottom. "Such a perfect ass. The shape, the feel of it in my hands…"

She moaned into her pillow again, still anxious but charmed by his praise.

He leaned over and kissed her on the lips, exploring her mouth with his tongue as his fingers caressed and teased her pussy, which was getting wetter by the second. He rubbed her clit, increasing her excitement, and just when she thought she couldn't take any more, he moved his hand lower, pressing his finger against her tight rosette.

She gasped softly, her body resisting the invasion as his finger slowly slipped inside. The feel of it was totally foreign, naughty and unsettling—and she froze.

His kisses became more passionate as he distracted her with his tongue as his finger sought even deeper access.

"Relax…" He took her by the waist and rolled her on top of him, continuing the deep kisses as his hand traveled back to finger her ass.

She gazed into his eyes as they kissed. Those mesmerizing eyes called to her, urging her to submit to his need. Although she was curious to know the feel of a man inside her in this extremely intimate way, the truth was, she also wanted to be possessed, to abandon herself completely to his carnal needs.

Between kisses, she whispered, "I'm yours."

He grunted in response, rolling her back onto the bed so he could unbutton his pants. He removed his clothes, throwing them off the bed.

She couldn't help staring at the stranger before her. The hair on his well-built chest complemented the dark pubic hair that framed the most handsome cock she'd ever seen. If a girl was going to give away her virginity, that cock was definitely worthy to take it.

"Where's your lubricant?"

She blushed. The question made what they were about to do that much more real. She giggled nervously, pointing to the nightstand.

He reached over and opened the drawer to retrieve it. "Give me your hand."

She held it out for him and he squeezed a coin-sized amount into her palm. He then pressed her hand to his cock. "Rub it all over."

Her heart skipped a beat when she touched his naked shaft for the first time. It was rock hard, but the head was smooth and kissable. Before she covered it in lubricant, Brie leaned over and kissed the tip. It twitched in response, obviously liking her attention.

She wrapped her hand around the length of his and began an up-and-down motion as she coated him with the slippery substance. He placed his hand over hers and forced her to squeeze harder. "Like that," he instructed.

It was so sexy being directed how to please him. Normally guys left her guessing and she could only hope she was doing a good job.

He took his hand away from her and watched as she continued to stroke him, covering the head of his shaft all the way down to the base with the clear, odorless gel. After she was done, he put a small amount on two of his own fingers. He rubbed the gel between them with his thumb, then scooted next to her, reaching around to play with her ass.

She bit her lip as he coated the outside of her sensitive area with the lube, then slipped his finger back inside. Just like the first time, her body resisted the infiltration. He kissed her again, his probing tongue demanding her full attention. Tingles of fear coursed through her as he pushed a second finger inside her, stretching her taut muscles.

"Oh God, your ass is tight," he growled lustfully.

She whimpered into his mouth, aroused by this naughty thing they were doing. Knowing how excited and turned on he was made the act that much more exhilarating.

Her loins contracted with fearful pleasure when he instructed her to get on her hands and knees. She did as he'd asked, but it felt surreal when she felt the bed shift as he positioned himself behind her, grabbing onto her waist.

"No other man will feel what I am about to feel."

She let out a nervous sigh. He was right. She was giving this stranger a part of herself no one else had known. It was both thrilling and disconcerting. He massaged her ass with both hands, relaxing her body as he prolonged the moment of penetration. She stiffened when she felt his cock settle in the valley of her ass cheeks.

Brie didn't realize she'd stopped breathing until he said, "Don't hold your breath. It tenses the body."

She let out it out, whispering apologetically, "Sorry."

"I can empathize—this is a singular moment."

He wrapped one hand around her throat and pulled her head back to kiss her, pressing his hard shaft against her taut hole.

She cried out when her body opened for him and his cock slipped into her ass. "Nice," he murmured as he gently thrust.

Brie closed her eyes, concentrating on the fullness of his shaft. Being taken this way felt completely different from being taken vaginally. The sensitivity and tightness was intoxicating, but she was unsure how much of his cock she could take.

"Please be gentle."

"Of course," he assured her as he tightened his grip on her throat, "but you are taking all of me tonight."

A feeling of reckless abandon washed over her.

He was in control.

She lifted her chin towards him and was rewarded with the feel of his warm lips on hers. His thrusting became more pronounced as his shaft pushed farther in, stretching her achingly. The guttural noises he made as he fucked her turned her on even more.

Of all the men she'd known, he was the first to make her feel this way—wicked and dangerously sexy.

He let go of her throat, placing his hands on her hips for more leverage. His thrusts became even deeper, demanding she relax to take all of him, but he kept the rhythm slow and easy. It was as if he were making love to her.

She soaked in the sensations, embracing the resistance, the deepness of his penetration and the feeling of utter possession. She was his in that moment.

She looked back and watched his face as he fucked her ass, a look of impassioned hunger in his eyes. She wondered what he was thinking, what he was playing out in his mind as he took her.

"You're so tight, I don't think I can last much longer," he announced.

Knowing her body was such a turn-on to him heightened her own arousal and she wasn't ready for it to end. "Don't stop," she begged.

He lowered himself, wrapping his arms around her as he grunted into her ear. "I want you to come for me."

She whimpered as he changed the angle of thrust and hit a new area of stimulation. It slowly built as he rolled his hips in measured, rhythmic motions.

The feeling soon became overwhelming, but she fought against it, wanting her climax to build until it exploded with power. That was when he bit her neck and all reason left her.

She arched her back, inviting deeper access as her body convulsed with delicious release. He murmured huskily, "That's it, virgin, come for me."

She was speechless, her whole body shuddering after the climax had passed, completely spent by the passion and emotion behind the act.

"And now it's my turn…"

He lifted himself up and placed his hands on her shoulders, pushing his shaft so deep inside her that she gasped.

"My come is going to bathe your virginal ass."

She held her breath so she wouldn't miss a second of the experience. He didn't move a muscle as he orgasmed. Brie felt the pulsing of his manhood and the rhythmic release of his warm seed inside her.

Sir's low, subtle cries of passion took her back to their first night together—the night he'd claimed her anal virginity and her heart. The night he'd exposed that vulnerable side of himself for the briefest of moments.

As he lowered himself onto her now, with his shaft still buried deep inside, Brie reflected on how far they'd come. Sir nuzzled her neck, wrapping his arms back around her to hold her tight.

Condors forever…

Magic in the Air

E ven though it didn't feel like Christmas, with sunshine and warm weather, Brie couldn't wait to celebrate her first Christmas with Sir.

"I just love Christmas, Sir! All the decorations, the cookies, the Christmas carols…stockings hung on the mantel, wrapped presents with bows, all made complete with a twinkling tree." She sighed contentedly. "Nothing beats the magic of Christmas."

He looked at her somberly. "I hate to tell you this, Brie, but I don't do Christmas."

Her smile faltered. "What do you mean, you don't *do* Christmas?"

"The holiday is meant for children. I put away childish things long ago."

She tried to hide her severe disappointment. "Not even a tree?"

"No. Look around this place. A dying tree would only disrupt the aesthetics of our home."

Even though she preferred real trees, she offered, "Why don't we get an artificial one? That way it won't drop needles on the marble."

"That's not the point. It would be an eyesore."

She could tell by the tone of his voice that he would not entertain a tree no matter how much she begged. "Can I at least hang up twinkling lights?"

"Brie," he glanced around the apartment for emphasis, "Christmas lights would take away from the calm serenity I have created here. I prefer things the way they are."

Her hopes dashed, she replied unenthusiastically, "Only if it pleases you, Sir."

Sir put his hand on her head. "Sorry to disappoint you, my dear, but I prefer to work through the holidays. It gives me an edge over the competition. While others take off two weeks at the end of the year, I burn the night oil. I suggest you do the same."

Brie sighed in resignation. "I can see how it's a sensible choice, Sir, but it doesn't seem very...fun."

"Life isn't all fun and games, babygirl. Surely you understand that."

"I do," she said in a lackluster voice.

"Do I need to remind you that you partnered with a man, not a little boy?"

She looked up into his magnetic eyes and smiled boldly, unwilling to give up just yet. "Still, Sir, I would like to get to know that little boy."

He shook his head. "That boy died long ago. Best if you get that notion out of your head."

"What about a candle, Sir?" she pressed.

He glared at her, but she met his gaze bravely. Finally, he rolled his eyes. "Fine. One candle—pine scented so you can satisfy your need for a tree."

Brie felt a sense of victory, but hid it by lowering her head and stating humbly, "Thank you, Sir."

"Bah, humbug," he said, retiring to his desk, but she detected a hint of amusement in his voice.

Brie was grateful that Sir was allowing her the small privilege of a candle. It gave her hope that he would not be angry when she presented him with her Christmas present. Whether he *did* Christmas or not, giving a present on Christmas morning was important to her. More than he could ever know.

Brie waited in the notorious—at least to her—Room forty-two at the Submissive Training Center. Marquis Gray had set up the arrangements, fully supportive of her choice of a Christmas gift for Sir. He'd declined to assist her, due to time issues, but had assured her that his replacement would do an exceptional job. She was extremely anxious about meeting the person Marquis felt worthy to instruct her.

She heard manly footsteps approaching and held her breath as the door opened. The impressive male who walked into the room had Brie grinning from ear to ear.

"Boa!"

"Hello, Brie."

"I had no idea you were a chef!"

"I'm not classically trained, but I've worked in a restaurant." He shut the door behind him and handed her one of the aprons he was holding. "I was told we're limited to short lessons, so let's get started."

"Sounds great." As she put on her apron, she asked, "Did you run your own restaurant?"

"No, I was a sous chef. I actually met my Mistress there."

"Oh, do tell," Brie encouraged.

"Not until I test your cooking skills."

She looked at him apologetically. "I don't have any. Didn't Marquis tell you?"

He chuckled. "I'd like to see for myself. Let's make it something simple. Prepare parmesan noodles for me."

"Like just noodles, some butter and cheese?"

"Sure."

Boa stood beside the cooking station and asked her to begin. Brie took a deep breath before leaving him to search the pantry for the needed ingredients. Once she'd found the spaghetti noodles, she grabbed a stick of butter and a shaker of parmesan cheese.

His eyes followed her every movement in the kitchen, making even simple things like filling up the pot with water a little intimidating. To pass the time while she waited for the water to boil, she cut the stick of butter into tiny pieces, hoping it would impress him. Then she stood and watched the pot, silently willing it to boil faster.

"So, Boa, where did you learn to cook Italian food?"

"When I was a senior in high school, I transferred to Italy for a semester. It was there I learned my passion for cooking, and the importance of simple ingredients."

"You believe you can really teach me how to make Sir's favorite dish?"

"I have no doubt."

She said dreamily, "All I want on Christmas morning is to see Sir eat my *ribollita* and say 'It reminds me of my fathers'." Tears came to her eyes just thinking about it.

"I don't know if we can get him to say those exact words, but your dish will taste authentic."

Brie smiled at Boa. "That's all I ask."

When the rolling bubbles started, she took the dried pasta and broke it in half to fit in the pot. She set the timer to ten minutes and minced the butter into even finer pieces.

When the timer went off, she took the pot off the stove and strained the noodles. Taking out a separate bowl, she threw the cooked pasta inside and sprinkled the tiny pieces of butter on top. Happily, it didn't take long to melt when she stirred it.

She portioned out a bowl for him to taste and shook a layer of parmesan cheese on top. It looked really bland, so she ran to the pantry and grabbed some parsley, throwing it in the bowl.

Brie smiled nervously as she handed the steaming pasta to Boa. "*Bon appetit.*"

He removed the parsley, stating, "Totally unnecessary." He then took his fork and twisted several noodles onto it, staring at the forkful briefly before tasting it. He chewed it for several seconds before swallowing. "Do you normally cook pasta for Sir Davis?"

"He prefers to cook that himself."

"I'm not surprised."

She smiled sadly. "I did warn you that I have no skills."

"Let me first go over your choices for the dish. Although I can understand why you chose dried noodles based on your limited skills, I have to wonder why you didn't salt the water. Your noodles lack flavor."

"I thought salting the water was supposed to make it boil faster, which I've heard is untrue."

"You salt the water to give your noodles taste."

She blushed. "Ah…"

"I also noticed that you relied on the timer to determine whether they were done. Do you know of any other method?"

"Well, I've heard of people throwing the pasta at the wall to see if it sticks, but that seems a little silly to me."

He laughed. "Unless you like your walls covered in starch and your noodles overcooked, I don't recommend it."

"So how *do* you get perfectly cooked noodles?"

"It's a closely guarded secret, but I will share it with you." He motioned her close, as if he was going to tell her a coveted secret. Brie leaned in eagerly and heard, "You taste them."

She snorted. "Very funny, Boa."

"I'm completely serious. You take one out and taste it. If it has an undercooked texture, wait a little longer. If it's mushy, throw the batch out and start again. While you can use a timer for guidance, you should never serve noodles you haven't sampled first."

He handed her a fork. "So taste the ones you served me and tell me what you think."

She twirled the noodles onto her fork and took a bite. Two noodles were stuck together and almost crunchy in texture. "Undercooked?"

"No. You failed to stir the pot, so they stuck together. Personally, I wouldn't eat this if you paid me."

"So you want me to start again?"

"No, I want to teach you how to make fresh pasta. Your Master should never have to eat dried noodles. It's a waste of calories."

Boa gathered flour, eggs, salt, a clove of garlic, oil olive and a wedge of parmesan cheese and set them before her. "Simple, fresh ingredients."

He piled up a mound of flour on the cutting board and made a well in the center. He cracked in the eggs, sprinkled a little salt and added some olive oil. Then, with his bare hands, he began to mix the ingredients.

While he mixed and kneaded the dough, he asked if she had any questions.

"Personal or cooking-related?"

"Either."

"You said you met your Mistress at a restaurant. What's the story?"

Boa's eyes twinkled when he shared. "Mistress came to eat at the place I worked. She raved about the appetizer she'd had, and asked to see the chef." He shrugged. "It happened to be the only dish of mine that my boss allowed on the menu. When she realized the chef hadn't created it, she insisted on meeting me."

"And that was the beginning of you two?"

He chuckled. "Actually, it took a bit of convincing on her part. You see, I considered myself a manly man at the time. Took a while for Mistress to introduce me to my more submissive side."

He put his muscle into the kneading of the dough, moving with a fluid, thrusting motion. The movement was almost sexual in nature. She took a peek at his crotch area and noticed a very large bulge.

"You really get into cooking, don't you?" she commented.

"Yes. I think that's why I never made it past sous chef. I intimidated the other men in the kitchen with my passion for cooking."

Glancing at his bulge again, Brie thought to herself, *That's not the only thing that intimidated them.*

"Normally you let the dough rest for an hour, but I will just roll it out because of the limited time."

Boa got out a small manual pasta machine and rolled the dough through it several times, making it thinner with each pass. Then he changed the setting and cut it into thin strips.

"It takes a lot less time for fresh pasta to cook." He separated the noodles as he put them in the salted water and stirred it. While it boiled, he put some olive oil in a small sauté pan and used a garlic press to add several cloves of garlic to the oil. A minute later he pulled it from the heat, strained the noodles and put them in a large bowl. He drizzled the heated oil over them, added the parmesan and tossed the noodles lightly.

Boa handed her a fork and they both served themselves from the serving bowl. He added a final sprinkling of cheese, stating apologetically, "The pasta would be lighter if it had time to rest."

She took a bite and purred. Such simple ingredients, but the texture of the noodles along with the tang of olive oil and toasted garlic was amazing. "I can make this?"

"Of course, you saw how easy it was."

She laughed. "Marquis makes omelets look easy—that doesn't mean they are."

Boa patted her on the shoulder. "By the time I'm done with you, you'll have several Italian dishes under your belt that I guarantee your Master will enjoy."

He looked up at the clock. "Looks like we're out of time here."

After they'd cleaned up the kitchen, Boa escorted her to the school entrance. "So what does your Master think you're doing right now?"

"I told him I'm using the Center's resources to work on my documentary for the next two weeks, which is totally true. I just haven't mentioned the extra time for cooking lessons."

"Oh, the hoops a sub must jump through in order to surprise her Master."

She grinned. "It's not easy, I tell ya."

He winked as she walked through the door. "Until tomorrow, then."

Brie was in for her own surprise on Christmas Eve. She came home to find Sir standing in the hallway waiting for her—a mischievous smirk on his face.

"What's up?" she asked cautiously, putting her camera equipment down.

He nodded his head towards the coffee table. Brie gasped when she saw what was sitting on it. She approached the tiny Christmas tree, squealing with delight.

"I won't have dead things in my home, but I have no objection to a living piece of art."

Brie stared in awe at the miniature tree, perfect in every way.

"It's a twenty-six year old Christmas bonsai," he explained.

She shook her head in amazement. "It looks exactly like a full-grown pine tree, only in miniature form." She stroked the delicate limbs. "It's like a little miracle."

"I'm glad you like it."

She stood up and hugged him. "I love it, Sir!"

"I enquired and was told that you can put miniature lights on it without harming the tree." He took a box of tiny lights out of his pocket and handed it to her.

She looked up at him, bursting with joy. "Thank you, from the bottom of my heart, Sir." She bit her lip and said, "I bought you a little something, too. Can I get it, Sir?"

"It's not a present, is it?"

"Oh no, Sir. It's just something to get you in the mood."

He raised an eyebrow. "In the mood, you say? Then you have my permission to get it."

She ran to the bedroom, quickly retrieving her wrapped gift from the closet.

Brie walked back to him and knelt at his feet, trying hard to hide the silly grin on her face as she handed over the gift.

"I thought you said it wasn't a present," Sir admonished.

She shook her head and peeked up at him. "It's not, Sir. I just like wrapping things at this time of year." She watched with bated breath as he unwrapped her gift. He pulled it from the paper and looked at it oddly.

"It's a Santa hat, Sir."

"I can see that."

"May I have it?" she asked.

He handed it to her.

Brie rocked off her heels and placed it on his head, adjusting it to a charming angle and moving the fuzzy ball to the side. She stood back to admire how adorable he looked. "It's perfect!"

He tilted his head, frowning. "Seriously, Brie."

It made him looked even more adorable, and she beamed with delight. "You make a stern, wise old Santa, Sir."

"Wise?"

She covered her mouth.

"Come here," he said, sitting down and pointing to his lap.

She was feeling particularly naughty and blurted, "If I lie on your lap, can I tell you what I want for Christmas?"

He gazed at her sternly, shaking his head as he pointed again to his muscular thighs.

Brie took a deep breath before lying down. He lifted her little red kilt and rubbed his hand over her ass. "This *wise* old Santa will show no mercy tonight."

With that, he swatted her ass hard enough that the sound of it echoed through the quiet apartment. She cried out in surprise at the power behind his hand, then giggled.

"Oh, my goodness, that hurt!"

Another, equally forceful swat followed. The sting of it radiated from the area of contact and the electricity of it traveled straight to her pussy.

How did he do that?

Spankings never felt as good as when Sir delivered them—even Headmaster Coen's skill did not compare. She gasped as he continued to spank her naughty little ass, bringing tears to her eyes while making her equally wet with desire.

When he finally stopped, she squeaked, trembling on his lap.

"Do you have anything to say?"

"I'm sorry for my disrespect, Sir. I did not mean to call you wise."

He swatted her with extra force.

She squeaked. "What was that for?"

"Willful misrepresentation. You led me to believe this item would get me in the mood."

Brie smiled up at him, her ass still stinging from his hand. "I meant in the mood for Christmas, Sir."

He gave her a crooked smile, chuckling in disbelief at her brashness. "You are a naughty girl, Brie Bennett."

"Speaking of naughty, I've always fantasized about eating Santa."

He looked properly shocked. "You *are* wicked."

Sir took off the hat and placed it on the coffee table before lifting her off his lap and ordering her to strip. Brie smiled as she slipped off her panties and flirtatiously flipped her little red kilt, letting him catch a glimpse of her bare mound.

"Very nice."

Giving him a curtsy, she turned away and slowly unzipped the kilt, letting it fall to the floor. She pulled off her blouse next, wiggling her hips as she did, so that he could admire her red little ass. Brie undid her lacy bra and flung it behind her, impressed when he deftly caught it in his hand.

She turned to face him again and presented herself, hands behind her back, her legs slightly spread where she stood to show her willingness for play.

Sir unbuttoned his slacks and smiled lewdly. "Come and put those naughty lips around this cock."

Brie sauntered up to him and gratefully sank to the floor, opening her mouth to take his manhood, but Sir stopped her. "Wait."

He retrieved the hat from the coffee table and placed it on her head. "Begin."

She smiled up at him, the soft furry ball of the hat tickling her cheek. Brie opened her lips and took his shaft into her mouth, purring as she flicked and licked the head of it. The tanginess of his pre-come played on her tongue. Tasting his excitement always had an erotic effect on her, making her pussy ache to satisfy his manly desire.

When he took her head in his hands and guided her deeper onto his shaft, she moaned in pure bliss.

"Remember the first time you took my cock in your mouth?"

She pulled away to answer him, smiling sweetly. "Of course I do, Sir."

"As I recall, you had to have your hands tied behind your back, but look at you now…" He guided her back onto his cock and she relaxed her throat to take him deep. She swallowed the length of his shaft, then slowly pulled back before returning to the base in short, slow movements. It was the same move she'd used when she'd deep-throated him for the first time.

The motion helped to constrict her throat, giving him the tightness he enjoyed. It also left her in control, allowing her to lavish love on his cock at her own pace.

Sir surprised her by holding her head against him for several moments before releasing her. It forced her to quiet herself as she felt her heart start pounding from the temporary lack of oxygen.

Brie took in several deep breaths before eagerly taking him again, excited by the power play. She rode up and down his shaft until he held her still, her lips buried in his dark pubic hair.

He took longer to release her this time, forcing her to concentrate on him. "Next time, I will come," he informed her as she pulled away.

She shivered with anticipation, taking long, deep breaths to ready herself for the challenge. She wiped her mouth with a playful smile. Oral sex had a way of making both partners powerful at the same time. She knew he struggled not to come as she deep-throated him, and he knew he had complete control of her mouth. It was an exciting exchange between Dominant and submissive.

She nibbled and teased the head of his shaft with her teeth and tongue, drawing out his final release. The fact that Sir allowed it meant that he was enjoying the anticipation as much as she.

Taking one last deep breath, she opened her lips wide and took his rock-hard shaft into her mouth. Sir groaned as his cock traveled down her tight throat. He held her head in place against him, then began thrusting slowly.

His build-up was slow, forcing her to be patient and to trust him as her heart pounded and her lungs burned. But then the moment came, the swelling of his cock just before the rhythmic release of his seed. Both groaned in ecstasy as his come shot down her throat—the exchange complete.

"I'm not done with you yet, naughty girl."

Brie giggled as he picked her up and slung her over his shoulder, slapping her ass hard before carrying her towards the bedroom.

Christmas Kink

B rie woke up early on Christmas morning and tried to roll out of bed without waking Sir, but he wrapped his arm tightly around her. "Where are you going at four in the morning?"

"You gave me permission last night, Sir. Remember, it's a surprise. Go back to sleep."

He took his arm away. "Fine, leave your Master cold and alone."

She leaned over and kissed his cheek. "You'll thank me later, I promise."

"I can't imagine anything can equal your warm body pressed against mine."

Brie smiled as she tiptoed out of the room, closing the door quietly behind her. She hurried to the kitchen, hardly able to contain her excitement. She put on a frilly apron to protect her naked body as she cooked, and laid out the tools required for the dish.

For the first time in her life, Brie felt confident in the kitchen, knowing exactly what she needed to do to create the special dish Sir loved. She put on headphones and turned up the volume, dancing and twirling to Christmas music as she cooked.

Every ingredient was professionally and lovingly handled as she recreated the *ribollita*. She thought of Sir's father making this dish for his family, and could relate to the love and joy he must have felt. She was grateful for that love, even though it had ended in tragedy, because Sir was a direct result.

She thought back to her own childhood, remembering with fondness the excitement of Christmas morning. She'd wake up far too early, waiting for sounds of her parents. Her father never failed to awaken at an ungodly hour, as excited as she was for the magic of Christmas to begin. Before she was allowed to unwrap presents, however, they would have hot chocolate together as a family—a special cocoa that was reserved only for Christmas morning. The three of them would spend that time reminiscing about their best and worst Christmas memories.

Brie suddenly had an image of Ruth. Instead of lying in a hospital bed covered in tubes, she was a young mother in love. *I bet you giggled on Christmas morning when your little boy got up and raced to the tree to discover what Santa had brought for him.*

A tear escaped, but Brie brushed it away. Christmas morning was not a time for crying. She smiled instead as she put the final touches on the dish and waited for Sir. Luckily, her wait was not long.

"What's this I smell?" Sir asked as he walked down the hallway towards her.

Brie quickly took off her apron and earphones. She took a proper stance as she waited for him, her heart racing with excitement. When he rounded the corner, she directed him to sit at the kitchen table, which she had already set with red napkins, gold bowls and a small poinsettia as the centerpiece.

She explained, "When I was a girl, we would always come to the table early on Christmas morning for hot chocolate. I thought it would be nice if we changed the tradition a little." With nerves threatening to do her in, she took the large pot from the stove and placed it before Sir. She took a deep breath before lifting the lid and presenting it to him.

He stared at her dish with a look of astonishment. "Is this what I think it is?"

She nodded eagerly, grabbing olive oil and freshly grated parmesan cheese and placing them on the table.

"Did you make it?"

Again she nodded vigorously.

"All by yourself?"

"It's my gift to you."

"It smells delicious." He spooned a healthy amount into his bowl and drizzled olive oil over it, adding the parmesan last.

Brie couldn't breathe as she waited for him to take a bite, clasping her hands against her chest as she watched. She stared at his luscious lips as he blew on the spoon before taking that first taste. Her gaze traveled up to his eyes and she was surprised to see that they were watering.

"Is it not good enough, Sir?"

"It's perfection, Brie."

She felt as if she was going to burst with happiness. "I'm so glad, Sir."

He took another spoonful and asked her to taste it. As she swallowed the savory Italian stew, he told her, "You are tasting my childhood."

She looked at him gratefully. "Thank you, Sir. I'm honored you feel that way."

"No, thank *you*, Brie. I cannot think of a more fitting Christmas gift."

He took her in his lap and the two of them shared his bowl. It was the most romantic thing ever.

When he was done, he kissed her on the lips. "I told you that I don't do the whole Christmas scene."

"I know, Sir. That's okay. It's the giving part I like the most, anyway."

He smiled knowingly. "That doesn't surprise me, little sub."

She grinned at him, laying her head on his shoulder.

"However…" He slipped a small red envelope onto the table.

Her eyes widened as she took it. "What's this?"

"Open it and find out."

She hurriedly ripped the tiny envelope open, pulling out a handwritten note in Sir's exquisite penmanship.

Many people decorate for Christmas.
Open the front door to retrieve my favorite kind of decoration.

Brie looked at him questioningly. "Sir?"

He said nothing, waiting for her to follow his instructions.

Brie went up to the door and looked through the peephole, not seeing anything or anyone. Completely naked, she unlocked the front door and opened it a crack. The hallway was silent because of the earliness of the hour.

She opened the door a little wider and squealed with joy when she spied a large plastic candy cane leaning against the wall.

Brie grabbed it, noticing there was a note attached. She quickly shut the door and opened it.

Return the cane to its owner and proceed to your reflection.

Brie ran back to Sir, tickled by his little scavenger hunt.

She formally held out the decorative cane with both hands. He took it from her and placed it on the table. She thought she knew where to head next, and ran down the hallway towards the bathroom, giggling like a little girl. On the counter she found two snowflake ornaments trimmed in gold, with clips to attach them to the tree. She wondered whether they represented the two of them, and gave each a kiss before reading her next note.

Return the ornaments and explore my place of work to find your next surprise.

She was curious what the next one might be as she handed Sir the beautiful snowflakes. "They're so pretty, Sir."

He had a definite smirk on his face when he placed them on the table.

Brie went to his desk, expecting to see a gift waiting for her, but it was as clean and tidy as it always was. She looked at her note again and realized he'd instructed her to explore the area.

She started opening all the drawers, a sense of excitement building as she searched for her surprise. Inside the bottom drawer, she found a spool of thick velvet ribbon. She took it out along with another note.

Return my ribbon and find the stick of mint where food is stored.

She walked back to Sir and handed him the ribbon, which he carefully put beside the other items. Brie disappeared into the pantry next, but second-guessed herself when she couldn't find anything. Surely it had to be the place he meant. She searched again, being more thorough, and was rewarded when she found a huge peppermint stick hidden amongst the dried herbs.

Brie gazed at the unusually large candy, wondering where Sir had purchased it. The thought of him spending time and energy finding these unique gifts for her was humbling and sweet. She read the note attached with a sense of deep appreciation.

Return my peppermint stick and go to the room that gets the least use to find something that twinkles.

She came out of the pantry with both hands wrapped around the thick peppermint stick, and handed it to him. She noticed the sparkle in his eye and suspected she knew where it might be going later.

Brie skipped down the hall and opened the door to the spare room. Sir was right; it rarely got any action, having become a makeshift storage room for the things she hadn't been willing to part with, but never used.

She had a much harder time finding the gift because of all the places it could be hidden. She checked under the bed, in all the dresser drawers, and then headed to the closet. Up on the highest shelf she found what she was looking for—two boxes of LED Christmas lights, one red set and one white. She pressed them against her chest. Sir knew her love of twinkling lights. She pulled out the note from the envelope, smiling like a fool.

Return the lights and head to your favorite spot after a long day apart.

She skipped back to him and knelt, handing him both boxes. "Thank you, Sir."

"You are not done yet, little sub."

She looked up at him. "I hope you know what this means to me." She rocked off her heels gracefully and hugged him before heading off to her next surprise.

The first spot she checked was the area in the hallway where she would await his return. There was nothing there, so she headed towards the couch. It was the place where she would kneel while Sir stroked her hair. Sure enough, on the floor she found sprigs of pine bundled together with a red bow. She held them up to her nose and breathed in their aromatic scent. He'd thought of everything.

Underneath the pine was another red envelope. She ripped it open and read its contents.

Return the pine and find the needed item in the storage of textiles.

She returned to her Master and handed over the pine bundle before running to the linen closet. She was rewarded with an ivory-colored hand towel sporting a candy cane pattern at the bottom. She picked up the red envelope attached to it.

Return my towel and find your next gift nestled in a safe place in the hallway.

Brie grinned when she handed the Christmas towel to Sir. He winked at her, laying it on the table. She left to look up and down the hallway, examining each painting and sculpture mounted to the wall. Nothing…

She scanned the area again, her eyes resting on his suit jacket hanging on the hook. A smile spread across her face. Bingo! She stuffed her hands into each of the pockets, finally finding her prize in the small inner breast pocket. Brie pulled out a miniature chocolate Santa wrapped in foil, along with the next red envelope. The clue was especially alluring.

Return Santa to me and find the place your fantasies lie.

Brie walked back to Sir and gave him the tiny Santa. She bit her lip as he placed it on the table. Just what did Sir have planned with that single piece of chocolate?

"Go forth and find," he commanded.

She skipped off to the bedroom, thinking that Sir's Christmas was like Christmas on steroids.

The first place she checked was the closet. It was the place which held all the tools responsible for making her fantasies come true. But after searching through it twice, she still hadn't found anything unusual. It didn't help that Sir hadn't stated in his note what she was supposed to look for.

Sir raised his eyebrow when she returned empty-handed. She was slightly embarrassed when she admitted she couldn't find the gift.

"I'm disappointed."

Oh, that cut her to the quick. Of course he'd expected she'd know where her fantasies lay. Was it Sir? She nonchalantly peeked between his legs.

"No, Brie. Not there, but I'm flattered."

She blushed. "I *will* find it," she assured him as she headed back into the bedroom.

It had to be there—she was certain of it. Brie checked around the bed and under it before returning to the closet. This time, she checked each tool carefully in case there was a new one she'd missed.

Having had no luck, she left the closet and glanced around the room again. That was when her gaze landed on her nightstand. A smile spread across her lips as she walked over to it and opened the drawer.

On top of her fantasy journal was a single condom and another red envelope. She picked up the condom and stifled a giggle when she saw that it was a special mint flavor.

She opened the envelope and read what would appear to be her last note.

Your hunt is almost over, my dear.

Return the mint and find your gift in the place that remains cold all year.

Brie stared down at her beloved journal, relieved to see that Sir had opened it. It meant that all was right with the world again. She walked back to Sir, proudly holding up the condom.

As with the other items, he placed it on the kitchen table and waited.

The last hint only stumped her for a second. She opened the freezer but did not find anything. She opened the refrigerator next, and squealed when she found a little black velvet bag.

Brie took it out and looked inside. She shivered as she pulled out a crystal-blue butt plug. She looked at him, suddenly worried. "This is cold,

Sir."

His wicked smile gave her extra chills. "You may return it to the fridge, then kneel at my feet."

Brie put it back in the velvet bag and placed it on the shelf, shutting the door as goosebumps rose all over her skin. She went back to Sir and knelt as he'd commanded.

"Do you know what we have here?" he asked her, gesturing to the items on the table.

"Christmas fun?"

He chuckled. "Yes, that's one way to put it."

Sir picked up all the items and instructed her, "Go and freshen up, téa. Your Master is about to celebrate Christmas."

Brie literally ran to the bathroom, unable to rein in her excitement. She quickly washed up, brushed out her curls and spritzed Sir's favorite perfume on her wrists.

She returned to the living room to the sound of Christmas music filling the air. Sir was standing beside the Tantra chair, holding the velvet ribbon in his hands.

"Oh, Master…" she sighed as she glided over to him.

"Hands behind your back, téa."

He began the slow process of binding her arms with the soft ribbon, starting at her forearms and tying all the way down to her wrists. He ended it with a pretty bow she could barely see looking back over her shoulder.

"A gift wrapped for my enjoyment," he said, guiding her to lean her knees against the lower end of the Tantra chair, leaving her ass exposed and poised for play.

Sir disappeared for a moment, returning completely naked except for the red Santa hat she'd given him. He stood before her proudly, a smirk on his face. "Santa's come home from a long night of work and is ready to play."

She looked up at him, overcome by how sexy and adorable he looked. "How can I please you, Santa Claus?"

"You will find I am a demanding old man," he warned, picking up the large, decorative candy cane and examining it thoughtfully. "Who knew people decorated their yards with BDSM tools?" He smacked it against his palm. "They make the perfect toy." Sir patted the cane lightly against her butt.

She giggled. "Oh, if my dad only knew…he was so proud of his Candy Cane Lane when I was a kid."

"I bet he was."

Sir smacked her ass hard enough to make it sting, causing Brie to cry out.

He carefully moved the ends of the velvet bow out of his way and began softly stroking her with the cane, slowly building up the force behind each stroke. The plastic material of the decoration made it more flexible and stinging—a challenging tool to take.

"Would you like marks from Santa, little girl?"

"If it pleases you, Santa."

The next series of strokes took her breath away.

Sir stood back after he was done. "Beautiful. Now your naughty little ass is striped like a peppermint stick."

Brie looked back at him, her eyes watering. "Thank you, Santa."

One of his hands lovingly caressed the reddened area, while his other untied her from the velvet. Once she was free, he lifted her up and lay down on the tantra chair, commanding her to lie on him. The new position gave him free access to continue caressing her sore ass.

Sir reached over to the coffee table and picked up the two pretty tree decorations. "Santa had to look far and wide to find ornaments with the correct tension in the clip to provide a proper bite."

He played with her left nipple, pulling and rolling it between his fingers to make it ready. She stared down in fascination as he opened the clip and placed the sparkling snowflake on her erect nipple. Brie moaned with pleasure as the ache the pressure caused traveled down to her groin.

Sir looked at her with a twinkle in his eyes as he applied the other ornament. She threw her head back and took in the wicked sensations his unique nipple clamps created as Sir massaged her breasts. Her pussy throbbed with pleasure from the attention, coating his cock with her juices.

He grabbed her hips and pushed her against his hard shaft. "I think it's time to treat Santa to a little show. Let me watch you ride Santa's pole."

Brie settled down on his cock, taking in the fullness of him. She loved that he watched her—the lust on his face as she moved up and down on his shaft was incredibly erotic. He continued to play with her breasts, tugging on the snowflakes for added stimulation.

Her heart skipped a beat when Sir threw his head back and let out a frustrated groan. He grasped her hips tightly and ordered her to stop. Brie didn't move a muscle as he struggled not to come.

Finally, he opened his eyes and stared at her. "Santa doesn't seem to have much restraint with you."

She moved slightly, taking him in a little deeper.

He immediately slapped her aching ass. "No moving, naughty girl."

Brie was thrilled by the power she had over him. Just another slight movement and her Master would be coming inside her against his will. The thought of that was intoxicating! But she was a good sub and didn't want to steal his power…at least not on Christmas Day. He was far too good a lover to play that kind of game.

"I believe a lesson is in order," he announced. Sir lifted her from him and stood up. He ordered her to lie stomach-first on the highest point of the chaise longue.

Brie stepped onto the curvature in the middle of the chair and lay against the soft leather, keeping her legs together. She loved how the chair supported the position. Her breasts rested on the highest curve, keeping them exposed for his play while giving him full access to her backside.

He picked up one of the strands of lights. "Time to restrain my naughty plaything." Sir started at her feet, wrapping them at the ankles, then brought the strand of lights under the chair to meticulously bind her wrists. He started with the second strand, but surprised her by binding the exact same areas.

Sir left her to turn out the overhead lights, then headed to the electrical outlet, stating, "Let there be light!"

When he plugged in the Christmas lights, he suggested that she look at the window. Brie saw in the reflection that she was bound in stripes of red and white, much like her striped ass.

"I love Santa," she purred.

The low temperature of the LED lights and the loose way he'd tied her made it a secure but comfortable binding. She was now officially a present tied up for Santa's kinky pleasure.

Sir unwrapped the large peppermint stick from the cellophane and asked, "If yard decorations make good canes, and ornaments are really nipple clamps, what do you think this is?"

She blushed when she answered hesitantly, "A dildo?"

He shook his head, tsking. "No, my dear. Candy should never be used for play in the nether regions. Unless, of course, you enjoy yeast infections." He lovingly caressed her mound. "One must always protect the chemistry of a woman's body."

Brie was deeply grateful that her Master was vigilant in his creative play.

Sir laid the Christmas towel next to her head and smiled wickedly. "Open."

Brie had to open wide, stretching her jaw muscles to take the circumference of the peppermint stick. She wrapped her lips around it, so the large stick wouldn't slip out. The mint had her instantly drooling onto her pretty towel.

Ball gags had always brought on a sense of humiliation for Brie. It wasn't just losing her voice during a scene, but losing the ability to control her body that made the experience unpleasant for her. However, Sir had made it sexy by using a tasty treat, along with his thoughtful placement of the towel. She embraced the loss of control and allowed her minty secretions to fall freely.

"Close your eyes, little girl," he growled softly in her ear.

Brie closed her eyes and listened for Sir. He moved around the chair, admiring the scene he'd created; his devoted sub tied in lights, gagged with a peppermint stick, while snowflake nipple clamps invited him to play. Oh, how she loved her Master's creative mind.

She suddenly smelled the distinctive scent of pine before she felt the needles lightly brushing against her cheek, sending chills through her. He used the pine sprigs as a sensation tool, gently caressing her with the needles without scratching the skin.

"A light touch is needed," he murmured. He went for the sensitive areas, including her bare feet. Brie squirmed and wiggled, goosebumps rising on her skin. When his warm lips landed on the tingling areas he'd created, she instantly stilled.

"Good plaything."

Her pussy contracted with pleasure. Nothing was more erotic and satisfying than hearing words of praise spoken by her Master.

"You know, I've heard it's cold in Nebraska."

Sir left her again, then she heard the sound of the refrigerator opening. Brie shuddered. The idea of the cold crystal butt plug made her tremble with fear and expectation as he approached.

Sir smoothed warmed lubricant over her sphincter, adding to the temperature play about to happen. Brie moaned in response, dribbles of mint dropping from her lips.

"I want you to experience a true Nebraskan Christmas," he stated as he pushed the cold crystal against her tight ass.

Brie held her breath.

"Keep breathing," he reminded her, "and bear down for me."

She took in a deep breath before bearing down. Immediately, the ice-cold plug slipped inside her resistant hole. Her nipples contracted achingly from the sudden chill radiating from deep inside her, but her whimpers were muffled by the peppermint stick.

"That's it, naughty girl. Take that cold crystal for Santa," he murmured, removing the peppermint gag and wiping her lips with the towel.

Brie groaned with surprise when he kissed her. Sir tasted of rich chocolate, making a delicious combination of cocoa and mint. She lost herself in it, her body warmed by his passion as it was chilled by the toy.

After claiming her mouth, Sir stood before her so she could watch as he unrolled the mint condom over his rigid cock. "Are you ready to be fucked, plaything?"

Brie nodded eagerly. "I want to be fucked by your huge minty stick, Santa."

Sir chuckled as he positioned himself behind her. "Now we can both experience a cold Nebraskan winter." He eased his shaft into her tight pussy, made that much tighter by the cold crystal inside her ass.

His warm, thick shaft contrasted sharply with the cold butt plug, and they cried out in unison. "Fuuuuck! You're like ice," he growled lustfully, reaching around to play with her nipples.

He let her feel the tingling of his mint-covered cock before grabbing her hips and thrusting. The vigorous friction caused by his impassioned strokes began to counteract the cold between them.

Brie looked back at the reflection in the window, noticing that the sky was just starting to pinken with the approaching dawn as the song *It's Beginning to Look a Lot Like Christmas* played in the background.

She had to stifle a giggle. There she was, tied in twinkly lights to a tantra chair, ornaments on her nipples, being pounded hard by her Master wearing a Santa hat. She knew she would never think of that song in the same way again.

Sir pulled out momentarily to remove the condom before diving back in. After several hearty thrusts, he became completely still, coming hard inside her. Brie cried out as his hot seed coated her chilled depths. In response, her pussy immediately clenched his shaft, milking him with her own powerful orgasm.

"Oh…my…Santa…" she panted.

Sir didn't move until the last pulse of her climax had ended. He pulled out slowly and rained kisses on her ass as he carefully removed the crystal. Then he unbound her. Once she was free, he lovingly unclamped a snowflake and sucked on her nipple to ease the pain of its release. He looked at her with a wicked grin as he removed the second one. Brie moaned with pleasure, enjoying the mixture of pleasure and pain the snowflakes caused.

Finally, Sir gathered her in his arms and cradled her against his chest, petting her hair gently in time with the music. Brie lay there, completely and beautifully spent, listening to the Christmas music and thinking that this had been the best Christmas ever—and then she saw it.

Mine

B rie spied a small box under the tiny Christmas tree.

"Sir, is that another present?"

He looked in the direction of the Bonsai tree. "One has to wonder."

Brie grinned. "May I go and look?"

Sir released her from his embrace. "By all means, but first you have to kiss me."

She traced his lips with her finger before leaning in for the kiss. "And here I thought you didn't do Christmas." She got up and retrieved the thin box before returning to Sir's arms.

She slowly opened the lid of the red velvet box and put her hand to her lips when she saw what was inside. "Oh, Sir…"

He reached in and pulled out the strand of dark pearls. "They're Tahitian black pearls."

Brie took the necklace from him, looking at the iridescent sheen of the multicolored pearls. "I've never seen anything like them before. They're exquisite, Sir."

He took the necklace from her and looped the strand once, putting it over her head and resting it between her breasts. "Knowing our history with pearls, I thought we might enjoy a fresh start."

She stroked the beads appreciatively. "This has to be the most wonderful Christmas gift I've ever gotten."

"That's not all, Brie."

She looked back in the box and saw a red envelope. "More?"

He nodded, a curious grin on his lips.

Brie picked it up and pulled out the card inside. She smiled as she looked at the card, but when she read the words, her bottom lip began to tremble.

You are MINE

Yet two things still separate us

A date

And a place

She opened the card and read:

You are cordially invited to the wedding of

Brianna Renee Bennett

and

Thane Lorenzo Davis

June 25

Brie stared at it, tears coming to her eyes. She whispered in disbelief, "We have a date."

"Yes."

"And the place?"

He caressed her cheek. "That, my beautiful sub, will remain my secret."

Brie would have protested, but she was far too thrilled knowing the date had finally been set for their wedding day—a dream come true.

She sighed happily. "June 25th…"

"Come hell or high water, we will be wed on that day," Sir assured her, laying Brie's head back against his chest. She closed her eyes, reveling in the sound of her Master's strong heartbeat.

In six months they would be man and wife—it was official now.

Merry Freakin' Christmas, Brie…

Brie's Montana Dreams

A Meal With Master

B rie stared into Sir's eyes as they lay together. He looked so serious…
She sensed that he'd made an important decision but was still
grappling with it. Their little 'holiday' from their problems hadn't fixed the
issues they faced, but it had reconnected Brie to him on a soul level—and
that was vital. They could survive anything as long as they remained
connected to each other.

"Did I mention I loved spending Christmas morning with you, Sir?"

He smiled, brushing a strand of hair from her eye. "Yes, a number of
times."

She turned and spooned against him, snuggling closer. "Spending time
with you was the best present of all…"

Sir held her tight as they lay watching the sun slowly breach the horizon on the first day of the New Year, flooding the room with light. He
gently nuzzled her ear with his lips before stating hoarsely, "I've decided to
begin the process."

A dark current of fear coursed through Brie. It was disconcerting
when she knew it was a good thing that Sir was ready to take action. "With
your mother?"

"Yes. I'm meeting with Thompson tomorrow. My mother has a mass
of outstanding debts and I would like to know the full extent and nature of
them."

Brie turned to face Sir, caressing his cheek lovingly. "This is a big step
for you."

"I've given it an inordinate amount of thought. Initially, I believed it
best to remember her as the woman I knew as a boy. However, I've come
to the conclusion that I cannot let her die without understanding the
woman she's become."

"That's courageous, Sir," she told him, but shuddered inwardly at the thought. "I worry that you may find out things that will upset or hurt you."

He gently traced his thumb over her downturned lips. "I'm the kind of person who prefers to know the truth rather than have things that are unpleasant kept from me. Unlike most people, ignorance is not my bliss."

She smiled, loving the ticklish feel of his touch. "Yes, I've learned that about you the hard way."

He chuckled, leaning over to kiss her on the lips. "But at least you learned."

Brie couldn't shake the ominous feeling associated with Sir and his mother and it confused her. She knew he needed to move forward, and the only way to do that was to wade through the mess his mother had made of her life. "I'll be with you every step of the way, Sir."

"I expect no less from my condor."

She settled back in his arms and sighed as she stared at the sun bathing the city with its golden light. It was impossible not to feel hope.

"Happy New Year, Sir…"

Brie stood in Mr. Holloway's office a month later, anxious to show him what she had filmed so far. She glanced down at the diamond ring on her finger and the pleasant butterflies started. She would be marrying Sir in less than five months…

Unfortunately, that left her little time to get all the filming complete for her second documentary. Wasting time going in a direction Mr. Holloway would not support was not an option for her, which was why she'd requested the special meeting.

Brie noticed that he watched Headmaster Coen's entire spanking scene while wearing a slight smirk on his face. Afterwards he turned to Brie, shaking his head. "This one is flirting with an XXX rating, Miss Bennett. I counted four orgasms, possibly five."

"While I know it's obvious to you and me, I doubt the audience will pick up on it. I find most people are ignorant of the orgasms happening around them."

"It *is* uniquely provocative, but I want you to edit portions of it, possibly film a few extra shots if you can't make it less obvious. I'm interested in keeping the segment, but we don't want your work confused with a pornographic film."

Brie felt the heat rise to her cheeks. "I'll work on the edits and talk to Headmaster Coen if needed."

Next she showed him her flogging scene with Marquis.

Mr. Holloway studied it with great interest, giving Brie reason to believe he'd enjoyed the scene. However, he stunned her when he announced afterwards, "This will *not* be included in your film."

"Bu—"

"End of discussion."

Brie hated the thought of telling Marquis Gray that his scene had been cut. It was a beautiful encounter, and was significant to her on a personal level. The scene was every bit as provocative and artful as the spanking scene, and Brie felt the urge to defend it. Yet when she studied the producer's face, his expression let her know there would be no budging on this point.

"Can I have an explanation, please?"

Instead of answering her, Mr. Holloway stated, "You mentioned a meeting with the head trainer of the Dominant course at the Center. How did that go?"

Brie saw the challenge in his eye, daring her to ask again about Marquis' scene. She reluctantly accepted the change of subject, not wanting to lose her documentary over it, although she feared it would be a disappointment to Marquis Gray, a Dom she highly respected.

"Master Nosh was busy, but I was told he might be willing to do an interview with me."

"I leave it up to you whether you want to pursue that further. I'm interested in what he has to say, but am unsure if it will have any relevance to your film. Where are you headed next?"

"I plan to visit Mr. Wallace and Miss Wilson at the Sanctuary in Montana. I sent a wire, since I am unable to contact them by phone, and received confirmation a few days ago that I would be welcome to join the commune for a two-week stay."

"Now *that* I am interested in. Send me the raw footage when you're done."

Brie was unsure why he was so fascinated with the commune, but thought it might have something to do with Mary. He'd shown an interest in her story when Brie was filming her first documentary. At the time, she'd assumed it was for purely professional reasons. Now she wasn't so sure...

"Certainly. I'll send it to you first thing, Mr. Holloway. As for the rest, I plan to have all the shooting done and the basic editing complete before June."

"Before the wedding, then? A wise choice, Miss Bennett. I have no patience for people's personal lives interfering with business."

"It won't, Mr. Holloway. I assure you. Sir Davis and I are agreed that the filming comes first."

"Fine, then you may see yourself out."

She stood up and nodded respectfully to him before walking towards the door.

"Don't forget, Miss Bennett, I want that footage as soon as possible."

Brie smiled to herself. He really must have a thing for Mary. Too bad the girl was already taken…

Since Sir was meeting with his lawyer in the same area of town, they met for lunch afterwards. She felt that familiar flush as she spied him sitting at a corner table. He looked so confident and handsome sitting there alone. It humbled Brie knowing that Sir was waiting for her, and the smile on his face when he spotted her across the room absolutely melted her heart.

"Please sit," he said, guiding her to the chair beside him. "I've already ordered an appetizer."

While Brie munched on the fresh fruit and cheeses he'd ordered, she explained how she'd fared in her meeting with Mr. Holloway. Underneath the table, Sir hiked up her skirt so he could stroke her smooth thigh.

"It sounds as if he's interested in your latest endeavor."

Brie smiled, unwilling to share her suspicions concerning Mr. Holloway's true motivations. Sir hated gossips. Unless she had indisputable evidence, it was best to say nothing. "Yes, he continues to be interested in the documentary, but I'm really disappointed I'm losing the flogging scene."

"That is a shame, Brie," he replied, slipping his hand between her legs. "I had hoped your father would see it and come to understand his daughter better."

She opened her legs to him, allowing her Master greater access.

"Me too, Sir. It was a powerful scene on many levels." Brie stopped eating, distracted by the electricity caused by his sensual touch.

"Have another slice of apple," Sir commanded gently as he swirled his finger over her clit.

She suppressed the squeak that burst forth as she took a slice and bit into it. Sir was so wickedly bad.

The waiter came up and smiled at Brie. "Miss, have you decided on a plate?"

She looked at Sir, the heat rising to her cheeks as he increased the delightful pressure on her clit. "I…umm…"

"We'll share a plate of your cock stuffed with brie."

"Do you mean our stuffed chicken breast, sir?"

"Exactly," Sir replied with a smirk.

"A fine choice," the waiter complimented, turning to Brie and giving her a wink before leaving.

"He seems to be smitten with you, my dear," Sir growled, slowly sinking his finger into her. Brie held her breath and remained still, every fiber of her being concentrated on the pressure of his finger. "Eat," he reminded her.

She lifted the slice of apple to her lips, her gaze locked on to Sir's. In a crowded restaurant, in the middle of the day, he was having his way with her. It was insanely sexy.

When the waiter returned with their dish, Sir pulled his finger from her and sucked it in front of the man. "I do enjoy the taste of Brie in the afternoon."

"Certainly, sir." The waiter placed the dish in front of them, adding, "The creamy texture of a good brie enhances the culinary experience."

Brie giggled, looking at Sir as she quipped, "So I've been told."

"If you require anything else, miss, please don't hesitate to ask."

She felt her Master's hand return between her legs and let out a satisfied sigh. "Thank you, but I have everything I need."

"Very well," the waiter answered, obviously discouraged by her dismissive tone.

After he left, Sir leaned over and whispered in her ear, "I do believe you just broke his young heart."

The heat in Brie's cheeks increased as Sir resumed his forbidden caress. "Cut off a piece of that breast and feed it to me, téa."

She picked up the fork and knife with trembling hands, and attempted to slice through the bird while her pussy caught fire with need. She bit her lip in concentration as she brought the piece of succulent meat oozing with brie to his lips.

"Look into my eyes," he said before taking the bite.

Brie gazed into them, a chill settling on her as her body primed for release.

He nodded slightly, giving her permission…

With a tiny squeak, she gave in to the fire. Her whole body shook as a wave of intense pleasure washed over her.

Sir swallowed his bite and smiled. "Good girl…"

He sucked his finger again, relishing her taste before taking the fork and knife from her. "Let me cut you a piece now."

Their meal was sensual and private, even though they were in the midst of a crowd. Sir had that unique and beautiful effect on her. She was sad when the check was paid and they were forced to go their separate ways.

"I want you to set up your travel arrangements for the Montana trip when you get home. Unfortunately, I will not be able to join you."

"Traveling is much more pleasant when you're with me," Brie said, silently pleading he would change his mind.

"However, it's not a reality for us. As a film director, you will often find yourself traveling alone. The secret lies in how we structure our time apart."

Brie nodded, sighing with resignation.

"You must keep a tight schedule if we are to wed this June," he reminded her, taking Brie's hand and kissing the ring on her finger.

"Well, when you put it that way, Sir... I'll be sure to make those arrangements as soon as I get home."

"That's better. We'll discuss the logistics of our separation tonight."

As she walked to her car once they'd parted ways, Brie fought off the sense of sadness that washed over her. Any time apart was hard on her, but she was determined to succeed with this second film. The world would be a better place because of her sacrifice and dedication; she had to trust and believe in that.

Big Sky Country

A lthough she faithfully wrote to Tono Nosaka every week, it was rare for him to respond. She impatiently opened his letter, anxious to learn how Tono was faring in Japan.

Dear Brie,

It pleases me to hear your meeting with Mr. Holloway went well and that you've been given the green light to continue filming. Naturally, if we should meet again, I would be honored to film a session of Kinbaku for you, although the opportunity seems highly unlikely at this point.

Despite my best efforts, my mother has become more discontented with time. To preserve my sanity, I took your recommendation to continue working on my modern take on Kinbaku. Chikako and I have made steady progress. It's brought me much-needed peace and I thank you for being forthright in your suggestion.

Against my mother's wishes, I have passed on my father's studio to a well-respected bakushi, a man worthy of continuing my father's legacy. I have neither the time nor the interest to run it. If I am completely honest, I did not want the responsibility, knowing it would cement my fate here in Japan. Although I fully accept my duty, I still hope to return to America someday. It is a purely selfish desire, but to deny it would be foolish.

I have not said anything until now, but I find it touching that you wear my orchid whenever you film. As you know, I admire your talent and am proud to be a part of the process—even if only in spirit.

Please continue to send your letters. They are something I have come to look forward to each week.

Enjoy your time at the commune. I'm certain it will be a fascinating experience. I trust Mr. Wallace will behave himself while you're there. I would be remiss if I did not admit my concern. However, I know your Master is invested in your wellbeing and would not put you in harm's way.

In all things, I wish you continued growth and peace. Give my best to Sir Davis.

Respectfully,
Ren Nosaka

Brie sighed as she placed Tono's letter inside the silk satchel, along with the others he'd sent. She saw a vision of his warm, chocolate-brown eyes and smiled.

"I'm praying you return home, Tono."

To her delight, Sir had insisted on taking her to the airport despite the earliness of her flight. He reached out as he drove, tenderly caressing her cheek. "Don't fret. It is only a temporary separation."

"I know, Sir, but I dislike leaving you, especially now because of what's happened to your mother."

"Although I appreciate your concern, I'll be fine."

"But if you need me to return for any reason, do you promise to contact me?" she pleaded. "It's going to be hard enough not talking to you while I'm at the commune, but I won't be able to focus on this assignment unless I'm certain you will let me know if things get worse."

"If her condition changes, I will send for you," he assured her.

"Not having daily contact with you is going to kill me, Sir."

"However, we must abide by the rules of the commune," he reminded her. "It's not as if we haven't been down this road before, when you were under Nosaka's care, and we have our protocols set. It will not be as difficult as you think."

Brie wiggled in her seat, feeling the comforting presence of her jewelry as it pressed against her clit. Wearing the intimate jewelry would definitely help to comfort her when she found herself longing for him.

"Keep your eye on the prize, Brie. I expect you to pursue it with dogged vigilance."

"I will, Sir," she said, smiling sadly, "but my heart will be pining away for you."

"As long as it doesn't affect the quality of your work," he chided teasingly.

"I promise to come back with footage that will amaze and astound you."

Sir chuckled as he parked the Lotus. "Mr. Holloway is the only one you need to impress, babygirl."

Before he left her at the airport, Sir kissed her deeply, prolonging the kiss so that all her attention was focused on him and nothing else. When he finally broke the contact, he smiled down at her.

Brie sighed. "Your kisses are like magic for my soul."

He grazed her lips with his fingertips. "I'm in agreement with you."

Sir walked away, moving through the airport with a confident stride that caught the attention of those around him. She allowed herself a moment to mourn their separation before turning away and walking in the opposite direction with an equally confident stride. She was a film director. All her energy needed to be centered on that for the next two weeks. There was no time for sentimentality.

Brie was surprised how far out the commune was from Whitefish, Montana. Truly, no one would stumble upon the place by accident. She knew she'd finally made it to her destination when she saw the gate, but there was no signage other than a warning posted on the gate that stated, *Trespassers will be shot.*

She was unsure whether it was meant as a humorous warning or a serious threat.

Brie saw there was a rusty intercom, and rolled down the car window to press the red button on the keypad. It crackled to life and a male voice with a distinctive drawl said, "State your name and order of business."

"Hello, I'm Brianna Bennett. Master Gannon is expecting me."

The intercom went dead. After several agonizing moments, it crackled again. "You may enter."

The gate creaked and complained as it slowly swung open. The secluded environment, the warning sign, the old equipment along with the thickly wooded area made Brie think of the movie *Deliverance*. She suddenly wondered if she should be concerned for her safety as she drove through the rusty gate.

As Brie drove down the winding dirt road, images of rustic cabins, rocking chairs and men with overgrown beards crowded her mind. When she rounded the last bend, the wooded area opened up and revealed a delightful surprise.

The commune was not a rundown cabin community at all. Oh, no…this establishment looked like a first-class resort. The main building was covered in scenic windows, multiple balconies and an elaborate stone patio that surrounded the entire structure.

When she saw two men approaching her on the road, she slowed the car to a stop and unrolled her window again. "Is either of you Master Gannon?"

"No, I am one of the Gatekeepers. Hand over your keys and your cell phone. Both will be returned to you when it's time for you to leave."

Brie was startled by the demand, but got out of the rental car, grabbing her suitcase and camera equipment before handing over her keys.

"Rajah will help with your luggage."

Rajah looked nothing like the mountain men she'd expected to see. He was tall and tan, with long dark hair and mischievous green eyes. Without asking permission, he grabbed her luggage and all her equipment before starting towards the building.

The Gatekeeper noticed the concern on Brie's face and assured her, "Rajah will take care of your belongings."

"But my camera equip—"

"Gannon is waiting for you, Miss Bennett."

Brie understood that to mean she was wasting Master Gannon's time. The last thing she wanted was to make a poor impression on the leader of the commune. It had been highly unusual to be invited as a guest, so she hastened towards the building.

An older man who looked to be in his sixties stood waiting for her on the steps. He had the unusual combination of one brown and one blue eye, which instantly drew her attention. She had to force herself not to stare in order not to appear rude. Brie held out her hand and was relieved when he shook it cordially.

"Thank you for letting me visit your commune, Master Gannon."

"That's simply Gannon to you."

"Yes, Gannon," she replied, immediately correcting herself.

A large black cat came up to him and rubbed against his legs. Master Gannon smiled as he picked it up. "So, Miss Bennett, what do you think of my utopia?"

She glanced up at the impressive building before her. "The Sanctuary is nothing like I imagined."

"This has been my lifelong vision," he stated proudly.

"You have an exquisite imagination, sir."

"I knew it would become reality, but I had to be patient and invite the right people to share in my dream. Although I've agreed to let you join us for several weeks, you are not allowed to shoot footage of any of the buildings on the estate. I want to promote the idea that we live a simple life to the outside world."

"What am I allowed to film, then?"

"Any outdoor activities. You may also interview interested members. However, the lush accommodations, as well as the exact location, must remain secret. I do not want our way of life disrupted by the curious and unvetted."

"Can I ask why you've agreed to let me film here if you want to keep your privacy?"

"I hope my vision will inspire others like it. America has been bound by laws created by prudish misfits. It is time to open our minds and bodies to something greater."

"It seems you're talking about more than just sexual freedom."

He cocked his head and smiled as he petted the cat. "You're perceptive, Miss Bennett. Before I subject you to a political lecture, I suggest you seek out your friends. I believe they are waiting for you in the garden."

Brie turned in the direction he'd pointed to and spied Faelan standing next to a large fountain. She excused herself, giving the cat a scratch under its chin before leaving the Master.

Todd Wallace looked leaner than she remembered, and she noticed a wildness in his eyes that she hadn't seen before. It made the young Dom even more striking, but it unsettled her on a gut level she couldn't understand. There was nothing sexual about his feral look.

Mary, on the other hand, looked totally relaxed and in her element. Brie had never seen her friend exude such easy confidence. Unlike the Blonde Nemesis of her training days, Mary seemed comfortable and *very* content.

"Well, look what the cat dragged in…"

"Hey, bitch," Brie answered good-naturedly. "Too good to contact me just to let me know you're okay? I assume you're free to leave the commune to connect with friends and family on occasion."

Mary looked around, gesturing to several shirtless men in cowboy hats walking past, and shrugged. "If given the choice, I would pick staying here and playing with them every time. In fact…I have."

Brie glanced at Faelan, curious whether he was jealous hearing Mary speak like that. She was surprised to see Todd's expression change as he stared at Mary. It was a protective but loving look, and made Brie reconsider her initial unease about him. Maybe this commune *was* a healthy environment for them both.

"Why did I even bother to come?" Brie teased.

"I don't know. It's not like I asked you to visit."

Faelan put his arm around Mary. "Now, now…" He looked at Brie with those mesmerizing blue eyes and said, "Don't let her bitterness fool you. She's been anxious for your arrival."

Mary elbowed him in the gut. "Shut the fuck up, Faelan."

He raised his eyebrow. "What did we say about the word 'fuck'?"

She let out an irritated sigh. "We only use it as a verb."

"That's right," he replied smoothly. "Drop and give me twenty."

Mary put her hands on her hips. "Don't do this. Not in front of Stinky Cheese."

"We agreed," he answered her.

Mary huffed as she reluctantly got down on the ground and began counting out twenty pushups. Brie had to cover her mouth to keep from laughing seeing Mary submit so readily to Faelan.

"Who the hell is this girl, and what did you do with Mary?" Brie demanded.

Faelan smiled charmingly. "Same girl, different attitude."

Mary continued with her pushups without adding her own snarky remark, but in her attempt to hurry, her pushups became shallow. Faelan put his foot on Mary's back, forcing her to lie still on the ground.

"Try that again. Nose to the dirt—don't half-ass it."

To Brie's surprise, Mary didn't argue as she started counting from one again.

Brie looked wide-eyed at Faelan, her mouth agape in sheer disbelief.

Mary looked up. "Hey, stop gawking at my man."

"But I've never seen you so…domesticated. This place is starting to remind me a little of the *Stepford Wives*."

Mary hesitated for a second, but Faelan reminded her, "Unless you want to start over, I suggest you continue."

Mary completed her set and got back up, wiping her hands on her skirt. Instead of verbally flaying Brie, she turned to Faelan. "I…apologize, Faelan."

"Kiss me," he ordered.

Mary leaned in to him and they kissed for several long, drawn-out minutes. Normally, Brie would have been irritated being forced to watch Blonde Nemesis play tonsil-hockey for such a long time, but it warmed her heart to see the two so hot for each other.

When Faelan pulled away, he brushed his finger over her lips. "Pedestrian curses only taint this beautiful mouth."

A smile tugged on Mary's lips.

"It appears commune life agrees with you, Mary Quiet Contrary," Brie complimented.

She nodded in agreement, not taking her eyes off Faelan. "You have no idea."

"So show me around the place. I want to discover what makes it such a transformative setting."

"Yes, why don't you take Brie for a tour of the grounds?" Faelan suggested. He grabbed Mary's chin possessively and kissed her again before letting go.

Mary shuddered in reaction to his impassioned kiss. "Fine, I will."

Faelan turned his attention back to Brie. "I look forward to hearing what you think of the Sanctuary once you've seen all it has to offer."

The Sanctuary

M ary pointed towards the main lodge building. "That's where we all live and do most of our play, but let me show you the estate first."

"You know," Brie said as they walked, "when you told me you were living at a commune, I had images of log cabins and old hippies running around. I wasn't prepared for it to be a high-class resort."

Mary scoffed. "Just because we're self-sufficient doesn't mean we have to live deprived lives."

"So how do you guys support a place like this? Were you required to invest your own money to join?"

"Hell, no. Master Gannon built it before the stock market crashed in 2001. He used all his investments to build the entire estate. Since our community lives off the grid, each of us is required to help maintain the grounds and make enough to meet the needs of all of the members."

Brie was impressed. "So how does one become a member?"

"Master Gannon hand-selects the people he wants to populate it. The vetting process is quite lengthy. Not only does the couple have to be experienced kinksters, they have to possess additional skills that can be utilized by the community. We're all expected to volunteer our time and expertise in order to keep the commune running efficiently."

"So you're required to work every day solely to support the commune without getting paid?"

"Our payment is getting to live here."

"So what specific skills did you and Todd bring to the community?"

"The commune recently lost their pharmacist, so I was a shoe-in when the man left to start a family. As for Faelan, he had his physical brawn and multiple BDSM skills to bring to the table."

Mary pointed to a huge, wooden barn. "The livestock and horses are kept there. Not only do we breed and train horses, but every morsel of meat we consume is born, raised and butchered on this property."

She pointed out a huge vegetable garden and orchard, with rolling wheat fields behind it. "Every vegetable, grain and fruit consumed comes from our own garden. It's empowering to be responsible for every aspect of our lives."

Brie looked at the snow-covered peaks in the distance. "How does the community support itself through the winter?"

"Nothing is cooked out of season, unless we've canned or preserved it." Mary pointed to another large structure west of the barn. "We also make BDSM furniture to sell."

"So you're kind of like the Amish."

Mary snorted. "Sure…but with awesome sex and modern conveniences thrown in."

Brie giggled, catching the attention of several males as they walked by. She noticed they nodded to Mary but completely ignored her. She found it curious but wasn't necessarily surprised. Having hung out with Mary in the past, she was used to Mary's power of attraction.

Fucking blondes…she thought, shaking her head in amusement.

"Out in the woods we have different areas designed for kinky play."

Brie looked at her oddly. "But you don't seem the nature type to me."

"Oh, I've screamed in the woods multiple times. But you're right, I prefer to stay indoors. You'll understand why when I show you…" Mary led Brie through the large doors of the main building.

The entrance opened up into a giant room with vaulted ceilings, an impressive fireplace made of river rock and a ridiculously long sectional couch in the center. Various play furniture lined the walls, including several styles of tantra chairs—one of which was currently in use.

"Oh, Mary! This is a kinkster's dream palace," Brie whispered.

"Yes, it is."

Mary smiled at the couple fucking on the chair as she led Brie to the other side of the spacious room.

It was strange. Mary was acting so… pleasant and normal. It was hard to believe she was the same person Brie had trained with at the Center.

"And downstairs we have the bedrooms," Mary informed her, pointing to a set of stairs.

"Can I see yours?" Brie asked, curious what they looked like after seeing the impressive main room.

Mary shrugged. "They're nothing special, Brie. We just sleep there, so they're small and unadorned. Master Gannon wants us interacting as a group during the day." To Brie's delight, Mary changed direction and led her down the long flight of stairs, walking past numerous doors of various colors in the narrow hallway.

Mary abruptly stopped and turned, opening a blue one. "This is Faelan's and my room."

Brie walked inside and whistled. There was only enough space for the king-sized bed, a closet and a private toilet. Brie's luggage had been piled in the corner, taking up the remaining space. The only design element of any interest was the impressive mirror mounted on the ceiling.

"Wow, girl. You weren't kidding about these rooms being small. It's reminiscent of a college dorm."

"Yes, but the beds are designed for fucking."

Brie jumped on the large bed and fell backwards, testing it out by rolling and gyrating on it.

"What the hell, Brie?"

"Just testing it out for myself. I have to agree, the bed seems sturdy enough for Todd's brand of spirited play."

Mary gave her a knowing smile. "Yeah, but the bed's barely strong enough for the two of us." Then she huffed in irritation. "But unfortunately for me, I'm stuck housing you for the next two weeks."

"What? All three of us here?" Brie asked, suddenly concerned.

"No, you twit. Faelan's been invited to join another couple. Damn, I wish it were me, but no…I get stuck sleeping with you."

Brie jumped off the bed, feeling relieved. "Hey, you'd better not get any ideas. I'm not into women, especially not bitchy blondes."

"Hah! Like you would ever be good enough for me."

As they walked back down the hallway, Brie asked, "Does it bother you that Todd will be with others at night?"

Mary stopped and stared at her as if she were a simpleton. "Are you kidding me? This is a commune—we share everything. Besides, you see the way Faelan looks at me. He may fuck the other girls here, but that boy's heart is all mine."

Brie nudged her. "I did notice that, and it seems to go both ways."

Mary gave her an irritated look. "I'm not you. God, why do you always have to assume I'm as lovesick and stupid as you are?" She tromped up the stairs, forcing Brie to run to catch up. The bitch might have changed in many ways, but she was still just as impossible.

Mary nonchalantly pointed out the large dining room. It was truly impressive, with a single, incredibly long table and all the numerous chairs that surrounded it. "Master Gannon insists we eat dinner together every night, no exceptions. He says mealtime is when familial connections are made and cemented."

She opened two swinging doors just right of the table. "And here is the kitchen. Everyone in the commune is required to cook. Tonight happens to be my night, but I warned them not to let you anywhere near the kitchen."

"Shows how much you know," Brie stated smugly. "I can cook killer dishes these days."

Mary snorted. "Killer is right."

"They're delicious. Even Sir approves. Boa took me under his wing and taught me."

"You mean under his cock?"

Brie giggled at the reference to the sub's colossal shaft. "Bet you didn't know Boa is a patient teacher. Far more patient than Marquis Gray."

"Yeah, I'll never forget the look on Marquis' face when you kept presenting him with your crappy omelets."

"Yours weren't any better."

"Hell yes, they were. I beat you out of the kitchen that day, didn't I?"

Brie rolled her eyes. "Well, now I can cook several authentic Italian dishes, but because of what you just said I'm not going to cook them for you—ever."

"Thank God," Mary said with sarcastic enthusiasm.

"I'm shocked they let *you* in the kitchen."

"I'm perfectly capable of prepping, and…I provide 'release' for the chefs."

"Ah, your true worth revealed."

Mary grabbed a large knife and waved it teasingly at Brie. "Unlike you, I have many talents."

Brie held up her arms in mock surrender. "Look, I'm not into knife play, but if you insist…"

Mary dropped the knife back onto the counter just as a fine-looking cowboy strutted into the kitchen. He took one look at Mary from under his wide-brimmed hat and tsked disapprovingly. "You're to treat the instruments of this kitchen with the respect they deserve."

Mary immediately picked up the knife and carefully slid it into the wooden block, looking sheepishly at him. Brie loved it. For all her bravado, Mary was still as much of a goof as she was. It was comforting to know.

"Yes, let me show you the equipment upstairs now, Miss Bennett," she said in an official tone, leading Brie out of the kitchen under the intense stare of the sexy cowboy. "It's my favorite place to play because of the view and exposure."

They climbed a long spiral staircase that led up to a row of separate play rooms. The first had a medical theme, complete with examining table, a wall of medical equipment, and scrubs. Brie shuddered and quickly made her way to the next room. Her heart skipped a beat when she saw the variety of floggers and the binding post. It appeared each room had its own theme with corresponding instruments and furniture to match, very similar to The Haven.

"Nice…" Brie complimented.

Mary smiled mischievously as she led Brie into the third room. Brie stopped short when she saw the wall of knives, needles and piercing equipment.

"Here we can enjoy blood play all we want. No restrictions other than safety."

Brie slowly backed out of the room. "I think I'll pass."

"You're such a baby."

"And proud of it," Brie stated.

"But this is the best part," Mary told her, dragging her out onto the balcony.

Brie caught her breath. The view overlooking the lake was magnificent, absolutely stunning. The beauty of the snowy peaks surrounding them was reflected in the still water. "Oh, wow…"

"There are four balconies up here, each facing in a different direction," Mary informed her.

Brie did not miss all the binding equipment stored in the glass case next to her. Before she could ask about it, the cowboy from the kitchen appeared beside Mary.

"Remove your panties, go to the railing and kneel facing me."

Mary instantly obeyed, as if it were Faelan who'd commanded her. After removing her thong, she knelt with her legs spread apart in an inviting manner, the shortness of her skirt exposing her blonde pussy to him.

The Dom grabbed nylon rope from the case and took her wrists, binding them together before securing them to the railing so she was immobilized.

"Open," he commanded, tilting his hat back so he could observe her.

Mary obediently opened her crimson lips, glancing up at the man with a sexy look of fear and anticipation—the perfect submissive.

He unzipped his pants and pulled his erect cock from his jeans, easing it into her mouth. "Deep-throat it, darlin'."

Brie remembered Mary's skill at sucking cock, and was impressed yet again as she watched her friend take the length of the man's shaft down her throat. He fisted her long blonde hair and thrust deeper, then began pumping vigorously as if he were fucking her pussy. Mary took it with grace, never losing eye contact as he thrust into her mouth. It was actually beautiful to watch, but it was his grunts of satisfaction that deeply affected Brie.

She felt a trickle of excitement travel past her clit jewelry and down her leg. It was definitely going to be hard living in the commune for the next few weeks, knowing she would be a witness to all kinds of kinky fun with no outlet for release. Sir had specifically ordered her not to masturbate while they were apart.

Damn…

The cowboy pulled out and caressed Mary's cheek. "I could fuck your lips all day, darlin'."

She smiled up at him. "I would be honored to service you."

He shook his head. "Unfortunately, there's a filly that needs breaking. I'll have to be satisfied with this for now." He rubbed the tip of his cock over her lips before taking her mouth again. This time he grabbed Mary's head with both hands and pumped forcefully into her, crying out when his orgasm finally hit.

Brie swallowed hard, looking out over the lake as she tried to concentrate on the beauty of the scenery rather that her own sexual need.

Missing you, Sir.

After he'd finished, the cowboy untied Mary and helped her to her feet. He tipped his hat to her. "Tomorrow, same time and place."

Mary nodded demurely.

The Dom kissed her well-used lips, all smeared with red lipstick, before leaving the girls alone on the balcony.

"So that's a common occurrence?" Brie whispered.

Mary wiped her mouth with her forearm, a smirk on her lips. "Any Dom can take you at any time. It makes daily life on the commune most enjoyable for a sub."

"Are you allowed to say no?"

"Naturally, but why the hell would I?" Mary pointed to a charming bridge in the distance. "I need to clean up. Why don't I meet you down there?"

"Sure," Brie answered. She admired the view from the other three balconies before following a second spiral staircase down and heading outside. The blueness of the Montana sky reminded her of Colorado and made her think of Lea.

"Girlfriend, I think you would go nuts here," Brie said out loud, laughing to herself.

She followed the dirt path to a footbridge that crossed over a stream, which fed into the mountain lake. She soaked in the sounds of rushing water as jays chirped above her in the pine trees. It was truly a relaxing environment…

"Strip and present yourself to me."

Kinky Fun

B rie opened her eyes and turned slowly to face the Dom who had commanded her. She was shocked to see Faelan staring at her lustfully. Although she knew such practices were common here, she'd never expected anyone to demand that of her as a guest of the commune—least of all Faelan.

She didn't make a move.

"Are you refusing a direct command?"

Although she was still aroused from Mary's recent encounter and her body naturally responded to his animal magnetism, she wasn't about to submit to him.

Brie held her head high and answered with a defiant, "Yes."

Faelan's demeanor completely changed. She'd expected anger; instead he started laughing. "Mary insisted I have a little fun with you, and I couldn't resist when I saw you here alone." He shook his head. "That look on your face was comical." He continued to laugh at her expense as he leaned against the handrail beside her.

"Very funny," she growled, not enjoying being the butt of Mary and Faelan's joke.

"Just so we're clear, Brie, I would have refused you if you had stripped. In this community you're considered untouchable until you've gone through Initiation. You're basically invisible to all the Doms here."

So that explains why I've been treated like a ghost.

Brie was used to Doms sizing her up before checking her neck to see if she was wearing a collar, but the Doms here had made her feel as if she didn't exist. It'd reminded her a bit of her tobacco shop days—before Sir had found her and changed everything.

"Just so *we're* clear," she told Faelan, wanting to put him in his place, "I never considered stripping for you."

"Oh, I saw that moment of hesitation when you considered it."

"Your arrogance never ceases to amaze me."

"Don't worry, I won't tell."

"There's nothing to tell!"

He chuckled again. "It's good to see you again, blossom. Mary's missed you, even if she refuses to admit it."

Brie should have protested the use of his pet name for her, but the way he said it was casual, like a nickname between old friends. It felt comfortable.

"Somehow I doubt she missed me."

"You have more influence on her than you know."

"She seems quite happy here. Happier than I thought she was capable of, truthfully."

"Yes, I think she gains strength from being here at the commune." Brie noticed a brief look of pain flit across his face and wondered at the cause of it. Before she could ask, Mary strolled up.

Faelan wrapped his arms around Mary and kissed the top of her head. "I heard Marcus was looking for you."

She smiled. "Oh...he found me."

"Good. I like having the sub everyone else wants to enjoy."

"I like being that sub," she replied conceitedly.

"I bet you do," he growled, nipping Mary's shoulder.

Brie was pleased to see how relaxed and attentive the two were towards each other. It would have been obnoxious if it hadn't been so genuine. Despite the challenges of having an open relationship, they seemed to be flourishing in this environment.

"So on a scale of one to ten, how would you rate commune life?" she asked Mary.

Mary snuggled against Faelan. "If you'd told me life could be like this, I would have socked you in the jaw for being a f—" she looked warily at Faelan and corrected herself, "...a liar."

He fisted Mary's hair. Her old habit of flinching caused her to cower momentarily in fear, but she soon relaxed when he grabbed her chin and kissed her deeply. "Yeah, I've got no complaints about this place," he said gruffly.

"So what about you, Brie?" Mary asked. "How's the vanilla world treating you these days?"

Brie couldn't hold in her excitement when she told Mary, "Sir and I are getting married in June!"

"Oh God, can you get any more vanilla than that?" Mary complained, rolling her eyes.

Brie laughed. "You can dis me all you want, bitch, but I'm one happy little sub." She looked at her ring, the diamond sparkling with an allure similar to Sir's eyes.

"Do what makes you happy, blossom," Faelan replied, sounding sincere.

"Thanks. I am happy, but I'll be even happier once I get this second documentary finished."

"Your time isn't going to be all work here, is it?" Mary complained. "I have a few things I want to share with you that are much too scandalous to make it into your vanilla BDSM documentary."

Brie ignored her teasing. "Sure. I'm hoping to spend time alone with you too."

Mary laughed. "Oh, Brie, you really are a twit."

Before Brie could take offense, Faelan spoke up. "Mary is in serious need of some girl-time. She hates to admit it, but you keep her grounded."

Now it was Mary's turn to be offended. "Grounded? What the f—" She regained her composure and asked, "What do you mean by that, Faelan?"

He patted her on the shoulder. "And on that note, I'll bid you *adieu*." He chuckled to himself as he walked towards the barn.

Mary stared at Brie with her lips pursed. "I don't need grounding, bitch."

"I wouldn't give it to you even if you asked."

Blonde Nemesis broke out in laughter. "Damn, Brie. I forgot you were funny. Always lump you in with Lea and her pathetic attempts at humor."

They sat on some boulders beside the stream to talk. "Admit it, Mary, there are times you laugh at Lea's silly jokes."

"No…I laugh *at* her, not with her."

"Someday I will get you to confess your love for Lea *and* her lame jokes." Seeing she wasn't going to convince Mary of that anytime soon, Brie asked, "So you mentioned wanting to share something with me?"

Mary's eyes lit up. "Oh, yes! I have three guys interested in trying it with me and I want you to film the event. But you can't use it for your damn documentary—this is for my private use only!"

"What exactly do you want me to film?"

She grinned, looking like a naughty schoolgirl. "I want to do a foursome."

"What's the big deal?" Brie was less than impressed.

"I want to take all three cocks at the same time."

Brie was imagining a DP with a little oral action. "So?"

Mary leaned in close. "I want to take two cocks in my pussy and one up my ass."

Brie looked at her in disbelief. "Oh, now that *is* different."

"Yeah…" Mary said with a self-satisfied smile.

"Is Todd—"

Mary waved off the question before she'd even asked. "He doesn't care to scene with other Doms."

Brie tried to wrap her mind around the idea. "How can your body take it? I mean, is your twat so huge you can handle two shafts?"

"Are you just trying to bait me so I beat the shit out of you?"

Keeping her smile to herself, Brie answered, "No, I'm honestly curious."

"I don't have a giant cunt, bitch. It's going to be a real challenge for me, but that's why I like the idea."

"That's all kinds of unnatural stretching."

Mary's eyes took on a dreamy look. "Being rammed by three cocks at once… Fuck, does it get any hotter than that?"

Brie shook her head. "I can't even imagine it, but I guess I won't have to."

"So you're willing to film it?"

"Sure, why not? As long as Todd's cool with it."

"Fuck, he's open to me trying anything."

"Hmm… I notice your language slips when he's not around. Should I enlighten him?"

Mary tilted her chin up and sneered. "I only clean up my language for him. You, on the other hand, don't matter to me."

"It's no wonder you don't have any girlfriends here, based on the way you treat me."

"I like putting you in your place—someone needs to," Mary huffed.

"I feel the same way about you."

"Because deep down I know you're jealous of me, Brie."

"Jealous of what?"

"My not having to deal with idiots who judge me and having the freedom to explore my wildest desires. What's not to be jealous about? You're missing out, and you know it." Mary put an arm around her. "I actually feel sorry for you, Stinky Cheese."

Brie forcefully removed Mary's arm from her shoulder. "Just because this is right for you doesn't mean I would thrive here. I like knowing Sir and I are exclusive…for the most part," she added with a grin, reflecting on their threesome with Rytsar.

Mary crinkled her nose in disgust. "Being stuck with the same person for the rest of your life? I can't think of a worse punishment."

"I find knowing Sir on such an intimate level—one that no one else shares—is the greatest turn-on of all."

Mary patted Brie's cheeks, making a kissy face at her. "Oh, my poor little Brie, you're still such an innocent."

Brie pulled away from her, unamused. "I still maintain that you're the one who's secretly jealous. Face it—you can't stand the fact that I'm collared and you're not."

"As if… Faelan and I are having the time of our lives. Why would we ruin it with a collar?"

"You really don't want to wear his collar?" Brie asked, not quite believing it.

"Hell, no! It would feel like a noose around my neck."

"Well, I can't argue with you, because whatever you two are doing seems to be working. I'll admit, you seem more content than I thought possible."

Mary eyed her suspiciously. "What the hell do you mean by that?"

Brie laughed. "You seem sweet together…like an old married couple."

"Old married couple! Do you think you could be any more insulting, bitch?" Mary looked ready to deck her, but Brie didn't flinch.

"I actually meant it as a compliment, Mary."

"It's not!"

Brie rolled her eyes. "Okay, I take it back. You're not sweet together."

Mary wasn't satisfied, and decided to throw Brie a curveball. "So what's the real story between you and Sir? Something's up, I can tell. Not everything is sweetness and light in Brieland."

Brie did not appreciate Mary's intuitive nature, and skirted the issue. "Both of us have been extremely busy, so that's made it hard to connect as much as we want."

"And?"

"And…things have happened."

Mary scooted closer. "Ooh, do tell! It's got to be juicy."

Brie wasn't about to expose herself to Blonde Nemesis after all her razzing. "Seriously, why would I tell you? It's obvious you'd just use it to harass me."

Mary frowned. "Hmm…you may be right. Let's forget all this sensitive, girly crap and talk about my scene."

Brie took a deep breath, reminding herself why she'd come to the commune. It wasn't about reconnecting with Mary, or Faelan, for that matter. Her sole purpose was to film segments for her documentary.

Although the scene Mary wanted to film would not be part of that, it might make the other participants more open to filming with her later.

"First, tell me where you plan to do this foursome, so I can plan how best to film around it."

Mary grinned, throwing her hands up in the air and gesturing to the sky. "Out here in the great outdoors."

Brie raised her eyebrow. "You? Out here in the open?"

"No, there is a perfect rock dubbed the Gang-Bang Altar that's the perfect height for what we have planned."

"I think I need to see this legendary rock."

"I can take you there now," Mary said, standing up. "We can map it all out now so you won't distract me with stupid questions when the time comes."

As they walked through the woods, Brie asked her, "Todd mentioned an initiation for subs. Can you give me details, or is it a big secret?"

Mary's laugh was insulting. "It's not like we're part of a cult, Brie." She gave a wicked smile when she added, "The Initiation… OMG, it's the hottest thing ever. I swear every woman should experience it—including *you.*"

"Fine, you've got me curious. Spill the beans."

"Before they can be accepted into the community, every submissive is required to go through the Initiation while his or her Dominant watches without participating."

"That sounds kinky."

"Trust me, it *is*." Mary spoke about it as if she were retelling a favorite fairytale. "First, you fast for twenty-four hours. Then they cleanse you to make you 'pure' for the community."

"What does the cleansing entail?"

"A bath, a thorough shave and an enema."

"I bet that enema was fun," Brie chuckled.

"*Everything* they do on that day is sensual and decadent," she insisted. "You're made to feel like a queen, with several attendants to take care of you for the day."

"So after you're made whole and pure, then what happens?"

"You're introduced to the community by your Dominant. He binds you to the ceremonial bed and then sits down to watch as you are tested."

"Tested? Okay, now you have my mouth watering."

Mary nodded. "I haven't even shared the best part. Your Dominant sits directly in front of you, so he can observe your reactions as every Dom in the commune scenes with you."

"What? Like a giant gang-bang?"

Mary shook her head slowly, a smile curling on her red lips. "Oh, no—

they play with you one at a time with a specific goal in mind."

Brie felt goosebumps rise on her skin. "You're killing me, Mary. What's the goal?"

"Each Dom uses his unique set of skills to try to get you to orgasm, but the catch is that if you come, you will be punished."

Brie stopped walking in the middle of the trail to face her. "Holy crap. Did you come?"

Mary's smile grew wider. "I came again and again."

"On purpose?"

"Fuck, no! The punishments hurt like hell. But as much as I didn't want to, it just made my orgasms that much more intense. Knowing I was going to be severely punished each time I peaked with an orgasm..." She visibly shuddered. "Yeah, that's a feeling I'll never forget."

It was easy to see that Mary relished her memories of the experience, but then, the girl had been weird to begin with. "What kind of punishments, exactly?"

"Paddles, canes, nipple clamps, anal hooks, suspension, humiliation...you name it. They want it to hurt, because they want you to be scared when you orgasm."

Brie's heart raced at the thought. "I can't imagine. It sounds terrifying, but kinda hot too."

Mary patted her on the shoulder. "Even you, my wimpy friend, would love Initiation. Every Dom showcases his or her skill on you, determined to make you orgasm in front of the community. In one night, I scened with every Dominant in the commune. The ceremony is pure genius!"

"Genius how?"

"I connected with every Dom on a personal level, experiencing their expertise as well as their favorite form of punishment. In one night, I became a real member of the community."

Brie could see how it was brilliant for the submissive, but what about their Dom? She imagined Faelan watching Mary orgasm under the hands of other Dominants, only to see her repeatedly punished for it.

"I don't understand what's in it for the initiate's Dominant. I mean, how did Todd benefit from it?"

"It's an honor to share your submissive with the commune, Brie," Mary said in a condescending tone. Then she elbowed her in the ribs, adding, "It also doesn't hurt that he gets to play with every future sub who joins the commune. Whereas we poor subs only get one glorious night, the Dominants get to join in every single Initiation."

"And you don't have a problem with that?"

"Why would I? It's only right that the new subs get to enjoy the same experience I had. And guess what? We're having an Initiation next Friday. Although you're not allowed to film it, Faelan has already discussed it with Master Gannon, and he has no issues with you watching as long as you don't intervene in any way."

Brie kicked at a rock on the trail. "I wonder if I can handle it."

"Better bring a couple of towels. I'm telling you, Brie, you've never seen anything more erotic. Only thing sexier is being the lucky girl herself."

Brie realized she was far too possessive to ever enjoy it, but having the opportunity to watch? Well, that would be a rare treat indeed.

"After you see an Initiation, you won't want to leave here..."

That evening, Mary and Faelan asked Brie to join them at the communal fire after dinner. She had watched the entire commune come together and share a meal, talking and laughing like a giant family. Although no one spoke to her directly, there was still a feeling of belonging as she consumed the meal the community had grown, harvested and prepared together. Brie understood why Master Gannon insisted on these community dinners. It allowed the group to connect on a different, less formal level.

She joined Mary and Faelan behind the main building, around a giant fire pit encircled by rows of comfortable chairs. The group seemed even more relaxed and friendly as they shared stories and sang songs to the strum of a lone guitar.

It reminded Brie of nights spent at summer camp, except for one major difference. Throughout the night, couples openly played with each other. Some left the group to finish their scene alone, but most stayed by the fire to play in front of the group.

Brie watched covertly with lowered eyes as a couple beside her began their sexual dance. It started with a simple command for the sub to put her hands behind her back. The man ran his hands over her breasts, complimenting her on the feel of them. The woman moaned into Brie's ear, making her an accessory to their scene.

He nibbled on the sub's neck while he continued to massage her breasts. Brie saw his hand slip under her pants. The sub's wiggles and jerking motions let Brie know he was hitting just the right spot.

Soon the clothes became too limiting for him, and he slipped her pants down below her knees, commanding her to lean on Brie's chair for support. Brie continued to stare at the fire, but all her senses were focused on the couple. Brie soon heard the slippery sound of the sub's excitement as her Dom began pumping her with his fingers.

The woman purred into Brie's ear, begging him to use her. The Dom was cruelly playful and continued to stimulate his sub's clit with only his fingers, taking her close to climax without allowing her to come. It was not just his sub he was teasing, because the woman's close proximity and her eager noises had Brie just as invested in her sexual release.

Brie glanced to her left and saw that Mary and Faelan were playing with a female. Mary was kissing the girl passionately while Faelan used a small switch he'd found in the woods to make the sub squeal and wiggle as he whipped her fleshy ass.

Looking up at the bright stars twinkling in the clear mountain air, Brie thought this would be heaven on Earth if she wasn't alone and unplayed-with. To survive, she took on the attitude of a film director, noting the sounds and sights around her. Master Gannon had mentioned that she could film outside. If she could get a couple to agree, filming by the fire might prove the perfect way to capture the erotic nature of the outdoor play she was experiencing now.

She suddenly had an image of Rytsar taking her by the fire on the night of her first auction, and her pussy began to pulsate around the glass of her clit jewelry. Was it possible to come without any type of physical stimulation? Brie remembered how susceptible she was to games of the mind and suspected that if she wasn't careful she could unwillingly defy Sir's order not to orgasm, and on her very first night here.

Oh, the humiliation!

The sub on her right was commanded to straddle the Dom and their sexual dance became a rock-and-roll session. He thrust his cock deep into her as she rolled her hips in sensual circles, stimulating his shaft more intensely. The two let out groans of passion as they played with one another.

Brie diverted her attention back to Mary and Faelan, which wasn't any help. Mary was under the girl, the two making out enthusiastically while Faelan plowed his cock into the sub. Both girls moved in unison to the rhythmic impact of his thrusting, which was a visual turn-on for Brie. The fact that Faelan stopped every now and then to admire the two girls and to play with Mary's clit was too much.

Brie stared at the fire, but the sounds of passion were impossible to ignore. She got up and hurried into the woods, needing the silence of the forest. However, she quickly stumbled on a noisy threesome and decided to head for the bridge, hoping the rushing water would drown out any sound.

What a wild place this commune was! Brie hadn't expected that she would be so profoundly affected by it. Being free to play without any judgment or restrictions really did make for an erotic environment. She looked up at the night sky. *More than ever, I'm missing you, Sir.*

Brie jumped when she felt something at her feet, then giggled when she saw it was only the black cat. "You scared me, big guy."

She picked up the large cat, surprised he wasn't heavier. She turned him to face her. "Are you made of just fur?" The cat meowed, so Brie cradled him in her arms and started to pet him, grateful for the company. His whole body vibrated with a deep purr.

The sound warmed Brie's heart, and the feelings of loneliness and desperation slowly eased. When her teeth started chattering from the cold night air, Brie put the cat down and made her way to Mary's bedroom.

To her delight, the cat followed her into the room and jumped onto the bed. "I have something I have to do," she explained to the beast.

Brie took off all her clothes, except for the jewelry snug against her clit, and knelt on the floor, facing the direction of LA and her beloved Master. She placed her hands behind her back and thrust out her chest proudly for him.

She closed her eyes, imagining Sir standing in front of her. He had instructed her that the moment she felt his touch on her head, she could go to sleep. Brie concentrated on her vision of him, imagining him moving throughout his day, going to the meeting with his lawyer, eating meals alone, taking a hot shower to end the day... Her heart ached that she had missed that time with him. "I love you, Sir."

The instant the words left her lips, she felt the warmth of his touch on her head. She opened her eyes in surprise, half expecting to see him there. The room was empty, but his presence lingered with her.

Brie stood up and slipped under the covers, the black cat curling up beside her. She felt content on a level she hadn't expected. Sir had been right; this simple nightly protocol would bring her needed connection with him.

Mary came bounding in, scaring the cat out of the room. "Oh, my God, I love it here!" She let out a happy sigh as she started stripping in front of Brie. "So sad you can't partake of the fun, Stinky Cheese. Sure hope you brought your Hitachi, 'cause you're sure going to need it the next two weeks."

Heading off to the communal showers, Mary called behind her, "There's an outlet on the right side of the bed, just in case you feel the urge."

Brie wasn't about to tell Mary about her orgasm restriction. That girl would cause her no end of grief if she knew. Instead, Brie curled up, wrapping the blankets tightly around her. After a long day of travel and the activities of the commune, it didn't take long before she was sound asleep.

Mary's Triumph

Mary shook Brie. "Get up, sleepyhead!"

Brie grumbled and turned over, trying to ignore her. All week, the girl had been hounding Brie to get up at the break of dawn. Just once, she wanted the chance to sleep in, but Mary refused to leave her alone.

"You have to get up. I've arranged a breakfast with all the Doms who are scening with me today. I want them to feel comfortable around you, so you aren't a distraction during my scene."

When Brie didn't stir, Mary ripped off the blankets, exposing her to the cold mountain air. Brie scrambled to get the blankets back, but wasn't quick enough and finally conceded defeat, heading to the showers. Although Brie cherished her privacy, having communal showers had helped her to get to know a few of the other submissives.

"Hey, Ariel, how's that calf muscle?" she asked, knowing the girl had strained it in an extremely challenging suspension position the day before. Brie had filmed the outdoor session, enchanted that the Dom had used the branch of a tree as support.

The brunette pixie got on her tiptoes and did a ballerina twirl. "Good as new."

"I have to say, suspension in the wilderness certainly adds an element of magic to the whole experience."

Ariel smiled. "I do enjoy it whenever we have outdoor sessions. Being naked and bound in the warm sunlight is definitely arousing."

Brie looked down at her own white mound and laughed. "Unlike your tanned self, my pussy would have burned to a crisp with that kind of exposure."

Arial winked. "Oh, I remember the first time I experienced an intimate burn. Holy crap, that was intense!"

"Stop with all the jibber-jabber," Mary griped. "The men are waiting for us."

Brie hadn't seen Mary so anxious or excited before. She hoped the scene would live up to Mary's expectations and not end up being a painful disappointment recorded on film. Mr. Gallant had warned them during training that there were some fantasies that might seem erotic, but were really train-wrecks waiting to happen—and Mary was famous for her train-wrecks. Brie dreaded witnessing another one.

Mary's three Doms were eating breakfast at a table on the patio. Brie instantly recognized two of them. Rajah, one of the Gatekeepers she'd met on her first day, and the cowboy, Marcus, who had partaken of Mary's lips. The third man was a lean, dark African. The three men stood up as they approached, and for the first time since she'd been there, all three Doms acknowledged Brie by looking her directly in the eye. She instinctively wanted to lower hers, but realized that she needed to behave like a film director, not a sub. Brie met their gazes and smiled as she shook each of their hands.

"Thank you for allowing me to film you today, Rajah, Marcus and..."

The third Dom took her hand in both of his and nodded formally. "I am Kamau."

She bowed instinctively—she couldn't help herself. "Thank you, as well, Kamau."

The entire party sat down, with Mary placing herself in between two of the Doms, looking mighty pleased with herself.

Rajah took Mary's hand and turned it so her wrist was exposed. He lowered his head and bit down on it lightly as he stared at Brie with those mischievous green eyes. "We appreciate that our efforts will be recorded today. Not many women have the fortitude to attempt such a challenge."

"I can't wait," Mary said, her eyes flashing with lust and excitement.

Marcus asked Brie, "Will you be filming several different angles for us?"

"I plan to film three. Two stationary cameras will capture all the action, one from underneath while the other will focus on Mary's face to capture her reaction to your multiple attentions. I'll film the action as well, using a wider angle."

"Good," Kamau stated. "I want to see her expression when I fuck her in the ass with two cocks already buried inside her pussy."

Brie's stomach fluttered at the thought, but she remained professional as she explained, "The most important shot is capturing that moment when the head of your shaft breaches her entrance for the first time. Once I have that shot I will pull back to film the three of you thrusting into her."

Brie's pussy responded just talking about the scene about to take place, and she felt a blush creep over her cheeks. "I also want to capture your individual facial expressions."

The three men looked at each other and nodded. Marcus spoke for them. "That's acceptable to us, Miss Bennett."

"Excellent." She turned to Mary. "Does that sound good to you?"

"Enough talk, already. I just want to get started, damn it."

Brie noticed that Mary hadn't eaten anything for breakfast, and assumed she was on a twenty-four hour fast to prepare herself for this three-cock invasion. While Brie liked the men well enough, there was no way she would ever have agreed to taking them all at once. However, she had a perverted sense of curiosity, wanting to know whether Mary would be able to handle them all.

The men finished their light meal, taking their time, knowing it was thoroughly testing Mary's patience. It was obvious to Brie that they enjoyed the power play.

To Mary's credit, she didn't hound the Doms to rush, but she kept glaring at Brie as if she were to blame.

Faelan came up before they were done and shook the hands of all three men before pulling up a chair to join them. "Is she chomping at the bit?"

Mary sat there silently while the men laughed.

"Foolish question, I know. This girl of mine hasn't talked about anything else for the past week."

"Do you plan to watch?" Brie asked him.

Faelan smiled, shaking his head. "No, this little stunt is between Mary and these fine gentlemen. However, I do plan to watch the video."

Brie wondered what Faelan was thinking. Was he really as okay with this scene as he appeared?

"It's something all of us have been looking forward to," Marcus said, touching the brim of his hat and nodding toward Mary.

The sexual tension between the group was palpable, and Brie found herself squirming in her seat because of it. It did not go unnoticed by Faelan, but he just winked at Brie. "Well, I will leave you all to your little experiment." He slapped Kamau on the back. "Be gentle with her—I want my girl back in one piece when you're done."

Faelan walked over to Mary, who stood up to receive his kiss. "Don't push yourself too far. You're more important than this little fantasy of yours." His eyes glinted with that wild look Brie had seen before as he ran his hand down Mary's front and cupped her pussy. "I consider this *my* property. Do not harm it."

Mary purred in pleasure.

Faelan gave her one last kiss before leaving the group to help round up the horses. Marcus was the first to stand and he offered Mary his hand. "Let's find out how much you can take, darlin'."

Brie ran to get her equipment and followed the foursome into the woods. Her heart was racing by the time they made it to Gang-Bang Altar. She felt almost as excited as Mary about the kinky scene about to take place.

As Brie set up the equipment, she found herself amazed that the rock truly looked as if it had been created with naughty sex in mind, with natural divots in the rock acting as hand-and-foot-holds to support different positions. She asked Mary to lie on the rock so she could get the right angle for both her stationary cameras. Once all her reflectors were set and adjusted, she announced to the group, "You can start any time. I won't speak, and will do my best to stay out of your way."

"Good," Mary said. "As far as I'm concerned, you don't exist." She ran her hands over the chests of all three men before taking the standing position of a sub ready to be commanded.

Marcus looked at Brie and tipped his hat, signifying that she was to begin filming. Brie trembled slightly when she hit *record*, focusing the camera on Mary. The three men removed their shirts before descending on her like hungry but well-mannered wolves—each one taking turns pulling at her clothing, sucking exposed parts and running their hands over her shapely body.

They circled Mary like predators as they played, all three men teasing her with their sexual caresses and forceful kisses. Brie moved slowly with them, catching the rawness of their lust and Mary's shameless enjoyment of it.

Mary moaned loudly while they played, inviting them to use her roughly. Brie noticed a change in their dynamic as the three men fed off each other's rising need for her. The air became more sexually charged as time went on.

Kamau was the first to strike, pulling Mary to him and ripping the last remnants of her panties away. He thrust his dark fingers inside her as he kissed her passionately. The other two watched as he finger-fucked her, forcing her first orgasm.

Kamau let go of her and Mary stumbled, struggling to remain on her feet. Marcus swooped in and picked her up, laying her on the rock and removing her remaining clothing. He stood back to admire her naked body. "Are you prepared to be ravished by three men, darlin'?"

She growled seductively and nodded.

Marcus pulled her arms above her head and began sucking on her breasts, before leaving a trail of kisses from her stomach down to the feminine swell of her mound. Marcus was more gentle than Kamau, but no less aggressive in his enjoyment of her. Mary squirmed and moaned, her passionate cry echoing in the woods when he induced a second orgasm with his tongue.

Rajah was the last to play with her. He took her left wrist and lifted her arm, nibbling and biting down the length of it. Mary squealed when his teeth landed on her nipple. He chuckled, leaving a new trail of bite marks from her breast to her hip bone. By then, Mary was visibly trembling with desire.

He lifted her from the altar and told her to stand, being careful not to knock over the camera as he took off his clothes and lay down on it, motioning Mary to him. "Wet my *lund* with that needy *chut*," he growled huskily.

Mary used the natural divots in the rock to climb back up and straddle him. She coated his shaft with her eagerness, grinding shamelessly against his cock. He aided her by grabbing her ass cheeks with both hands and sliding Mary's dripping pussy up and down on his rigid shaft.

Meanwhile, the other two men undressed themselves and started stroking their cocks in anticipation. After Brie caught them on film, she focused back on Mary, certain the first penetration was close at hand.

Rajah held his cock in position as Mary slowly descended onto it. She groaned with pleasure when his lengthy shaft slipped inside. He gripped her ass, forcing her up and down on his stiff rod, then held her still, commanding her to grind harder. "Do not stop until you come."

Mary was in control of the speed of his cock rubbing against her mound, but Brie knew the pressure he was placing on her clit was making it far more intense. Mary braced herself and started grinding hard and fast. Rajah lifted his head and bit her neck.

Mary moaned passionately, "Ooh...ooh...OOH!"

Wetness covered his balls, announcing her third orgasm to the world. Brie pulled the shot back as Marcus moved into position between her legs.

Mary's pussy was glistening and swollen, making it slippery and ready for Marcus' unnatural invasion. "You're going to take all of me, darlin'." He held on to his shaft and began pressing against her full cunt. He rocked his cock against her, pressing even harder. Brie held her breath, wondering what it must feel like and if it was similar to taking Boa's massive shaft.

"Harder; I need it harder," Mary begged.

Marcus' shaft slowly stretched and then breached her resistant hole. She moaned loudly as he pushed in deeper. The two men coordinated their thrusts, pushing into her as one unit. Rajah grabbed her hips as support as he thrust deeper.

Mary began crying loudly, "Fuck yeah! Oh, fuck yeah..."

Kamau was the last, but before he mounted her, he asked, "How does it feel?"

She panted. "God...it's amazing... Feels like...I'm being ripped in two...but I fucking love it!"

"Are you ready for a third?"

She tilted her head back and offered him her lips as the other two continued to fuck her overstretched pussy with rhythmic thrusts. Kamau traced her lips with his tongue before kissing her deeply.

"And now I am going to make your fantasy complete." Kamau launched himself onto the rock with the grace of a gazelle. His was the hardest position, because he had to straddle Mary without getting in the way of Marcus, but this man was incredibly limber.

He got into position, stroking his lubricant-covered cock. It was deliciously dark, with a round head and long, thin shaft. Brie felt tingles course through her as he pressed the head of it against Mary's bright pink rosette.

Marcus directed Kamau verbally to ensure he got the proper angle. "Lower. Right there, you got it, you got it..."

Brie gasped softly when she saw his dark shaft slowly slip into Mary's tight ass.

Rajah groaned as he gripped Mary's buttocks. She tilted her head back and cried, "Oh, yes! Oh, my God, yes!"

Kamau grabbed her hair, using her to brace himself for better control. "Can you take more?"

"Fuck, yeah..."

He tried to push deeper into her, but her body resisted and he made no progress. It took the coordination of all three men to get his shaft to sink in farther. The excitement of the group was tangible.

Marcus grasped Mary's thighs. "You look sweet all filled up, darlin', but now we're going to make you scream."

"Do it, do it," Mary begged.

Brie had stopped breathing at this point, her heart pounding in her chest as the three men started thrusting into Mary.

Mary let out a low, primal moan that sounded more animal than human. The three men continued fucking her, their grunts of satisfaction and effort echoing in the woods as they worked together to ensure the deepest penetration. Brie watched in fascination as Mary's body accepted the onslaught, her ass muscles clutching onto Kamau's dark shaft, seeming unwilling to let it go whenever he pulled back.

Soon the woods filled with Mary's screams.

The men slowed their strokes, and Rajah kissed Mary. "So sexy…" he murmured. Her whole body relaxed as she started to fly, allowing them to take her even more deeply.

Kamau came first. Lifting his head, he let out a warrior's cry as he orgasmed. He pulled out his dark shaft, a gush of white liquid dripping from her stretched ass. Marcus pulled out and commanded Mary to play with his balls as he squeezed her buttocks together and fucked the valley of her ass. Her perfectly manicured nails grasped his balls as he let loose, his essence covering her entire back.

Rajah now had free access to her pussy and grabbed her buttocks with both hands, pumping her hard as he came. His guttural cries affected Brie, causing her clit to throb against her jewelry.

The two other men helped Mary off Rajah and lay her on the altar. They caressed her skin, giving her light kisses as they praised her accomplishment. She was unable to speak, but Brie could see the smile on her face from where she stood. She zoomed in, knowing Mary probably wouldn't remember this part of the scene.

The care and respect shown to her by the three men was touching, and demonstrated to Brie how much the community at the Sanctuary cared for one another. She stopped filming and quietly put her equipment away, not wanting to disturb Mary's aftercare.

Marcus tipped his hat to her as she left. She smiled and nodded, knowing that she would once again become a ghost to him now that the scene was over. She accepted her fate, grateful for this glimpse into their intimate world.

The Initiation

B rie had been anticipating the Initiation ever since Mary mentioned it. The idea of every Dom participating in the ceremony completely blew her mind.

Initiation was a huge deal for the community. Instead of having a communal dinner, the group gathered for breakfast, knowing that the evening would be taken up by the event. Every person there seemed energized, eager to bring two new members into the fold.

Faelan had explained to Brie that the community was in charge of culling the applicants to a select few, but it was up to Master Gannon to make the final decision. It meant no one knew who was going to walk through the gate to join their extended family except Gannon.

Brie wasn't allowed to participate in the preparations, but the moment the room was ready, Mary dragged her in to see it. When Brie stepped into the main room, she had to stop for a moment to take it all in. The huge room had been completely transformed.

In the center was a four-poster bed. It was opulent, with carved wooden posts and gossamer material flowing from the top of each post in a canopy of white. The bed itself was covered in a virginal white coverlet with a variety of uniquely shaped pillows to aid in various sexual positions.

To the right were several tables covered in different tools, running the gamut of BDSM play. On the left were common pieces of kinky furniture, including a tantra chair, a spanking bench, and an iron cage.

Just behind the bed sat an impressive throne, intricately carved, with upholstery of rich red velvet. Mary led her over and told her to stand beside it. "This way we get to see all the action up close. If you want a good spot, you have to come early or you'll end up standing in the back and missing all the good stuff."

"Is there anything I'm expected to do?"

"You're only here to observe. That means no talking, and if you must leave, you'll need to go through the back." She pointed in the direction of the kitchen. "It's common for couples to leave for a temporary break throughout the ceremony."

"I bet it is."

"Actually, it's expected and encouraged, but not for poor Brianna Bennett. She gets to stand here through the whole ceremony and burst into flames, a victim of spontaneous human combustion."

Brie hit Mary's arm. "That's the part I am *not* looking forward to. So how long does an Initiation take?"

"Hours and hours…"

"Oh, great."

Mary opened the large purse she was carrying. "That's why I brought plenty of water and," she pulled out a small hand towel, "something for you."

Brie laughed. "Thanks for thinking of me."

"No problem. Feel free to wipe your snatch whenever you feel the need."

Brie stuffed the towel back in Mary's bag when she saw Faelan approaching through the gathering crowd. "I'm sure I'll be fine."

But Blonde Nemesis wasn't letting her go that easily. "No really, if you want you can stand on the towel. That way you won't get the floor all messy, little Miss Moist-a-Lot."

Brie elbowed Mary. "You suck."

"Better than you…"

Brie didn't miss Faelan's amused snort, and she protested, "I'm positive Sir would disagree."

"Oh, really?" Mary laughed. "Why don't we ask him? He certainly seemed to enjoy my lips during training."

Brie had never forgotten being forced to watch Mary go down on Sir when she'd had the DP session with Master Coen, but Brie pretended she didn't care and answered lightly, "Obviously Sir preferred my lips, and that's why I'm collared."

Mary raised her eyebrows. "You wear that thing as if it's something to be proud of."

Brie fingered her collar and smiled knowingly. "Jealous…"

Mary hit Faelan in the shoulder. "I told you she was an idiot."

"It's not our place to judge," he replied, standing behind Mary and putting his hands on her shoulders. Mary rolled her eyes in irritation.

"I saw that," he stated. "Should I make you do a set of twenty?"

Mary shook her head.

"Fine. Apologize for rolling your eyes and disrespecting your friend."

Mary's jaw fell open.

"Drop or speak, it's your choice."

Mary sighed in frustration, but complied. "I'm sorry for rolling my eyes, although I have no idea how you saw it, and—"

Everyone suddenly became silent around them as the crowd turned to face the large doors. Brie followed their gaze and watched as the new couple entered the room.

"That's the initiate," Mary whispered with reverence.

Brie watched the curvaceous woman in a bright crimson dress walk into the room escorted by her Dom, who was dressed in a black tux. She murmured, "I didn't expect it would be so formal."

Faelan whispered, "This is their chance to impress us."

Brie looked at the woman again, with her perfect hair, perfect red lips and those ample breasts spilling out of her tight bodice.

Well, I'm impressed.

The Dom led his submissive to the large bed and pulled her head back roughly, kissing her on the forehead before picking her up. He lay her on the bed and began tying her to the posts using quick, skillful knots.

It looked to Brie as if the initiate were being presented as a sacrifice. She could feel the excitement in the room rise, every eye on the couple.

Once the submissive was secure, her Dom turned to the group. Brie breathed in sharply and felt Mary stiffen beside her. The man was older, with sharp features and cold, hard eyes. His intimidating confidence gave Brie chills.

He announced to the assembly in a gruff voice, "I am Razor. This is my submissive, null. I give her to you tonight as a sign of my trust, and her willingness to please."

Brie did not care for the pet name of Razor's submissive, but understood its meaning. The submissive was nothing, and Brie suspected the Dominant was null's chosen instrument of pain.

Brie couldn't help shuddering as he approached, and lowered her eyes when he glanced in her direction before sitting down. She suddenly wished Mary hadn't insisted on standing so close to the throne. The fierceness of his confidence rolled off the man in waves, making it hard for her to concentrate. She noticed that Mary was equally affected, and was not surprised when Faelan instinctively wrapped his arms around his woman.

The dramatic sound of a large drum announced the beginning of the ceremony. It gave a welcome solemnness to the occasion. When it stopped, all eyes turned to their leader.

Master Gannon spoke to the community in a somber voice. "We accept the gift of your submissive tonight, Razor. We promise to instruct her well in the practice of self-denial."

Razor replied, "May she prove worthy of your attention."

Master Gannon removed his shirt before picking up a cane. "I am Master Gannon, null. I am the leader of this commune. Tonight you will be challenged by each of the Dominants, but you retain the right to stop an activity with the safeword 'red'. What is your safeword?"

"Red, Master Gannon."

"Very good. Then let us begin. You are not allowed to orgasm, null. Disobedience in this area will be met with immediate and severe punishment. Do you understand?"

Brie was close enough to see the bound sub's chest rising and falling rapidly, but she nodded as she answered, "I will obey, Master Gannon."

He snorted. "I *will* make you come."

Mary let out a sigh beside Brie, and whispered, "Yes, he will…"

Master Gannon placed the cane in null's mouth. "Hold this until I punish you."

He went to the table and picked up two clover nipple clamps. Brie knew they were the most painful kind of clamps. He also grabbed some weights, tossing them in his hand as he approached.

"I heard you like these."

The sub nodded lustfully.

He knelt on the bed and unbuttoned her bodice, pulling the material down to expose her large breasts. He massaged and teased them before he attached the first clamp to her nipple. The girl remained silent, giving no indication of the intense pressure the tool provided. He bent down and sucked on her other nipple before attaching the second clamp.

Master Gannon then undid the bindings and had her stand up for him, the cane still in her mouth. He tied her wrists together and bound them above her head to one of the foot posts of the canopy bed. He smiled seductively as he added weights to each clamp.

Null whimpered softly in response.

"Now that I have you primed, I am going to make you orgasm."

He knelt down on one knee and pulled off her panties, having her step out of them. He took the bottom hem of her dress and tucked it inside her open bodice to expose her shaved pussy to the community.

"Open those pretty legs," he commanded.

Null obeyed, spreading her legs apart as she balanced in her high heels. Master Gannon looked up at her and said forcefully, "Do *not* come."

Mary nudged Brie, the smile on her face letting Brie know the girl was about to disobey that direct order.

The voluptuous sub moaned when Master Gannon began playing with her pussy. When he had enough natural lubricant covering his fingers, he forced three inside and began pumping inside her in an almost violent manner. The aggressiveness of his hand quickly produced wet sounds as her body unwillingly gave in to the stimulation. Null threw her head back and let out a low cry that quickly increased in pitch. She groaned against the cane in her mouth as her sex pulsated and a huge gush of watery fluid escaped from her slick pussy.

Master Gannon stood up and walked over to the table, casually wiping his hand on a towel as he stared at her. She stood there squirming under his forceful gaze when he approached.

"Open."

She parted her lips and the cane fell into his hand.

As he pulled off the nipple clamps, Brie saw null grimace in pain but she made no sound. Then he untied her wrists and asked, "What did I tell you?"

"That I would be punished if I came."

"Bend over the bed so that you are facing your Master. Lift your skirt and take your punishment."

Null looked at Razor briefly and then quickly lowered her eyes. He wore a slight smirk on his lips as she bent over and lifted her skirt for Master Gannon.

The commune leader stood behind her, the cane cocked and ready. Gannon rubbed the soft swell of her ass appreciatively as he explained, "I will be quick and thorough." With that, he whipped the cane repeatedly across her ass. Null whimpered and squirmed, only crying out twice. Afterwards, he caressed the welts he had left before commanding her to stand.

Master Gannon cupped her chin and kissed her on the lips, telling null, "See that you learn your lesson well tonight."

He walked over to take a place in the crowd, while another Dom took his place with null. This man was dressed in black jeans and a dark shirt with a breast pocket, the sleeves of which had been rolled up to show off his tattoos. Although Brie had not met him personally, she'd been told he was the resident blacksmith. He certainly fit the part, with his large arms and rough five o'clock shadow.

He approached the sub with a serious expression that let her know he was not one to be trifled with. "You will call me Wayland. You are not allowed to orgasm. Disobedience will result in immediate and severe punishment. Do you understand, null?"

She nodded, but her voice wasn't as certain as it had been the first time when she answered, "I will obey, Wayland."

He pulled at her bodice to more fully expose her breasts to the crowd before ordering, "Move over to the spanking bench."

She shuddered, her ass already red and painful from her first punishment, but dutifully walked over to the bench.

"Mount it and bare your ass to me."

Null climbed onto the furniture and pulled up her dress, showing off the marks left by the cane.

"I like my submissives to feel helpless. I want them to know there is nothing to stop me from taking my pleasure." Wayland went to the table and returned with an anal hook. He smiled as he held it up to her. "I made this one myself. I was told you are familiar with the tool."

Null answered, "I am, Wayland."

"Good." He coated the metal tool with a liquid lubricant and stood beside her, separating her ass cheeks with his other hand. "I made the end extra-large. Do you think you can take it?"

She looked behind her at the round ball at the end of the large hook— the part that was to go inside her—and nodded.

"Let's see if you're right. You may want to bear down for this one." He used his strong arm muscles to slowly force the large metal ball inside her ass. Null took it, purring as the huge ball finally slipped inside.

"You do like these, don't you?" Wayland complimented. He twisted up her hair into a long rope with his hand and secured it with a leather strip. He tied the rope of her hair to the anal hook and tightened it so she had to keep her head back in the stretched position.

Wayland took out a cigar from his breast pocket and lit it, breathing in the smoke and slowly exhaling as he watched her strain in her bonds. He stared at her amorously for several moments before moving to her head and squatting so his lips were level with hers, just inches from her face. "Breathe in," he commanded.

Wayland slowly exhaled, and the wisps of smoke seductively swirled between them as null breathed it in. Brie couldn't believe how sensual the simple act was, and shifted uncomfortably where she stood.

He stood back up and picked up a vibrator that looked suspiciously like a mini Hitachi wand from the table. He placed the buzzing vibrator against her clit. Null struggled, but the anal hook effectively kept her in place. He slowly moved it up and down her clit, reminding her that the punishment would be great if she came. Null started whimpering and then cried out in fear when her body betrayed her and her pussy pulsed against the wicked toy.

Wayland immediately turned it off, saying nothing as he put the vibrator down. Before he punished her, he meticulously cleaned all her exposed skin. Then he walked back to the table and put on a thick leather glove, sliding a white plastic container next to the bench with his foot. "As a blacksmith, I have a particular attraction to burning metal." White mist rose out of the bucket when he opened the lid. He pulled out a metal rod with a brand on the end and approached her. "I will not leave a permanent mark, but you will experience the burn."

Null looked at him, her eyes wide with fear, but she was helpless to avoid her punishment.

"Why are you being punished, null?"

"I disobeyed your command and came, Wayland."

Wayland nodded. "Yes, you did, and now you must pay." He branded her left ass cheek first, leaving the brand there for several seconds. The sizzling sound of cold metal meeting skin made Brie tingle with excitement and fear, remembering her own branding.

Wayland picked up another brand from the bucket. Null looked at him wildly as he moved to face her, the brand inches from her face. "No, I would never mark that beautiful face," he assured her.

He placed the brand on her exposed breast, chuckling softly to himself when she whimpered. "It burns, doesn't it?"

Brie noticed that Wayland was careful to press the brand only lightly, leaving it there for just a few seconds so she would feel the burn but it would not permanently harm the skin. He moved around her, branding different areas, leaving her right buttock for last. "Learn your lesson well tonight." He pressed it against her ass, leaving it on a little longer so she would not forget.

Brie noticed the woman's increased breath, and understood that null was breathing through the discomfort. When he'd finished, he knelt and kissed her. "You received your punishment well, null."

While she was still quivering from her last orgasm and punishment, Faelan left Mary's side and approached the spanking bench. "You will call me Faelan. You are not allowed to orgasm. Disobedience will result in immediate and severe punishment. Do you understand, null?"

She looked up at him and swallowed hard. "I will obey, Faelan."

He smiled at her charmingly as he undid her bindings and removed the hook. "I'm sure you will try."

The girl trembled, but her eyes were locked on him. Brie could tell she was already under Faelan's spell. Brie glanced over at Mary, surprised to see her staring at Razor instead of watching the scene. Brie bumped shoulders with her, and Mary jumped as if being caught doing something wrong. Brie gave her a questioning look.

Mary responded by mouthing the word, "bitch".

What the hell is your problem? Brie wondered, shrugging it off.

She chose to ignore Mary and focused her attention back on Faelan. He'd freed null of her dress and laid her on the bed. He unbuttoned his shirt slowly before taking it off, making her wait for him to begin.

The boy had grown in confidence and skill since Brie had scened with him at the Center, but Faelan still maintained that primal element that brought out the animal in a woman. There was no doubt he held that power over null as she panted and growled, inviting his rough play.

The poor girl was completely captivated when Faelan brought out the knife and began teasing her with it, pressing the sharp edge of it against her most sensitive areas and dragging it across her skin with enough pressure to scratch, but not to break the surface. Her eyes were wide and her breaths shallow as she watched the deadly knife caress her skin.

"Are you scared?" he asked.

She looked at him with trembling lips, and nodded.

He brought the knife up to her neck, pressing it against her jugular. "You should be."

With the rush of adrenaline caused by the edge play, Brie knew it wouldn't take much to send null over the brink. She watched in anticipation as he dragged the knife back down over her curvaceous body, ending at her swollen mound.

"Do you know what I am about to do?" he asked.

Null answered hesitantly, "Make me come?"

Faelan moved between her legs, grinning when he confirmed her answer. "Yes, null." He pressed the point of the knife to the top of her mound. "If you move, you will cut yourself."

With that warning hanging in the air, Faelan began to eat her pussy, relentlessly applying that skilled tongue to her erect clit.

The danger of the knife had null on such a sub high that she came almost instantly.

Faelan pulled back, a charming smirk on his lips. "Null, you disappoint me."

"I'm sorry, Faelan."

"Although I accept your apology, it is my duty to punish you." He left the bed to get his chosen tool of punishment, a violet wand. The way null stared nervously at the instrument let Brie know she was very familiar with it.

Null looked up at him repentantly, quietly accepting her fate.

"Stand in front of your Master," Faelan commanded.

She followed his order, but kept her head down as she faced Razor.

"Look in him in the eye, null."

She slowly raised her head and stared bravely into the eyes of her intimidating Master. Brie could only imagine what she was feeling.

Faelan stood behind the sub and turned on the device. The crackling sound of the wand added an element of danger to the punishment scene.

"I can tell you are a dedicated sub, null," Faelan growled into her ear, "even though you disobeyed a direct command."

Brie appreciated that Faelan was giving null words of empowerment, even though she had failed in her task—a task she was *meant* to fail.

Faelan turned up the intensity of the wand before touching her with it. Null involuntarily flinched, but stayed in place. He dragged it down from her ribs to her hip, stating, "It feels like the edge of a knife cutting into you, doesn't it?"

She nodded, looking nervously to her left, anticipating the next pass. He did not disappoint, shocking her sensitive skin with the intense current. He held her to him as he made a pattern of concentric circles on her belly. Brie could see her muscles contracting as they came into contact with the stinging instrument.

Faelan turned off the wand and a profound silence followed. He kissed her neck gently and murmured, "Your pussy looks neglected, null."

She stiffened in his arms when the buzzing started up again. Faelan wrapped his arm firmly around her waist and brought the wand to within an inch of her swollen mound. He waited several moments before he grazed it against her clit.

Null let out a frightened gasp but made no more sound, gritting her teeth and accepting the sting of the instrument without complaint.

"Good null..." he said, shutting off the device. He turned her chin towards him and kissed her deeply. Brie did not miss her passionate whimper when he broke away.

Faelan returned to Mary, obviously turned on by the scene he'd just finished. He ran his hands over her body while nibbling on her ear whispering nasty things to her. Before long, Mary was dragging him through the crowd, towards the back door.

Brie sighed in frustration, attracting the attention of Razor. He glanced up at her with those dangerous, steel-blue eyes and she stopped breathing for a moment. He was all kinds of scary.

Without the reassuring presence of Mary and Faelan, Brie decided to leave the ceremony. She escaped to Mary's room, where she undressed and crawled into bed after performing her assigned nightly ritual.

Sir's presence seemed to remain in the room, tempting her. Brie was excited by the activities she'd witnessed and slipped her finger between her legs, stroking her clit jewelry. "Oh, Sir, if only you were here."

The subtle throbbing was tempting her like a siren's call to let go and stop the terrible ache in her loins.

Just a little more pressure…

The creak of the door stopped her cold. With her heart pounding in her chest, Brie opened her eyes and saw the door ajar, but no one standing in the doorway. She sighed in relief, but let out a squeal of terror when the black cat jumped on her bed.

"Oh, thank goodness it's just you!" she cried, holding out her hand to the cat. He sauntered slowly up to her, rubbing his cheek against her in a possessive manner. She gathered him in her arms, laughing at herself. "You scared me to death, you bad, bad boy."

He began purring, oblivious of the fright he'd just given her.

Brie scratched him under the chin, grateful for the distraction. "I guess I should thank you. You just saved me from disobeying my Master."

Her Challenge

B rie was surprised when Rajah came up to her during breakfast and told her that she needed to meet with Master Gannon directly. She excused herself, giving Mary a confused look before she followed Rajah to Gannon's office.

"Miss Bennett, please sit down."

She sat, folding her hands in her lap to hide her nervousness. "What's this about, Gannon?"

"I normally do not allow phone calls, but Sir Davis has asked to speak to you. Because of the unusual circumstances, I have granted him the favor. You may call him on my private phone. Get me when you're done."

It felt as if the ground was falling out from under her. Something bad had happened to Sir's mother, she was sure of it. However, she kept her voice calm as she took the phone from him. "Thank you, Gannon."

He left the room, shutting the door quietly behind him.

Brie stared at the phone, afraid to make the call to Sir but dutifully calling nonetheless. Her stomach fluttered on hearing his voice.

"Hello, this is Thane Davis."

"Sir."

"Ah, Brie. It's good to hear from you."

"Is everything all right?" she asked uneasily.

"Yes, babygirl. There's no need to be concerned."

"Then why the phone call, Sir?"

"Gannon contacted me a few days ago and made a suggestion that I have been mulling over. I've decided you would benefit from the experience and have given him my permission."

She felt a thrill of excitement. "Permission for what, Sir?"

"I've been told they are having a dungeon event."

"Yes, it's tonight! It's a quarterly event at the Sanctuary. Quite the to-do I've been told."

"Tell me more."

She smiled, happy to share the details with him. "They transform their main room into a dungeon, and give each of the subs a role to play."

"What kinds of roles?"

"Some get to clean the equipment after each use, a few serve food and drink throughout the event, there's even a group who act as toys, but the rest get to be dungeon playmates."

"It sounds like an interesting setup."

"I agree, Sir. I was afraid I'd have to miss out, because I hadn't even been invited to observe the event."

"Gannon firmly believes you cannot fully appreciate the importance of what the Sanctuary provides to its community unless you are a participating member, and he does not want you leaving there without getting a taste of his vision."

"Did he tell you how he wanted me to participate tonight?"

"He did, Brie."

She giggled nervously when he did not explain further. "And how am I to participate, Sir?"

"It will be a challenge for you, téa."

Her heart raced when he used her sub name. "What is being asked of me, Master?"

"You will act as a toy tonight."

She couldn't breathe. It was the last thing she'd expected to hear. "I'm not sure I can. I mean—"

"Think of this the same way as you would a lesson at the Center. I want you to experience something you've never faced before and learn from it."

"But Sir, the toys are open to all the Dominants of the commune."

"I want you to be aware that I've spoken to Gannon about Wallace and you will be off-limits to him."

Although Brie was relieved to hear it, she still struggled with the idea of taking on the role of a toy. "Master…"

"I believe you will gain valuable insight from this experience, téa. I am commanding you to present yourself tonight for the festivities. I want you to embrace it, to relish it for the once-in-a-lifetime encounter it is."

Brie swallowed hard, choking on the lump that had suddenly formed in her throat. This felt exactly like the time he'd asked her to serve under a new Master. She whispered into the phone, "What if I say no?"

"I will be very disappointed."

His words cut her like a knife. She didn't want to refuse him, but to give herself away like that...

"Brie, you *must* trust me."

Calling her given name had great power over her. Sir was asking her to trust him on a deeper level, as her Master *and* partner.

Brie closed her eyes. Did she trust Sir to further her submissive journey—or not?

While she did trust him, it was with great reservation that she answered, "I will do as you ask, but only if it pleases you."

He laughed, knowing she was politely voicing her unwillingness. "It *does* please me, téa," he assured her.

"Then I will join the event, Sir, because that is what you have commanded of me."

"Don't just *do* it, Brie. I want you to give yourself over fully to it, as if you were giving yourself to me. I want your pussy dripping with anticipation for any hand that touches you."

She trembled listening to his directive. His words made her long to please him, to embrace her role as a plaything, to make him proud of her service even though it would be in the hands of another.

"What are you going to do for me tonight, Brie?" Sir asked, making her voice his command out loud for his benefit—and hers.

She took a deep breath to calm the butterflies in her stomach. "I am going to please the Dominants with the same enthusiasm I reserve for you, Sir."

"Yes," he growled seductively. "Hold nothing back. I expect a full account when I speak with you next."

Brie let out an uneasy sigh as she hung up.

Would she truly be able to give herself over in both mind and body to fulfill Sir's challenging command? For the first time since being collared, Brie was haunted by a sense of doubt, worried she might fail.

Brie was grateful for Mary in a time like this. If there was anyone who could snap her into the proper frame of mind to play out her assigned role, it was Blonde Nemesis.

Because so many subs were preparing for the dungeon event, Brie and Mary had to shower in the same stall together. Although Brie had seen Mary naked plenty of times, it was a little odd when they kept touching as they soaped up.

It didn't help things when Brie felt Mary's hand rub against her pussy.

"Be sure to lather up good there. It's going to be used a lot tonight."

Brie automatically smacked her hand away before pushing her out of the stall. Mary screamed and scrambled back in, throwing Brie up against the shower stall. "What the fuck, bitch?"

"You freakin' touched my snatch! I don't remember giving you permission to touch it."

"Oh, my God, Brie. It's not like it's the eighth wonder of the world. Hey, everyone, I touched Brie's cooch, now I'm eternally blessed."

The subs in the other shower stalls started laughing hysterically.

"Screw you, Mary." Brie couldn't help it; she joined in their laughter. "But for future reference, my sacred pussy is off-limits to the likes of *you*."

Mary rolled her eyes as she rubbed the bar of soap over her tanned breasts. The rest of their shared shower experience was performed in silence, but the two snuck amused looks at each other while the rest of the subs continued to break out in spontaneous giggles.

As Brie toweled off, she glanced around and noticed that the other subs, both male and female, had perfect tans. Nude sunbathing seemed to be the norm at the commune and their even skin tones certainly made for a pleasant look. Brie glanced down at her swimsuit lines, realizing she would stand out among the others tonight looking *very* vanilla.

However, she knew confidence was key as a submissive. Instead of seeing it as a liability, she decided to embrace her multi-shading. It made her unique, a rarity among the submissives here. She wasn't one of them, which would make her more attractive to some of the Dominants.

Brie still hadn't gotten used to the fact that none of the Doms had looked at her in a sexual way since she'd entered the commune. She understood the reasons why, but hadn't realized until now how much she depended on that sexual tension to give her energy. Being a ghost was not freeing for her. On the contrary, it had proven to be completely exhausting.

"Girls, as you know, this is Brie's first time as a toy. Any advice for her?" Mary asked, in a show of unexpected kindness.

One of the girls answered, "Being a toy always takes me into subspace. There is just something about being treated roughly with no regard that's a total turn-on for me."

"Yeah, I second that," an older woman agreed. "I like the feeling of being used. You mean nothing and everything to them in that moment, simply for the release your body can provide."

"That's sexy to you?" Brie asked.

"Objectification is hot. Have you tried it?"

"I was a platter once."

All of the submissives chuckled at her answer—really, she couldn't blame them.

"A platter, huh? Well, you aren't going to be experiencing platter action tonight, little girl," a male chimed in, snapping his towel on Brie's ass.

Brie squealed and the group laughed again.

"Enough of this racket," Master Gannon barked, walking in on the group.

For a fraction of a second, Brie almost covered herself with her hands, but resisted the urge when she noticed everyone standing to attention. She straightened her back and put her hands to her sides in an open and inviting manner.

"The dungeon is nearly ready. Have yourselves prepared to join me in five minutes." He looked briefly at Brie, infusing her with a sense of responsibility and excitement. This wasn't just about her experiencing objectification for her own benefit; her role tonight was to please the Doms of the commune who would partake of her.

"You will be on the farthest end, Miss Bennett."

She nodded and looked at her feet, a feeling of exhilaration coursing through her for the first time. This truly was something she had never experienced—never dreamed of experiencing.

In order to honor Sir's command to give herself over to this with no reservations, she knew she had to change her state of mind and told herself, *I am a submissive. My very nature is to serve, and I'm being asked to serve the Dominants of this commune. It is my pleasure to serve and please them. I will embrace my duty with an open mind and full heart. This is what my Master commands of me. This is his desire—and mine.*

Mary bumped her shoulder. "It's time. Hell, this may be the most exciting thing you ever do, Brie."

The interior of the lodge had been completely altered. The long sectional couch in the middle was gone, replaced by all kinds of different play furniture from spanking benches, whipping posts and St Andrew's crosses to wooden A-frames and cages. Some of the furniture Brie had never seen before, and could only guess at its use. There were also rows of tables with various tools spread out, and areas specifically set aside for aftercare. Brie liked the light, airy, spacious feel of this particular dungeon environment.

"You will proceed to the beds," Gannon instructed, pointing to the row of beds lined against the farthest wall. They all had iron headboards, but these beds were thinner than a normal twin and each was covered in a plastic sheet. It was obvious their sole purpose was for fucking.

Brie's stomach fluttered when she noticed the strands of red rope that had been placed on each bed. The last one—the one meant for her—also had a small table beside it, with lubricant and a variety of condoms laid out.

Brie was grateful that Mary came up from behind and chose the bed beside hers. Doing this challenge was intimidating but having a friend there, even if it was Mary, gave her more confidence.

The naked submissives each stood at the foot of a bed, hands behind their backs, legs spread apart, patiently waiting their turn. Brie quickly followed suit. Naturally, Master Gannon started with the girl on the other end.

Brie watched covertly as the sub was commanded to lie on the bed on her back with her head at the edge. Brie had to smile; it was the perfect height to offer oral stimulation. The girl's wrists were secured to the legs of the bed. He then moved to the headboard and told her to spread her legs. With rapid movements, he tied her ankles to the metal. Master Gannon returned to the end of the bed and gently smacked her cheek before leaving her. "Good girl…"

The first toy was bound and ready for play.

The King Returns

Master Gannon moved on to the next submissive, who happened to be the male who'd snapped Brie's ass with a towel. He was ordered to lie on his back, with his wrists resting against the headboard. Gannon secured them tightly, then bound his ankles to the legs of the bed. Just that simple contact of being bound had the submissive's cock rising to attention. Gannon slapped the sub's masculine thigh before moving on.

Each submissive was tied into a different position so that the Dominants would have their choice of play without having to remove or change the rope bindings.

When Master Gannon finally reached Brie, she was a quivering mess of nerves. This was it—she was about to become a toy.

Unlike with the other submissives, Master Gannon talked to her before he began. "Are you prepared for this, Miss Bennett?"

She nodded. "I am, Gannon."

"You will not be released from your bonds until the end of the play session. This is not only a test of your submissive nature, but your endurance. We do not choose our toys lightly. Consider this an extreme honor."

His words helped her to focus on what was being asked of her, and she answered confidently, "I do, Gannon."

He pulled out a sash from his jeans pocket. "Turn."

Brie was surprised and wondered if she was being blindfolded because she was not a member of the commune. Thankfully, blindfolds gave her a sense of power, and she accepted it graciously.

"On the bed, toy, with your knees under your torso."

She felt for the bed and settled down onto it, tucking her knees in, knowing the position lifted her buttocks at a pleasing angle to allow access to both her pussy and ass.

Master Gannon took her left ankle and wrapped it several times in rope before securing it to the bed post. He bound the right next, spreading her legs farther for easier access. With exact movements that spoke of his years of experience, Master Gannon tied her wrists together, then pulled hard so that she was stretched out seductively, her cheek resting against the mattress as he secured her hands to the headboard.

Gannon slapped her on the ass before he left. All the toys were now bound and ready for play…

"Having fun yet?" Mary whispered.

Brie smiled, purring, "Actually, yes. You know how I love the feel of rope."

Mary chuckled. "Yeah, you're a total freak about it."

"So when will the Doms come to play?"

"Not for another half-hour or so. Master Gannon wants the toys eager for their attention."

"Shh," one of the other subs cautioned.

Brie understood that this forced waiting period had multiple purposes. It encouraged each submissive to reflect on what was about to happen. It also helped to put them in the right frame of mind—as objects of pleasure, they were there to meet the Doms' needs. A toy's satisfaction and enjoyment were based solely in fulfilling those needs.

For Brie, however, it went far deeper than that.

This extra time allowed her to ponder how similar this was to her first night at the Submissive Training Center. To be under the power of a stranger was both unsettling and exhilarating.

Just as she had when she'd scened with Ms. Clark for the first time, Brie decided to imagine that each Dom who came to her that night was *her* Dominant, the one she'd willingly given her body and heart to. It made the connection meaningful to her, and would translate into a more pleasing exchange for them both.

From the other side of the beds, she heard a distinctive and familiar sound. The loud buzzing of a Magic Wand cut through the heavy silence in the room. Soon the moans of the first toy followed, announcing her orgasm.

Brie whispered to Mary, "What's going on?"

"Master Gannon wants the toys eager and wet."

Brie listened to the erotic sounds as each sub orgasmed under the power of that wicked instrument, knowing her turn was coming. She stiffened when she felt a hand on her thigh and then the touch of the wand, but there was no escaping its merciless vibration or the immediate fire it incited.

"Don't fight it," she was told.

Brie willingly obeyed, and the juicy sound of her wet excitement joined the energetic hum. She cried out when her pussy pulsed in heated release.

Nothing was said, but the Magic Wand stopped buzzing and pulled away. With her wet clit still throbbing, she listened to the sounds of people making final adjustments to the playroom equipment before the room fell silent.

Brie's loins contracted in fearful pleasure—soon the Dominants would be coming to play…

Mary had explained that the Dominants warmed up using the toys before the other submissives were allowed to join the event. Releasing their needs beforehand allowed the Doms to concentrate fully on their BDSM scenes rather than their sexual urges. If at any point during the event they felt the need to release again, they could return to one of the many waiting toys.

Mary admitted to Brie that she preferred to be a playmate rather than a toy, but had bitten the bullet just for her. It was little things like that which let her know Mary considered her a friend, no matter how much the woman denied it. Blonde Nemesis was not one to normally sacrifice for another.

Brie whispered, "Thanks for doing this with me."

"Hey, I wasn't about to deny you your one chance to live."

The sound of low, male voices and the sultry pitch of females filled the massive room as the Dominants entered the dungeon.

"Welcome to the Dungeon, my fellow Dominants," Master Gannon announced. "The Toy Station has been primed and is ready for use."

Brie felt a moment of panic, but Tono's gentle command resonated in her head and she slowed her breathing, calming herself. This was not an experience Sir wanted her to 'survive', this was something he expected her to enjoy and learn from.

"Well, well, are you hard for me, toy?" a Domme asked down the line. Brie heard the sound of slapping and the primal grunts of the sub in response. Her pussy pulsated in reaction to their erotic exchange.

Soon the sounds of grunts, creaking beds, and moans filled the dungeon. Yet both Mary and Brie remained untouched.

How humiliating would it be *not* to be chosen the entire event?

"I knew you would be waiting for me," a gravelly voice stated, dripping with masculine arrogance. It sent chills down Brie's spine. She breathed an audible sigh of relief when it was Mary, not she, whom Razor chose to play with.

Mary cried out unexpectedly.

"That's right. I am going to treat you like the slut you are."

Mary purred, before the sound of slapping skin and whimpers ensued. Brie lay there helplessly, listening to the Doms and Dommes enjoying the other toys. After a while, she resigned herself to the fact she was only going to be a forgotten observer.

Then the steady footsteps of a man in boots approached her bed, the smell of his unfamiliar, musky cologne surrounding her. Brie slowed down her breathing even more as she willing gave in to her role.

This is it...

She experienced a moment of disappointment and partial relief when he moved away. However, it wasn't long before the footsteps returned. She gasped when she felt the touch of a wooden paddle on her ass. He caressed her skin with it for several moments before he lifted the instrument. She bit her lip, waiting for the impact.

It came down hard, harder than she was used to, and she yelped in surprise from the sting of it. Several of the Doms beside her chuckled, causing Brie to clam up. The last thing she wanted was to make a poor impression.

The paddle came down again and she grunted, her ass burning from the contact. He continued to rain down a volley of swats. Brie whimpered quietly, willing it to end. When he'd finally stopped, he resumed caressing her ass with the paddle.

Brie let out a sigh, appreciative that the pain quickly dissipated into a warm ache. She could tell the man playing with her was a skilled Dom, and it helped to ease her fear when he started up again.

Tears soaked her blindfold, but she did not cry out. When he stopped the second time, she heard him place the paddle on the table beside her. As she lay there trembling, she heard the distinctive sound of pants being unzipped, which was soon followed by the slight crinkle as he tore the wrapper off a condom.

There was a moment of panic—and Brie almost called her safeword.

However, she couldn't deny that she was excited by the slippery sound of lubricant being slathered over a hard cock, her body pulsed with the need to be filled by it, so she said nothing as the Dom moved to the edge of the bed.

He pressed his shaft against the valley between her ass cheeks and Brie let out a soft whimper of surrender. When his hands glided over her skin, she felt an unexpected jolt of electricity.

"Sir?" she whispered.

He leaned down and growled into her ear. "No, I am your Khan, and you are my final virgin for the evening."

She shivered in pleasure as it dawned on her that this was his version of her fantasy: all the subs tied up, waiting to be taken just like the virgins in her story, the giving of herself to a stranger, the King—or in her case, her Khan.

Brie kept in character, receiving his caresses as if they were from her sovereign Lord, but truly there was no need for her to roleplay. His unexpected visit had her on an emotional high that she couldn't contain.

She knew he would be rough with her, because that had been her fantasy, and oh, how she *wanted* to be used by her King. This environment was the perfect set up for it.

"I desire to claim this pink little ass," he said, chuckling arrogantly as he slapped her buttocks. She was taken by surprise when he stuffed her mouth with a cloth. "But I don't want to hear your screams when I fuck your virginal hole."

He positioned his cock against her anus and plunged in without any warning, letting her know he was taking his role as Khan very seriously. She groaned into the cloth, forcing her body to accept the full length of him. He pushed her face down into the mattress as he thrust deeper and harder, grunting with effort.

Brie's ass was on fire. He fisted her hair and pulled her head back, challenging her body with his rough handling. She panted into the dry cloth, surprised by the force and fierceness of his claiming but reveling in the first flutterings of subspace. She moaned when he let go of her hair, clutching her waist to thrust at a new, more demanding angle.

Reality blurred as she became focused solely on his royal shaft. Every part of her was concentrated on the fiery buildup he was creating as he pounded her without mercy.

So this is what it feels like to be possessed by a king...

Just when she felt she was on the precipice, he pulled out. Brie whimpered, suddenly feeling lost and desperate. He removed the cloth from her mouth and growled into her ear, "But I do want to hear your screams when I fill you with my seed, girl."

She heard the sound of a condom being removed and was soon rewarded with the head of his naked shaft against her aching pussy. He pressed his thumb into her sore ass, asserting his authority over her body.

Changing tactics, he took her pussy slowly, making her feel every inch of him as he buried his rigid shaft in her. "I will ruin you for other men."

With that pronouncement, he began stroking her pussy with long, slow thrusts as he pressed his thumb deeper. She moaned loudly, wanting him to hear the depth of her desire. The initial pulsing of an impending orgasm began deep within her core, growing in power as he coaxed it with his skillful manipulation.

She whimpered again, afraid the intensity of it might prove too much, but she was helpless to prevent what was coming. Her Khan was in control…

"Feel the heat of my pleasure, girl," he roared, his thrusts coming hard and fast as he released his seed deep within her. It started a chain reaction as her nipples contracted into hard buds while her pussy clenched his pulsing shaft, milking it with her own orgasmic release.

Brie screamed as she lost herself to the power of it, almost losing touch with reality as she came with violent force. She couldn't stop shaking afterwards, her body still reverberating from the fierceness of the release. "Oh, my God…oh, my God…" she whispered repeatedly, overwhelmed by the intense experience.

Sir began untying her, rubbing his hands over the marks on her skin caused by the tight binding. She smiled lazily when she was finally freed from the last of the rope, her hair damp from tears and well-earned sweat.

"I love you, babygirl," Sir whispered as he lay on the bed and positioned her rag-doll body on top of him. He untied her blindfold, then began stroking her hair, sending delightful shivers down her spine.

"I'm floating…" she murmured, nestling against him as she closed her eyes.

She heard Faelan beside them, taking his turn with Mary. It was an erotic exchange, animalistic and primal, but through it all she sensed the undercurrent of love between them.

As Brie lay in Sir's arms, she felt as if she were flying on a cloud of contented ecstasy, listening to the sounds of all the dungeon-play around her. The lashing of whips, the clanking of chains, and the cries of passion and pain—it felt like home to her.

Before Faelan left the Toy Station, he addressed Sir. "Glad you could make it, Sir Davis."

"This has been a remarkable experience, Wallace."

"You two can retire to our room, if you would like," Faelan offered.

Mary spoke up. "Wait, where am I—?"

Faelan put his fingers to her lips. "I've already arranged our evening, toy. Another outburst from you, and you'll be reported."

She looked up at him and smiled, then turned to Sir, nodding respectfully to him.

Sir acknowledged the gesture but did not speak to Mary. Instead he lifted Brie off him and commanded her to kneel. To her surprise, he left her alone there, not explaining his actions.

Brie knelt beside the bed, her hands behind her back, her chest out and her head bowed, but she couldn't keep from smiling. Sir was here…

He returned minutes later with a sponge, towel and bowl of soapy water. She purred as the warm sponge glided across her skin.

"Our rambunctious play has left you a bit untidy."

The best kind of messy, Brie thought as she spread her legs wider and felt his essence trickle down her leg.

He smiled to himself as he meticulously washed every inch of her skin. Once he was done, he gently toweled her off. The act was intimate and tender, his own brand of aftercare following his rough use of her.

Sir handed over the sponge, bowl and towel. "Return the items and meet me downstairs."

Brie walked through the dungeon, naked and proud. Maybe the Doms only saw her as a ghost, but she knew who she was. She was Sir's collared submissive.

Her heart swelled with pride when she walked into Mary's bedroom and found Sir waiting for her with open arms. "Come to me, Brie."

She glided to him, grateful to be in his embrace.

"Did you enjoy your fantasy?"

"It was a perfect interpretation, Sir. I am in awe."

"You didn't suspect I was coming today?" he asked, as he wrapped his arms around her. She curled up against him, laying her head on his chest.

"No, not for a second."

"I was actually concerned you might call your safeword before I had a chance to play with you."

"I came close, Sir," she admitted with a giggle. Brie traced the muscles of his chest with her finger, loving the feel of his rough hair. "You are a very devious Master."

His smirk let her know he had something else up his sleeve.

She propped herself on his chest. "Okay, what aren't you telling me, Sir?" she demanded playfully.

"I have an unexpected trip to make."

"Can I join you?"

"I'm unsure you'll want to. Unless, of course, you fancy the taste of vodka."

"Russia, Sir?" Brie squealed in delight.

Sir chuckled. "My Moscow client has encountered a problem I must address. I also was told that a certain Ruski holds out hope of being part of your documentary, so a Russia trip may actually prove useful to you."

"That would be incredible!" she said, bubbling over with excitement. "I was hoping to film the dynamic between a sadist and masochist."

"Well, now you'll have that opportunity." He pulled her against him and inhaled. "I miss the smell of you when we're apart. I find the fragrance of Brie intoxicating." She giggled as he began sniffing her body, but those giggles quickly quieted when he moved between her legs and his tongue made contact with her sensitive clit. "I think this Brie needs to be consumed."

"Oh, Sir…"

Broken

F aelan sought Brie out the next afternoon. "Have you seen Mary?"

"She left after lunch. Didn't tell me where she was headed, though." Brie could feel his anxiety, but was unsure of the cause. "What? Is something wrong?"

"I suspect she's with Razor right now."

Brie had noticed Mary's unnatural attraction to the fierce Dom. It wasn't a sexual attraction, but something darker and more insidious. "I'll help you look for her."

After searching the main building and barn, they headed out towards the woods. When they heard Mary's screams, they sprinted in the direction of her cries and found her bound to a tree. Razor was slapping her face with such force that it was already leaving bruises.

"Stop!" Faelan demanded.

Razor looked at him with surprise, but stepped away, growling, "I'm only giving the lady what she wants."

"I understand. It's not you I have an issue with." Faelan said, ignoring Razor as he approached Mary. She was slow to respond, the endorphins having kicked in from their violent play, but she turned her head to face Faelan with a look of defiance.

"Why are you going down this path again?" he asked, sympathy coloring the anger in his voice.

Mary frowned, and replied with disdain, "Fuck you, Faelan."

"I won't do this again. You were free of your father's influence; why are you choosing to return by playing out your past now?"

Her lip trembled for a moment, but she shook it off and lashed out angrily. "You don't know what I want or need!"

Faelan began untying her from the tree. "You are like an addict, incapable of staying away from the one thing that will destroy you."

"Don't be so overdramatic, asshole. And stop treating me like a child."

As soon as she was free, he pushed her up against the tree. "I told you *never* to do this again and yet you defy me?"

Her answer dripped with insolence. "Yes."

"I can't—I won't do this anymore with you." He let go of her. "You have a choice, Mary. You can stop pursuing your past or drown in it."

She shot daggers of hate in her gaze as she raised her chin defiantly to him.

"Fine." Faelan backed away from her slowly, with a look of resignation and overwhelming sadness in his eyes. "Goodbye, Mary."

The words sounded so final that it frightened Brie. "Don't do this. You're both upset. Why don't you discuss this when you've had time to calm down?"

Faelan looked at Brie, his blue eyes communicating his resolve. "She made her choice the moment she sought Razor out for this scene. There is nothing more to say."

He walked away, not looking back when Mary called out to him. When he didn't respond, she turned to Brie and rolled her eyes. "Such a fucking drama queen…"

"Go after him," Brie implored.

"He'll be back."

"No, Mary. He won't."

Mary gave an insolent laugh. "Oh, he'll be back. The poor boy can't get enough of me."

Razor chuckled as he grabbed her roughly by the throat. "Then let's finish what we started, slut." He spat in her face as he slammed her against the tree.

"Hit me again."

Brie turned away. It was heartbreaking that Mary was encouraging her own destruction. She watched in desperation as Faelan disappeared into the woods.

"Damn it, Mary. If you don't go after him right now, you'll lose him."

When Blonde Nemesis acted as though she hadn't heard, Brie started after Faelan, shouting behind her, "You're a fucking fool, Mary!"

"And you're a stupid bitch!"

Brie could not catch up, and lost Faelan long before she made it back to the lodge. She saw Sir talking to a group of Dominants and ran to him, panting for breath.

Sir excused himself and led Brie to a private spot, obviously concerned for her. "What's wrong, Brie?"

"Todd's run off. Mary defied him and he says he's done with her." Tears started to fall when she confessed, "She needs him, Sir."

Instead of becoming concerned, Sir pulled Brie into his arms. "I was afraid it would end this way."

She looked up at him in disbelief. "Why would you say that?"

"Wallace spoke to me about Mary's attraction to the newest Dom. Unfortunately, the man bears a striking resemblance to her father."

Brie suddenly felt nauseated. "Oh no…"

"Wallace is doing the right thing. Her defiance of his direct command cemented her fate."

"But they love each other," she insisted.

"Wallace has done what he can to ensure her well-being. Now he must concentrate on himself."

Brie felt a prickling on the back of her neck. "Sir, is there something wrong with Todd?"

The seriousness of Sir's expression confirmed her fears. "It's not for me to say. If Wallace wanted you to know, he would have shared it with you."

Brie's heart beat wildly, a feeling of panic setting in. "He can't leave Mary now. She has no idea, Sir. I'm sure of it."

"He didn't want to burden her, and ultimately it *is* his choice."

"But she would never let him go if she knew. It's not fair to her. I have to tell him!"

"I don't believe it would do any good."

The desperation she felt was overwhelming, and she begged, "Please, Sir."

He took pity on her, and told Brie, "Wallace went downstairs to pack. You may speak to him if he is still there."

She raced into the lodge and burst through the door to see Faelan closing his suitcase.

"There's nothing to be said, Brie," he barked.

"Whatever is wrong with you, Mary deserves to know."

His eyes narrowed. "What are you talking about?"

"I suspected something was wrong, and Sir just confirmed it but wouldn't tell me what."

He chuckled angrily. "Leave it to *you* to notice, when Mary didn't."

"She would never let you go if she knew, Todd."

"It makes no difference and wouldn't have changed what happened today."

"Trust me, if Mary knew—"

"This is something I have to face alone. She doesn't need to know and neither do you." He looked at Brie sternly. "I don't want Mary to know anything about it."

"But—"

"Do not defy me in this."

His tone took her certainty down a notch or two. Faelan was right. This was his life, his decision. It wasn't her place to intervene. "Fine, Todd. I won't."

"At this moment, Mary is basking in the belief that she has one-upped me, but once she realizes what she's done, she's going to fall hard." He looked at Brie with compassion. "If she reaches out to you, promise me you'll support her."

"But I'm so pissed with her now!"

"Feel free to hit her between the eyes with how you feel, the same way she would you, but be there for her nonetheless. I'm afraid she has chosen a path she won't recover from."

The look of loss on Faelan's face undid Brie. She walked over to him and placed her hand over his heart. "I'm sorry."

He looked at her with ocean-blue eyes haunted by deep sorrow. "I don't understand why I was spared on the day of the crash, because nothing I've done since has amounted to anything."

"No, that's not true," Brie protested. "I'm grateful to know you, and Mary is a better person because of you. Don't doubt that—never doubt that."

He shrugged. "Just be there for her, Brie. You're the only real friend she has."

"Of course. Can I at least ask where you're headed?"

He smiled sadly, shaking his head. "No, that's just between me and the powers above." He slung his duffle bag over his shoulder and grabbed the suitcase. "See you, blossom."

Tears blurred her vision as she watched him go, the lump in her throat making it impossible to speak.

But in her head she was crying, *Don't leave!*

Skeletons

Mary avoided Brie like the plague the last few days of her stay, choosing to bunk with another couple in a room at the other end of the lodge. Whenever an accidental meeting occurred, she treated Brie as if she didn't exist, although she acknowledged Sir.

"You are being very patient with her," Sir complimented Brie.

"I understand Mary. Despite her bravado, she knows she messed up—and bad. She just isn't ready to admit it yet, especially to me."

On the last day, however, Mary sought her out while Brie was taking in the mountain scenery from the bridge; the same bridge where Faelan had met with Brie on the first day.

"So you're headed back into the vanilla world, huh?"

"Yes, but I'm going to miss this place."

"Yeah, you're going to wish you could come back here, I bet."

Brie smiled, glad they were talking. "I'm sure I will."

Mary shifted uncomfortably on her feet. It took her several minutes before she built up enough courage to say, "If you see Faelan, tell him I'm sorry."

"I will." Brie didn't have the heart to tell Mary that she had no way to pass on the message.

Mary looked broken when she confessed, "I don't think he's coming back."

Brie felt tears prick her eyes. "No, I don't think he will."

Mary glanced around and stated, "Here I am, living the dream, and it doesn't mean a damn thing without him."

"Brie," Sir said, walking up to them, "Gannon wants to speak to us before we leave."

"Certainly, Sir." She reached out to hug Mary and clasped her hand instead when the girl tried to pull away. "Look, I'm here for you. You can call if you need to talk, even though you'll have to head into Whitefish to do it."

Mary rolled her eyes. "Whatever."

Brie took the arm Sir offered and they headed towards Gannon's office. Mary called out to her, "You'd better accept the charges if I call, Stinky Cheese."

Brie turned around and laughed. "I make no promises, Mary Quite Contrary."

Master Gannon had an unexpected surprise for them when they reached his office. Brie had assumed he wanted to go over last-minute issues concerning the footage she'd shot. Instead, he handed Sir a large envelope. "It just arrived."

Sir took it from him and looked at the address of the sender. He glanced at Brie. "It's from my lawyer."

Brie held her breath, afraid she already knew what it said. Sir tore open the envelope and read through the first letter with a questioning look. He shook his head and handed it to her while he read the second.

She looked it over with a growing sense of dread.

```
Dear Mr. Davis,

I didn't want to bring this issue to your
attention until I was certain it was a legitimate
concern. I received this letter a week ago and
requested she submit a genetic test to verify her
claim. Normally, that is enough to deter scam
artists, but she has agreed to the test.

    I await further instructions at your earliest
convenience.

Harold Thompson, Attorney at Law
```

Brie looked up and saw Sir with an expression of disbelief on his face. He read the letter again before handing it to her. Brie didn't want to take it, based on the look he gave her. She was sure it could only mean one thing—he was a father.

Brie noted that the woman's penmanship was as exquisite as Sir's.

Dear Thane Davis,

It is with a racing heart that I pen this letter to you. I have lived my life believing I was an only child. My mother, Ruth

Elizabeth Meyers, never spoke of you, never once mentioned her life before my father, Jake Robert Meyers.

I can hardly think straight, and apologize if this letter makes no sense. I only just learned that my mother lies dying in a hospital in China. Even worse, I have been told that you may be seeking to end her life.

I beg you to spare her. Whatever your relationship was with my mother, you should know that she has always been good to me. I love her with all my heart, and cannot bear to lose her.

I hope you will agree to meet with me. Hopefully, we can come to a mutual decision concerning her future care and unravel the secrets she's kept hidden from us both.

I have no idea why she kept her past from me, but now that I know you exist, I feel desperate to meet you.

With earnest sincerity,
Lilly Meyers

Brie was stunned, and handed the letter back to him listlessly. He took it and read through it a third time.

Sir has a sister…

Why did that fill her with such foreboding?

Sir kept his cool, shaking Master Gannon's hand. "Thank you, Gannon. We have both enjoyed our stay here. You've created an environment for true community and sexual freedom that I didn't think possible. I'm impressed."

"I believe it should be the norm, not the exception." Master Gannon stated. He turned to Brie and shook her hand. "I hope the exposure you bring to my vision will incite change."

"That is my hope as well, Gannon. I will do my very best."

"I expect no less."

When they left Master Gannon's office, Rajah was there to meet them. Brie looked down when she felt the black cat rub against her leg. She smiled and picked him up, scratching under his chin.

Rajah looked at her strangely.

"What's wrong?" she asked, squeezing the cat against her.

"Shadow doesn't come to anyone but Master Gannon."

Brie smiled as she continued to pet the cat. "Really? He's been my friend during the entire stay here."

Rajah raised his eyebrow. "Master Gannon will find that fascinating."

Brie tried to hand the cat to him, but Shadow jumped out of her arms and ran out of the door. She giggled and shrugged. "Cats..."

"Pussies continue to remain a mystery to me," Rajah replied with a poker face as he handed Brie her car keys and cell phone. He then addressed Sir. "I've put your luggage in the trunk as well, Sir Davis. You are free to leave."

Brie asked Sir, "Didn't you drive here?"

"No, my dear. I flew in by private plane and landed a few miles from the commune on the morning of the dungeon event. Gannon picked me up personally. You had no idea that I was speaking to you from inside the main building when you called from Gannon's office?"

Brie shook her head. "A man of many surprises."

He looked at the papers in his hand. "Some I'm not even aware of."

Once they were on the road and could talk privately, Brie asked, "Do you think there's a possibility the woman's telling the truth, Sir?"

He glanced at her, shaking his head. "Frankly, I was expecting a false paternity suit."

Brie didn't want to admit she'd immediately assumed he was a father. She felt guilty now, knowing it showed a lack of trust in his honor that Sir did not deserve.

He continued, "Having a sibling was never a consideration. I will not give it another thought unless the test results confirm her claim."

"Do you want to head back to LA, then?"

"Brie, there is no need to concern ourselves about this when all we have to go on is a simple letter. The world is full of unscrupulous people. No, we move forward with our lives as if nothing has happened."

"As you wish."

"I've been looking forward to seeing Durov again, and we have yet to make use of the birthday present he gave you," he said, taking her hand and putting it to his lips. "Which is long overdue, babygirl."

Brie's Russian Treat

The Parents

O nce they were in the air, Sir explained that he had a short detour planned for them. Brie was elated, thinking that not only was she getting a trip to Russia, but an additional surprise as well. Those happy feelings died when she started noticing the familiar landscape of Nebraska outside the airplane window.

"We're visiting my parents, aren't we?"

"Yes. Although we've spoken to them about the wedding date, your parents deserve to be part of the planning process. It's tradition, is it not?"

"Yes, but normally the bride knows *where* she's getting married."

Sir smiled charmingly. "Nothing about us is normal, babygirl."

"You aren't planning on telling them the location, are you?"

"Naturally."

"How is that fair?"

"This is not about being fair, Brie." He kissed her hand, grinning with a mischievous glint in his eye. "It's about planning an event that will enchant you."

"But I hate surprises."

"No, you don't," he corrected. "You hate having to wait."

A young boy peeked his head over the seat and stared at them.

Sir continued, "As I am a responsible Ma—" he looked at the child and amended his next word, "...man, I must provide you with lessons in patience."

"You try my patience, Sir," Brie replied, pouting.

He chuckled, nodding to the child who was staring at him so intently. "I must continually provide her with lessons because she's such a stubborn pupil."

The little boy's eyes grew wide at actually being acknowledged by Sir, and he quickly popped back down in his seat.

Brie grinned. It was heartwarming to see her Master interacting with a child.

Sir turned to Brie. "I firmly believe in the saying 'Spare the rod, spoil the child'." He kissed her on the lips and whispered huskily, "But it may be because I enjoy using my rod on you—repeatedly." Her stomach fluttered at his words.

She could only giggle when the little boy popped his head up again.

As they pulled up to her parents' home, Brie's stomach trembled for a different reason. "This should be a good visit, right?"

Sir held out his hand and helped Brie out of the car. "I'm unsure. Although your parents have accepted your choice of husband, I don't get the impression they're happy about it."

"Then, Sir, may I ask why you keep putting us through this?"

"I believe in showing people the respect owed them. Your parents did a fine job raising you and deserve to be a part of your life now. Just because they dislike me, should not preclude them from seeing you."

"But it hurts my heart when they're rude to you," she said, stepping reluctantly onto the porch.

"I'm quite capable of handling their displeasure, Brie. Don't let that be a concern. I trust the bonds we create now will eventually mend the rift between us."

Brie shook her head. "If my parents understood how wonderful you truly are, they would greet you with open arms and a bottle of champagne."

"Possibly," he said with a smirk as he rang the doorbell.

Brie's mother opened the door, smiling shyly at Sir. "Please, won't you come in?"

"Mom!" Brie cried, stepping inside to hug her.

She felt her mother's muscles relax in her arms as they embraced. After a couple of seconds, Brie relaxed as well—it felt good to be in her mother's arms again.

"It seems like ages since we've seen you, Brie," her mother complained lightly as she took Sir's jacket and Brie's purse. She nodded them towards the living room. "Please make yourselves comfortable."

Brie was embarrassed to see her father sitting in his chair, purposely choosing not to stand up to greet them. Her father's slight did not deter Sir. He walked straight over to the man and held out his hand. "Pleasure to see you again, Mr. Bennett."

Her father could not take Sir's intense stare and stood up, shaking his hand. "Forgive me if I seem less than excited to see you, Mr. Davis. My experience has been that your visits only herald bad news."

"Wait," Brie piped up. "The first time I came I introduced my new boyfriend to you, and the second time I told you about my documentary."

"Exactly. If you look at it from our perspective, neither was exactly good news—now, was it?"

Brie stepped back, deeply hurt by his answer, but her mother put her arms around Brie's shoulders. "Your father is mistaken. Meeting Thane was certainly a shock, but we are both pleased to see you so happy. As for the documentary, although it was followed by much unpleasantness, we are proud of your accomplishment."

Her father looked as if he was about to say something, but wisely changed his mind and sat back down. "Pardon me if I'm not anxious to hear what you have to tell us today."

Sir sat down and pulled Brie next to him when she sat on the couch. "As you know, we have a date set for the wedding and would like you to be a part of the planning process."

Brie's mother's eyes lit up. "Really?"

Sir's smile was engaging and genuine when he told her, "Yes, Mrs. Bennett—it would mean a lot to Brie and I."

"Oh, you can call me Mom if you want to," her mother replied, blushing profusely.

Brie's father cleared his throat. "I do not think I could ever get used to a man nearly my age calling me Father."

Sir turned to him. "And yet you will." He took Brie's hand in his. "Family is important to us."

"Look, I know why you're here, Mr. Davis. You act all formal and superior, but the reality is that you came to ask us to pay for this wedding."

Sir shook his head, amusement on his face. "As you so eloquently pointed out, I am *old* enough to finance our wedding. No, your involvement would be purely your choice—with Brie's approval, of course. In the end, it is the bride we all seek to please."

Brie felt heat rise to her cheeks. Hearing Sir refer to her as his bride was all kinds of romantic.

"Brianna, do you plan to come back here to marry?" her father asked.

"Actually, Dad, I have no idea where we're getting married."

Her father turned on Sir, his voice tainted with self-righteous venom. "Is this another example of you controlling my daughter, Mr. Davis?"

Sir patted Brie's hand gently. "No. I enjoy surprising Brie, and in this case it's strategic. While I devote my attention to the wedding, it gives Brie time to finish filming her documentary."

Now all her father's attention was riveted back on Brie, his tone stern. "What documentary, daughter?"

"Dad, I was asked to film a sequel."

"Not again!" he bellowed. "Didn't you put us through enough hell the first time? We've just barely recovered from the humiliation. What is this, Marcy?" he exclaimed, turning to Brie's mother. "Why must we continually be disgraced by our only child?"

Her mother wrung her hands nervously. "Another film, Brie?"

"I thought you would be happy for me, Mom. Although the first one met with some resistance, overall it was received positively by the film industry."

Her father frowned. "It was *not* a positive experience, young lady. Maybe for you, but certainly not for us." He turned savagely on Sir. "Why the hell are you letting her do this again? You *know* what happened last time."

"Mr. Bennett, this is your daughter's career, not mine. As her fiancé, I support her decision to do this second film and will help her complete the project in any way I can."

Her father was not pleased by Sir's reply and turned to Brie. "Brianna, time and time again you have proven how childish you are. It's as if you go out of your way to test us. Why? Aren't you too old to play the rebellious teenager?"

Brie's lip trembled as she fought to keep back the tears. She wanted to respond, longed to put her father in his place, but she sat there mute—as helpless as a baby.

"Brie," her mother said kindly, "Are you sure this is the best direction for your career? I know you once dreamed of making romantic comedies. If you do this second documentary, what chance have you got of being taken seriously?"

"Mom, I was a kid when I told you that. Things have changed since then—my dreams have taken a new direction. Trust me when I say that this film is important to me. I'm proud of my work and I believe in it so strongly that I'm willing to face your disappointment," she turned to her father, adding, "*and* unfair judgments."

"I can't believe we're being forced to go down this road again," he growled.

Sir squeezed Brie's hand. "Family is important to us, Mr. Bennett, and I trust it is important to you." Brie heard the raw emotion in his voice, and looked up at Sir in concern when he shared, "You know that I lost my father years ago. I can't tell you what I would give to have him in my life now, and yet here you are, throwing away your relationship with Brie as if it means nothing to you."

"I believe in tough love, Mr. Davis. You don't coddle people when they're making bad decisions."

"Then I have to ask, who do you see when you look at your daughter? I see an intelligent woman, full of compassion and grace, working hard in her career but also seeking to build a fulfilling life outside it. Isn't that good enough for you?"

"Damn it, man, I'm not the bad guy here!"

Sir's voice remained calm, despite the implied insult. "Although your daughter has chosen to pursue a path you don't agree with, it doesn't change the fact that she is still your daughter. Is your love and acceptance based solely on what you think she should be?"

Brie's father's angry laughter filled the room. "Oh, that's rich coming from the man who controls my daughter's every move as her 'Master'."

"What you fail to understand is that I hold Brie in the highest regard. If she wanted to stop with the film and move in another direction, I would fully support her in that. Let me be perfectly clear, Mr. Bennett, Brie is in control of her life. I simply enjoy tweaking some of the details."

"And he's wonderful at that," Brie answered, wrapping her arms around him and kissing Sir on the cheek.

Brie knew the show of affection was difficult on her father, and wasn't surprised when he snapped, "I still maintain that her life would be *very* different if she hadn't met you."

Sir nodded. "I do not disagree. The question you must ask yourself is if that 'other life' you so desperately cling to is worth losing your daughter over."

"Brie *is* very happy, dear," her mother declared bravely, siding with Brie. "And they came to us to ask us to help with the wedding. Weren't you saying just last week how disappointed you were that we weren't being included?"

"No need to bring that up in front of these two," her father huffed in irritation.

Brie couldn't help but smile. Sir had been right. Her parents did want to be part of the wedding, despite her dad's bullheaded attitude.

"It would mean a lot to me," Brie confessed, putting her hand on Sir's knee. Then she corrected herself, "…to *us* if you would help plan the wedding." She turned to her father. "Please, Daddy."

For the first time that evening, her father's expression softened.

Her mother dabbed her eyes. "I can't believe my little girl is really getting married."

Brie stood up and walked over to her. "I would love it if you'd help me pick out the wedding dress, Mom." Her mother became a puddle of tears when Brie wrapped her arms around her.

When Brie turned and approached her father, he rose back to his feet. "Dad, having you walk me down the aisle means everything to me."

He held out his arms, squeezing her hard when she ran into them. "I'm your father—of course I'll walk you down the aisle." He kissed the top of her head. "That's my job, little girl."

Brie's mother joined them and they shared an impromptu group hug. "Your happiness is all that counts to your father and I."

Her father pulled away, furrowing his brow. "But that doesn't give you permission to become a Bridezilla."

Her mother laughed. "A what?"

"A Bridezilla. I've seen them on TV. It's disgusting."

Her mother shook her head, playing with a strand of Brie's hair. "Our little girl is no Bridezilla, Bill. I don't know why you even brought that up."

"Mr. and Mrs. Bennett," Sir interrupted, "I would like to fill you in on the specifics without Brie being present. Can we retire to the study?"

Brie refrained from whining when the three headed towards the study, but she was delighted when her mother looked back and announced, "Bill can fill me in later. I'll just spend time with Brie while you men talk."

"But Marcy…" her father implored.

She laughed, patting his arm. "You don't need to be afraid of your future son-in-law, honey. He isn't going to bite."

Brie wondered what Sir thought of being called 'son', but his expression didn't change as he followed her father into the room and shut the door. She trusted the conversation would be far more agreeable than the last one they'd had in that study.

"So, sweetie, tell me all about this second film…"

Brie spent the next half-hour nervously glancing at the door as she shared about Tokyo and Denver, the LA sessions and the Montana commune with her mother.

Her mom took it all in, shaking her head in disbelief. When Brie finished, she replied hesitantly, "It sounds fascinating, dear." Brie found the response cute coming from her mother.

Both women jumped when the study door finally opened.

Brie looked to Sir first, and was glad to see a pleasant expression on his face. "Then we're agreed. We'll have Mrs. Bennett fly down in a month to help Brie pick out a wedding dress."

"What's this?! I get to visit you in LA?" her mother asked with glee, then she immediately scolded Sir. "You really have to start calling me Mom."

Brie thought she saw a flush of color on Sir's cheeks when he answered, "Yes…Mom."

"That's more like it, dear," she said, giving him a maternal hug.

The bemused expression on Sir's face when he looked over her shoulder at Brie was freaking adorable.

Before they left for the airport, Sir handed her father a memory stick. "This is a piece Brie filmed that will not be included in the documentary. It involves a flogging scene with Marquis Gray. Your daughter not only filmed it, but was part of the scene itself. I hope you will consider watching so you can see the beauty of the exchange."

Her father hesitantly took it from him.

Sir continued, "Marquis Gray is an undisputed expert with the tool, but you'll see how exceptional your daughter is as well."

"He doesn't have sex with her, does he?"

"No, it's simply a flogging scene," Sir assured him.

Her father stared hard at the memory stick. "Mr. Gray did say it's therapeutic, that flogging 'thing' he does…"

"Therapeutic and breathtaking," Brie agreed.

Her father set it on the coffee table. "I'll consider watching it."

"Good." Sir held out his hand to him. "Until we meet again, Mr. Bennett. Before we leave, can you tell me if there's a carwash nearby?"

Brie was pleased that her father didn't hesitate to shake his hand this time as he answered, "Yes, a new one just opened two blocks south of here. You can't miss it."

"Perfect." Sir hugged Brie's mom, telling her, "And I'll see you in a month, Mom."

Brie's mother giggled like a young girl. "Oh, I can't wait!"

When they got into the car, Brie let out a long, happy sigh. "That went *way* better than I thought it would." She snuggled up to Sir before he started the car. "But only because you're brilliant, Sir."

"Brilliant may be overstating things a bit. The truth is your parents are easy to read. It's apparent that they love you, so my mission is to remind them of that whenever we steer off-course."

"Like I said, brilliant!" Brie insisted. He brushed his hand against her breast as she leaned over to playfully kiss him on the nose. The light touch caused tingles throughout her body.

Sir stared at her for a moment and then looked back at the house. "There's one more stop we need to make before we head off to the airport."

Never

Sir pulled up to an automated carwash and Brie broke out in giggles as he painstakingly inserted his change, hitting the Deluxe Wash setting after he was done.

"Why are we washing a rental car, Sir?"

"Due to the lack of time before the flight *and* the lack of privacy on this particular plane, I have a challenge for you, téa."

She raised her eyebrow, smiling seductively at him. "Your wish is my command, Master."

Sir pulled the car onto the rails and set the vehicle in neutral. The machine gently guided the car along without the need of assistance.

He took his hands off the wheel and adjusted the seat back. Then he slowly unbuttoned his pants. The tingling she'd felt earlier traveled lower as she watched him free his cock from his boxers.

"Do you think you can bring me to completion before the car finishes the cycle?"

"It would be my honor." Brie got on her hands and knees, straddling the console to lean over Sir's rigid shaft. She looked up just as the soap bubbles covered the car in their rainbow colors. Giggling softly, she took his cock into her mouth, licking his frenulum teasingly before taking him deeper.

Sir groaned and pressed her head down farther onto his shaft. Knowing her time was limited and Sir's restraint was legendary, she began rapidly bobbing up and down, taking him deeper each time until her lips were nestled against his dark pubic hair.

She held herself there for several seconds, then pulled up to take a breath. Without missing a beat, her lips were back on his shaft. She started gagging as she tried to force it down too quickly.

"Slower, babygirl...I don't want you hurting that pretty throat."

She wiped away the tears that had formed from her efforts and tried again, being more careful to relax as she deep-throated him.

"Time's almost up," he warned gently.

She arched her back, thrusting her ass in the air. It was more enticing for Sir and gave her throat a new angle. In addition, she began moaning on his shaft, remembering what Mr. Gallant had taught her at the Training Center.

It was enough to push Sir over the edge...

He groaned loudly as his hips rhythmically thrust his cock deep into her throat. After the last burst of come, he pushed her off of him. "Hurry, there are towel dryers."

She had no idea what he meant, but immediately flopped into her seat and swiped her mouth with her sleeve.

Sir didn't have time to zip up his pants, and casually pulled his white shirt over his open fly as two smiling attendants started hand-drying the car.

Brie looked at Sir in disbelief. "I barely met that challenge, Sir."

He hurried to adjust the seat back. "Neither of us was prepared for an audience at the end."

She waved gleefully at the men as they pulled away from the carwash, and watched in the side-view mirror as the two started ribbing each other. Brie suspected they knew exactly what had just transpired.

"I appreciate the opportunity to please you, Sir. You know I love it."

"I have another request."

"My pleasure, Sir."

"At the airport, after we have passed through security, I want you to take my belt and go to the restroom. Secure it under your dress, right about here." He touched the lower part of her abdomen just above her mound, making her heart race with the simple contact. "Make sure it's tight. I want you to feel the pressure of it the entire trip."

It was a wickedly cruel but sexy command. The last time she had flown to Russia, Sir had given her a lesson on belts in a private cabin. She would be reminded of that lesson the entire flight, without any hope of release.

"You know, I'm a tad surprised that Rytsar didn't insist on sending a jet for us, Sir."

"I left a message when I couldn't find a better flight, but he never called back. I have to assume he wasn't able to make arrangements on such short notice."

"But he does know we're coming?" Brie asked, remembering how

Tono Nosaka had been surprised by their visit.

"He does, and I'm expecting his normal shenanigans when we get there. That could be the reason he hasn't returned my call—he's too busy planning his next prank. However, this time you and I are prepared. It's a waste of time on his part, but nothing can deter Durov once his mind is set."

Brie giggled, looking out the car window as they approached the Eppley Airfield. "I wonder what it will be this time…"

Numerous times during the lengthy international flight, Sir slid his hand behind her back and lightly pulled on the belt under her dress. It hit just the right spot to cause a pleasant pressure in her loins, which further teased and excited her.

"Tweaking the details," he murmured in her ear, "and later today I will grab on to that belt and fuck you like a slut, téa."

She shivered, smiling to herself. Yes, Sir was an expert at tweaking the details.

It was a surprise to Brie when they got through Russian security without any hassles. Even more surprising was the fact that Rytsar was nowhere to be found once they were out.

"He's still not answering his cell," Sir griped as he thrust his phone into his pocket. "I guess we'll take a cab."

Sir lifted his hand to hail one. It took a while before a taxi finally pulled up. While Brie climbed into the vehicle, the driver put their luggage into the trunk and asked Sir where they were headed. The instant Sir stated the address, the man's face fell. Without explanation, he unloaded the luggage and shook his head.

Sir spoke to the man in Russian, but he just kept repeating, "*Nyet.*" He gestured Brie out of his cab, then sped off as if the hounds of hell were following him.

"Well, that was odd." Sir put his arm around Brie as he hailed another one.

After a few minutes, another cab pulled up. Before Sir let him take the luggage, he explained where he wanted to go. This cabbie looked alarmed, glancing around nervously before jumping into his vehicle and driving off with no explanation.

"Okay, now I am getting irritated," Sir complained. "What is Durov up to?"

Sir hailed a third cab and explained where they were headed. The cabbie hesitated for a moment, but then nodded. Sir breathed a sigh of relief. "Good. Keep your eyes open—Durov has to be around here someplace laughing his Ruski ass off."

The cabbie exited the airport, but was silent for the entire drive, even when Sir spoke to him directly. It was eerie.

"I don't understand where Durov is going with this ruse, but I don't find it particularly funny. Do you?"

Brie shook her head. "Not at all, Sir."

She felt chills as they rounded the corner of Rytsar's street and she heard Sir's intake of breath. She couldn't see anything yet and asked, "What is it?"

He did not respond, a frozen expression of shock on his face. As they pulled up to Rytsar's mansion, Brie understood why. The top half of the structure was gone, looking as if it had been physically ripped off, and what was left had been gutted by fire.

The cabbie quickly unloaded the luggage and demanded payment. Without counting the money or even looking back, he jumped back into the cab and hit the gas, leaving them standing in front of the ruins.

The shock of the scene held Brie speechless as she took in the devastation. She shook her head, not wanting to believe it. She followed silently behind Sir as he walked around the mansion. The back of it told the story. The entire side had been blown away as if by some tremendous explosion. Sir walked through the huge hole, carefully stepping over the rubble.

Brie finally found her voice and asked, "Do you think Rytsar survived?"

"I don't know."

"What's happened, Sir? What could have caused this?"

"It looks like a bomb, but as far as I know, Durov didn't have any enemies."

"Is it possible he got tangled up with the Russian mafia?"

"The Durov family does not engage in *Bratva* activities."

"Could he have become a target because of that?"

Sir's voice was empty when he answered. "I can't say." He walked farther inside, trying to make sense of the destruction around them.

"Rytsar…" Brie whimpered.

"This wasn't survivable," Sir stated dully.

"But he must have gotten out," Brie insisted, needing Sir to reassure her.

"I haven't heard from him for three days." Sir closed his eyes, his breathing becoming labored.

Brie grabbed on to him, tears falling silently as she glanced around at the burnt wreckage that had once been Rytsar's home. "He can't…"

"If this is related to the *Bratva*, then it explains the strange behavior of the cab drivers." Sir put his arm protectively around Brie. "We need to leave—we're not safe here."

"But we have to find out what happened to Rytsar," she cried desperately.

Sir grabbed her shoulders and shook her. "No one could survive this."

Brie's lip trembled.

He let go of her, the look of devastation on his face gutting her. Sir looked around the ruins, shaking his head in disbelief. "He's gone…"

"But not forgotten," a jovial voice announced behind them.

Brie turned around, her mouth agape as Rytsar walked up, a huge grin on his face. "It was truly beautiful to see your heartfelt concern for your old comrade, but not to fear. I am alive and well."

Sir stared at him for several seconds before he punched Rytsar square in the face. The large Russian crashed to the ground.

"You never joke about that!"

Rytsar's entourage advanced on Sir, ready to restrain him, but Rytsar got back to his feet, rubbing his jaw slowly. "Stop, no need," he said, calling back his guards.

Sir's eyes burned with anger as he stared down the Russian Dom.

"I'm so touched, *moy droog*. You—"

"You *never* joke about death." Sir turned away, his jaw quavering slightly.

Rytsar's jovial expression disappeared. "I'm sorry…" He tried to touch Sir's shoulder, but he jerked away from the Russian.

"Never."

Rytsar nodded. "You're right. It was a cruel joke." He reached out and grabbed Sir in a bear hug, refusing to let go. "I am heartily sorry."

Sir let out an angry sigh. "Don't ever fuck with me like that again."

Rytsar pulled back to look him in the eyes. "It was only meant in jest, but I won't, *moy droog*. I give my solemn promise."

Sir pushed him away, straightening his jacket with quick, jerky movements. "See that you don't."

Rytsar turned to Brie next, brushing away the remaining tears from her cheeks. "I apologize to you as well, *radost moya*. I did not appreciate how deeply you felt."

"Liar," Sir snarled.

The Russian Dom shook his head sadly. "I did not mean to cause a rift between us, brother."

Sir's lip twitched. "I don't forgive you, but I will look past this."

"Good, because I lost everything when the gas main exploded," Rytsar said, gesturing at the ruins around him.

Sir nodded in new understanding. "So that's what happened here."

"That's terrible, Rytsar," Brie cried. "What a horrible loss for you."

"Generations lost," he growled angrily.

Brie remembered all the heirlooms, the fine paintings, numerous antiques—the sheer amount of history that had been lost in the explosion was devastating.

"Mercifully, it happened on a Sunday when my staff was away," he explained.

"Where were you?" Brie asked.

He raised his eyebrow. "I was…occupied at the time."

She blushed and looked down at her feet, trying to hide her smile.

"Certain friends of mine pressured the local government to rebuild it, since a home of such rich historical significance was destroyed due to a faulty gas line. Construction will start once the area has been shored up and deemed safe. It is a testament to my forefathers that the foundation of my ancestral home remains solid."

"What about the items lost in the fire, Durov?" Sir asked.

Rytsar snorted in satisfaction. "I am being adequately compensated."

"But all your family heirlooms, all those memories…" Brie lamented.

"*Da*, but something of great value to me was spared."

"Really?" Sir remarked with interest.

Rytsar started walking farther into the interior of the building, waving his hand for them to follow.

Brie turned to Sir. "Is it safe?"

"Probably not."

Sir followed the Russian anyway, and since he hadn't forbidden Brie, she followed behind him.

"As you know, Father and I never had much in common, but even he would have been pleased."

Rytsar led them down what remained of the stairs and opened the thick door that led down to the dungeon. Brie gasped as she stepped inside. It looked completely untouched, as pristine as the day she'd visited it last. The walls were lined with lit torches, hinting at the fact that he'd planned to show them this little 'miracle' all along.

"I can't believe it's unscathed, considering the violence of the explosion," Sir said in amazement.

"It is truly a *chudo*," Rytsar agreed. He walked over to the wall of instruments. "My men have been thorough in checking for damage, but have yet to report any. I have, however, discovered one pleasant byproduct left by the fire that raged above." He picked up his cat o' nines and dragged it under his nose, breathing in deeply. "All of my instruments retain the scent of the smoke. I find it an alluring addition."

He held out the cat o' nines to Brie. "Wouldn't you agree?"

Brie walked over to take a whiff, but her body shivered being so close to the instrument, having experienced its ferocious bite. She smelled the leather, taking in the aroma, and looked up at him in surprise. "I do find it pleasing."

He caressed the cat o' nines sensually and asked, "Would you like another session, *radost moya?*"

Brie backed up to Sir, distancing herself from the Russian. "No, once was more than enough. Thank you."

Sir chuckled. "I think you have effectively cured my sub of that desire."

Rytsar put the tool back on the wall. "Such a shame," he said wistfully, stroking the length of it. "It's one of my favorite pastimes."

"So, Durov, where have you been staying since the explosion?"

"I have several apartments in Moscow. Housing is not a problem, only an inconvenience."

Brie crinkled her brow in confusion, wondering why he would have multiple residences when he lived in a mansion.

"There's still one thing I can't wrap my head around," Sir said. "Why did the drivers behave so strangely at the airport? It makes no sense, given that this was only a gas explosion."

Rytsar slapped him on the back, laughing. "I informed the taxi companies of your arrival and offered a healthy sum if they refused to take you. All but one driver, of course. Were they convincing? I promised an extra bonus if they were."

"Yes, Durov, they were," Sir stated dryly. "You should dig deep into your wallet. I hope it hurts."

"That is good to hear," he answered with a satisfied grin.

When Sir frowned, Rytsar immediately realized his folly and said, "Let's forget the unpleasantness and concentrate on the rest of your stay here. I assume you will be headed to the cabin."

"Actually, I had planned to stay at your home. Because of what's happened, I suppose I can send Brie ahead until my business in Moscow is completed."

"Excellent! I will act as her host while you stay at my apartment, *moy droog.*"

Sir eyed him suspiciously. "Before I let you have her, I'll have to write down a list of what you can and cannot do in my absence."

"Only if you feel a list is necessary."

"Imperative."

"Don't you trust your longtime comrade?"

"After this last stunt? No."

"That hurts," Rytsar said, placing his hand over his heart. "But I will make it up to you both," he promised solemnly. "Come—we will stuff our bellies, drink a bottle or two of vodka, and go over this list together."

Pink or Blue

R ytsar took them to the modern side of Moscow, famous for its towering skyscrapers and twisted glass buildings that looked more like art than offices.

"Moscow is such a cool city," Brie exclaimed, looking up at the tall structures, in awe of their varied architectural design.

"It is a rare gem among the great cities," Rytsar stated proudly. "Moscow has a long and rich history."

He took them to a newly built apartment building made of glass and steel. It was a marvel of modern conveniences and artful design—the exact opposite of the historic mansion he'd grown up in.

"I can better understand why you have multiple dwellings, Rytsar," Brie said, adding, "it gives you the chance to enjoy the old and the new."

"*Da*, I truly had the best of both worlds," he agreed sadly.

Brie realized that she'd just stuck her foot in her mouth by mentioning the mansion, but before she could apologize, he changed the subject. "To go along with that theme, there is a new restaurant that opened recently. Let me tantalize you with the traditional foods of my forefathers tweaked with a modern flair."

She eagerly agreed, as she took a moment to survey his spacious apartment. The windows overlooking the scenic downtown reminded Brie of Sir's home, but instead of art covering the walls, Rytsar's place was decorated with BDSM tools, many of which looked cruel and menacing. As she glanced at the various instruments, she couldn't help wondering if they were strictly for ornamentation or actual use.

Rytsar kept his word and they did end up stuffing themselves, but Brie never got to partake of the vodka. A full stomach, after a long plane trip and an emotional scare, had her drifting off before the night had even started.

Brie was bereft when she woke up in an empty bed early the next morning.

"Sir?"

When she got no answer, Brie slipped out from under the covers, and was flustered to discover she was completely naked. She looked around the room, grateful when she spied her clothes folded on a chair. She trusted that Sir had been the one to undress her but wondered, *Why didn't he join me in bed?*

After donning her clothes, she peeked her head out of the room. There sat Sir and Rytsar, chatting away with glasses of vodka in their hands.

"Drinking in the morning, Sir?" she chided playfully when she emerged from the bedroom.

He looked at his watch and winked at her. "Nope, we never stopped."

Rytsar nudged Sir and asked, "Want to toast to the morning?"

"Why not?"

Rytsar poured two large glasses.

Brie stared at them in shock, surprised that they had nearly finished off two bottles of vodka. "What did you two do all night, besides drink?"

"There was much discussion, my little sub." Sir took the glass Rytsar handed him, and picked up a pickle before toasting. "To my bastard of a friend, who doesn't deserve to lick my boots."

Rytsar's low laughter filled the apartment. "To my grouchy comrade, who needs to find where he misplaced his humor."

The two clinked glasses and chugged. It was perversely interesting to watch, considering how much vodka was already flowing in their veins. They slammed the glasses down and consumed their pickles with gusto.

Sir turned to Brie afterwards. "I'm glad to see you're awake. I've missed your presence."

Brie knelt on the floor beside him and laid her head on his lap, purring when he began stroking her hair. "I'm sorry I missed your conversations, Sir."

"It was for the best, *radost moya*," Rytsar assured her.

Brie didn't feel that way at all. She wanted to learn everything there was to know about these two, and knew vodka made them unusually open and talkative. "So…what *did* you discuss, Master?" she asked provocatively, rubbing her hand against his inner thigh.

He looked down at her with a mischievous smile that hinted at secrets unknown. "We talked about our college days and a certain list that needed to be made…"

"Oh, you tease me so."

"I like to keep you on your toes, téa. It keeps you strong and focused."

She turned to Rytsar. "He definitely keeps me on my toes. Did he tell you about his latest challenge at the commune?"

Rytsar nodded. "I could imagine your pussy quivering for a stranger as he lubed up his cock for you."

"It wasn't just my pussy that was quivering." Brie laid her head back on Sir's thigh. "But my Master never steers me in the wrong direction. I trust him completely."

"It is equally met, little sub," Sir replied, lifting her chin. "You force me to face emotions I'm unwilling to confront."

"We're the perfect team," she said, kissing his hand.

"I would find you two sickening but for the fact you are my good friends."

Sir chuckled. "I would find us nauseating as well. However…" He paused, looking down at Brie. "I can't get enough of her."

Rytsar held up the nearly empty bottle of vodka, but Sir declined. The Russian poured the last of it into his glass and downed it. He snapped his fingers, and from seemingly out of nowhere, his bodyguard, Titov, produced two packages.

"As you know, I have been waiting for this day with impatience ever since you told me you had news to share, *moy droog*." He added with a glint in his eye, "It's taken you long enough."

Rytsar nodded to the guard, and the man handed Brie one of the gifts. She tore at it excitedly, wondering what pre-wedding surprise he had picked out for them. She was a tad shocked when she pulled out a tiny dress of excessive pink lace.

Brie couldn't help but laugh, and shook her head at him.

"No?" he asked in surprise. "Not a problem." The bodyguard handed her the second gift and Brie dutifully opened it.

It was a miniature tux of blue. Brie blushed, shaking her head again.

Rytsar looked utterly devastated and turned to Sir. "No *malyshka*?"

Sir stood up and put his hand on the Russian's shoulder. "No, my friend. I was simply going to ask you to be the best man at my wedding."

Rytsar gave Sir a look of disgust, then turned to Brie with a charming grin. "*Radost moya*, you would have a round belly and we would be anticipating our first *dotchka* if you were mine."

Brie giggled. "Rytsar, I'm not ready to have babies yet!" She held up both baby outfits and shrugged. "Seriously, I'm only twenty-three and I have a film career to think about."

Rytsar motioned her to him. Brie stood up and walked over, leaning close when he said in a secretive tone, "The sooner you start your little family, the sooner they fly the nest." He added for emphasis, "Your Master isn't getting any younger."

"I heard that."

"I only speak the truth, *moy droog*. If your little sub is to stand any chance of being a mother, you need to start making your fucking count."

Brie burst out in a giggle.

"I think I will withdraw your best man status," Sir snarled.

"If you are a man who cannot handle the truth, then yes, by all means withdraw the honor," Rytsar challenged with a wicked grin.

"If you are so anxious for children, why not impregnate one of your subs? I'm sure there are several who would be happy to carry your child."

Rytsar shook his head. "I'm far too young for such commitment, but not to be a *dyadya.*"

"You're a year older than me, my friend."

"Ah, but you have found 'the one' and I have not. A child should be conceived in love, no?"

Sir grunted in agreement.

Rytsar held his massive arms out as if he were cradling a baby. "To hold and spoil a tiny version of *radost moya…*" he said wistfully.

"And if it's a boy?" Sir questioned.

"It won't be."

"All this talk of babies has me craving a pickle," Brie said, grabbing one off the tray and munching on it.

"The day you refuse my vodka is the day I'll know you are pregnant." Rytsar snapped his fingers and Titov fetched a new bottle. "Will you have a drink with me?"

Brie looked at Sir.

"Do as you wish."

Not wanting to be left out, Brie nodded. "Please, Rytsar."

"Although that is not the answer I wanted, I am pleased to fill your glass. Zyr has become my vodka of choice. Let me know what you think."

She downed the fiery alcohol at the same time as Rytsar, surprised that it went down so smoothly, far more easily than she'd been expecting, with only a hint of bitterness afterwards.

"What do you think, *radost moya?*"

She smiled. "It's surprisingly smooth!"

He held his pickle to his lips, so she did the same and they both bit down on the salty treats. Brie giggled as she chewed on the pickle while looking into Rytsar's eyes.

"Do you think you can handle Durov for a couple of days?" Sir asked her.

Brie turned to her Master and replied solemnly, "If he has agreed to the terms you have set, then yes. I trust your judgment completely." She embraced the warmth the vodka caused and added proudly, "I would do anything you asked, Sir."

"Count yourself lucky I do not have a wicked heart, because that statement could get you in a lot of trouble, Miss Bennett," Sir teased.

Brie liked the easy banter that alcohol seemed to bring about.

"I will make the best of the limited access I've been afforded," Rytsar murmured resentfully.

"A tight rein is the only way I would allow you control over her. I know you, Durov."

"*Da*. At least you have agreed to the club."

Brie's interest was piqued. "Club?"

Rytsar's grin was roguishly intimidating. "A favorite underground BDSM club of mine, with a decidedly sadistic slant."

Brie turned to Sir in surprise, her mouth agape.

"You did just say you would do anything I asked."

She trembled as she nodded.

"My requirements of Durov are very specific."

"Too restrictive," Rytsar complained.

Sir assured Brie, "You will not be compromised, but you will be tested." He handed Rytsar all the items off the coffee table one by one, then commanded her in a sensuous tone, "Undress and lie on the table for me, téa."

Brie smiled as she slowly removed her clothes for her Master, wanting to entice them both with her disrobing without making it a blatant striptease, which Sir had not asked for.

He helped her onto the table and ran his hand over her body. "I think we bite her."

Rytsar moved to the other side. "Agreed."

Brie held her breath as both men leaned down and took a bite of her thighs. Neither was gentle as they bruised her skin between their teeth, and she gasped.

"Too much?" Sir asked.

"No, Master."

"I will start at her toes, you go for the neck," Sir instructed his friend.

Brie whimpered when Rytsar stared at her with those penetrating blue eyes before nestling his warm lips against her throat. He started out so tender, lightly kissing and teasing…

The instant Sir bit down on her sensitive arch, Rytsar sank his teeth into her, sucking hard as he bit. The dual sensations at opposite ends were too much, and she instinctively tried to twist out of their reach.

Strong hands held her down, her action only inciting more of their delightfully cruel play. Brie whimpered as Rytsar took samples of her neck, breasts and torso as Sir moved from her toes to her thighs and up to her quivering pussy.

They licked, nipped and bruised her most sensitive areas with those wicked teeth, making her crazy with desire even as she squirmed beneath them to avoid the momentary pinpoints of pain.

Master knew her attraction to being bitten, but to be bitten by these two men—to be marked by their passion—what more could a girl want?

With a husky voice, Sir announced, "She's exceedingly wet."

"We may have a masochist yet," Rytsar said, biting harder until she yelped. Brie shook her head. He chuckled as he moved to a new spot to torture with his lips and teeth.

Sir rimmed her wet opening and she moaned in pleasure as he slipped two fingers inside, but Brie soon stiffened when Rytsar's fingers push their way in too, stretching her tight.

It so closely reminded her of Mary's encounter that her pussy began to pulsate in response to their attention.

"No coming, téa."

Brie groaned as she fought off the urge while both men forced their fingers deeper inside her. She was ravenous to be overfilled by them, and bucked her hips upwards. They obliged her need and began pumping her in unison, rubbing vigorously against her G-spot.

She instantly realized her mistake and tried to pull away, but Rytsar dug his fingers into her waist, preventing her escape.

Brie tossed her head back and forth, and begged them to stop. "Please, no more. No more, Master…"

Neither man listened to her desperate pleas. In a last-ditch effort, Brie stilled herself and tried to concentrate on a spot on the ceiling. She *almost* succeeded, until each man grasped one of her wrists with his free hand and bit down on her sensitive skin.

She. Was. Lost.

Brie came hard, her body clamping down on the four fingers inside her as her pussy gushed with watery come.

Tears rolled down her cheeks from the intensity of her climax and the knowledge that she had failed to obey Sir's command. She lowered her hips to the table in resignation as they pulled out their wet fingers and looked at each other, saying nothing.

What will happen to me now?

"Why did you disobey me?"

Brie did not offer any excuses. "I was greedy, Master."

Rytsar broke out in laughter. "I appreciate her honesty."

Sir couldn't hide his smile as she explained, "I wanted it too much and then I couldn't stop myself when I needed to pull back."

"How shall we punish such wanton behavior, téa?"

Brie swallowed, unsure if her answer would be well received but feeling too giddy to stop herself. "Make me come again?"

This time Sir was the one who laughed.

"You have a cheeky sub, *moy droog*," Rytsar said, chuckling along with him, but then he became scary-serious. "She must be punished."

The smile on Brie's lips disappeared when Sir replied, "I agree, Durov."

Brie whimpered as each man undid his buckle and slid his belt from his pants. "I'm sorry, Master. I was trying to be funny. Please..."

"What you consider humor, I call insolence," Rytsar replied coldly. "This will hurt you far more than it will hurt me. Kneel on the table with your hands behind your neck."

Brie looked at Sir and he nodded. Shocked by the turn of events, she pulled herself up into a kneeling position and clasped her hands behind her—her whole body shaking with fear.

Instead of hitting her with the belt, Sir fastened his around her neck, pulling tightly so that she felt the constrictive pressure of it.

"That is a pretty picture," Rytsar complimented.

Sir reached over and pulled on the belt, forcing her head back. He kissed her deeply, keeping his hold on the belt so that she felt the pressure and knew who was in control.

Damn if her pussy didn't pulsate with desire. She was hopeless in the hands of these two.

Rytsar forcibly bound her knees together with his belt, announcing, "There will be no more release for you."

The men unzipped their pants and presented her with their rigid cocks.

"You will pleasure us at the same time."

Brie beamed inside, realizing they'd only been teasing her, but she continued to act the part of a repentant submissive. She gazed up at them with a remorseful expression, eager to pay for her disobedience.

Grasping both shafts, she began stroking and was rewarded by their low grunts of pleasure. Her pussy ached with sexual desire. She leaned over and licked the pre-come from Sir's cock, then began sucking his shaft while keeping the same rhythm with her hand as she stroked Rytsar.

The luxury of two cocks was deliciously extravagant, and Brie moaned as she moved to Rytsar's shaft, not wanting either man to feel neglected. She looked up as she took him into her mouth.

Rytsar did not move or make a sound as he watched her. It was unnerving, the way he gazed at her so intensely. She knew she'd failed to please him orally the first time they'd scened together, and was determined to show him the full extent of her expertise.

Brie relaxed her throat and took his shaft deeper. Still there was no reaction from the man, just an intensive stare that challenged her. What more did he want?

Her attention to Rytsar did not go unnoticed by her Master, who pulled on the belt around her neck. She disengaged from the Russian and returned to Sir. He pulled back her head as he applied pressure to the belt.

"The challenge is to please us both at the same time," he reminded her. "Not an easy task."

She nodded, amping up her hand motion on Rytsar's cock as she flicked her tongue under the ridge of Sir's shaft.

"Deeper," he commanded.

Brie opened her lips wide and took his entirety.

"Good girl…" he growled.

Brie moaned on his shaft, loving his praise. She added a little twist to her wrist action with Rytsar so he would know she hadn't forgotten him, and was rewarded with a release of pre-come. It lubed his cock, allowing for more energetic handling.

Sir pulled on her belt, forcing her to disengage.

Brie stroked his manhood, using the twisting motion as she returned to the Russian. She started down at his balls, licking, nipping and sucking her way up the length of his shaft. Although his expression remained stoic, she noticed a slight upturn at the corner of his mouth. It was all she needed…

Brie took him into her mouth and began slowly taking him deeper, making him anticipate the constriction of her tight throat around his shaft. She played him as she continued to stroke Sir's shaft vigorously. Opposite ends of the spectrum—one slow and deliberate, the other fast and furious.

When her lips encircled the base of his shaft, Rytsar actually let out a low groan as he looked down at her.

Triumph!

She slowly pulled away from him and returned to Sir. It pleased her greatly to tease Rytsar as she took her Master deep, giving him what Rytsar had only tasted for a moment.

Brie took the fullness of Sir's shaft to the base and then did her signature shallow pumping to tighten her throat around him.

"That's it, babygirl."

She changed the rhythm of her stroking of Rytsar to match the movements of her mouth on Sir's cock. Slow, deep, gentle...

"*Hvatit*," Rytsar snarled under his breath.

Without warning, he pulled on the belt, prying her from Sir's cock. He then forcefully guided her lips onto his shaft and held her head with both hands as he pumped her mouth.

So much for teasing the sadist.

Brie relaxed her throat and looked up at him, taking his hard thrusts with the same grace she'd seen Mary achieve.

I am your vessel of pleasure...

But she had not forgotten her Master, and stroked his shaft with the same intensity that Rytsar was pumping her mouth. She knew that as Sir watched, the sensations of her hand would mimic the feeling of being deep-throated.

"Fuucckkk..." Sir groaned.

Rytsar pulled away from her and commanded, "Stroke it until I come."

She stroked both men with long, tightfisted caresses. She opened her mouth and stuck her tongue out in anticipation and was rewarded with their tangy release. She licked the heads of their cocks, taking as much of their seed as she could. Her chin and breasts were covered in their white reward by the end, despite her best efforts, and the fresh smell of come filled her nostrils. Brie moaned in satisfaction, grateful for the honor.

Sir pulled on the belt and she tilted her head up to look at him.

"Go clean up, babygirl, and present yourself to me when you're done."

Rytsar undid the belt around her knees while Sir released her from the one on her throat. She felt a sense of loss when it slid from her, appreciating the submissive feeling the belt had evoked.

Before Rytsar let her leave, he pulled her to him and murmured, "You are much improved, *radost moya*. Much improved..." She blushed as a smile crept across her lips—gratified that he had noticed her enhanced skills.

Brie hurried down the hallway to the bathroom to take a quick shower, readying herself for more play. She was curious what else the two had in mind, but was disappointed when she returned to discover Rytsar lying on the couch, snoring.

Sir was nowhere to be seen, so she headed to the bedroom and found him lying on the bed working on his laptop.

He saw the disappointment on her face and smiled, motioning her over to him. "Losing his ancestral home has affected Durov more than he will admit. It's exacting an emotional toll he refuses to acknowledge."

"He's lost so much," Brie agreed, curling up beside Sir on the bed.

"Having you here will prove a good distraction. I've asked him to take you out tonight to film a session with one of his subs."

"Thank you, Sir. Will you be joining us too?"

He chuckled. "No, I'll be sleeping." He stroked her hair and Brie felt the familiar tingles down her back start.

She glanced at his computer screen, but it meant nothing to her because it was written in Russian. The fact that he was fluent in the language was just another aspect about Sir she admired.

As the minutes passed, her curiosity got the best of her and she asked, "When did you learn Russian, Sir? Before or after you met Rytsar?"

He said nonchalantly, as if it were a common occurrence, "Soon after I met Durov. It only seemed natural once we became blood brothers."

Brie shook her head, now with a million more questions she wanted to ask, but Sir put his finger on her lips. "I'm not up for a question and answer session right now, Brie. I suggest you plan out tonight's shoot. Rytsar said he was open to anything you wanted to see."

It was with great effort that Brie switched gears, her head still swimming with the knowledge that Rytsar and Sir had a rich history she knew little about. She hoped the Russian would be more forthcoming about their past once she got him alone.

Brie grabbed a pad and pencil from the nightstand and snuggled up to Sir, grateful to have this quiet time together. The fact he enjoyed her presence as much as she enjoyed his was of great comfort to her.

Wicked Sadist

R ytsar was raring to show off his skills for the camera, and wasted no time once he had awakened from his nap. Brie shared her ideas for the scene, but he disagreed.

"No, we start with something simple. It is always best to start that way."

She shrugged. "You're the expert, but I *had* hoped for footage that people wouldn't be able to stop talking about."

He smiled confidently. "No need to fret, *radost moya.*"

His guard, Titov, escorted Brie into the vehicle and then loaded all of her equipment, while Rytsar called to make the necessary arrangements with two of his subs. Brie was taken to an apartment on the other side of Moscow.

"One of my girls is setting up the scene at my old apartment so we can begin immediately," he informed her.

"Great," Brie answered, forcing herself to calm the nerves that had started. She wondered how she would handle watching Rytsar from behind the camera lens. This was a first for both of them.

His sub met them at the door and bowed low at Rytsar's feet. Without verbally greeting her, he touched the sub on the head on his way in as acknowledgement, then began barking commands. The older woman rocked off her heels and quietly closed the door before responding to his numerous requests.

Brie looked around the apartment, noting how small but comfortable it was, with female touches such as flowers on the kitchen table, frilly pillows on the couch and paintings of animals on the walls. Not Rytsar's tastes at all. She wondered if this was a 'perk' to being one of Rytsar's preferred subs.

While the sub busied herself with last-minute details, Brie got out her equipment and starting positioning the reflectors. Rytsar disappeared into the bedroom, leaving the women to their respective jobs. They worked together in silence, but Brie was struck by how comfortable she felt in the presence of the woman, despite their language, age and fetish differences. His submissive seemed almost regal in the way she held herself, but there was no arrogance radiating from her. Rytsar certainly had good taste in women.

The Russian Dom came out a short time later, dressed only in brown leather pants and dark boots. Brie had to admit the dragon tattoo stood out prominently on his left shoulder, only adding to his sex appeal. She was convinced the audience would love him.

When the doorbell rang, Rytsar turned to Brie. "Start filming. Say nothing, just observe what I do. I will explain as I go."

Brie nodded, her heart racing as he opened the door to a young, petite woman. The first thing Brie noticed was her stunning crystal-blue eyes and sensually arched eyebrows. The girl looked to be the same age as Brie, a sharp contrast to the other sub in the room.

Rytsar invited her inside, speaking in Russian. The two seemed to have a casual vanilla conversation as she undressed down to her underwear in front of him. He wasn't even looking at her as they spoke, because he was too busy preparing his instruments for the scene.

The way they interacted was so relaxed that Brie imagined they were talking about the weather or some equally mundane topic. She got so caught up in listening to the lilt of their conversation that she was caught off-guard when the girl suddenly bowed and he directed his other sub to grab her wrists.

What had started out as vanilla and routine quickly took on a kinky tone, as the new girl was forced onto her feet and dragged to the St. Andrew's cross in the corner of the room. Rytsar explained to Brie, "She does not care for other women, and wishes I would bind her to the cross myself." His smile was dangerously charming when he added, "Howev-er...I prefer to see her challenged. She needs to be reminded who's in control."

Rytsar walked up to the girl and spoke to her in English, although it was obvious from her blank reaction that the sub couldn't understand a word he'd said. It reminded Brie of her first encounter with Rytsar when he'd only spoken to her in Russian—adding an element of mystery and intrigue to their initial scene together.

Brie could appreciate how it was adding to this sub's experience. Being filmed by an American she didn't know while her Master spoke to her in that foreign language—it was the stuff fantasies were made of.

Rytsar smiled at the girl as he murmured tenderly, "Ksana, you and I have a unique relationship. Your extremely low tolerance for pain makes our scenes together far too short, and yet…unbearably sweet."

The other submissive barked a command and the girl obediently lifted her arm to be secured to the cross.

Rytsar told Brie, "It turns me on to watch her willingly give herself over to my submissive, despite her inner objection, simply because ksana knows it pleases me."

He walked around the cross, taking in the erotic scene of the nearly naked submissive being bound to the wooden cross by another of his women. Brie could appreciate the sensual power play this was for the Dom. He certainly knew how to push boundaries while still making his submissive hungry to please him. Brie had experienced it herself, and was inspired by the sexual confidence he was showing now.

Rytsar explained, "Whereas ksana has a low tolerance for pain, Dessa has a very high tolerance. It allows me to release my passion without fear of harming her. In fact, Dessa and I can play for hours. Can't we, my sweet?" he stated proudly, caressing the older woman's cheek. "Lift your dress so they can admire our last play session."

Unlike the girl, this sub understood English, and stopped the binding process to lift her dress above her head. She turned her back to the camera to show off her marks.

Brie had to hold in her gasp as she focused the camera's lens on the dark red marks covering the woman's shoulders and curvaceous buttocks. Just seeing them caused goosebumps on Brie's skin.

"Aren't they beautiful?" Rytsar stated affectionately, lightly caressing the marks he'd left during a previous session.

Dessa smiled at Rytsar after pulling down her dress, and he kissed her tenderly before leaving her to return to her task of binding the girl.

Rytsar approached ksana with a ball gag in his hand. "You will be screaming, slave, and we don't want to disturb our neighbors." He lifted the large rubber ball to her mouth. "Open."

The girl didn't have to understand English to know what he wanted. She opened her beautiful pink lips and accepted the gag, her chest rising and falling rapidly as he secured it around her head.

Rytsar turned to Brie. "She's scared. She knows I will hurt her today, and yet she cannot resist the craving. It is…intoxicating for us both."

He stood back to admire her. The girl's nipples were hard, indicating both her fear and anticipation. "You look exquisite bound to my cross, as you wait for my pleasure."

Rytsar left her to pick up an instrument Brie had never seen before. The long, thin wand was red and triangular-like in shape, but she had no idea what it was used for. As soon as the submissive saw it, however, she started whimpering, struggling against her bonds as tears formed in her eyes.

Brie noticed that the girl's eyes were riveted to the tool when he turned it on. Rytsar caressed the girl's wet cheek with his other hand. "Yes, you remember this wand well, don't you?"

He shared with Brie, "I allowed her to experience the jolt of the device last time we met, and she didn't care for it." He smiled, turning back to the girl and crooning softly, "Did you, pet?"

The girl shook like a leaf when he brought the tool near her face. She turned her head away, but her eyes remained locked on the tool.

Brie almost felt sorry for her, but reminded herself that ksana had come here to play, knowing full well Rytsar's brand of kink. She figured there must be some addictive aspect to the pain that this girl responded to. Why else would she choose not to end the scene when she was obviously terrified?

The Russian stroked ksana's cheek again and murmured, "She doesn't know it yet, but she will press her breast into it of her own free will today."

The girl whimpered in relief when he turned it off and put the instrument down, replacing it with the Magic Wand.

Brie felt her loins tingle pleasantly seeing the stimulating vibrator in his hand. The girl visibly relaxed as Rytsar knelt on one knee and placed the wand against her lacy panties, pressing it against her pussy. He looked up at his sub and said something in Russian.

The girl nodded.

Rytsar informed Brie, "I explained to ksana that when she orgasms, it will signify her permission for me to continue with the other tool."

Brie licked her lips, now deliciously nervous for the girl. When Rytsar turned on the Magic Wand, its loud buzzing called to Brie. She sighed to herself, wishing she could partake in its wicked vibration.

Ksana closed her eyes, determined to resist the intense tool, but there was no escaping the vibrations, bound as she was. Rytsar growled seductively, saying aloud, "You cannot stop what is about to happen, pet. Fight all you want, but you *will* come for me, and when you do, I will ask you to press your sensitive nipple against the electric prod."

The girl whimpered when Rytsar turned the Magic Wand to the higher setting. She threw her head back, moaning as she fought against the building orgasm.

Rytsar grunted in satisfaction when her thighs began to quiver, and he said proudly, "See how she fights it? She knows that intense pain will follow her pleasure and it terrifies her, yet she is unwilling to prevent it."

All three watched silently as the girl shook her head, trying to stave off her impending orgasm. Her body became drenched in sweat from the effort as her thighs shook with more violence.

Rytsar boasted, "She's stubborn and I admire her for that. Fear of pain is a powerful motivator, but it also causes the orgasms to be that much more intense."

Brie was impressed by the girl's tenacity. There was no way she could have lasted as long under the relentless vibration of the Wand on its highest speed. Finally, there was a deep groan from the young sub as her body tensed for an orgasm that could not be denied.

Rytsar stared at the girl's mound with uninhibited lust.

Her cries were muffled by the large ball gag as she stiffened, just before a gush of juices soaked her panties and Rytsar's hand with her powerful climax. It was damn sexy to watch.

Afterwards, he stood up and picked up his wicked tool, turning it on. The girl started whimpering again.

"You know what you must do."

She stared at the tool, tears falling freely.

He put the instrument near ksana's left breast, her nipple poking through the thin material of her bra. Rytsar nodded his head towards it and smiled encouragingly to her.

The girl hesitated before lifting her shoulder so that her tender nipple came into contact with the end of the tool. Her muffled scream stirred something in Brie.

"Again," he told her, moving the device to her other breast.

The girl pleaded with her eyes, shaking her head, but Rytsar was silent as he waited patiently for her to comply.

The sub gulped between sobs as she slowly brought her right nipple into contact with the electricity.

"Good girl," Rytsar praised when her muted scream filled the apartment. He immediately turned off the device and grabbed her throat, biting her neck passionately. The girl seemed to melt into him, her tears suddenly forgotten.

"Turn off the camera, *radost moya*."

Brie pressed the off button as Rytsar took off the ball gag, wiping the excess spittle from ksana's mouth before bending down and releasing her ankles. He unbuttoned his pants and pulled out his hard shaft.

With her wrists still bound to the cross, he lifted her knees to her chest, then pushed aside the lacy material of her thong.

Holding her in that position, Rytsar penetrated her dripping-wet pussy. They both cried out in pleasure as he sank his cock deep into her and began thrusting. He growled something into her ear as he pounded the girl with vengeance, his muscles churning from effort as he fucked her.

Good lord, that's how he looks when he takes me, Brie thought to herself.

She found it too erotic to watch, so Brie shifted her gaze towards the kitchen and thought of omelets…

The Lake

Rytsar drove with Brie to the cabin the next morning. It was difficult to leave Sir behind, the only consolation being that he would join them as soon as his meetings were finished.

"Be good, babygirl."

"I don't think I'm the one you have to worry about, Sir."

He chuckled and pulled her to him. "I'd trust that man with my life."

She stood on tiptoes and kissed her Master gently on the lips. "If you trust him, then I trust him."

"That isn't to say I didn't set strict parameters for Durov. I may trust him, but I'm not an idiot."

"I disagree," Rytsar stated, coming up behind them and slapping Sir hard on the back. "Based on your extensive list, there is little trust between you and I."

Sir laughed. "I relish the idea of you struggling to meet your needs under the confines of my limits."

"You are no friend."

Sir looked down at Brie. "I want you to be open to his lessons, téa. He is not your Master in my absence, but I have given him permission to train you."

Brie's stomach did a flip. "I will do my best to learn, Master."

Sir played with the collar around her neck. "Be true to yourself—it's all I ask."

Tears filled her eyes. "I love you."

He kissed her, drawing out the tenderness of the connection before letting her go. "Until we meet again…"

Rytsar was unusually quiet on the drive up to the cabin. She wasn't sure if he was contemplating the days ahead or if he was preoccupied by the loss of his familial home. Either way, she wanted him to know she was there as support. She did not stare out of the window but sat quietly, her eyes on her lap but her focus completely on Rytsar.

He cleared his throat and took her hand, placing it on his muscular thigh. There was no other contact made and no words shared, but that simple act touched her deeply.

When they pulled up to the secluded cabin—his birthday gift to her— Brie let out a surprised gasp.

Rytsar smiled as one of his guards opened the door, and helped her out of the vehicle.

"What's this?" she asked the Russian Dom, staring at an elaborate wooden swing set with a big slide and jungle gym attached.

"I made the assumption my comrade had done right by you, and simply wanted my little niece to have her own swing set when she comes to visit her *dyadya*."

Brie burst out laughing. "Even if I were pregnant, it would be a while before she was old enough to use this."

He led her to the equipment. "Ah, but it is made strong enough for adults." He pointed her to one of the swings.

When Brie sat down on it, he began pushing her. She let out a trill of laughter, feeling as lighthearted as a child.

"I see that you enjoy my equipment, *radost moya*."

She grinned, noting the sexual innuendo behind the comment and answered, "Yes, I enjoy it very much, but that shouldn't surprise you."

Rytsar's eyes glinted with mischievous delight as he held the swing still and ordered her to follow him. They walked beside the shore of the lake in silence.

"Did your Master tell you what is on the list?" he asked.

Brie sighed nervously. "No, he didn't."

Rytsar nodded his head thoughtfully. He led her out onto a wooden pier, his expression solemn and somewhat frightening when he told her, "I was instructed to challenge you."

"I was afraid of that."

"One area in particular."

Brie swallowed hard, dreading his answer. "Which one?"

"Watersports."

She stared at him in shock. "But Sir knows I struggle in that area."

"Precisely."

"It's not even something I'm interested in."

"I am quite aware of that."

Brie stared at the calm lake water, feeling anything but serene.

"You should know that your Master has kept that side of himself hidden, knowing how you feel."

She shifted uncomfortably beside him. It suddenly made sense that Sir hadn't explained what would happen at the cabin. He was ashamed of his own desires. Yet, it was a fetish she'd never imagined Sir enjoyed—not in a million years.

"It must be important to him," she mused out loud.

Rytsar said nothing.

Brie was put off by the idea of watersports and had no desire to pursue it. Still…if it was something that turned Sir on, shouldn't she at least keep an open mind? Wasn't that her duty as his collared submissive *and* lover?

"Be gentle with me, Rytsar," she pleaded. "You know this is uncomfortable territory for me."

"Gentle? I'm sorry, *radost moya*, I cannot be gentle."

Brie screamed when he swept her off her feet and tossed her into the water. She came up sputtering and gasping for air to the sound of Rytsar's boisterous laughter.

It wasn't until then that she understood. Brie ignored the hand he held out to her and swam all the way back to shore. She'd stomped halfway to the cabin before he caught up with her.

"Now, now…" he chuckled, encircling her in his arms.

Brie struggled, but could not break free. She pounded his chest with her fists out of frustration. "That wasn't nice!"

The low timbre of Rytsar's laughter was sexy, but insulting in its mirth.

"I can't believe you did that to me," she cried, pounding harder.

Rytsar grabbed her wrists and held them up so that her face was inches from his. "I am not to blame, since I've been forced to derive pleasure based on the strict limits your Master's given me."

"But to joke about that?"

"Admit it was funny."

Brie shook her head violently, droplets spraying everywhere. "No, it wasn't!"

"It was," he insisted.

She looked up at him and repeated, "No, it wasn't."

"Watersports…"

Brie's frown slowly cracked into a smile against her will, as a drop of water traveled from her bangs down her cheek. "Yeah, watersports." She giggled as he escorted her to the cabin.

Before they reached the door, she asked, "Just so we're clear. You're not going to start peeing on me, right?"

He stopped and answered seriously, "Only if it would turn you on."

Rytsar said it with such conviction that she wondered if it was a kink he practiced himself. For a fraction of a second she actually considered it, but shook her head, shocked at his power over her.

She suspected that the Russian Dom could convince her to try anything, no matter her level of opposition. It made the man dangerous in her eyes.

Rytsar informed Brie that he was taking her to the underground BDSM club that evening. "Part of the reason I chose to buy this particular plot of land was the proximity to the club which meets a half-hour from here." He chuckled wickedly. "This is like nothing you are used to in America. It's been in existence for over a hundred years and distinguishes itself with its authoritarian rules."

Brie was intimidated at the thought of facing such a foreign environment, terrified that she would fail. She was desperate not to disappoint Rytsar—or Sir. "What are the protocols?" she asked him. "Just how authoritarian are they?"

Rytsar chuckled again, enjoying her discomfort far too much. "In this club you must stand three feet behind me, and keep your gaze down at all times. They will respect your collar, but won't hesitate to physically punish any sub who steps out of line."

Brie's anxiety increased two-fold.

"No need to worry," he said soothingly. "Unless, of course, you forget yourself and make eye contact."

"You're not helping," Brie groaned. "You know what a challenge that is for me." She looked at him suspiciously and asked, "This isn't another one of your jokes?"

Rytsar shook his head. "No, *radost moya*, this is very serious. I will not be able to protect you if you insult one of the other Dominants at the club."

"Why take me, then?"

"Were you not the top of your class at the Submissive Training Center?"

His question both challenged and grounded her. Brie hadn't been in a formal setting in months, but she understood her place. Although she was afraid of accidentally breaking protocol, she was a competent submissive. She smiled at him, feeling her confidence grow when she answered, "Yes, I was."

"They will be observing your every move tonight."

The thought of accidentally making a mistake and being punished by a sadist frightened her. Rytsar read the fear playing across her face and grasped her chin, forcing her to look into his pale blue eyes.

"It is very simple. Keep your gaze focused on the heel of my boots, and your hands behind your back. Do not speak. Although my friends will be admiring your body, they will not engage you." She breathed a sigh of relief until Rytsar added, "In my circle, eye contact is a grave sign of disrespect and will be brutally punished."

Brie felt the panic start to rise again.

"But you will not fail in this," he stated firmly. "Even when we scene tonight, you will keep your gaze down at all times."

She squeaked out, "We're scening together?"

"Naturally my comrades want to observe you at play."

"What kind of scene?"

"One you're already familiar with," he assured her.

"But which one?" she pressed, frightened it might be his cat o' nines.

His lip curled into a seductive smile. "The cane."

Brie wasn't sure if a cane was any better than the cat o' nines in the hands of Rytsar. "I can still call out my safeword, can't I?"

"Of course, *radost moya*, but you will not. Tonight I'm going to teach you to enjoy the pain."

Brie trembled at the confidence behind his words. She had no doubt that she would be crying out in both passion and pain this evening. Although she feared what the Russian Dom had planned, the prospect of scening with him again was thrilling.

Rytsar smiled at her. "You are agreeable, then. That pleases me."

She felt the butterflies start. Why his praise had that kind of effect on her was a mystery, especially knowing his brand of kinky play. However, she had to silently thank Rytsar. By placing her in a new environment and setting up a challenging scene for her, he'd effectively sent Brie back to her training days.

It was strangely exhilarating to find herself in unknown territory again.

Savior

B rie was a bundle of nerves when they pulled up to an ancient stone building that looked suspiciously like a church, with its lone spire and stained glass windows lining each side. Had Brie been a simple tourist driving by, she would never have suspected that sadistic kinkiness happened within its majestic walls.

Rytsar helped her out of the vehicle with a devilish twinkle in his eye. "Are you ready to make me proud, *radost moya?*"

She smiled demurely, even though her entire body was buzzing with apprehension. She followed behind him at the required three-foot distance, while his entourage took their place behind her—a wall of protection she deeply appreciated.

Before they entered the building, Rytsar stopped and took off Brie's coat, grabbed the material of her bodice and pulled it down to expose her breasts. Her nipples instantly hardened, not liking the cold night air.

He smiled mischievously. "It's a requirement of the subs here."

Brie understood that nakedness was an effective method of humbling a sub, so she accepted the exposure with grace. She was determined not to draw attention to herself, but to keep her confidence nonetheless.

Rytsar used the huge iron knocker to announce their arrival, and the air reverberated with the deep sound of it as it shook the wooden door. A peephole immediately opened, and Brie dropped her gaze to the ground. Rytsar was asked a series of questions in Russian. After answering them, the heavy door swung open and he was invited inside.

The Russian Dom walked over the threshold without looking back. Brie's heart raced as she dutifully followed, staring hard at the heels of his boots. The conversation in the large gathering suddenly stopped, and Brie felt the heavy stare of everyone in the room as Rytsar spoke to the assembly.

Although she could only understand a few words, she did pick up Sir's name and 'American'. There were several manly grunts, then Rytsar strode to the back of the building. Brie struggled to keep up, disappointed that his men stayed behind, guarding the entrance. She suddenly felt vulnerable without them.

Keeping her eyes glued to Rytsar's boots, she still managed to catch glimpses of what was happening around her in her peripheral vision—there was a naked girl locked in a cage on the left, and a whipping pole with two scantily clad subs attached on the right.

From the sounds of the play, this environment was much rougher than anything she'd imagined. Brie's nipples hardened in fear when she heard a girl gagging as if being choked to within an inch of her life.

Yes, it was *much* darker play…

Rytsar strode up to an area in the back, where he stopped to talk to several men, leaving Brie free to observe covertly while she maintained her assigned stance.

To her immediate right, she saw the sweaty thighs of a woman. Her legs were spread wide and secured tightly with leather bindings. The sub was grunting from effort and discomfort as her Master slowly forced his fist inside her. Brie had never witnessed a fisting and found herself riveted to the spot.

It seemed crazy that people were engaged in normal conversation around her as this woman strained to take the unnatural girth of the man's large hand. Brie inched a fraction closer, wanting to get a better view.

She noticed the sub's pussy lips were glossy with lubricant, but stretched unbearably thin as her body tried to accommodate him. The woman lifted her hips, pushing against his hand in an attempt to break through her body's resistance.

He murmured low, nasty Russian words to the woman as he used a twisting motion to loosen her as he pushed farther in. Brie struggled to breathe as she watched his huge hand slowly disappear inside her pussy.

What does fisting feel like? she wondered.

Brie had never bothered to ask Mary, because she'd found the practice too kinky for her tastes, but being here and seeing it happen in front of her eyes suddenly had Brie curious.

The woman began tossing her head wildly, grunting as the thickest part of his hand slipped all the way in, yet she never called her safeword. Brie assumed the scene was nearly over, but his hand continued its relentless progress until his wrist disappeared into her as well.

Brie swallowed hard when he started pumping his fist.

303

The woman's scream was muffled by a gag. Brie dared to glance up momentarily and saw that the sub's eyes had rolled back in her head. Brie looked back down at Rytsar's heels again, disturbed yet turned on by it.

The man did not slow down, mercilessly thrusting as the sub continued her muffled cries. It shouldn't have been sexy, but Brie felt wetness between her legs. The girl's willingness coupled with the man's ruthless desire was strangely arousing.

Brie could appreciate that when a sadist and a masochist got together, it was a fierce but sexually alluring dance.

She noticed Rytsar move away from the group of men and she obediently followed, still affected by the impassioned cries of the woman behind her. Rytsar led her to another section of the building, where a scene involving a stockade was in progress.

The sub was locked into the wooden device, but not in the normal kneeling position. She was facing upward in a pose much more difficult to hold. Brie instantly recognized the beauty of it for the Dom, because it left the sub's mound exposed for punishment.

"Higher and wider," the burly Russian barked. Brie was surprised to hear English and had to fight off the urge to look up. She wondered if he was doing it for her benefit, as Rytsar's guest.

She watched as the girl repositioned herself and lifted her pussy higher, her leg muscles straining with the effort. A flogger snapped across her bare mound, and the girl flinched. The strokes came faster and harder, reddening her pussy and thighs.

The sub's legs began to quiver as she forced herself to stay in place and take the wicked lashing. When her hips dropped just a fraction, he stopped and commanded her to reposition before starting up again.

If the sub's pussy hadn't been so wet, Brie would have considered his play too ruthless. However, she could not deny that the girl was not only taking her Master's punishment but enjoying it, based on the lustful expression on her face.

Rytsar had assured her that he would be able to train her to enjoy the pain. Brie shuddered as the flogger fell again, desperately hoping he was right.

There was a knock on the large door. After a short exchange, a new man wearing a superior smile entered, followed by his cowering sub. She removed his coat first and then hung up her thin shawl next to it, revealing that she was completely naked underneath. He led her to the center of the room by a leash and jerked roughly on the chain. She obediently fell to her knees.

He barked a command in Russian.

Those near her moved to allow the girl room as she listlessly leaned forward until her ass was in the air with her chin touching the stone floor. She grabbed her buttocks and pulled them apart to display herself to the men.

Rytsar's full attention was focused on the Master, not the girl. He stepped back and put his hand on Brie's shoulder and commanded, "Stay."

As Rytsar approached the new visitor, he asked warmly, "What do we have here?"

The man grinned. "I have a slave in need of a Master. Notice how tight it is." He pointed to the girl's sex. "Sewed it myself. Makes for a more satisfying claiming."

Rytsar stared at the girl's pussy as if he were genuinely interested. Brie squirmed, not caring for his interest in the girl. It was painfully obvious the sub was very young. However, it wasn't just her age that was disturbing. There was no expression of pride or joy on her face. The girl only conveyed resignation—and fear.

"Is she willingly compliant?" Rytsar asked.

The man stated proudly so everyone could hear his answer. "Oh, it obeys flawlessly. Would even die for me if I asked." As proof, he stepped on the girl's head, grinding her face into the stone floor.

The girl didn't move or make a sound, but when he pulled away she said, "Thank you, Master. Your pleasure is my pleasure."

Rytsar snorted, unimpressed. "Is she only motivated by fear?"

"This one has grown to love me over the past several weeks," the man declared, pulling on the leash. The girl stared up at him, her eyes communicating dread with a hint of longing.

Rytsar laughed amiably. "Survival instinct isn't love, idiot."

The man shrugged. "Who cares why it submits, as long as it obeys every command impeccably?"

Brie gasped when the man kicked his submissive hard in the ribs. The girl only grunted, returning to her position. "Thank you, Master. Your pleasure is my pleasure."

The man smiled at Rytsar. "See? The perfect slave."

Rytsar walked around the girl, studying her carefully. "How long did it take to break her?"

"Wasn't much of a fighter. Not long."

Rytsar nodded as if he liked the answer. "So how much are you asking?"

The man's triumphant smile sickened Brie as he explained, "I had to travel a distance to attain it, and then there was the training…"

"How much?" Rytsar repeated.

"For you?" The man grinned confidently as he leaned forward and whispered in Rytsar's ear.

Upon hearing the price, Rytsar immediately snapped his fingers and one of his bodyguards came up, handing over a wallet stuffed with bills.

The girl's Master held out his hand, a condescending smirk on his face as he anticipated what looked to be a healthy payment.

"Before I conclude our transaction, tell me how you acquired the girl. I want to know her history."

"Simply an exchange student from Kazan."

"And her given name?"

"What does it matter?" the man scoffed.

"I'll pay you extra for the information."

The man pulled out a small notebook and flipped through the pages. "Stephanie."

The girl twitched but remained silent at his feet.

Rytsar stared down at her with a grave expression, then asked the man, "Do you feel any remorse for what you do?"

"What?" He laughed, looking at Rytsar as if he were joking. "I only provide what my comrades want." He glanced around at the women chained to equipment and huffed. "It's no different. I do not see victims in the world, only opportunities. If it's stupid enough to fall into my trap, it deserves its fate."

Rytsar's voice was deceptively pleasant when he said, "I agree, comrade. If you are foolish enough to walk into a trap, you deserve no mercy."

The man laughed, slapping Rytsar on the back. "*Da!*"

Rytsar handed the money back to his guard, looking down at the girl again. "I never play with a broken puppet. I find them disgusting, but the man who commands one is beneath contempt."

The man snorted angrily. "What do I care what you think? I have thousands who would pay good money."

"And each one is as vile as you."

"*Yeb vas,*" the man snarled. "I refuse to waste any more time with you." He called out to the others, "Who wants to bargain? You won't be disappointed by its service." He repeated himself in Russian when no one responded.

"A man without a soul endangers us all," Rytsar stated coldly.

Without warning, Rytsar hit the man with a sharp uppercut to the jaw, snapping his neck around severely. He crumpled to the floor like a ragdoll and did not move.

"No mercy," Rytsar spat as he walked away. He snapped his fingers, bloody from the impact, and two of his guards grabbed the man's arms and started dragging the lifeless body towards the entrance.

The tension in the room began to rise and angry murmurings began as the shock of what had just happened sank in. Rytsar faced them, his eyes flashing as he shouted to the crowd in his native language.

Rytsar turned to Brie, watching with satisfaction as his guards carted the man's prostrate body away. Under his breath he growled, "I refuse to condone human trafficking by standing idly by." He glanced at the cowering girl, still spreading herself out for the men.

"Kneel," he commanded as he walked up to her. The girl hesitantly got up from her display position and knelt at his feet, visibly shaking. He placed his hand on top of her head. "I am your protector. You are safe now."

She let out a tiny gasp as tears fell down her cheeks, but she dared not look up at him.

No one moved or spoke as the seconds passed, the gravity of the situation hanging over them like a dark cloud. When the two guards returned, the severity of their faces confirmed that the man was dead. Brie noticed that Titov held the man's notebook in his hand.

She shivered, unsettled that Rytsar wielded that kind of power. It made him far more dangerous.

He told Titov, "Look through the notebook. If you can't find what you need, call our contact in Kazan to find out who she is. I want her family contacted and their flight arranged. Also, ready my surgeon. Those stiches are to be removed when you reach Moscow."

Rytsar looked his men in the eye before instructing them. "I want both of you to go. Don't leave this one unattended—not for a second. They are fragile at this point."

"Understood," Titov answered gravely, picking up the whimpering girl from the ground and cradling her in his arms. Rytsar escorted them out, lightly touching the girl's forehead and whispering something to her before they left. The girl turned back to stare at Rytsar with a look of blind adoration as she was carried out.

After they were gone, Rytsar called Brie to him. Her heart raced as she approached the Dom, her eyes riveted to the ground. He grasped the back of her neck with the same bloodied hand that had just killed a man, sending spine tingling chills through her.

"We are done here," he announced grimly.

The Dominants gathered around Rytsar and pounded their chests three times in unison. He nodded solemnly to them. Brie took it to mean what had happened would remain between them.

Once outside, Rytsar took a deep breath as he gazed up at the stars.

Brie wondered what he was thinking, but was too shaken to speak. The remaining guard helped Brie with her coat and asked Rytsar, "Should I call for another vehicle?"

"No, we will walk," Rytsar replied, starting forward.

Brie knew the cabin was a fair distance away, and the night air below freezing, but she did not offer any complaints as she attempted to match his stride. His guard followed them at a distance.

Walking silently on the dark country roads of Russia with Rytsar beside her was surreal. Brie had just witnessed a side of the Dom she'd never seen—never known existed—and although she felt completely safe beside him, there was now an element of danger about him that frightened her.

After several miles, she finally found the courage to ask, "Do you think the girl will be okay, Rytsar?"

He acted as if he hadn't heard her. Instead of an answer, the crisp sound of their footsteps breaking through the icy snow filled the night air.

Eventually, however, he did speak. "It is a long, treacherous road. Some do not survive."

"Why not?"

He spat on the ground, snarling angrily under his breath, "They take their own lives, *radost moya*."

Rytsar's tone stopped any further conversation. Brie had never seen his dark and brooding side, and found it impenetrable. They walked the remainder of the trip in silence. She wondered about his past and how he knew of such things.

To keep from irritating him with further questions, Brie concentrated on the moon-bathed countryside, finding solace in the icy landscape. But when the warm light from the cabin cut through the trees, she squealed and started walking faster.

"Come, Rytsar," she encouraged, breaking into a run. She jogged the last hundred yards, arriving at the cabin coughing out the frigid night air that burned her lungs.

"That was foolish," Rytsar scolded as he walked up.

He helped her out of her coat and boots once they were safely inside. "Bathe to warm yourself," he ordered, smacking her hard on the ass as penance for her rashness. She was grateful to see a glimmer of the old Rytsar when she looked back at him.

Brie escaped into the bathroom and spent a long time soaking in the tub as she tried to come to terms with what had happened. It didn't seem real and she struggled to wrap her mind around the fact a man had been killed and a young girl rescued right in front of her very eyes...

After she'd toweled off and redressed, she went to find Rytsar, but stopped abruptly in the hallway.

The Russian Dom was seated in the main room, hunched over a single pillar candle as he lit it. His low voice drifted through the hallway as he whispered something over and over again while staring at the flame, lost in thought.

Brie understood it was a private ritual, and chose not to disturb him. Instead, she tiptoed to the bedroom and took refuge under the heavy blankets, still feeling unsettled by the evening's events.

Falling asleep proved impossible for her, but partway through the night Rytsar joined her. He pulled Brie to him with his strong, muscular arms and held her tight. His thoughts still seemed a million miles away, so Brie concentrated on slowing her breathing to help him relax. It took a while, but eventually his breath synced in time with hers, and soon after he was snoring quietly in her ear.

It brought tears to Brie's eyes when she heard it.

Whatever dark secrets Rytsar held, she would keep them safe. It was what Sir would want, and what her heart desired.

This Will Hurt

Brie woke up alone the next morning.

Rytsar's guard directed her outside when she asked where he was. She found Rytsar beside the cabin, chopping wood. He was silent, not addressing her even when she called out to him.

Taking the hint, Brie headed back inside, unsure what to do with herself. She was tempted to call Sir to ask for advice, but it proved unnecessary when the Russian Dom returned, noisily kicking the mud from his boots.

"Come here," he demanded in a gruff voice.

Brie quickly made her way over to him and automatically bowed at his feet because of the forceful tone of his command.

"Last night we were to scene together. That was taken from me. We will do it—now."

Brie looked up, a warm flush on her cheeks, remembering Sir's requirement of remaining true to herself. "You told me that you would make me enjoy the pain, but that frightens me, Rytsar."

For the first time since the incident, Rytsar broke into a smile. "Your fear is like sweet ambrosia to me."

Again, Brie was struck by the unsettling fact that her fear acted as an aphrodisiac.

"This will hurt, *radost moya*."

He said it so causally, as if it were a romantic invitation.

"I'd be lying if I didn't admit I was scared to scene with you."

"Frightened but willing?"

Her heart raced when she answered, "Yes."

"Then undress and lie on the bed. I will get my tools."

Brie felt lightheaded as she slowly walked to the bedroom. It seemed unreal that she was about to give herself over to the Russian Dom.

She quickly stripped off her clothes and laid them in a neat pile on top of the nightstand before crawling onto the bed. Brie lay there, suddenly feeling naked and afraid. Goosebumps rose on her skin so she hugged herself, trying to keep her courage as she waited.

Rytsar did not hurry, purposely dragging out her anticipation—and dread.

Brie whimpered when he finally entered the room. She noticed that he was holding his hands behind his back so she could not see what he carried. The fact he was hiding it meant he was not going to use a cane for the scene.

Oh, hell, what did that mean for her?

"There are several things I expect from you during this session," he informed her. "First, you will be brave. Second, you will be honest. Third, you will trust me."

Brie took a deep breath, sifting through her misgivings before she replied with conviction, "Yes, Rytsar."

He then surprised her by requesting, "What would you ask of me?"

She had to think for several moments before she came up with her answer. "I understand it will hurt, Rytsar, but I don't want to be permanently damaged physically *or* psychologically." She added with a hesitant smile, "I want to still like you when we're done."

"Hah! You will like me even more when we are finished, *radost moya*," he stated brazenly.

Rytsar laid his instruments on the dresser on the other side of the room, still keeping the items a mystery to her—all but one. He held up his Hitachi and raised an eyebrow. "This will open you up to enjoy my unique attention."

She licked her lips nervously and blurted the first thing that came to mind as he approached the bed. "I remember that you told me once that my body was like a child learning to walk and it needed your guidance."

He nodded slowly, a pleased expression on his face. "I'm impressed you remembered that. It's true. I can help change your body's response when it comes to the pain I inflict."

When the bed shifted with his weight, it suddenly became real to her so she asked another question, stalling for time. "Before we start, can I ask why you enjoy hurting people?"

He paused, tilting his head charmingly. "For me, it is the highest form of submission—relinquishing one's own instincts of self-preservation and self-gratification to satisfy the cravings of another. It is the ultimate power exchange, but means nothing unless it is given willingly. A sacred part of

the person, a part they never share, is handed over to me in the exchange."
He smiled lustfully at her. "I find it my drug of choice."

His words had a hypnotic effect on her. She longed to know the intimacy of that exchange and to share it with the man before her.

Rytsar turned on the Magic Wand and the familiar buzzing filled the room. "First, I reward your willingness." Rytsar placed the vibrator against her clit. She turned her head away, embarrassed by how quickly her pussy responded to the vibration.

"Eyes on me the entire session," he commanded.

She looked at him and lost herself in the intensity of his pale-blue gaze. Her first orgasm followed a short time later.

Rytsar pulled the wand away, telling her, "That is a good start." To her surprise, he placed it back on her clit and ordered, "This time you will come harder."

Brie often found it difficult to come consecutively, but forced her body to relax so that the sensation of the vibrator could take over and carry her on to another orgasm.

Rytsar was talented with the tool, watching her intently and pulling the wand back whenever her pussy started to pulsate with need. He was determined to build the second climax, and was highly skilled at the process, so in tune with her responses that it was as if she were guiding the wand herself.

Brie moaned when he pulled it away again, desperate to enjoy the aching release he'd produced with his tool.

"We are close," he assured her.

She nodded, relaxing her muscles and willing her thighs to stop shaking. When he placed it back on her clit, however, they started trembling again. Brie knew it was going to be a powerful orgasm.

"Come for me, *radost moya*."

Her eyes rolled back in her head as she let go and allowed her body to embrace the climax it had been fighting. Brie's hips lifted as her body came hard against the vibrating wand.

Rytsar murmured passionate words in his native tongue as she orgasmed for him, enhancing the experience and turning her on even more. Afterwards she lay there like a ragdoll, already spent, and they hadn't even begun yet.

"Now that we have your body primed, I will introduce you to the process."

Rytsar left her side and returned with a beautiful set of clover nipple clamps attached together with a heavy chain. She was familiar with them because she'd seen them used at clubs, but she had never experienced them herself because they were notorious for being extremely painful.

Brie looked at Rytsar fearfully.

"You know the bite of this clamp?" he asked.

"Only by reputation. I've never wanted to play with them."

"They *will* demand all your attention."

Brie looked at the clamps warily, whispering to herself, "I hope I can handle this…"

Rytsar grabbed her chin and stated in no uncertain terms, "You will be brave."

She faced his intense gaze and nodded.

Rytsar released his hold, laying the clamps on her stomach. She jumped and then giggled nervously, surprised by the chilliness of the metal.

He pulled a length of rope from his back pocket and bound her wrists together, securing them above her to the headboard. Then he began caressing her breasts with both of his large hands. "Your body is already flowing with endorphins. It's hungry."

She stiffened when he began pinching her left nipple, making it hard and erect. Brie knew he was readying it for the evil clamp, and starting breathing more rapidly.

"Yes, I want you to anticipate the pain."

Brie realized that Rytsar was the opposite of Tono Nosaka in a scene. Whereas Tono knew how to bring peace to her soul as he carried her along, Rytsar enjoyed the thrill of her fear and encouraged it.

Polar opposites with the same end goal.

She cried out when he picked up the clamp—before he even brought it anywhere near her poor nipple.

Rytsar's chuckle was low and charming as he grasped her breast with one hand, squeezing it so her nipple protruded while he opened the clamp and placed it on either side of her innocent nipple. She stared at it in dread, knowing he was about to let go.

"Look at me."

Brie looked up as he slowly released his hold on the clamp and it closed around her tender flesh. Her eyes widened as the pain registered, and she whimpered. She'd promised Rytsar she would be brave, so she silenced her cries, although tears formed as she fought through the sharp, throbbing ache it caused.

"I know your low tolerance for pain, *radost moya*," he murmured as he kissed her on the lips and then left a trail of fiery kisses down her throat to her other breast. "I appreciate the sacrifice of your will as you struggle to obey."

All Brie felt was the sharp pain of that clamp. It took over every thought but one as he pulled and pinched her other nipple.

Oh, God, he's going to do it again…

Brie felt the same wild terror she'd witnessed when filming his sub, as he picked up the attached clamp and dragged the chain across her skin, bringing it to her other nipple. She fought the urge to look and kept her gaze locked on him.

Rytsar's eyes shone with unbridled lust. She'd never seen him look at her that way before and it moved the submissive in her. She longed to please him—to be fully pleasing to him.

Knowing he valued her willingness, Brie forced herself to lift her right shoulder, offering her nipple to him even though everything inside her was screaming to push away.

The smile he bestowed on her was worth the sacrifice.

He lowered the clamp and released. Shooting pain erupted from the contact and she closed her eyes, trying to prevent the tears that now streamed down her face.

"Open."

She forced her eyes open, letting out soft mewing sounds as she struggled with the unbearable pain. "It hurts."

"I know."

The lustful confidence in his voice stirred her loins, and she felt a trickle of wetness. She looked up at the ceiling, doubting she could stand the pain for long.

"I want you to listen to my voice as you come, *radost moya.*"

Brie was unsure if climax was even possible, but Rytsar had commanded her to trust him, so she nodded.

The pleasant buzzing of the Hitachi started up. She opened her legs wider when he placed his hand on her thigh.

"Concentrate on the vibration and my voice."

Brie's clit was sensitive since she had come twice already, but she didn't fight the toy as it pressed against her. Rytsar began murmuring to her in Russian, words she did not understand, but the tone of which was sensual and intimate.

She had been down this path before when she'd tasted Master Anderson's bullwhip. She'd been able to transform the pain into pleasure, but it had been for a brief moment, not with sustained stimulus like this.

Brie laid her head back on the pillow and focused on the vibration of the Hitachi, letting Rytsar's voice carry her as she gave in to the demanding toy. The tone of his voice changed as he sensed her impending orgasm. Instead of pulling the wand away, he pressed it harder against her, coaxing a greater climax.

For a brief moment she forgot about the nipple clamps as the rush of her orgasm crashed over her. Brie let out a long, satisfied moan, basking in the heated release.

"Very good," Rytsar complimented as he turned off the wand and laid it to the side.

She was still floating on the aftereffects of her climax when he reached up and lightly pulled on the chain.

Brie cried out in surprise as a shockwave of pain coursed through her body, all of her attention suddenly back on the clamps.

"These are cruel devices, *radost moya*. When I pull on them, they tighten." He gave another gentle yank and Brie about jumped out of her skin, reacting to the viciously sharp pain.

"Please don't, please don't do that again," she begged, squirming away from him.

"But I must."

"No, Rytsar," she pleaded. "I can't take any more!"

"You are brave," he assured her. He pulled on the chain with a little more force and all her resolve left.

"No more, no more," she cried, desperate for the pain to stop.

"You will come as I slowly pull them off."

"No, I can't!" she cried.

"But you will," he answered with confidence.

She started to panic and begged, "Please don't make me do this, Rytsar. Please!"

"Trust."

Brie choked down her protests. She had desired this experience with him, but now that it was real she wanted to run from it. She glanced down at her nipples, dark red from the tight squeeze that the clovers had on them. She was surprised how beautiful her breasts looked, bound by the cruel metal as her chest heaved from fear and pain.

With tears still falling, Brie looked up at Rytsar again and said, "I trust you."

He caressed her tear-stained cheek and kissed her tenderly on the lips. "*Radost moya.*"

He left the bed momentarily and returned with a shirt in his hand. "When training the mind, one needs to entice all the senses."

He laid the shirt over her eyes. Brie smiled, taking in a deep breath. It smelled of Sir.

Even as she lay struggling with the intense pain, she could appreciate the thought Rytsar had put into this scene. Her wrists were bound, which was something he knew brought her a sense of security. Her eyes being covered gave her a deeper sense of confidence. And now Sir surrounded her with his masculine scent. The pain remained as acute as ever, but mixed with it were these pleasant stimuli she could hold on to.

Rytsar pulled her legs down and lay on top of her, still fully clothed. The pressure of his chest resting against the clamps was excruciating, but she was soon distracted by his insistent tongue as he kissed her deeply.

The Russian was aroused on a level she had never experienced with him. It was almost as if his kisses sucked the life from her soul, and she was willing to be emptied completely.

The hardness of his cock pressed against her mound through his pants as Rytsar began biting her, leaving a trail of painful kisses down to her collar bone. He grabbed her throat with one hand and came back to her lips, his kisses aggressive and demanding as he ground his cock against her.

"Oh, Rytsar…" Brie panted, caught up in his ravenous desire.

"Are you ready?" he growled.

"Yes."

The Hitachi came back to life as he repositioned himself between her legs and pressed it against her swollen pussy.

"No matter how painful it becomes, know that the clovers will not break the skin."

Brie nodded in understanding, taking in deep breaths of Sir as she gave over her will to Rytsar, letting him have his way. He teased her cruelly with the Hitachi, bringing her to the edge only to whisk it away, making her crave the release he refused to give.

She knew he was waiting for her. Waiting until she couldn't take any more and begged for the pain.

"You are a fighter," he praised, "but I will not lose." He switched the wand to the higher setting.

"Mercy," Brie cried when it vibrated against her clit.

Rytsar chuckled under his breath, showing her none.

He's right, Brie thought as her body longed for release, *this is the ultimate power play.*

To experience release she had to submit to his pain, something she would never willingly do under normal circumstances. With her thighs quivering uncontrollably and her body covered in a sheen of sweat, she finally gave in to Rytsar's will.

"Please."

He began pulling on the clovers as he repositioned the Hitachi. The clamps squeezed like devilish vise grips as the raging fire below caught hold.

"Let it happen…"

The intense pain overwhelmed her and a terrified scream escaped her lips when he gave the clovers a final tug, ripping them from her body. In that moment of excruciating pain, she orgasmed with such delicious violence that everything went black.

She heard Rytsar's voice calling her name, but she wasn't ready to come back quite yet, still flying on the cloud of ecstasy he'd created. The Russian called her name again, lightly slapping her face.

With determination, she opened her eyes for him.

Rytsar shook his head as he wrapped his arms around her and nibbled on her shoulder. "Your Master mentioned your propensity to fly, *radost moya*, but I didn't realize you soar as deeply as some of my masochists."

Brie slowly floated down from her sub high, listening to Rytsar whisper to her in Russian in his husky voice. It was a beautiful way to come back to Earth.

She turned to face him and gazed into his pale blue eyes. Rytsar seemed unguarded in that moment. Ever since she'd first met the Russian he'd been daunting and mysterious, but now she saw a glimpse of the man behind the tough exterior.

He wiped away a remaining tear from her cheek. "You were brave."

She glanced away, his praise unsettling—but in a good way.

Rytsar lifted her chin, forcing her to look at him. "I'm impressed."

Heat rose to her cheeks as she admitted quietly, "That pleases me."

He gazed into her eyes, saying nothing. It was an exchange unlike any she'd had with the Dom because it was intimate and real.

"I have known you from the beginning, when you were new and uncertain."

She giggled. "Yes, you have."

"You've grown since. Yet even then I understood my comrade's fascination with you."

"I'll never forget how you made my fantasy come true with such thoughtful accuracy, like a craftsman." Brie laughed to herself. "Of course, I found out you were a sadist months later. I felt kind of sorry for you."

"No need. Taking you so early in your training was a privilege."

"I was shocked when Sir told me that you were friends and that he'd specifically invited you to bid on me."

"We are brothers, he and I. The only person I trust."

Brie smiled sadly. "I'm sorry to hear that."

Rytsar stroked her cheek with his rough hand. "I do not trust easily, and yet I expect it from my subs."

"You are demanding, but you earn that trust."

"Trust begets trust. Therefore I will allow you one question."

In the Woods

"I can ask you anything?"

He nodded solemnly.

Brie looked into Rytsar's intense blue eyes. "What were you like as a child?"

He laughed. "I tell you to ask me anything and *that* is what you choose?"

She shrugged. "I always wonder that when I meet people."

Rytsar rubbed his bald head, a slight grin on his face. "I was precocious. My mother had her hands full."

"What was she like?"

"Only one question."

"But your mother is a part of your childhood," she protested.

He gave her an exasperated look, but his eyes shone with tenderness when he told her, "I would describe my mother as beautiful. Stunning in looks, but it was her passionate soul—and endless patience—that I remember most."

"Did you take more after her or your father?"

"So many questions," he growled.

"But still related to your childhood," she reminded him.

Rytsar frowned, but she noticed the twinkle in his eye when he answered, "The Durov line runs deep, obliterating any genes that cross with it."

"So you look like your father?"

"A spitting image of my father."

"He must be a handsome man, then."

Rytsar's eyes narrowed. "Are you flirting with me?"

Brie shook her head. "No, just stating the obvious."

"Hah!" he exclaimed, but she saw the flash of a smile. "My father was well known for his looks, but it was my mother who stole people's hearts."

"Then you *do* take after your mother."

"You are playing a dangerous game, *radost moya.*" He laughed, then looked away, sighing. "I wish I could show you a picture of her, but the fire destroyed all my memories."

"Then describe her to me," Brie encouraged. "Help me see her in my mind."

"Ah, well, she had extraordinary pale gray eyes and playful arched eyebrows that could charm the bitterest man. Her high cheekbones complemented those soulful eyes, but it was her smile that bewitched and conquered all who met her."

"She sounds stunning."

"Her looks only hinted at the exquisite soul underneath." He looked at Brie with a serious expression. "But nothing could withstand my father's will, not even her. You see, a woman does not choose a Durov, she is chosen. Needless to say, when my father met my mother, her fate was sealed."

Rytsar abruptly changed the direction of the conversation. "If it weren't for her patience and understanding, I would be a different man, *radost moya.* Never underestimate the power you will have as a mother."

Brie blushed, embarrassed he was bringing up the prospect of her motherhood again.

"I have brothers," he told her. "Did you know that?"

Brie shook her head.

"*Da,* four of them."

"Wow, I can't even imagine." Brie was enchanted by the thought of there being four more Rytsars in the world, but wondered why she had never met them. Not wanting to lose this rare peek into his life, she said, "Your mother must have been an exceptional woman to raise so many strong-willed men."

"You will be too," Rytsar stated confidently. "I look forward to seeing you with your offspring."

"So where is she now?" Brie asked, secretly hoping he would offer to take to her to meet his mother.

"What has that got to do with my childhood? We're done."

"But—" She wasn't ready to give up her aftercare so soon and quickly changed tactics, laying her head on his muscular chest. "Thank you for guiding me through the scene, Rytsar."

A low rumble of satisfaction emanated from deep within his chest. "Now that you've made it to the other side, what are your thoughts?"

"It was an incredible rush, but equally frightening."

"Although I find your tears as charming as your smile," he murmured gently, "with a little patience I could condition your body so that you would come to anticipate my pleasure, not fear it."

Brie lifted her head from his chest and grinned. "Still determined to convert the non-masochist?"

He shrugged. "You are an itch I can't scratch."

She was shocked to hear those words coming from Rytsar. They were the exact ones Ms. Clark had used with her.

"What?" he asked when she stiffened.

Sir had warned Brie never to bring up Ms. Clark to Rytsar, so she quickly answered, "It's nothing."

Rytsar grasped the back of her neck and squeezed, demanding, "What's wrong?"

"I'm not allowed to talk about it," she explained.

"There are no secrets when it involves me," he said, becoming noticeably irate.

"Trust me. It's not worth repeating, Rytsar."

His grip became tighter. "No games, *radost moya.*"

"Ms. Clark said the same thing once."

His tone became cold and guarded. "About me?"

"No, she said it to me off camera, during my documentary interview with her."

Rytsar growled. "Does your Master know what she said?"

"Of course."

"And he still lets you interact with her?"

"Yes, I saw her in Denver during my last visit…"

Brie was afraid to say more and stopped, for fear of upsetting him, but he wouldn't have it and demanded, "Go on."

"She's working at Master Anderson's Training Center now."

He snarled, "I must talk to *moy droog.*"

"Rytsar, Sir believes she's changed, and I would agree after seeing her this last time."

His nostrils flared. "She is not to be trusted, especially not with you. Just because he helped train her, Thane feels responsible, and that blinds him to the truth."

Brie wasn't sure if Rytsar was being overly protective, or if he perceived something Sir could not.

Rytsar asked in a deadly serious tone, "Do you trust her?"

She frowned. "No, not completely." But then she quickly added, "Still, I trust Sir's evaluation of her."

"I appreciate your loyalty, but I will be speaking to your Master when I see him today."

"What do you mean, *today?*"

"I called him this morning to collect you."

Brie was taken aback. "Why?" She was heartbroken to hear that her Russian trip was ending so soon.

"You cannot be associated with what happened last night. No one knows you are here other than my men and those at the club. They will not talk. However, I cannot risk your further exposure."

"So you really killed that man?" Brie asked in the barest of whispers.

"I killed no man, only a maggot."

Brie shuddered, remembering the cowering girl at the club. "I can't believe a person could treat another human being that way."

"The soulless don't have a place on this Earth."

She recalled the look the girl had given Rytsar as she was carried out of the club, and asked, "What did you say to the girl?"

He pulled Brie against him, smashing her face against his broad chest. "I told her that she was never a puppet, only a survivor."

Tears came to her eyes. After the horrors the young woman had experienced, Brie could only imagine how empowering those words must have been to her. "You're a good man, Rytsar."

"Enough," he growled, squeezing her tighter.

Rytsar ordered Brie to ready herself for Sir's return and then meet him outside next to the woodpile.

Knowing that her Master was coming, Brie pulled out all the stops. She took a long bath in scented oils, styling her hair and dressing in her sexiest outfit, even taking extra time applying her makeup.

When she met Rytsar out at the woodpile, he laughed at her. "All that extra primping was unnecessary. Now strip down to your snow boots and take out that fancy doodad in your hair."

"But it's cold," she protested, while still dutifully unzipping her skirt.

He pointed to a large tree and stated with amusement, "It's not cold in the sunlight, *radost moya.*"

Brie undressed, laying her clothes on a fallen log before placing her decorative comb on top. She stood beside the large tree he'd indicated, wearing nothing but her fur-lined boots. Her tender nipples hardened from the chill in the air.

"Much better," Rytsar praised, as he approached her with three long strands of leather in his hand.

She looked at him warily. "We aren't having another lesson on pain, are we?"

He laughed without answering, as he pressed her against the rough bark of the tree trunk and lifted her arms above her head. Rytsar secured her to the tree with the leather, tightening it firmly around her wrists.

The second one he wrapped around her torso, just above her mound. He kissed her on the lips as he cinched it tight. It was deliciously sexy, and she purred when he pulled away.

Rytsar smiled seductively as he instructed Brie to place her feet together, then knelt to bind them to the tree. He ran his hands over her body when he was done, starting from her bound ankles, over the swell of her womanly hips up to the curve of her breasts. Then he stepped back to admire her more critically.

"Yes, a very nice form to be greeted with," he stated, before moving back over to the woodpile. He started chopping again.

It was curious to be bound to a tree, completely naked in broad daylight, waiting for her Master's arrival. Brie looked at the birds in the trees above her and wondered if they found it equally odd.

Rytsar's remaining guard came out and spoke to him in Russian. As he turned to leave, the man glanced briefly at her. Although his overall expression did not change, she could have sworn she saw him lift his eyebrows as he walked by.

She looked back at Rytsar, who was wiping his brow of the sweat caused by the strenuous work. It seemed he was putting all of his unspent sexual energy into the act. When he put down the ax and took off his shirt, Brie was tempted to let out a whistle of appreciation.

He looked in her direction as if he could feel her admiration and nodded with a smirk on his lips before picking up the ax again to chop the next block of wood.

Brie studied his rippling muscles every time he swung the ax. The man was impressive in both form and confidence, as he precisely cut the wood into quarters and stacked them up.

She vividly remembered what he'd looked like when he'd been fucking the sub during her shoot in Moscow and shivered. Soon that would be her—with Sir.

Trinity

When Rytsar had cut all the wood, he slammed the ax into the chopping block and grabbed his shirt. He looked at her with a mischievous grin before walking into the cabin.

Brie couldn't believe that he was leaving her bound and alone in the woods. She looked around nervously, certain the Russian countryside had huge, fearsome bears. Suddenly the sounds of the forest became almost sinister as she imagined a giant Kodiak meandering through the woods, heading towards her.

"Rytsar," she called out. When she got no response, she yelled toward the cabin, "Rytsar, please don't leave me ou—"

It was then that she noticed he was standing by the window, silently watching her as he chugged down a glass of vodka.

Of course...

This was another experience he wanted her to have, to embrace, while he watched over her protectively.

Feeling his eyes still on her, she lifted her head, standing up straighter so that she kept a long, lean line, while she pressed her shoulders against the tree so that her back arched slightly, thrusting her breasts forward.

If she was to be his bound captive, then she wanted to be the best-looking sub he'd ever tied to a tree. Brie closed her eyes and lifted her face towards the sunlight, relishing its warm caress on her skin.

She stayed in that position for what seemed like hours, fighting against the ache in her muscles as she listened and became connected with the nature around her. She secretly hoped that the two men would play with her outside. It would be exhilarating to know that kind of uninhibited freedom.

In the far-off distance she heard the faint rumbling of a car engine.

Her heart rate increased.

Master is here!

What would he think when he found her here, bound outside in nothing but boots? Brie purred at the thought, her eyes glued to the vehicle when it rounded the bend. Sir got out of his car and looked her up and down with appraising eyes, but she was startled when he headed towards the cabin without saying a word to her.

She watched in disbelief as Rytsar opened the door and invited him in, leaving her outside—alone again.

A taste of objectification.

Brie looked at the cabin and felt butterflies when she saw both Rytsar and Sir watching her from the window. She could see their lips moving as they spoke to one another. Knowing they were talking about her as they admired her bound form was incredibly arousing.

The two came out a short time later, both shirtless and holding tools in their hands. She wanted to squeal with happiness, tickled it *would* be an outside session with them.

Sir laid his assortment on the hood of his car and approached Brie with a dark purple flogger in his hand. Brie bit her bottom lip, anxious to feel its caress on her skin.

"Hello, téa."

"Good afternoon, Master."

"Did you miss your Master?"

"I did, very much! Although I was well cared-for."

"I'm glad to hear it." He ran his hands over her tender nipples and she cringed. "I see Durov worked you over this morning."

She agreed, "It was a very challenging session."

"But I heard you did well." He brushed her cheek with his free hand. "Always growing, always expanding your horizons…" Sir bent down and kissed her firmly on the lips, slipping his tongue inside her mouth. Brie groaned, lost in the sensuality of his kiss.

He pulled away and began swinging the flogger back and forth. "Because you have been good, I think you should be rewarded with a flogging."

"Thank you, Master." Brie gazed longingly at him, ready for the session to begin.

He moved her hair back before he started stroking her lightly on the stomach with the flogger, smacking the leather on one side and then the other in a fluid motion. Sir slowly started up her torso, caressing her skin with the multiple tails as he advanced towards her breasts. They bounced erotically when he reached them, sending shockwaves of pleasure to her loins.

Without missing a beat, he started back down, going past her hips down to her thighs. His lashes were becoming stronger, but remained pleasant as he warmed up her skin with the tool. Then Sir suddenly grabbed the tails and stopped.

"Rytsar?" he called.

The Russian came up from behind, holding a wooden crop with accents of black leather and a short tail of gray horsehair on the end. It was a beautiful tool in its own right and she was curious how it would feel.

"We use these on our horses," Rytsar informed her with an impish grin.

Rytsar started by tickling her with the instrument. Goosebumps rose on her skin, the light sensation of the horsehair almost too much to take. She squeaked as he brushed over her stomach and breasts, lightly tickling her forehead and lips, causing delicious tingles that traveled straight to her loins.

Rytsar moved even lower, grazing her mound with the unique tool. Brie moaned softly, liking its gentle caress. That was when he introduced her to the other characteristic of his unique crop, whipping it against her leg.

Brie squealed at the sting of the pretty whip and squirmed against the tree as he continued to lash her with it. Who would have known a tool could be so sugary-sweet and cruelly stinging? She continued to flinch and giggle as he flicked the crop across her skin.

Sir returned with his flogger and Rytsar respectfully stepped out of the way. Her Master swept away the lingering sting by replacing it with the pleasant thud of his sensual flogger, and she purred in delight.

"You like that, don't you, babygirl?"

"I do, Master."

The woods filled with the sound of leather against skin, of soft squeals and whimpers as she took the onslaught of his flogger. He played with different sensations, creating caresses that soothed and lashes that challenged, all the time keeping her enthralled and hungry for more.

Before he finished, Sir smiled at her wickedly. With quick, deft movements he lashed her sensitive nipples, first the right and then the left. Brie cried out in surprise, her tender nipples contracting achingly. He leaned over and licked them both before leaving her side, announcing, "I'm not done with you yet."

Sir retrieved something from the hood of his car and returned to her. She looked at his hand and shivered when she saw the small purple toy was partially made of ice.

"Your nipples look so sexy, all hard and pink. Let's see if we can make them even harder."

They were already so sore from her session with the clovers that Brie begged, "Please, no...Master."

Sir raised an eyebrow, shaking his head in disappointment. "I distinctly heard the word 'no' come from those sweet lips."

Brie realized her error and corrected herself, "I meant only if it pleases you, Master."

"That's what I thought you meant to say." He shrugged at Rytsar. "So, shall we see how hard we can make them?"

"*Da.*"

Brie couldn't breathe as the men descended on her. Rytsar grasped her throat and growled into her ear, "This is what happens to subs who say no."

Sir slid his hand between her legs. Brie struggled against her bonds when she felt the cold ice. The tool had little icy nodules on the end to add to the stimulation. And then...it started buzzing.

Rytsar kissed her hard as Sir rubbed the freezing-cold vibrator against her clit. Her poor nipples contracted into tight buds ripe for sucking. The men took notice and descended on her breasts at the same time, each taking a nipple into his mouth.

With Rytsar's hand still against her throat, Brie's cry was muted when the men began sucking on them. She pressed against the trunk of the tree, overcome by the conflicting sensations coursing through her body—the warmth of their mouths, the chill of the vibrator, the soreness of her nipples and the overwhelming knowledge that both men were going to take her.

Tears ran down her cheeks as the first chilly orgasm hit and her body surged with forbidden pleasure. The men pulled back and stared at her critically.

"First she says no and then she comes without permission," Sir remarked, sounding as if he was stunned.

"You have a very undisciplined sub, *moy droog.*"

"Apparently. Shall we see if we can make her come again?"

"Let's."

Brie shook her head, but Rytsar grasped her throat again, tightening his hold until she offered no further resistance.

The ice-cold vibrator was applied to her clit, and she gasped when Sir turned it back on. The men studied her face while they lustfully squeezed and caressed her breasts, so when that first pulse hit, they both knew it.

Sir tsked. "She seems to have no self-control today. What did you do to her?"

"I made her fly."

Her Master looked at her with sympathy. "Have you been played with too much, téa?"

Brie shook her head vigorously. However, her pussy would not be denied and she came again.

Sir took the toy from her and examined the ice vibrator. He seemed amused. "The heat of your orgasms seems to have melted my instrument, téa."

"I'm sorry, Master."

"I'm impressed, but before we play with you further, you will have to be punished for your transgressions."

Sir undid the leather around her wrists while Rytsar released her ankles. The Russian Dom took the two strips of leather and walked over to the car. Sir stayed to undo the last one, around her torso. As he untied it, he told her, "I enjoyed driving up and seeing you bound, in nothing more than snow boots."

She smiled. "I enjoyed waiting for you, Master."

He led Brie to the car and told her to bend over the hood. She lay against it and glanced hesitantly at the leather straps as Rytsar handed one to Sir. They folded them over like belts and stood behind her on either side.

Brie looked at the reflection in the windshield and held her breath as the two bare-chested Doms cocked their arms back to begin her punishment.

"Why are you being punished, téa?"

"I said no, instead of a proper submissive response."

"What else?"

"I came without permission, Master."

"Correct. Now take your punishment like the good girl you are."

Brie nodded, readying herself.

The two men worked as a team, starting on her ass and smacking her alternately as they moved down her legs with each strike. When they reached the sensitive area behind her knees, she cried out and bounced up and down on her tiptoes from the sting of it. They switched back up to the fleshy part of her ass again and started back down again. Brie hid the fact that she actually liked the feel of the leather and was super turned on by being the sole focus of these two extraordinary Doms.

Once Sir felt she'd been punished enough, he put down the leather strap and picked Brie up, slinging her nonchalantly over his shoulder. He headed towards the cabin with Rytsar following, staring at her like a hungry wolf.

The Russian Dom hadn't been able to satisfy himself with her earlier in the day, and looked determined to make up for it now. She glanced down and noticed just how ravenous he was.

"Yes, *radost moya*, that is for you."

She let out a little gasp and quickly looked at the ground, shivering with excitement. *Hell yeah, this session is going to be hot!*

Little did she know just how hot...

Sir set her down on the kitchen island and both men stood back to look at her while they talked. "I was thinking of starting with fire," he told Rytsar.

"Fine. You light her up while I partake of that generous mouth."

"Done."

While Sir readied the materials, Rytsar walked over to undo her boots, sliding them off and setting them on the floor. He then moved to her head, pulling her closer to him so that her head fell from the edge.

"She's never experienced fire play while giving oral sex," Sir commented as he dipped the large cotton swab into the alcohol.

Rytsar looked down at her. "Good. I like being a first."

Brie squeaked when the cold alcohol touched her skin. Her heart started beating faster in anticipation of the flames that would soon follow.

"Take her slowly so she doesn't move."

She heard the unzipping of pants and opened her lips when Rytsar brought his rigid cock to her mouth. Just as Sir had ordered, Rytsar was excruciatingly slow as he forced his shaft down her throat.

Brie moaned when the heat of the fire raced up the trail Sir had made between her breasts. Rytsar growled in response, liking the extra constriction it caused in her throat as Sir tapped the flames out.

Sir dragged the swab against each thigh next, coming dangerously close to her bare mound. Rytsar pulled out to let her catch her breath momentarily, before slowly plunging back in.

Brie's muffled moan filled the kitchen when Sir lit each trail and allowed them to burn a little longer. After he'd swept the flames away, Rytsar held her head still, forcing the entirety of his shaft down her throat.

The rush of her heartbeat filled her ears as he kept her there.

Sir tapped the alcohol on each of her nipples and lit them on fire. She remained motionless, relishing the feel of heat on her nipples and the fullness of Rytsar's cock in her mouth.

This is what it means to trust and be owned. What a glorious feeling!

Sir cupped her breasts with both hands to put out the fire while Rytsar pulled his shaft from her mouth. She gasped for oxygen, tears having formed in the effort.

"Color?" Sir asked.

"Green," she croaked. "I want more…"

Sir continued with the fire play while Rytsar fucked her mouth with excruciatingly unhurried strokes. She was in pure heaven, and it was evident from the wetness of her pussy when Sir slipped his hand between her legs.

He grunted his approval. "Why don't we try a real challenge? I'll bring her off while you come in her throat."

"*Da*," Rytsar said gruffly, his cock twitching as he pulled out, obviously liking the idea a little too much.

"Téa, you cannot move," Sir reminded her.

She lifted her head and nodded, desperate to meet his unusual challenge.

Placing the container of alcohol beside her, Sir cleaned off his hands before moving between her legs. He gently slipped his fingers inside her moist pussy, then nodded to Rytsar.

Brie laid her head back and opened her lips for him. Just as the head of Rytsar's cock grazed the back of her throat, Sir's fingers began their magic. She struggled not to move as he quickly brought her to the edge.

Her whole body stiffened in response as she willed herself to remain still. Having come so many times already, she knew it was going to be quick and dirty. Brie moaned when she began to climax, feeling Rytsar's warm seed release in her throat, his cock pulsating with each burst.

That was when Sir encircled her bellybutton with a trail of alcohol and lit her on fire. With Herculean effort, she kept her hips from lifting as she came for them—fire, cock and pleasure her only reality.

Sir swiped away the flames with his free hand as Rytsar slowly pulled his spent shaft from her. She whimpered in pleasure, her pussy pulsing one last, glorious time around Sir's fingers.

"I love feeling you come, babygirl," Sir whispered huskily.

Brie pushed back her damp bangs, wiping the sweat from her face. "You are too much for me, Master—I love it."

Sir smiled to himself as he gently cleaned her skin, removing the residue left by their play. Meanwhile, Rytsar grabbed three glasses and filled them up with vodka. When Sir helped Brie off the counter after he was finished, Rytsar immediately handed them each one.

"To my comrade and his lovely submissive."

Brie lifted her glass and easily downed the smooth Russian vodka. She enjoyed the heat of the liquor as it went down, and mused that she was finally becoming a Russian at heart.

Sir led Brie to the couch and had her sit at his feet while he played with her hair. He asked Rytsar to explain what had happened at the club. Afterwards, he questioned, "How is Titov handling it?"

Rytsar sucked in his breath, shaking his head. "It isn't easy, but this experience has been therapeutic—for both of us. If you cannot save the one you love, saving someone else is the next best thing."

Sir put his hand on his friend's shoulder. "So true."

"The girl has a strong spirit and was not in the hands of the maggot for long. There is hope it will not end like it did for Tatyana."

Brie wondered what the story was behind Tatyana and Titov, and how Rytsar was involved. She hoped Sir would shed some light on it later, when they were alone together.

"I don't expect any trouble, *moy droog*. No one will report that the maggot has gone missing, and the girl doesn't even realize he's dead."

"No chance Brie will be associated with this?"

"No. I kept her away from the girl, and my comrades at the club will never speak of it. It's as if it never happened." Rytsar glanced at Brie. "However, I don't like to take any chances with her."

Sir pulled her hair back to gaze into her eyes. "Are you doing okay after what happened?"

Brie licked her lips, still unsettled by the events from the night before. "I'm in shock, Sir, but grateful Rytsar did what he did."

"Unfortunately, it means we'll be heading out tonight. I was hoping to spend more time here at the cabin."

Rytsar stood up and put his hands on his hips, showing off his impressive chest muscles to Brie. "Since that is the case, I would like to sample more of your Brie, *moy droog.*"

Sir nodded and looked down at her. "Are you ready to be fucked, téa?"

The butterflies started as Sir stood up and offered his hand.

Brie trembled as she took it. "Please, Master."

They took her into the bedroom, where both men undressed before her. She swallowed hard, stunned by this rare chance to take in their handsome physiques. Sir, tall and striking, and Rytsar, all muscle and brawn—a girl's fantasy.

It was obvious the men had already talked about how it would play out, because Rytsar lay on the bed, stroking his cock as he watched her.

"Kiss me," Sir commanded.

Brie glided over to him, her body already aching with excitement. Standing on her tiptoes, she leaned up to kiss her Master. He took her face in his hands and kissed her hard, groaning as their tongues intermingled.

Oh, the taste and sound of Sir…

While they kissed, he took her hand and placed it on his hard cock. Brie moaned, loving the feel of his physical excitement. She lost herself in him, floating on an emotional and sexual high as she stroked his manhood.

Her manipulation proved pleasing, as Sir's cock became slippery with pre-come. Brie forgot herself in the joy of his tongue and cock, and started stroking him a little too vigorously. He abruptly grabbed her wrist.

"Too much," Sir growled, biting her on the shoulder as his cock pulsed in her hand.

Once he had successfully averted the orgasm, he gave her one more kiss and then pushed her towards the bed. "Please him, téa."

Brie moved with sensual grace, knowing both men's eyes were on her. She crawled onto the bed like a cat and straddled Rytsar.

"*Radost moya*, kiss your Russian."

Rytsar wrapped his muscular arms around her and kissed her fiercely, taking out his pent-up arousal on her lips. She met his kisses with equal passion, her pussy longing to be taken.

Lifting her waist while not giving up her lips, Rytsar pressed his cock against her wet opening, guiding her down onto his shaft. She opened her eyes and gazed into his pale blue eyes as she took his length. The connection was so powerful that her heart fluttered unexpectedly.

Sir came up from behind, lathering his cock generously with lubricant. He placed his hand on her ass and guided his cock to her tight hole, but once there he stopped.

"Look back at me."

Brie broke the kiss with Rytsar and turned back towards her Master. He swept her hair to the side so he could see her face clearly.

"There's my beautiful girl," he said soothingly, pressing his cock against her anus. "You have such a fine ass, my little sub." He ran his hands lightly over her flesh, which was still pink and tender from her punishment, before grasping her hips and pushing into her.

Both men groaned as the head of his shaft forced its way in. Sir grabbed her throat, kissing her as he rocked his hips, driving his cock deeper.

Brie had forgotten the challenge of taking two men at once and had to mentally relax in order to accommodate the fullness of them. It took several minutes, but once Sir was deep inside her, Rytsar wrapped his large hands around Brie's waist and began thrusting.

"Oh, yes," she purred, when Sir met those thrusts with alternating strokes.

Hearing the guttural grunts of both men as they took their pleasure in her was powerful, and Brie joined in the chorus—the three of them caught up in the erotic union.

Submissive bliss…

Soon, however, the men changed their focus, concentrating their efforts on rubbing her G-spot with their shafts at opposite angles as they stroked her in unison. It was too much stimulation, and she cried out for them to stop.

"Relax," Rytsar commanded, caressing her cheek.

Brie gazed into his eyes again. Did she trust them enough to give over control even when her body was violently fighting against it?

Yes.

She let out a long, drawn-out breath and consciously untensed her muscles, moaning loudly when they amped up their efforts again. Soon her breaths came in sharp, panting gasps as the overstimulation built a raging fire within her. Without warning, her body exploded in fierce, rhythmic waves as she gushed in watery release.

"Fuck, that was a good one," Sir commented, pulling out to look at her still-dripping pussy.

"Again," Rytsar demanded.

Brie whimpered as Sir plunged back into her and they started up again, increasing the tempo as they got her close to the edge. She threw back her head and screamed the second time her pussy rushed with her come.

She couldn't stop trembling after the second orgasm, her mind and body shocked by the intensity of it.

"One more time," Sir suggested.

"I can't…"

Rytsar insisted, "Once more."

This time they did not slowly build up the tempo, but started off fast and furious. The sound of skin against skin filled her ears, and Brie saw stars when she climaxed the third time, covering both men in her sweet-smelling come.

"Good girl," Sir praised, collecting her limp body in his arms and pressing her back against his chest. He nuzzled her neck and kissed her sweaty skin as Rytsar played with her breasts, pulling and tugging on her erect nipples.

"And now we will be gentle," Sir whispered gruffly.

He lightly pushed her back down onto Rytsar's chest and the two began thrusting slowly. Their hands explored her body as they stroked her with their cocks, but they were so tender in their taking of her that it felt as if they were making love.

As Rytsar leaned up for a kiss, Brie was caught by the openness in his gaze. This was the man, not the sadist, who was being intimate with her. Sir lay down on top of Brie as the two men finished off, Rytsar biting her neck on the left as Sir bit her on the right. In that delicious moment, she felt both men come inside her.

It was then that Brie realized Sir had carefully orchestrated this intimate moment between them, and her heart overflowed with love.

A Call for Help

It was with regret that Sir and Brie left Rytsar at the cabin later that evening. As they pulled away, the Russian Dom pointed to the swing set.

Brie grinned while waving both her hands back and forth vigorously in a gesture of no.

"Why is there a swing set at the cabin?" Sir asked her.

Brie giggled. "Well, Sir, that's for the baby he thought we were having."

"Good Lord."

Brie threw Rytsar one last kiss, then snuggled up to Sir in contented silence as he drove them back to Moscow.

"I assume you want children," he stated later, as the city lights appeared on the horizon.

She looked up at him in surprise and smiled. "I do, Sir. When we're ready."

He let out a prolonged sigh, which frightened her a little.

"You want kids, don't you, Sir?"

He turned to her. "I'm not fit to be a father."

"Of course you are!" she assured him, squeezing Sir's arm in encouragement.

"Hell, Brie, I struggle enough with you. What child needs an emotionally distant father?"

"No parent is perfect, Sir, but you have a good heart. That's all a child needs."

He chuckled sadly. "If only it were that simple."

"I firmly believe a child created in love is blessed."

Sir shook his head. "Are you forgetting my mother?"

"No. I can never forget all that you've suffered. However, I'm selfish when it comes to you." Brie kissed Sir on the cheek. "If your parents hadn't fallen in love, I wouldn't be so deliriously happy now."

"To be honest, the idea of children scares me. It scares Durov too, which is why he wants us to have one so he can be an uncle, and not endure any of the complications of parenthood."

"Sir, I think it's normal to be unsure whether you'll be a fit parent or not. All we can do is strive not to repeat the mistakes of our parents, but hold on to the things they did right."

"So you've been thinking about this a lot, have you?"

She shook her head, giggling. "No, it was only Rytsar's incessant baby talk that had me pondering it."

"But you definitely want children."

"Yes." She laid her head on his shoulder, hearing the tension in his voice. "But not until you want to start a family. There's no reason to worry about it now."

Sir kissed the top of her head, saying nothing. Brie was still flying high from the day's events, and randomly burst out in a fit of giggles.

"What's so funny?"

"Oh, nothing. I just love everything about you, Sir."

While Sir finished up with his clients the next day, Brie packed for their long trip home. She looked around Rytsar's stylish apartment and sighed to herself. It was really a shame they had to leave so soon, but she was extremely grateful for what Rytsar had done.

Not many would risk themselves to help another, especially a defenseless girl. In her eyes Rytsar was a hero, but no one would ever know that except the girl, Titov and Brie.

Her thoughts were interrupted by the ringing of her cell phone. It was an unfamiliar number, so she picked it up hesitantly. "Hello?"

"Brie, is that you?"

"Yes." She couldn't recognize the woman's voice because it was so shaky with emotion. "What wrong?"

"They're kicking me out. They say I can't stay here anymore."

She was shocked when she realized it was Mary. "Who's kicking you out?"

"The commune! Master Gannon says I need…" Mary let out a painful sob, "professional help."

"Where are you now?"

"I'm still here, but he wants someone to get me as soon as possible." She started sobbing again. "I don't have anyone...so I called you."

Brie could hear how close to the edge she was, and took charge. "Mary, I'll talk to Sir and see if we can stop by to get you on our way home from Russia."

"How long will that be?" Mary cried.

"We're leaving today. I'll have Sir call Master Gannon once the arrangements are set. Trust me, we'll be there as soon as we can."

"Brie...I need Faelan."

Brie held back the tears, knowing that was not an option. "Don't worry, we'll be there soon."

Mary's voice was listless when she answered, "Okay..." Then she hung up.

Brie stared at her phone, stunned. It'd finally happened. Mary had hit rock-bottom. Brie desperately hoped they would be able to pick up the pieces.

She immediately called Sir and explained the situation.

"You call the airlines, while I find a suitable place for her to stay in LA."

"Sir, Mary's a mess. I don't think she can handle staying with strangers."

"I called Gallant about my concerns with Miss Wilson after we left the commune. He suggests Captain might be a viable option, should she need a safe haven."

"Yes! That's a perfect solution."

"It remains to be seen if Captain is up for such a challenge."

"But he likes Mary, and Candy is a survivor in her own right." For the first time since getting the call, Brie felt a glimmer of hope. "Thank you, Sir."

"The Center always looks after its graduates," he stated with compassion. She heard some men talking in the background and Sir said, "Look, I need to finish up here. Are you done packing?"

"Almost, Sir."

"Don't pack my extra belt."

Brie smiled to herself, suddenly anticipating the long flight home.

She spent the rest of the afternoon going over her footage from both Montana and Russia, having no doubt that Mr. Holloway would be pleased.

However, her mind kept drifting back to Sir. He'd explained to her father that he enjoyed tweaking the details of her life.

Well, that man tweaked them in the most delicious ways...

Brie's City of Angels

Pieces

Brie arrived at the Sanctuary with Sir just as the sun was setting. It had been a long flight from Russia, full of delays and unexpected layovers. Both were exhausted, but Brie felt her nerves hit when they drove up to the rusty gate. What would Mary be like, and could Brie handle her, given her current mental state?

The intercom crackled to life, and the rickety gate opened as soon as Sir stated his name. "Park your car and make your way to Master Gannon in his office, Sir Davis. He's expecting you."

"What about Miss Wilson?"

"She's with him now."

Sir drove directly to the main building, where they found Rajah waiting for them. "Please follow me," he instructed, glancing at Brie briefly with a look of concern. She picked up her pace, troubled by his unease.

Master Gannon greeted them at the door and ushered the two into his office. Mary was looking out of the window, sitting on a chair, curled up in a protective ball.

As soon as Brie saw her, she called out, "It's okay, Mary. We're here now."

She slowly turned to Brie, a look of desolation on her face. Brie raced to her, and was surprised when Mary offered no resistance to the hug she gave her.

"What happened?" Sir asked Master Gannon as he sat down next to the girls.

He took his time to answer. "The community has endured several incidents with Miss Wilson, which leads me to conclude professional counseling is necessary."

Mary buried her head in Brie's chest.

"What was the nature of the incidents?" Sir asked.

"On numerous occasions she hassled and threatened one of our newest members, at one point even assaulting the man."

Sir turned to Mary. "Is this true?"

With her head still buried in Brie's chest, Mary nodded.

"Why, Miss Wilson?"

Mary did not answer Sir's question, choosing to remain silent.

Sir addressed Master Gannon again. "I'm sorry to hear that one of our graduates has behaved in such an intolerable manner, but I wonder if she was provoked."

"He was apprised of Miss Wilson's instability, and immediately stopped all private contact with her. We wanted her to succeed here, Sir Davis. I even took her under my wing once Mr. Wallace left, but Miss Wilson has become unruly, and the entire commune has suffered her irrational rants. It wasn't until she became physically violent that I made the decision to dismiss her."

Sir nodded.

"Unfortunately, this problem is much bigger than we can address here at the commune. I'm sure you agree that she needs professional help and I cannot further compromise the wellbeing of the community."

Mary groaned into Brie's chest.

"We will see that she gets the professional help she requires," Sir assured him.

Master Gannon called to her in an authoritative tone, "Mary."

She pulled away from Brie to face him, answering meekly, "Yes, Master Gannon."

"Although you are being sent away, you are important to this community. You will be welcomed back, should you want to return, but only after your counselor deems you fit and you have a partner who can join you."

Mary sucked in the sob that looked ready to burst forth, and nodded to him.

"All of her belongings have been set beside your vehicle," Master Gannon informed Sir. "I think it's best that you leave now. The sooner Miss Wilson starts on the road to recovery, the sooner she can move forward with her life."

"Agreed." Sir stood and took his outstretched hand. "Thank you for your care in this matter, Gannon."

Mary was slow to stand up, but quietly followed Sir out. While he put her luggage in the trunk, Brie was visited by Shadow. The cat rubbed against her leg, letting out a single meow.

She bent down to pet him, whispering, "It's good to see you too, my friend."

The cat sauntered back to its master, who stood watching the encounter from the porch. "I was told that Shadow had an affinity for you, Miss Bennett."

Brie smiled up at Master Gannon. "He was a great comfort to me while I was here."

He stooped down and picked up the large black cat, cradling it in his arms. "I'm convinced he is an old soul with exceptional intelligence."

"I don't doubt it. I got the distinct feeling he could read my mind."

Master Gannon chuckled. "I feel that way myself at times. The fact that he comes to you when he is skittish around everyone but me, I find utterly fascinating." He scratched the cat's chin. It looked up at him, closing its eyes in blissful pleasure. The strong bond between the two was easy to see. "There are times when I wish he could speak, but I suspect it would lessen our connection."

"I can appreciate that," she agreed.

When Sir slammed the trunk shut, Brie headed towards the passenger-side door, but Mary stopped her. "Sit in back with me. I don't want to be alone."

Sir nodded his approval.

After saying their goodbyes to Master Gannon, the two women piled into the back seat. "Make sure you're both buckled in," Sir ordered as he slid into the front seat and started the engine.

Mary dutifully snapped on the belt, but slipped the shoulder strap behind her so she could curl up and lay her head on Brie's lap. It reminded Brie of the night at the Center when Mary had suffered a trigger while scening with Tono, which had left her an emotional wreck.

Brie stroked her long, blonde hair, knowing what a comfort it was when Sir did it to her. The drive to the airport was uneventful and quiet, almost peaceful.

Sir informed Mary, "You will be staying at Captain's home. Dr. Reinstrum has agreed to begin counseling you again, since he's familiar with your situation and feels he can help."

Mary only grunted in response.

"If you have any objections, you can stay wherever you wish."

Mary said nothing. Brie stopped petting her head and was surprised when Mary quietly pleaded, "Don't stop, Brie."

Brie looked at Sir in the rearview mirror, worried about the girl. This wasn't the Mary she knew. It was as if the life had been sucked out of her.

It wasn't until the airplane was on its final descent into LA that Mary began acting more like her old self and shared some of what had happened with her.

"After you left, I kind of lost it, I guess. God, I needed Razor to take the pain away, but the asshole refused. He avoided me like the plague—like I wasn't worth his time anymore."

"You know that's not true. He was instructed to leave you alone."

She rolled her eyes at Brie, growling. "All I know is how it made me feel…still makes me feel."

"They were only trying to protect you."

Mary snarled in disgust. "The fact that Faelan could just abandon me like that… What the fuck?"

"Don't even go there, Mary," Brie warned. "You disobeyed his direct order and were insolent when he called you on it. I'll never forget the look on his face."

"Don't," Mary snapped, tears forming in her eyes.

Brie took solace that Mary was showing some emotion at least. "You're lucky."

"I'd sure like to know the fuck how," she growled.

"You've got the entire Training Center behind you."

Mary pressed her forehead against the airplane window and said in a defeated voice, "You don't understand. Sometimes a person can be so fucked up there's no coming back…"

"The trainers believe in you. Captain does too. You're not alone, woman."

"What about Faelan?" Mary asked.

Brie hated to be the one to break it to her, but it had to be done. "You have to face the fact that his journey is no longer part of yours."

She turned to Brie, her stoic expression crumbling as she started to sob. Brie wrapped her arm around her and murmured softly, "Shh…shh…"

The people around them started to get visibly uncomfortable as Mary's sobs became louder.

"Miss Wilson," Sir said quietly from the seat behind them. "Although there is a time and a place for tears, now is not one of them."

Mary nodded, taking a deep breath before accepting the tissues he handed her. Brie looked back at Sir, at a loss for how to comfort her friend.

It was a helpless feeling.

Sir wasted no time getting Mary into the hands of Captain, driving straight to his home from the airport. Candy greeted them at the door with a welcoming smile. "Please come in, Sir! It's wonderful to see all of you again."

She took Mary's hands and squeezed them. "You especially, Mary."

Candy guided them into the sitting room, where Captain was waiting. Brie was shocked to see a collar in his hand.

"Before I allow you into my home, Miss Wilson, I insist you wear a protection collar. By accepting it, you are agreeing to follow my house rules, and I am agreeing to care for and protect you. I will only warn you once if you break any of my commands. A second infraction will garner swift punishment, and a third will be cause for dismissal. I do not tolerate disrespect in my home."

Mary stared at him in disbelief as she stared at the collar, but regained enough composure to ask, "What are the house rules?"

"You will not leave this house without my permission, you will perform duties to keep this household running smoothly, you are to remain in my presence at all times unless I command otherwise, *and* you will show the utmost respect to my submissive and myself. Do you understand?"

"I do."

"Do you agree to live under these rules?"

Mary looked apprehensively at Brie.

Brie understood how hard this was for her, and was relieved when Mary answered with a quiet, "Yes."

"Then kneel at my feet and accept this collar."

Brie held her breath as she watched Mary slowly kneel. The girl had never worn a collar—claimed she couldn't stand them—and yet there she was, kneeling at Captain's feet to receive the one he offered.

Captain looked down at her with sympathy, and in that moment Brie thought he was truly the handsomest man on Earth. After he'd fastened the black leather collar around her neck, he put his hand on her head. "Until the day I remove this collar, you are under my protection and care. You are to address me as Vader for the duration of your stay."

Mary gave him a questioning look. "Why?"

"My heritage is Dutch. As I am head of this house and caretaker to you, it is fitting you should address me as father."

The significance of the moment was not lost on Brie. Captain was taking on that role in Mary's life so he could help her to replace the cruel memories of her past with new, healthier ones. However, Brie was stunned to see tears streaming down Mary's face when she lifted her head and said in the barest of whispers, "Thank you, Vader."

Captain spoke to Sir. "Thank you for delivering her to me. My pet and I look forward to aiding in her reeducation."

"Dr. Reinstrum will call you soon to set up her counseling sessions."

"I've already contacted him and it has been arranged."

"Perfect."

"Since you've had a long day, why don't you head home? She will be fine here."

Before Sir agreed, he asked Mary, "Miss Wilson, are you comfortable with us leaving?"

She wiped the tears from her eyes. "Yes. I am, Sir."

"You understand the rare privilege Captain has bestowed on you. I expect you to take full advantage of this opportunity for growth."

Captain placed his hand back on Mary's head. "Between my pet and I, I'm confident we can help her to overcome the barriers that hold her back."

Candy looked up lovingly at Captain. "My Master has a very big heart."

With his hand still on Mary's head, Captain cradled Candy's chin. "You are a pleasure to spoil, pet." He kissed her gently, fingering the collar around her neck.

It was a romantic scene that melted Brie's heart. Yes, there was hope for Mary in this home. Captain was a stern Dom and would not put up with her insolence, while Candy understood the pain of abuse. Together, they could prove to be exactly what Mary needed.

"Pet, you may tell your friend goodbye."

Candy walked over and hugged Brie. "It's so good to see you again. I hope we'll see more of each other from now on."

"Me too, Candy."

Captain looked down at Mary. "*You*, I need to think of a name for." He stared down at her for several moments and said with finality, "Your name will be *lief* in my home."

"What does it mean, Vader?" Mary asked.

"Before I answer, I want you to tell me what you think it means."

She blushed with humiliation when she answered. "Lost?"

He shook his head, smiling kindly at her. "I thought you might say something like that, but you would be wrong. It means well-behaved child. Now, *lief*, say goodbye to your good friend."

Captain lifted his hand from her head and Mary rocked on her heels and stood. The expression on her face was a mixture of relief and fear as she approached Brie.

Brie could appreciate her concerns. Captain had placed the burden of extremely high expectations on Mary, and the girl was unsure she could meet them. Brie whispered in her ear, "It's going to be okay. You're home."

Mary gasped softly, only nodding in response.

Brie had never seen Blonde Nemesis like this before—humble, weak and vulnerable. It was actually endearing, and made her want to hug the crap out of Mary. She surprised Brie even further when she didn't resist the embrace, resting her chin on Brie's shoulder and hugging her back.

Brie closed her eyes and smiled, filled with a sense of real hope.

Ice Goddess

It was wonderful to return to their own apartment. Brie had missed its familiar smells.

"Undress," Sir commanded as soon as he'd shut the door.

She was delighted to shed her clothes, all except the belt she'd worn the entire trip. She had forgotten about it after picking up Mary, but was very much aware of it now as she presented herself to Sir, kneeling at his feet.

"It's good to be home," he said, sighing with contentment as he lightly touched her head. "Stand and serve your Master, téa."

Brie stood before him, purring when he caressed her cheek.

"I have teased you, but now the time has come to satisfy you," he stated as he pulled on the belt around her waist.

"I've been looking forward to this moment ever since we boarded the plane in Russia," she confessed as they strolled down the hall together.

Once they reached the bedroom, he ordered, "Stand behind the bed, legs spread, hands behind your back."

A few minutes ago, Brie had been ready to collapse on her Master's bed and fall asleep. Now she was staring at it with tingles of anticipation coursing through her body.

"I like having an array of familiar instruments at my fingertips," Sir called out as he scavenged through his tools in the closet.

"I like it too, Master."

She grinned when she heard his low, manly laughter.

Sir returned with a spreader bar, leather cuffs, and a bundle of rope, which he laid on the bed before her. He lit a single candle on the nightstand and took off his shirt, exposing his handsome chest covered in dark hair with the lowercase 't' resting prominently over his heart. The sight of him melted hers.

With tenderness, he placed the leather cuffs on her wrists, making sure they were tight, then attached them to the spreader bar. "Lift your arms," he commanded huskily.

This was new for her. Normally Sir used the spreader bar on her legs. She lifted her arms above her head and he took the rope, tying it to the bar. Then he strung the rope through a ring above her head and pulled tight.

"Oh!" she gasped, liking the feel of the restraint.

"Keep your legs spread," he commanded as he pulled tighter, causing her to tiptoe for him. He finished off the knot and stood back to admire her.

"Wait…"

He rifled through their luggage and produced her fur-lined snow boots. "I liked seeing you in these." He slipped them on and laced them up. "There. Now you look the part of my sexy ice goddess."

She basked in his gaze, her stomach fluttering as his hands traveled over her body, purposely avoiding her most sensitive areas and driving her wild because of it.

How was it possible, after all this time, that she still reacted so intensely to his touch? Brie never imagined that love could be this tangible and real—a part of her being. This wasn't lust that would dull over time; this was a penetrating love that now defined her.

"I love you, Master…"

"I love you, téa." Sir turned her head to face him and kissed her passionately on the lips. She swayed in his embrace, losing her balance but completely supported by her bindings—a willing but helpless plaything for her Master.

Sir took full advantage of her helplessness, telling her, "There's one more thing needed to make this scene complete."

He left her side and she listened to his echoing footsteps as he walked out of the room and down the hall. Brie shivered in expectation, wondering what surprise he had for her when she heard his footsteps return.

Sir pressed his body against her back, leaning forward to lightly nibble on her ear. "You're so hot, téa."

She shrieked when she felt ice against her clit and automatically clamped her legs shut, trying to protect herself from the cold.

"Tsk, tsk…"

"I was surprised, Master," Brie explained. "I'm sorry." With determination, Brie repositioned herself, leaving her legs wide open to suffer his wicked attention.

"Did you like Rytsar's ice vibrator?" he asked, pressing the ice against her pussy. "I could always order one for the closet."

Brie panted, forcing herself not to move even though her body violently resisted the spine-tingling chill the ice caused. "I prefer a hard cock and hot come, Master."

Sir chuckled in her ear as he slowly forced the half-moon of ice deep inside her. "Close your legs, téa. Let it melt. I plan to thoroughly fuck my ice goddess."

Brie looked upwards, biting her lip as she crossed her legs together, keeping the ice from slipping out as it chilled her from the inside. Her nipples became hard while goosebumps rose on her skin. Sir took notice and started tugging on her pert nipples.

She leaned her head back, hanging from the bar and moaning as water dripped from her pussy onto the floor.

"You like having your nipples played with."

Brie moaned louder as he rolled them between his fingers and answered, "You know how to send an electrical current straight to my sweet spot, Master. I'm desperate for you, even though I hate the cold."

"I, on the other hand, am anticipating it. Your chilled pussy is going to take a pounding."

More of the water spilled out in response to his words.

Sir played with the rope, loosening it so she was left bent over the bed but not quite touching it. He secured the rope again and stood behind her. "Seeing you bent over like this is such a turn-on, téa. Your perfect ass displayed and your pussy dripping for me."

Brie purred as the last of the melting ice trickled to the floor.

Sir moved into position behind her and fisted her hair, pulling Brie's head back. "Grab on to the bar and prepare to be royally fucked."

Brie wrapped her cuffed hands around the bar for greater support and closed her eyes when Sir grabbed her waist with his other hand, using it for leverage. He waited, building up the anticipation before plowing his hard cock into her.

The warmth of his shaft shattered the icy cold and Brie cried out in pleasure.

Sir's groan was low and primal, stirring the flames of her desire. Bound as she was, their movement was not hindered by friction from the bed, and she rocked into him with every thrust. He pulled her head back farther as he ramped up the pace, and soon the thrusts came so hard and fast that Brie felt the flutterings of subspace.

Sir suddenly pulled out and let go of her hair. Brie whimpered in protest.

"Come for me," he ordered, slipping his finger inside and simply resting it against her G-spot. His energetic thrusting had made her hypersensitive, and that simple pressure caused her to come around his finger. She let go of the bar and lost herself in the intensity of it.

"Good. I'm going to fuck you again. Hold on to the bar."

Brie grabbed the bar as he took her hips with both hands and pounded her with much greater force. Sir's breath came in short, raspy grunts from sheer effort as he gave it everything he had.

Brie began screaming nonsensical words as she took the onslaught, loving the carnal brutality of it. Never wanting it to end…

Sir stopped again, and with quick movements he untied the rope, lowering her onto the bed, his cock still buried inside her. Sir pressed the full weight of his body against her as he came. Brie moaned, feeling his cock pulse with each powerful release.

Her eyes fluttered closed and she came for him—again.

"Get your ass over here. I have to get out of this place now!" Mary screamed into the phone. It hadn't even been twenty-four hours, but she was already begging to leave.

"What happened? Did Captain hurt you?" Brie asked, genuinely concerned.

Her question grabbed Sir's attention and he stopped working to listen.

"Yes, I have been forever scarred by what I have seen. It was totally gross!"

Brie looked over at Sir, shrugging to let him know it wasn't serious. "What happened exactly?"

"Those two…together…they're horrifyingly cute, in a sickening way that makes me want to puke."

"What did you see?"

"Oh, my God! Here he is, this badass Dom, and he's petting Candy all the time, telling her how pretty she is and spoiling the bitch with little treats."

Brie couldn't believe Mary was being so rude and disrespectful of both Captain and Candy. "What the hell is your problem, Mary? You have no right to judge them!"

"Forgive me. I forgot I was talking to the biggest cheeseball of them all. Of course you would defend their behavior."

"Here I thought something serious had happened, and you're crying uncle because they're being sweet to each other?"

"It's disgusting, damn it! And he makes me sit in the corner and watch."

"What? Watch them having sex?"

"Hell, no. I could handle that. Instead, I'm forced to observe while he feeds her little bites from his plate, strokes her hair whenever they watch TV and kisses her goodnight before he chains her to the bed. OMG, it's more than any sane person can take."

"Before you say another word, answer me this. Has Captain mistreated you in any way?"

"Other than scarring me for life?"

Brie was not amused.

"He's been a complete gentleman—too much of a gentleman for my tastes."

"Why the heck are you calling me, then?" Brie asked. "You *do* realize how lucky you are that they took you in, right? You should go to Captain right now and bow at his feet. Thank him for taking in such an unworthy, sniveling worm."

"Shut up, Brie. You're such a fucking asshole!"

"You're the one out of line here, bitch. Anytime *anyone* shows you a lick of kindness, you stomp all over them like they did something wrong." Brie was shaking with repressed anger and growled, "I still can't get over what you did to Todd."

"What *I* did?!"

"Yes. You disobeyed a direct order, one he only had in place for your sake—and yet, before he left, he told me to take care of you. Even after all the shit you put him through."

"Oh, boo hoo… What else did he tell you?" she demanded.

"He said he was leaving the commune, but refused to tell me where he was headed."

"Hah!" Mary grumbled. "I don't fucking believe you. Yeah, I bet the two of you had a grand old time going over a long laundry list of my faults."

"You're a real piece of work, you know that? You don't deserve him, Mary. All Todd ever did was put your needs above his, and all you can do is bitch about him."

Sir took the phone from Brie. "Miss Wilson, this conversation has gotten out of hand. Is Captain treating you well? Fine, then show him the respect he deserves and don't call here again until you have learned something worth sharing."

Sir handed Brie the phone back with a disappointed look on his face.

"She just gets me so riled sometimes," Brie complained.

"With Miss Wilson, you must tread lightly. She already feels worthless, which explains her defensive tactics. When you tell her things such as she doesn't deserve Mr. Wallace, you only feed into her fears of worthlessness. Is that what you intended?"

Brie frowned. "No, but I just want her to admit she's wrong to treat people that way."

"I chose Captain to watch over her because of his background. He won't be swayed by her outbursts. Let the man do his job without undermining his efforts."

She hated that she'd made a mess of things, and bowed at his feet. "I'm sorry, Sir."

"Look at me," Sir commanded.

Brie looked up hesitantly, her lip trembling.

"I understand your anger towards Miss Wilson. She's been disrespectful to your friends and you felt the need to lash out. What she needs, however, is something you can't provide. Step back and let Miss Wilson work through her issues under Captain's guidance. Don't answer the phone if she calls again. She's been instructed to call me if she's being mistreated."

"Yes, Sir."

"Rather than worrying about Miss Wilson, I want you to unpack our things while you concentrate your thoughts on tonight's outing."

She looked at him questioningly. Sir answered that look with a smile, telling her, "I'm taking you to The Haven, my dear. And I have wicked plans for you." Sir held out his hand and helped her back to her feet.

It was like magic.

Like the night before, Sir had completely changed her mindset within a matter of seconds. Brie had expected to putter around for the next few days, recovering from their weeks of travel. Instead, Sir had them moving on with life, headed in a most delightful direction.

Triggers

B rie hadn't visited The Haven in over two months. She was excited at
the prospect of seeing old friends and meeting new members who'd
joined recently. The club had seen a significant influx in membership after
the documentary, and had become the happening place in LA for
kinksters.

She glanced at the mirror as she dressed in the vinyl outfit Sir had
gifted her. The top was a sexy combination of a black corset with laces up
the front and a hood in the back, attached to a high-low skirt that flowed
like a long cape. The bottoms of the outfit consisted of simple short
shorts, which were scandalously tiny. She felt like a vinyl priestess when
she put it on, and twirled several times to admire the flow of the skirt. The
outfit was outside Sir's normal tastes, but she liked it very much.

When Brie emerged from the bedroom, Sir let out a long whistle.
"That looks killer on you, babygirl."

After twirling for him, she gushed, "Thank you, Master. I love it."

He held out his hand and she took it, standing gracefully before him.
"My pleasure, téa. I like showing off my sub. Others can look, but they
can't touch."

"Will we be scening tonight, Sir?"

"Yes," he said with a smirk, "I thought a little violet wand might add
some spark to the evening."

She grinned. "Not only are you a talented Master, but a skilled come-
dian as well."

He swatted her butt. "Sarcasm will only get you in trouble, my dear.
Expect to pay for that."

"I'm unsure whether to be excited or frightened."

The lack of amusement on his face made her heart skip a beat. Maybe she would pay dearly for her jest… It was the not knowing that thrilled her. Oh, how she loved his devilish humor!

Sir seemed to be in a particularly playful mood, and drove the car with gusto, taking sharp corners and punching the gas so that she was thrown back in her seat. Brie giggled for the entire ride, enjoying his expertise behind the wheel. She caressed the dashboard lovingly after he screeched to a halt once they reached The Haven's parking lot, appreciating the wildness the car brought out in him.

Brie waited for him to help her out of the car once he'd grabbed the duffel bag from the back. She walked confidently beside him, grateful that The Haven was nothing like Rytsar's club. She didn't have to worry about breaking some simple protocol and suffering punishment in front of everyone. Although Sir would certainly call her on a breach of protocol, *no one* would ever be allowed to touch her, much less punish her, without his permission.

She was surprised at the long line to get into the club, and stunned by the sheer number of people once they finally made their way in. The middle area was standing room only. It had the feel of a concert venue rather than a kinkster gathering.

Trying to make it to one of the alcoves proved challenging as Sir forced his way through the crowded room. Instead of taking Brie to watch a scene, he went directly to the club's owner.

"Is it normally like this, these days?" Sir asked.

"Fridays and Saturdays are the worst. If you want a less crowded evening, I suggest coming Tuesday or Wednesday."

"I'll keep that in mind in the future. Do you still have us down for tonight?"

The owner looked over his sheet. "Yes, I have you down for eight, Sir Davis. Try to make it there at least fifteen minutes early. It gets a little crazy whenever a scene ends and the crowd starts moving."

Sir glanced around at the sea of people. "Looks like you might want to expand."

"Funny you should say that. We are opening up another club north of here in a few months."

"A wise move. I'd be willing to drive farther to avoid the crowds."

"You'll find everyone is respectful of making room for the scenes. We added extra staff, so there's someone stationed between every adjacent alcove. Even I find this level of activity uncomfortable, although the profits have been staggering. I have you and your sub to thank for that."

Brie blushed, pleased that her film had had a positive impact on the club.

Sir put his hand on the small of Brie's back. "All the credit goes to Miss Bennett, but I'm sure we're both glad to hear The Haven is seeing a positive benefit from the film. Can you tell me if Mistress Luo is scening tonight?"

"As a matter of fact, she's up now at the same alcove you'll be scening at. You should still be able to catch her."

Sir guided Brie through the mass of people, ignoring the number of subs who bowed as he passed. He might not have noticed, but Brie sure did. It only helped to highlight the influence Sir still had in the community, despite having stepped down from his position at the school. It made Brie feel proud—and a little remorseful.

He found a spot where Brie could easily observe the scene, and they were treated to the sight of Boa naked and bound in rope. Brie purred to herself, aroused by the vision of the man kneeling, his arms bound together from the forearms down to his wrists with his palms facing upwards in a sign of surrender. Mistress Luo had bound his arms to his thighs and was finishing it off by wrapping the rope around the back of his neck so that, as she tightened the rope, his head was pulled down into a bowing position.

Because Boa had such a strong, masculine body, Brie found it particularly sensual to see him subdued in rope. His Mistress picked up a candle burning on an elegant metal stand and poured wax over his shoulders and down his back.

He visibly shuddered and let out a low grunt.

"You like that, don't you, Boa?"

"I do, Mistress."

She picked up another candle and proceeded to pour more wax over his back. He groaned even louder.

"This one burns a little hotter."

"It does, Mistress."

"Would you like to try another?"

"Please."

A mischievous smile played on her lips as she poured the third candle's wax onto his shoulders, letting it slowly drip down his back. He let out a low, tortured groan.

"Challenging?" she asked sweetly.

"It is," he answered, his head still bowed.

"One more?"

"Yes, Mistress."

She picked up the fourth candle and held it higher above him. Brie understood that it would help to control the temperature of the wax as it fell. He said nothing when the first drop hit his skin, but as she lowered the candle, he began to shift in his bonds, then let out a deep, masculine moan.

She was certain he must be fully erect, but his impressive shaft was hidden by the placement of his arms. *Such a shame,* she mused. It was crafty of Mistress Luo to tease not only Boa, but the entire audience with her choice of body position. Such a cruelly gifted Domme.

Mistress Luo set down the candle, and knelt beside Boa, whispering something. Brie saw a slight nod from him. Mistress Luo kissed him with her ruby lips, leaving her mark on his cheek, then stood, motioning over one of her other subs. A female sub came up and held her ruby-red cat o' nines out with both hands.

Brie shivered, looking at its wicked knots. *Poor Boa!*

Mistress Luo positioned herself behind him. The first swing from the whip released a cascade of hard wax from his skin. With precision, she lashed his back with enough force that she soon had all of the wax covering the floor.

His Mistress nodded to her waiting sub, who brought rubbing alcohol and a towel. It was then that Brie understood the whipping had only just begun. Boa's Mistress carefully cleaned off his back and dried it before handing the towel back to the female.

Brie watched with trepidation as Mistress Luo positioned herself again, stating, "I am going to count down from five. When the last number leaves your Mistress' lips, your rapture will begin."

Brie's stomach churned when Boa answered, "Thank you, Mistress."

The Asian Domme might have been small in stature, but she was an expert at playing the audience. Everyone watched with bated breath as she cocked back her arm and counted down slowly in her seductive voice.

Brie could barely watch when Mistress Luo finished her countdown and took the first swing. Boa's whole body stiffened upon impact. His Mistress continued to stroke his back hard with the cruel instrument, her rhythm consistent and even.

Instead of focusing on Boa, Brie kept her eyes on Mistress Luo, studying her expression as the Domme released a torrent of lashes. There was a look of deep concentration and affection on her face. This wasn't simply a BDSM scene for all to see, but a chance to witness the deep connection between the Dominant and sub.

It was a powerful exchange; one Brie would not have been able to appreciate before her recent encounter with Rytsar.

By the end of it, Boa was panting with low grunts from the intense character of the instrument.

Mistress Luo stepped back to admire her work before handing the cat o' nines to her attending sub and returning to Boa. The Domme gently ran her hands over Boa's sweaty shoulders and arms, humming softly as she caressed him with her skillful fingers.

"The marks suit your level of submission," she complimented him, loosening the rope around his neck. She lifted his head to kiss him deeply.

"Thank you, Mistress," he replied in a hoarse voice. Brie didn't miss the lowered lids as he looked at his Domme, an indication of a good sub high.

Mistress Luo knelt beside him, and with sensual movements, slowly released Boa from the rope. Her light touches, along with the erotic way she slid the rope over his skin, were arousing to watch. Brie appreciated that the Mistress treated the end of the scene as skillfully as the beginning.

For the sub who was still flying, such treatment accentuated the entire experience. It was the loving actions after a scene that made a submissive feel cared for and cherished.

Sir wrapped his arm around Brie's waist and pressed her against him. It seemed her Master also appreciated Mistress Luo's work.

One of the staff members walked over to the Mistress and announced their time was up. While the female sub quickly cleaned up the alcove, the tiny Domme helped Boa to his feet and walked him out of the alcove, heading towards the back of the club, presumably for extended aftercare.

Brie glanced at Boa as they passed by, and shuddered when she saw the numerous slashes covering his upper back. No blood had been drawn, but the marks were angry and red, attesting to the onslaught he had endured.

The next couple had already started setting up their scene. Sir leaned down and whispered in Brie's ear, "We're after this."

She nodded, curious what this scene would consist of. She was not familiar with either the Dom or sub, but figured their scene would be a messy one because of the large plastic tarp that had been placed on the floor. The young female placed a chair in the middle of it and stood by as she waited patiently for her next command.

Her Dom was an impressive male with skin like dark chocolate, something Brie found particularly attractive. She watched with fascination as he laid out tiny instruments on a pedestal with his large hands. Although she couldn't see what the objects were, she was excited to find out. It wasn't often she got to observe something new.

Once he was ready, the Master told his slave to undress and straddle the stool, facing the wall so her back was to the audience. She did so, exposing the beautiful complexion of her dark skin. The girl rested her hands against the seat, spreading her legs apart and arching her back so that her round buttocks were displayed beautifully for the crowd. Her pose alone was art.

Brie watched with growing interest as the Dom cleaned off her entire back, from her shoulders all the way down to her shapely ass, swiping it once with a cloth to make sure it was completely dry. It wasn't until he put on surgical gloves that Brie was first alerted to the nature of the scene.

Her heart rate increased when he picked up a long, golden needle.

"Sir, I thought they didn't do blood play here," she said in a worried tone.

Sir looked over at the waiting staff member, who seemed unconcerned. "It appears their policies have changed."

The Dom approached the slave, making sure she saw the needle before he moved to her back. He lightly patted her right ass-cheek with his free hand, letting his slave know the first area of play.

Brie started hyperventilating, visions of Darius holding her down as a child springing to mind.

"What's wrong, Brie?" Sir asked.

"Oh nothing," she said, giggling to hide her apprehension.

When the Master pinched the flesh of his slave and started inserting the long needle into her skin, Brie stopped breathing but failed to notice.

"You're shaking like a leaf," Sir said with concern.

Brie heard blood pounding in her ears just before everything went black and she crumpled to the ground.

Sir picked her up and fought the crowd as he carried her to the back of the club. They met Boa and Mistress Luo, who were on their way out. The Domme smiled at them as they passed, but the smile froze on her lips when she noticed the expression on Brie's face.

Mistress Luo led them to the first open room and quietly shut the door behind them. Sir tried to let her down, but Brie clung to him, whimpering as she pressed her face into his chest—desperate to make the images of Darius go away.

"Shh…shh…it's okay, babygirl."

The pain and humiliation she'd suffered under the bully's hand as a child came rushing back in a tidal wave. Even with Sir holding her tight, she couldn't stop reliving the beatings, the feeling of utter helplessness, and the dread as he'd picked up the needle and started towards her.

"Talk to me."

Brie forced herself to say his name. "Darius…"

"The boy from elementary school," Sir stated rather than questioned.

Brie nodded, not understanding why her emotions were raging out of control after so many years. "I thought I was over it, Sir. Baron helped me get over this."

Sir pressed her against him. "Memories are funny things, babygirl. They can lay dormant for years and then spring up when we least expect it."

The tears started again as she relived Darius repeatedly stabbing her with the used hypodermic needle.

Sir sat her down, understanding that she was locked in her visions of the past. "Look at me."

She forced herself to look into his eyes, feeling unbearable shame when she did.

Sir surprised her with his raw anger. "I wish I could go back in time and smash the face of that boy before he ever laid a hand on you, but I can't. I can't change the past—nobody can. But you are safe now. No one will hurt you again."

"I know, Sir," she choked.

He cradled her face in his hands. "I want to make sure you're okay. Triggers should never be ignored. They indicate something deeper we must deal with."

She nodded, leaning in to kiss him on the lips, but an image of Darius forcing her lips apart before spitting into her open mouth made her shudder. She refused to break the embrace, concentrating all her attention on Sir's firm lips.

Sir gently scolded her when she broke away. "You failed to be honest with me out there."

Brie slumped in his arms, knowing she had pretended that nothing was wrong—even told him so when he'd specifically asked. "I'm sorry, Sir," she whispered.

"Why did you do that?"

Tears brimmed over as she attempted to explain. "I didn't want past fears to affect the evening we had planned."

"In some ways you're similar to Mary—just as stubborn and fool-hardy."

Oh, the humiliation of being compared to Mary. However, Brie could not deny the comparison and shrugged in resignation, smiling sadly at Sir.

"Babygirl, you can't move forward unless you confront the past. Weren't you the one to tell me that not that long ago?"

She sighed, slightly amused her own words were being used against her. "I did say something similar, Sir."

"Lying to me, and yourself, will only lead to trouble."

She looked down at her lap. "I'm sorry I lied, Sir. I know I deserve to be punished for putting you in that position."

Sir lifted her chin. "Tonight you learned something valuable, and I don't believe punishment will add to that knowledge. Let's go home."

"Please, Sir, I still want to scene with you tonight."

"I don't think it would be wise."

"But I need it, Sir. I need to feel your loving dominance over me. It acts like a protective blanket for my soul."

He stared into her eyes, penetrating her with the intensity of his gaze.

"It's *vitally* important to me, Sir."

He nodded, releasing his hold on her. "I understand the reason for your request."

Her lips trembled with gratitude. "I'm so grateful you understand."

He traced his thumb over her bottom lip. "If we do this, you must be completely open with me. No repeating what just happened."

"It won't happen again, Sir. I promise."

"It will be a simple bondage scene, accented with electricity."

"It sounds perfect."

"If you are certain you're ready, then I'll check to see if the last scene is over. You won't be allowed to join me until everything has been cleared."

Brie shivered, hugging herself when Sir left the room. She'd never understood the deep emotional impact a trigger could cause. It had been as if she'd been dragged back in time to a dark place she never wanted to visit again.

It was easy to have more sympathy for Mary now. Yet her own experience left her wondering why Mary was intent on inviting triggers that pushed her into those dark places.

When Sir returned, he graced her with a reassuring smile. "The area is being cleaned as we speak. People were asking about you. Naturally, your friends are concerned."

"Then it's good we're going ahead with the scene, Sir. There's no reason for them to worry about me."

"You're sure about proceeding with this?"

"Absolutely, Master."

"Then prepare to be shocked."

She looked up at him in surprise, then giggled to herself. "That's funny, Sir."

He chuckled as he opened the door. "At least it made you smile."

Sir led her to the middle of the alcove and helped her out of her vinyl corset. Brie looked out into the crowd, feeling her confidence grow as she spied familiar faces.

"Stand on the X and put your arms up, téa."

Brie settled over the large X and put her arms up, looking at the ceiling as the chains were lowered. She appreciated the calming blue hue of the walls and the familiar scent of the ocean breeze floating in the air. Oh, how she loved this particular alcove.

There had been a time in her life when clinking chains would have scared her, but they now brought a welcome thrill. Sir took his time, lavishing her with caresses as he took her wrist and buckled it into the cuff, tightening it until she felt secure. He did the same with the other, leaving trails of ticklish kisses up her arm before buckling it into the cuff. The sensuality of his slow and purposeful movements lured her into his seductive spell.

Sir kissed her on the back of the neck before leaving her side to open the case that held the violet wand. He purposely kept in her line of sight, explaining, "I want you to see what I do. No surprises tonight."

Brie appreciated that he was ensuring she would not feel apprehensive during the scene, safeguarding her success.

She bowed her head in gratitude.

After taking out the violet wand and inserting the rounded glass rod, he plugged it in. Sir nodded to the staff member standing by. The lights were lowered in the alcove, adding to the sensual atmosphere of the scene. When he turned on the wand, the real show began.

Along with the buzzing, came the sparkling purple light. There was excited murmuring in the crowd. Brie figured a few of the new members hadn't seen the electrical toy before, while others knew its delicious feel and were jealous.

She jumped the instant the wand touched her skin, even though it felt good. There was something about the buzzing and sparks that had all her senses on alert.

"Color, téa? Sir asked, obviously concerned she wasn't as prepared to scene as she'd thought.

"Green, Master," she purred. "The wand has a lot of bark, but not any bite."

With permission given, Sir tickled her with the electricity as he lightly grazed her left side, from her wrist down to her ankle, and then up the right. The light sensation was so enjoyable it was difficult not to squirm in pleasure.

"And now for the chest."

Brie moaned softly when he guided the wand over her breasts, resting momentarily on each nipple, causing them to grow hard as the tool buzzed and crackled with gentle electricity.

"I can tell your body enjoys the stimulation," he murmured in her ear.

She turned her head, hoping to kiss him, but Sir teased her further by coming close enough to her lips that she could feel the warmth of his breath before he pulled away to play with the wand some more.

Brie sighed in pleasurable frustration, loving the way her Master enticed and tortured her.

"I wonder if your pussy is hungry for it too. It's a shame it's covered in vinyl, babygirl. Perhaps some other night..." Sir teased her thighs and stomach with the electric wand, making her wet with desire.

"More, Master," she begged.

"More current?"

"Please."

Sir turned off the wand and switched out the end of the tool, slipping the contact pad into his pants pocket. He slid metal tips onto each finger of his right hand and smiled wickedly at her when he turned the violet wand to a higher setting. "Ready for some real fun?"

She moaned as he approached, knowing Sir was now electrified and that his metal-tipped fingers had the ability to shock her with the current that ran through his body.

"Head back, téa," he ordered. He brushed her hair away and grazed her neck with the metal tips, sending tingles throughout her body. Brie swayed in her chains, moaning loudly in response.

"Color?"

"Violet."

He chuckled. "I take it that's a variant of green."

"Yes, Master," she purred in agreement.

Brie held her breath as he moved his hand, hovering over her right breast. The suspense was excruciating as she waited for him to touch her.

"Watch," he commanded.

She looked down and watched as his fingers cupped her breast. She gasped as the sharp points dragged across her skin as he closed his hand, ending at her erect nipple—which received the stimulation of all five fingers at once.

A ragged moan escaped her lips as the intense current seemed to go straight from her nipple to her groin. Her pussy pulsed in readiness.

Sir moved his hand to her left breast, and smiled as he encircled it with his fingers a quarter-inch from her skin. "What do you want, téa?"

"I want you to touch me, Master," she groaned, her loins aching with need.

"Are you sure?" he teased.

"Please."

"Kiss me."

As she leaned forward to receive his kiss, the metal tips touched her. She moaned into his mouth as he closed his hand, pinching her nipple with his electrified claws.

Those evil hands excited her body, making her jump and squirm as he leisurely explored her skin with the sharp pinpoints of current. The audience loved it, their murmurings of enjoyment competing with the buzz of the violet wand.

"Oh, God, I want you so badly," she whispered when he turned the toy off.

"It's a good thing you have those vinyl panties on, téa, or I would be ramming into you right now."

"Rip them off..." she begged him.

Sir shook his head, but he teased her by getting down on his knees, his lips only inches from her mound. He took a long, appreciative whiff and looked up at her. "I smell your need, babygirl." He kissed her quivering stomach before getting back to his feet and carefully putting his tools in the case.

Brie, along with the crowd, were left hanging with a burning need for release—a release he denied them all.

Blessed Release

I t wasn't until they returned home that Sir made good on his seduction at The Haven. With tender hands and gentle lips, he stoked the burning embers he'd created during their scene together. When he finally pulled off her shorts, they literally dripped with her excitement.

"I think both of us are in need of a shower," Sir told her.

He led Brie into the bathroom and ordered her to stand while he adjusted the temperature of the water. He looked back at her with a charming grin. "I don't want cold water ruining your heat, babygirl."

She twisted where she stood, desperate to put out the flames raging inside her. Her poor pussy ached for him. Being a good submissive, however, she did not complain. She knew the release would be worth the wait.

When Sir was satisfied with the temperature, he stripped down and held out his hand to her. "Shall we?"

Brie moaned with pleasure as the warm water cascaded down her skin, the tiny droplets stimulating her body even more. Sir stepped in behind her and grabbed the bar of soap. Gliding it over her skin, he murmured, "First I lather you, then I bend you over."

Brie moved with him as he covered her body with the luxurious bubbles, the manly scent of his soap an added turn-on. However, what was driving her absolutely wild was his rock-hard cock pressed against her back, announcing his need.

She gasped when the welcome words came as he put the soap down and placed his hand on her back. "Bend over."

With sensual grace, she followed his command, loving the feel of his palm on her back. She braced herself against the tiled wall and looked back at her Master, opening her legs to him.

Sir forced himself inside, bringing tears to Brie's eyes as he filled her aching need with his rock hard shaft.

"I needed that, oh, how I needed that..." she groaned.

"I know," Sir said, grabbing her shoulders to fuck her deeper.

Cupping one hand over her mouth, he increased the tempo of his thrusts, releasing his pent up desire on her body. In a gruff voice he commanded, "Come for me, Brie."

The use of her given name in that passionate moment made her release more powerful and prolonged.

"Oh, damn..." Sir cried, finding himself coming inside her before he wanted. He grabbed her hips and added depth to his final thrusts. Then he lifted her back into a standing position and wrapped his arms around her, his cock wedged inside her still-quivering pussy.

"I wanted to take it slow with you, but there was no denying my lust tonight."

Brie tilted her head back to look at him. "I'm glad you didn't, Sir. I was about to burst into flame."

"The smell of you..."

"I thought for sure you were going to take me right there at The Haven."

He ran his hands over her skin, washing the remaining soap from her body. "I spent too many years fucking trainees in front of a panel. When it comes to taking you...I prefer to be alone."

"I think you stole a year of my life with that little stunt. I feel completely drained, you lust-vampire."

He let his cock slip out of her and turned Brie around, laughing. "Lust-vampire? That's one I've never been called before."

She looked up at him, the hot water still cascading down her back and over her well-spent pussy. "You've earned it, Sir—in spades." She stepped out of the shower, feeling a little faint from the encounter and hot steam.

Sir stayed behind to finish rinsing off. "Go lie down, Brie. I'll join you shortly."

She sprawled out on the bed, feeling utterly and beautifully used. When Sir walked out, he smiled at her. "Did I tucker my little sub out?"

"Completely, Sir."

He crawled into bed and gathered her into his arms. "You never cease to amaze me, Brie. I thought you were mistaken to continue with our plan to scene tonight. Yet here we are, having experienced a very successful evening together."

She caressed his strong jaw, admiring his handsome face. "It's all because of you, Sir. You were so romantic during the scene at The

Haven." She propped herself up and looked at him seriously. "I'm grateful that wasn't stolen from me because of what happened."

"It came down to a matter of trust—for both of us."

"Yes." Brie settled back down and thought about the first time they met. "I think I've trusted you from the very beginning, even before I knew who you were."

"Foolish girl," he chided.

"Sir, can I ask you a question?"

"You know my standard answer. You can ask me anything, but that doesn't mean I will answer the question."

"Fair enough. You see, I've been wondering about my entrance video lately."

He raised an eyebrow. "Go on…"

"I think the other trainers must have seen the video I submitted."

"Why do you ask?"

"Well, Lea and I got to talking about it when the trainers in Denver were looking over video submissions during my last visit. It made me wonder about my own video because, up to that point, I'd always assumed you were the only one who saw it."

"The panel always goes through the videos together. It ensures we have a balanced class of submissives." Sir brushed the wet hair from her face. "However, yours was truly a piece of art, Brie. I'd never seen anything as charming as that smile when you threw your socks into the laundry basket."

Brie snuggled up to him, enjoying his flattering critique of her video submission.

"We were all impressed that you did the entire video facing away from the camera with your clothes still on. No entrant had thought to do that before." He glanced at her. "I found it…enchanting."

Brie felt heat rise to her cheeks as she blushed, but she didn't want him to stop. "Was that all you liked about it, Sir?"

Sir chuckled. "No. I also enjoyed the enthusiastic way you sucked the plastic phallus, but it was the look on your face when you penetrated your virginal ass that charmed me the most."

"Charmed you?" Brie felt a twinge of embarrassment thinking back on that moment—her first self-administered anal penetration.

"Based on the form you filled out, it was a shock for all of us to see you perform that act. However, the look of surprise when it slipped in… Ah, well, that was classic. I determined then that I would be the one to introduce your virginal ass to a real cock."

Brie felt pleasurable tingles on hearing his confession. "How did the other trainers react when I called out your name?"

He shook his head. "That little slip almost cost you the spot, babygirl. None of the trainers were pleased, but Gray was especially troubled because he was convinced you must have known me personally."

"But you explained we were strangers, right?"

"I did, but it only seemed to provoke him further. The fact that you were fantasizing about a trainer before you even started the program was a major concern to him." Sir tilted his head and shrugged. "Looking back on it now, I suppose he had a point."

"What did *you* think when I called out your name?"

He grinned. "It was gratifying, Miss Bennett."

"I still can't believe I was brave enough to do the video with that tiny phallus, especially when I…" She blushed profusely, remembering making the entry video for him. "Truly it was only because I was thinking about you that I found the courage to do it. I felt this deep stirring in my soul whenever I thought of you."

"Which brings validity to Gray's initial argument. Luckily, Samantha fought hard for your inclusion into the training program."

Brie looked up in surprise. "What?"

"You heard me correctly." He chuckled, thinking back on it. "Samantha fought to keep you, despite Gray's vehement protests, and was even able to convince Coen that you would be a good fit for our program."

"And they both lived to regret it," she said, laughing to herself.

"No, Brie. Coen respects you, and Samantha…I'm convinced she suffered with issues of jealousy, which clouded her professional judgment. However, she's come to appreciate your abilities and talents."

"Rytsar told me at the cabin that he wanted to talk to you about her."

"And he did, but I do not agree with him."

"What are your thoughts on it, Sir?"

"My friend was damaged by his encounter with Samantha. It's understandable that he still harbors strong feelings against her. It stands to reason that if he can't trust her himself, then he's unable to trust her with anyone he cares about."

"So you aren't concerned about Ms. Clark?"

"Samantha has striven to change her behavior and better herself. She's not the same undisciplined woman she was in college. With that in mind, I have to answer no. I do not worry about her with you, although I completely understand why Durov feels that way. I'm certain I would as well, if it had happened to me."

"Sir, Rytar asked me a question that has haunted me since."

"What's that?"

"He asked if I trusted her, and I can honestly say that I don't. I trust all of the other trainers, but I don't fully trust Ms. Clark."

Sir nodded sadly, accepting her assessment. "Unfortunately, Samantha has never given you a reason to trust her. Trust must be earned, and she's failed in that regard with you."

"I accepted she was harsh as a trainer, and respected her even when she was harder on me than the others. Knowing how much Lea cares for her, and then learning about your own relationship with her, has helped me to keep a more open mind."

"How did you feel when you met her in Denver?"

"It was *very* different. She seemed easygoing, less abrasive, although just as intense."

"Did you feel differently when you were alone with her during filming?"

"The truth is I always feel uncertain around her, Sir—even now. I definitely enjoyed filming her scene, but I also felt a bit like a mouse being played with."

"That is an interesting way to put it. Although I know Samantha insists on having the upper hand with subs, I felt the unusual tension between you. As you know, I was forced to call her on it several times, even after your training was over."

"Sir, I never understood her obsession with forcing me to keep my eyes down until this last trip to Russia. After going to Rytsar's club, I can appreciate why eye contact was so important to her. I believe her desire to please him played out in her training of the students."

"You may be right, but Durov doesn't particularly care about eye contact when it comes to his own submissives. He demanded it from Samantha because she was a Dominant, and it pleased him knowing it ate her up inside to obey."

"Always the sadist."

Sir frowned. "I still can't reconcile what happened between them…but I would never willingly put you in harm's way. Rytsar may be blinded by what happened between them, but I'm not. I can see both sides and have seen the devastation it caused. However, if you do not feel safe around Samantha, I will make sure you are not left alone with her again. I trust your instincts, babygirl. I always have."

"If I ever feel unsafe, Sir, I promise to let you know."

Sir mused aloud, "I suppose in the end it comes down to whether you believe people can change. I do, up to a point. Put in the same situation with the same stimuli, most will revert back to the way they were. It's the reason I encouraged Samantha to give up on Durov. There was no hope and never could be, given their history. Since then, she has matured and found her place within the BDSM community." He looked at Brie and asked her solemnly, "Do you believe people can change?"

"Of course, Sir. I'm not the person I was before I met you."

He gave her a sly smile. "I've never admitted this to anyone, but I kept your submission entry. I couldn't delete such a masterpiece."

Brie laughed, shocked but pleased by his admission. "I can't believe you kept my video, Sir."

"I was reckless when it came to you—right from the start. Tell me, babygirl, would you like to revisit that moment in your life?"

"Please, Sir."

Brie snuggled up to him when he settled back on the bed with his laptop. She smiled to herself when she saw he had named the file 'MasterpieceAKABrie'. As soon as he hit play, she could tell just how nervous she'd been by the way she'd smiled at the camera and then looked away shyly.

Brie buried her head in his shoulder, embarrassed to watch. But when she heard her own laughter, she looked back at the screen and saw herself licking the tiny phallus.

"It was so incredibly small, Sir."

"It was meant not to intimidate the entrants."

It was hard not to burn with mortification when she started making mewing sounds as she attempted to deep-throat the thin tool. However, Brie's juices started flowing at the sound of her own moans as she watched herself lay down on the bed and masturbate with it.

"I enjoyed hearing your unique noises. It made the experience that much more intimate and personal."

Brie cuddled closer to him, very much enjoying his take on her video.

There was a pause in the action when she went to buy the lubricant from the corner store. When the camera flipped back on, Brie saw herself pulling off her socks. She distinctly remembered throwing them into the hamper and yelling, "Score!" when she made the basket.

Sir stopped the video when she looked back at the camera and smiled. "This is the exact moment you stole my heart. That open smile in the middle of a sexual scene." He shook his head, his eyes warm with affection. "It was perfect."

He hit play, and Brie had to suffer the embarrassment of watching herself coat the tiny phallus with far too much lubricant and then tell herself out loud to relax as she tried to push it inside her anus without success.

"I thought you were done here—we all did—but then you..."

Brie blushed as she watched herself get on all fours, now facing the camera. She knew what was coming and buried her head in his shoulder again.

"Watch," he commanded gently.

Brie looked back at the computer just as the toy slipped inside, and she heard herself gasp.

Sir stopped the video again. "That tiny gasp and the surprised look on your face sealed my fate."

Brie covered her eyes, humiliated by the humorous expression captured on the screen. Sir pulled her hand away and forced her to look at herself. "It was your reaction right after this that convinced us all you had real potential. You closed your eyes, deciding if you wanted to continue." Sir smiled tenderly at her. "Despite your fears and inexperience, you chose to go on. You weren't playing for the camera, you weren't forcing yourself to do something you didn't want to do. No, you were being true to your nature and we all recognized that strength in you."

"I remember it like it was yesterday, Sir. I was scared to introduce a foreign object into my body, but all I had to do was imagine that it was you. I wanted to know what it felt like to have you deep inside that forbidden place."

Sir placed his hand on her upper thigh. "That desire came across loud and clear in your video."

She giggled. "To think I have Ms. Clark to thank for my acceptance into the program…" Remembering back to those beginning sessions, Brie stated, "I do remember that she was complimentary in her critiques the first couple of days, before she grew to hate me."

"It wasn't until my claiming of you that I noticed her claws come out. She felt very protective of me, although there was no reason for it."

"How did she find out when it was done in private?"

"The Center has cameras in every room, Brie. I fully expected the trainers would see it. However, I'm a man who knows what he wants and refuses to play the coward by hiding his actions. I wanted you, so I claimed you before anyone else could fuck that fine ass of yours." Sir lightly caressed her buttocks with his hands before grabbing them possessively.

"That was all I wanted, Sir. In fact, I was upset when the class ended that second night and I thought you weren't going to keep your promise to me."

"Ah, but I wasn't about to ruin our intimate moment by inviting a live audience." He pressed her body against his. "No, I wanted our first time to be as private as possible."

"Even at the cost of losing your position at the Center…which eventually *did* happen, Sir." Brie let out a heavy sigh. "I hate that you had to give up your job to collar me."

"Some things are worth the sacrifice." Sir kissed her on the lips as he slipped his fingers between her legs…

His cell phone rang, and Sir's hand instantly froze. "That is Thompson's ringtone," he explained as he disengaged to reach for the phone.

Brie watched his expression carefully as Sir talked to his lawyer. Although his voice remained calm, she noticed his lips twitch several times during the conversation.

"Interesting… I suggest you set up a meeting at your office if that's the case." He paused for a moment, then replied, "Fine, I'll pay for the flight. Thursday will work for me. We'll speak then."

Sir stared at Brie after he hung up, looking a bit stunned. "The test results came back positive. It appears I have a half-sister."

Brie wasn't sure how she felt about the news, but forced herself to reply optimistically. "That's amazing, Sir."

He shook his head, a smile playing on his lips. "To think I have a sibling I never knew about…"

"I take it you're meeting her this week, based on the part of the conversation I heard."

Sir took Brie's hands in his. "*We're* meeting her this week."

"How strange it will be to meet her in person. Oh, my gosh, I wonder if she looks like you."

Sir surprised her by growling under his breath, "I hope for her sake Lilly looks nothing like her father. I don't think I could handle it, given the part he played in my father's death. In fact, the idea of meeting her brings back memories I'd rather not deal with."

"But we'll face them together, Sir," Brie vowed, putting her hands on his chest. "This is a positive step forward for you."

He shook his head slowly as he gazed at the lock of her brown hair he was rolling between his fingers. "Although I'm curious about this girl, there are still so many questions that have yet to be answered."

Lilly

M eeting Lilly at Thompson's law office reminded Brie of the last meeting Sir had had with his mother. She sincerely hoped it would be the *only* similarity.

"I don't care if it seems odd or cold to her," Sir stated as they rode up on the elevator. "I still have my reservations, and a professional environment will help to remove emotion from the equation if this goes poorly."

"I understand your caution, Sir, given what you've been through."

Sir hesitated with his hand on the doorknob to the meeting room. "Why do I have the unsettling feeling this is going to change my life in ways I can't imagine?"

Brie put her hand on his. "Because it will. You have family again."

Together, they opened the door and walked inside. Sir immediately stopped and stood silent as he glared at Lilly.

The girl stood up to greet him, a pleasant smile on her face—an eerily familiar smile.

"I can't believe it!" she cried, running up to Sir with her arms open wide. To Brie's horror, the girl was a perfect replica of Sir's mother.

Sir kept his arm outstretched, keeping his distance as he shook the woman's hand in a stiff manner. "There can be no doubt that you are my mother's daughter."

Lilly looked up at him, smiling. "And you! No doubt you are the son of a handsome Italian."

Sir dropped her hand abruptly and turned to shut the door.

Brie understood the emotional jolt he'd suffered, and spoke up to relieve some of the tension in the room. "Hi, I'm Brie Bennett. It's nice to meet you, Lilly."

The girl took Brie's hand, but then enfolded her in a hug. "Yes, I've read all about you. I haven't seen your film yet, but I certainly plan to someday soon."

Brie was taken aback when Lilly kissed her on the cheek, but she didn't have time to react, because Lilly was back on Sir, grabbing his hand and pulling him towards the table. "There's so much to talk about!"

Lilly sat down and covered her face with her hands, exclaiming excitedly, "Oh, my God, you're really my brother. This is so weird…"

Sir was slower to sit down, and pulled out the seat beside him so Brie could join him. "I admit this is a shock for me as well."

"Why in the world would Momma keep you a secret?"

Sir looked at her solemnly. "I assume you are aware of our past."

"Well, naturally I've looked you up on the internet, but still… I don't get why she would want to keep you and me apart like that."

He answered without any emotion, "I'm a part of her past she wanted to forget."

Lilly shook her head, smiling at Sir. "But I don't get it. She loved being a mother. I can't imagine her abandoning you like that."

"The two of us did not end on good terms."

Without asking, Lilly grabbed his hand and squeezed it. "You know, I read about the tragic death of your father. Both Mom and you must have been devastated. I've heard unexpected deaths can break families apart."

"He didn't die tragically; he killed himself because of her," Sir stated, pulling his hand away.

But Lilly would have none of it, and grabbed it back. "I can't believe Momma could be so cruel as to leave you behind, Thane. It was wrong for her to do that."

Sir looked down at her hand gripping his but, to Brie's surprise, he didn't pull away. "I do not know the person you claim her to be. My experience with Ruth has shown her to be a heartless human being, and she proved that to me time and again."

"Thane…I hope you don't mind if I call you that," Lilly said with an infectious grin.

"I'm not opposed to it."

"Thane, I can't explain my mother's actions, but I sincerely hope you and I can become friends and break down the walls she built. Neither of us should be alone in this world."

Sir glanced at Brie. "I'm not alone."

Lilly smiled, quickly correcting herself. "No, that's not what I meant, but surely you'll agree it's wrong to be deprived of family."

"You should talk to your mother about that, but unfortunately she can't face your justified wrath."

Lilly patted his hand before withdrawing hers. "I don't hate her; I just want to understand her reasons for doing this to us. Momma was only loving and kind to me. Whatever she did to you, that was not how she treated me." She smiled at Sir apologetically. "But we should leave that for another day. Really, all I want to do is get to know you better."

"Agreed."

Lilly raised her eyebrows playfully. "So I read that you run your own consulting company and that you used to be headmaster of a school. That's all fine and good, but what do you do for fun?"

Sir looked at her oddly and did not reply.

"I mean, what are your hobbies? What do you do in your spare time?"

"Spare time? What the hell is that?" Sir laughed.

Brie wrapped her arm around his and smiled at Lilly. "The two of us are always on the run. If we aren't working, we're…doing things together." She laid her head on Sir's shoulder.

"I get that you two are a couple, but seriously, Thane. What do you enjoy doing on your own? Surely a man as independent as you are has other interests."

Brie felt a twinge of resentment. It felt as if the question was meant to be a jab against her, not asked out of simple curiosity.

"Although we haven't had the time recently, I do enjoy the opera."

Lilly's eyes lit up. "I do too! Have you seen Carmen? It's my favorite one."

Sir shook his head. "No, I have not. Its storyline reminds me too much of my mother. I could only wish she had ended like that."

Tears formed in Lilly's eyes. "How could you say that? I…"

Sir sighed before reaching over and taking her hand. "I'm sorry. I think both of us must tread lightly when talking about her."

Lilly dabbed her eyes with a tissue and nodded. "Still, I really think you should see it. I love that opera."

"I will keep it in mind, Lilly," Sir said kindly.

"So other than our mutual love of opera, what else do we have in common?"

When Sir failed to answer, Brie chimed in. "He's a talented cook."

Sir shook his head. "Talented is a stretch. Let's just say that I enjoy my time in the kitchen."

Lilly grinned. "I grew up in the kitchen with Momma. She was always experimenting with new dishes."

Sir seemed interested in that fact and asked, "What did she cook?"

"Oh, every French dish under the sun. Momma always said the more butter and cream, the better."

"No Italian then?"

"No, Momma said she hated Itali—" Lilly's face fell and she immediately apologized. "Oh God, I'm sorry."

Sir shook it off. "That's fine. I think we're done here."

"Done? But we've barely started. I'll be more careful with my words, Thane. I *need* to get to know you better. Please don't brush me off."

He could not be swayed by her pleas, and informed her, "This is enough for now. We've established communication."

Lilly got up from the table and rushed over, wrapping her arms around him. "I want so much more than that. Please, Thane."

It was surreal to see a younger version of his mother hugging Sir so tightly. Brie hoped it brought him comfort, because it made her skin crawl.

"I'm staying at the Rayburn hotel for the next couple of days. I would love to get together again. Please say yes."

Sir broke away from her and stood up, holding out his hand to Brie. "Miss Bennett and I have a busy week ahead, but I'll consider it."

"Thanks again for the plane ticket and hotel," Lilly blurted. "I can't tell you how much this means to me."

"Don't give it another thought."

"Well, I'm sure you heard from your lawyer that I'm a junior accountant in New York and can barely make ends meet even with a roommate." She laughed. "So getting the chance to come to LA is a dream come true for me, but meeting my long-lost big brother totally blows my mind!"

"It is equally unsettling for me."

Lilly shook her head, giving him a humorous look. "No, Thane, it's not unsettling. It's wonderful!"

He chuckled lightly. "Fine, it's wonderful."

The next morning, an envelope arrived for Sir via courier. Inside was a note and a smaller, golden envelope. Sir read it out loud to Brie:

Dear Thane,

Just talking about Carmen got me excited. Imagine my surprise when I found out it's playing here! It took some doing, but I obtained tickets. Please think of it as a thank you for the travel, and a chance for you and I to get to know each other in a less formal environment.

Love,

Lilly, your little sis

Sir opened the second envelope and pulled out a single ticket. He looked at her apologetically.

Brie smiled as she put her arm around his waist. "It's for the best, Sir. You should spend time alone together."

"Unfortunately, it's on the same night as Mr. Gallant's party. I had hoped to speak to Miss Wilson there to see how she's faring. Even though I trust Captain with her care, as her former trainer, I feel responsible and wanted to check in."

"I'll talk with her, Sir. I suspect she'll be more open with me anyway."

"Keep it civil this time."

Brie blushed, remembering her last phone call with Mary. "I won't attack her, no matter how rude she is."

Sir's voice took on a softer tone when he asked, "What are your impressions of Lilly, Brie?"

She collected her thoughts before answering, not wanting to put a negative spin on something so personal to Sir. "To be fair, I've only met her once."

"And…"

"I'm unsure."

"As am I. I'm trying not to be suspicious of Lilly's intentions, but her look is uncanny and quite disturbing to me."

"I know what you mean," Brie confessed, grateful he'd been the one to bring it up. "But it's unfair to judge a person by their appearance. Although I understand that, it's hard not to think of your mother whenever I look at her."

"I was surprised by her financial situation."

"You mean that she's living modestly like any normal person her age? I was surprised by that too, Sir. I naturally assumed your mother would have raised a spoiled brat, but maybe she honestly wanted to give Lilly a fair chance in the world."

"Or maybe Lilly recently lost all her money and has always known about me," Sir speculated.

Brie hated to even go there. The last thing Sir needed was another Ruth in his life. "Did Mr. Thompson find out anything on her that contradicts her story?"

"No, everything checks out, but…"

Brie was relieved to hear it. "You just need time, Sir. Time to get to know Lilly so you can see her for the person she really is. That's all." She kissed him on the lips. "You're a good judge of character. Trust your instincts."

Sir shook his head, growling angrily. "When it comes to my mother and anything associated with her, I find myself assuming only one thing."

Brie took the ticket from his hand. "Maybe, just this once, you should let down your guard and get to know your sister."

"Sister…what an odd concept."

"But your new reality."

Mary Quite Un-Contrary

Sir left for the opera an hour before Brie was to leave for the party at Mr. Gallant's. Just before he headed out the door, Sir handed her a red box. "Open it."

Brie lifted the lid and took out the delicate red mask that was nestled in tissue paper. "It's beautiful, Sir, but what's this for?"

"The Gallants are requiring masks for the evening."

"Really?" She looked it over, suddenly intrigued.

"Yes, his wife thought masks would add to the festivities tonight."

"Oh, Sir. Now I'm really unhappy you won't be joining me."

"I had this shipped from Italy," he told her, taking the mask and placing it over her eyes. He tied it into place and turned her back around to admire her. "You look stunning, babygirl."

It was important that he spend time with his sister, Brie knew that, but the chance to see Sir wearing a mask would have been such a rare treat. It was hard not to pout.

Sir kissed her on the lips. "Rest assured, we'll have our own private mask party."

Brie purred. "Good, because I want to make love to you in a mask."

He pinched her butt. "Aren't you the kinky one?"

She giggled, but the merriment ceased the moment he shut the door on his way out. Going to this gathering without him would be a depressing ordeal, no matter what the reason for it.

Standing on Mr. Gallant's doorstep a short time later, Brie sighed self-consciously. It wasn't easy being there alone wearing her mask. It just felt odd without Sir.

All that changed when Ena answered the door wearing a breathtaking mask of gold. "Miss Bennett, don't you look lovely? Thank you for coming tonight. Please, won't you come in?"

Brie was greeted by the sound of laughter echoing from deeper within the house.

"We've been waiting for you," Ena explained. "You're the last of our guests."

Brie had come fifteen minutes early and was surprised to hear it, but automatically apologized. "Oh, I'm sorry."

"Don't be. You came exactly on time."

Mr. Gallant's wife escorted her into the main room, where Brie was overjoyed to see some of her favorite people. Not only were Captain, Candy and Mary there, but also Marquis, Celestia, Master Coen, as well as his three female subs. Rounding out the group was a tall, copper-toned man Brie instantly recognized as Nosh, the head of the Dominant Training Center.

Mr. Gallant walked up to Brie wearing a silver mask, which made him look even more distinguished and refined in her eyes. "Welcome, Miss Bennett."

"It's wonderful to see you again, Mr. Gallant! Is it okay if I hug you?" Brie asked, fighting the urge to throw her arms around him.

"As I only acted as your teacher, I see no breach in protocol."

Brie grinned as she hugged her tiny but formidable teacher. To her delight, Mr. Gallant's two girls came bouncing into the room. "Must we leave, Daddy?" the oldest protested sweetly. "Everyone looks so beautiful."

"This is an evening for adults, girls," he gently reminded them.

The youngest pushed out her bottom lip. "Please, Daddy?"

Mr. Gallant tweaked her nose. "If I hear no more complaints, we'll treat you and your friends to a masked gala of your own."

The girls squealed and showered him with kisses. Ena came up and told them, "Now girls, your ride is here. Promise me you won't keep the Hendersons up giggling until all hours of the night."

"We won't, Mommy," the two answered in unison. The youngest turned to Brie and said, "I like your mask best," before skipping out the door.

"Hurry along," Mr. Gallant said, picking up their overnight bags. "We don't want to keep your friends waiting."

Ena turned to Brie and tsked good-naturedly. "My girls have their father wrapped around their little fingers."

"It's quite charming," Brie confessed. "It's nice to see serious Doms can still be doting fathers."

"And devoted husbands," Ena added, smiling as she shut the door once Mr. Gallant had walked back in.

Her former teacher explained to Brie, "Although we can relax a bit, we keep things relatively vanilla even when the girls are gone. Should one of our children walk through the door unexpectedly or neighbors happen to look through the window, we don't want them to be shocked by what they see."

Brie smiled, respecting his wish to protect his family. "Understood, Mr. Gallant."

She spied Mary kneeling in the corner and excused herself to find out what Blonde Nemesis was up to. As she approached, she couldn't help admiring Mary's sparkly emerald mask.

"Nice eye wear, woman," she complimented, then whispered, "Are you being punished?"

"No, bitch. Vader said I struggle with not being the center of attention. Now go away," she hissed without looking up. "You're going to ruin it for me."

"Whatever…"

Brie scooted in the direction of Candy and Celestia, who were waving her over enthusiastically. Candy wore a sapphire mask that matched Mary's emerald one, while the art that graced Celestia's face was of midnight black, accented with pinpoints of crystal around the eyes. It reminded Brie of a night sky, which was poetic, since that was the name Marquis had given her.

Brie asked Candy in a confidential tone, "Is Mary being punished?"

Candy smiled, glancing over at her. "No, what you see there is a woman who wants to impress."

"Impress Captain?" Brie asked, unable to hide her surprise.

"She's grown close to my Master, and takes what he says to heart," Candy explained. "Mary has made significant strides since joining our household." She added with a laugh, "It almost makes up for everything she put us through the first few days."

"Oh, my," Celestia exclaimed.

Brie snorted. "I can only imagine."

Candy looked over at Mary with pride. "Surprisingly, she has a deep philosophical side to her, and a gentleness few see."

"Gentle? Mary?!" Brie scoffed. "That is *not* a word I would ever use to describe her."

Candy smiled in Captain's direction. "My Master sees right through walls. You'd be surprised what he discovers when he tears them down."

"Well, I for one never imagined Mary would try so hard," Brie said, giving Candy a grateful squeeze. "Thank you for letting her invade your home. My friend really needed you."

"It's been our pleasure, Brie. You helped me, and we've been able to help someone else. That's how it's supposed to work, right?"

"Yes, but let's face it, I had it a lot easier than you." Brie turned to Celestia, not wanting her to feel left out of the conversation. "So tell me, how has life been treating you lately?"

"I've been doing well, and would love to tell you all about it over a cup of coffee sometime."

"We should all get together more often," Candy suggested.

"Sounds great, but I can't make any plans until after the wedding. Once the raw footage is shot and the wedding is behind me, *then* I'll have a more open calendar."

Candy nudged her playfully. "Sure you will…"

Brie grinned. "It's been freaking crazy lately, but thankfully it'll all be over in a few months."

"Yes, it will, Miss Bennett," Marquis said, strolling up to join them. His mask was like Celestia's, but all black, perfectly framing the dangerous glint in his eyes. "If you have any reservations about the upcoming nuptials, now would be the time to state them."

She felt heat rush to her cheeks. "No, Marquis Gray. The wedding, I'm looking forward to. It's everything *before* the wedding that's getting to me."

"Like Sir Davis's dying mother?"

Brie gasped. Leave it to Marquis to hit the tenderest mark without warning or mercy.

"We're working through it, Marquis Gray."

"And his sister?" he pressed.

"He's coming to know her."

"I'm curious, Miss Bennett. What were your first impressions of the girl?"

Brie knew she needed to step carefully with Marquis, or she would invite a cascade of difficult questions she didn't want to address. "It's really too soon to make judgments."

Marquis raised his eyebrow. "I asked for your first impression."

"To be fair, I find that she looks too similar to Sir's mother for me to judge."

"So if you *were* to make a judgment, it would not be favorable at this point."

Brie shook her head. "No, that's not what I meant…"

Master Nosh walked up to the group. The chiseled, masculine mask he wore hinted at his Native American heritage, but it was the long, painted black tears that drew Brie's attention. She was startled to find he was staring intently at her from under the mask.

Mr. Gallant moved in to formally introduce them. "I don't believe you've been properly introduced, Miss Bennett. This is Master Nosh, Head of Dominant Training. Master Nosh, this is Brie Bennett, former student of our school and resident film director."

Brie bowed. "It is an honor, Master Nosh."

She remembered the Master from her training days, when she and the other submissives had been given the unique opportunity to critique training Doms at the Center. That had been the same day Faelan had impressed her with the power of a simple feather.

The intimidating Dom only nodded to Brie, saying nothing.

"Master Nosh is a man of few words," Master Coen announced, joining them with his arms draped around two of his submissives. His smile was barely visible underneath the metal mask that covered three-quarters of his face. It gave him a distinctive gladiator vibe.

His girls each wore the same style of mask, made of colorful cock-feathers which contrasted nicely with the cold metal of his mask.

"I was told you never had a chance to discuss your film with Nosh, Miss Bennett, but he is a wealth of knowledge."

Brie appreciated Master Coen's lead-in, and took the opportunity to address the Master personally. "I hope you will consider sharing some of that knowledge with me, Master Nosh. I know many fans of the original documentary hoped for a peek at the Dominant Training Center."

After an extended pause, the man spoke in a voice so deep it made Brie's insides tremble. "I will consider it."

He turned to Master Coen and put his hand on his shoulder, silently gesturing to the rest of the group.

"Yes, I suppose now is as good a time as any," Master Coen conceded, speaking to the entire room. "Master Nosh and the Gallants already know the news I'm about to share."

Mr. Gallant kissed Ena lightly on the back of her hand and nodded to Master Coen in encouragement.

He stunned the room with his next pronouncement. "I am stepping down as Headmaster."

Silence settled over the room.

"Don't look so glum. I've been recruited to head the first sister school in Australia."

"Oh, now that *is* interesting…" Marquis Gray remarked.

Mr. Gallant gave Master Coen a congratulatory pat on the back. "Reason enough for celebration tonight."

Ena disappeared into the kitchen, returning with a small but decadent-looking chocolate cake. "Who would like a piece?"

It seemed to break the dazed spell Master Coen had caused, and Captain requested a large slice. He proceeded to sit down on the couch, placing the plate on the coffee table. "Pet, *lief*, come."

Brie watched Mary stand up and walk over to him, gracefully kneeling on one side of Captain while Candy knelt on the other. He waited until the entire party had been served before he cut a small piece for Candy and then another bite for Mary. Darned if Blonde Nemesis didn't demurely eat from the fork Captain offered with a slight blush on her cheeks.

Mr. Gallant told everyone, "Although this is a vanilla affair, try to have a little fun tonight."

Master Coen wanted nothing to do with the cake, but for personal entertainment he insisted his submissives share a piece without using utensils. He watched with obvious pleasure as they seductively licked the frosting off each other's fingers.

Mr. Gallant watched with amusement and swiped his finger over the top of Ena's cake, spreading the rich chocolate over her lip. "Charming," he praised. "You look good enough to eat." He leaned over and removed the offending chocolate with a sensuous lick. "Delicious…"

Brie smiled to herself, nibbling at her cake.

"Oh, Brie, do you remember when you brought over the custard?" Celestia asked, giggling.

Brie whimpered, "Must we bring that up?"

Celestia leaned in and whispered, "You'll never know how much that endeared you to Marquis. He enjoys seeing his students humbled. He believes everyone needs a little grounding now and then." She nodded discreetly at Mary, who was looking up at Captain with adoration as she accepted another bite. "Whenever one of their students overcomes an obstacle, it is a victory for the entire staff."

Brie smiled. "I agree with that sentiment. Seeing Mary dig herself out from her violent past is truly inspiring."

Celestia mused aloud, "You can't help but wonder what Faelan would have thought…"

Mr. Gallant cleared his throat, making both Brie and Celestia jump. Brie was sure she was about to be reprimanded for gossiping when he took her to the side to speak to her alone.

"Captain and I believe you and Mary should talk."

"I would love to, Mr. Gallant."

"Please use our bedroom upstairs for privacy's sake. It's the last door down the hall."

Brie walked over to Mary to ask her to join her upstairs, and was pleasantly startled when Mary deferred to Captain. "May I leave the room, Vader?"

He placed his hand on her head. "Yes, *lief*. Enjoy your time with your friend."

"Thank you, Vader." Brie was stunned that Mary seemed genuinely content under Captain's rule. She turned to Brie and smiled. "Lead on, Stinky Cheese."

"Mr. Gallant said we could use his room upstairs," Brie informed her as they walked out of the room.

"His bedroom? Now that sounds naughty, doesn't it?" Mary murmured, placing her hand on the railing as she headed up the stairs.

"You're not going to do anything weird, are you?"

Mary tossed her hair back and shrugged. "We're just going to talk. Right?"

Mr. Gallant's bedroom had impressive double doors that opened into a large room complete with an oversized bed, a reading nook and a wet bar. Mary looked around, running her hands over the oak counters of the bar and the red leather of a chair next to a bookcase. "Talk about a *Master* suite."

"We're not here to snoop in Mr. Gallant's room," Brie warned. "We're supposed to be talking."

"You're such a wet blanket, Brie" she pouted, flopping onto the king-sized bed and looking up at Brie. "So talk."

"I'm not saying a word until you sit on the edge of the bed. Show Mr. Gallant and Ena a little respect, damn it."

Mary spread her hands over the comforter as if she were making a snow angel. "Just think, Brie. Our illustrious teacher fucks his submissive on this very bed."

Although it was an alluring thought, Brie didn't want to start down that path with Mary. "That's it," she snapped. "We're sitting on the floor—a place you're used to."

Mary rolled her eyes, but flopped onto the floor, crossing her legs. She kept looking around the room, fascinated by it. "I bet we're the first students ever to see this hallowed place. Why do you think he has a bar in his bedroom? Don't you think that's a bit strange?"

"I don't care, Mary. Talk to me about you. How have things been going with Captain?"

Mary let out a long sigh. "Getting all serious on me, huh? You're no fun."

"Well?"

She looked away when she answered. "It's fine. No, actually it's better than fine."

"So what's been going on since we last talked? Did he stop making you watch them kiss and snuggle?"

"No," Mary said with a slight grin. "I'm...getting used to that."

Brie nudged her shoulder. "I knew it! You're an old softie inside. I couldn't believe that you let him feed you in front of us tonight. It looked like you actually enjoyed the attention."

"Shut the fuck up."

"Deny it all you want, but it was obvious to everyone in the room and I found it sweet."

"Now I know you're just trying to piss me off."

"No." Brie put her arm around Mary. "I'm not. There's a real change in you. Why can't you just admit it?"

Mary paused, suddenly getting serious on Brie. "I don't want to jinx it."

"Jinx what?"

"At first, being around them was nauseating. But the more I saw how Captain was with Candy, how he genuinely cared for her, the more..."

"The more you wanted it for yourself?"

Mary snarled, "I'm not lusting over Candy's man, if that's what you're implying."

"No, you twit. I meant you want to be treated that way by another man."

Mary rolled her eyes again. "You totally don't get it."

Brie growled in frustration. "Then explain it to me."

"I..." Mary seemed to struggle with the words. "I feel accepted for the first time in my life... I've never felt that way before, and I don't want to lose it."

"Accepted you how? Because Todd accepted you, fangs and all. What's different?"

"They accept me for me, damn it," she said, pointing to herself. "Just me. Not for my looks or how great I can give a blow job...and I'm far better than you—just saying."

Brie ignored the jab, realizing the importance of what Mary was sharing. "So they accept you as a person, not as a sex object?"

"No, you idiot! What I'm trying to tell you is that they accept me as..." She could hardly say the word, and just whispered, "....family."

Brie felt a chill go through her and goosebumps rose on her skin. It took everything not to cry, but she knew how much Mary hated tears and valiantly fought them off. "That's profound, Mary."

"I know. A few times at their home, when we were just hanging out there, not doing anything special, I felt whole." Mary's lips trembled. "I've never felt that before, Brie. Ever."

"You deserve to feel that way, my friend."

She shook her head. "I was afraid Captain might be a mental-case making me call him Vader. I was sure he was planning to act out some Daddy fantasy on me, but fuck it, he really means it. He's been respectful to me this entire time—no wandering touches, no flirtations or sexual glances. You know what I mean. Those stolen glances that let you know where their mind's really at."

"Sure."

"In the past I would have been offended that he was ignoring me. Hell, that's how I relate to all men. But staying with Captain has been different. I really feel a connection to him that has nothing to do with sex."

"Like a father figure."

"Exactly."

"What about Candy?"

Mary smiled. "My relationship with Candy is just the icing on the cake. I see every woman as competition, but she's the first one who doesn't bring out my cutthroat nature, and it's not because she isn't hot. It's just that...I don't feel the need to compete with her."

"Wow, that's huge."

"See, I thought of all the people I know, you might understand. It is huge—it's *fucking* huge! Even my shrink is impressed."

"So I take it that your counseling is going well?"

"Reiny, that's my pet name for him—God, he hates it—he tells me I've been much more open this time around. Seems hitting rock-bottom has that effect on the strong."

"Did he say that or did you?"

"Well, maybe not in those exact words, but let's just say he's impressed with my progress."

"That's great, Mary. Really great. Sir will be thrilled to hear it."

"Yeah," she growled. "Don't think I'm unaware that everyone's been talking about me behind my back."

"Seriously, you're not *that* important. People are concerned, yes, but Miss Wilson isn't the main topic of conversation."

"Sure I'm not..."

Brie let out a snort. "I can't tell if you're fucking with me or being serious."

Mary grinned, her eyes sparkling mischievously.

"Well, at least it's good to see you acting like yourself again."

"Brie, I have to ask..."

"What? Anything."

She paused for a long time. "How's Faelan? I haven't stopped thinking about him, not for a second since he left."

Brie frowned, wishing she had something positive to share with her. "I'm really sorry, Mary. I have no idea where he is and I haven't heard from him since we left the commune."

"Don't you think it's fucked up? I'm finally getting my shit together, but he'll never know I love him?" A tear escaped, but Mary brushed it away angrily.

"He knew that, Mary," Brie assured her, trying to stop her voice from quavering. "I believe that's why he never gave up on you."

Mary buried her face in her hands, trying unsuccessfully to hold back tears.

Brie looked away, knowing she was about to fall apart herself. She was angry that fate had been so cruel to them.

Mary took a couple of deep breaths, brushing away her tears. "Well, I'm done talking."

They stood up together, but Mary walked over to the dresser mirror to fix her face and fluff her hair before presenting herself to the group again. She turned and smiled wickedly at Brie. "Since this is the only time I'll ever be in here…"

Before Brie could stop her, Mary went behind the bar and tried to open the cupboards. "They're all locked! I bet this bar is really just a cover to hide all his toys from the kids." She slapped her hands on the counter in frustration. "Damn, I was hoping to see what kind of kink he's into."

"OMG, Mary, get away from there! You have no decorum whatsoever."

Mary held her arms up in surrender. "Fine, but don't tell me you weren't curious." She shut the double doors to the bedroom, murmuring, "Some other time, Gallant…"

Brie would never admit it to Mary, but she *was* curious. Mr. Gallant was a compelling mystery that she'd often contemplated, and it appeared the man was destined to remain that way.

Darkness

B rie arrived to an empty home, even though she didn't get in until after two in the morning. She wasn't surprised, however, knowing Sir and Lilly had a lifetime to catch up on.

She drifted into the bedroom and was getting ready for bed when she noticed Sir's journal open on his nightstand. She inadvertently glanced at it, wondering if it might hold a fantasy of his. When she saw the word 'Mother', she immediately picked it up to read, wanting to know what he was feeling.

Mother

You are darkness

You seek to destroy

Betrayal as your heritage

Cruelty your legacy

And yet

I care

Forever damned

By the love that ruined me

Yet haunts me...

Still

Brie sat down, rubbing her hands over the words, wishing she could remove the profound pain expressed on the page. She knew Sir still struggled with memories from the past, and meeting his sister had only helped to stir the nightmares he'd kept buried deep within.

She closed his journal and kissed it, placing it back on the nightstand. "May tonight bring you a new level of peace, Sir."

Not being the least bit sleepy, Brie decided to wander back out to the couch with a large blanket to cuddle in. She turned on the TV for background noise and whipped out her laptop to work on her film while she waited for Sir's return.

She was in the middle of reviewing the footage between Rytsar and his young sub when she could have sworn she heard his name on the TV. She glanced up and turned up the volume when a picture of him flashed across the screen.

"…Rachel, I have a little tidbit about the man we've been hearing so much about."

"Do tell!"

"I did a little digging and discovered our Russian hero is the very same Rytsar Durov from that naughty underground hit last summer."

"Get out!"

The two women giggled as they fanned themselves.

"Of course, it's tragic what happened to the girl, but how dreamy it must have been to be rescued by him."

"Those big buff arms…"

Brie quickly googled Rytsar's name and was shocked to find a recent news article detailing the captive girl's ordeal. Upon further investigation, she found that the culprit of the leak was the girl herself. Apparently she had fallen for the Russian Dom and wanted the whole world to know of his heroism.

Brie started hyperventilating, afraid this young woman's zeal might end up costing Rytsar his freedom or even his life. She picked up the phone and called his private cell, a feeling of unease setting in when he didn't pick up quickly enough.

"Hello?" he finally answered in his thick Russian accent.

"Rytsar, have you heard what's happened? Stephanie, that young girl you saved, just told the world who you are and what you did."

He cursed under his breath. "Titov specifically told her and her family to remain silent. Why would she do this?"

"I'm not sure, but I think it might be a case of hero-worship. This girl's going on and on about how you saved her from the bad guys. Luckily, the only substantial information I've been able to glean from the internet is your name and your main residence in Moscow. Get ready, though—the phone is about to start ringing off the hook."

Rytsar snorted. "No, the landline was destroyed in the fire, *radost moya*. They will not be able to reach me, and only those I trust have this number."

"What if you get in trouble because of this?"

"The girl knows little," he assured her. "Titov spoke to her extensively before they left the Motherland. Besides, without a body or witnesses, there is no crime. Do not fret—you will not be tied in any way to the event."

"That's right, you don't know! They've already associated you with my documentary."

Rytsar sounded amused rather than upset. "You Americans and your fascination with the men of Mother Russia."

"This isn't a laughing matter!"

He lowered his voice, speaking calmly to her. "I do not foresee it being an issue for you—I will ensure it."

"What about you?"

"Huh! If something were to befall me, I would not alter the course of my actions. I am at peace, *radost moya*. There is no reason to be concerned."

Brie's lip trembled when she confessed, "I couldn't handle it if anything were to happen to you."

"It won't."

Not willing to end their phone call and still longing to know about his past, Brie prodded hesitantly, "Rytsar?"

"*Da?*"

"Can I ask you what happened to Tatyana?"

The phone went silent.

"Rytsar?"

He whispered softly to himself, "Tatyana..." It seemed as if simply hearing her name had flooded him with images and memories. "Yes, *radost moya*, I will tell you of her."

Brie turned off the TV and wrapped the blanket around her, chilled by the haunted tone of his voice.

"I wouldn't have known her if it weren't for Titov. We were boyhood comrades, he and I, making trouble in the streets of Moscow. The two of us got into many scrapes together." He chuckled to himself. "You wouldn't believe the numerous whippings I suffered under my father's belt because of our mischief—all worth it."

Brie giggled, imagining the little hellion Rytsar must have been.

"But as often as I hung around Titov, I never really noticed his little sister until she turned sixteen. I'd been invited over for dinner one evening, and she greeted me at the door. It was then that I was confronted by those dangerously arched eyebrows and blossoming curves." He grunted with pleasure at the memory. "It was as if a light bulb had suddenly been switched on and I was consumed by only one thought: *MINE!*"

Brie smiled to herself, imagining that moment.

"However, Tatyana told everyone she was saving herself for the right man. She purposely ignored me, inviting the chase. But I was content to bide my time, in no particular hurry to settle down just yet."

He growled under his breath. "It wasn't long after that Titov started running with a different crowd—people I refused to associate with. I warned him, but he was young and foolish, full of ambition. He and I went our separate ways, but I never forgot about Tatyana. I knew she was waiting for me to claim her."

"On her eighteenth birthday he came banging on my door, shouting that Tatyana had gone missing. We looked everywhere for her only to discover that one of his new 'comrades' had amassed a huge gambling debt. The boy had needed to turn a quick profit or lose his life as payment. Rather than face his fate, the maggot kidnapped Tatyana and sold her to a foreign buyer. The two of us beat the shit out of him to get the information, only to miss rescuing her by mere minutes—*minutes!*"

A tear ran down Brie's cheek at the thought of the young woman being kidnapped and raped repeatedly, believing she'd been forsaken, never knowing how close she'd come to being saved...

"We were forced to spend the next five months playing a perverse game of cat and mouse as we tracked her from owner to owner." Rytsar's tone became more subdued when he told Brie, "She was broken, just skin and bones, huddled in a corner, high on heroin the day we finally caught up with her. When Titov approached Tatyana, she offered herself to him, begging her brother to be gentle. We foolishly thought we'd saved her when we brought her back home, but what did we know?"

"But you did save her," Brie insisted.

"*Nyet.* We failed to understand how shattered she was. Her family and I bought her smiles and assurances, and took heart when she forced herself to start eating again. The reality was that she was appeasing us, just biding her time—whether she knew it or not."

Brie felt chills when she heard his next words. "I'll never forget the day she killed herself. I'm not a man for sentimentalities, but I bought her yellow flowers. It was a national holiday and I was in a rare mood to celebrate." He paused, his voice becoming bitter. "Now I only associate yellow with blood... I hate flowers."

"Why did she do it when she had so much to live for?"

"Tatyana told me once that she was tainted beyond repair, and it made me furious. I swore to her that anyone who dared tell her that would answer to me personally. I failed to listen, *radost moya.* She was not talking about other people's perceptions of her, but her own."

Brie heard the heartbreak in his voice when Rytsar confessed, "You cannot fix the broken, no matter how much you want to. She was the *one*—my mate and the future mother of my children. When that maggot took her, he not only stole her future, but mine and that of generations to come."

Rytsar pounded his chest, howling in rage, the sound of sickening thuds carrying over the phone line. Tears rolled down Brie's cheeks as she listened, knowing there was nothing she could do to ease his suffering or the unbearable loss he felt.

When the terrifying sounds stopped, an eerie silence followed.

"Rytsar?" she cried out softly.

His hoarse voice cut through the darkness like a beacon of hope. "That's why this girl is important. Titov and I need her. We need her not only to survive—but to *live*."

Those words haunted Brie after they hung up. She put her computer away, no longer able to work. Instead she folded the blanket, laying it on the arm of the couch before heading off to bed. Just as she flicked off the lights, she heard the ding of the elevator in the hallway.

She didn't know what possessed her, but she jumped into bed and pretended to be asleep.

Sir lingered out in the hallway for an unusually long period of time. Finally his welcome footsteps started towards the bedroom and she buried her head in the pillow. She heard him step inside the threshold, but then stop.

After several long, agonizing moments, Brie snuck a peek to see what was going on. Sir was standing in front of her, looking down with a knowing smile on his lips.

"Just wake up?"

She looked up at him guiltily. "No, never fell asleep."

He chuckled as he started loosening his tie. "I noticed the blanket was still warm in the other room, and you don't usually sleep with your face smashed into the pillow."

She pulled back the covers and invited him to bed. "How was the opera with your sister, Sir?"

The sparkle in his eye said it all. "It went far better than I'd hoped. Tell me, how was the party?"

"It was wonderful, Sir."

"Since neither of us feels like sleeping, why don't we fill each other in on the night's events? Waiting until morning only ensures we'll forget a detail or two."

"Did you hear about Rytsar and the girl?"

Sir nodded. "Durov texted me. I'll be watching the situation closely, but for now all we can do is wait, trusting it will blow over without incident."

"Rytsar told me about Tatyana."

"Such an unfortunate loss," Sir stated, a sad look in his eyes. "Although it spurred him to come to the States as an exchange student, it's sobering to think that his loss became my gain. I wouldn't be where I am today if I hadn't met Durov in those early college years."

"Life is a strange journey."

Sir grunted his agreement.

Brie wanted to lighten the mood, so she fluffed up the pillows and propped herself against the headboard, snuggling against Sir when he joined her in bed. "Why don't you tell me all about Lilly?"

To her delight, he shared everything. Not only what they'd discussed, but his thoughts and impressions throughout the evening. Any concerns Brie had had about being left out disappeared as Sir detailed the entire night. What struck her most was how excited he seemed. Sir radiated energy, as if he were riding on an emotional high.

"Until tonight, I can't say I would have understood when you shared Miss Wilson's assertion that one could feel whole again. But it seems, for a brief moment, I experienced that this evening."

Although Brie found that admission surprising, she was completely unprepared for Sir's next revelation.

"Brie, in the spirit of feeling whole…" He pulled her closer. "I have a serious question for you."

"Of course, Sir. You can ask me anything."

He cupped her chin and smiled. "For this conversation, call me Thane."

Brie's interest was piqued, and she leaned in to kiss him. "My pleasure…Thane." She loved the way his given name rolled off her tongue when she said it—so sexy and romantic.

"There's something that my grandfather did on his wedding night. He spoke of it as if it was the greatest experience of his life. One not to be missed."

"Oh! You have my mind spinning now. I can't even imagine what you're about to say."

Sir gently stroked her cheek, causing tiny, tingling jolts of electricity to run over her skin. "My grandfather said the most beautiful moment of his life was when he made love to my grandmother on their wedding night. He said it was knowing they *might* conceive a child from the union that made it so singular."

Sir continued, tracing her lips with his fingertip. "My father hinted at the same thing. It's tradition for our family—no contraception allowed on the honeymoon. Simply a man and his woman, committing their lives in the most intimate way."

He gently pressed her head to his chest, stroking Brie's hair as he looked down at her. "You've mentioned you want children, Brie."

She nodded, but added softly, "When you're ready."

"Durov was not wrong to point out I'm not getting any younger. I feel, if this is truly the direction you want to go, we should start a family sooner rather than later. There's no sense in putting it off."

Brie lifted her head. "While I can appreciate what you're saying, S— Thane, I have my documentary to think of, and you're still building your overseas business."

"True enough, which is why you must be absolutely certain this is the path you want to take. I'm willing to have children, but only if we begin now."

The reality of what he was suggesting was both thrilling and frightening to her. "*Now?*"

"If we conceive quickly, which is no guarantee, I will still be in my mid-forties by the time the oldest is barely ten. It's now or never, Brie."

She bit her lip, adrenaline flowing through her veins as she seriously considered his proposal. "A family when I'm still just a kid myself?"

"My grandmother was nineteen when she had her first child, and my mother...only twenty-two."

Brie took a deep breath as reality began to sink in. "I would have to put my career on hold."

"Probably, at least for a few years once you get pregnant. If we do this, I want you to take care of yourself and the baby. No late nights, and no last-minute deadlines."

She shook her head in disbelief. "I have to admit, when you started the conversation tonight, this was so *not* the direction I thought it was headed."

"Durov made a nuisance of himself in Russia, but it made me think. He was right to push the issue. If you wish to be a mother, we need to begin soon."

Brie stroked his jaw, rough with morning stubble. "Do you really want to have a baby with me, Thane Davis?"

The tenderness in Sir's eyes melted her heart. "Yes, Brie. I want you to have my child." He smiled as he wiped away a tear that had formed in her eye. "But there's something you have to do for me."

"What's that?"

"You need to stop taking your birth control pills, and we won't be having intercourse again until our wedding night."

Her jaw dropped. "For two whole months?"

Sir nodded, grinning when he saw her look of shock. "When we make love again, Miss Bennett, it will be as man and wife."

"I can't even imagine…"

"Now, that's not to say we won't enjoy each other's company. It just won't be in the traditional manner."

"Oh, thank goodness! I think I'd shrivel up and die otherwise," she said laughing. Then Brie looked at Sir seriously. "In case this is our last chance for a while, I'd like to make love with you tonight."

Sir kissed her on the lips, slipping his tongue into her mouth. "Let's…"

Brie scooted out from under him. "Did you buy a mask for tonight's party?"

He nodded towards the nightstand. Brie opened the drawer and pulled out a black mask lined in silver. "I like this very much, it's so stylish. Do you mind if I put it on you?"

He lifted his head and she slipped it over his eyes. She sat back to take in the sight of Sir lying naked in the bed, wearing nothing but the sexy mask. "You are one handsome man, Mr. Davis."

He smiled and held up his hands. "Have your way, Miss Bennett."

Brie growled lustfully at the invitation and climbed onto him, straddling his already hardening cock. She grabbed his wrists and forced them over his head. "Resistance is futile."

She put pressure on his wrists, using them for leverage as she slowly slid her wet pussy over his shaft. "I want you to feel how much I love you." She kissed him on the lips and left a trail of kisses down his chest. "I cherish every part of you."

Sir groaned when she flicked her tongue over his nipple. She moved to the other and nibbled lightly before flicking her tongue again. "Do you want me, Thane?"

"What do you think?" he replied, thrusting his pelvis upwards so she could feel the hardness of his shaft.

Brie smiled as she lifted up to slowly descend on his cock. She threw her head back and moaned as she took the fullness of it. "You feel so good inside me." Taking her time, Brie rolled her hips, purposely moving slowly so he would feel every movement, every slight tilt of her pelvis.

Sir stared up at her, totally infatuated with her dangling breasts. They proved too much of a temptation, and he reached up to play with them.

"God, you're beautiful," he murmured. Brie purred, loving the feel of his hands on her nipples, caressing and tugging on them. Sir leaned up and took a mouthful, grazing her nipple with his tongue before sucking it.

"I crave your mouth," she moaned, pressing herself against him.

He amped up the suction as he showered equal attention on each breast. Brie rewarded his attention with deeper penetration and faster pelvic thrusts, which drove both of them to the edge.

Brie suddenly stopped and laid her head on his chest, listening to his wildly beating heart. She smiled up at him once it had slowed back down to a normal rhythm. "I treasure that heart."

She sat up again, wiggling her pussy against his base as she caressed his body with her fingers, from his muscular thighs and toned stomach to his hairy chest and talented hands.

"Every inch of you is sensual and pleasing," she confessed.

"Show me how much I please you."

Brie bit her lip, bracing her hands against his chest as she began rolling her hips again. "I will not stop this time," she warned him. "I'm going to use your gorgeous body for my own pleasure." She took him at just the right angle to rub the ridge of his shaft against her G-Spot. With quick, short strokes, she built up the delicious tension until chills coursed through her.

"I'm close," she whispered, throwing her head back and concentrating on his cock rubbing against that sweet, swollen area deep inside her. Her breath became shallow as her body tensed for release.

"Let me make it easy for you," Sir growled huskily. He reached around, teasing her clit with his fingers. She moaned in pure bliss, creeping ever closer to the edge. When she was on the precipice, he slowly slipped his finger inside her ass.

Brie cried out in ecstasy as her body began its rhythmic dance around his cock. "Come with me, Thane."

He pulled her down on top of him, wrapping his arms around her as he thrust his pulsing shaft into her, filling her with his seed.

Brie lay there panting afterwards, smiling. "I love when you come inside me."

He gave a contented sigh. "I do too, babygirl."

They lay in each other's arms as the sun peeked over the horizon, bathing their bedroom with its light.

"Welcome to a new day, Sir."

He leaned forward and kissed the top of her head. "Brie."

She immediately looked up, responding to the serious tone of his voice.

"I want you to carefully weigh what we've discussed. This decision will change the course of our lives—not only our careers, but our relationship as well."

The gravity of the decision was not lost on her. She curled up under the comforter as Sir got up to pull down the shades. The complexity of their situation was overwhelming. She was about to change what they had—the perfect life she knew and loved—to grasp for something out of reach.

It was risky.

But when she closed her eyes, she saw herself holding Thane's child and she knew peace...

The Mission

A few days later Sir sat Brie down, explaining that he had an important mission for her. "Lilly would like us to fly to China to visit our mother together. However, I need you to return to Denver."

She felt a twinge of jealousy that Lilly was trying to leave her out. "My documentary can wait, Sir."

"It's not about the film, Brie. Mr. Wallace needs at least one of us to be with him right now."

The mention of Faelan completely stunned her and she gasped, fearing the worst. "Is he dying?"

"Yes...and no." Sir took her hand in his. "He will die without intervention, but a donor has been located and Wallace has finally been given a date for surgery."

"A donor for what, Sir?"

"He lost a kidney in that car accident years ago. Unfortunately, his remaining kidney was also damaged in the crash and has begun to fail."

"So he's getting a kidney replacement?"

"Yes, but because of his blood type that has proved a difficult issue."

"Couldn't his parents just donate one of theirs?" she asked naively.

"No. He has the particular honor of being O negative, which means he is a universal donor but can only receive organs from another O negative patient. They are extremely rare."

"But you said a donor *has* been found?"

Sir nodded. "Yes. In the most unlikely of places. After Mr. Wallace apprised me of his situation while we were at the Sanctuary, I began contacting people who might be able to help within our community back in LA. When no donor was found, I expanded the search. Naturally, donors are less likely to give up a healthy kidney to a complete stranger.

The surgery itself requires months of recovery, extreme pain, and the very real loss of a functioning kidney."

"That must be why Todd gave up all hope."

"The likelihood of finding a donor in time was next to impossible, but fate has been generous and a man overseas has agreed to donate his organ. The surgery will take place next week, but I want you to be there for Mr. Wallace now. I've been told he's not doing well, physically or mentally. For this procedure to succeed, he must be as healthy as possible going in to the operating room."

"Of course I want to help, Sir, but my preference is to be there for *you*."

He kissed her tenderly on the lips. "I cherish your support which is why I plan to fly with you to Denver, before I continue on to New York to pick up Lilly."

Brie could not hide her disappointment at being left behind. "I wanted to be there when you saw your mother again."

"I wish that were possible, babygirl. Sometimes life pulls us in different directions and we have to do what's best for all concerned."

"Will you two be deciding whether to let her die?"

"I hope to convince Lilly that it's time. However, she refuses to even discuss it until she sees our mother in person. I can't blame her; it's not easy to end a life."

"But if you decide to pull the plug, you *will* send for me."

"Brie, you are a part of me. I will need you there when the time comes."

She laid her head against his shoulder and sighed. "I hate that there is so much going on at once, and none of this is easy."

"Life isn't easy, I learned that a long time ago. We must each find our happiness during the hardships if we are to survive." Sir took her hand and kissed it. "*You* are my happiness."

"And you are mine, Sir."

"Before we start this unwanted separation, I have a pleasant task for you to complete. I've arranged for your mother to come this weekend. Do you think you can find a wedding dress in two days, my dear?"

Brie squealed, overjoyed at the prospect of visiting with her mother and finding *the* dress. "I will leave no stone unturned."

"I have only two requirements for the gown."

She raised an eyebrow, curious what they might be. "Please share."

"I want it to be pearl-white and have a low, swooping back." He rubbed the small of her back sensually with his fingertips. "I hope to see a hint of your brand."

She blushed, pleased by his requests.

"Money is no object. However, I do have an added challenge for you and your mother—to add to the thrill of the hunt. I'm giving you ten thousand."

Brie's jaw dropped. "Ten thousand dollars?"

"Yes, but what you don't spend can go to the charity of your mother's choice."

"I love the nature of this challenge, Sir," she said, giddy with excitement.

"Good, but don't feel any shame if you end up giving five dollars to your mother's charity. I want you to purchase the dress of your dreams. One that makes you feel elegant inside and out."

Brie threw herself at Sir. "Man, I can't wait to marry you!"

He chuckled. "On a more serious note, have you given any more thought to having children?"

Brie nodded, answering his question by marching into the bathroom and bringing back her two packets of pills. She knelt at Sir's feet and held them up to him. "I stopped taking them last night."

He took the two cases from her and deftly tossed them. They made a satisfying clunk when they landed in the wastepaper basket. Sir took her hands and kissed each upturned palm. "You and I are officially starting a family, babygirl."

Brie's mother came late that Friday night and the two began mapping out the dress shops they wanted to visit. "Let's go for the big wedding shops in outlying cities first—they should have the best selection of discount racks—and then we can concentrate on the smaller boutiques if we need to."

Sir interjected, "I don't want you to find a bargain deal, Brie. Your dress should be as exquisite as you are."

Her mother cooed. "Oh, I love that you talk to my daughter that way." She placed her hand on his shoulder. "But you must trust me that I will not fail in this duty I've been given."

Brie grinned at Sir. "Getting my mom on the case was a wise decision. She has a nose for quality bargains."

"As long as you're happy with the dress," Sir replied.

"Don't worry, Thane. She will be, but you shouldn't expect to see us until late tonight. There's no rest for the wicked."

He smiled charmingly at her mother. "I hardly consider a mother and daughter shopping for wedding dresses as being wicked."

"Oh, you don't know me at all, son," her mother quipped. "This woman is going *whole* milk in her latte today."

Sir laughed. "I'll be sure to warn the cops."

As they were leaving, her mother confided, "I like your man, sweetie. A sense of humor goes a long way in a marriage."

"He and his friends are all kinds of funny, Mom."

She shook her head. "I can only imagine. Actually…" She giggled. "I'm afraid to."

They spent the day running from shop to shop, trying on many beautiful gowns, but not one stirred Brie's soul. She came back that night feeling defeated, until she smelled the enticing aroma of Sir's *ribollita* floating from their apartment.

"What?! He cooks too?" her mother asked in astonishment as they walked through the door.

"Thane's a true Renaissance man, Mom. Maybe now you can understand why I love him so much."

Sir had set the table simply and let them dish up their own bowls, but he insisted on finishing their dishes. Brie's mom was taken by surprise when he sprinkled her bowl with aged parmesan and a swirl of olive oil.

"Oh! I've never had anyone put oil on my stew before," she said, giggling.

"Trust me, it makes the dish," Brie assured her. The dinner was accented with many sounds of pleasure as her mother enjoyed the fruits of Sir's labor.

He wore a pleased smile as he watched the two women consume the meal he'd made. "So no dress today, Brie?" he asked, once he'd finished his bowl.

She put down her spoon and shrugged. "I'm sorry."

"Do I need to repeat that getting a bargain is not the goal? I don't want my challenge to stop you from buying the dress you want."

"It wasn't that. It's just…I never found one that felt right. There was one this afternoon that was close, but something was missing. I didn't love it."

Brie's mother patted her hand. "Don't worry about it, Brianna. Tomorrow we'll try the smaller shops. I'm positive the dress you're looking for is out there. We will find it, *and* at a price that will make you sing."

Brie smiled, accepting her mother's promise. In typical 'mom' fashion, she insisted on doing the dishes when Brie stood up and started to clean off the table.

Sir protested and tried to stop her. "You're a guest in our home."

"Nonsense. We're practically family, and family helps out. Besides, you cooked the meal. It's the least I can do."

He nodded graciously, consenting to her offer and retiring to the adjoining room. Brie smiled every time she glanced at Sir while hand-drying his cooking tools.

"I wish your father could see this," her mother stated wistfully.

"He will someday, at a holiday gathering, when he's bouncing his grandson on his knee."

Her mother stopped scrubbing the pot to look at Brie. "Are you planning on having children?" she asked in a hushed whisper.

Brie smiled shyly and nodded.

Her mother's eyes suddenly filled with tears. "I never dared hope…"

Brie wrapped her arms around her mom and they both started crying. It wasn't until then that she fully understood the dreams her parents had given up in their desire to be supportive of her marriage.

"Is everything okay in there?" Sir asked from the couch.

They smiled as they wiped away each other's tears. "Everything is perfect, Thane," Brie answered. She looked at her mother and they started laughing.

"Good. I prefer laughter to tears."

Her mother elbowed Brie. "A keeper for sure."

The next morning, the two women started out early, driving over an hour and a half to get to a little shop south of LA. It was in an older area, and the shop was so tiny that Brie wasn't sure she even wanted to stop, but her mother insisted.

When they entered the establishment they were greeted by an elderly couple. "Welcome, ladies! Which one of you is getting married?" the old gentleman asked.

Brie's mother giggled. "Aren't you so cute?" She pushed Brie forward. "My daughter is looking for a dress, but she has specific requirements, so why don't we cut to the chase and not waste any time?"

The grandmotherly woman took both of Brie's hands. "What are you looking for, dear heart?"

Brie blushed, moved by the woman's gentle eyes. "My future husband requested a pearl-white dress with an exposed back."

The woman's eyes lit up. "Do you like lace?"

"I do," Brie answered enthusiastically.

She turned to her husband. "It finally happened."

"What?" Brie's mother asked, laughing nervously at their odd behavior.

"Go get the gown," she said to him in a reverent tone.

The old man smiled and disappeared into the back of the shop. While he was retrieving the dress, the shopkeeper explained, "Years ago, a young women ordered a beautiful wedding gown but she never returned to claim it."

He came back out with the dress and smiled as he lifted it for Brie to see. The woman continued, "The front is covered in Italian lace, but the silk sheath underneath will flatter your figure because of its princess neckline. So modest and elegant."

She led Brie into the changing room to help her into the gown.

"Momma," Brie called once it was on, grazing the delicate lace with her fingertips.

Italian lace…

When her mother entered the fitting room, she stopped short and put her hand to her lips, tears welling up in her eyes.

Brie slowly turned to behold the splendor of the back as the shopkeeper shared, "The back has a simple but beautiful scoop line, and just look at that train… We took a hard hit when the young woman never showed up, but I always trusted the right bride would come along."

Brie smiled at she looked at the dress in the mirror. It accentuated her back, still in keeping with the elegance of the front, and the gown showed off her curves with tasteful sensuality. The best part—the one she knew Sir would appreciate most—was that it showed the slightest hint of her brand.

"Of course, it will need to be fitted, but oh…" the old woman sighed, holding her hands over her heart, "this dress was made for you."

The woman called out to her husband, "Honey, you *have* to see this!" She hit his arm excitedly when he pushed back the curtain. "Didn't I tell you it would find a home?"

He smiled looking at the dress and then up at Brie before turning to his wife. "Yes, you did, dear. I should never have doubted you."

Brie played with the pearl buttons that ran up the length of her arm, loving that little touch. "So now I must ask the dreaded question. How much?"

The woman smiled hesitantly, clasping her hands together in a nervous manner. "Twenty-five hundred."

It was far cheaper than Brie had expected. She looked at her mother and smiled, an inspiration coming to her. "Do you have a veil to go with this?"

"Oh, I have the perfect one. It will complement the dress but won't detract."

While the couple hunted for the veil, Brie whispered in her mother's ear. To her delight, her mom nodded in enthusiastic agreement.

The couple returned a short time later with a simple handmade veil. The old woman placed it on Brie's head with a loving touch as she smoothed out the fine lace. "There!"

Brie turned and looked at the mirror. She was overcome with a prickling sensation she knew well. It suddenly felt real, all of it—the wedding, a life with Thane, growing old together.

Without any hesitation, Brie told the shopkeepers, "I would like to pay twenty-five hundred for the veil."

"No!" the old man scoffed.

"Consider it a finder's fee. You've had this dress waiting for me for years. I won't take no for an answer. You've made me unbelievably happy today," Brie gushed.

Her mother chimed in, "That's true for both of us, and I'm sure a certain groom will be thanking you later."

The woman blushed, waving away the praise, but then she asked timidly, "Would you mind sending us a picture of the wedding? It would mean so much to us."

Brie's mother grabbed a business card from the counter. "Consider it done."

On the drive home, Brie took a detour to the area above the city where Sir had taken her on several occasions. Even though it held difficult memories, it was a stunning view of the city she'd grown to love, and she wanted to share it with her mother.

Brie pulled to the side of the road and they got out to take in the expansive city below.

"So you really like it here?" her mother asked.

"I love it, Mom. I couldn't be happier."

"I can appreciate that better now. For us, everything was overshadowed by our own shock. But now...now I've seen you two together in your home, with no strained conversations, no guards up, I can see how truly happy you are."

"It's kind of hard to do that around Dad."

"You know he means well, and it'll make him happy to know how well this trip went. Brianna, he only wants what's best, and you can't blame us for being uncomfortable with this whole...BDSM thing. I mean, who wants to know what their children do in the bedroom?"

Brie blushed. "Although I can appreciate that, our lifestyle choice is so much more, Mom. There's a community of people we can count on, and lifelong friendships that have changed me for the better. Most people my age walk around in a daze, coming home from work to waste time on their phones, watching TV or playing on their computers." She stated proudly,

"But I don't waste my time, Mom. I'm constantly challenging myself to grow as a person with Sir's—I mean Thane's—help."

Her mother wrapped her arm around Brie. "You can call him Sir around me, sweetie. Your father finds it disturbing, but it doesn't bother me in the least."

Brie smiled as she pointed in the direction of the tobacco shop down below. "I was sitting in a dead end job, just trying to make ends meet while filming shorts on the weekend. I would still be there if it hadn't been for Sir."

"No, honey. I believe you would eventually have found your way into the industry."

Brie shrugged. "I guess we'll never know, but what I *do* know is that I love the path I'm on, and I wouldn't change a thing. How many people can say that?"

Her mother looked over the city as she squeezed her daughter. "Not many, Brianna. Not many."

Although it was hard to see her mother head back to Nebraska, it was even harder watching Sir pack for his trip to China.

"I don't want you to go, Sir," she lamented as he folded a shirt and laid it in his suitcase.

"You need to start packing too, babygirl."

"I know, but I've been putting it off because I don't want us to be separated again."

Sir stopped what he was doing and walked over to her. "Mr. Wallace is struggling. He needs your encouragement, and I must go to China."

"I understand…" Brie sighed. "We can't change what is happening, but I hate these separations."

"It's amusing you feel that way, since you're a film director by trade. You did *know* it requires a lot of travel."

"Yeah, yeah…"

"In that vein, I suggest you use any free time in Denver to film missing elements while you have people at your disposal. Time is running out."

"I know, because soon we'll be getting married!" she squealed with joy.

"Yes, we will, Miss Bennett." He grabbed a fistful of hair and pulled her head back, kissing her deeply. "So let's get through this difficult part, focusing on the fact that the best is yet to come."

When Brie lay in his arms that night, she could barely keep her eyes open.

"Go to sleep, babygirl," Sir whispered.

She dutifully closed her eyes and images of her bridal dress came to mind. Brie could just imagine walking down the aisle, seeing Sir's expression when he beheld her in the gown for the first time...

Tono's smile took her breath away. "Are you ready, toriko?"

She smoothed out the exquisite dress, admiring the lace details of the ivory gown before looking up at him and answering confidently, "Yes, Tono."

The Asian Dom held out a piece of jute and she purred, willingly offering her wrist to him.

Tono gently wrapped the rope around her delicate wrist, creating a decorative pattern of rosettes.

Brie examined it closely when he was done, sighing in contentment. "It's beautiful." She looked up at him, tears in her eyes. "It's perfect, just like you."

He took her hand and gently kissed the rope. "No tears, toriko."

She wiped them away, giggling. Brie pushed her shoulders back and lifted her chin as the music began to play. She clutched the bouquet of orchids and smiled. Her moment was at hand...

Brie started when she woke.

"What were you dreaming about?" Sir asked, stroking her cheek. "I was watching you and saw a hint of a smile on those sweet lips."

"I was dreaming about my wedding." Brie blushed, confused about why she'd been dreaming about Tono. Thankfully Sir could not see the flush on her cheeks.

"Good," he said in a low, soothing voice. Sir tucked her against him. "Now try to go back to sleep. We both have a long day ahead."

Brie nodded, but she lay there wide awake, pondering her dream. Why was she dreaming about Tono, and what the heck did it mean?

Brie's Mile High Club

Departure

Brie boarded the plane headed to Denver, along with a bunch of groggy passengers. It was four in the morning and, other than the businessmen, the majority of travelers were slow-moving and sleepy. She waited patiently for people to stuff their luggage into the upper bins, but had to quell her irritation when some of them took far too long to do that simple task.

At one point, an older woman tried several times to lift her baggage above her head to slide it into the bin. When the man in front of Brie refused to extend his help, she pressed past him to offer her assistance.

"Thank you, dear."

"My pleasure, ma'am."

"It's so rare to find gracious young folk these days."

"They're still around, ma'am. They're just harder to find at four o'clock in the morning."

The woman laughed, insisting that Brie stay as she dug in her purse and produced a piece of wrapped candy. "It's from my secret stash. Best chocolate in the world," she stated proudly, handing it to Brie.

Brie thanked the woman before moving farther down the aisle, curious where Sir could be hiding. She was surprised to spot her handsome Master at the very back of the plane.

"Fancy finding you here," she said when she reached him.

Sir winked as he took her bag and placed it in the bin above. He took out a blanket and a small pillow, handing them both to her.

"Oh no, Sir. There's no way I'm going back to sleep."

He leaned in and said in a seductive whisper, "Trust me, téa, you're going to need it."

Her heart quickened at the use of her sub name in public. "Ah...well then, thank you." She scooted to the window seat and buckled herself in, placing the two items on her lap. "I've never ridden at the back of a plane with you before, Mr. Davis," she teased flirtatiously.

"When I noticed this wasn't going to be a full flight, I decided we should take advantage of the fact," he replied, grazing his finger under her chin.

"I must say I like your way of thinking," she replied, adding in the barest of whispers, "...Master."

He sat down and commanded in a low voice, "Lay your head on the pillow and cover up with the blanket."

Brie grinned to herself as she followed his directions, propping the small pillow against the window, wondering what he had planned for her.

After the plane had taken off and the lights had been turned off so the passengers could sleep, Sir instructed her to close her eyes. She was thrilled by the mystery behind his unusual requests, and lowered her eyelids, refusing to open them even when the *ding* above her announced that the seatbelt sign had been turned off.

Brie heard Sir take out his computer, followed by a light clicking sound as he started to type.

It was pure torture sitting there with her eyes closed, not knowing what he was up to, but she remained still, as per his command. When a stewardess passed by, Brie heard Sir stop her and explain, "We would prefer not to be disturbed for the rest of the flight, but I would appreciate a glass of water."

"Certainly, sir."

Brie giggled to herself, never tiring of hearing service people unwittingly call him by his title.

After the woman returned with his water, she heard him pull down her tray and placed the plastic cup on it before lifting the armrest between them. "Now, téa, unbuckle yourself. Place the pillow on my shoulder and lay your head against it while you cover my lap with an extra portion of your blanket."

They released their belts at the same time and Brie nonchalantly switched her position, settling her head on Sir's shoulder. She noticed a movie playing on his computer screen and noted that he was wearing earphones to make it appear as if he were actively watching the show.

Brie dutifully closed her eyes again, waiting for her next set of instructions.

After several minutes, Sir murmured, "Slowly, so no one will notice, slide your hand under my boxers and take hold of my cock."

Her pussy contracted pleasantly upon hearing his command. With measured movements, she headed towards that sacred spot between her Master's legs. Sir had already unfastened his slacks, allowing Brie easy access to his shaft. Her fingers slipped under the elastic band of the boxers and grasped his rigid shaft.

"Don't move."

She remained still as she felt his hand move ever so slowly under her skirt and beneath her lace panties. He rested his hand over her mound and stopped.

They stayed like that—neither moving—but each deliciously aware of the other's hand resting on their sex.

Finally, Sir directed her, "Slight movements. Don't attract attention."

Brie pressed herself closer against him to get a better reach and gently squeezed and released his cock in her hand. Sir met the challenge by separating her outer lips and lightly fingering her clit. She was already moist due to the nature of her task, and he whispered appreciatively, "Nice and wet."

Brie remained silent, keeping up the ruse of a sleeping partner as she explored his shaft with imperceptible movements. She was rewarded with drops of pre-come on the head of his shaft, announcing his enjoyment to her without words. She used the coveted liquid as lubricant, rubbing it over his shaft as she stroked him ever so slowly, his manhood throbbing in response.

Not to be outdone, Sir increased the tempo of his fingering, causing her to unconsciously arch her back.

"Stay still," he warned.

Brie nestled her head against his shoulder, squeezing his shaft tighter as she stroked him, longing to make the challenge as difficult for him as it was for her. She heard the stewardess pass by again and froze. When Sir assured her that the woman hadn't given them a second glance, she started up again.

Brie relished the fact that this was their first 'official' encounter since deciding to have a child. He had warned her there would be no intercourse until their wedding night, but he'd also promised they would enjoy alternative activities while they waited. Never in a million years would she have guessed they'd be pleasing each other miles above the Earth—in the presence of strangers, no less—the very next morning.

Wicked, wicked Sir.

"No one is near. Stroke me harder, téa."

Brie grasped his cock and pumped it with real gusto until he gripped her wrist tightly. She heard someone pass by and whispered, "Close."

"Closer than you think," he groaned, his cock pulsing in her hand with denied release.

After the individual had returned to their seat, Sir ordered, "You're to remain still, a pleasant expression on your face, with your eyes closed. Anyone walking by will only note that there's a beautiful girl sleeping beside me."

Brie gave a slight nod.

Sir proceeded to roll his finger over her clit, wetting it with her own excitement. He teased her opening with his middle finger while he occasionally flicked his thumb over her clit. The randomness of that additional contact had her body hyper-sensitive. Each time his thumb rubbed against her, a burst of electrical energy headed straight to her core, building her sexual desire.

When he determined she was primed and ready, Sir started stroking his finger from her entrance up to the tip of her clit in slow, rhythmic motions that mimicked his long, tantalizing lick. She let out a soft gasp and he stopped.

Keeping her eyes closed, she pretended to yawn and pressed against him, hoping he would continue. After several minutes, the stroking started up again. Brie could think of nothing but the sensations his touch evoked, and the only way to assure it would continue was not to respond in any way.

Every time she heard someone pass by in the aisle, it added an extra thrill to the experience, increasing her arousal exponentially.

Normally such subtle attention would not result in an orgasm, but the exhibitionistic aspect with the added risk of being caught was an aphrodisiac for Brie. When she could take no more, her body tensed for its release.

Sir noted that she was close and started rolling his finger over her clit again, bringing her to a glorious, drawn-out orgasm. Not a peep did she make, nor did she move, as her pussy contracted and released, wetting his finger.

She felt his cock stiffen in her hand, exposing the pleasure he gained whenever he orchestrated her climax. It was intoxicating to feel the hard physical evidence of just how much he enjoyed pleasing her.

Brie opened her eyes to sneak a peek and saw Sir staring at his screen with a bored expression on his face. No one would ever suspect the naughtiness going on under the tray tables beneath their little blanket.

Her natural inclination was to return the favor but, while still watching the screen, Sir commanded under his breath, "Remove your hand from my cock, téa."

She did so, reluctantly, because it was a direct order, but she was sad not to have the opportunity to please him more fully. Once her hand was back on her lap, Sir removed his and licked his fingers as if he'd just finished eating a delicious snack while watching his movie. He then took the water from her tray and drank it, a smile playing on his lips.

Brie quickly closed her eyes when he turned his head in her direction. She did not dare stir again until the airplane began to descend and Sir shook her shoulder.

"Wake up, my dear, the plane is about to land."

She opened her eyes to gaze into his. "Thank you, Sir," she purred.

"My pleasure, babygirl."

"You're such a sexy man…"

"And you are a very sleepy girl."

"Only for you, Sir," she answered with a grin.

"Are you ready for today?"

Brie grimaced. "I'm nervous about visiting Todd, Sir. He's such a spirited individual; I can't imagine seeing him in a hospital bed, dying."

"Brie, he cannot see your fear. You must put on a brave front, no matter what condition we find him in. He needs our strength. Anything less would be a disservice to him."

She looked down at her lap, sighing. "I hate hospitals. No… I hate the pain that happens in hospitals. They only represent death to me."

He lifted her chin. "You must be brave."

Those words reverberated through her. They were the very words Rytsar had used during their last scene together. She'd been brave then. Brie held on to that, determined to be brave now.

Faelan

B rie hesitated at the hospital entrance, frightened of what she would find inside.

"Come, Brie," Sir insisted, guiding her through the open double doors. After receiving instructions on the location of Faelan's room, they headed towards the elevators.

You must be brave... she reminded herself, straightening her posture and nodding to Sir when the elevator doors opened. He led her through several hallways until they found the room number. Outside the door stood an elderly couple, holding on to each other in a desperate embrace. Brie couldn't help wondering if they were Faelan's grandparents.

Sir walked up to the couple to introduce himself. "Mr. and Mrs. Wallace?"

They looked up, expressions of misery and hopelessness coloring their faces. The man answered matter-of-factly, "I'm Mr. Wallace."

Sir held out his hand. "It is good to finally meet you, sir. I'm Thane Davis. We've talked on the phone several times."

The woman's face lit up. "Mr. Davis?" Without warning, she threw her arms around him.

Sir embraced her, patting her lightly on the back. "Your son is going to be fine, Mrs. Wallace. He will recover from this."

It wasn't until then that Brie realized these were Faelan's parents, *not* his grandparents. The revelation was shocking, but she suspected the hardships they'd faced over the years must have taken a physical toll on the poor couple.

"Things are not well, Mr. Davis," Mr. Wallace corrected. "At this point, we're uncertain he'll even go through with the surgery."

Sir seemed surprised by the news. "What do you mean?"

Mrs. Wallace broke the hug, tears coming to her eyes. "It's like Todd's lost his will to live." A sob escaped her lips. "He refused dialysis, and now he says he doesn't want the surgery. I'm losing my boy, Mr. Davis, and there's nothing I can say or do to prevent it."

Brie swallowed the lump growing in her throat and fought off the tears, knowing that Sir was watching her. If she was going to act courageously, this was the perfect time to prove it.

"Mrs. Wallace, I'm Miss Bennett, a friend of Todd's. He has an entire community back in LA pulling for him. You're not alone."

The woman tilted her head. "You wouldn't happen to be Mary, would you?"

Brie was startled by the question, but smiled warmly. "No, my name is Brie, but Mary and I are friends as well. Has Todd mentioned her to you?"

The woman shook her head. "No, but sometimes he calls out her name when he's asleep."

Brie had to close her eyes to keep back the tears. She opened them and smiled once she had them under control, stating with conviction, "I know we can help Todd regain his strength together. You've had far too much to handle on your own."

Mrs. Wallace broke down, sobbing as she cried on Brie's shoulder. "It's been so hard watching him…fade away."

Brie wrapped her arms around the frail woman, conveying her strength as she held her. Mr. Wallace cautioned in a low voice, "Hush, Ada. You don't want Todd hearing you through the door."

She choked back her sobs and nodded, pulling away from Brie. "I don't want to lose my son, Miss Bennett. He's been through enough in his young life. It's not fair that he's having to face this now."

"Let's concentrate on the fact that a healthy donor has been found and the operation takes place next week," Sir encouraged them. "We've come specifically to support your son. You're no longer alone in this endeavor."

"I thought Todd mentioned he had a sister," Brie said, troubled that the couple was facing this without family support.

"Lisa is in the last month of her pregnancy," Mrs. Wallace explained, new tears forming as she shared. "The doctor has restricted her to bed rest. I'm afraid the pressure of everything has gotten to her. We can't risk losing the baby too…"

"Of course not," Brie agreed, hugging her again.

"Come, Ada, let's get some coffee while Todd's friends visit," her husband suggested, taking her hand. Mr. Wallace glanced back at Sir, his face conveying a look of defeat.

Sir took Brie's hand and squeezed it. "Are you ready for this?"

He will *recover. He* will *live a long life,* she silently repeated, steeling herself for the reunion. She looked up at Sir and answered with confidence, "I'm ready, Sir."

Although Brie had thought she was ready, as the door swung open and she saw Faelan for the first time, she had to struggle to breathe.

Sir whispered, "Remember why we came."

Brie quickly pulled herself together as she took her first step into the room. Faelan looked gaunt, his face sunken and hollow. With his eyes closed, it looked as if he might already be dead—the sound of periodic gasping the only sign of life.

"Mr. Wallace," Sir said loudly. "Mr. Wallace, Miss Bennett and I have come to see you."

His eyelids fluttered for a moment, but he did not move or open them.

Brie spoke up. "Todd, it's me. Sir and I have come to visit you." When he did not respond, she called out, "Faelan."

Todd slowly opened his eyes.

Brie sucked in her breath. Those magnetic blue eyes that had always drawn her in were now dull and lifeless.

"Go away," he rasped.

Even though a chilling sense of doom fell over her, Brie stubbornly held on to her mantra. *He* will *recover. He* will *live a long life...* She shook her head, laughing softly as she took his limp hand. "Oh no, you aren't getting rid of me that easily. I'm here to stay."

He turned away slowly, a pained expression on his face. "I don't want you to see me like this. Go...now."

Brie didn't move.

"Although I appreciate how you feel, Mr. Wallace, we won't be leaving," Sir said with compassion. "You'll have to dig down deep to find the strength needed to survive this surgery, and we've come to support you in that cause."

Faelan snarled, "I don't want your help. I never asked for it."

"Friends don't wait to be asked," Brie told him.

He closed his eyes in an attempt to block her out. "I don't even want this damn operation."

"Why not?" Brie cried.

With his eyes still closed, Faelan stated coldly, "There's no point in a perfectly healthy man losing a kidney. I'm dying. Hell, I've been dying since I was sixteen. Just let me get on with it."

"You have too many people who care about you," she protested.

He laughed bitterly. "Right..."

"Don't you realize how desperate your parents are, thinking they might lose you? You can't do that to them," she insisted. "And what about your poor sister and her baby?"

He opened his eyes and glared at Brie. "They'll be better off. They *all* will."

She knew he was including Mary in that statement. Playing on his sympathy for others wasn't working, so Brie changed tactics. "What kind of legacy are you leaving if you give up now? You can't end on a cowardly note."

"I'm no coward."

"Exactly," Sir answered. "Which is why you will suffer whatever is needed to survive this. You're neither a coward nor a fool. When fate has granted you a second chance, you grab it with both hands."

When Faelan remained unmoved, Sir added in a grave tone, "You have no idea of the devastating consequences such a cowardly act would have on your family and friends."

Brie wondered if Sir was referring to his own father. Was there a part of him that resented his father for taking his life and leaving Sir behind? Her thoughts turned to Mary. Brie was concerned that if Mary ever found out Faelan had chosen to die, it might destroy her.

Without asking permission, Brie lowered the rail on the bed to sit beside Faelan. She took his hand back in hers and squeezed it. "You've touched too many lives to have the luxury of giving up now. Think who will suffer if you do—your parents, your sister, your friends…and Mary."

For the first time, she saw a flicker of light in his eyes, but he turned his head from her. "I'm tired, Brie. I just want to stop fighting." He let out a long, agonized sigh. "I just want to die in peace."

"Too fucking bad," she stated, standing back up. "I'm here now and *I* won't let you."

Faelan glanced at Sir and said in an ominous tone, "You don't want to know what I'll do to her if she stays."

"What? Are you going to throw insults at her? Because God knows you're too weak to throw anything else."

Faelan's expression darkened. "Not that long ago you wouldn't have let me near her, and *now* you're willing to risk her staying alone with me?"

"If I am brutally honest, Mr. Wallace, there's no risk involved, given your current state."

"Fuck…you."

Sir smiled. "Is that the best you can do? Brie should have no problem, then." He turned to her. "You're in charge of getting him to eat regularly and forcing him to exercise his limbs. A gratitude journal might also prove beneficial."

"You have to be shitting me," Faelan growled.

Sir replied with a straight face, "I never shit, Mr. Wallace—unless I'm in the bathroom."

Brie covered her mouth to keep from laughing.

Faelan stared at him, a look of disbelief on his face. Out of the blue, he started laughing, but it soon became gasping breaths and he turned from them in humiliation. When he finally regained his composure, he commanded hoarsely, "Go…"

"We will," Sir informed him, "but only because I need to help Brie settle in. Rest assured, Mr. Wallace, she will return tomorrow with the donor. It will give you a chance to meet the man who has graciously agreed to save your life."

Faelan stared at the window, his voice devoid of emotion. "Save us all the trouble, Mr. Davis, and buy the poor bastard a return ticket home."

His words cut Brie to the bone, but she kept her mind firmly on her mission. "So, Todd, start thinking about what you're grateful for so you can fill up your gratitude journal. Oh, and you'd better inform the nurses what you want to eat, or I will choose something for you—and I'm feeling rather spiteful at the moment."

"Go to hell, Brie."

As they exited the room, Sir smiled at her. "That went well."

"But, Sir, you saw him…"

"Mr. Wallace still has enough fight in him to give us grief. That's encouraging. I was worried for a moment."

Brie took his assertion to heart, and was able to keep a genuine smile on her face when Sir spoke to Faelan's parents. "Not to worry, Mr. and Mrs. Wallace. With Brie's caring ways, I'm certain he will not only agree to the surgery, but will recover quickly from it. You'd be surprised what's possible when you have the right people behind you."

Faelan's father shook his hand vigorously. "Thank you, Mr. Davis. Not only were you instrumental in finding our son a donor, but your support now means the world to us."

"Please save your gratitude for the donor."

"And he'll be coming tomorrow?" Mrs. Wallace asked.

"Yes. In fact, Miss Bennett will be picking him up after she drops me off at the airport. I expect he'll be here at the hospital by ten tomorrow morning."

"We'll be sure to look for him when he arrives," Mrs. Wallace assured Sir.

"Good. May I suggest you both get some rest tonight? Your son has some serious soul-searching to do, and such tasks are best done alone."

"We'll certainly take that under consideration," he replied.

Mrs. Wallace blushed as she broke away from her husband and gave Sir another hug. "Despite what you say, I can't thank you enough. You have given him—all of us, really—hope again."

"I simply made a few phone calls."

She stated shyly, "Mr. Davis, I make a strawberry jam that has won several blue ribbons at the county fair. I would like to make you some as a thank you."

He smiled down at her. "That is very kind of you. Sadly, I leave to-morrow, but if you give it to my fiancée, she'll make sure I get it."

"Very well, Mr. Davis," she agreed, returning his smile.

While they were driving to Master Anderson's home, Brie told Sir, "I love how compassionate you were with Todd's mother."

He shrugged. "I understand it's difficult to receive help without giving something back. They are such kindhearted people; it makes me curious how they will handle the gift of the donor."

"Maybe a case of strawberry jam?" Brie suggested.

Sir chuckled, ruffling her hair.

"So, Sir, did I hear that I will be picking up the man tomorrow?" Brie ventured.

"That's correct, babygirl. His flight comes in two hours after mine leaves. I must warn you, though, English is not his first language."

Brie furrowed her brow in concern, afraid of losing the hapless man in the large airport.

Sir noted Brie's expression and grinned. "No need to worry. I told him what you look like, so the pickup should go smoothly. Simply help the man with his luggage and drive him to the hospital. The staff will take it from there."

Brie nodded, satisfied with the arrangements. "Sounds simple enough."

"I've tried to make this as easy as possible for you, since I won't be here." He stared towards the impressive mountain range. "I find it extraordinary that there are people in the world willing to make that kind of sacrifice for another. Although his airfare and hospital stay are being paid for by the Wallaces, he's refused any other compensation."

Brie felt tears come to her eyes. "We're all indebted to him for this."

"Yes, we are," Sir replied, with a hint of melancholy in his voice.

Brie touched his shoulder. "Are you okay?"

"I'm sorry I won't be here, Brie."

She could tell he was genuinely distressed about it. "I'll be fine, Sir."

"I know you will," he said, gracing her with a smile. "Did I tell you

Brad has an entertaining night planned for us? Something he says will take our minds off our concerns for a while."

"Oh, my! With Master Anderson, that could mean anything." Brie giggled.

"Which is exactly why I'm looking forward to it."

Brie wondered if it would be a session in the backyard with bullwhips, or free rein over the entire Academy. Oh, the kinky possibilities!

Beta

S ir whistled as they drove up to Master Anderson's home nestled in the foothills. "He really has some view up here, doesn't he?"

"Being in the mountains overlooking the city of Denver does seem like a little slice of heaven. Boy, I can only imagine what it looks like in the winter with all that snow."

Sir snorted humorously. "The fact that I can't drive my car in the winter kills the allure of this place. He can keep his mountain paradise."

They rang the doorbell several times, and Sir banged on the door, but got no response. Brie spied Master Anderson's nosy neighbor peeking around the corner of his garage. The woman cleared her throat before stating, "Mr. Anderson is in the back, weed—" She stopped midsentence when Sir turned to face her.

"Thank you," he replied in a pleasant but formal tone.

Courtney blushed from head to toe, her attraction to Sir painfully obvious to Brie. "Are...are you a friend of Mr. Anderson's?"

"Yes, we're long-time friends. Now if you'll excuse us." Sir put his hand on Brie's back and guided her past Courtney, heading towards the backyard.

Darned if the woman didn't blush a deep shade of red as he passed, her eyes drifting down to stare at Sir's sexy ass. Brie shook her head, stunned by the woman's brashness.

When Sir opened the backyard gate, Brie saw Master Anderson stand up in all his bare-chested glory, a handful of weeds gripped tightly in his fist. He glanced briefly at Courtney, then dropped the weeds and brushed off his hands.

The smile he bestowed on Sir as he approached was quite...beguiling.

"I don't believe it! It's really you after all this time!" He reached out to

Sir, his arms outstretched.

Sir tilted his head, confused by Master Anderson's odd behavior. "I—"

"No, don't. I don't care why you left me. The only thing that matters is that you're here with me now." He wrapped Sir in his beefy arms, grabbing his ass firmly with both hands.

Sir gripped his wrists and forcefully removed the offending appendages from his butt, shaking his head with a bemused look on his face.

"Don't be like that, lover," Master Anderson scolded.

Brie heard Courtney inhale sharply behind her, and she turned to see the woman staring at the men, her mouth agape. Playing along with Master Anderson's ruse, Brie smiled nervously at Courtney as if they'd caught the lovers in a stolen moment. She slowly closed the gate on the stunned woman, blocking her from continuing to gawk.

"Come into the house," Master Anderson insisted. "I need to show you how *deeply* you've been missed." He winked at Brie as he led them into his home.

"I don't even want to ask," Sir remarked once the door was shut.

"Welcome to Ms. Courtney, the neighborhood snoop."

"Is she still trying to set you up?" Brie asked, fondly remembering the little prank they'd played on Courtney the last time she'd visited.

"I can't tell if her interest is still for others or for herself these days." He looked at Sir. "That's the reason I *had* to take advantage of your arrival."

"I hate to break it to you, Master Anderson," Brie said, laughing, "but I think you only raised the hot factor for her. I definitely saw Courtney staring with lust in her eyes when you grabbed Sir's fine ass. She might even make it her task to convert you now."

Master Anderson slapped his forehead. "I can't win with that woman."

Sir shook his head. "I don't know how you get yourself into these predicaments. I've never had any issues with my neighbors."

"Of course not. You stay in your apartment like a hermit, while I go out and actively engage my neighbors."

"More like provoke them," Sir answered, glancing at his bare chest.

Brie giggled.

Master Anderson frowned at her. "You find this humorous, young Brie?"

"Yes, I find your situation very entertaining, Master Anderson."

He grumbled as he went to wash his hands in the sink. "Let's forget about Ms. Courtney and focus on my plans for tonight." Nodding at Brie, he said, "You'll be wearing a corset and mini-skirt for the event, and *you…*" He faced Sir. "I want you wearing dress slacks and my favorite tie, loverboy."

Sir raised an eyebrow. "What kind of place is this?"

"Ha! You're going to have to trust me, bud."

"You *are* aware I don't trust you."

Master Anderson grinned, throwing the wet hand towel at Sir. "Which is what makes this all the more fun for me."

Sir caught it nimbly and set it on the counter. "Maybe I should change my plans and take the last flight out tonight."

"Don't you dare! It's taken me *how* long to get you to come to Denver? You're not bailing out on me now."

Brie could tell Sir enjoyed having the upper hand, but also knew he liked Master Anderson far too much to follow through on his threat.

"Fine, but no more groping."

Master Anderson put his hands up the air in a gesture of surrender. "Agreed. Now why don't we head on over to the Academy? I'm anxious to show you what I've done with the place."

As they were walking out to Master Anderson's massive truck, he whispered to Brie, "Is she watching at the window?"

Brie looked back. "Affirmative."

With a sly glance at Brie, Master Anderson pinched Sir's butt.

Sir swatted his hand away in irritation. "Better watch it, Brad. I'll kiss you in front of that neighbor of yours. By the time I'm done with you, she'll be hounding you every minute of every day."

Master Anderson grinned. "I always knew you had a crush on me."

Sir laughed as he opened the passenger door for Brie. "I think it's the other way around, cowboy."

Brie giggled as she jumped into the truck, settling between the two men. How lucky was she? She didn't miss her chance to wave enthusiastically at Courtney as they drove away.

When they arrived at the Denver Academy, Sir exited the truck and stood quietly, admiring the large converted warehouse. "Okay, I am officially impressed by the size of the building."

Master Anderson took them inside, showing off the many amenities of his training center as he explained in detail everything he'd done to the place.

"Brad, this is exceptional," Sir stated when the tour was finished. "Every kind of play is possible here. What a brilliant facility."

"And the cost of the building was next to nothing," Master Anderson declared proudly.

"Your business degree certainly paid off for you."

Master Anderson nodded. "Best decision I ever made, heading back to college."

"Are you sure you can give the place up?"

Brie turned to Sir, startled by the question. Her eyes drifted over to Master Anderson as she waited for his response.

"I'd be lying if I said this was going to be easy." He caressed the back of one of the leather seats of the auditorium. "I was able to perfect what you had in LA."

"I see that."

"However, it's been difficult heading the business side of things as well as the program itself. There's a real appeal to serving only as Headmaster."

Brie stared at him, almost afraid to breathe. Was she hearing him right? Was Master Anderson coming back to the Submissive Training Center as Headmaster of the school?

"As worthy as your work here has been, there's no way to create a life outside of it. Time is your enemy, my friend."

Master Anderson raised his eyebrow. "Actually, time has been my ally."

"In avoiding life."

He chuckled. "I resemble that remark."

Sir slapped Master Anderson on the back, and they both laughed. "You've been missed, old friend, and I know the Submissive Training Center will benefit from your leadership. I said that the first time I recommended you for the position."

"Were you surprised that you weren't asked?" Master Anderson inquired as they headed back outside.

"Of course not. I stepped down from the position because I broke protocol—there's no recovering from that."

Brie looked up at him sadly, knowing she was the cause.

"Oh, no, Brie," Sir admonished. "There's no reason to feel remorse. I wouldn't give you up for a hundred Headmaster positions."

Brie said nothing, but she bound those words to her heart.

Sir turned his attention back to Master Anderson. "So what about your staff? Are any returning with you?"

It was the question Brie had been longing to ask the minute she'd heard he was returning, and she waited with bated breath to hear his answer.

"Ms. Clark is going to stay. Her previous experience at the Center makes her invaluable to this program. As for Baron, he jumped at the chance to return home."

"What about Lea?" Brie blurted.

Master Anderson smiled down at her, a look of sympathy on his face. "Ms. Taylor is still deciding."

Brie did her best to hide her disappointment. It was obvious that, as much as Lea loved her as a friend, she loved Ms. Clark more. It was a difficult truth for Brie to wrap her heart around, even though she understood it.

"Will you be returning to LA soon?" Sir inquired.

"Yes. The Training Center hasn't given me much time. Luckily, my Academy has already garnered notice in Denver, and I have a group of investors lined up to meet with me this coming week."

Sir glanced around the stylish auditorium. "Will you be able to give this up when the time comes?"

Master Anderson gave him a smug look. "Actually, I'll be renting the facilities to the buyer at a reasonable price, while keeping the option to buy back the school at a later date."

"Smart, but you won't be returning."

"Why do you say that?"

"My gut says you aren't coming back to Denver."

Master Anderson let out a snorting laugh. "When have you ever listened to your gut?"

Sir looked down, smiling tenderly at Brie. "At least once."

"Well, I suppose if I find balance in my life, I wouldn't have a reason to come back," Master Anderson conceded.

"Precisely."

Brie trembled beside Sir while the two men talked. The mere thought of having her best friend return to LA had her all wound up, but it was the very real possibility that Lea *wouldn't* be returning that consumed her.

"Have you done any events here?" Sir asked. "This is a large enough space to take advantage of opportunities like that."

"Yes, I held a charity event not too long ago. I sponsored it with Adam Montague, co-owner of the Masters at Arms Club."

"Ah, yes, I've heard of him. A military man, correct?"

"Correct. Adam is a serious individual, but a real pleasure to work with. He even allowed his wife Karla to sing at the event—a huge hit with the donors. Sure was great seeing her on stage again..." Master Anderson shook his head, chuckling to himself. "But I have to say, babies sure change a man. I don't recommend it."

Sir cleared his throat in response to the last statement. "I assume the event was a success overall?"

"Naturally," he stated with pride. "Raised a significant amount of money for our charity. It's part of the reason I have investors chomping at the bit now."

Sir placed his hand on Master Anderson's shoulder. "I must admit, I'm looking forward to your return to LA."

"I am as well, Thane. It'll give me a chance to check on those herbs I gifted you."

Sir said nothing and looked up, appearing to examine the equipment suspended above the stage.

"Don't tell me you killed them."

Sir gave a disinterested shrug. "What did you expect? With all the traveling we've done recently, they didn't stand a chance."

"Thank goodness you aren't planning on having children," Master Anderson joked.

Brie glanced at Sir with the slightest of smiles. Although Master Anderson missed it, Sir did not, and he laughed. "Me, have children? What a ludicrous thought."

Before heading out for the evening, Sir informed Brie that he had something special to add to her outfit as he handed her a small vibrator. It was unusual, because of the silicone piece that was made to slip inside the vagina so it would fit snugly against her clit.

He explained, "Having no idea what we're doing tonight, I plan on entertaining myself." He kissed her on the lips, adding seductively, "This will *not* be a lesson in orgasm denial."

Brie quivered, knowing that meant a night of excess, and hoped she was up for the challenge. "May I put it on now?"

When he nodded, she started towards the bathroom.

"No, téa. I want to watch."

She smiled as she settled on the edge of the bed, pulling up her skirt and shimmying flirtatiously out of her panties. Brie played with herself as she glanced demurely at Sir. It was such a turn on having him watch, and soon she felt the welcome ache between her legs that made her wet enough for the toy. She picked up the vibrator and slowly slipped it inside. It rested against her pussy, much like her clit jewelry.

Sir pulled a device from his pocket and smiled at her as he switched it on. Brie jumped and then giggled as the vibration took over. She forced herself to relax as she embraced the wicked tool.

Before she could give in to the building pulsations, however, Sir turned it off, stating, "That was just a taste, babygirl. No more fun until we reach our mystery destination."

Oh, how Brie loved it when he teased her!

"Thank you for the taste, Master. I can't wait until the main course." She slipped her panties back on and stood, bowing. "I wait with impatience, but with a respectful attitude."

Sir chuckled, resting his hand on her back as he led her out of the bedroom.

Master Anderson whistled when he saw the two approach. "Now that's what I'm talking about, loverboy. The way those pants hug your tight ass is sublime, and that tie...I recall fondly what we did with that tie."

Sir fussed with the knot of his tie, grumbling, "Not sure why you insist on continuing the ruse when your neighbor isn't present to listen."

"It's all about getting into the role. Has Brie taught you nothing? She's the perfect partner when it comes to pranks. A natural at it."

Sir looked at her proudly. "Is she now?"

"Yes, and her talents are completely wasted on you."

"No," Sir replied smoothly. "I utilize those talents for a higher purpose."

"What's that?"

Sir took Brie's hand and kissed it as he stared into her eyes. "For my own pleasure."

She felt her loins contract around the toy and smiled, anxious for their night to begin.

"Enough with the lovey-dovey looks, you two," Master Anderson scolded. "It's time to roll out."

He drove them out of the foothills and into the heart of downtown Denver. The historic buildings mixed with modern chain restaurants and shopping malls were an interesting combination. He parked in a large lot that was open, but they had to walk down several streets to get to their final destination.

The old brick building was blaring music from inside, and Brie saw a long line of people wrapped around it. She noted a small, unassuming sign hanging from the entrance, which simply read: 'Beta'.

Master Anderson walked past the line and straight up to the entrance guarded by several hunky men. One of them smiled at him in greeting. "Ah, Mr. Anderson, back so soon?"

"I have a couple of out-of-towners who have yet to enjoy the Beta experience."

"Understood. I just need to look at their IDs, but you're free to enter."

Brie looked back at the extensive line, grateful that Master Anderson had some pull. The moment the doors of the club opened, Brie was blasted with the delicious deep bass of a dubstep song. The vibration of it reverberated through her, causing her stomach to tremble with the beat.

Oh, yeah…

The thin hallway opened onto a giant concert hall. It was packed with people gyrating to the sexy beat, with laser lights and a giant disco ball above filling the room with dancing color.

Brie looked up and saw that there was a second level crowded with people looking down on them. She heard an explosion, and a flurry of confetti floated like feathers down from above.

"I love this place," she said.

"What?" Master Anderson asked, leaning closer.

She shouted, "I freaking love this place!"

Master Anderson's smile was enchanting when he replied, "I was certain you would."

He led them up a long flight of stairs to the second level. On one side of the large opening there was a line of people leaning against the railing, watching the action below, while on the other side there was a section of tables and booths, with scantily clad ladies tending their VIP clients.

Master Anderson pointed to the middle table, where a hot redhead was waiting for them. She smiled as they approached. "Mr. Anderson, what a pleasant surprise to see you again."

"You know me, Sasha. Can't resist a killer drop. The deeper the better."

She giggled sweetly. "May I ask what I can get for you and your friends?"

"I'll take my usual beer, my friend over here would like a dirty martini, and…" He looked questioningly at Brie. "What you would like?"

"I'll take a shot of Zyr vodka," she announced.

Sir nodded. "Change my order. I'll have the same."

Master Anderson looked at him in surprise. "Well, hell, if that's the case, make it three shots, Sasha."

"My pleasure."

Master Anderson sat back and smiled at them. "Have you ever been to a dance club like this?"

"No, never," Sir replied, glancing around to take it all in.

"I want to live here," Brie exclaimed, loving everything about the club—the music, the lights, as well as the erotic energy of the place.

"You have the right connections to get in most nights."

"Well, I'm glad I know you, then," she replied.

The deep, driving beat reminded Brie of Faelan and the chocolate dance they'd shared. She wondered if this was where he'd learned to love the music. Suddenly, an image of him lying in the hospital bed alone came to mind.

Sir noticed the change in her demeanor and quietly corrected her. "No, Brie. You're not allowed to think of anything but me tonight. Tomorrow will come soon enough." He reached into his pocket and she felt the buzz of the vibrator. The gentle vibration between her legs caused delicious chills to course through her body.

Brie took the shot glass Sasha handed her and looked at it critically, thinking, *A shot is a whole lot bigger in Russia.*

"Here's to a night we won't forget," Master Anderson toasted, clinking glasses with her. After she'd raised her glass to Sir and was downing the shot, her first orgasm hit. Brie squeaked, sputtering vodka.

"Straight vodka too much for you?" Master Anderson asked with amusement.

Sir smirked, turning off the vibrator. "She's perfectly fine." He kissed the remaining vodka from her lips and ordered another round.

After the second shot, Master Anderson suggested they stand by the railing to enjoy the music. Brie eagerly agreed, and was thrilled to have a chance to look down at the massive crowd below. It was one giant dance, everyone moving in rhythm to the deep bass that shook the entire building.

Brie was unaware that she was gyrating her hips in harmony with the beat until she overheard Master Anderson tell Sir, "She's sexy when she dances."

Sir said with an appreciative smile on his lips, "This music agrees with you, téa."

"I *love* this kind of music, Sir! I can feel the energy rising up from the crowd. It's almost too much…"

He leaned down and ordered lustfully, "Dance, then, while you come for me."

Brie groaned as the vibrator caressed her clit with a new, slow, pulsating rhythm. She shuddered, not expecting the difference in vibration but responding favorably to it. Closing her eyes, she gave in to the erotic nature of the beat and swayed hypnotically to its call.

"That's it, babygirl, seduce me."

Sir's encouragement radiated through Brie. The warmth of the vodka, the tension of the vibrator and intensity of the erotic music had her floating on a sensual high, and she quickly peaked, welcoming the sensation as she orgasmed for her Master.

"Good girl," he purred in her ear. She continued to dance as the two men moved back to their seats to observe her and talk—but she noticed they did very little talking as she took on the role of exotic dancer for her

Master, enticing him with her sensual moves. It was empowering, knowing she had his complete attention and the ability to drive him wild.

As she was dancing, Brie was struck by an idea she thought Sir would enjoy, so she walked over to him and whispered in his ear. He nodded his approval as he stood, moving back to the railing as he watched her leave. Brie made her way around to the other side of the large opening and threw Sir a kiss. He responded by pulsing the vibrator several times.

Brie giggled in delight, grabbing the rail to begin her seduction of him from afar. This time, laser lights of orange and yellow played across her skin, as if lighting her on fire. It was beautiful, reminding her of their fire play.

The music changed from a lively beat to one that was more slow and primal, so her movements changed accordingly. She was determined to captivate him with her alluring, cat-like grace.

Master Anderson stood beside Sir and they watched as she moved to the erotic beat. The vibrator turned back on and Brie moaned softly, giving in to Sir's desire. It was so wickedly hot to come in front of everyone, even if there was only one person watching who knew it.

Brie gripped the railing as she threw her head back and came for the third time. Afterwards she swayed her hips slowly, watching the laser lights playing across her skin and clothes as she recovered from her climax. When she looked up again, she noticed that Master Anderson had gone missing.

Sir nodded to her and gestured, but she was unsure of his meaning. Taking it as a command to keep dancing, Brie started up again, her focus solely on him. She felt someone brush up beside her and turned to see a young man wearing a black T-shirt and a lustful stare. She scooted to the left but he followed her, pressing even closer.

All of a sudden, she was encased by two strong arms grasping the railing on either side of her, effectively trapping her. She would have been concerned, but she knew those arms well.

"Scram," Master Anderson told the boy. "This one's mine."

The young man looked up at his impressive stature and shrugged, disappearing into the moving mass of people without a word.

"We saw him descending on you," Master Anderson informed Brie.

"I was oblivious."

"We could tell."

Brie giggled and looked back to ask him, "Should I head back?"

"No, your Master wants you to dance a little longer."

She looked over the expanse and saw Sir nod. Brie started up again, but with less hip action, conscious of Master Anderson being so close.

The vibrator buzzed back to life, and she moaned in surprise.

Master Anderson bent down. "What was that?"

She shook her head as the buzzing increased. Sir gestured that she should continue dancing. As she began to sway, Master Anderson moved with her, the two becoming one unit as they responded to the deep, pulsing bass.

It was erotic to be in the protective embrace of Master Anderson as she danced for Sir. Every now and then their bodies touched briefly and the slight contact sent shivers through her.

When the vibrations increased in power, Brie knew Sir was demanding an orgasm from her. Although Master Anderson was close, Brie licked her lips and let the delicious feeling take hold. She lost herself in it, letting her carnal desire take over her reservations, the music almost demanding it.

Brie whimpered when she started to come, then felt Master Anderson crush her against the railing, growling, "As per your Master's orders."

The rigidness of his erect cock pressing against her ass caused Brie to climax powerfully. He wrapped her in his arms until her trembling stopped, before pulling away and offering his hand to her.

"Shall we return to your Master?"

Brie was a little unsure on her feet, so Master Anderson held her tight, providing the extra support needed to walk.

"Lovely," Sir complimented as Master Anderson handed her over. "I enjoyed watching that little scene play out."

"Fortunately, I got there in time," Master Anderson stated.

Sir smiled at Brie. "She can get a little distracted when she's determined to please me."

Master Anderson shifted his tight jeans, his impressive erection visibly straining against his pants. "Why don't I order you another round while I search out a girl to…dance with," he said with a cheeky grin.

"By all means, my friend," Sir agreed.

When Sasha brought them another round of vodka, Sir raised his glass to Brie. "Here's to our small attempt to get Brad back in the game."

Brie clinked her glass against his in admiration. "You are a clever one, Sir."

They didn't return to the house until the wee hours of the morning. Master Anderson seemed unusually quiet and content on the drive home—a good sign, Brie thought.

When she finally made it to the bedroom, Brie felt an overwhelming need to jump on Sir. "Let me please you as much as you pleased me, Master."

"Oh, you will," he assured her. "I've just been priming you for the event. Two days of making you come while denying myself has made me a ravenous man."

She stood and watched as he undressed, starting with his tie. He was slow and deliberate in his movements. Brie literally shivered as she watched him slide it off, then unbutton his shirt.

"What's wrong, babygirl?"

"I want to please you so badly, Sir."

He smiled. "Orgasming multiple times wasn't enough for you?"

"Not when you couldn't join in the fun."

"Come, then, and show me the level of your desperation."

Having his permission, Brie held nothing back as she pushed him against the wall, struggling to undo his pants. Sir lifted her chin and kissed her forcefully as she tugged on his boxers, releasing his cock from its confinement.

She fell to her knees and grasped his shaft in her hand, gratefully wrapping her lips around it as she began to bob up and down on his cock.

Sir was a bundle of tense muscles and she could feel him shuddering as she released her passion on his manhood.

"Brie…"

She looked up at him, his shaft still in her mouth.

"Slower."

She smiled as she released his cock and nibbled and licked up the side of it and back down. She took his balls in her mouth one at a time and sucked lightly, before grazing the length of his shaft with her teeth.

His growl of lust made her pussy even wetter. She opened her mouth and took the fullness of him down her throat, but he pulled her back. "No, we're not going there tonight. On the bed, all fours."

He pulled her up and pushed her towards the bed. She presented herself to him, knowing her pussy was wet and swollen with need. She didn't look back, waiting for him to take her, wondering if Sir had forgotten his vow in his desire for satisfaction.

He grasped her ass with his powerful hands, bruising her flesh as he ripped the vibrator from her. But he suddenly stopped, growling to himself. "Fuck!"

She heard Sir frantically rummaging through his suitcase. "Where is it, damn it?" When she moved to get up to help, he commanded, "Stay there—don't you dare move."

Brie returned to her position, arching her back just a little more to entice him. He murmured his approval. "Very nice. Play with yourself while you wait for me."

Soon she heard the slippery sound of lubricant and smiled to herself.

He was not breaking his vow, but she was grateful he would be fucking her deeply. He played with her ass using his thumbs, spreading her cheeks apart to admire the pink rosette that would soon take the length of him.

Sir sucked in his breath as he pressed the head of his cock against the tight muscles of her sphincter. Her burning desire for him was sated as he slowly slipped inside. "I love watching your ass take my shaft."

Brie closed her eyes as he pulled out only to push in again. "Master, I love the feeling of possession it evokes."

He thrust deeper. "Then feel the fullness of my possession."

When Brie cried out, Sir covered her mouth and warned, "We're not at home, babygirl."

He kept his hand on her mouth as he ramped up his thrusting. Brie's muffled moans filled the bedroom as Sir made demands on her body. He fucked her hard, being completely selfish in his taking of her, and Brie savored it.

When he let out a low, guttural cry, Brie felt Sir stiffen as he filled her ass with his seed. He collapsed on top of her afterwards, panting, "I needed that more than you know."

She turned her head and smiled. "I did too, Sir, more than you know."

He kissed her on the lips and lifted himself off, lying down beside her. "This separation may be harder than I anticipated." He tenderly caressed her face. "Damn, I will miss you."

A tear rolled down her cheek as she nodded in agreement.

"Only two more months," he reminded her.

"Two months."

"And then I'll make my fucking count."

Brie burst into giggles and hugged him.

The Donor

B rie sighed heavily the next day when the moment came to say goodbye at the security line.

"Keep in mind your purpose, Brie. You're exactly what Mr. Wallace needs right now. Trust your instincts. Others have caved under the weight of his situation, but you know him better than most and you understand what he has to live for."

"I won't forget that, Sir, no matter how difficult it gets."

"As for me, I hope for a quick resolution with Lilly concerning my mother, but that is probably wishful thinking on my part. It'll be a shock when she sees the Beast, and there's that whole process of letting go…"

"How long do you think you'll be there?"

"I'm hoping not more than a week. However, if she decides to end her life, I'm afraid we'll be there much longer while she comes to terms with that choice."

"I don't know which I should hope for, Sir."

"I would prefer to end her life, no matter how long it takes. This holding on when she's already gone has been torture for me. I don't wish that on Lilly." Sir looked at his watch. "I need to go."

"I know," Brie choked out, trying unsuccessfully to hold back the tears.

Sir wiped them away. "No crying, babygirl. Be strong. At night, when you are alone and your thoughts are with me, *then* you can cry freely into your pillow. Connect with me whenever you feel sad and I will be your comfort."

She nodded, lowering her head so he wouldn't see her tears. Sir lifted her chin and kissed the remaining ones away. "Enough," he whispered. His gentle attention and feather-light kisses made her smile, despite her sorrow.

"That's better, babygirl."

More for herself than for him, she declared, "I will not fail, Sir."

"I have no doubt you will succeed and you have others here you can lean on, but remember I am your man—the rock you can count on. I don't want anyone else playing that role for you."

"Yes, Sir."

"While waiting to pick up the donor, I want you to eat something. I noticed you didn't touch your food this morning."

She laughed sadly. "I never feel hungry the day you leave."

"Nevertheless, you will eat now, and I expect you to continue to eat three meals a day while I'm gone—whether you're hungry or not. Agreed?"

She nodded, loving him all the more for caring so much.

Brie watched Sir go, comforting herself with the thought that she could cry later that night. She waited until he'd disappeared down the escalator to the underground transport train before she made her way to the food court. Even though the thought of eating made her nauseous, she dutifully bought a salad and ate it with the plastic fork provided. She stared at the instrument afterwards, imagining Sir raking it down her back like a Wartenberg wheel. It made her smile, so she stuffed the utensil in her purse.

She felt a sense of renewed confidence, certain she would prove worthy of Sir's faith in her. The sobering fact was Faelan could not afford her to fail.

When the time came, Brie headed toward the exit area for the arriving passengers and waited nervously for the donor. Sir hadn't told her what he looked like, so she was counting on the fact that he would recognize her. Every time a new group of people emerged from the underground station, she searched their faces, hoping to see a spark of recognition.

Two young children, who were waiting for their father's plane to arrive, started running in circles around Brie out of sheer boredom. The little boy accidentally bumped into her, causing Brie to stumble where she stood. He looked up at her in alarm and then ran behind his mother for protection.

"Tell the nice lady you're sorry for running into her," his mother demanded.

The little boy shook his head.

Pulling him from behind her, the mother said in a harsher tone, "Do it, *now*."

Brie felt sorry for the boy and knelt down, saying, "It's okay. I was getting bored too."

The boy smiled, his ears turning a shade of pink, before he darted behind his mother again.

Brie stood up and assured the woman that further apology was unnecessary, but stopped mid-sentence when she heard her name called behind her.

"Brie…"

Her heart skipped a beat as she turned and looked into those warm, chocolate-brown eyes she knew so well. She shook her head, not quite believing he was standing there before her.

Tono Nosaka walked around the barrier and took her hand, shaking it formally. "It is a pleasure to meet you, Miss Bennett."

"Are you Todd's donor?"

He smiled with a glint in his eye. "It seems fate has brought us together again."

She couldn't stop smiling as she led him to the baggage claim area. There was so much to ask, so much she needed to know, but she couldn't satisfy her curiosity in such a public arena, so she was forced to wait.

To bide her time, she kept glancing at him, blushing whenever he caught her staring. The Asian Dom was still just as handsome as she remembered, with his long, dark bangs and gentle smile.

She couldn't believe Tono was here. *Sneaky Sir,* she giggled to herself, knowing he had purposely orchestrated this surprise for her.

Once the luggage had been loaded into the rental car and they'd both buckled up, Brie turned to Tono and begged, "Please tell me everything!"

He chuckled. "Everything? Why don't I condense it down for you?"

"As long as you don't leave out any important parts, like what happened to your mother, and how did Chikako take the news of you leaving, and are you here to stay? Please say you are!"

He shook his head, his eyes sparkling with amusement. "I will tackle them one question at a time, but I suggest you start the car or we'll never leave this place."

Brie turned the key and revved up the engine, heading out of the parking garage before declaring, "Okay, you can begin."

"You're aware my mother remains a forceful personality, and I'm unable to bear it like my father did. Things had gotten so bad between us that I spent most of my time away from the family home simply to avoid the constant bickering."

Brie looked at him with compassion. "I'm so sorry, Tono."

"Slow down, Brie," he said in a quiet, unruffled voice.

She turned to look at the road and had to slam on her brakes to avoid hitting the car in front of her that had switched lanes unexpectedly. With her heart racing, she let off the brake and hit the gas again.

"Please continue."

"Keep your eyes on the road."

"Yes, yes. I will," she promised.

With her verbal assurance given, Tono continued. "When Sir Davis called to inform me of Wallace's condition, I was at a loss. I knew our blood types matched, which is exceedingly rare, but I was unsure if I was in a position to help. When I broached the subject with my mother, something very odd but fortuitous happened. She refused to talk to me for a week. I naturally assumed she was angry and would forbid me from shirking my duty to her." Tono smiled, shaking his head. "But I couldn't have been more wrong."

His words were like music to her ears. "Oh, my goodness, what did she do?"

"Brie, look ahead," he cautioned.

She glanced back in time to see a family of ducks crossing the road. She instinctively swerved to miss them and nearly hit the car beside her.

"That's it!" she cried in frustration.

Brie took the next exit and parked on the shoulder, positioning the car so they were facing west, towards the outline of blue-and-white peaks in the distance. "I can't wait to hear this until we get to the hospital, and I'll kill us if I continue driving."

He chuckled softly, nodding his agreement. "Always impetuous, but only because of your true heart."

Brie grasped his arm, begging, "Please, Tono, tell me what happened with your mother."

He smiled, but the emotion did not transfer to his eyes. "When she finally spoke to me, I was told I had never been a good son."

Brie sputtered in disbelief. "But...but..."

"It wasn't said in anger, it was simply her truth. I was never what she wanted or needed. She and I are like oil and water."

"But you've done *everything* she's asked. You sacrificed your life for her!"

"It was a healthy revelation, Brie. I did not mind hearing it."

"You have to know what she said is untrue, Tono. You are an incredible son, and a remarkable person."

He caressed her cheek, releasing the tension from her face. "The beauty of that admission is that it set me free. There was no more point in trying to please her."

"But she's wrong," Brie insisted.

"No, Brie. It is her reality, as well as mine. She's never been the mother I needed. When she insisted I leave Japan, it was the first time I didn't resent submitting to her will."

Brie growled in justified anger. "But she should have thanked you for everything you've done, all the sacrifices you made."

"Letting me leave was enough. Who knew that the Boy would end up being my ticket to freedom?" Tono's genuine smile lightened her heart. "Life is a beautiful mystery."

Brie looked deeply into his eyes, noting the joy as well as the sorrow she found there. "How did Chikako take the news of your leaving?"

"That was not easy," he said. Tono looked towards the mountains as he confessed, "We'd grown close, working together. There is an intimate bond created with the jute."

"I know," Brie said with quiet conviction.

He had a look of remorse when he said, "I think for the first time I understand the dynamic you share with the Boy. I care for Chikako, and I thoroughly enjoy her company, but…"

"What?"

"I will never love her."

"Your parting could not have been easy for either of you."

The pain in his voice tugged at her heart. "No, it wasn't. For the first time, I know what it is to break a heart."

"Still, you were kind."

Tono frowned, shaking his head. "There is no kind way to break a person's heart."

She reached out, touching his shoulder in sympathy. "Does that mean you left on bad terms?"

"Chikako saw me off at the airport and assured me she was okay…but I know better."

Brie gazed deep into his eyes. There was so much left unsaid, things that could never be spoken between them.

"As to your last question, I will be staying. I'm unsure where I will settle down after the surgery, but Japan is not in my future."

"I'm glad, Tono."

He stared at her, those gentle eyes expressing a torrent of emotion. Finally, he spoke. "So now we must go and see if the Boy will accept my offer."

"Wait! Todd doesn't know you're the donor?"

"Sir Davis and I agreed it was best, considering the past history I shared with the Boy. The simple fact is that Wallace has no more options. We've placed him against the wall, knowing he will resist." Tono smiled at her tenderly. "Which is where you come in."

"I don't have that kind of power over Todd. Not anymore."

"You have more than you think. Used in the right way, it may prove lifesaving."

"But if I fail..."

"There's no fear of that. You and I will convince the Boy that his life is more important than his willful self-pity."

Brie started up the car again, but said one more thing before she started off. "I'm worried for you, Tono. This isn't an easy operation and there are risks." She turned to face him. "Even if it goes well, you won't be able to perform your art for months after recovery. And worse, what if years down the road your remaining kidney fails?"

"I understand what lies ahead for me, and I accept the risks."

Tears came to Brie's eyes, but she held them at bay. "Your mother is blind, Tono. You are an exceptional human being." She backed up and threw the car into drive, speeding towards the hospital—and what would become Tono's destiny.

Faelan's parents met them in the downstairs lobby.

"Mr. and Mrs. Wallace, this is Ren Nosaka," Brie said, introducing him to the anxious couple.

Mr. Wallace shook Tono's hand energetically. "I can't tell you how grateful we are. What you are doing for us is... Words can't express the depth of our gratitude."

Before Tono could respond, Mrs. Wallace held out a jar of preserves. "I can't..." She broke into tears and thrust the jar at him.

Tono took it and gently placed his arm around her shoulder. Brie saw the woman begin to relax, responding to the peace he exuded. "It is my pleasure to help a friend."

Faelan's mother looked at him, shocked. "You know my son?"

"I do. He's a good man."

"I'm sorry to say he's never mentioned you to us."

Tono's smile was charming when he replied, "I'm not surprised. Although your son is a good man, he is also exceedingly arrogant."

Faelan's parents broke out in unexpected laughter and Brie joined in. It felt good to laugh under such stressful circumstances.

"How did Todd seem to you today?" Brie asked his mother, once the laughter died down.

"He wouldn't speak to us, but he seemed calmer. More at peace than he's been in a long time."

Tono nodded. "Good. If you don't mind, I would like Miss Bennett and I to speak to him alone. If all goes well, we will invite you to join us later."

"By all means," Mr. Wallace answered.

Tono went to the nurse's desk first, and was handed a huge stack of papers to fill out. He spoke to the staff for quite a while before nodding to Brie to join him.

"It looks like Wallace has indicated to the staff that he will decline my offer. Shall we go change his mind?"

"Let's," Brie answered, feeling more confident with Tono beside her.

The look on Faelan's face when Tono walked through the door was priceless. "What the hell are you doing here?"

Brie smiled to herself as she shut the door behind them. Those were the exact words she'd used the day Faelan had surprised her at the Training Center. She took it as a positive sign.

"I am your donor, Mr. Wallace."

"Like hell you are," Faelan said, struggling to sit up on his own.

The difference in him from yesterday to today was startling. Anger seemed to be a good motivator for Blue Eyes. Brie walked over to help him, but he glared at her with those ocean blues. "Get away. You should have told me."

"I just found out myself," she protested.

Tono sat down and stared at Faelan, waiting patiently for him to calm down.

"Come join me, Brie," Tono suggested, pulling a chair next to his.

Brie left Faelan's side and sat down, unable to hide the smile that threatened to escape.

"What are you grinning about?" Faelan snarled.

"I'm just glad to see you're feeling better today."

"I'm not feeling better, I'm dying. Are you really that dense?"

Brie giggled.

Faelan punched the controls on the bed so that he slowly moved into a sitting position. "Laugh at me again," he demanded.

A remark Mary would make came to Brie's mind, but she kept it to herself, struggling to keep her smile from widening even more.

"You're unbelievable, Brie," Faelan growled.

"What's unbelievable is that you're planning to turn down the surgery," Tono stated.

"Yes, I decided last night. I don't want someone else's kidney and I refuse to spend my life on dialysis. What I really want is to die."

"And yet you have a willing donor and the chance to reverse your circumstances. Why would you turn that away?"

"I didn't ask for your help, old man."

Tono smiled. "You must be referring to the difference in maturity between us, since I'm only five years your senior."

"Brie, get him out of here," Faelan said, glaring at her.

Tono answered evenly, "But I wish to help."

"I don't want it!" Faelan insisted, pounding his fist on the bed.

Tono's demeanor did not change. "Explain why."

Faelan gave him an icy stare. "I want to die, damn it! I already told you that."

"But you don't have to."

Faelan roared furiously, "I said I don't want your help!" When he broke into a fit of coughing afterwards, he scowled at Tono as if it were his fault.

"Why are you refusing a new kidney, which will ensure your health and prosperity?"

Faelan looked at Brie, those big blue eyes beseeching her to agree with him. "It's not worth the risk to him." When Tono argued the point, he snarled, "Do I have to spell it out to you? *I'm* not worth the risk."

"Tell me why."

Faelan growled in frustration. "Go and live your life, Nosaka. Have kids, get old and croak at the age of a hundred. That's what you are meant to do."

"And you?"

"I was supposed to die years ago. I shouldn't be here, and fate has finally seen fit to finish the job."

"Mr. Wallace, you are as stubborn and strong as you were the day I met you. Nothing has changed except your attitude."

"You have no idea what you're talking about."

Brie broke in. "I disagree. That man who came to me at the Training Center and introduced himself as Faelan sits before me now. It's the same man who earned the respect of the subs in our community despite his lack of experience. The very same man who won my friend's heart."

Faelan's eyes flickered with pain at her mention of Mary.

Brie continued, "You have no idea the number of people you have influenced and who genuinely care about you."

"It is your duty to go through with this operation," Tono maintained. "Fate saved you the day of the crash, and has saved you again with a suitable donor. To give up now does not honor the man you've become."

Faelan clapped his hands sarcastically. "Oh, those are very pretty words, Mr. Nosaka."

Brie stood and walked over to the bed, deciding now was the time to lay all her cards on the table. "You should know that Mary left the commune. She's been going to therapy and working hard to break the chains of her past."

Faelan's eyes softened as he asked, "Mary's okay, then?"

"Yes and no."

"Why? What's wrong?"

Brie's lips trembled. "She misses you."

He rolled his eyes. "Well, she'll get over it."

"No, she won't. Mary confessed that she's in love with you."

Faelan closed his eyes and laid his head back on the pillow.

"If something happened to you…" Brie's voice broke and she needed a moment to regain her composure. "I don't know if she could survive it. That's why you can't give up. You just can't!"

He didn't respond to her plea, so Brie sat back down next to Tono. They waited in silence, letting Faelan war with his soul.

The Wolf Surrenders

B rie lay down that night, surprised that she didn't feel the need to cry. She had been certain when she'd watched Sir leave that morning that her pillow would be stained with tears that night. Instead, her heart was full of joy because Faelan had agreed to go through with the surgery.

Brie had been given specific instructions by Sir for her nightly ritual while in Denver. It started with journaling to him, but *not* in her fantasy journal. He had stressed that this time apart would be challenging for them both, and it was vital they stay connected.

"I don't want to miss the varying emotions you'll experience while I'm gone. The only way for me to know them is if you share them faithfully each night. I promise to do the same for you." Sir had handed Brie a new journal and held up his as well. "This is our commitment to each other while we're separated."

Brie took the new journal from the nightstand and opened it to the first page. It comforted her to know that Sir was doing the same on the other side of the world.

Dear Sir,

Today was quite a rollercoaster! I'm sure you were grinning on your trip to China, knowing how surprised I would be when I saw Tono. Such a flood of emotions, Sir happiness at his return, anger that his mother was so unkind to him, fear about the surgery ahead, and sadness that he is still alone. I found out it did not work out with Chikako I was secretly hoping it would.

We tried to talk in the car on the way to the hospital, but it proved too challenging for me so I had to pull to the side of the road to ensure no ducklings were harmed in the driving of the vehicle.

When Tono shared his plans to remain in the States, I wanted to shout for joy! I don't think he's had a moment of peace since his father died. He tries to hide it, but I can tell the toll it's taken, and my heart hurts for him.

As much as I wasn't prepared for Tono, you should have seen Todd. Wow! He became irate (which I found amusing). In a matter of seconds he went from being the sick and weak individual we saw to an angry bull.

It took Tono's wisdom and patience for Todd to finally agree to go through with the surgery. I'm so thrilled right now I can barely contain myself. He was ready to give up, and now he is getting ready for the fight of his life.

But all this makes me think of you, Sir. How you are facing the exact opposite situation with your mother. Know that my heart is with you, my love surrounds you, and my thoughts are yours.

Love, Brie

Brie closed her journal, laying it back on the nightstand. Sir had given her a second task for her nightly ritual. With a nervous smile, she opened the drawer of the nightstand and pulled out the Hitachi.

Sir had handed her the Magic Wand along with a small box of toys. "You must choose a different instrument to challenge yourself with each night. Imagine your Master controls it, and discover the one that brings you the most pleasure. When I return, it will be the first one I use on you."

His sexy promise made her giddy to try, even though he had picked some demanding instruments. She opened the box and grinned as she examined her choices. She was about to grab the shiny metal clothespins, but her hand drifted over to the Wartenberg Wheel. She knew Sir personally enjoyed the tool, and wanted to see if she could learn to appreciate its spiky caress.

Brie got up and went to her suitcase, pulling out a T-shirt of Sir's. She'd brought it so she could sleep with Sir's scent every night, but she'd enjoyed the way Rytsar had employed it in Russia.

She figured it would enhance the experience and draw her even closer to her Master. Brie plugged in the Magic Wand and laid the shirt on the pillow. She then picked up the wicked little wheel and scrutinized it. "Your job is to bring me pleasure."

Taking a deep breath, she pulled down her panties and turned on the vibrator, placing it against her clit. The delicious vibration sent instant shivers through her. Her body knew this toy well and responded quickly as soon as she imagined Sir was watching over her.

She pulled it away, scolding herself. "Not so fast, woman."

Brie placed the Hitachi back on her mound, and closed her eyes so she could fantasize as she played with the challenging caress of the wheel.

Sir wanted to take her in the garden…

He escorted her to the center of the huge rose garden and laid out a blanket on the grass. "Take off your clothes, téa."

It was a beautiful Colorado day with blue skies and warm sunshine. As she undressed, Brie noticed a slight breeze and her nipples hardened in response.

Sir noticed and commented. "Your nipples are anticipating our play, I see."

"My whole body anticipates your touch," she confessed.

"Lie down, then, so I can begin."

She lay on his blanket, opening her legs expectantly as he removed his shirt.

"No, téa, close those lovely legs. I have something else in mind."

She was surprised by his command, but demurely closed her legs and waited.

Sir pulled out shears from his pocket and started cutting the stems of the most stunning roses in the garden. He seemed very particular about the ones he chose. After gathering a number of them, he stuffed the shears in his back pocket and meticulously removed the leaves from each stem.

She watched in fascination, wondering what he had planned for her. When he was done, Sir laid the flowers beside her and sucked the blood from his fingers. "Roses are beautiful but treacherous flowers."

"They are, Master," she agreed.

"Are you ready to be caressed by such a treacherous blossom?"

She nodded eagerly. "Please."

He picked up a large pink bloom and put it to her nose. "Take in its scent. Know its full character."

She breathed in its fragrance deeply, intoxicated by the sweet perfume.

Sir lightly trailed the soft petals over her stomach, causing a delightful tickling sensation. She purred with pleasure, anxious for more.

Brie rolled the wheel across her stomach and goosebumps rose on her skin. She laid her head back, breathing rapidly, pretending that Sir was dragging the large thorns of the rose across her stomach, causing her to squirm and whimper.

"I told you it's a cruel flower."

He leaned forward and kissed the area that had received its harsh attention. His warm lips caused her stomach to tremble in pleasure.

Brie felt the very real pulsation between her legs announcing her body's enjoyment of the fantasy. She pulled the wand away and forced her heart rate to slow back down. She was determined to make her body work for that orgasm, just as Sir would.

She stared at the spikes on the wheel, deciding that she could take more pressure if she prepared herself for it.

Pressing the vibrating Hitachi harder against her clit, she closed her eyes again, imagining Sir kissing her on the lips as the sun beat down on her skin, his tongue running over her teeth before darting in and claiming her.

Brie moaned, the pressure of his lips and the taste of his mouth very real to her.

Sir picked up another rose, a light purple one with tiny thorns. "A wicked thing, this one. So delicate and inviting…" He let her smell it, the fragrance spicy, like cloves.

The silky petals teased her as they skimmed across her breasts, especially when he ran them over her nipples. However, a cold chill followed, knowing that the thorns would soon take their place.

"Are you ready, téa?"

She turned her head and smashed her face into his shirt, taking in Sir's scent as she moved the Wand to the perfect spot to make her come quickly.

Sir kissed her breasts before he trailed the tiny thorns across them…

Brie ran the wheel over her breasts and gasped each time it came into contact with her sensitive nipples. "Oh!" she moaned. Brie lifted both instruments from her, panting from the effort.

One more pass and she knew she would come. She deeply inhaled Sir's scent before she gave in to the sensation of the wheel and wand. "Oh, oh, ooooooohhh…." she cried, tears coming to her eyes as she allowed the powerful release.

"Good girl," he whispered in her ear.

Brie opened her eyes. She could have sworn she'd heard his voice, but was disappointed to find herself all alone. She turned off the Magic Wand and laid the wheel beside her, panting with pure satisfaction.

That was when she heard the subtle squeak of a floorboard outside her room. She turned her head to see the movement of a shadow under the door before it disappeared.

Brie blushed, wondering how loud she had been. She quietly put her toys back in the drawer but kept Sir's shirt beside her, curling up in the bed and sighing.

"Good night, Sir. Until tomorrow night…"

She woke up to the savory smell of Tono's favorite breakfast and emerged from her room to find him dishing up a bowl for her.

"Good morning, sleepyhead."

She looked at the clock and protested, "It's only six in the morning, Tono. I don't think that qualifies me as a sleepyhead."

"We have too much to do to waste even a minute," he said with a gentle smile as he handed the bowl to her.

Master Anderson stumbled into the kitchen, rubbing his eyes. "Why the racket at this ungodly hour?"

Tono proceeded to dish him up a bowl as well. "I did my best with the ingredients on hand. I hope you enjoy it."

Master Anderson stared at the mixture of rice, egg and vegetables. "There is no doubt I appreciate a hearty meal in the morning, but not this early."

"Brie needs to get to the hospital to check on Wallace. I was also wondering if I might use your facilities in the next day or two. I only need a single room. I would like to show her what I've been working on."

Brie perked up. "Oh, Tono, do you mind if I film it?"

"Not at all. I'd be honored."

"I suggest you use the auditorium so it can be filmed on stage."

She turned to Master Anderson and beamed. "That would be perfect! Thank you."

"I have another favor to ask," Tono said.

"Certainly," Master Anderson replied agreeably.

"Could I use Lea, or will she be working this week?"

"She does have work all week, but if you do it in the afternoon, there's no reason she shouldn't be able to take part. Of course, you'll have to run it by her first."

"I'll phone her," Brie piped up. "I have to give her a hard time for not calling me yet."

Master Anderson gave her a guilty half-grin. "That would be my fault, young Brie. I asked her to leave you alone the first two days. Thane wanted it to be just the three of us the night you arrived, and I knew yesterday the Boy would need extra tending after meeting with his donor."

"You're lucky you said something, or I would have ridden Lea's ass for being a crappy friend. Dang, she's probably as anxious as I am to get together."

Master Anderson slid his phone over to her with a sly grin. "Let's find out."

Brie knew he was counting on the earliness of the hour to be a deterrent for Lea's enthusiasm, but she was curious as well to see how her best friend would react to such an early call. She picked up his cell phone and dialed the number.

When it went to voice mail, she hung up and called again. Just before it switched to voicemail again, Lea picked up and cried, "Nooooooooo-ooooooooo!"

"No what?" Brie giggled.

"Wait. Brie? Is that you?"

"Yeppers. What the hell are you sleeping in for?"

"I didn't go to bed until two-thirty, girlfriend."

"Three and a half hours of sleep should be more than enough."

Lea gave her a long raspberry.

"Dang, I've missed you, woman," Brie confessed.

"I missed you too, although I forgot what a pain you can be."

"Don't blame me—Master Anderson was the one who told me to call."

"No wonder his number showed up on my phone."

Master Anderson told Brie, "Inform Ms. Taylor that any plans for retribution had better be tempered by the knowledge that I am allowing her to film with you."

"What was that?" Lea asked.

"Master Anderson is going to let you scene with Tono!"

"Wait… Did you say Tono? What's he doing back in the States?"

"He's Todd's donor."

"Get out!"

"Seems they share the same rare blood type," Brie told her, smiling at Tono.

"Man, Faelan's been so negative about the transplant I didn't think he was going to go through with it."

"Luckily, Tono is a very convincing man."

"Oh yes, he is," Lea purred.

Brie grinned into the phone. "Lucky for you, he wants to show off his new rope tricks. Do you mind if I film the session?"

Lea squealed. "Of course not, Brie! But you'd better hang up now, because I'll need my beauty sleep if I'm going to be on camera. Last thing I need is to have the dark circles under my eyes distracting people from my gorgeous boobs."

"Diva," Brie teased. She stared at Tono critically and commented, "You know, Tono doesn't have dark circles, and he's suffering from jetlag."

"I need my sleep, Stinky Cheese."

"Fine, but you'd better be perky when I see you, Miss Thing."

"No worries, I'll be perky like virgin tits."

Brie giggled. "Before I let you go, I have a joke for you."

"No way. Lay it on me, girlfriend."

"How do you know you're kinky?"

"Tell me, tell me!"

"You know you're kinky if your favorite dessert is hot-cross buns and you don't even like sweets."

Silence met her punch line.

Brie protested. "Seriously, Lea, I laugh at your stupid jokes."

"Oh wait, was that supposed to be the joke?"

"You weenie!"

Lea giggled hysterically.

"You're a butt. Go back to bed," Brie said, hanging up on Lea's wild laughter.

She shook her head, sliding the phone back to Master Anderson. "After all the bad jokes she's made me endure…"

"In her defense, it wasn't funny," Tono stated.

"It's not supposed to be funny, Tono. That's the whole point."

Master Anderson chuckled. "She got you good."

"You're as evil as she is," Brie grumbled, shoveling rice into her mouth, but inside she was laughing.

One point for you, Lea the Lame.

Before they left for the hospital, Brie made one more quick call. "Hey, Autumn, it's Brie. I know it's early, but I'm in town and a dear friend of mine has agreed to do a Kinbaku demonstration for my film. Only hitch is that it'll be happening in the next couple of days. I would love for you to see it. Lea is going to be his partner for the scene, and I think you would enjoy seeing her in action."

"Oh, my goodness, Brie, thanks for the invitation, and I don't want to seem ungrateful, but I don't want to be in your film."

Brie laughed. "Don't worry, the camera will be focused solely on Tono and Lea. Let me sweeten the pot by promising no one else will be there."

Autumn asked hesitantly, "Are they going to have sex?"

"No, this is simply bondage. His rope art is breathtaking. You don't want to miss it."

"You're sure I won't get in the way?"

"Not at all. You'll be keeping me company while they perform."

"Well, if that's the case, I would love to come. I've got a few days of vacation left from work, so it shouldn't be a problem. Just tell me where and when."

After talking to Autumn, Brie grabbed her purse so she could leave with Tono, and they headed to the hospital.

Faelan was in a foul mood when Brie arrived. While Tono met with the surgeon performing the operation, Brie faced the angry brute alone.

"Good morning, Todd. I see you haven't eaten yet," she stated, looking at his untouched tray of food.

Faelan glared at her. "Turn around and leave."

"What's all the hostility for?"

"I feel like shit and I want to be left alone."

"I'll be happy to leave after you eat a solid meal."

"I'm not hungry," he growled.

"Hungry or not, you have to give your body the nutrients it needs to heal after the operation."

"Fine, I'll eat later," he said dismissively.

"Fine, you'll eat now," Brie answered, taking his fork and stabbing the rubbery eggs with the tines. "Here you go…" she said, handing him the fork.

He folded his arms and glared at her.

"Now, Todd, we can do this the easy way or the hard way. You can eat these eggs like a big boy, or I will be forced to take drastic measures."

His glare burned like acid, but Brie met it without cringing. "Last chance or suffer the consequences, big guy."

When he didn't budge, she put the fork down and left. She heard him snort in triumph as she closed the door. Did he seriously think he'd won?

Brie talked to the nurse in charge, who readily agreed to her request. "His refusal to eat has been a sticking point with me. If this works, I'll thank you personally."

A few minutes later, Brie returned with a covered dish and smiled sweetly at Faelan. "Do you know what happens to big bad Doms who refuse to eat their food?" She removed his breakfast tray, replacing it with her new dish. Brie lifted the lid with a flourish. "They get spoon fed like a little baby."

He looked down at the oatmeal and snarled in disgust.

"Last chance, Todd. Will it be eggs or oatmeal?"

"Neither," he huffed, looking towards the window.

"Fine, oatmeal it is."

Brie scooped up a spoonful and made airplane noises as she brought it to his lips.

"Get that away from me."

"Come on, Wolffie, don't make me bring out the big guns."

He clamped his mouth shut and ignored her.

Not in the least bit discouraged, she rolled the tray out of the way and lowered the railing on his bed. Being mindful of the many tubes and monitors connected to him, she carefully mounted the bed and straddled him.

She heard the beeping of the heart monitor increase, and hoped it wouldn't trigger any alarms at the nurse's station.

Faelan stared at her in disbelief as she leaned forward and sensually grazed his lips with the spoon.

"Come on, open those pouty lips and eat this for Mary."

His blue eyes stared at her, unblinking.

Brie was sure he was going to call security and order her to leave, but to her relief he slowly parted his lips. She smiled as she fed him the first bite. "Good job." After he'd finished the whole bowl, Brie pulled out the piece of candy she'd been saving.

"For being so good, you deserve a piece of chocolate," she announced, holding it out to him. Chocolate held a special place in her heart after her auction session with him. She'd never forgotten the driving beat as they'd performed their chocolate dance together.

Brie proceeded to unwrap the candy and put it to his lips. "You earned it." When he wouldn't take a bite, she bit into the decadent chocolate and purred, "Best chocolate in the world…"

She lifted it to his lips again and was pleased when he opened his mouth, taking the bite.

"Isn't it sooooo good?"

He chewed it and swallowed, his eyes never leaving hers. "Brie."

"Yes?"

"Why are you doing this? Why has Davis bothered to do all this for me?"

She stared at him in shock. "Not only are you my friend, but you trained with Sir. We both care about what happens to you."

He rolled his eyes, but she could tell it meant something to him.

Brie licked her fingers to get the last of the rich chocolate and smiled at Faelan. "When I saw you and Mary together at the commune, I was so happy."

"How is Mary—really?"

"She's working hard to be whole again, but as strong as she is, she cries whenever she talks about you."

"I want to believe it, Brie."

"I would never lie to you."

He touched her cheek lightly. "No, blossom, you never have."

Ghosts of the Past

"**B**rie, there's something I feel I must do before I leave Denver, but I would like you to join me," Master Anderson stated.

She tilted her head, curious what he was asking of her. "Of course, Master Anderson, I would love to. But what's this about?"

"Thane suggested closure would help me break away from Denver cleanly."

She looked at him with sympathy, "Is this about Amy?"

Master Anderson closed his eyes. When he opened them again, she saw intense pain reflected in his jade-colored gaze. "Not just Amy."

"Do you mean her husband?"

He nodded.

"That's a huge step," she said, feeling only compassion for the man.

"The move is forcing it on me. If Thane's right, it must be done before I leave."

"I think you're doing the right thing."

"I don't want her feeling sorry for me, so that's where you come in. Since Amy already believes we're a couple, do you mind continuing that ruse a while longer?"

Brie smiled. "Not at all, Master Anderson. I'll speak to Sir about it tonight."

"Good. I've set it up to meet them at lunch tomorrow. I should warn you that their baby will be joining us."

"Aww…"

"Not 'aww'," he reprimanded. "It will only be a distraction."

She shook her head. "I must respectfully correct you, Master Anderson. The baby is not an *it*."

He smiled, his green eyes showing a hint of the old spark. "Fine, the child is not an *it*, but he'll be a distraction."

"Oh, so they had a little boy and not a girl?"

Master Anderson nodded, complaining, "I hope it doesn't cry through the whole damn lunch."

Brie gave him a disapproving look.

He sighed angrily. "I meant he."

"I know you did," she said with a gentle smile. "I think this meeting is long overdue," she added, wrapping her arms around Master Anderson's muscular waist.

Master Anderson took Brie to the Italian café where they'd run into Amy before. He explained as he helped her out of the truck, "I figure I might as well confront her at our favorite restaurant."

Brie took his hand in hers. "You're not confronting Amy, you're letting her go."

She saw the flicker of pain return, but he nodded. "That's right, I'm letting her go."

The redhead waved the two over as soon as they entered the establishment. Master Anderson escorted Brie to the table, whispering, "I want you to address me as Master."

Brie was surprised by the request but answered amiably, "Of course, Master."

Amy and Troy stood as they approached. There was no disputing that they were a striking couple. Amy, with her long red hair, sun-kissed freckles and big green eyes, and Troy, who was her perfect complement with his dark hair, dark eyes and five o' clock shadow. But it was the man's smile that caught Brie's attention—it was genuine and kind.

Troy shook Master Anderson's hand first. "It's good to see you, Brad." He looked at Brie and took her hand with a warm, firm grip. "And a pleasure to meet you, Miss Bennett."

She smiled, responding to his natural charm. "Please call me Brie."

Amy walked over to Master Anderson and gave him a tentative hug. "I can't tell you how glad I am that you asked us to lunch, especially at our favorite restaurant."

Brie saw him tense as she hugged him, but Master Anderson forced a smile. "It's good to see you again, Amy. Been far too long."

Amy hugged Brie next. "Great to see you again, too."

"Likewise. I see your bun is out of the oven."

Amy giggled. "Yes, he is!"

Troy lifted the baby carrier, saying apologetically, "I'm sorry, he just fell asleep."

Brie peeked under the hood of the carrier and grinned, whispering, "What a handsome little guy." She looked up at Master Anderson, who was staring warily at the baby. "Don't you think, Master?"

She noticed that Troy shifted uneasily upon hearing her call Master Anderson by that title.

"Yes, Brie, he looks to be a healthy child. That's what's important, right?" Master Anderson said, chuckling uncomfortably.

Brie suspected the forced laughter stemmed from his uneasiness, so she joined in by giggling, hoping the others wouldn't notice. "Yes, and he's a cutie, Amy. A real charmer."

"Such a good baby too," Amy said proudly, looking down at her sleeping child. "Brandon has been a dream come true for us."

Troy carefully placed the carrier on the chair between the two of them before asking, "Would either of you care for some wine?"

"Please," Brad answered without hesitation.

Troy raised his hand and the server immediately came over. "Yes, Mr. Dawson?"

"Our friends would like some wine."

The waitress stared brazenly at Master Anderson when she asked, "Which would you prefer, sir?"

She actually blushed when he turned his full attention on her. "I've always been partial to the house wine here."

The woman bowed her head slightly, a flirtatious smile spreading on her lips. "You wouldn't happen to be Brad Anderson, would you?"

"I am. Do I know you?"

"No, but one of our servers does. Mandy described you to a T." The girl laughed coyly. "Oh, won't she be crying tomorrow when she finds out you were here."

"Please give Mandy my best regards." Master Anderson turned and asked Brie, "And what you would like, my pet?"

The waitress stared unabashedly at the collar around Brie's neck. There was no doubt she knew *exactly* who he was.

Brie smiled affectionately at Master Anderson, wanting everyone at the table to know how much she cared for the man. "I'd be honored to have whatever you're having, Master."

"Perfect. Bring a carafe and glasses for everyone."

Amy held up her hand. "Please, none for me." When Master Anderson questioned her on it, she explained with a blush, "I'm still breastfeeding."

"Ah…" He glanced at Brie, looking chagrined.

"So, you still have quite the reputation here," Brie said after the waitress left, wrapping her arm around his muscular one. "I'm not sure if I should feel jealous or proud, Master."

Master Anderson kissed the top of her head. "No need for jealousy, my pet. No one holds a candle to you."

Troy's unease increased and an uncomfortable silence settled over the table until Amy burst out, "Oh, my goodness! Is that an engagement ring I see on your finger?"

Brie looked down at her glittering diamond and then at Master Anderson, curious how he would handle it.

He smirked, obviously thrown off by the discovery but not one to back down. "It's true, a marriage is in our near future."

Amy grinned. "I'm so happy for you both! It's plain to see how much you're in love with each other."

Brie blushed when Master Anderson took her hand and kissed it. He looked deeply into her eyes and said, "Brie's a rare gem."

Troy interrupted. "Brad, I don't mean to sound rude, but this feels like a setup to me."

Master Anderson nodded, a look of newfound respect on his face. "You're right, Troy. I do have an ulterior motive for this meeting."

"Which is?"

Master Anderson kissed Brie's hand again before setting it on his muscular thigh. "I'm moving to Los Angeles and doubt I will return." He glanced at Amy. "I wanted to clear the air between us before I left Denver."

"I've wanted that too, Brad. I care about you and hate having this 'strangeness' between us," Amy said, relief on her face.

Master Anderson turned back to Troy and stated, "I owe you an apology."

Troy seemed taken aback. "That's probably the last thing I expected you to say."

"Well, I've had a lot of time to think. Although I can justify my actions back then, the fact is I acted dishonorably and it has haunted me since."

Troy stared at Master Anderson as if he were seeing the man for the first time. "Again, you surprise me."

"I suppose you could say that I've gotten a little older and wiser."

"Brad," Amy said with compassion, "I understood why you did what you did, based on the little you knew of Troy. Every time you and I got together it seemed like I was recovering from losing him."

"I only wanted to protect you, Amy."

Her smile held a hint of sadness when she answered, "I know."

Master Anderson addressed Troy again. "It appears you really are as good a man as she claimed."

Troy seemed troubled by the admission, and took a sip of wine before replying. "I suppose I owe you an apology as well."

"How so?"

"Amy always insisted you were acting in her best interests, but I didn't believe it. I've never liked you."

Master Anderson actually smiled. "Understandable. We *were* rivals."

"It was more than that." He glanced at Brie and asked, "Do you mind if I speak frankly?"

"Not at all," Brie encouraged.

"Brad, I've never forgiven you for what you did to Amy. When I saw the bruises I wanted to kill you."

Master Anderson threw back his head and laughed. "Finally, the truth comes out."

"It was no laughing matter to me," Troy stated angrily.

"You do realize it was consensual."

Troy glanced at Amy. "She said as much, but I've never understood it—how a man could hurt a woman like that."

"Maybe I can provide some clarity," Brie offered. She lifted Master Anderson's strong, masculine hand and held it in both of hers before continuing. "This man has the unique ability to please a woman on a level she never knew existed. It is done with respect and a deep-seated desire to please her. Any marks left behind are something to be cherished, because they remind her of that special encounter."

This time it was Amy who shifted uncomfortably in her seat. Brie knew she must be remembering her encounters with Master Anderson and thought, *Poor girl, you probably haven't known that kind of satisfaction since.*

"Thank you, Brie," Troy said. "I've never had it explained to me that way before." He looked apologetically at Amy. "Although you tried to tell me that on several occasions."

"I'm grateful Brie was able to shed some light on it," Amy said, a blush creeping over her cheeks.

Troy addressed Master Anderson again. "So I must apologize for hating you. It appears there was no cause."

Master Anderson shook his head. "Let's be honest. You had a legitimate reason for hating me. I did everything in my power to win her over." He looked directly at Amy while still speaking to him. "And if I'm completely honest, I'm still in love with her."

Amy gasped, tears filling her eyes as she abruptly stood up and murmured, "If you'll excuse me." She ran off to the bathroom before Troy could stop her.

He sat back down, glaring at Master Anderson. "What was the point of that?"

"I wanted to be open, to lay it all out there so Amy and I could experience the closure we both seek."

"Did you honestly think that confession would help any of us?"

Master Anderson shrugged. "If you think for one second she doesn't know I still love her, you're only kidding yourself."

"What about Brie? Don't you have any regard for your fiancée's feelings, or is she supposed to accept it because you're her *Master*?" Troy said with disgust.

"She knows exactly how I feel, Mr. Dawson. Just because I still care about Amy doesn't change how I feel about Brie. That is one important skill you lack. I know how to communicate openly with my partner."

Troy's eyes narrowed. "I beg to differ."

"I'm curious, Dawson," Master Anderson said. "Why did you agree to meet with me today?"

"Because I love Amy and I knew she needed this."

"Admirable."

Amy returned to the table, smiling apologetically. "I'm sorry about that."

After she sat down, Troy took her hand. "Were you aware he still had feelings for you?"

She cringed, but answered, "I wasn't sure…"

"Come on, Amy," Master Anderson urged.

"I *did* suspect there might be something," the redhead admitted, looking down at her lap, her face turning a deep shade of crimson.

"Does it affect how you feel about Troy?" Master Anderson asked.

Her head popped up and she answered defiantly, "Of course not."

"Then why did you run?" Troy asked gently.

"It was so uncomfortable, my love. I didn't want you to be hurt by his words." She kissed Troy on the lips, then glanced at Master Anderson. "And I hate knowing I hurt you."

She shifted her gaze to Brie. "I'm sorry for hurting him."

Brie grinned. "You followed your heart, Amy. There's no reason to apologize for that."

She smiled gratefully. "Thank you for saying that, Brie, because you're right, I had no other choice. I *had* to follow my heart."

Master Anderson pushed his chair back. "So there we have it, the truth laid out in all its ugly yet glorious beauty."

"What are we supposed to do with it?" Troy questioned.

"Accept it, I suppose. I will always love Amy, but I have a new respect for you and I'm glad to see she's happy."

Amy nodded. "And I'm glad that you're getting married soon and will experience the same happiness. Who knows? Our kids may even play together someday."

"Oh no, we're *not* having kids." Master Anderson stated, grasping Brie's chin and kissing her passionately on the lips. "She and I have no interest in messy diapers."

Amy laughed at his assertion. "We'll see about that..."

The waitress came up with the check and whispered to Master Anderson, "If you ever need an extra partner or anything, my number's inside."

He opened the check and handed back her number. "I could never do that to Mandy. I hope you understand."

The woman took the paper, muttering, "Of course," before she rushed off.

Troy raised his eyebrow. "Does that happen often?"

Brie laid her head on Master Anderson's beefy shoulder. "More than you know, but he always lets them down gently."

Troy grunted. "I suppose I had you pegged all wrong, Brad. Thank you for this meeting today. It has been enlightening, to say the least."

"For me as well," Master Anderson agreed.

As soon as the baby started to fuss, Master Anderson stood and held out his hand to Troy. "So, we'd better be going. I wish you both well."

Troy took his hand and shook it heartily. "I wish you success in your marriage, as well as the move to California."

Amy picked up her crying child, cradling him against her chest, and the boy instantly quieted. Brie thought the interaction was beautiful and smiled at Amy.

"We would love an invite to the wedding," Amy begged.

Master Anderson shook his head. "Sorry, Mrs. Dawson, the wedding won't be held in Colorado. However, I appreciate the sentiment."

His casual statement caught Brie's attention. Was it possible that Master Anderson knew where her wedding would be? Surely, Sir must have told him... "I'm curious about the location, Master..."

Amy's eyes sparkled with intrigue. "You mean you don't know where your own wedding will be?"

Brie shook her head, smiling at Master Anderson. "But I'd *sure* love a hint."

Master Anderson laughter filled the restaurant. "My lips are sealed, pet. I'm not spoiling the surprise for you."

"Drat," she pouted.

When the baby fussed again, Brie walked over to Troy. "It has certainly been a pleasure meeting you, Mr. Dawson. I must say you have a lovely wife and the cutest little boy."

"Thank you. I've enjoyed sharing lunch with you. I hope our paths cross again."

"Me too," she said with sincerity.

Brie hugged Amy next, the baby between them. "You have a beautiful family."

"Thanks, Brie. It's been a real treat getting to know you better."

"I feel the same way."

"Come, pet," Master Anderson commanded.

Brie played with the collar around her neck so that Troy noticed, and purred, "My pleasure, Master."

She trusted Troy would take the hint, hoping Amy might enjoy a little side of kink in the near future...

Tono Experiences Flight

B rie was shaking with excitement as she pulled up to the Academy.
Tono laughed beside her. "You're behaving like a little kid at Christmas."

"That's exactly how I feel, Tono," she giggled. "You know me so well—you always have." She reached over and opened the glove box, pulling out the small container that held the orchid comb he'd given her. "I never film without it."

Tono opened the box and lifted out the delicate white orchid, admiring the flower. "Do you mind if I put it in your hair?"

"Please, it would be my honor."

He smiled as he carefully placed it in her hair, his lips coming dangerously close to hers in the process. In another time and place, she would have leaned forward to kiss those lips, but neither of them made a move towards the other.

Tono sat back to admire it when he was finished. "It looks as good in your dark hair as I'd hoped."

Brie lightly touched the petals and smiled. "Thank you, Tono. I've gotten many compliments on it."

"It's unique, like you."

She gazed into his chocolate-brown eyes, trembling with joy. Something was going to happen today, she could feel it in her bones.

He looked at her questioningly. "What's got you so anxious?"

"I'm not sure. Maybe because I get to film you today? I never thought I would have the chance again and you know I love watching you in your element. The icing on the cake is that I get to hang with Lea and you get to meet Autumn. I think this is mounting up to be the perfect storm of happiness."

Tono looked at her curiously. "I didn't realize Autumn was coming."

"I hope you don't mind. I invited her as soon as I knew you would be partnering with Lea." Brie got out of the car and popped the trunk, handing Tono his heavy duffel bag full of jute. He slung it over his shoulder and offered to take some of her equipment while Brie explained, "This is a rare chance for her to see what Lea does. Plus Autumn is such a graceful person on the ice, I'm certain she'll fall in love with your art."

"If you think she'll enjoy it, I'm fine with her watching."

Brie stopped pulling out her camera equipment from the car for a moment to warn him, "She's *really* shy, Tono. Autumn has never seen bondage of any kind, so this is a huge step for her. Don't be offended if she hides from you."

Tono gave her a half-smile. "I'll keep that in mind when we meet."

Brie picked up the rest of the equipment, bumping shoulders with him. "I can't believe you're really here with me!"

As they walked towards the school, she thought back to the dream she'd had about Tono a few nights earlier, and realized that it must have been her soul hinting at their upcoming reunion. The soul connection she had with him was truly rare and beautiful.

While Brie set up her camera equipment in the auditorium, Tono laid out all his rope on the stage. He then hung the black lights that would add to his unique performance. "I've chosen a toned-down version of my act, since you'll be filming it for the documentary."

"That's perfect, I thin—"

Hands covered Brie's eyes as big boobs pressed against her back. "Guess who?"

"Pamela Anderson?"

Lea giggled as she turned Brie around. "Aren't you cute?"

Brie noticed that Lea was wearing the red kimono she'd worn for Brie's twenty-third birthday surprise. Seeing it brought back a flood of pleasant memories involving the three of them… She grabbed her best friend, squeezing the breath out of Lea. "Oh, I've missed you!"

Lea gave as good as she got, and the two were left gasping for air by the time they were done.

Then Lea turned to Tono, bowing formally. "I'm thrilled to be working with you again, Tono Nosaka."

"I'm looking forward to it as well, Ms. Taylor."

Lea grinned, bursting out, "By the way, I've got a joke for you."

Brie groaned. "Why am I not surprised?"

Lea was not deterred by her lack of enthusiasm. "So, God, in all His wisdom, promised the Dominants that good and obedient subs would be found in all the corners of the Earth…then He made the world round."

Tono chuckled lightly.

"A+ for me!" Lea squealed.

Brie teased her, "Forced to grade your own jokes these days?"

"Hey, I'm the only one who judges them fairly."

Brie hugged Lea again, her heart overflowing with happiness. She wanted so desperately to beg Lea to come back to LA, but knew the decision was not an easy one for her friend. In the end, what Brie honestly wanted was for Lea to remain true to her heart, even if it meant staying in Denver.

"So, Tono Nosaka, is there anything I need to know about this scene today?" Lea asked.

He led her up onto the stage and went over the progression of the rope ties. Brie went back to setting up. She looked through the camera's lens, focusing it on her best friend, and watched Lea nod enthusiastically while Tono explained the scene to her. Brie felt a twinge of jealousy knowing that her girlfriend was going to experience flight with the jute Master.

Once again, woman, you owe me one.

Brie nearly jumped out of her skin when she felt an unexpected tap on her shoulder. She turned to see Autumn, dressed in blue jeans and a T-shirt, wearing a thin veil that covered the lower half of her face.

"I'm sorry, Brie. I didn't mean to startle you like that."

"Oh, no, that's okay." She giggled, hugging Autumn tightly. "I'm glad you made it!"

"Me too. I've wanted to see what Lea does here."

"Well, you're in luck, because you'll also get to see Ren Nosaka, a world-renowned Kinbaku artist. Since they're going over the scene right now, why don't you sit beside me and we can chat while I finish setting up?"

Autumn quietly took a seat, admiring the comfortable leather auditorium chair. "I didn't realize the school was going to be such a fancy place."

"Master Anderson believes in quality."

"I see that." Autumn watched as Brie finished making the final adjustments to her equipment, and commented, "You must enjoy making films."

"I love it!" Brie answered, not holding back the excitement she felt towards her craft.

Lea heard them talking and looked down from the stage. "Is that Autumn?"

"In the flesh!"

Lea let out a joyous squeal as she ran down the steps. She hugged Autumn tight, looking over her shoulder at Brie. "You sneaky devil."

Brie shrugged. "Once in a lifetime opportunity. Couldn't let Autumn miss out, now, could I?" She then asked, "Autumn, would you like to meet the man who is going to make Lea fly today?"

She seemed startled by the suggestion and sat back down. "Oh no, I would prefer not to, Brie. Let me just sit here and watch."

"If you're sure," Lea stated, "then it's time to get this party started!"

"Let's," Brie agreed. She called up to Tono, "Are you ready?"

He gave her a thumbs-up, looping the first rope through the hanging metal ring above him. While Lea rejoined Tono on the stage, Brie readied the auditorium lights with a remote control, turning them down except for one solitary beam that shone from above, highlighting the couple.

She whispered to Autumn, "I'll need you to be quiet through the entire performance. My mic will pick it up anything you say."

"Got it."

Even though Tono hadn't given the signal to start, Brie turned on the camera to capture this moment. It was one of her favorite parts whenever she'd scened with Tono—the process of becoming in sync with each other before the formal scene began. Brie suspected movie-goers might find it as romantic as she did.

Lea knelt on the jute mat he'd placed on the floor, and Tono settled behind her with his hands on her shoulders. He leaned forward and whispered in her ear. Brie knew that he was instructing her to breathe with him, as he slowly embraced her in his arms. Brie closed her eyes, slowing her own breath, and soon felt soothing peace enter her soul. She was amazed Tono still held that kind of power over her.

Brie opened her eyes to find him staring at her through the lens, waiting for her to begin the countdown. She blushed, held up her fingers and silently counted down from five before cuing the music.

The musical piece Tono had chosen for the performance was a combination of traditional flute and low bass drums. It started off dramatically but soon slowed to a sensual beat, drawing Brie into its erotic spell as Tono and Lea swayed to the captivating rhythm.

Brie adjusted the lighting, dimming it to a soft glow as she turned up the black lights, so the dyed jute could reveal its intense colors. She bit her lip as she watched Tono pick up the first bundle of rope and begin binding Lea in a rope harness of fluorescent purple. His movements were graceful, sensuous and precise.

Brie's skin tingled as if she could feel the jute caressing her own skin with its magical touch.

The next color Tono chose was a bright pink, which he used to bind Lea's wrists and legs. He pressed her gently to the floor, continuing his binding by tying Lea in a pose reminiscent of a dancing ballerina.

Tono stood, grabbed the glowing yellow rope from the metal ring above him, and secured Lea's bonds to it. Brie leaned over, whispering to Autumn, "Lea's about to fly."

The two watched with rapt attention as Tono took the strands of rope and pulled on them with such skill that Lea was lifted gracefully from the ground, as if floating by her own power. He tied the jute off and cradled her face, kissing her on the lips before pushing against her shoulder to start her twirling in circles.

"Head back," he commanded.

Lea threw her head back and the pose was complete, the ballerina caught in mid-air.

Brie heard Autumn gasp loudly, and smiled to herself. She didn't reprimand the girl, because the vision before them was extraordinary and poignant. Gasping was a totally appropriate response that the audience would echo.

Tono continued, binding Lea in several different positions. Each was reminiscent of the last but building upon it, becoming more complicated and challenging as he progressed. The bindings the Asian Dom created accentuated Lea's sexuality while remaining elegant, artfully emphasizing her female form as she floated gracefully above the stage.

The entire performance was breathtaking and romantic, enhanced by his occasional kisses and light touches throughout the scene. By the time Tono finished, Brie had fallen completely under his spell—along with Lea.

Brie turned off the camera and sighed quietly to herself. *That was pure perfection, Tono...*

Autumn clapped enthusiastically, the moment Brie stepped away from her camera. "Bravo, bravo!"

Lea was still coming down from subspace after the scene, and was a little slow as she attempted to walk down the steps of the stage. Tono took her by the arm and guided her, sitting her next to Autumn.

"Mr. Nosaka, that was incredible!" Autumn gushed, standing up to face him. "I've never seen anything like it, never imagined anything like it even existed."

Tono held out his hand to shake hers. "Thank you for the kind words. I'm Ren Nosaka."

She tilted her head, looking questioningly at him. "But Lea always calls you Tono Nosaka."

"That's my title because we work together. Tono means Master in

Japanese."

"Oh!" She giggled nervously. "Well, that explains that."

To ease her obvious embarrassment, Brie asked, "What did you enjoy most about the performance, Autumn?"

"All of it! The rope, the music, the overall character of the dance—and it did feel like a dance to me. But what I loved most is that it also possesses the effortlessness found in ice skating."

Brie noticed Tono staring intently at Autumn, and then he did something she would never have imagined the gentle Dom would. Tono reached over and gently tugged on Autumn's veil so that it fell to one side, exposing her face.

"That's much better," he complimented.

Autumn stared at him in shock, but no words of protest escaped her lips. She automatically went to cover the scar on her face with her hand, but let it drop to her side.

"Brie told me you're like poetry on the ice," he said kindly. "I would like to see you skate sometime."

She laughed, shaking her head. "I'm not nearly as graceful as you made Lea today."

"I could teach to you to fly, Autumn."

Her eyes widened as if she was enamored by the thought, but she quickly backpedaled. "Oh no, Mr. Nosaka. It wouldn't be the same." She knocked on her artificial leg. "I would look ridiculous up there."

"You wouldn't wear it," he said with a confident smile.

A flush crept up Autumn's face when she answered, "I couldn't possibly, Mr. Nosaka."

"Please call me Ren."

"Okay...Ren," she said, nervously twirling a strand of her hair with her finger.

Brie turned her attention to Tono and was struck by the change in his countenance. His eyes were sparkling and his smile melt-worthy. Was it possible a new romance was budding before her eyes?

Oh, please, please let it be so... she thought.

The Cat's Out of the Bag

It had been a particularly hard day, fighting to keep Faelan's spirits up the day before his surgery. Brie returned to Master Anderson's home early, collapsing on his couch.

"Bad day?"

"Sometimes I think Todd actually beats me in the stubborn department, and that's saying a lot," she groaned, dragging her hands over her face in frustration. "That boy is killing me…"

Master Anderson sat down beside her. "Maybe you need a nice bull-whip session to get the tension out."

"I hate to break it to you, Master Anderson, but I find your bullwhip is a tension-maker, not a tension-taker."

He laughed. "A cooking session, then?"

"Again, tension-maker."

"A sure-fire tension releaser is rough sex, but since a good romp in the hay is out of the question, how about joining me in a practical joke?"

"We're not pranking Ms. Clark again, are we?"

"No, my plans are far bigger, young Brie."

She looked at him warily, but the distraction was desperately needed. "Count me in."

"Good. You'll be acting as my plant to help engage the others involved. I simply need you to react to what you see—overreacting would be even better."

"Am I required to wear a ridiculous outfit?"

"No, but you'll need to dress in businesslike attire. You're going as one of the investors I'm meeting with tonight."

"Sounds a tad boring."

"Boring?" He laughed. "Never! I live for this stuff."

"Hmm... I suddenly understand why you prank others so often. You're in serious need of a permanent sub. By your own admission, 'If a romp in the hay is not an option, pranking is the next best thing'."

He shook his head, grinning. "Touché, young Brie, touché."

Due to the upcoming surgery, Tono chose to remain at Master Anderson's house to meditate. "I must ready my mind and body," he explained, when Brie asked if he wanted to join them.

"Of course, Tono. Would you rather I stay here with you?"

"No, a solitary evening would be beneficial to me."

"I support whatever you need," Brie said, letting out an anxious sigh.

"Why the heavy heart?" he asked, tucking a stray curl behind her ear.

"I'm worried about you—about both you and Todd."

"Whatever happens is supposed to happen," Tono assured her. "I've lived that truth my whole life."

She was hesitant to express her deepest fear to him. "But Tono, this surgery carries serious risks."

"There is no point in worrying about what *might* happen. If tomorrow is my last day—"

Brie was about to protest, but he put his fingers to her lips. "What would you want to say to me?"

Her lip trembled. She didn't want to contemplate the worst out loud, but when he lifted his fingers she took the opportunity to speak from the heart. "Knowing you has changed my life, Tono Nosaka. You've become a part of me."

"As you are a part of me. I tell you this with a full heart. If I were to die tomorrow, I would have no regrets. I've lived a full life. There would be no reason to mourn."

"But I would mourn, Tono."

"And you would look back on this day and know that I'm okay."

Brie closed her eyes, struggling not to cry. Tono responded to her unspoken pain by whispering, "No regrets..."

Brie arrived at the Denver Academy with Master Anderson an hour before the Submissive Training course began. "It's imperative that I have everything ready," he explained, "but you can't help, because I want your reaction to be as genuine as possible."

"What do you want me to do until then?"

"Keep Baron company. He's extremely allergi—No, never mind. Just go to the teacher's lounge. You'll find him there."

Brie liked the assignment he'd given her and asked no more questions. She found Baron reading a newspaper while sipping a cup of coffee. He put the paper down when she entered the room. "What a pleasant surprise."

"Master Anderson sent me. He said you might be a little bored while he sets up whatever this thing is that he's setting up."

Baron smirked. "That man is always hatching something. We're lucky he doesn't possess an evil bone in his body, or we'd all be in serious trouble."

She sat down next to him, scooting her chair closer. "A little bird told me you're planning to return to LA."

He folded his newspaper and set it on the table. "I am. I was willing to stick it out here with Master Anderson, but the moment he informed the staff he was heading back to California, I volunteered to follow."

"I can't tell you how happy that makes me. LA hasn't been the same without you."

"I miss the old haunts, and never really found my groove here."

"Will it be hard returning to the places that remind you of Adrianna?"

"I plan to move somewhere new—a fresh start in the city where she and I fell in love."

Brie smiled, putting her hand on his. "She would like that."

There was a sneeze on the other side of the door just before it opened. Ms. Clark waltzed in, her high heels clicking rapidly as she hurried to grab a tissue before she sneezed again. "Why does he do this to us?" she grumbled, wiping her nose.

Baron's chuckle was deep and easy. "I can't complain—Anderson keeps things interesting here."

Ms. Clark gave Brie an unexpected smile. "So, Miss Bennett, I see you're back with us."

"I'm only here tonight to help Master Anderson. I'm planning on being at the hospital most of this trip to look after Mr. Wallace and Tono."

"We're all praying for them, kitten," Baron said compassionately.

"Thank you. I'm sure it will go well, but—"

"There are no buts, Miss Bennett. They will both be fine," Ms. Clark interjected.

Brie nodded, knowing there was no solace to be found with Ms. Clark.

The Domme changed the subject by asking her, "Are you almost done filming the second documentary?"

Brie didn't mind the shift in the discussion and answered, "I'm close." She turned to Baron. "That reminds me. I would really love to film you, Baron. Would you be willing?"

"Let me think on it. I saw how Faelan was hounded by desperate subs after your first film came out. I'm not interested in that kind of attention."

"I'll respect whatever you decide," Brie answered, still hoping he would consent.

"Miss Bennett," Ms. Clark barked, "I would like to have a private conversation with you at some point while you're here."

Brie's heart rate shot up when she turned to face the Domme, Rytsar's warning coming to her mind. "What about?" she asked lightly.

Ms. Clark inclined her head toward Baron. "It's *private*."

Stalling for time before she gave a definitive answer, Brie replied, "Before I commit, I'd like to talk to Sir."

"If you feel you must," the Domme stated dismissively, before sneezing into her tissue. "The hell I put up with working under that man."

Baron laughed. "You know you love it, Samantha. Why else would you join in?"

"I only do it because I respect Brad as my Headmaster," Ms. Clark said defensively, but then her lips curled into a dangerous smile. "Of course, seeing the reaction of his intended victims is always entertaining."

Master Anderson popped his head in, addressing Brie. "Are you ready? The show is about to begin." He handed her a pair of glasses, as well as a tablet and stylus. "We need you looking the investor part. Just write down anything that sounds important while I give my sales pitch.

"As for you, Baron," Master Anderson added, "remain here until Lisa confirms the facility has been cleared. You'll be heading the panel during my absence tonight."

"Good luck," Baron replied.

"With fifty—" Master Anderson looked at Brie and stopped short, shrugging his shoulders. "What could possibly go wrong?"

"Not a thing," Baron said, chuckling.

When Brie slipped on the plastic frames, Master Anderson whistled in appreciation. "I knew you'd make an enchanting geek, Miss Bennett." He rushed her out of the room, explaining, "The first of the investors should be arriving any minute."

Master Anderson escorted her to the front entrance, telling his secretary, "Lisa, I have a last-minute addition to our list of investors. A Kristoffer Larson will be joining us."

"Certainly, Master Anderson."

He smiled mischievously when he shared, "Gunnar Larson and I have an 'accidental' encounter planned. It should prove entertaining."

"Of course," Lisa answered, grinning to herself as she dutifully added the name to her list.

He whispered to Brie, "We have a little love connection in the works. Gunnar suspects Kristoffer and one of our current students—a cute little redhead named Pamela that I've had my eye on—might be the perfect match. Gunnar's hopeful a nudge in the right direction might set things in motion for these two unsuspecting colleagues. Tonight, we'll see if his instincts prove right."

"That's so romantic," Brie cooed.

"But it's not why you're here," Master Anderson explained. He opened his mouth to say more, then groaned, as if not telling her was a great sacrifice to him. "No, I can't say another word, damn it!"

She laughed, loving that he was fighting not to divulge any more of his devious plan. "I can't wait to see what you've got planned, Master Anderson."

Brie took on her businesswoman persona the moment the first investor entered the school. She held her back straight and crossed one leg in front of the other to make for a more pleasing form to the eye.

Master Anderson strode over to greet the first man, his whole demeanor suddenly morphing into that of a serious business owner. "Welcome to the Denver Academy, Mr. Rodriguez..."

Brie watched in admiration as he interacted with each individual as they came in. They not only responded to his obvious knowledge of the business, but his natural charisma. She noticed, however, that he kept glancing towards the front doors, stalling for time.

The moment a middle-aged gentleman with a solemn disposition entered the school, Master Anderson strode over, holding out his hand. "Ah, you must be Kristoffer Larson. Glad you could make it—I was beginning to worry. I know Gunnar voiced particular interest in this property."

The man did not smile as he shook Master Anderson's hand. "I apologize for being late. There was a five-car pileup on I-70 near Georgetown. It couldn't be helped."

Brie watched covertly as they talked. She was struck by the contrast between the two men. Master Anderson was tall and muscular, with jet-black hair, chiseled good looks, and a winning smile, whereas Mr. Larson was leaner, but toned, with shoulder-length blond hair slightly gray at the temples, furrowed brows, and a somber expression on his handsome face.

Observing the man more closely, however, Brie noticed that Mr. Larson seemed unsettled, as if something were weighing on him. When he caught her staring, his gaze held hers because of the intensity of those piercing blue eyes—a Dom for sure.

She smiled apologetically, pretending to adjust her glasses before turning her focus back to Master Anderson. There was no doubt in Brie's mind that the serious-minded man could benefit from Master Anderson's friendly nudging. *Oh, Mr. Larson, you have no idea what you're in for tonight...*

"Before we enter the school proper," Master Anderson said, standing at the front to address the group, "let me explain the concept behind the Denver Academy. While we run both a Submissive and a Dominant Training Program, tonight I will focus solely on the submissive aspect. Our training consists of an intensive six-week course that tests and refines the men and women chosen to attend our classes. Each night they begin with a formal lesson, then they move on to a practice session critiqued by a panel of Dominants, and finish with a personalized practicum centered around the individual's interests and talents. At the end of each week of the course, we hold an auction attended by vetted Dominants from the community. They take our students for an extended excursion outside the walls of the school, where the submissives receive additional practice and a written critique by the winning Dominant. In every way, we strive to prepare our students to become skilled submissives who are not only confident in their talents, but also highly sought-after by the BDSM community worldwide."

"Isn't there a school like that in California?" one of the investors asked.

Master Anderson nodded. "You are correct, and our curriculum is based off of that highly successful program."

The man who'd asked the question scribbled in his notebook, so Brie followed suit, using her stylus to type in the information on her tablet, hoping she would appear like a serious investor.

Master Anderson continued, "We take the privacy of our students seriously, but I've informed the class of tonight's agenda and they've graciously agreed to allow an observation of the lesson."

Brie trembled as Master Anderson led them down the hall to the first classroom on the right. She fondly remembered the excitement of being a student, and warm feelings of nostalgia washed over her as she listened to the teacher's confident voice lecturing on the other side of the door.

Master Anderson instructed in a low, commanding tone, "Please line up against the wall to the left as you enter, and remain quiet. I'll answer any questions you have *after* we exit the room." He opened the door and the group was treated to an anatomy lesson—one that Brie remembered well.

Pamela, the pretty redhead Master Anderson had spoken of, was standing in front of the class beside a muscular male. Both were completely naked.

Brie snuck a peek at Mr. Larson, who seemed to be scanning the classroom and making mental notes, until he spied the redhead and his eyes opened wide in surprise. He shifted his feet, which inadvertently garnered the attention of the woman. When their eyes met, a pink hue crept over Pamela's face. She quickly turned back to face her classmates, pretending she hadn't recognized him, and Brie didn't miss the worried look in her eyes or the slight frown on her lips before she set them in a firm, straight line.

"Mr. Avery, please come up to the front of the class and name the anatomy of both sexes."

One of the male submissives stood up from his desk and took the wooden pointer the teacher handed him. Brie smiled to herself, recalling when Boa had stood before her as she'd pointed to his impressive manhood while naming each part.

To Pamela's credit, she showed the same confidence Boa had. Any sign of her earlier distress was gone as she focused on the back wall of the classroom, her head held high but at a respectful angle.

Brie stared at Pamela unashamedly, admiring the beautiful contrast of her red pubic hair against her pale white skin. She suspected Mr. Larson was appreciating that triangle of curls as well, or perhaps that Mr. Avery was pointing out the pink areola of her breast near her very erect nipple. Mr. Larson surreptitiously loosened his tie before undoing the first button of his collar. The attraction he felt for her was obvious to Brie, and she couldn't help wondering how things would play out between them when they met again outside the school walls.

The group was ushered out of the room once Mr. Avery had successfully named the various body parts of both sexes. Brie noticed that Mr. Larson was the last to leave, and smiled to herself. While Master Anderson answered questions in the hallway, she casually glanced at Mr. Larson again. The man's attention returned several times to the door they had just exited. Even though he hadn't been taking written notes during the tour, he was obviously no longer making mental notes either.

Master Anderson noticed his distraction as well, and winked at Brie.

The next stop on the tour was the row of practice rooms specially furnished and designed to accommodate specific kinds of play. "You will note that a fully functioning kitchen is utilized in our training as well. We want every graduating student to please their Master's full range of appetites. I have seen firsthand that some of the submissives we train are in dire need of such instruction." Master Anderson glanced briefly in Brie's direction, chuckling loudly as he continued down the hall.

"And this is my crowning glory," he announced, as he opened the doors to the luxurious theater-in-the-round. The dramatic reveal was met with appreciative whistles from the crowd.

"The practicums are the heart of this training program. It was important for me to invest accordingly. We have state-of-the-art lighting and sound systems, as well as fine leather seats for the students and trainers. If you look above the stage, you will notice a variety of equipment hanging from the ceiling, which is lowered for use as needed during training."

"This is quite a remarkable setup you have," Mr. Larson stated, once again engaged with the tour.

"Thank you. It's my belief that to create superior graduates, you must utilize superior equipment and hire only the best trainers. There's no reason the Denver Academy can't become as renowned as the Submissive Training Center in LA."

For the last part of the tour, Master Anderson guided them to a large, open room with an impressive assortment of BDSM furniture and suspension equipment. "Unlike the Training Center in California, this warehouse is large enough to include a dungeon area especially designed for the use of the bullwhip. The area itself is perfect for community gatherings and special events, and can be an added revenue generator when classes aren't in session."

A stern-looking female raised her hand and asked, "Does all this equipment come with the school?"

"Yes, everything you see here is included with your purchase of the Academy. As an added bonus, you will also receive the experience and talent of the staff members who remain."

Mr. Larson tucked a strand of his blond hair behind his ear before asking, "Will training continue for the current class of students if the center changes hands within the next six weeks?"

"Rest assured, Mr. Larson, as Headmaster of the school I will not be abandoning my current students. Only after this class has graduated will the transfer of ownership take place."

The object of Pamela's attentions narrowed his eyes and nodded curtly. Brie was certain his interest in the future of the students was for purely personal reasons.

Score!

There was quiet murmuring among the investors when Ms. Clark walked into the room, dressed in a slim, black business suit, her high heels clicking seductively as she joined the large group.

Master Anderson introduced the Mistress to the potential investors. "This is Samantha Clark, a long-standing faculty member of the Submissive Training Center. She understands the program inside and out, and will remain part of the training panel after I'm gone." More murmurs erupted and Master Anderson responded by adding, "You need to be aware that I've asked several staff members to stay in order to ensure the quality of the program remains consistent. As part of the contract, I will also have the program evaluated each year to confirm that the Denver Academy continues to meet the high standards I have set."

"That's highly unusual," a shorter man wearing thick plastic frames complained beside Brie.

Master Anderson smiled broadly. "This is a highly unusual school."

Suddenly a door opened on the far side of the dungeon and a hefty man entered carrying a large cardboard box—followed by a steady stream of cats.

"Not again!" Master Anderson cried in frustration.

"What the hell?" the man beside Brie exclaimed.

Brie looked around in utter shock as at least fifty cats stormed the dungeon. Master Anderson growled, barking commands to his staff. He sounded properly exasperated when he apologized to the group. "Could you please excuse me for a moment?"

Brie feigned a look of horror, even though she was giggling inside. *Cats? Really?*

One of the staff members picked up a bullwhip from the wall and started swinging it at the creatures.

Master Anderson yelled at him, "For God's sake, Ryan, put that down now. You might hit one of the damn things."

An orange tabby rubbed against Brie's leg and she screamed loudly, clutching the short man beside her for protection. "I hate cats," she whined. "They're too much like giant rats!"

The group of investors became more agitated with her antics as the entire Academy staff—minus Baron—arrived to descend on the cats.

Ms. Clark picked up a crop and tried to herd the cats in one direction, hissing, "Shoo, shoo…"

"Ms. Taylor," Master Anderson yelled at Lea, "I need a little help here!"

Lea grabbed two paddles off the wall and tried to direct the clowder of cats back into the far corner, where Master Anderson stood ready to grab them. She waved the paddles wildly, saying in a deep, manly voice, "This is your captain speaking, please find your way to the nearest exit."

"Make the awful things go away," Brie begged, continuing to cower against the man next to her while she watched the reigning chaos with delight.

To her surprise, Mr. Larson took her antics seriously and reached down to remove the cat from her ankle, idly stroking its neck while he watched the bedlam around them. She noticed a wedding band on his finger and wondered why Gunnar Larson and Master Anderson were trying to hook up a married man.

But the cats soon distracted her again as they scattered, some even climbing onto the equipment to avoid capture. Brie noticed a fluffy white Persian sitting primly on a spanking bench, licking its paw as if it didn't have a care in the world. Ms. Clark tried unsuccessfully to sneak up on the beast, but her high heels gave her away. The moment she was close enough to grab it, the cat jumped down dismissively and disappeared under the bondage table.

Finally, the man who had let the cats in managed to catch one standing on the top of a St. Andrew's cross. He held it up proudly for all to see.

"Good job, Nathan," Master Anderson called out.

The man walked to the door, struggling to hold on to the squirming creature. When he opened the door to throw it out, three more cats ran in to take its place.

Mr. Larson shook his head, smiling for the first time. "Herding cats? You can't be serious, Mr. Anderson."

"What?" Master Anderson asked innocently, holding two mewing kittens in his muscular arms.

Larson raised his eyebrow, a knowing smirk on his face.

Master Anderson handed the tiny felines over to Ms. Clark and pointed at him. "I *knew* I liked you for a reason." He reached out to take the tabby from Mr. Larson's hands, before whistling loudly.

A new door opened and, as if by magic, the cats headed towards it. When Master Anderson set the tabby down to follow its comrades, the feline rubbed against Mr. Larson's dark pants leg, leaving a patch of white-and-orange fur to mark its territory.

Before it left, Mr. Larson bent to give it one last ear-rub with his large but gentle hand, almost making Brie want to purr herself. To his credit, he didn't even attempt to brush the fur from his once-impeccable suit.

Turning her gaze toward the retreating cats, Brie nearly lost it when the Persian sauntered past Ms. Clark, its head held high in a dismissive manner as it strolled towards the door.

Master Anderson crossed his arms, staring intently at the group of investors as the door closed with a resounding clang. "This was simply my way of illustrating how investing can be a lot like herding cats unless you know what you're doing. This Academy is growing, and will continue to grow at a steady rate with the right person heading it. You may think that you came tonight to decide whether this is the right investment for you, but you'd be only partially correct. I will not hand over this business unless I feel confident that you are worthy to own this training center."

"Well played, Mr. Anderson," Mr. Larson replied, clapping his hands in admiration. Brie joined in the applause with everyone else, impressed by the meaning behind his little stunt.

It was easy to see that Master Anderson had won them over with his unconventional methods, and he was peppered with questions as he led them to a meeting room to lay out the numbers in black and white.

Master Anderson was absolutely brilliant, so that by the time he'd finished, many of the investors had voiced interest in becoming the new owner of the Denver Academy. Brie noticed, however, that one investor kept glancing at the door. It appeared that Mr. Larson was far more interested in a certain red-headed trainee within the walls of the school than in Gunnar Larson's financial future.

Brie gave Master Anderson a slight bow of her head when he looked in her direction, wanting to show her gratitude at being included in the evening's events.

It had been exactly what her heart needed.

A Good Day

B rie arrived home late from the Academy and knew the next day was going to be brutal. Still, she faithfully wrote to Sir in her journal, adding a brief fantasy rather than challenging herself with a toy. She hoped Sir would not only understand, but employ it at some future date.

The Intruder

I'm woken by a strong hand covering my mouth.

"Don't scream, or I'll hurt you."

My mind sifts through the fogginess of sleep, quickly becoming alert when it registers that this man does not smell or sound like my fiancé.

"Please don't hurt me," I plead when he takes his hand away.

"Lie still and I won't have to."

I start trembling, my body thrown into the primal fight-or-flight instinct when he rips the blanket from me and whistles his admiration at my nearly naked body.

The hand returns to my mouth as he starts to caress me with the other. I can only stare at this frighteningly beautiful stranger as he invades me with his touch, squeezing my breasts and pinching my nipples before his hand heads lower.

I feel him tug at my panties, but I refuse to cooperate, squeezing my thighs together. It proves to be of no consequence, as he rips the material from my body and tosses it aside. I whimper in terror and hear him chuckle in response.

Knowing that he hungers for my fear, I remain silent, even when he forces his fingers between my legs.

His middle finger grazes over my clit, demanding entrance into my sex, but my pussy is dry and tight. I attempt to bite the hand covering my mouth, but he growls in anger and moves it from my mouth to my throat, pressing against my windpipe.

The action effectively quiets my protests.

"Open those legs."

I resist until the blood starts pounding in my ears, my body desperate for the oxygen it needs. I spread my legs for him and he rewards my obedience by easing the pressure around my neck.

He forces his fingers inside, and I squirm but make no sound.

"Good girl," he praises, as if I am his pet.

My body is initially resistant to his manipulations, so he changes tactics, unzipping his pants. He repositions himself, straddling my chest and presenting me with his rigid manhood.

When I turn my head, he responds by increasing the pressure around my throat. "Come on, baby, open that mouth and suck that cock like a good girl."

I shake my head, but when the pressure on my throat increases, I open my mouth reluctantly.

"That's it," he murmurs, forcing his large shaft between my lips. "I want to see it disappear down that pretty little throat."

He releases his hold on my neck, grasping my hair with both hands as he forces me to take all of him. I am left gagging on his cock, and try to pull away, but he holds my head still, telling me, "I want you to choke on it."

To my horror, he reaches between my legs and discovers I am wet. He looks at me, a knowing smile on his lips, but says nothing.

When he tires of my mouth, he announces, "I'm going to fuck you hard."

"No!"

He laughs wickedly. "I never leave a wet pussy unsatisfied."

The man grabs my wrists in one hand and lifts them over my head as he settles between my legs. I feel the head of his penis pressing against my opening and I cry out.

"Make no mistake, I'm going to give this body exactly what it wants…"

Brie closed her journal and slipped it under her pillow, wanting to feel closer to Sir. She closed her eyes and eventually drifted off to sleep.

The alarm went off far too soon, but Brie dutifully dragged herself out of bed and dressed. Checking her phone, she was relieved to see a text from Sir, sent while she was sleeping.

Thinking of you today. Be strong.

She texted back.

I will, Sir. Love you.

She stuffed the phone into her purse, then walked out of the room, looking for Tono. She found him sitting cross-legged out on the patio. She opened the sliding glass door and asked, "Do you mind if I join you?"

"Please," he answered, patting the ground beside him.

She knelt down and looked at the colors of dawn making their appearance in the eastern sky. The vibrant hues were spectacular, but did little to calm Brie's nerves.

"How are you?" she asked.

"At peace. And you?"

She smiled sadly. "Not so much."

"Clear your mind," he ordered gently.

She closed her eyes and listened to the birds singing as they greeted the new day. It was easy finding peace beside Tono, and it didn't take long before her spirits were lifted.

"Thank you, Tono."

"Today will be a good day," he stated, as he leaned over and gave her a hug.

She wrapped her arms around him, resting her chin on his shoulder. "Yes, it will," she agreed.

They headed to the hospital early so that he could be prepped for surgery. Once Tono was settled in his room, Brie left to check on Faelan.

She noticed he had a grimace on his face when she entered the room, but it disappeared as soon as he turned towards her. "Well, look what the cat dragged in."

At the mention of the word cat, she laughed softly. "Did you hear what happened last night?"

"Yes. Lea called to wish me luck and filled me in."

Brie shook her head, thinking back on the night's events. "It was nuts, Todd."

"Sounds like it."

She took his hand, gazing into those ocean-blue eyes, and saw a look of foreboding in them. "How are you doing this morning?"

"I don't want to do this, Brie. I'm only consenting for the sake of others, not myself."

She lifted his hand to her cheek and admitted, "I don't care what your motivation is as long as you go through with the surgery."

"How is Nosaka doing?"

"He's at peace. There's no doubt he wants to do this."

Faelan broke eye contact and looked out of the window. "He's a brave man."

"Yes, he is. I think his courage comes from knowing this will save your life."

He looked at her again. "I don't like being on the receiving end."

She kissed his hand and laid it back on the bed. "I know."

"If anything happens…"

Brie shook her head. "Don't."

He ignored her plea. "If anything happens, let Mary know she was my last thought."

Brie looked at the ceiling to hold back the tears. Once she had them under control, she looked him in the eye again. "I promise to tell her if needed, *but* I won't have to. The surgery is going to be a success."

"And one more thing."

"What else?"

"Thank you."

Brie smiled. "I'll have you know there'll be a piece of chocolate waiting for you when you wake up."

"I'd prefer to wake up to heavy bass."

She winked, giggling. "I'm sure that can be arranged as well…"

Faelan's parents entered the room, so Brie took her leave, hugging them both on her way out. She could see the excitement and hope radiating in his mother's eyes.

"This is really happening," Mrs. Wallace exclaimed.

"Yes, it is!" Brie answered, matching the woman's enthusiasm.

"We can't thank you enough for all you've done."

"Ren Nosaka is the hero here."

Mr. Wallace spoke up. "We just finished visiting with him, Miss Bennett. What a remarkable young man."

"I wholeheartedly agree," she said. "I'm headed back to him now."

As she was leaving, Faelan called out, "Brie." She turned and smiled at him. "Don't forget what I said."

She knew what he was referring to, but refused to consider that he might not survive the surgery, and answered, "Heavy bass. You've got it!"

Brie returned to Tono and found him surrounded by jars of preserves. "Wow, Todd's mother sure has been busy."

Tono chuckled as he looked them over. "It's a virtual fortress of fruit."

She picked a jar up, examining the homemade label crafted with care and smiled. "This appears to be a fortress of fruit protection made with love."

"I like that sentiment."

"His parents are so excited, Tono. I don't think they believed this day would ever come."

"How is the Boy?"

"Struggling, but still going through with it." Brie put the jar down and walked over to him. The reality of what was about to happen hit her full force.

"How are you, Brie?"

"Good."

He laughed softly. "Why do you bother lying to me?"

Brie shook her head, tears welling up in her eyes.

"It's okay. You can voice it out loud."

"I'm still afraid for you."

Tono stared at her for a moment, then motioned Brie to him. "Listen to my heart." Brie pulled down the railing and rested her head lightly on his chest. His slow, steady heartbeat resonated in his chest, declaring his vitality and strength. The sound of it soothed her growing fears.

She lifted her head and smiled at him. "It's strong."

"Remember that when you sit in the waiting room." Her fears suddenly seemed foolish as she stared into his warm gaze. He reminded her, "I will be okay."

Brie nodded.

She gave him one last kiss on the cheek for luck when Flora, one of his attending nurses, came in and announced that he was being taken to the operating room. Brie headed to the waiting room still riding high on Tono's confidence, and burst out in giggles when she saw Master Anderson, Lea and Autumn waiting for her.

"I didn't expect you guys to be here!"

"Before he left, Thane insisted I stand in his place today," Master Anderson explained.

She ran to hug him, thankful for his added strength while she waited through the dual surgeries.

Brie looked upwards and silently said, *Thank you, Sir!* before giving Lea and Autumn both hugs. "You guys are the best."

Autumn held up two 'Get Well' signs she was holding. "I thought we could hang these up in their rooms."

Lea looked at them and grinned. "Hey, we could have a little fun decorating their hospital rooms. What do you think?"

"Sounds a lot more fun than sitting around here worrying," Brie replied.

"We should go to a party store if we want to do this properly," Lea insisted.

Master Anderson sat down. "I'll stay here and hold the fort."

Brie's eyes lit up. "Fort? Oh, that gives me a great idea for Tono."

The girls giggled and chatted as they made their way to the elevator. Two hours later, Brie was placing the final touch, a little flag on the top turret of the fortress she'd created out of Tono's jars of preserves. "He's going to love this!" she stated proudly, stepping away from the windowsill to admire her creation.

"Brie," Master Anderson said, walking into the room, his voice tense with worry. "You need to come. Something's happening. I'm noticing a lot of activity."

Brie's stomach sank, her whole body becoming numb as she rushed out of the room. She ignored the shouts of the nurses as she scooted through the closing doors of the restricted area and ran down the hallway until she found the operating room with all the commotion.

She stared through the glass window to see Tono surrounded by a crowd of nurses and doctors. Alarms were blaring as they rushed about, but her eyes were glued to the heart monitor—her worst fears realized as she watched the straight line move across the screen.

"Tono…"

Time stopped. She felt the numbness consume her body while she watched helplessly as the paddles were brought out. His chest lifted from the table as the electricity was applied, but he lay back down limp and unmoving, the line continuing with cruel conviction.

Brie turned away and slowly slid down the wall, hugging her knees to her chest as she struggled to breathe. All thought faded into darkness as fear took hold of her. She heard faint voices insisting she leave the area, but she did not respond until she felt the strong arms of Master Anderson lifting her.

"He's gone," she whimpered.

Master Anderson said nothing as he carried her to the waiting room and cradled her in his protective arms. Lea and Autumn sat on either side of her, crying silently, but she was in too much shock to shed a tear.

Tono.

Master Anderson understood his role well and held her even tighter, sharing his strength while reminding her that she was not alone.

A short time later, Flora came into the room and walked straight over to Brie. She stood up to face the nurse, even though she was afraid of what Flora had to say.

"The surgeon wants you to know that Mr. Nosaka has been revived and his vitals are reading normal. Dr. Shepherd will speak to you later, once the surgery is complete. He expects Mr. Nosaka should be moving to the recovery room in the next hour or so."

"Can I see him then?" Brie managed to choke out.

"No, I'm afraid not—he'll need to be closely monitored—but once the doctor gives his consent, you will be sent for."

Brie touched her arm, needing her reassurance. "He's okay, Flora?"

"Everything appears normal, Miss Bennett. Mr. Nosaka is a healthy man, and Dr. Shepherd remains optimistic he'll make a full recovery."

Once the nurse had left the room, Brie finally broke down, letting out all the pent-up fear and pain that had been building inside her. It was a cathartic release in the arms of her friends.

Both surgeries were successful, but it was hours later before Brie was allowed to see Tono. He was still being closely monitored, but the surgeon surprised her by agreeing to let her visit him briefly.

She moved the curtain aside and was stunned to see Tono gracing her with a faint smile, tubes running everywhere from him. The nurse monitoring his vitals pointed to where Brie could stand.

She moved to his side, her heart in her throat as she stared down at him.

He gazed up at her—the two speaking volumes without words. When he lifted his hand weakly, she grabbed it, holding on to it with both hands.

Brie swallowed hard to get rid of the lump in her throat so she could speak. "You left me, Tono."

"But I came back," he whispered hoarsely.

Brie kissed his hand, covering it with fresh tears. "I was so scared."

"It's okay."

Her lip trembled as she nodded.

"The Boy?"

"He's in recovery too."

"Good."

"It's best that you keep this short," the nurse said curtly. "The doctor only agreed because Mr. Nosaka insisted on it."

Brie leaned over and gently kissed him on the cheek. "Thank you."

"I could feel your fear."

"Now you will only feel my healing thoughts."

After she left him, a second nurse directed her to another bed in the recovery area. "Mr. and Mrs. Wallace have asked that you speak to their son."

When Brie pulled back the curtain, she was shocked by the contrast between Tono and Faelan. His skin was ashen in color, and he looked despondent.

"The surgery was a success," she reminded him.

Faelan looked at her with such agony that she hurried to his side. "What's wrong?"

"Nosaka almost died."

"I was just with him. He's fine. You don't have to worry."

"He should never have taken the risk."

"But he did, and now your body has a healthy kidney. This is a good day," she insisted.

"How can you say that when his heart stopped on the operating table?" Faelan closed his eyes, the devastating pain easy to read on his face. "I almost killed another man today."

The overwhelming guilt he carried hit Brie. "Todd, don't."

He opened his eyes. "I'm not worth another man's life."

"Tono believes you were worth the risk."

"And he almost died because of it. I'm nowhere near as good a man as he is. Not even close."

For the first time since knowing Faelan, Brie heard humbleness—not arrogance—coming from his lips. "You most definitely were worth the risk he took, based solely on what you just said."

"What?" he growled. "You enjoy seeing me grovel?"

"No, I like seeing you humble. It's a positive step."

He gave her an icy stare. "Get out."

"Normally I'd be offended, but I kind of like it when you're feisty."

"Out. Now."

"Fine, but heavy bass and chocolates are waiting in your room. Not that you deserve it."

He snarled as she left, but it was music to Brie's ears. She was convinced that Faelan would be okay.

Brie dug her phone out of her purse, needing to hear Sir's voice, and was disappointed not to have any messages or texts from him. She tried to call, but it immediately clicked over to voicemail, so she was forced to leave a message.

"Please call, Sir. I *need* you."

After spending time with Lea, Autumn and Master Anderson at an old-fashioned diner across from the hospital, Brie excused herself. Food held no interest for her—all she could think of was Tono.

"I hate to cut this short, you guys, but I'm heading back to the hospital."

"Wait, Brie," Lea said. "Before you go I have a little funny you can share with Tono."

Brie knew it would be bad, but suspected Tono might appreciate it. "Hit me."

"I love *everything* about pain play except for one thing."

"What's that?"

"The pain part."

Brie snorted as she shook her head. "Is that even a joke?"

"It made you laugh." Lea grinned.

Autumn giggled. "Hey, I liked it."

Brie looked at her incredulously. "But Autumn, you like all of her jokes."

"Because they're funny!"

"Girl, I need to take you to see a real comedy act. You have no idea what funny is."

Autumn looked shyly at Brie. "I have one I think he might like."

Brie assumed it would be terrible, but urged her to share anyway. "I'm sure Tono will enjoy it. Give it to me."

"What's round and tastes like an orange?"

"Hmm…" Brie thought for a moment, but nothing came to mind. "You've got me stumped."

"An orange."

Master Anderson burst out laughing. "I like that, Miss Autumn. Simple but effective. You have my seal of approval."

Brie shook her head in disbelief. The fact that Lea and Autumn were equally unfunny was astonishing to her.

After promising Master Anderson she would return to his house soon to get some rest, Brie made her way back over to the hospital. She was happy to find that Tono had been taken to his room by then—a positive sign.

When she walked in, she noticed that most of the tubes and monitors had been removed. "You look more like yourself, Tono."

He nodded, managing a pained smile. "Don't feel like it yet."

"It really hurts, huh?"

"The drugs help, but it only takes the edge off."

"I wish I could do something to help you."

"I know what would help."

"Anything, Tono."

"Come lie with me."

She looked back at the door, worried. "Do you think it's allowed?"

"I don't care."

Tono grunted as he scooted over to make room for her. His heart monitor shot up, but quickly calmed down as he worked through the pain.

"Oh, Tono," Brie whimpered. "I can't stand seeing you in agony."

"Come, then," he insisted.

Brie lowered the railing and carefully lay down, covering them both with the extra blanket before settling down beside him.

"I feel better already, toriko."

She noticed he'd used her sub name, but at that moment it was exactly what she needed to hear. She'd almost lost him…

As she lay there with Tono, listening to the reassuring rhythm of his heartbeat, she was haunted by the image of his lifeless body lying on the operating table and the tears started to flow.

"There's no reason to cry," he gently chided.

"Today I came face to face with how fragile life is."

"It *is* fragile, which is why every moment must be savored."

Brie looked up at him. "This experience highlighted just how much you mean to me." She settled back, laying her head lightly on his chest.

He kissed the top of her head. Again the heart monitor jumped as he worked through the pain caused by the effort, but it quickly returned to its slow, steady beat.

"Have you decided where you'll be headed after you recover?" Brie ventured.

"I'm beginning to think Denver might be a good place to settle."

Brie snuck a peek at him. "Is that because a certain ice skater lives here?"

He chuckled, then groaned loudly. "Laughing hurts."

"Then I'd better save Lea and Autumn's jokes for another time."

"Feel free to share them."

"No, although they aren't funny, I would never risk hurting you." Brie grinned knowingly at him. "So you *like* Autumn, don't you?"

He smiled. "I would like to know her better."

"I bet you're unaware that she helped decorate the room. She made that for you."

He glanced at the sign that read, *Get Well Soon, Master Ren Nosaka!*

"Did she now? That was thoughtful of her." He looked over at the fruit fortress Brie had built on the windowsill. "I appreciated my fortress of protection as well."

"It seems you really needed it today." Brie settled back down again, smiling to herself. "Considering all that's happened, this has ended up being a good day."

"A very good day," he agreed, holding her closer.

"Tono?"

"Yes, toriko?"

"The world is a much better place with you in it."

When Brie returned to Master Anderson's home, she found a big bowl of soup waiting for her. "I want to warm your belly before I put you to bed, young Brie. I noticed how little you ate at the diner."

She smiled apologetically. "But I'm not hungry."

Master Anderson pulled out a chair and directed her to sit. "Still, you will eat my soup even if I have to force feed you. I can't shirk the duty Thane entrusted me with."

Brie frowned as she took out her phone to check it again. "You know, I haven't heard from him all day."

He handed her the spoon. "Take a bite and I'll tell you why."

Brie brought a spoonful of the warm soup to her lips and slurped it, purring at the soothing meld of broth and herbs swirling on her tongue.

"One more," he insisted.

She would have protested, but it tasted so good that she obliged.

"I got a call from his sister this evening. Apparently Thane's phone disappeared—most likely stolen—although the tracking on it shows that it's still in the hotel. The theft wasn't discovered until late in the afternoon, after they returned from visiting his mother. He's torn apart his room looking for it. From the little his sister shared, it sounds as if things are going badly over there."

Brie's heart dropped at the knowledge Sir might have experienced a day as difficult as hers. She hadn't considered it, and felt terrible now for being short-sighted. "How is Sir?"

"I don't know. The connection kept cutting out, so we had to keep the phone call short. Thane has no idea what happened with Nosaka today, which may be for the best—considering."

Brie's concern showed on her face.

"Another bite," he insisted.

She swallowed another spoonful, pondering what he'd said. "I wonder why Sir didn't call me using her phone?"

"I was told he tried several times but the calls failed to go through."

It relieved Brie to know that Sir had made an attempt. She looked down at her soup, the day's events weighing heavily on her. "I don't know how I would have survived today without your strength, Master Anderson."

"I'm grateful to have been of service, but I also owed you one. It's fortunate Tono Nosaka survived the operation. Not only because he is a good man, but because losing him would have devastated many people in my circle. Hell, I don't know if the Wolf Pup could have survived the guilt."

"You're not kidding. He's taking it hard enough as it is."

"I hope he doesn't waste Nosaka's sacrifice."

"I'll do everything in my power to make sure that doesn't happen, Master Anderson."

He took the utensil from her and fed her himself. "This must come from him. You are not responsible for what happens."

She nodded, taking the next spoonful he offered her.

"After I finish with you here, I want you to take a warm shower and go straight to bed. That's an order."

She smiled. "Thank you, Master Anderson. For everything."

"You have been strong, but I have a feeling you will be tested even further by Thane's situation. Don't lose heart, and if all else fails, eat a good soup. It will see you through."

He wiped her mouth with a napkin once the whole bowl had been finished, then dismissed her. Brie did as he commanded, and was surprised when he came to tuck her in.

"Straight to sleep," he ordered as he covered her with blankets.

Brie called out as he was leaving, "Sweet dreams, Master Anderson."

"Same to you, young Brie." He gave her a wink before turning off the light.

Once the door was shut, she turned on her phone for added light and pulled out her journal so she could write. She told Sir everything that had happened that day from the moment she woke up to now, sharing her hopes and fears to the smallest details, like Lea and Autumn's awful jokes. She wanted him to feel he had been there with her the entire day, and desperately hoped he would do the same for her.

Afterwards, she grabbed Sir's shirt and pressed it against her cheek. Brie was fearful of what was coming, but she fell asleep determined to meet it with courage.

Brie Lives Her Fairy Tale

Positive Force

B rie woke up to the subtle sound of her phone vibrating. She checked
it and saw that Sir had texted her from Lilly's phone. She dialed the
number immediately.

"Sir, I'm so glad to reach you!"

"Shouldn't you be asleep?" he asked. She was instantly alarmed because the tone of his voice sounded distant, cold.

"I was asleep, Sir, but I've been waiting for your call and woke when
you messaged me."

"I didn't mean to wake you," Sir said irritably, as if he regretted texting
her.

"But I'm *glad* you did. I needed to hear your voice."

He paused for a moment before replying, "Last night was rough. I'm
still recovering from it."

"What happened?"

He chuckled angrily. "I don't know what kind of local concoction I
drank, but I'm suffering from an intense headache today, and my memory
of the evening has been compromised."

Brie was deeply concerned. Sir wasn't the kind of man to drown his
sorrows with liquor. "Were you with Lilly last night?"

"She insisted we get out of the hotel and celebrate."

"Celebrate what?" Brie was surprised having assumed things were not
going well.

"Lilly saw my mother open her eyes briefly." He let out a low groan.
"It's the last thing I need, Brie—the possibility that the Beast might
recover."

She couldn't help questioning Lilly's claim. "Do you think it's possible
she might have imagined it? We both know how close she was with your

mother."

"I have considered it, trust me. However, the only way to be sure is to have another scan for brain activity. I can't cut life support until that question has been resolved. Based on Lilly's excitement yesterday, I'm afraid she'll be crushed when the results of the scan come in—and I can't even consider the alternative."

"It's so sad, Sir. Either way, one of you is going to suffer."

"Yes."

When Sir didn't say anything more and didn't ask about the surgeries, Brie decided to share what had happened to Tono. Her voice caught when she said, "We…almost lost Tono."

"What do you mean you almost lost him?"

"His heart stopped on the operating table." Tears rolled down her cheeks as she thought back on that moment. "They were able to revive him, but—"

"But what?"

"I saw it. I saw Tono's lifeless body, Sir." She broke down sobbing, unable to say more.

"I trust Brad was with you."

She swallowed hard several times before she could quiet her sobs. "He was, Sir, and he was wonderful support. However, he isn't you."

Sir didn't reply. As the silence stretched, Brie feared the phone connection had been lost.

"Sir?"

"I'm sorry I wasn't there for you."

She suddenly regretted saying anything because of the pain she heard in his voice. "I'm fine, Sir. I don't know what I would have done if Tono had died, but he didn't."

"How is Nosaka now?"

"When I left him last night he was in pain, but in good spirits."

"And Wallace?"

"The fact that Tono's heart stopped has really messed him up."

"I'm not surprised. Wallace has lived with the guilt of that young man's death for most of his life. I can only imagine what effect Nosaka's own brush with death has had on him."

"It's bad, Sir. He looked so despondent after the surgery. I don't think he'll ever forgive himself."

"If anyone can center Wallace, Nosaka is the man to do it." Sir abruptly changed subjects. "Have you had time to work on the film?"

"I've filmed Tono's scene. I hope to shoot Baron in the next day or two, but he says he needs permission from you."

"Why would he require permission?"

"Baron wants to reenact the scene he and I did together the second day of training. He says it will involve the swing and clitoral stimulation with a toy, but no penetration."

Another long pause followed before he answered. "I trust Baron, but question whether you would you be able to use the footage in the film."

"I believe so. I will be wearing clothing to cover the important parts, and if it's shot properly, the action can be alluded to instead of shown."

"Call Holloway to confirm it. If he gives you the green light, Baron has my permission to proceed with the scene."

"Thank you, Sir." Brie paused before asking, "I would also like permission to speak with Ms. Clark privately."

"In regards to what?" he asked, sounding slightly annoyed.

"She wouldn't say because Baron was present at the time."

"You already know how I feel about Samantha, but if you'd rather not speak to her, you can tell her I would not allow it."

"To be honest, Sir, I'm curious to find out why she wants to talk, but I can't help thinking about Rytsar's concern."

"I highly doubt Samantha means you harm."

Again, she noted the irritation in his voice and wondered at the cause. "You're right, Sir. Thank you."

"Let me know how the conversation goes. Is there anything else?"

He was trying to end the phone call, but she wasn't ready to let him go, so she asked, "Do you mind if I read you my journal entry from yesterday?"

Her request was met with silence, but to her relief he finally said, "Please do."

Brie read her emotional entry, choking on her tears several times as she read it to him. She waited to hear his response, hoping he would comfort her. Instead, she heard detachment in his voice when he confessed, "I was unable to write anything last night. I don't even remember how Lilly and I made it back to the hotel."

Goosebumps rose on her skin knowing Sir wasn't engaged with her. She was certain something was fundamentally wrong with him. "Please talk to me, Sir."

But he did not allow any further conversation, stating, "There's nothing to talk about. Start your day, Brie."

"I want to fly out to you."

"I left you with a duty to perform. Give Nosaka my regards," he ordered before hanging up.

She headed to the shower, needing to eliminate the cold chill that had settled over her. Afterwards she sought out Master Anderson, seeking his wisdom as a long-time friend of Sir.

Even though it was still early, Brie knocked lightly on his bedroom door. She heard nothing and was about to return to her room when the door opened. Master Anderson stood before her in nothing but his pajama bottoms.

When he saw the look on her face, he insisted that she come in, sitting her on his bed. "What's going on?"

Brie looked around, suddenly distracted, never having been in his bedroom before. Unlike Sir's bedroom back home, there was nothing here that hinted at the BDSM lifestyle. She noticed family photos on the dresser but was too far away to see the faces of his kin. There was a feeling of intimacy being in his bedroom, as if another layer of the man was being peeled away.

"What's this about?" he asked as he sat down beside her. "I assume you must have spoken to Thane."

She nodded sadly. "You mentioned that Sir and I might be tested, and based on my conversation this morning, I'm afraid you're right. Something's wrong with Sir."

"Tell me what happened."

"I guess Lilly claimed that his mother opened her eyes, and she's convinced the Beast is recovering. Naturally the idea of that has Sir in a tailspin."

"I can only imagine..." Master Anderson muttered.

"But even more disturbing is the fact that Sir went out drinking with his sister last night and totally blacked out. That doesn't sound like Sir at all."

Master Anderson's eyes narrowed. "I'll see if I can't talk to him myself. It could be that he doesn't want to burden you with his problems after what happened to Tono."

"I'd be grateful to hear if he shares anything more with you, Master Anderson."

He growled under his breath. "Something is definitely wrong."

"I know." Brie's bottom lip trembled as she fought back her tears.

Master Anderson held out his arms to her and she settled into them, soaking up his strength and comfort. He squeezed her tight, chuckling softly. "You are a tiny thing to carry so much weight on your shoulders. Would you like me to make you some more soup?"

She shook her head, a giggle escaping at the suggestion, even though she was upset. "I can handle whatever comes our way as long as I know *what* it is that I'm facing."

Lifting her bodily from the bed, Master Anderson put her down facing the door. "Get yourself ready to head to the hospital. I'll speak to Thane today and let you know what I learn."

Brie left his room feeling more confident with Master Anderson on the case. She felt certain he could get Sir to confess what was really going on.

"Good morning, Tono."

He looked up from his arm, where the nurse was drawing blood, and smiled at Brie. "Every new morning is a good morning."

She nodded in agreement. "How are you feeling today?"

"Actually worse than yesterday."

Brie frowned. "I'm sorry to hear that."

Tono shrugged with a grimace. "It's to be expected."

"Well, if that's the case, I hate to think how Todd is doing today."

"I'm going to walk to his room so I can see for myself."

"But you just had surgery!" she protested, not willing to have him sacrifice his health further.

Flora, the nurse, explained as she finished taking the last vial of blood, "Miss Bennett, it would be best if Mr. Nosaka starts walking today. It aids significantly in recovery."

Brie frowned at Tono, still concerned. "But you're already in so much pain…"

"And yet I must walk."

Brie sighed in frustration, lamenting, "I wish I could take some of the pain—that I could help somehow."

"You can. Once Miss Flora is done, take me for a stroll. Based on how I feel today, I have a suspicion that Mr. Wallace is in serious need of company."

Flora glanced up with a look of concern on her face at the mention of Faelan, but quickly looked back down, continuing her work.

Tono told Brie, "And that's all the motivation I need to get on my feet."

Brie watched helplessly as Flora helped Tono to stand. Although he grimaced in pain several times, the Asian Dom never made a sound, but she noticed his white-knuckled grip on the IV pole.

Tono took a couple of deep breaths before asking, "Would you help me, Brie?"

She hurried over, offering her arm as support, but cringed when she heard his sharp intake of breath as he took his first step. Tono wobbled momentarily from the pain, but straightened his back and willfully took another.

"Excellent!" Flora praised from behind him. "With that kind of determination, you'll be walking out the hospital doors in no time."

He gave her a slight nod. "I'm certain that under your exceptional care, my recovery will be doubly quick."

Tono took it slowly, halting several times to rest and regain his composure, but not giving up until he was standing in front of Faelan's hospital room. It was no surprise to Brie that Todd's parents were standing outside it, looking bereft.

Mrs. Wallace looked at Tono in shock. "How? How are you walking so soon after surgery?"

"It's a requirement if I am to heal."

She shook her head, tears falling down her wrinkled cheeks. "My boy is in no shape to walk. He seems even worse today than yesterday."

"That is why Mr. Nosaka came to speak to him," Brie said, putting her hand on her frail shoulder, instinctively wanting to comfort the woman. "He knows the pain your son is suffering and can help him to fight through it."

Brie hadn't been prepared to see Faelan in the same condition he'd been in on her first visit. His eyes were closed and he was breathing in short, shallow gasps.

"Mr. Wallace," Tono called.

When he got no response, Brie begged, "Faelan, please open your eyes."

His eyelids fluttered open, but when he saw who was standing before him, he closed them again, growling as he scratched weakly at his arm. "The itching won't stop."

"I'm sure you've been told that once the kidney starts functioning fully, the itching should cease."

Faelan opened his tortured blue eyes and stared at Brie. "It's driving me crazy, Brie. I can't make it stop."

"There is a solution," Tono informed him.

Faelan's gaze rested back on Tono, his tone desperate. "What?"

"Get out of the bed and start moving."

Faelan's nose crinkled into a sneer. "Are you out of your fucking mind, Nosaka? I can barely move, much less walk." He scratched angrily at his chest, snarling more loudly.

"Trust me, the pain of moving should take your mind off the itching. It will also speed the healing process."

Faelan huffed in resentment. "You may have donated your kidney, but you have no idea how much I'm suffering right now."

Tono sat down slowly, sucking in his breath as he did so. Once he'd settled into the chair, he looked at Faelan and smiled. "I agree. I do not know the level of your suffering."

Faelan stared at him, the anger in his eyes slowly transforming into guilt. "You almost died."

Tono nodded. "I stopped breathing, it's true. However, I was fully present. I saw the doctors working to revive my body and I felt the presence of Brie with me. It was a remarkable experience."

Brie turned to him, stunned to hear he'd had an out-of-body experience. And yet…it gave her considerable comfort too. Even in death, they'd been connected.

"Why do you do that?" Faelan complained. "Why do you put a positive spin on everything?"

Tono raised an eyebrow. "It's how I have chosen to lead my life. How have you chosen to lead yours?"

Faelan looked away, unable to meet Tono's candid stare.

"You've been given a rare opportunity, Mr. Wallace. A second chance ripe with possibilities. What you decide to do with it is totally up to you. You are in control."

"You make it sound so easy, Nosaka, but you have no idea how hard I've had it."

"And you have no idea about me," Tono stated firmly. "Still, you can choose to be a positive force in the world or a negative one. I see no point in wasting my life being negative."

Faelan looked at Brie and said in an accusatory tone, "I suppose you subscribe to the same philosophy?"

"It comes naturally to me."

He rolled his eyes. "Well, it doesn't for this man."

Tono struggled to stand, accepting Brie's help when she offered it. Once he was on his feet, he straightened his back with great effort. "It's as easy as that. I choose to stand, even though it hurts. I accept the assistance of others because it eases the journey."

He held out his hand to Faelan. "Stand with me, Mr. Wallace."

"There's no way I can walk," he retorted.

"I'm only asking you to stand. Each obstacle you overcome will make you stronger."

Inspired, Faelan attempted to swing his legs over the edge of the bed after Brie lowered the side rail. He grunted in pain and frustration after several attempts, then lay still. When Brie tried to help, he slapped her hands away irritably.

"Get away, I can do this." After resting for several minutes he tried again, but the pain proved too much. "I can't," he finally cried, laying his head back in defeat.

"Why didn't you take Brie's hand?" Tono asked.

"I'm a man, damn it, not a mouse."

"You look like a mouse to me."

Faelan's nostrils flared in anger. He gritted his teeth as he lifted himself again, letting Brie help him to swing his legs over the edge of the bed. He reluctantly took the hand she offered as he pushed himself off. The jolt when his feet made contact with the ground caused him to grunt in pain, but he slowly straightened his back and glared at Tono, eye to eye.

The Asian Dom bowed his head in acknowledgement. "A good effort. The next few weeks will forge your character in ways you cannot foresee, and will solidify why you were spared those many years ago."

Tono had purposely exposed Faelan's greatest fear—the burden of surviving, which he had carried all his adult life. The look of vulnerability on Faelan's face when he stared at Tono nearly did Brie in.

"You believe that, Nosaka?"

"I *know* it for a fact. You were meant for great things, Todd Wallace, and this was the path you were destined to take in order to prepare for it."

When Brie saw Faelan wobble slightly on his feet, she took his arm and helped him back onto the bed. He continued to stare at Tono, as if he were afraid to believe him.

"You can endure pain, and you can do the same with disappointment, because both will hone your spirit. In some ways they are our greatest allies, even though we resent their company."

"Is that what life is to you, Nosaka? A constant struggle?" Faelan asked, shaking his head. "What's the point of going on if we're only meant to suffer?"

"I don't feel that way at all. I'm simply sharing my philosophy on living a satisfying life. I invite the lessons of pain and disappointment so that I will not dwell on them. Without resentment, I am free to enjoy the many facets this life has to offer." He looked at Brie. "Including deep and abiding friendships."

Brie looked at Tono, overcome by a feeling of love and gratitude. Faelan noted the expression on her face.

"Are you truly happy, blossom?"

She met his gaze and smiled. "Yes, I am."

Faelan tilted his head slightly as he studied her. "That must be why I found you attractive when we met. I never understood my obsession with you until now."

She gave him a questioning look. "I'm not quite sure how to take that."

"You are a positive force in the world."

She blushed under the intensity of his magnetic blue eyes and murmured, "Thank you."

Faelan growled unexpectedly as he started scratching again. "God, I hate this constant itching. It's going to be the death of me."

"Think of it as purposeful torture." Tono suggested. "You are being tested to prove which is more powerful—the discomfort, or your will."

Faelan breathed in deeply, forcing himself to stop scratching. After a few seconds he snarled, his body twitching in discomfort. "It'll require everything I have to fight against it."

Brie encouraged him, "Then let it take over. *Don't* fight it. I know it goes against your nature, but by submitting to the sensation—mentally allowing it—you'll tap in to a different kind of strength... At least, that has been my experience as a submissive."

"Sage advice," Tono agreed.

"I suppose if that fails," Faelan snorted angrily, "I'll try standing again, 'cause that hurts like a motherfucker."

Tono chuckled, then groaned in pain. "On that note, I will return to my own bed, but I don't plan on remaining there long." Tono grasped his IV pole and started towards the door.

Faelan called out, "Nosaka."

Tono turned slowly to face him.

"I appreciate it." Although he was obviously uncomfortable expressing himself, Faelan continued, "The kidney, the risk you took... This second chance—I won't let you down."

"I know your character, Mr. Wallace, and never questioned your success."

Faelan surprised Brie by putting his hands together and bowing his head to Tono.

Tono let go of the pole and returned the bow, a look of mutual respect on his face.

Brie felt lighter in spirit as she followed Tono out of the room, sincerely impressed by both men. Tono had the ability to strike at the heart of a problem, but in a way that empowered the individual, while Faelan remained young and stubborn, but showed an inner strength few possessed—now it was laced with a newfound humility that would carry him even farther.

She walked alongside the Kinbaku Master as he made the arduous trek back to his room. Brie stared at him in wonder as they walked, blurting, "You saved a life—literally. There aren't many people who can make that claim, Tono."

"To have that kind of opportunity is rare," he agreed, smiling even though he was panting with effort from the walk.

"Todd is lucky to have you in his life," she said, wrapping her arm around him in support, "but not half as lucky as me."

Baron's Sultry Session

B rie was surprised to come across Ms. Clark just outside the hospital when she was leaving. "What are you doing here?"

"I came to pay my respects. Why so shocked, Miss Bennett?"

"I suppose I'm not used to seeing you outside the school setting, Ms. Clark," Brie muttered, feeling completely unprepared for a confrontation with her.

The Domme put her fingertips together, highlighting her long, blood-red nails. "I wanted to inform you that I will be present when you film with Baron."

"That's not necessary," Brie assured her, feeling her hackles rise at the suggestion.

"Nonsense. You need someone to film the tight shots, don't you? I'm the best option you've got if you want it to pass Mr. Holloway's exacting standards."

"You have experience shooting film?" Brie asked her in disbelief.

Ms. Clark's eyes twinkled with unsettling merriment. "There's so little you know about me, Miss Bennett. If you would prefer someone else, I'll respect your wishes. However, I guarantee you'll compromise the shoot if you do." Ms. Clark gave her a nod and walked into the hospital without allowing Brie a chance to respond.

Unfortunately, Ms. Clark's assertion proved to be right. Brie was unable to find anyone comfortable enough with the camera to take over the shoot for her. She lamented the fact to Master Anderson that night.

"You should be grateful. It's rare for Samantha to offer help of that nature."

"Well, it doesn't feel like an honor to me. It feels like she's spying on me because Sir's not around. Speaking of Sir, were you able to reach him today?"

Master Anderson shook his head. "I left several messages on Lilly's phone and eventually ended up calling the hotel. Although I speak very little Chinese, I established that he was out for the day, as was Lilly."

Brie frowned.

"Until we hear differently, let's assume that whatever is happening has his full attention. I'm sure he'll call later when he has the time and inclination."

Brie grudgingly took his advice, but found it difficult to concentrate as she drove to the Denver Academy. She arrived an hour early, not thrilled about having to scene with Baron in front of her former trainer. She was certain the Domme would be looking for flaws to point out to her later.

She had convinced herself that Ms. Clark didn't care for the idea of her being alone with Baron, even though Sir had given his permission. The thought of that provoked Brie to no end, but there was little she could do. Mr. Holloway had made it clear in her last meeting that she needed different angles and plenty of close-ups capturing facial expressions in each scene. Brie was afraid the lack of those elements had been the reason Holloway nixed Marquis' compelling performance. With so little time left, she couldn't afford to make the same mistake twice.

She placed Tono's flower in her hair and calmly waited for the Domme. When she heard the clicking of heels out in the hallway, Brie lifted her chin. She greeted Ms. Clark with a smile when the formidable woman entered the theater.

"Miss Bennett, it's fortunate we finally have a chance to speak alone."

"I'm sure you won't mind if I set up while we talk," Brie answered, wanting to establish that the film was her primary focus.

"We're both professionals here," Ms. Clark replied coolly, but Brie didn't miss the hint of annoyance lurking behind her tone.

It might have thrown Brie off in her earlier days, but she took a deep breath and set to work placing her reflectors. "What do you want to talk about, Ms. Clark?"

Her answer took Brie completely by surprise. "I want to speak to you about Lea."

Brie stopped what she was doing and stared at the Domme.

Is Ms. Clark about to confess her love?

"What about Lea?"

"I'm sure she's mentioned her feelings for me."

Brie nodded.

"Although I'm fond of the girl, it's recently become an issue."

Brie suddenly felt ill. "What do you mean, an *issue?*"

"As you're aware, Master Anderson is going to head the school in LA and Baron plans to join him, but I've gotten the impression that Lea plans to stay for my sake."

Feeling the need to protect Lea, Brie kept her answer vague. "She hasn't decided yet. I know she likes Denver, and her friend Autumn lives here."

Ms. Clark narrowed her eyes. "Miss Bennett, don't be coy with me. Lea has declared her love on several occasions."

Brie stared at her numbly, feeling certain her best friend was about to get her heart broken by the Domme.

"As I said, I...care about Lea," Ms. Clark stated, a red hue coloring her cheeks. Maybe Brie had misread the situation. "Because of that, I need you to do me a favor."

"Go on."

"Since you are such good friends with Lea, I was hoping you could convince her to return to LA when Master Anderson leaves."

Brie's jaw dropped. "But you just said—"

"Lea is an extraordinary person, but she's still young. I want to see her take full advantage of her potential while she remains free and unattached." There was a hint of regret in her voice when she added, "I've wasted too many years chasing ghosts. Lea should not suffer for it."

"So you love Lea?" Brie asked hesitantly.

The Domme shot Brie a look that let her know she had overstepped her bounds by asking. However, Ms. Clark surprised her by responding to her question a few moments later. "It's the reason I'm letting her go. She wouldn't leave if she knew my true feelings—you and I both know that."

For the first time, Brie felt empathy for the woman.

"You need to make a strong case for Lea to return to LA. It's best if she feels she made the decision to leave. It'll comfort her if she has moments of doubt later on."

"What about you?" Brie asked, realizing this would be the second time Ms. Clark had lost out on love.

"I'll be taking charge of the Dominant Training at the Academy. I need to focus on my skills rather than relationships."

The Domme's candidness left Brie mute. She returned to setting up her equipment. "I'll do what I can, but you know Lea has a mind of her own. She's held out hope you would collar her."

Ms. Clark surprised Brie by coming up behind her, so close that she could feel the woman's warm breath on her neck. "I'm depending on you to release her from that dream, Miss Bennett."

Brie didn't move, her heart suddenly racing. She turned to face the Domme and found herself staring at Ms. Clark's sensuous red lips.

"I'll…do my best." It was unsettling having those bright-red lips so close to hers. Why on Earth did she have the urge to kiss them? Brie shook her head and scooted away. This wasn't the first time she'd felt an uncharacteristic stirring for her former trainer.

What was it about the woman that inspired such an instinctual—albeit unwanted—attraction? She found herself blushing and turned away, hoping Ms. Clark hadn't noticed.

"Succeed, Miss Bennett, or I will be forced to hurt her, and I don't want it to end like that between us."

Brie could better understand her friend's obsession with the Mistress now that she knew Lea's affections were returned, but she wondered if it was possible to break her of such a powerful attraction—especially if there was any chance Lea suspected Ms. Clark's true feelings.

It seemed like an impossible task, but for Lea's sake, she would try.

Baron entered the theater, a playful smile on his lips as he asked in his deep, baritone voice, "Are you ready for me, kitten?"

Brie felt familiar chills as memories of their first encounter together flooded her mind. "Baron!"

Ms. Clark picked up the camera, pretending to look over the equipment as she composed herself. Brie caught the Domme staring at her intensely on several occasions as Brie talked to the Dom. She wondered if Ms. Clark regretted being so open with her. She'd certainly exposed a side of herself Brie had never seen before.

While Baron waited, Brie changed into simple black lingerie that showed skin but did not bare any intimate parts. She covered up in a silk robe before double-checking her equipment. Brie was definitely curious how he was going to play out the scene this time around.

Back when she'd first known Baron, he had frightened Brie because he reminded her of the violence she'd experienced as a child in grade school. Yet he had been so gentle that night, he'd been able to make a difficult lesson one she still looked back on with fondness.

Before they began, Baron explained, "I want you to think back on how you felt the second night we scened together. Let *those* feelings play out as we scene today. I'm striving to evoke the same emotions a new sub experiences when punished for the first time under the caring hands of a Master."

"I've never forgotten that lesson, Baron," Brie admitted. "It spurs me daily not to disappoint Sir."

Ms. Clark focused the camera on Brie and replied snidely, "And yet you still do, Miss Bennett. Maybe a second lesson *is* necessary."

Baron shook his head at the Domme. "Don't insult my kitten, even in jest."

Brie loved Baron for his protective nature!

After going over the details of the scene with Ms. Clark, Brie slipped off her robe, shedding her director's persona as she bowed at Baron's feet.

He rifled through his tool bag, retrieving an item before ordering her to stand before him. Brie let out an audible gasp when she looked up, caught off guard by the dark leather hood he was wearing.

Of course… Baron had worn a similar mask for that second session, and just like that night, it made the dark Dom seem dangerous and foreboding. She instinctively lowered her eyes.

"Look at me," Baron commanded.

Brie gazed up into his hazel eyes and was reminded again of their calming effect.

He handed her a tiny vial. "Rub five drops of this on your clit before you join me." He left her to her task as he made his way onto the stage and waited.

Brie dutifully poured a few drops from the vial onto her fingertips and slipped them under her panties, covering her clit with the oily liquid. She did it a second time to apply all five drops her Dom had commanded.

She already knew the effect it would have, and was not surprised when heat started building between her legs. There was no doubt that Baron wanted to make this simple lesson a challenge for her.

She wiped her hands on a towel before joining him on the stage. As she approached the masked Dom, she felt familiar fears from her past take hold, and she willingly embraced them.

She needed to be scared.

Thinking back to that second day of training, she'd had no real connections with Sir, Marquis or even Tono at that point—there had only been the dark Dom, the stage and her own desire to explore her submissive nature.

She ascended the stairs with that in mind, meeting Baron as an inexperienced sub unsure of herself on her second day at the Center. When she reached him, Baron gave the order, "Turn and face the camera, kitten."

Brie turned away from him, looking at the camera with an expression she hoped conveyed both anticipation and fear. In truth, her heart was beating rapidly, just as it had that night.

Ms. Clark held up her fingers and counted down before hitting the record button. Baron took the cue and wrapped one arm around Brie's torso, highlighting the contrast of their skin tones. He placed his other hand over her heart and chuckled. "It's beating fast..."

Brie nodded.

"Have you ever tried a sex swing before?"

"No, Baron," she answered, as she had during her initial session with him.

"Good," he replied in a deep, soothing tone. "I enjoy introducing subs to new devices."

From above, the equipment began its descent. Brie watched, her eyes growing wider when the swing stopped descending level with her.

She laughed nervously when Baron swept her off her feet. He looked down at her with that black leather mask covering half his face. Although she had long since come to trust him, Brie purposely tapped into dark memories of her childhood—Darius, the boy who had tortured her daily—and the fear became very real for her.

Darius had tainted her innocence and stolen a part of herself she would never get back...

"Trust me, kitten."

Brie was grateful for Baron's reminder. "I trust you," she said aloud for the camera.

She relaxed in his arms as he placed her in the swing, helping her to put her feet in the stirrups. The swing comfortably supported her body as she lay suspended above the stage. Brie had forgotten how freeing a swing could be, and that it had a slight Kinbaku feel to it.

Since pleasuring him orally was not part of the scene this time, Baron had planned a different challenge for her. He leaned down and took Brie's face in his hands. "Kiss me."

When she lifted her head to kiss him, he pulled the swing closer so that her lips were only centimeters from his. The heat between her legs heightened her desire, and she ached for the simple contact—but Baron was in control.

Just before their lips met, he pushed her away. Brie giggled in surprise as she slowly swung away from him.

"I said kiss me," he teased in a low, chocolatey voice that sent shivers down her spine.

Brie tilted her head back this time and he let their lips brush for the briefest of moments before pushing her away again. It was a playful game of cat and mouse.

Baron drove her wild with their *almost* kisses as her pussy continued to burn with building desire. The anticipation he created using simple denial was deliciously effective, and had her whole body trembling with need.

"Do you feel the heat?" he growled seductively, staring at her mound.

Brie moaned softly in response.

He moved away from the swing, stating, "Now it's time I test your level of obedience, kitten."

She lay there, swaying gently, knowing he was intent on making her fail his new test. Although she'd come quickly on the first night, Brie was an experienced sub now. For the film's sake, she would eventually give in, but this time she was determined it would be on her *own* terms.

Baron returned with a confident smirk on his kissable lips. She saw that he held a portable version of what looked like a Magic Wand. He stood between her open legs and turned it on. "I plan to torture you with pleasure."

Brie took a deep breath, realizing he wasn't going to let her pretend for the camera. This was meant to be a worthy challenge for an experienced sub. She knew she was at a disadvantage because of the addictively helpless feeling the sex swing evoked. Brie was unable to resist when he placed the vibrator on her lace-covered mound and began moving it slowly up and down the length of her pussy.

Already hot and swollen from the generous amount of oil she'd applied, Brie threw her head back, more determined than ever to fight off the sensual vibration—but to no avail. In less than a minute, she cried out as her first climax hit.

Baron chuckled. "I'll let you have the first one for free. Now you have to wait for permission to orgasm."

Brie was mortified by her utter lack of control and smiled sheepishly up at him. "Yes, Baron."

The experienced Dom had correctly gauged her overconfidence and what was needed to strip it away. With renewed determination, Brie braced herself as he pressed the vibrator against her sensitive clit.

"Look at me, kitten."

Brie lifted her head to gaze at Baron. Those gentle hazel eyes behind the leather mask drew her in with their lust. She was caught like a rabbit in the hypnotic gaze of a predator, unable to resist what was about to happen. Baron licked his lips as he skillfully employed the vibrator, making her thighs shake as she tried to ward off the next orgasm.

She groaned, struggling to resist the pull of those magnetic eyes as he turned the vibration up. Then he changed the angle of the wand and all was lost. Baron's smile spread—he knew she was close.

"Nooooooooooo!" Brie panted as her body orgasmed again.

Baron tsked as he turned off the vibrator. "Now you must be punished for failing to obey a direct command."

He left her swaying in the swing, alone on the stage, waiting for punishment. It was embarrassing that she hadn't lasted any longer than the first time, but she couldn't help admiring Baron's skill at playing her so well.

Baron walked back onstage holding a large flogger in his hand. Although she normally loved the touch of the instrument, when used for punishment it took on a whole different feel.

"I'm sorry, Baron."

"What did you do wrong, kitten?"

"I came without your permission."

"As a responsible Dom, it is my duty and privilege to punish you for your disobedience. Lean back and lift your legs higher."

She longed to close her eyes and take her punishment silently, but she knew Baron would not allow it. Instead, she kept her eyes on him and reluctantly lifted her legs to give him free access to her ass.

Originally, Baron had only lashed her once with the flogger, but this time he gave her five solid strokes. She whimpered, but took his punishment willingly. When he left the stage again, she recalled the ache she'd felt the first time, knowing she had disappointed Baron. She connected with those feelings now, letting the tears fall.

When she finally heard his footsteps on the stairs again, Brie wiped her eyes.

"Are you ready to obey me?"

"I *want* to obey you, Baron."

"Then focus on me."

Baron had the small wand clutched in one hand and rope in the other. He placed the vibrator against her clit and tied it securely, using creative rope work so that it remained snug against her pussy giving her no chance of escaping it.

He smiled at her as he turned it on. "A challenge worthy of a good sub."

Brie jumped in the swing and then giggled when she felt the vibration, unsure how long she could outlast the constant stimulation.

The dark Dom moved up to her head and commanded with a smirk, "Kiss me."

This time he did not push her away when she lifted her head and their lips met. Brie was grateful for the connection, but soon understood the danger of it when his tongue entered her mouth. Her pussy began pulsing again, needing release.

Brie moaned, but was determined not to fail this new challenge. Baron was ruthless as he plundered her mouth while the vibrator he'd secured teased her relentlessly. Even though she squirmed and moaned in desperate need of climax, she refused to come.

Eventually, Baron took pity on her and ordered her to orgasm.

Brie closed her eyes, letting the vibration consume all her senses. Her body twitched in the swing, releasing her sexual tension in rhythmic waves as they kissed.

She opened her eyes afterwards and purred, "Thank you, Baron."

"My pleasure, kitten."

Come to Me

B rie felt really good about the shoot with Baron. She'd gone over the footage that very night and was extremely pleased by the shots Ms. Clark had been able to capture. The raw connection and struggle that had defined her original session with Baron had translated well in the new scene, yet the creative camera shots kept it tasteful and artistic.

Brie was in the middle of editing it when she heard her cell phone ring. She'd left a message for Lea earlier and knew the conversation was going to be a tricky one, so she let it go to voicemail, promising herself she'd call her friend back as soon as she was finished. She was determined that Lea was *not* going to end up with a broken heart.

Once the rough edit was complete, Brie gave herself a mental pep-talk before retrieving her phone from her purse. She wanted to scream when she saw that the missed call had actually been from Sir. His calls normally had a particular ringtone that she responded to immediately, but he'd had to call her from Lilly's cell.

Brie hit play and put the phone to her ear. She closed her eyes when she heard Sir's voice, ragged with emotion as if he'd been grieving.

He only said three words. "Come to me…"

She burst into tears and tried to call him back. Although she dialed the number multiple times, he never answered. Brie shivered, overcome with cold reality.

Sir needs me.

She left her bedroom, desperate for company, but Master Anderson was at the Academy heading the submissive training for the evening. She went out into his backyard and sat down in the exact spot Tono had taken on the morning of his surgery. Brie looked out over the Denver skyline, taking a deep breath to quell the rising fear inside her as the same thought kept echoing in her head: *Sir needs me…*

Brie knew Tono would be able to handle if she left, but she was deeply concerned about Faelan. Would he give up if she suddenly disappeared?

Closing her eyes, she slowed her breathing down even further. There was a solution. She just had to discover it. When it finally came to her, she felt a prickly sensation course through her body.

It was perfect—for everyone.

Brie pushed herself off the ground and hurried back to her room. She contacted Mr. Gallant, although the hour was late—too nervous to approach Captain with her idea until she'd run it by her former teacher. Although Mr. Gallant was agreeable to her plan, he was unsure if Captain would feel the same and suggested she call him straight away.

Brie dutifully called Captain next. She worried that he was already asleep when he didn't answer, but she hung up and tried again, knowing time was of the essence. Her second attempt met with success, although he sounded annoyed. "Explain yourself."

"Captain, I'm sorry to wake you but I need to ask your advice and a favor, if you're agreeable."

He listened patiently as she explained the situation with Faelan and her need for a substitute. "I've talked to Mr. Gallant, but he said only you would know if she's ready."

Captain took a long time to answer. "I would never have considered such an idea, but I understand the reason for your request. Before I say anything further, I need to talk to Miss Wilson."

"Of course," Brie agreed. "Due to the urgency of the situation, I'm going to go ahead and purchase her tickets, whether she uses them or not. Please stress to Mary that her wellbeing comes first."

"Rest assured, Miss Bennett, my loyalties lie with Miss Wilson. I will only agree to what's in her best interests."

"Good," Brie said, grateful for his frankness. "If Mary *does* agree to come, send me a text tomorrow and I will meet her at the airport."

"Either way, I will call you, Miss Bennett."

"Thank you, Captain." An overwhelming sense of gratitude for the kind man caused Brie to choke up. "No matter what you decide, I will never forget your willingness to help."

"Think nothing of it. Finish what you must do, and get some rest. You won't be any good to your Master if you are dead on your feet."

"Thank you. I'll do my best to sleep," she assured him, although she knew she was too wound up to rest.

Brie booked the flight for Mary and then called Autumn. To her relief, her friend was still up and answered quickly. "I'm actually surprised you're still awake, girl."

"I was watching anime on my computer," Autumn confessed. "It's kind of an obsession of mine."

"I love anime too, so your secret's safe with me. However, I do have a favor to ask."

"Sure, Brie. Ask away."

"I have to leave for China as soon as possible, but Tono still has weeks of recovery ahead. He'll be staying at Master Anderson's once he's released from the hospital, but he still needs someone to take him to doctor appointments and look after him. I'd ask Lea, but she's in the middle of training, with no one to take her place. I know it's a lot to ask, Autumn, but is there any way you could help out?"

Without hesitation, she answered, "I'd be happy to. In fact, if Tono wants to, he can stay at my place. I have a guest room that's just gathering dust, and I'm sure my boss would have no problem with me working from home for the next few weeks."

Brie let out an inner sigh of relief. "I can't tell you how happy you just made me!"

"Actually, it's you who's doing me a favor," Autumn asserted. "I don't know if I would have gotten up the nerve to talk to him, and now I have the perfect excuse to talk to him twenty-four seven."

"That's music to my ears."

"So I'll talk to my boss in the morning and stop by the hospital tomorrow to see how Ren Nosaka wants to handle it."

"Awesome. You've just taken a huge weight off my shoulders."

"No problem, Brie. Hey, if you need anything else, give me a call. I mean it."

"I could just hug you right now!"

"And I could just hug you back, little missy."

After Brie hung up with Autumn, she was haunted by Sir's desperate plea. It spurred her to start packing even though she could barely keep her eyes open.

I'm coming, Sir…

Captain called Brie at the break of dawn to let her know that Mary had agreed to come. "I not only believe that Miss Wilson is ready, but I suspect she will also benefit from the task. I wasn't sure after speaking with you, but she and I had a long conversation. I'm releasing her from her collar with full confidence."

"That's wonderful, Captain! Of all the people Mr. Wallace could have as support, Mary is the only one he truly needs. I've been a pale replacement."

"You were what was needed at the time, Miss Bennett."

"You are very kind to say that." Her debt to him was so great, she felt the need to add, "I promise to thank you and Candy properly for everything the next time I see you."

"No need," he assured her. "Watching Miss Wilson grow into a more fully actualized person has been a rare gift for us both."

Brie was touched by the respect and admiration he held for Mary. She couldn't wait to see for herself just how much Mary had changed.

Brie was on pins and needles while she stood waiting at the airport. She literally squealed when she saw Mary emerge from the crowd. Brie scooted around the barrier to meet her, squeezing the breath out of Mary in her enthusiasm.

"You're here!"

"Yes, Stinky Cheese, I'm here," she said with an amused look on her face, as they started walking towards baggage claim.

"Who would have guessed the Three Musketeers would all end up in Denver?"

"Can't say it was ever a dream of mine."

Brie giggled, nudging Mary while they waited for the luggage. "Bet you can't wait to see Todd again, huh?"

Mary frowned. "Let's get one thing straight, here. I'm really pissed at you."

"Why?"

"You never said a damn word about what was going on with Faelan— not one fucking word."

"I was told not to," Brie answered defensively.

"So? I'm your friend, bitch. You should have told me."

"I wanted to tell you, but Sir said it was Todd's right to keep it from you. And after how you treated him at the commune…"

"It didn't give you the right to play God, damn it."

"I didn't play God, Mary. I only did what Todd asked."

Mary pulled her luggage off the carousel in a huff. "You're damn lucky he didn't die. I would never have forgiven you. Ever."

"And I never would have forgiven you for treating him like crap, so we're equal on that point."

Tears pooled in Mary's eyes and she swiped them away angrily.

"Look, I'm sorry it hurt you, Mary. However, I still stand by my decision."

Mary pursed her lips. "Fuck you, Brie."

Brie snickered. "Funny, that's just what Todd said when he saw me."

Mary's demeanor changed once they were in the car. "Shit... I wasn't sure I'd ever see him again. I'm nervous about it." She rolled her eyes. "I feel so stupid right now."

"I'll share something that should ease your mind. His mother told me that Todd calls out your name in his sleep."

"He does? Hell...the poor boy is worse off than I thought."

"He's really struggling to recover from the surgery, but now that you're here I wouldn't be surprised if he starts to walk."

Mary's smile suddenly disappeared. "You're telling me Faelan can't walk?"

"Yeah, the surgery really took a toll on him. But now that you're here—" Brie could tell that Mary was thrown off by the unexpected news, and patted her on the arm, confident everything would work out once Mary and Faelan were together again.

Her confidence slipped when Mary stopped at the entrance of the hospital, looking ready to bolt. Brie remembered feeling the same way, and grabbed her hand, pulling her inside. "The look on Todd's face is going to be priceless."

When they reached the room, she swung the door wide open and shouted, "Ta-da!"

Faelan rolled his eyes as he turned to face Brie, then froze as if he'd seen a ghost when he spied Mary.

They seemed both seemed frozen in time as they stared at each other, neither speaking.

Brie giggled, surprised by the odd reaction. "It's true, Todd. Your eyes are *not* deceiving you. It's Mary, here in the flesh."

The two continued to stare, ignoring Brie.

"It's good to see you again, Mary," Faelan said, finally breaking the ice.

Mary only nodded, looking more than ever like she was ready to bolt.

Brie shut the door to block Mary's escape and pushed her towards the bed. "I have to leave for China, so Mary has graciously agreed to take over for me."

Faelan tilted his head, gazing intently at Mary. "How are you?"

Mary snorted sarcastically. "Better than you."

He answered with a charming smirk. "Well, that wouldn't be hard, now, would it?"

Mary's smile seemed forced, and she took a step back from him. Brie saw the look of pain flash in Faelan's eyes.

"Where have you been? Brie told me you left the commune."

"I've been staying with Captain. He took me in."

Faelan stared at Mary in disbelief. "Were you wearing Captain's collar?"

She shrugged. "Temporarily."

"But you told me you would never wear a collar."

Mary raised her eyebrow, saying in a defiant tone, "Truth is, I would only wear a collar for one man."

"Who? Captain?" he spat.

She snarled angrily. "You're a fucking idiot, Faelan."

"And you're a cruel, heartless bitch."

Mary turned to Brie and shouted, "I shouldn't be here. This is your fault!" She ran out of the room, a flurry of curses flying from her lips.

Brie reluctantly faced Faelan and his accusatory glare. She explained, "The answer to your question was simple. Mary would only wear a collar for one man—you."

He shook his head, not believing her.

"Captain agreed to take Mary on to help her work through her past. She did it so she could have a real chance with you."

Faelan stared at the open door, a look of sympathy on his face.

"But I have no idea why she acted so strangely when she saw you..." Brie admitted.

"I know why."

She looked at him sadly. "I'm sorry. I've made a mistake bringing her here."

"No reason to be sorry," he answered, letting out a heavy sigh. "Bring Mary back this afternoon. I have something I need to say to her."

Brie was desperate for them to meet up again, hoping the two could resolve their differences when it was obvious they loved each other. "I'll make sure she comes."

She left to find Mary, but didn't come across her until she went outside and spied her sitting next to a water fountain. "What's going on, woman? What happened in there?"

"This was a mistake, Brie. A *colossal* mistake."

"But I don't get it. You love Todd and he loves you. How can this be a mistake?"

"You're as big an idiot as Faelan. I hope to hell that ticket you got me is exchangeable, because I'm flying back to LA this afternoon."

"Oh no, you're not! You're not pushing him away again. I don't know what your problem is, but you'd better get your act together real quick or you're going to lose the only man who's ever loved you."

"Don't tell me what to do, bitch!"

A group of orderlies walking into the building stopped due to the loud commotion. Brie waved them on. "Just a friendly spat. We're fine here."

She tuned back to Mary once the orderlies had entered the building. "I'm going to fucking kill you if you break his heart again. But...if that's really what you intend to do, then you'll do it face to face. You don't get to play the coward this time."

Mary's glare could have melted steel. "God, I hate you!"

"Believe me, right now, I hate you too," Brie snarled.

"Just go! Leave me the fuck alone."

"Fine," she spat, "because some of us actually care about people, and I need to see Tono right now."

Brie marched into the hospital, so livid she couldn't see straight. Mary hadn't changed at all! How disappointed would Captain be when he found out all his sacrifice and hard work had been for nothing?

Brie escaped into Tono's room and shared with him everything that had transpired—from Sir's disturbing phone message down to Mary's rejection of Faelan.

Naturally, Tono struck at the heart of the issue. "Sir Davis comes first. You've done all you can here." Brie smiled weakly, grateful for his wisdom and encouragement. She noted the glint in his eye when he added, "Asking Miss Autumn to look after me was a stroke of genius."

She chuckled. "I'll admit I thought so too."

"Be confident in the fact that we all will be fine, including Mr. Wallace."

Brie's smile crumbled. "Tono, I can't stand it if Todd gets hurt again. It's the last thing he needs right now. I'll never forgive myself if it ends badly for him."

"I suspect there's more going on than we know, but whatever happens is fated. The fact that Captain agreed to release her should ease any concerns you have on that matter."

Brie looked at him tenderly. "You've always known how to speak to my heart."

He placed his hand on her chest, above the heart. "We speak the same language, you and I."

Brie took hold of his hand and lifted it to her cheek, gazing into his chocolate-brown eyes. "Tono, I—"

Mary burst into the room and stopped short. "Whoa, I didn't realize what I was walking into. Don't mind me, Rope Freak, I didn't see a thing…" She made an about-face and exited the room.

Brie let out an exasperated sigh.

"Go talk to her."

"Yes, I'd better. Knowing how Mary's mind works, I can only imagine what she's thinking right now."

"Safe travels, Brie. Know that my thoughts will be with you and Sir Davis."

"I appreciate that more than you know, Tono." Before she left, she bowed low to him, holding back tears as she walked out of the room.

With help from the nursing staff, Brie found Mary in the waiting room, banging on the candy dispenser and screeching, "The hell you're going to steal my money!"

"Stop, already," Brie said, grabbing her hands. "I'll buy whatever you want downstairs. Come on, before they throw us both out."

Mary gave the machine a resounding kick before consenting to leave. "Fucking deny *me* chocolate!"

Brie noticed the nervous glances of several older visitors there waiting, and quickly ushered Mary out.

"I need to head out to get something for Master Anderson before I leave for China tomorrow," she explained. "So I'll just leave you here in the cafeteria, where you can eat as much chocolate cake as you want."

"Can't I join you?"

Brie was surprised by Mary's request, "Do I have a choice?"

"Not really."

Brie took it as a good sign, until they got into the car and Mary asked, "So tell me, what was going on back there with Nosaka?"

"Nothing."

"*Nothing*… Okay, 'cause I swear I saw you gazing all lovey-dovey into each other's eyes. It makes me wonder if that's how you 'cared' for Faelan."

Brie slammed on the brakes and pulled to the side of the road. "Don't even go there."

Mary shrugged. "Hey, I only call it like I see it."

"Tono died on the table during surgery, Mary. I bet you didn't know that. Well, I still haven't gotten over the shock of it."

"Look, I don't care if you're two-timing Sir—I won't tell. But you'd better not be pulling that shit with Faelan."

"What would it matter if I was? I asked you to come to Denver to care for him, but you're planning to dump him instead? I don't get you at all!"

Mary glared at her. "Let it go, Brie… Get your fucking errand done so I can go back and get this over with." She looked visibly shaken and turned away to hide it.

Brie was at a loss, but remembered Tono's assertion that there were things she didn't know about Mary—and might never know. Pulling back onto the road, she continued on her mission.

"What the hell is this place?" Mary grumbled when Brie parked the car in an old neighborhood north of Denver.

"A no-kill animal shelter. I owe Master Anderson," Brie answered, without explaining further.

Brie headed straight into the large home that had been converted into a shelter for dogs and cats, leaving Mary behind. She stopped just inside to watch a glassed-walled room full of tumbling puppies. She figured Mary couldn't resist such adorableness, and smiled to herself when Blonde Nemesis walked through the door and stood beside her.

"Aren't they the cutest?" Brie asked, giggling when one of the pups nipped its own tail and started running in circles.

"They may be cute to look at, but they're a pain in the ass to care for," Mary answered.

"Puppies are a lot of work… Oh, my gosh, did you see that? The little Golden just fell into the water bowl." Brie giggled.

"Get whatever you came for so we can get the hell out of here."

Mary pretended she didn't enjoy the puppy's antics, but Brie knew better. As she walked away to talk to the staff, she looked back and noted that Mary chose not to return to the car, staying to watch the adorable puppies instead.

Animals are good for the soul, Brie thought, and it made her that much more excited about her gift.

She spent nearly an hour observing and playing with many of the tiny creatures, wanting to make sure she picked the right one for the sexy Dom, being in no hurry to return to the hospital with Blonde Nemesis.

When she was convinced she'd found *the* one, Brie talked to the owner personally to set up delivery for her special gift. She walked out grinning like an idiot.

"Don't tell me you spent all that time in there for no apparent reason," Mary complained when Brie showed up empty-handed.

"Actually, I found exactly what I was looking for and am having it delivered to Master Anderson tomorrow."

"You'd better pray he doesn't kill you."

"I'm sure he won't. I got *exactly* what Master Anderson needs, I'm sure of it."

"Says the girl who fucked with my life."

"How did I fuck with your life? All I've ever done is try to support you. Please explain what I did wrong here. I'd really like to know."

"I never have met Faelan if it weren't for you."

"And how was meeting him a bad thing?"

Mary's countenance changed. She shook her head and looked away, unwilling to look Brie in the eye.

"Talk to me, Mary. I want to understand."

Her voice was barely audible when she confided, "I finally give my heart to a guy…and he's going to die on me."

Brie put her hand on Mary's shoulder. "He isn't going to die."

Mary jerked away from her, turning on Brie, her eyes flashing with anger. "I saw him, bitch! Don't lie to me about that. You brought me here to watch him die."

Brie was stunned and just stared at her.

"So here's what's going to happen. You're taking me back to the hospital. I'll tell him goodbye and then I'm out of here—and you'd better hope to God I never come across you again."

Heartbreak

It was disturbing that Mary seemed serene as they drove back to the hospital, as if the task ahead meant nothing to her. It pissed Brie off.

Faelan needed support, and here Mary was intent on stabbing the poor guy in the heart when he needed her most—because she loved him.

"You'd better be kind," Brie warned as they entered the hospital.

"I'll be quick and to the point."

Brie groaned inwardly when she saw Faelan's parents standing outside his room, their faces glowing with excitement. Mrs. Wallace immediately walked up to Mary.

"You must be the girl. You're even more beautiful than I imagined."

Mary stood there, a look of panic on her face.

Mr. Wallace held out his hand to Mary. "What a pleasure to meet you, Miss Wilson. Although my son is close-mouthed about his personal life, it's easy to tell how much he cares for you."

Brie had to nudge Mary to take his hand.

Mary laughed nervously as she shook it, then looked back at Brie, a frozen smile on her lips.

Oh, hell, this was going to be so much worse than Brie had imagined.

Better to get it over with now—like ripping off a Band-Aid, she decided. "Mr. and Mrs. Wallace, Mary and I would like a chance to talk to Todd privately. I hope you don't mind."

Mrs. Wallace beamed with delight. "Of course not. He's expecting you."

Brie opened the door for Mary, but the girl stopped abruptly as soon as she entered the room, causing Brie to walk into her. "What the heck, Mary?" she complained, and then she saw the reason why…

Faelan stood before them, dressed in a suit, with his hand gripping the

IV pole.

"What the—?" Mary gasped.

Brie noticed the white-knuckled grip he had on the IV pole, and understood the sheer effort he was making for Mary.

"Mary Wilson," Faelan stated, "you are mine."

Mary shook her head slowly, opening her mouth to speak.

Don't do it… Brie silently begged.

"Faelan, I—"

"I know you're scared, Mary," he interrupted. "I could tell it when you came in this morning. You probably thought you were looking at a dead man, but you're wrong. I'm not going anywhere."

Tears filled Mary's eyes.

"Tono Nosaka donated his kidney so that I could have this second chance."

"I don't…"

"Bow at my feet," he commanded. "It's either now or never, Mary. Make your choice."

Brie could see the inner battle Mary was fighting. The risk of loving him only to lose him was more than she could bear.

With great effort, Faelan took a step towards her and commanded again, "Bow to me, Mary."

Brie held her breath as Mary slowly approached Faelan, her eyes locked on his. She paused for a moment before gracefully lowering herself to the floor, kneeling before him. As an added gesture of obedience, she lowered her head until her forehead touched his feet.

Faelan undid the belt of his dress pants. "Look at me," he ordered. With painful determination, he looped the belt around Mary's neck, pulling it tight.

Mary gazed up at him with an expression Brie had never seen on her beautiful face—a look of pure joy.

"You are mine. From this day forward, you answer only to me."

"Yes, Faelan."

"Stand now and kiss your Master."

He tugged on the belt when she stood, bringing her lips hard against his. While they kissed, Faelan let go of the pole to caress her cheek. "When I get out of this hospital, I will get you a proper collar."

Mary smiled. "I don't care."

He brushed her bottom lip with his finger. "But I do. I want the world to know you are my cherished submissive."

Mary kissed Faelan again, with such passion that Brie lowered her eyes. When she started towards the door to give the couple privacy, Faelan called out to Brie.

"Don't leave just yet."

Mary turned to face Brie, but her loving gaze remained locked on Faelan.

"You have been a true friend in every sense of the word, blossom. I thank you for your diligence."

Brie smiled, tears coming to her eyes. She thought back to the man who had stood so confidently before her, expecting to receive her collar on Graduation Night. She would never have guessed how things would turn out. "It's been my pleasure."

He tugged on the belt, forcing Mary to kiss him again. Brie took his cue and quietly exited. There was just one more task to take care of before she could return to Sir's side.

Lea did not have much time to spare before heading to work at the Academy, but she agreed to meet, knowing Brie was headed to China in the morning.

"Okay, okay…we have to start this on a positive note," Lea stated when Brie opened the door to let her in. "What do you call a Chinese billionaire?"

"You're kidding me. I haven't even invited you inside yet."

Lea grinned. "Come on, Brie. What do you call a Chinese billionaire?"

Brie rolled her eyes. "I have no idea."

"Cha-Ching."

"No, no, no…that was terrible!"

"Did you hear what happened on the opening day at the newest Chinese zoo?"

"I'm shutting the door now," Brie said, pretending to close it on her.

Lea stuck her foot out to block it. "It was Panda-monium!"

Brie laughed in spite of herself. "Barely redeemed yourself with that second one. I guess you can come in."

Master Anderson was finishing up his meal in the kitchen. "Don't be late, Ms. Taylor. You have a big scene to perform tonight."

"Don't worry, Headmaster. As much as I love me some Brie, work always comes first."

"I won't keep her, I promise," Brie assured him.

"See that you don't. Baron would look awfully silly trying to play the part of Lea in front of the training Dominants. I'm not sure he would ever forgive you." He pointed to a plate on the counter and smiled. "By the way, I made you brownies."

"Oh, thank you, Master Anderson!" Brie squealed, as both she and Lea descended on the plate.

"Have fun, ladies," he said, tipping an imaginary cowboy hat before leaving them.

"Isn't Master Anderson the best?" Brie purred, taking a huge bite of a warm brownie.

"Yes…oh yes…" Lea moaned in ecstasy, sounding freakishly similar to when she was having sex. "I'm sure gonna miss that man."

Brie jumped on the comment, a natural transition to the reason she'd called Lea over. "You don't have to miss him…"

Lea smiled. "I know."

"Have you seriously considered moving back to LA?"

Lea took another bite of brownie and finished chewing before answering her. "Sure, I've thought about it. I mean, LA *is* awesome, but I have my reasons for staying here."

"If it's because of Autumn, you may want to rethink that. Who knows what's going to happen with Tono now that she's caring for him for the next few weeks? I've definitely seen some sparks fly between them."

Lea sighed. "Yeah, I've noticed that myself. I'm happy for them, don't get me wrong, but whenever people hook up, friends seem to get the short end of the stick."

"It's a natural process, I suppose."

"You know, with Baron and Master Anderson moving to LA, that leaves Mistress Clark all alone in Denver. It might be the best chance I ever get."

Brie's heart started racing. She was terrified she would say the wrong thing and screw it up. "I know how you feel about Ms. Clark, but have you ever wondered why nothing's happened between you? I mean, you did tell her how you felt, right?"

"Yeah, I've told her a few times, but you have to understand that Mistress Clark isn't one to jump into relationships quickly—not after Rytsar."

It seemed hopeless. Lea was never going to give up on Ms. Clark. Brie put her brownie down and exhaled. "I can't lie—the idea of having you come back to LA thrills me to death. I've missed you so much, girlfriend."

"I've missed you too, Brie. You know that!" Lea leaned over and gave Brie a hug as she stole another brownie off the plate.

"Don't you miss the big city, Lea? There's nothing quite like Los Angeles. And the ocean…remember lying on the beach and listening to the waves come in?"

Lea took a bite and purred. "Oh, I *do* miss tanning on the beach. And all those hunks in swimming trunks…"

"You know, if Autumn and Tono hook up, they might end up in LA. He has a loyal following there. And as far as Ms. Clark…" Brie stepped carefully, formulating her next words. "You don't want to be that girl who pacifies a lonely heart."

Lea stated defiantly, "I love her, Brie."

Brie put her arms around Lea. "I know you do. I've never doubted it. Ms. Clark must know that too, which makes me question why she hasn't pursued the relationship. Damn it, Lea, you deserve a lover who will pursue you with dogged determination."

"She's hurt, Brie. It's not easy for her."

"Sir was hurt, but he couldn't let me go when I decided to walk away."

Lea's eyes lit up. "That's it! I'll tell everyone I'm headed to LA. When Mistress Clark realizes what she's losing, she's bound to make her move."

Brie frowned. "But what if she doesn't?"

Lea popped the rest of the brownie into her mouth. After swallowing, she shrugged and said, "Then I suppose it wasn't meant to be."

But Brie didn't miss the glint in her eye. "It's a crazy plan, Lea."

She smiled. "It's the crazy ones that usually work."

"So if the worst happens and Ms. Clark doesn't realize what an incredible catch you are, will you stay in LA?"

"Of course, but don't get your hopes up, 'cause I see a bright, shiny collar in my future."

She knew Lea's heart was going to be broken, no matter what she did. Her only consolation was that she could be there for Lea when it all came crashing down.

Brie tossed and turned that night, but eventually fell asleep secure in the knowledge she would soon be in Sir's arms.

"Brie, I want to try something new," he told her in a husky voice.

She trembled, loving the idea of exploring something new with her Master, especially when it was something he desired.

"I'm all yours, Master."

"This will challenge you in ways you've never experienced."

She was even more excited and purred, "I look forward to it."

"It demands your trust and complete cooperation."

"Of course, Master. You have both, without question."

He smiled seductively as he explained, "I plan to fist you tonight."

She gasped, her loins contracting in fear.

"Is your heart racing now, téa? Are you still willing?"

"I'm not sure…"

"I've heard it is a singular experience," he growled lustfully in her ear.

"Yes, Master," she answered, trying to recover from the shock of his request. The word 'singular' had different connotations—both good *and* bad.

"Will you submit to me?"

The act of fisting frightened her, but still…the idea of being completely filled in that way had its own dangerous allure.

"If it pleases you, Master," she finally consented.

His look of approval made it worth facing her fears. "I'm glad to hear it, my little sub. I've watched it performed on numerous occasions, but have never experienced it myself."

That fact alone made Brie all the more willing to submit to his uncommon desire. To be his first in *anything* was a cherished gift.

"I promise not to take you past the point of breaking, but I *will* bend you tonight."

Brie moaned softly. To be taken to the edge by her Master was an intoxicating experience.

He laid out the lubricant, Hitachi Wand and a digital camera before placing a towel under her buttocks. "I expect you will cover this bed with your sweet come multiple times this session."

Brie bit her lip, suddenly hungry for what he was about to do.

She watched with nervous fascination as he covered his hand with the lubricant before massaging her tight opening. It reminded her of the same process he used when he relaxed her sphincter before fucking her deep in the ass.

He was gentle but firm as he stretched her vaginal muscles. "That's it," he praised, "open yourself to me…"

Brie tilted her head back, giving in to his loving but demanding touch while he kissed and nuzzled her breasts with his lips. The thought of being completely filled by him in a way she'd never experienced before had her moaning fearfully in anticipation.

He continued to massage her inner muscles, making sure they were loose and ready for his invasion. When he shifted off the bed to change position, she felt a moment of panic.

He looked at her knowingly. "You need to relax, téa." He pulled her to the edge of the bed and leaned down, kissing her inner thigh. "Trust your Master."

Brie let out a gasp, but spread her legs wider in submission to his will.

"Concentrate on letting me in—allow me to push through your resistance."

"Yes, Master," she answered breathlessly.

He started with three fingers, easing them into her as he described what he was doing. "First, we start out slowly to acclimate your body for what's to come."

Brie took deep breaths as he began thrusting them inside her, helping to relax her further.

"And now I add a fourth finger."

Brie held her breath, then moaned as he started rotating his hand back and forth, further massaging her muscles as he slowly pushed all four fingers inside her.

She could barely breathe, the ache of his invasion taking over all thought.

"Good girl. Now, we're going to open that tight little pussy even more."

Master took his time, in no rush. He seemed to enjoy the process as he watched her resistant body slowly submit to his will.

"You might be frightened, but I can tell your body enjoys the unique challenge."

Brie licked her lips and nodded, moaning louder as he bit the flesh of her thigh.

"And now all five…"

He added more lubricant before adding his thumb, and he continued the twisting motion, forcing himself deeper inside.

Her young body opposed the unnatural invasion. To aid her, he turned on the Hitachi and pressed it against her pussy. With her clit stretched so tight, it didn't take long for her to climax. The moment her pussy began pulsing in release, his knuckles breached her opening.

Brie cried out in surprise, the ache of being filled beyond capacity almost too much.

Master turned off the Hitachi and placed it on the bed beside her. He waited several moments, allowing her to grow used to the new sensation, before continuing his conquest.

Brie made small mewing sounds as he persisted. Her body was being taken to its absolute limit…and that was when she felt the tingling start.

He leaned over and kissed her belly. "That's it, let go and fly for me."

Once he was wrist-deep with his hand curled up inside her, he started lightly thrusting. The intoxicating pressure on her G-spot was intense.

He smiled up at her from between her legs. "This is only the beginning."

She lifted her head and looked down to see Master's manly arm buried inside her. It was surreal and strangely erotic. She could feel every movement he made, no matter how slight.

Brie moaned, lying back down and throwing her head back when he began twisting his hand again.

"This will be an orgasm you will never forget," he murmured as he began thrusting his fist.

All of Brie's resistance disappeared as he forcibly stimulated her G-spot. The concentrated thrusts had her screaming as she released a gush of watery come.

"I'm not done yet," he warned her seductively, nibbling her quivering thigh.

Brie tensed as he settled back down between her legs. "I'm going to make you orgasm even harder."

The twisting motion started up again, loosening her before he started pumping his fist. Brie let out a long, primal cry as she began to shake uncontrollably, her whole body readying for the intense climax.

"Ohhh…my—" She stopped mid-scream as she gushed in release, coming long and hard.

He pulled his hand out slowly, reveling in the amount of liquid passion he'd been able to inspire from her. "That was a thing of beauty," he said, in a low voice ripe with lust.

Immediately following her powerful orgasm, Brie started shivering. He gathered her in his arms, pressing his hard cock against her thigh as he gently stroked her long, brown curls. "I am well pleased, wife."

Brie woke up with a smile on her face. The intensity of the dream had her panties soaking wet, but it was the feeling of intimacy that lingered in her mind.

It comforted her to know that today she would be in her Master's arms.

Cold Reception

B rie was still packing last-minute items when Master Anderson entered the guest room. "I have something for you."

He handed her a small mason jar of homemade soup. "Just in case you have need, young Brie."

Brie hugged the jar to her chest. "I hope to partake of your soup for no other reason than to enjoy its taste."

"That would please me," he said, smiling kindly. He then handed her a fistful of foreign bills. "I stopped by the bank yesterday and got some money exchanged for you—just in case."

"Thank you for looking out for me, Master Anderson."

"Thane entrusted me with your care, and I take the job seriously."

Brie took the money and slipped it into her purse, then carefully wrapped the jar in her clothing to protect it, placing them snugly against Sir's preserves. "At least I'm guaranteed not to starve while I'm in China."

Master Anderson put his hand on her shoulder. "No matter what happens, don't lose sight of how much you're worth to Thane."

She was about to reply when the doorbell rang.

"Who could that be this early in the morning?" Master Anderson griped as he left to answer the door.

Brie snuck a peek from her room when he unlocked the door and opened it.

"Mr. Brad Anderson?"

"Yes. What's this about?"

"I have a delivery for you."

"Sorry, you must be mistaken. I haven't ordered anything," Master Anderson stated, starting to close the door.

"I was told this is a gift."

"Fine," he muttered, as if it was an inconvenience. "Where do I sign?"

The courier handed Master Anderson a cardboard box with handles and tipped his hat. "Have a pleasant day, sir."

Master Anderson stared at the box for a moment, then called out to the man, "Wait! Why does this box have holes in it?"

Brie had to stifle her giggle as he cautiously set the box on the coffee table and sat down. He pulled out the note attached and read it aloud.

To Master Anderson

May you find your joy and delight in this box.

He looked warily at the cardboard box again, mumbling to himself, "What the hell…" After lifting the lid, he chuckled as a tiny orange tabby enthusiastically jumped out of the box but overshot it, meowing pitifully as it tumbled off the table. Luckily, Master Anderson had quick reflexes and caught the tiny thing in his large hands before it hit the floor.

"Brie!" he roared.

She left the safety of the room, approaching him slowly, unsure whether he liked her gift.

"Did you do this?" he asked in an accusatory tone.

She twisted nervously where she stood. "Maybe…"

"A kitten?"

"I know you have a thing for redheads, and she was a cute little red-head who needed a good man."

The kitten attempted to climb up Master Anderson's muscular arm as Brie was talking. He gave up trying to control the furball and let it crawl up his arm to his shoulder, where it stood fearlessly, surveying the new landscape from its high vantage point.

"The last thing I need is an animal to care for," Master Anderson complained as he gently rubbed under the tiny creature's chin.

"I couldn't stand the thought of you coming home to an empty house anymore, Master Anderson. Besides, kittens make excellent chick magnets."

"Did you forget I'm moving in two months?"

"She'll make the move much more interesting for you. Trust me."

The kitten rubbed up against Master Anderson's handsome chin, purring loudly.

"Oh!" Brie cooed, putting her hands to her heart. "You two look so cute together."

Master Anderson picked up the tiny kitten and looked it in the eyes. It let out a sweet little mew, and that was all it took—he was hooked. "Fine,

I'll keep her, but be assured I will do a far better job caring for *her* than Thane did with my innocent herb garden."

Brie burst out laughing. "Well, that's a relief."

He passed the kitten to her. "Hold on to the little thing while I get your luggage into the truck. No reason she can't take the ride with us."

"What are you going to call her, Master Anderson?"

He looked at the tabby with an amused expression. "I haven't decided yet. I want to get to know her first, so I can give her a title befitting her spunky personality."

While he was carrying the luggage to the car, Brie kissed the kitten's tiny pink nose. "Yep, you don't know what a lucky little pussy you are."

When Brie stepped off the plane in Chengdu, she was hit by culture shock as she made her way through the busy airport. There were not many foreigners, and few people, if any, seemed to speak English. Since she had not been able to reach Sir before she'd left, there was no one there to greet her. She was completely on her own, which was a real challenge, since she knew very little Chinese.

Luckily, both she and Sir had tracking devices on their phones. It allowed them to keep tabs on each other while traveling, and proved vitally important to her now. Knowing that his missing phone was still lost at the hotel, she was able to find the exact location.

Once she had all her luggage and had finally managed to hail a cab, she showed the driver the GPS map on her phone. He shook his head, indicating that he didn't understand. She tried to pronounce the name of the hotel, but try as she might, the man could not understand her. Brie could tell he was getting frustrated and was afraid he would kick her out of his cab.

In a last-ditch effort, she googled the translation for the name of the hotel and showed him the Chinese characters. The man smiled, nodding his approval as he hit the gas. Although she was afraid the translation might be off, she grew more confident that they were headed in the right direction once the dot on her phone began to move.

Brie thought how terrifying it would be to get lost in this giant city of fourteen million people without knowing the language. She fervently prayed that Sir would be at the hotel when she arrived.

The drive took almost an hour and there were several heart-stopping moments. The streets were full of bicycles, motorbikes, pedestrians and buses, as well as regular cars and taxis. It took much weaving and braking to avoid hitting the different modes of transportation gathered on the same roadways, and the crazy intersections seemed like accidents waiting to happen. To Brie's relief, they arrived at the hotel unscathed despite (or possibly because of) her cabbie's haphazard driving.

The driver handed Brie her luggage and eagerly took the yuan Master Anderson had given her.

Thank you, Master Anderson!

Brie entered the hotel and walked up to the counter. "Sir Thane Davis?" she asked, hoping his name would ring a bell. The clerk said something in Chinese, so Brie said it again more slowly, pointing at the different room keys hanging behind the woman.

The clerk smiled and repeated Sir's name with her thick accent. Brie nodded enthusiastically, thrilled the woman understood. She was surprised when the woman left her post to personally escort Brie to the room.

The clerk knocked on the door and called out his name, but it was not Sir who answered. Instead Lilly stood there, looking as surprised as Brie. The clerk seemed unhappy, looking at both women as if she was afraid she'd done something wrong by showing Brie to the room.

To alleviate the woman's fears, she held out her hand to Lilly. "It's good to see a familiar face."

Lilly accepted the handshake, but failed to invite Brie in.

The front desk clerk was satisfied, however, and left them to return to her job.

"Is this Thane's hotel room?" Brie asked, surprised to find her there.

"Yes. I'm waiting for him to return from his daily jog before we visit Mother again."

"Good," Brie answered, brushing past her to enter Sir's room. She put down her luggage and collapsed in a nearby chair, sighing loudly. "It's been a long flight and I'm totally exhausted, but if I take a quick shower to freshen up, I can join you two."

When Lilly didn't respond, Brie asked, "You don't have a problem if I freshen up, do you?"

"Of course not," Lilly answered, but she sounded less than pleased.

When Lilly made no move to leave, Brie asked bluntly, "Do you mind giving me a little privacy? I promise not to take long."

Lilly seemed reluctant to leave Sir's room, but made her way out.

Brie shut the door behind her and headed into the tiny bathroom. Realizing she had little time, she quickly undressed and sponged herself, reapplying her makeup and fixing her hair. Before she dressed in new clothes, she spritzed herself with perfume and felt adequately refreshed.

Brie knelt at the door waiting for him. It was only a few minutes later when she heard him slipping the key into the door. She looked down, smiling to herself as it swung open, anticipating their reunion.

Sir entered the room and shut the door, stating only, "You came."

She looked up and her heart skipped a beat. "I…I did, Sir." He had a haunted, cruel look in his eyes that was unsettling to her soul.

What's happened to him?

Rather than the normal protocol of releasing Brie to serve him, Sir stayed where he was. "I met with Lilly in the lobby. She let me know you were here."

Brie wondered why Lilly had felt the need to tell him and spoil her surprise. She looked at his troubled face and asked, "Aren't you happy to see me, Sir?"

There was a light knock on the door.

"Excuse me," he said curtly. Sir answered it, telling Lilly, "Give me a minute. I'll come get you when I'm ready to head out."

He shut the door again and stared at Brie. The cold look in his eyes reminded of her of the song "Demons" that he'd sung to her back in Tokyo, and his warning: *"When I shared that I have my demons, it was not simply idle talk, Brie. I am my mother's son."*

Brie could feel his hostility increasing. She was afraid she was about to meet his demons head on, but she held her kneeling pose as he approached, even though she felt like cowering.

In one solid motion, he lifted her from the ground and threw her over his shoulder, carrying her into the bathroom. There he stripped out of his jogging sweats and ripped her out of her clothes, pushing her against the shower wall. He turned on the hot water and let it cascade over them both.

Sir grabbed her hips so violently that she cried out. Instead of taking her, he wrapped his arms around her, holding Brie tightly against him—so tightly that she struggled to breathe. But she did not resist his restrictive embrace—she clung to him.

After several minutes, he began to shake as silent sobs wracked his body. Her own tears fell, her heart breaking for him.

Sir did not let go until the water became ice cold and Brie was shivering in his arms.

He shut off the shower and grabbed a towel, drying her in silence before taking care of himself. His expression remained just as tormented, but there were no telltale signs that he had been crying.

"We will leave when you're ready," he stated gruffly, exiting the bathroom.

Brie looked in the mirror, frightened by the change in him. With shaking hands, she wiped away her running mascara and applied her makeup for a second time. Brie slipped into her clothes and styled her hair simply.

She rejoined Sir, her hair still wet, hoping he would talk to her before they met up with Lilly again. It disturbed her that he would not look her in the eye.

"Sir…" she said, moving towards him.

He stopped her in her tracks with his accusatory tone. "What was the reason for the delay?" When she opened her mouth to answer, he snapped, "Never mind. Hand me your journal."

Brie immediately dug through her luggage and handed it to him. She wanted to explain, but stood silently, feeling guilty of a crime she was unaware she'd committed.

Sir sat down, not inviting her to join him as he starting flipping through her journal. Brie watched his expression carefully, hoping to see compassion. To her dismay, his face remained impassive, even though Brie had poured out her heart to him on every page.

It pained her to see him so cold and uncaring.

After he'd finished, Sir closed the book. "I have many questions for you, but not now. I have an appointment with the Beast. You are to remain here until I get back."

"But Si—"

He put up his hand to stop her protest. "Go to sleep. You've had a long day of travel. That's an order, téa."

Brie dutifully took off her clothes as he watched, and laid them in a pile on the nightstand before slipping under the covers of his bed.

She watched in disbelief as he walked out the door, leaving her alone in the hotel room while he joined Lilly.

What the hell is going on?

Brie felt certain Lilly was the cause of the disconnect with Sir. But the question she couldn't answer was why. What possible motive could Lilly have to do such a terrible thing?

As much as Sir wouldn't want to hear it, she knew it was time to voice her concerns about his sister, but Brie also understood that she'd have to tread lightly. Lilly was family and, in the short time he'd known her, Sir had grown to care about the girl.

Even though it was about to get ugly, as his submissive and future wife, Brie understood it was her duty.

Condors, Sir.

She eventually gave in to her exhaustion, falling into a fitful slumber. She dreamed of snakes and kittens, a wedding dress and black pearls…

Brie woke with a start. It took a moment to realize she was in Sir's hotel room. Just when her heart was slowing down, an unpleasant masculine scent assaulted her senses and then she heard movement.

Someone else was in the room.

Before she could scream, a strong hand wrapped around her throat pinning her to the bed. Brie struggled for her life, but her cries were muffled as her assailant squeezed her windpipe. His grip was hard and unforgiving as he strangled the breath out of her.

As she became lightheaded, her spirited thrashing quickly became feeble movements. Once she stopped fighting, recognition slowly dawned—*Master's touch.*

Even though his scent did not match because he was wearing the shirt of another man, it was Sir who held her by the throat.

Sir released the pressure of his grip but his hand remained tight around her neck. He growled ominously, "Don't make a sound." Sir ripped the blankets away, exposing her naked body.

He was playing out the scene she had written in her journal, but there was another element to it—a dangerous one that frightened Brie. She instinctively cried out, "Please don't hurt me."

Still keeping in character, he leaned down and whispered in her ear, "I won't unless you force me to."

Was it a threat or an invitation to play?

Sir's hands were unusually rough as he caressed her body, bruising and clawing at her in his raging lust. Brie whimpered under his touch, both turned on and frightened by his harsh treatment. He seemed like a man possessed.

Sir flipped her over and buried her face in the pillow as he rubbed his hard shaft between the valley of her ass-cheeks. He panted over her. "No lube this time."

Brie's frightened whimpers were muffled by the pillow as Sir positioned himself. She braced for his hard cock to thrust deep into her unprepared ass, knowing she had been the one to invite this scene.

She waited for his painful entry, but Sir loosened his grip and pulled away. His ragged breathing slowly returned to normal. "I thought I wanted this...but I don't."

Brie turned her head to look back at him. "Why?" she asked hesitantly, unsure if he was rejecting the scene—or her.

He stared at Brie, his expression unreadable. Then his eyes softened as he slid his hand over the curve of her ass. "I need to make love to you, Brie."

His unexpected answer melted her heart.

Sir gently turned Brie over and lay on top of her, smothering her with his large frame. He propped himself on his elbows and held her face in his hands as he gazed into her eyes. He said nothing, but Brie became entranced by his silent language.

Eventually, tears ran down her cheeks as she whispered, "I love you."

"I'm lost."

"We'll find the way back," she assured him, lifting her head and kissing him on the lips.

Sir nuzzled her neck. "This moment is the only thing that's real to me...my anchor in the storm."

"I will always be your safe haven, Sir," Brie vowed, trailing feather-light kisses down his neck.

Sir's impassioned groan reverberated deep in his chest. "Since I cannot make love to you with my cock..." She closed her eyes as Sir moved lower, tenderly kissing her thighs before concentrating on her pussy. In a world of kinky sex, with constant physical and mental challenges, she cherished such loving attention equally as much.

Brie ran her hands through his thick brown hair as his tongue and fingers made love to her for hours. It was his escape from the world, his stolen moment from the mounting pressure around him.

His lovemaking wasn't about how many orgasms he could elicit or how high he could make her fly—it was about expressing his love using only his touch and tongue.

Betrayal

It was obvious to Brie that Lilly was unhappy Sir had left her to visit their mother alone, because he received a scribbled note as soon as she returned from the hospital.

Thane, must talk.

Meet me in my room.

Lilly

Sir invited Brie to join him, the tension returning to his face. "Mother's situation has put a strain on our relationship, but I trust we can move beyond it after this is over."

After hearing his confession, Brie was surprised when Lilly opened the door with an inviting smile. That all changed when her eyes drifted down and focused on Sir's arm around Brie's waist. The light seemed to leave Lilly's face as her hands dropped to her sides, and she drifted over to the bed, not even bothering to invite them in.

It appeared that seeing Brie had triggered something dark in Lilly. The girl became silent and unresponsive even when Sir questioned her.

"Lilly, what's happened? Is it Mother? Talk to me."

The girl just sat on the bed with a blank stare on her face, as if she were a million miles away.

Sir shook his head, looking at Brie in confusion. "I can't explain it. I've never seen her like this before."

After a few minutes, Lilly seemed to come back to life. She nodded as if she'd made a decision, looking at Sir with deep sadness. In a hushed voice, she asked, "Are you going to tell Brie what happened that night?"

"What are you talking about?" he asked, sounding genuinely concerned.

"I've forgiven you, but will she?"

"I have no clue what you mean."

Lilly slowly shook her head, tearing up as she spoke. "I know you didn't intend to hurt me, Thane. I know it was the drink."

"What exactly are you accusing me of?" Sir demanded.

"Don't make me say it, Thane. Don't make me relive that moment." Brie could see that Lilly was visibly shaking, and wondered about the cause.

Brie looked questioningly at Sir.

Sir met her gaze. "I have no idea what she's talking about, Brie."

Lilly seemed genuinely distraught and looked on the verge of panic. "I forgave you, Thane. Please let it go…"

His nostrils flared in disgust. "You will not throw around veiled accusations, Lilly."

"Brie," Lilly cried piteously, "he must have been thinking of you when he grabbed me and forced himself…" She struggled to speak through her tears. "He…he…" She shook her head, breaking down in heart-wrenching sobs that pulled at Brie's heartstrings.

Brie looked back at Sir, the icy realization of what Lilly was accusing him of wrapping itself around her heart.

Sir's gaze remained fixed on Brie. "Even though I can't remember what happened that night, I could never do what she's insinuating. Never."

The look of agony on Lilly's face came from a place so deep it could not have been faked, but Sir…Sir could never hurt a woman that way, much less his own *sister*. The idea was too revolting to even contemplate.

"I don't know what kind of game you're playing, Lilly, but you are most definitely a carbon copy of your mother," Sir said with abhorrence, unmoved by Lilly's copious tears.

"How can you say that, Thane?" she sobbed. "You're the monster here, not me! Damn it, I forgave you. I forgave you that very night, when you broke down after realizing what you'd done."

Sir shook his head, but he had the look of an animal finding itself trapped. "Do you have any proof?"

Lilly cried, "I don't need proof! I remember what happened."

"You had as much to drink as I did…*sister*," he stated coldly.

"I know what happened, Thane."

"Then it comes down to your word against mine. I know myself well, and without any evidence proving otherwise, I stand by my assertion that nothing happened between us."

"But it did!" Lilly whimpered, covering her face with her hands as she sank to the floor.

Brie craved to comfort her, instinctively responding to her pain, but she didn't make a move. To do so would be a betrayal of Sir if Lilly was lying.

So she stood anchored to her spot, unable to think.

"Brie, I wouldn't do that to a woman, no matter how drunk I was. You know that."

"Normally you wouldn't…" Brie agreed, trailing off as her throat closed up, an image of him with Lilly coming into her mind.

"Don't go there," he warned. "Don't allow what she's said to filter through your thoughts. She's lying, Brie. There's no other explanation."

Lilly looked up at him, her eyes red and swollen. "Even now, I forgive you. I know you didn't mean it."

The response struck Brie as odd. If Sir had really done the horrendous thing she was implying, there was no way Lilly could still forgive him after he'd just accused her of lying about it. No woman would let a man get away with that. It made Brie wonder if this was all an act to garner her sympathy so she would take Lilly's side against Sir's.

If so, what possible benefit would Lilly gain by this vile ruse? She'd just alienated Sir, her only sibling, and she'd never shown any interest in Brie until now.

None of it made sense.

"I don't know what I think," Brie muttered, looking down at Lilly crumpled on the floor. The girl looked emotionally shattered.

"You have to believe me, Brie," Sir asserted. "I didn't… I wouldn't hurt her."

Brie couldn't leave Lilly lying there weeping, her pain too raw and real to be ignored. She lifted the girl to her feet and helped her into bed, covering her with a blanket. As they were leaving the room, Lilly called out to Sir with a look of regret. "I know you didn't mean to."

Sir snarled angrily. "Stop. Whatever game you're playing, just stop."

Brie was stunned. If Sir were guilty, his reaction to Lilly was unforgiveable. But if Lilly were lying—the betrayal to Sir was of horrific proportions.

Either possibility was unbelievably terrible.

They left Lilly's room, but when Sir reached out for Brie, she unconsciously stepped away, an unwanted image of Sir violating Lilly crowding her mind. "I have to get out of here," she cried. "I need time alone."

The look of hurt in Sir's eyes cut Brie to the quick, but it didn't stop her from running out of the hotel.

Brie walked the crowded streets of Chengdu, oblivious to the people around her. It terrified her that in one fell swoop, everything she'd believed in had been shaken to its foundation. Sir was an honorable man. Brie knew he would never do such a thing…and yet he had admitted to her on the phone that he had no recollection of that night, after liberally ingesting a local brew.

Was it possible that it had made him momentarily insane—unstable enough to hurt his own sister?

Brie couldn't get over the fact that Lilly had looked genuinely traumatized. Something terrible must have happened to her. Still, the girl kept insisting she'd forgiven Sir. Why? And why would she continue to stay with Sir if he'd hurt her like that?

There *had* to be something more—something Lilly was hiding.

Yet visions of what Lilly had accused Sir of flooded Brie's mind, and once the tears started, they wouldn't stop. People began to stare. Out of desperation, Brie sought escape, finding an isolated wooden bench. Once she sat down, she held her head in both hands and sobbed uncontrollably, oblivious to everything and everyone.

Breathe, Brie, breathe… she reminded herself.

Eventually a strange but welcome calm took hold, and her heartrate slowed as her breaths became deep and soul-satisfying. Once the panic fled, clarity took over.

Sir would never do such a thing.

With shaking hands, she pushed herself up and wiped away her tears. It wasn't until then that she realized she was hopelessly lost. She hadn't brought her phone and couldn't remember the Chinese name for the hotel.

A fresh sense of panic took over as she glanced around, unsure from which direction she'd come. That was when her eyes landed on Sir. He stood a little more than a block away, ever her protector, even when she was questioning his integrity.

Without hesitation, she started running towards him, but before she reached Sir she stopped, suddenly feeling ashamed.

"Come to me, Brie."

She melted into his forgiving embrace and immediately apologized. "It was wrong of me to leave."

"No," he insisted. "While it was foolish to walk the streets of an unfamiliar city alone, I respect your need to process. You and I are not that different."

Brie looked up at him. "I know you never could…"

"No," he assured her.

"But why would Lilly do such a thing? It doesn't make any sense."

Sir shook his head. He seemed gutted when he answered her. "I was an idiot to believe she was any different."

Brie hugged him tighter. "I'm sorry I encouraged you to trust her."

"I have only myself to blame," Sir closed his eyes, a look of agony on his face. "... and now I understand what I must do."

He did not explain as he took Brie's hand and guided her through the streets, leading her back to the hotel. It felt to Brie as if he were facing a firing squad, but instead of losing his life he was going to lose the last living connection to his mother. Now Sir would never know closure or peace.

Once they reached the hotel, Sir headed directly to Lilly's room. She immediately answered when he knocked. Although her eyes were still bloodshot from crying, she stepped to the side and invited him in as if she was relieved to see him.

"We can talk this out, Thane. Despite what happened, I can't bear losing you."

Sir was not swayed by her heartfelt plea.

"I came to tell you that I'm going to issue the order to stop all life-support. There's no point pretending she's going to recover after the results of the latest scan."

"Don't, Thane... Don't punish Mother for this."

"It's not an act of punishment."

"But she opened her eyes. I saw it! Are you trying to get back at me for daring to talk to Brie about what happened between us?"

His voice was as cold as ice. "You can stop with the act. I never hurt you."

Her laughter was tinged with hysteria. "Brie, he claims he wouldn't hurt anyone, but he's set on killing his own mother." She screamed at Sir, "You cold-hearted bastard!"

"The only reason I entertained your false hope regarding the Beast was that I cared about your emotional needs. That is no longer the case."

"Don't say that. You still care about me—I'm your fucking sister for God's sake!"

"I have no sister."

The panic in her voice rose to a fever-pitch. "No... You can't abandon me like that, and I'm sure as hell not letting you kill Mother! You're fucking with the wrong person, Thane!" Lilly grabbed her purse and rushed out of the room.

Sir's eyes narrowed as he watched her go. He shut the door and ordered, "Look for the phone."

It was a shock to Brie how cunning Sir was. The two siblings were dangerously adept at manipulating each other.

She rifled through the drawers while Sir tore through Lilly's luggage with no luck. Sir scanned the room. "Leave nothing unturned—it's got to be here."

He finally struck gold when he overturned the mattress. The cell phone had been hidden between it and the box spring, stuffed clear to the center where it could not be found.

"I *knew* it," he growled furiously, holding up the phone.

Finding his cell was important on many levels. Not only did it prove Lilly's malicious intent, but just as critical to Sir, it had all his business contacts, information and messages.

"What a fool I was," he growled in disgust, slipping it into his pocket, "and I played right into her hands."

"I wish I hadn't encouraged you to ignore your cautious nature."

Sir shook his head. "You only told me what I wanted to hear. I needed to believe that Lilly was different, and now I'm paying the price for it."

"Not everyone is untrustworthy, Sir. You shouldn't have to question the loyalty of family."

"I forgot one fundamental rule—only bad comes from *anything* associated with my mother."

Brie wrapped her arms around him. "I disagree, Sir. You're proof of that."

Sir kissed the top of her head before directing her towards the door. "It's essential we distance ourselves from Lilly and everything to do with her."

"So we're not going to the hospital?" Brie asked in surprise.

"No. We'll be headed back to LA on the next available flight. I need to meet with Thompson to discuss how to proceed from here."

"What about your mother, Sir?"

"The Beast can rot for all I care!"

The harshness of his attitude was understandable, but it still shocked her. Such hatred could only hurt Sir in the end.

He saw her look of concern. "I will deal with her later, Brie. Right now I need to leave, or I'm liable to kill the Beast's daughter."

Sir took the hotel notepad on the desk and scribbled a quick message. He handed it to Brie and asked her to sign it, before leaving it on the disheveled bed for Lilly to find.

The phone has been located. Go crawl back to the hole you came from.

Further contact is prohibited.

Sincerely, Thane C. Davis and Brianna R. Bennett

On the plane ride home, Sir put his roomy first-class seat back in a full recline position and had Brie snuggle on top of him. He covered her with a blanket and held her, saying nothing. Those twelve hours were some of the most emotionally intimate she'd experienced with Sir, even though no words were exchanged.

When they finally landed, Sir whispered in her ear, "My safe haven."

"Always, Sir. Condors forever."

"Do you think I should get that tattooed on my ass?"

She smiled, giggling when she answered, "Only if it pleases you, Sir."

Sir spent his first week back locked in meetings with his lawyer, while Brie finished editing her film for Holloway's presentation. Although it was only a rough edit, she was determined to impress the man with her sequel.

Unfortunately, Mr. Holloway was in a foul mood when she finally had the chance to meet with him. If Brie had a choice, she would have cancelled the meeting right then and there.

As it was, she was forced to weather out the storm when he opened the meeting with, "Miss Bennett, I hope to hell it's good. I'm not in the mood for amateur hour."

"You'll be impressed," she replied evenly, handing him the DVD. He slipped it into the player and sat back, an unpleasant scowl on his face.

"Would you like me to come back another time?" Brie suggested before her film started, hoping he would jump on the offer.

"Hell, no. I'm behind enough as it is."

Brie kept her disappointment to herself, knowing there was a very real chance Mr. Holloway could pull the project, making all her hard work mean nothing. She took a deep breath, trying to calm her racing heart.

The intro began with a dark screen and some heavy bass. He paused the film and frowned. "What's this crap?"

"It's called dubstep, Mr. Holloway. It's popular among young people."

"Pick something more classic, damn it. Our target audience is much broader, Miss Bennett."

She nodded, mentally noting where she could add dubstep farther into the film as she wrote down his suggestion. He was right, of course—this documentary *was* meant to be multi-generational. "Got it."

He huffed, growling to himself, "Why I have to point out the obvious is beyond me."

Brie hated falling short of his expectations, but suspected that anyone who had the misfortune of crossing paths with him today was guaranteed to suffer similar humiliation.

She noticed his keen interest whenever Mary came onto the screen. This wasn't the first time he'd shown interest in her, and Brie was curious why. Was it simply due to her good looks, or did she and the producer have some kind of personal connection Brie didn't know about?

Whatever the case, Holloway seemed disgusted when the documentary ended. "I specifically asked for more scenes with Miss Wilson. Where the hell are they?"

"They're all there, Mr. Holloway. There were some unforeseen issues at the commune, which limited her screen time."

He leaned forward, snarling, "And I bet those *issues* would make great film, wouldn't they, Miss Bennett?"

"No."

"Yet again you disappoint me. You're not a great film-maker, Miss Bennett. You don't have the instincts for it." He leaned forward and added harshly, "You're so concerned about people's *feelings* that you sabotage your own damn work."

Brie felt sick. It was clear that Mr. Holloway hated the film…and even worse, he was right about her. Her concern for Mary and Faelan were more important than the success of this documentary. "I'm sorry to disappoint you, Mr. Holloway."

"It's not just me who's disappointed. Surely you must be disgusted by this amateurish attempt. Such a shame your parents wasted their hard-earned retirement putting the likes of you through college."

Had it been a year ago, Brie would have been crushed by Mr. Holloway's words—but not anymore. She was confident in her abilities and wasn't willing to back down. "I have a good handle on what the viewers want to see, and this second documentary has it. Wouldn't you agree that Rytsar Durov's scene is a powerful piece of film?"

He raised his eyebrow as he thought back on it. "With the recent publicity concerning him, that might play out in our favor—but it's not enough."

"You didn't care for my scene with Baron?"

A slight smirk greeted her question, but he quickly squashed it.

His unconscious reaction let her know that her film hit closer to the mark than he wanted to let on. Brie was certain that her work was not the huge disaster he was claiming it to be. The challenge was getting him to admit it without pissing him off.

"I thought the session with Ms. Clark playing with her two subs was entertaining to watch."

He nodded. "The Domme is majestic on screen."

"I also believe the audience will go crazy for Tono Nosaka's modern version of Kinbaku."

Mr. Holloway took out a cigar and lit it, taking in a long drag before releasing the smoke slowly from his lips. "It has merit."

"Am I wrong in assuming that the issue you have with my film boils down to it not having enough drama?"

"No," he stated firmly, leaning towards her. "Not more drama, Miss Bennett. I asked for more of Miss Wilson. I couldn't have made it clearer—and yet you defy me." He pointed his cigar at her. "*That* is what I have an issue with."

Brie understood that the fate of her film was in jeopardy, and gently defended herself. "Defy is a strong word, Mr. Holloway. I *had* planned to get additional shots centering on Miss Wilson, but extenuating circumstances prevented it."

"As the producer, I'm not interested in excuses. Where is she now?"

"Mary is staying in Denver at the moment," Brie answered, not offering any specifics.

Mr. Holloway answered with a condescending smile, "Then I suggest you get on a plane right *now* and film Miss Wilson, like I asked."

Brie knew better than to argue with the man in his current state, so she swallowed her pride and stood up. "I'll take what you've said into consideration."

"No. You will do exactly what I say or I'll shitcan the film."

It took everything in her not to respond. Instead of jeopardizing the film further, Brie simply nodded and started towards the door, but she couldn't help looking back and asking, "What is your interest in Miss Wilson, anyway?"

The surly man glared at her. "Out!"

Brie smiled. Whatever strange hold Mary had over Mr. Holloway, it was enough to keep her documentary alive—for now.

Brie laughed to herself as she exited the building, pleased by how much she'd grown. Before Sir and the Training Center, a heated confrontation like that would have completely derailed her, but now she actually felt energized by it. There was a thrill in being challenged on work she was passionate about.

This was a different kind of confidence. For Brie it wasn't about fighting to save herself, it was about fighting for the project and all the people who could benefit from the film. Little did Mr. Holloway suspect he had unleashed the dragon inside her, and woe befall any man who got in her way.

The Limo Ride

Brie did not take Mr. Holloway's advice about running back to Denver. Instead, she started rearranging the scenes in the film, having been inspired by their meeting. She knew Mary and Faelan needed time alone, and frankly, so did she and Sir.

Sir was extremely busy with his business and their wedding plans, but surprisingly, rather than spend his nights working, which had been his norm, he made the choice to put away his computer every evening and revel in his submissive instead.

Each night Sir sat, drinking his martini, as he admired a new pose he'd requested from her. It was like a game between them—she was his canvas and he was the artist. It had the feel of objectification, except for the fact she was the center of attention.

It reminded Brie of nude models who posed for hours as the painter captured the image, except that Sir painted his picture with words rather than brush strokes, describing what he saw as he leisurely sipped his drink.

Sir often played the song 'Cinema' by Benny Benassi before they began the evening's entertainment. He said it expressed how he felt perfectly and every time Brie heard it, she was humbled and fell even more in love with him.

Tonight's pose had her naked on the tantra chair. She was lying on it, facing away from him but looking back over her shoulder. He had draped white silk around her, then adjusted it strategically so it exposed most of her back and just a hint of her ass.

"I like it when you are facing away from me, téa. Your coy expression as you look back at me moves your Master."

She smiled, a slight blush rising to her cheeks.

"But tonight's pose is especially erotic. I must applaud myself. Having the beauty that is your ass barely peeking out from the white silk… I could literally stare at you for hours and never tire of it."

She grinned. "How long has it been tonight?"

He looked at his watch and raised an eyebrow, admitting, "Already two hours and ten minutes. There's something alluring about having you displayed but not being able to partake of you that has my libido soaring."

"I feel the same, Master. I just want to turn around and open my legs to you."

He tsked. "Such a naughty girl." He pressed down on his slacks, adjusting his hardening cock. Sometimes Sir allowed her to play with herself to completion. On other days, he'd let her suffer.

Tonight was one of those nights when they were suffering together. Instead of driving her crazy, it seemed to draw her closer to him. Sir talked about the day, sharing moments he normally glossed over.

Rather than working hard on projects or having mind-blowing sex together, they were spending time communicating about the little things, which led into broader topics and impassioned discussions about life, politics and the future of society. The entire time, Brie stayed in her pose and Sir watched her from his vantage point.

On occasion, he commanded her to pleasure him with her mouth at the end of the evening. In those rare instances, Brie swore he gazed down at her with a new level of admiration that had nothing to do with her skills as a submissive.

Brie received a text in the afternoon, and naturally assumed Sir was giving instructions for her next pose, but she was in for a surprise when she read:

Limo will pick you up at 7:00. Pearls a must. No undergarments.

She should have been excited, but her two experiences with limousines had both ended in disaster. It was hard to forget, but ever the optimist, she was willing to try again with Sir.

Brie smiled as she picked up the red velvet box that held the black pearls he'd given her for Christmas. Sir had created such incredible memories, despite his aversion to the holiday. She trusted that he would do the same tonight, changing the dread she felt about fancy limousines.

She chose a form-fitting black dress with a high neckline, long sleeves and a short, flouncy skirt that would focus all his attention on her legs. Brie took the pearls from their box and slid them across her lips, imagining where else those pearls might end up that night.

Putting the long strand around her neck, she slipped it under her dress at the back—a little tease for Sir.

Brie was meticulous as she applied her makeup and styled her hair. She wore it up to show off her long neck and added a few inviting curls to encourage him to nibble her throat.

Fifteen minutes before seven, she headed downstairs and found the limousine already waiting for her. She giggled nervously as the driver opened the door, but was surprised that Sir was not inside to greet her.

Brie found a note waiting for her on the leather seat instead.

Tonight we break the curse of the limo.

She kissed the ink of the note, loving his beautiful handwriting. It added a thrill to the adventure knowing he was waiting somewhere else for her to arrive.

Brie stared out of the window as the limousine made its way to the coast. The driver dropped her off at a private beach and instructed her to follow the sandy trail to her destination. He handed her a flashlight. "In case you get lost in the dark."

Brie thanked him before setting off, ready for the adventure to begin.

Without the moonlight to guide her, she found her little flashlight invaluable as she navigated the thick vegetation out to the beach. When she saw a fire burning, she turned off her light and followed its romantic glow.

Brie was surprised that Sir was not waiting for her as she approached the fire pit, but she found a blanket with a picnic basket and a black sash. She spied another note and picked it up.

Take off your shoes, put on the blindfold.
Kneel towards the ocean and await your Master.

Shivers of anticipation coursed through Brie as she followed his instructions. She knelt on the blanket, the black sash secured tightly, and listened for his approach, but the smell of the ocean and hypnotic sound of the waves overtook her senses and she jumped when she felt his touch.

He chuckled warmly. "Did I scare you?"

"Surprised is more the word."

Sir paused for a moment, then asked, "Did you bring the pearls?"

"Of course."

He swept his hand over the material of her dress, finding the pearls she had hidden underneath. "Ah…" Each pearl tickled her skin as he slowly pulled the long strand out from under her dress. He caressed her hard nipples and commented, "I see your body remembers the pleasure of pearls."

"I have never forgotten," she purred.

Sir looped the strand several times before placing it over her head and tying a knot, so that layers of pearls rested tight against her throat.

A collar of pearls, she mused.

"Tonight you will try different aphrodisiacs and tell me which one turns you on the most, téa," he explained.

She grinned. "Sounds arousing, Master."

"The first has been an old standby for centuries." Brie listened as he opened the basket, then Sir growled huskily, commanding, "Open."

She opened her mouth to take in his treat and quickly regretted it as the salty sliminess of a raw oyster filled her mouth.

"Swallow."

With pure determination, she gagged the nasty thing down and opened her mouth again.

"Not a fan?" he asked.

She shuddered. "No. Nothing sexy about that, Master."

"Maybe this is more to your liking…"

She smelled its sweet scent before he brought it to her lips. *Strawberry…* Brie purred as the skin of the fruit broke between her teeth and its sweet juices washed over her tongue. "Oh, yes. This definitely does it for me."

He kissed her juice-covered lips after he fed the last of it to her. "So sweet."

Sir acquired a new item from the basket and explained, "Like the oyster, this has a *long* history of increasing desire."

Brie closed her mouth, now suddenly wary. She'd read once that balut, a fertilized duck egg, was considered an ancient aphrodisiac. After the oyster, she couldn't stomach the thought. "Please, Sir. It's not balut, is it? Please say it isn't."

His amused laughter was not promising. "Open, téa."

"Please don't make me swallow it if it is, Master."

"You will swallow everything I give you."

She opened her mouth to please him, but she could not stop from whimpering as she did so.

"Wider, téa. Stick out your tongue."

With trepidation, she did as he asked. The seconds dragged by as she waited, her innocent tongue defenselessly exposed to the mysterious aphrodisiac he was offering.

Brie cried out the moment the first drop made contact with her tongue, then giggled as sweet honey covered it. The complex flavors of the golden liquid teased her mouth, delighting her taste buds. Sir dribbled some onto her bottom lip so that it slowly dripped down to her chin, then he moved in and seductively licked it off.

Brie moaned in pure pleasure.

"I take it honey agrees with you?"

"Very much, Master." She sought out his lips again, kissing Sir deeply as she shared what was left of the honey.

He broke the kiss, mumbling to himself, "And you thought I was going to feed you balut…"

She felt his warm breath against her ear when he commanded again, "Open."

This time she willingly offered her mouth to him. The texture of the next food was creamy and smooth, although it was not sweet like the honey. "I didn't realize avocados were considered an aphrodisiac."

He growled into her ear. "Oh, but they are… Avocados are the only fruits that look like a testicle hanging from the tree and female genitalia when they're halved and pitted. Certain religions even banned them to protect their parishioners from sinful thoughts."

Sir placed another piece of it in her mouth. Brie appreciated the seductive feel of the flesh and its sinful creaminess.

"Your thoughts?" he asked.

"I have new respect for the naughtiness of the fruit, Master."

"Now for one that is a personal favorite."

Brie leaned closer to him, excited to know what he enjoyed most.

"Tilt your head up and part those pretty lips."

She moaned when she felt his warm lips on hers as he kissed her with wine in his mouth. She remembered the distinctive flavor of berries and vanilla, and it took her straight back to that day on the island when he'd 'kidnapped' her.

"Your father's wine," she said when he broke the kiss. "Definitely a powerful aphrodisiac."

"Brunello di Montalcino *is* a powerful force," he agreed. Sir left a trail of light nibbles on her neck before murmuring into her ear, "And to think one day I will be celebrating our child's rite of passage with it."

Brie's heart fluttered at the thought.

Our child…

Sir spoiled Brie with several long kisses, imparting more of the red wine and stoking the flames of her desire.

"I need you," she whispered.

Sir lightly caressed the pearls around Brie's neck. "Patience, téa. We still have one left."

He collected it from the basket, telling her to open her mouth. "Women swear by this," he said in a low, sultry voice.

Sir placed a small morsel in her mouth, and she closed her lips around it as the decadently rich taste flooded her mouth. "Chocolate…"

"Does it turn you on, téa? Does it make you want to throw all caution to the wind and give in to your desire?"

Brie moaned as she felt his teeth graze her neck just above the pearls before he bit down.

"I'm burning with desire," she groaned.

"Then I think it's time to christen these black pearls." Her breath quickened as he untied the blindfold and let her watch as he carefully loosened the knot, removing the pearls from around her neck.

Sir lifted her dress over her head, leaving her naked before him. He then began to undress himself, his hard cock announcing the level of his arousal. He lay down beside Brie, holding the long strand of pearls. "Pearls are said to represent purity and harmony." He interlaced the fingers of his right hand with the fingers of her left. "Both attributes speak to your character. The purity of your love sustains me and the harmony of your spirit heals me."

Sir slowly wrapped the necklace around their wrists once and slipped one end through the opposite loop, pulling it tight. He then continued binding her to him, using the necklace like rope. When he reached the end, he laced the pearls back through the binding, securing it tightly.

"I have bound us together for a reason, téa."

She looked at their wrists joined by pearls, charmed by his creativity. "Why, Master?"

"I plan to show you how quickly a goddess becomes a slut."

Brie's loins contracted in pleasure as he placed her free hand on his rigid cock. "Your challenge is to make me come before you do."

She leaned closer and growled in his ear, "I *like* this challenge, Master."

"Whoever wins gets to decide where we will honeymoon."

"Anywhere?"

"Anywhere your little heart desires—provided you win, of course."

Brie frowned, realizing his strategy. "Did you just stack the odds in your favor by feeding me aphrodisiacs?"

Sir winked at her.

"You're playing dirty."

"It's about to get a whole lot dirtier, princess." Sir grabbed her throat with his unbound hand and started nibbling on her ear.

She felt a trickle of wetness between her legs, her body reacting favorably to his dominance. Determined to win, she started stroking his cock.

Sir held his bound wrist above her head, effectively pinning her left arm there as he moved out of reach, leaving a trail of kisses from her throat down to her breasts.

"Not fair," she cried as his tongue rimmed the outline of her areola, before he took her entire nipple into his mouth and started sucking. "Really not fair…" she moaned.

Brie reached out blindly with her right hand, stretching to find his cock. To his credit, Sir did not move once she found it. She wrapped her fingers around his hard shaft. Apparently he liked this game as well…

Maybe a little too much, she thought gleefully, when she felt the wetness of his pre-come dripping from his cock.

The natural lube made pleasuring him easier, and she soon found her rhythm as she stroked his length in slow, twisting motions.

Sir groaned, enjoying her attention. He removed his hand from her throat and began to caress her wet clit, giving as good as he got.

Brie arched her back, trying hard not to succumb to the delicious flood of heat he was creating. When he slipped his finger inside and found her swollen G-spot, she knew she was in trouble.

With a tighter hold, she pumped his shaft, hoping to break him before he broke her, but hearing Sir breathe heavily was such a turn-on… Her pussy started to pulse and she struggled to get away, but being bound to Sir made it impossible.

"Please…" she cried.

"You want to come?" he growled huskily in her ear.

"No…oooohhhhh," she moaned when Sir swirled his finger over the swollen spot.

Out of desperation, she changed the tempo of her stroking, slowing down rather than speeding up, concentrating all her attention on the head of his shaft.

When he stiffened against her, she felt victory was near. That was when his lips sought out her neck and he whispered, "And she comes…my goddess, my slut," as he bit down, sending chills rocketing straight to her groin.

Brie tensed as the first wave of her orgasm rolled over her against her will. She threw her head back, crying in frustration, "Nooo…" but it felt so good that soon she was moaning, "Yes…oh, yes…"

Before she'd finished climaxing, Sir joined her, his whole body shuddering as the warm liquid of his release covered her.

"That was so hot," she sighed as she looked up at the stars.

"And I won," he added with a grin.

"Not by enough to count."

He turned his head, raising his eyebrow at her. "Close only counts in horseshoes, babygirl."

"Cheater."

"Winner."

She laughed and sought out his warm body as the cool night breeze played with the sweat on her skin. She lightly kissed the 't' on his chest. "Where will the honeymoon be?"

"As with the wedding, it shall remain my secret."

She giggled, feeling too content to care. She held up their interlaced hands and gazed at them thoughtfully. "I know it will be amazing."

"I hope to take your breath away."

"You already do, Sir."

Sir leaned over and kissed her before undoing their pearl bond. He gathered her into his arms and they lay there, listening to the soothing sound of the ocean as the fire crackled beside them.

"This is enough," she declared.

White Russian

B rie woke up to the sound of two male voices in the kitchen. She quickly donned her silk robe and made her way out of the bedroom. She immediately recognized the deep tones of the Russian's laughter.

"Rytsar! What the heck are you doing here?"

"*Radost moya*," he said, his arms outstretched.

Brie looked at Sir as she hugged the burly man, shaking her head in surprise.

"Rytsar has come to escort you to Denver before you meet me in China," Sir explained.

She was stunned by his statement. "Why?"

Sir's smile faded. "I need to go to New York with Thompson. There are a few items that must be ironed out."

"With Lilly? Then I should go with you."

He shook his head. "Thompson will act as my liaison, so there will be no face-to-face contact with the girl. You, on the other hand, need to get that last bit of footage for your film."

"But I've decided not to—"

"No, Brie. To defy Mr. Holloway would be a grave mistake. Wallace and Miss Wilson know the reason you are coming. I leave it up to you to work out the details of the shoot."

Brie frowned. "Sir, I don't want to be separated from you again. Not when it's so close to the wedding."

"I'm here to act as your Master's stand-in," Rytsar declared. "You will not miss him."

Brie giggled. "While I'm grateful, Rytsar," she looked at Sir, "I want to be with you."

"And you will be—for a lifetime. It's unfortunate that this extra step is necessary to end the Beast's life."

Brie walked over to Sir, wrapping her arms around his waist. "At least you won't be alone when it's time."

"Although she is already dead, I will be grateful to have both of you beside me when she breathes her last."

"You are doing the right thing, *moy droog*," Rytsar assured Sir, slapping him on the back. "Since I have known you, she has haunted your life. It is time."

Sir laughed uncomfortably. "I'm unsure whether I can handle the loss."

Rytsar's tone was sober when he answered, "You will be surprised how much you miss the weight on your shoulders initially, but trust me, *moy droog*, you grow used to it."

Sir nodded. "I look forward to that day, old friend."

"Are you sure Lilly won't fight you over this?" Brie asked.

Sir's voice became ominous. "She will have no choice. Thompson and I are seeing to that. Once the Beast is gone, all familial ties will be severed."

"And you will finally be free," Rytsar stated.

"A new life," Sir agreed, kissing Brie on the top of the head.

She looked up and smiled. "As man and wife."

"With a kinky white Russian," Rytsar added, grabbing her ass in his strong hands.

"Hands off, old friend. We are practicing abstinence."

Rytsar smiled knowingly, taking his hand from her ass and placing it on her tummy. "That can only mean one thing."

"Well, we're going to start trying, at least," Brie said, blushing.

Rytsar stared at Sir. "Thank you, *moy droog*."

"For what? This will be my child, not yours," Sir joked.

Rytsar shook his head and said solemnly, "For showing me what's possible."

Silence followed his statement.

Eventually Sir nodded. "You said yourself the defective should not accept a lesser life."

"*Da...*" He gazed at Brie wistfully, then smiled. "I amaze myself with my wisdom."

Brie discovered just how possessive Rytsar could be when they traveled to Denver. Although Master Anderson graciously offered his home to them, the Russian would have none of it. "When you are under my protection, no other man will care for you."

It wasn't a topic up for discussion, so Brie accepted it when they stayed at a hotel instead. She quickly learned, however, that it also meant she had to ask permission whenever it involved others—even a simple phone call to Mary.

She had just dialed the number and hadn't even said hello yet when he hung up the phone. "Who are you calling?"

"Mary! Why did you do that, Rytsar?" Brie protested.

"No calls without permission."

"But why? I'm not wearing your temporary collar."

"You are precious to me, *radost moya*. I must know where you are and who you are talking to at all times. I will not fail you or your Master while you are under my watch."

The passion in his voice touched Brie, so she did not question him again. "May I call Mary?"

"*Da*, but you must okay any meetings with me before you commit to others."

Brie gave him a chagrined look. "Fine."

"Fine what?" he asked in his sexy Russian accent.

"Fine, Rytsar."

"*Nyet.*"

"Fine, Rytsar Durov."

"*Nyet.*"

"What, then?"

"You may address me as Ruler of My Universe."

Brie giggled, but answered dutifully, "Fine, oh Ruler of My Universe."

"Better, but I could do without the giggling."

She broke out in a peal of laughter, shaking her head as she called Mary again.

Naturally, Rytsar insisted on being present during the filming, confiding to her, "I still do not trust Wolf Boy."

"Should I get a shotgun for you?" she teased.

"No," he answered, with a smug look on his face. "My 'nines should do nicely if he crosses the line."

Mary had informed Brie that Faelan was recovering well, considering where he'd started from, but that she was still concerned about the scene. "*You* are not worth his health, Brie."

"I agree. I wasn't even planning to ask, but Sir insisted. I've been thinking about it and I believe what I have in mind shouldn't put any strain on his body. Really, I have no idea why Mr. Holloway is so obsessed with you."

"Eh, it doesn't surprise me."

"Why? Do you know him?" Brie asked, hoping to sate her curiosity.

Mary laughed. "No."

"Oh, so you just naturally assume he's obsessed because of your charm and good looks."

"You know it, Stinky."

"Well, I think he must have a mental disorder, just like Todd."

"Odd…"

"What's odd?"

"You're asking me for a favor and yet you insult me."

"Hey, what are friends for?"

Mary scoffed. "I find friendship highly overrated."

"Says the girl with no friends…"

Brie met the two at the Denver Academy, with Rytsar glued to her side.

Faelan was *not* thrilled to have a fellow Dom observing him. As soon as he entered the room, he asserted his dominance over the Russian.

"You, over there," Faelan ordered, pointing Rytsar to a far-off corner. "You will not speak or offer direction while I'm scening today."

Rytsar snorted. "One inappropriate word or touch, and you will be crying to the moon, Wolf Boy."

"Why did you have to bring him?" Faelan complained to Brie.

"Rytsar is my escort, as per Sir's orders."

Faelan's blue eyes sparkled with amusement. "What? Is Davis back to worrying about me now?"

Rytsar growled under his breath and started towards Todd, who immediately backed away from Brie. "Calm down, old man. I have no need to fish elsewhere." Faelan turned to Mary, looping his finger around the ring of her new collar, pulling her close. "This sub suits my needs just fine."

Brie was impressed by how good Faelan looked. He moved stiffly, hinting at the pain he still suffered, but his color was good and his eyes were just as magnetic as ever. Faelan's recovery seemed like a miracle, and she felt certain Mary had everything to do with it.

She explained the scene to Faelan, "I want this scene to showcase a simple lesson many subs experience, while letting you basically just lie there without having to tax your body."

Mary teased, "Oh, I'll make sure he taxes something."

Faelan winked at her. "Tax it, baby."

Rytsar grunted in the corner, their silly banter too much for him, but

Brie was thoroughly charmed by it.

"I don't want you undressing for this scene, Todd. Keep your shirt and tie on, as well as your pants. Women love a well-dressed man, and it will hide your recent scars from the camera. Oh, and do you mind calling her 'pet' for the scene?"

Faelan looked at Mary with a smirk.

Brie instructed Mary, "You will wear only your heels, bra and panties."

"Nice," Mary commented. "What do I get to address him as? Mother-fucker?"

Brie laughed. "No, you get to call him by his title."

Mary sighed, but faced her man and asked, "May I strip, Faelan?"

"Of course, pet. I want you to show that scowling Russian over there what he's missing."

Rytsar kept his eyes locked on Faelan with a fierce look of distrust.

Watching Mary undress had a visible effect on Faelan. He loosened his tie and undid several of the buttons of his white shirt. His exposed chest would read well on the camera, along with his magnetic blue eyes. No doubt women would eat this scene up.

"Okay, Todd, you'll sit here in the leather chair. I'll be filming directly in front of you. Try to find a comfortable position, because you'll be staying in it for the entire shoot."

Brie felt wickedly clever. She hadn't liked feeling pressured by Mr. Holloway to get this last shot, so she'd created a scene meant to tease the producer—as well as the audience.

"Now, Mary, remember you're supposed to be new at this."

"Yeah, yeah…"

"Don't 'yeah, yeah' me. This is serious. I want you to come off as a believable novice."

"I got this, Brie."

"Do you have any questions for me?" Brie asked Faelan before they began shooting.

"Sure." His eyes sparkled mischievously. "How many times do you think I could make you come with just my tongue?"

Rytsar answered for her from where he stood, "None, because you would be picking up your teeth from the floor after I gave you a proper Russian hello."

Brie smiled at Rytsar as she positioned herself behind the camera. "Mr. Wallace, I believe Rytsar is trying to protect you from a sexual harassment lawsuit."

Faelan's laughter was cut short as he sat down. Brie noticed him gri-macing with pain and figured it only served him right for baiting Rytsar like that.

"Mary, if you could open his shirt a little more…yes, that's it. Perfect."

"He fucking is," Mary agreed as she got down on her knees between Faelan's legs. "How do I look?"

"The back of your head is pure perfection."

Mary glanced over her shoulder. "I *can't* believe you told me to spend extra time on my makeup."

Brie snickered to herself.

"Whenever you're ready," Faelan said. She nodded and started her silent countdown before hitting *record*.

Faelan began the scene by caressing Mary's hair.

"Undo my belt and unzip my pants, pet. I have a new lesson for you."

Mary looked down at his crotch and hesitated for a second before doing what he asked.

"Do you see how hard you make your Master?"

She nodded, her long mane of blonde curls moving alluringly up and down her back with the movement of her head.

"Open your lips and take it into your mouth."

Mary moved with a lack of confidence as she made an awkward attempt to free his cock from its confines and giggled softly from the effort. The sound of her innocent laughter was charming.

She took his shaft in one hand and stared at it for a second before slowly lowering her head.

Faelan sucked in his breath, indicating the moment her lips made contact with him. Brie felt the first stirrings of desire in her nether regions.

Crap, this might prove a harder shoot than I thought.

Soon Mary's head was bobbing up and down, but it wasn't enough. "Deeper," Faelan commanded gently.

She took it a little deeper, not really challenging herself. "Deeper," he ordered, his tone more demanding.

Mary lowered her head and made a choking sound, popping back up as if she were scared by the feeling.

"That was good, pet. Try that again, but don't pull away this time," Faelan encouraged.

Mary went back down on him, lowering her head until she started to gag.

"Good, keep it there. Get your throat used to the feel of my cock."

Mary only lasted a few seconds more before she lifted her head, pretending to gasp for air.

"Again," he told her.

Mary obediently went back down on him, but this time when she tried to pull away, Faelan pressed her head lower, "Deeper, pet. That's it…" He continued to hold her even as she struggled to breathe.

When he let go, she came up gasping for breath.

He wiped her mouth, looking down lustfully at her. "There we go—I want to see your mouth dribbling with more spit."

Mary moaned softly, indicating her excitement at trying to please him.

"Do you want to try again, pet?"

Brie really liked how Faelan was demanding more but still taking it slow with Mary—encouraging with his praise rather than forcing her to submit.

Mary nodded enthusiastically. This time she went much lower, taking most of him into her throat, but when he started to thrust she began sputtering and struggled to break free. This time Faelan held her down on his shaft, saying repeatedly in a soothing voice, "Take it, pet, take it…"

She coughed when he finally released her and wiped the water from her eyes.

"A challenge, yes?" he asked.

"Yes, Faelan, but I like it."

"Good, because this time I'm going to fuck your pretty face."

Mary took several deep breaths to ready herself before descending on his cock again. As she took him into her mouth, he fisted her hair, forcing his cock even deeper down her throat. It was actually a turn-on to watch Mary struggle as she instinctively pushed her hands against him as he thrust.

"Hands, pet," Faelan warned her.

Mary put her hands behind her back and continued to take his lustful face-fucking.

Brie had to give the woman kudos. She totally believed, based on Mary's performance, that this was her first time.

Mary moaned loudly when Faelan finally released her.

"You like that, don't you?" he growled, pulling her head back to look him in the eye.

"Yes," she whispered hoarsely.

"For being such a willing student, I will come in your mouth."

Mary stared into his eyes, neither of them saying anything for several moments, the connection evident during their intimate yet voiceless exchange.

"Are you ready?"

Brie felt her pussy react to Faelan's question and rolled her eyes, vowing never to let Mary know a towel would be necessary after the filming of their scene.

When Mary nodded, Faelan commanded firmly, "Open."

He took her head in both hands and forced her mouth up and down his shaft, grunting with pleasure. Mary moaned enthusiastically, her hair bouncing rhythmically on her back with each thrust. Finally Faelan's body stiffened, his hands gripping her head as he released his come deep in her throat.

"Swallow, pet."

Brie bit her lip, panning back to show Mary's beautiful body, her hands still behind her back in a perfect submissive pose as Faelan finished off inside her mouth.

Well done, Mary…

Once Brie was finished packing up her equipment, she went over to them with Rytsar standing protectively by her side. "That was amazing to watch. I totally believed you were inexperienced, woman. How did you pull it off so convincingly?"

"It was easy, Stinky Cheese. I just pretended I was you."

Brie looked at her in shock, then burst out laughing. "You're such an ass, Mary."

Brie spent the night in the company of her dearest friends. Autumn had invited her over to join Tono and Lea for dinner. Naturally, Rytsar joined her as well, acting as her charming yet intimidating bodyguard.

As soon as she entered Autumn's home, Brie was attacked by Lea. "Girl! How lucky am I? I didn't think I'd get to see you again until the wedding."

"Yeah, I can't believe you're going to be there with me. It's so far to travel, you know?" Brie answered, hoping to trick Lea into telling her the wedding destination.

"Nebraska's not that far from here."

Brie couldn't tell whether Lea was teasing her or not. "Right, Nebraska…"

A deep red blush crept from Lea's cheeks to her breasts, as if she had just realized she'd said too much. She made a funny face and blurted, "What's the difference between Nebraska and yogurt?" Lea didn't even wait for Brie to answer before giving away the punchline. "Yogurt has an active living culture."

"But that's not a joke, girl, because it's true," Brie replied, swatting Lea's butt. As they made their way into Autumn's kitchen, she was left wondering if she had just been played. There was no way her wedding would be in Nebraska—no way!

Brie was impressed by Autumn's cooking skills. The girl had truly outdone herself, having made four different kinds of pizza for them to try. The pies filled the kitchen with their heavenly aroma as the cheese bubbled under the broiler. Brie noted she'd made some of Tono's favorites.

The Asian Dom was the picture of health, and his soulful spirit seemed to take over the room. He stood up and bowed to Rytsar and then to her. "It is a pleasure to see you both again."

If he was surprised by the presence of the Russian Dom, he didn't show any indication of it, but Brie explained, "Rytsar Durov is taking me to China to meet with Sir."

Tono's expression saddened. "Has the time finally come?"

Brie nodded, unable to tell him all that had gone on during her first trip to China. She had no doubt that Tono could tell there had been terrible complications, but he only said, "I'm sorry for your Master, but I know you will be a great comfort to him."

His simple encouragement soothed her troubled spirit, and she bowed. "Thank you, Tono. I take great solace in that."

Autumn cried out as she pulled the last pan of sizzling-hot pizza from the oven and quickly placed it on the table, sticking two of her fingers in her mouth.

"Are you okay?" Tono asked, moving to get up.

She waved off his concern. "No, no… It's nothing, Ren. Please don't get up."

Brie didn't miss that Autumn was calling Tono by his first name. That was huge in the Japanese culture and spoke of a deeper level of friendship. It appeared that her caring for the Kinbaku Master after his surgery had progressed their relationship in a positive direction.

Autumn gave her a hug. "So glad you could come for a surprise visit, Brie."

"Yeah, it seems there's no rest for the wicked, but at least I get the perk of seeing you guys again. By the way, Autumn, I forgot to introduce you. This is my good friend—and part-time bodyguard—Rytsar Durov."

Autumn glanced apprehensively at the impressive Russian. "Are you really her bodyguard?"

"In spirit," he answered with a slight smirk. "It is a pleasure to meet you, Miss Autumn. Or as we would say in my country—Miss *Osen*."

"Oh, I like that way that sounds, Mr. Durov."

"Most things sound better in Russian."

Autumn laughed, then asked shyly, a blush rising to her cheeks, "Can I tell you a joke? I've been saving this one for a while."

"Please," he answered.

Brie stifled a giggle, knowing Rytsar had no idea what he was in for.

Autumn seemed really nervous, but forged ahead anyway. "I'm really starting to dislike those stupid Russian dolls."

He tilted his head and asked, "Do you mean the *matryoshkas?*"

"Yeah…" She paused for a moment. "They just seem so full of themselves."

Rytsar threw back his head and laughed. Not just a polite, forced kind of laugh, but an all-out rolling thunder of a laugh. The entire kitchen rocked with it, and everyone soon followed.

That was one of the best Brie had heard—and who better to share that joke with than Rytsar?

Goodbye

T he plane ride to China was such an excruciatingly long one that encouraged either sleep or deep conversation.

It was something that Brie actually appreciated, since she was with Rytsar. Once the stewardesses finished fawning over the Russian Dom and had retired to their stations, Brie turned to him and asked, "What happened with the girl from America after she revealed your name? Has there been any fallout from it?"

He shook his head, an amused look on his face. "You Americans…"

"What?"

"So tenacious."

"Why? What did she do?"

"It's not her, it's your damn reporters. Every few weeks, a new one shows up at my door begging for an exclusive interview."

"So they know where you live now?" Brie asked with concern.

"It was only a matter of time, *radost moya*. Thankfully, no serious professionals, just little girls sent from the entertainment side of your news. So strange, the fascination you Americans have with celebrities…"

Brie lowered her voice, "Have you heard from the Russian police?"

"*Nyet*. Although I'm getting too much attention, having young female reporters from America hound me weekly has only made me a target for jest."

Brie sat back in her chair, sighing with relief. "I'm glad to hear it, Rytsar. I've really been worried."

He confided, "I've been tempted to show a few of the obstinate ones my true interests when they flirt so outrageously, hoping to get an interview. However, I do not think they could handle it."

"I agree," Brie said, laughing. "Most girls think being tickled with a feather is kinky. They have no idea what they'd be in for with you."

Rytsar's expression changed when he shared, "The girl, Stephanie, did send me a letter. I have not answered it because it would only complicate matters, but I keep it with me." Rytsar pulled out his leather wallet and took out a folded note, handing it to Brie.

She unfolded the letter, noticing the perfect penmanship, and wondered how many times the girl had rewritten it, wanting it to be flawless.

Dear Rytsar Durov,

I have not been able to stop thinking about you and what you did for me.

It's hard being back home. I'm not the same person. No one understands me. Only someone who was there could know how I feel.

I know it's stupid, but every day I listen for a knock on the door, hoping you are there to rescue me from this strange existence. I feel so alone. You told me I am a survivor and that has helped me on those days when nothing makes sense.

I feel so ungrateful, because you have done so much for me. How can one person ever truly repay another for saving their life? I would do anything, give anything to do just that for you. Please, Rytsar, tell me what I can do. It would make me so happy to fulfill the debt I owe you.

Sincerely, Stephanie

"She is on the edge, *radost moya*. This letter is like taking a peek into Tatyana's soul." He glanced at the letter, stating, "It hurts me to read it."

Brie wrapped her arms around him. His whole body was tense, the muscles of his arms shaking with unreleased emotion. "She'll be okay," she assured him.

"I have sent a counselor to her, one who has much experience with freed sex slaves, but I'm uncertain whether it will be enough."

"You have done more than most people would ever do, Rytsar. You have to trust she can recover from it."

He looked at her, all his defenses down. "Do you know what my given name is?"

"No. Sir never told me."

Rytsar smiled. "He is a trustworthy comrade."

The Russian's intense blue gaze caused her to momentarily stop breathing when he spoke. "When my mother passed, I refused to be called by the name she'd given me, preferring my title instead." He looked down at her tenderly. "I would like to hear it spoken from your lips."

"What is your given name?"

"Anton."

Brie placed her hand on his square jaw and smiled when she said it. "Anton."

Tears came to his eyes. "Thank you, *radost moya.*"

Rytsar folded up the letter and placed it back in his wallet. He stared out the window, seemingly lost in a sea of past pain and regret.

Priceless one… Brie knew that was the meaning of his name and could appreciate the power it must have over him. His mother was gone—how or why was still a mystery to Brie, but she suspected it had everything to do with his father.

Don't give up, Stephanie, Brie called out in her head, sending positive thoughts to the girl he'd rescued. *People are counting on you to survive.*

Rytsar's demeanor changed once they landed in Chengdu. He stayed beside her, his hand gripping the back of her neck. It was a very possessive hold that let others know to stay away.

"It's okay, Rytsar," Brie said, looking up at him. "I've been here before. It's a safe city."

He shook his head. "*Nyet.* There are human traffickers looking for foreigners like you. You are *not* safe."

Brie quickly scanned the airport in shock, wondering as each person passed which one held evil intentions behind their stoic expression. It was a frightening thought that Brie had never considered.

She could not hold back her excitement, however, when she recognized a familiar face in the sea of Chinese. "May I?" she asked Rytsar.

He released his hold, and Brie ran straight for Sir, nearly tripping over herself in her haste.

"Slow down, babygirl."

Brie buried her head in his chest, sighing with relief.

"Did Durov treat you well?" Sir asked, sounding concerned.

"I was the model of decorum," Rytsar answered as he walked up.

"He was, Sir. I'm just thrilled to see you."

Sir shook Rytsar's hand. "Thank you for taking care of her. I've had enough to worry about."

"How did it go in New York?" Rytsar asked.

"It was worse than I imagined, but it's done. Time to face the last unpleasant task."

"*Moy droog*, keep your eye on the prize. You're to be married in a few days."

Sir looked down at Brie. "I hope it's everything you've dreamed of."

"If I'm marrying you, it will be."

He ruffled the top of her head. "Good, because I questioned the location, although I know it means a lot to your parents."

Brie shot a look at Rytsar, hoping to see a look of amusement, but he just smiled sympathetically at Brie.

Oh, wow, I really am getting married in Nebraska…

She sighed, realizing it didn't matter. Although she had hoped for someplace exotic, as long as Sir was the groom, she could have her wedding in the middle of a garbage dump and still be happy.

"What are the plans for today?" Rytsar asked him.

"We go to the hotel and partake of your favorite beverage. Tomorrow I will face my demons."

Brie took Sir's hand in hers and squeezed it. A silent reminder that she would be with him every step of the way.

Brie hadn't seen Ruth since the meeting at Mr. Thompson's office, and was unprepared when she walked into the luxurious private hospital room. Sir had spared no expense keeping the woman comfortable, despite her condition.

But it wasn't the accommodations that threw Brie off, it was Ruth herself. It was as if time had stood still, just as Sir had described—like Sleeping Beauty in the fairy tale. Ruth looked as if she were resting peacefully, a slight smile on her pink lips. It was disturbing on so many levels.

Brie could finally sympathize with Lilly for believing Ruth was still alive, because it truly seemed she might wake up at any moment. No wonder Sir had struggled with this decision…

A woman walked in wearing a crisp white outfit. She stopped short when she saw them and hastily explained, "I am here to do Madame's daily exercises."

"It's not needed anymore," Sir told her.

The woman bowed her head and left the room.

Brie felt tears threatening when she saw the look on Sir's face. It was killing him inside to do this. She put her arm around him in support.

"I hate you," he said, his voice full of venom as he stared down at his mother. "I hate that you are making me do this. I want to slap that fucking smirk off your face."

Rytsar slapped Ruth's face hard, the sickening sound of it echoing in the room.

"Why did you do that?" Brie asked in horror.

Rytsar told Sir, "She's not here, *moy droog*. You're talking to a ghost."

Sir nodded.

"Even though she is gone, if you would find solace in beating her, I will shut the door and let you have at it."

Brie's jaw dropped at the suggestion, but she kept silent in case Sir was seriously considering it.

"Beating a dead body would bring me no peace."

"Fine, but I do recommend screaming at it. There is great satisfaction to be had in letting your rage out."

Again Sir nodded.

"Would you like us to stand outside the door?" Rytsar asked.

"Yes."

Brie willingly went with Rytsar, although she was surprised that Sir wanted her to leave.

Rytsar shut the door, standing in front of it with his arms crossed while Sir's impassioned ranting began. Although Brie could hear the pain and anger in his voice, she could not make out his words.

The Russian looked down at her. "Do not feel bad that he sent you out. There are things that should remain between them. Memories too terrible to be shared."

"Why? Did he share them with you?"

"No, *radost moya*, I speak from my own experience."

"I'm sorry, Rytsar."

"There is no need to be sorry. It's not your burden to carry."

Brie frowned as she stared at the closed door, wishing with all her heart that she could share some of the burden Sir still carried. His tirade went on for what seemed like hours, then the room became deathly silent.

As the silence stretched on, Brie braved cracking open the door and found Sir on his knees beside the bed.

"Sir?"

When he did not respond, Brie entered the room and approached him hesitantly.

"Sir, are you okay?"

He did not look up, but answered in a broken voice, "No."

Brie knelt beside him and slipped her hand into his. "I'm here for you."

Sir looked up and questioned her. "Why do I still care? Why do I have any empathy for this beast of a woman?"

"She was a good mother when you were young. She loved both you and your father once."

"I wish I could forget," he snarled. "I don't want to feel any love towards her."

"You may hate me for saying it, but I don't want you to forget. I believe it's important to hold on to what was good, because it shaped you into the man you are today."

"It was all a lie."

"I don't think it was, but even if it was, you had a good childhood—you said so yourself. Hold on to it and let *that* be the legacy your parents leave behind."

Sir stood up, and stared at Ruth for several minutes before he took her limp hand. "Momma…"

Brie felt tears well up at the sound of love in his voice when he said the simple name.

"There was a time I loved you. It is my reality, although I wish I could deny it. I loved the games you played with me when we waited for Father's return. You let me rescue you from pirates and we explored the deepest jungles of Africa together from the safety of our living room. Your enthusiasm and creativity was something I cherished as a boy." He paused, looking at her frighteningly beautiful face. "It's hard for me to reconcile there was ever a time I felt safe and loved in your arms."

Tears began to fall as Brie watched Sir gather his mother's limp body in his arms and hug her. "But I'm still here, Momma. The little boy you once loved—your little *tesoro*. There's no reason to be frightened. The end of your suffering is here. It's time for you to let go…"

He laid her gently back down and said to Brie, "Tell Rytsar to get the doctor."

She silently exited the room, so choked up with emotion she was barely able to speak when she passed on the information to Rytsar. She returned to Sir, holding his hand in silent solidarity as they waited.

All three of them stood together and watched as the doctor began removing the tubes, saving the respirator for last.

"Are you ready, Mr. Davis?"

Sir closed his eyes, letting out a long breath. When he opened them again, his tone was resolute. "Yes."

Rytsar put his hand on Sir's shoulder as Sir wrapped his arm around Brie.

Once the respirator was turned off, Ruth's body started jerking as it fought unsuccessfully to take another breath.

"Go in peace, Momma. I forgive you…"

Brie began sobbing silently as Ruth's struggles ceased and the heart monitor went flat. The doctor checked her over before pronouncing her dead.

It wasn't until then that Sir cried. Brie knew he was mourning the death of the young mother he remembered, but Brie cried for an entirely different reason. Her pain came from knowing that Ruth would never have the chance to undo the wrongs she had done.

When the nurses came in to care for the body, Sir wiped the remaining tears from his eyes and announced, "We're done here."

They walked out of the hospital without saying a word. Rytsar hailed a cab and they went directly to the airport. He said his goodbyes as soon as they entered the building.

"I'm sorry to leave so soon, but I must run if I am to make my flight."

He leaned down and gave Brie a crushing hug. "I will see you in a few days, *radost moya*. Save a dance for me."

He put his hand on Sir's shoulder and grasped it tightly. "It will take time to adjust, but the worst is over, *moy droog*. Concentrate on the wedding, and deal with the lingering effects later. They aren't going anywhere."

"Sound advice, old friend."

Sir gave him a hug that lasted longer than normal, causing several passing businessmen to stare. The two men slapped each other hard on the back before letting go.

It was difficult to watch Rytsar walking away—it felt like part of their strength was leaving with him.

"Come, Brie," Sir said, handing her a plane ticket. She looked down to see if they were heading to Nebraska and was shocked to see the word "Italy" written on her ticket. Sir explained, "I thought it was important that we see my grandparents before we get married."

"I think we all need that, Sir."

"I agree, babygirl." Sir placed his hand on the small of her back as he escorted her through the busy airport. The despondent look on his handsome face was enough to break a girl's heart.

La Famiglia

B rie was just as enchanted by the island as she had been the first time they'd taken the boat ride to Portoferraio. She could see the change in Sir as they drew closer to his father's hometown. He faced into the ocean breeze coming off the water, a look of expectation and exhilaration on his face.

She felt it too—a sense of coming home.

Sir smiled and squeezed her hand as the ferry approached the port and docked. "It's good to be back."

"It's been too long," she agreed.

The sky was a brilliant blue and the sun shone down on them with its gentle warmth as they walked the narrow streets towards his grandparents' home. Brie was captivated by the bright magenta flowers that graced the walls and fences of many of the buildings.

"What are these called? They're absolutely beautiful, Sir." She took a branch in her hand to smell it and quickly let go, surprised that the flowers had nasty thorns.

Sir laughed as he brought her fingers to his lips and kissed them. "They're bougainvilleas. Beautiful to look at but painful to cuddle."

She giggled, taking his arm as they continued their trek up the steep hill. "Have you ever considered living here, Sir?"

He stopped and looked towards the ocean. "Maybe when we're older and life has slowed down for us."

Brie snuggled against him. "Wouldn't it be lovely walking these streets as a happy old couple?"

He gazed down at her and smiled. "Yes, it would."

Sir led her to the apartment with the vivid red door Brie remembered well, and he knocked. From inside she heard the excited voices of numerous people. "It seems they're expecting us this time."

Sir's Aunt Fortuna, whom Brie had met on their first visit, opened the door wide and grabbed him. "Thane!" A flurry of Italian words followed, which obviously meant she was glad to see him. She ushered them inside, directing the two upstairs.

At the top of the stairs stood Sir's grandfather with his arms out-stretched. *"Nipotino!"* There was excited chatter as other members of his family gathered around him, wanting to welcome Alonzo's son home.

Brie scooted to the side, watching the excitement, hoping someday she would be greeted with the same enthusiasm.

"Brianna," a gentle voice called behind her.

She turned to see Sir's grandmother grinning up at her. Brie bent down to give the frail woman a hug. Brie was surprised by the crushing strength of her embrace. She might be tiny and old, but the woman was *strong*—so much stronger than the last time they'd met.

"It is so good to see you again," Brie said. When she saw the look of confusion on the woman's weathered face, she said hesitantly in Italian, *"Buongiorno."*

The old woman smiled and grabbed her cheeks, kissing her on the lips. *"Buongiorno."* His grandmother then made her way through the crowd to greet her grandson.

It was beautiful to watch, this apartment full of people who were thrilled to be in the presence of Sir. Not because of his reputation and many talents, but simply because he was family.

Brie and Sir were taken up several flights of stairs, all the way to the roof, where tables had been set out for a meal. Brie and Sir were directed where to sit, and the men of the family sat down with them while the women disappeared back inside. They returned a few minutes later with platters upon platters of food.

When all the ladies had set down the food and taken their seats, silence ensued.

Brie looked at Sir and noticed that his head was bowed. She did the same and listened to the beautiful sounds of his grandfather's prayer. A hearty "Amen" followed from all, and everyone dug in. Unlike the dinner at Isabella's, Sir's family served themselves. It was much less formal and much more to her liking.

Although she could not follow much of the conversation, Brie kept hearing the word *'matrimonio'* thrown around. The word for wedding was being said with joy and excitement, but she noticed that Sir's grandmother was *not* happy. It showed in the woman's face and in her voice.

"What's going on with your grandmother, Sir?" Brie asked.

He sighed deeply. "We're at an impasse."

"What do you mean?"

"My grandmother wants us to get married in church. She's not happy about my decision to have a civil ceremony."

This was the first Brie had heard anything about the wedding, and she pressed. "Civil ceremony, Sir?"

"I see no point in getting married in a church when neither you nor I are believers. Hell, I'm still on the fence if there even is a God."

His grandmother started talking, the tone of her voice expressing her anger. Sir's grandfather started in, and then the entire family began adding their two cents. It seemed they were very passionate about having a church wedding.

His grandmother looked at Brie and said in disbelief, "No God?"

Brie didn't know how to respond but nodded her head. "I…believe there's a God."

"Church?" the grandmother asked plaintively.

Having never gone to church other than attending other people's weddings or funerals, Brie could only shake her head no.

His grandmother's eyes grew wide and she started back on lecturing Sir. He stood up, his eyes flashing with anger as he argued with the tiny woman. Brie was shocked to see Sir react in such a way to his grandmother.

What was supposed to be a joyous occasion seemed to be causing nothing but a terrible rift between them.

"Sir," Brie said quietly. When he didn't respond, Brie said more loudly, touching his arm, "Sir."

He sat back down and took her hand in his. "What is it, Brie?"

"If it would make your grandmother happy, I wouldn't mind getting married in a church."

Sir sighed. "I appreciate the sentiment, babygirl, but you don't understand. We are not allowed to get married in my grandparents' church unless we are practicing Catholics."

Brie grinned, the tension in the air momentarily forgotten. "Does that mean we're getting married *here*—in Italy?"

He kissed her hand. "Yes, Brie, it does."

She broke out in a smile, looking over at his family, bursting with love for them. Without explanation, she got up and hugged each and every one, saving the last hug for Sir. "We're getting married in Italy!"

The family was unsure how to react to her joy in the midst of a heated argument. Sir explained. "They had no idea you didn't know."

Brie smiled at them all, throwing together Italian words she knew, trying to express her joy. *"Grande famiglia, ti amo."* She hoped it meant "Big family, I love you," but their silence was disconcerting.

His grandfather stood up and put his arms out to her. Brie grinned as he enfolded her in his embrace. The conversation started up again, but with a much more loving tone. Brie looked over at Sir, her eyes brimming with happy tears.

After the meal, Sir sat down with his grandparents, pulling out some papers from his suitcase and handing a set to them and to Brie. He told her, "Read it over carefully. This is what will be said at the ceremony. There's nothing romantic about it, simply a dry list of what makes up a marriage. The government requires that it be recited in Italian, so I want you to read over the English version now so you understand what is being said."

His grandmother spat at the paper in disgust, handing it back to Sir, highly displeased.

Brie looked the paper over and was surprised that it sounded more like a list of rules than wedding vows. "Are there any other scripts we can choose from?"

"For our marriage to be legal, this is how it must be."

Brie looked through it again. There was only one point in the whole ceremony where she was expected to speak. "How do I say 'I do' in Italian, Sir?"

He smiled. *"Lo voglio."*

All of the women in the room let out an audible, "Awww…"

Brie blushed, repeating it several times until she had the pronunciation right. "So that's all I need to do, just say 'I do' and we're married?"

"For a civil ceremony, yes."

She looked sympathetically at his grandmother, better understanding her displeasure. "Tell her it's the love of the couple, not the ceremony that matters."

Sir translated her words.

"How do I tell her it's okay?" Brie asked.

"Va bene."

She smiled at the old woman and said with passion, *"Va bene."*

His grandmother shook her head sadly, patting Brie on the hand.

"Well, that went well," Sir joked when they left hours later.

"I love the idea of getting married here, Sir. It's worth the discord with your family."

"We're not getting married here, Brie."

Brie turned to face him. "No?"

"No. I have something very special in mind."

"The island where you and your father used to treasure hunt?"

He chuckled loudly. "No—that would have been a challenge to pull off."

"Where, then?"

"You'll have to wait and see, Miss Bennett."

They strolled down the street towards the dock in silence.

"Sir, does your family know what happened to your mother?" Brie asked.

"No, and I don't plan to tell them. At least, not for now. She caused my father's family too much grief as it is, and I don't want it tainting our wedding in any way."

She took his hand. "I'm sorry you've had to carry that burden alone."

"I'm not alone, babygirl," he said, smiling down at her.

Sir walked Brie to a small house on the beach. She was surprised to see it was full of people. "Your friends, Sir?"

He shook his head as he opened the door. "Not my friends—*our* friends."

"Surprise!" everyone shouted.

Brie looked at the group in shock, stunned to see her dearest friends. "I can't believe you're here!" she cried as she ran to hug Lea.

"I know—I never knew Nebraska looked a whole lot like Italy," Lea said with a snicker.

"You liar," she complained good-naturedly.

Brie looked over her shoulder at Tono, who was standing next to Autumn. "You guys are here too?"

"In the flesh," Tono replied. "Your fiancé insisted."

Brie turned to Sir. "I can't believe you did this."

"What's the point of a wedding if your family and friends aren't there to celebrate with you?"

"Brianna."

She heard her dad's voice and searched the room expectantly. "Mom, Dad!" she cried, running to them. "I can't believe this!"

"Your fiancé is an extravagant man," her father said, as her mother hugged Brie.

When her mother let go, Brie heard another familiar voice behind her.

"What am I, chopped liver?" Rytsar complained, picking her up and giving her a bear-hug. Brie struggled to breathe in his tight grip.

When he put her down, she laughed. "And I thought you were headed back to Russia."

"I am, *radost moya*—after my layover in Italy."

"Could you stack the cigarettes for me, Miss Bennett?" Mr. Reynolds asked beside her.

"I haven't seen you and Judy in ages," Brie exclaimed, breaking out in delighted giggles as she hugged him.

"You two have been busy little beavers," Judy said, giving Brie a squeeze. "I'm sure we'll see more of each other once you settle down."

"I hear you're planning for a bun in the oven," Mr. Reynolds whispered.

Brie blushed, surprised that he knew. "Sir told you?"

"He'll make a fine father. I think he just needed a little reassurance from his Unc."

She looked over at Sir and nodded. "I agree, Unc."

Brie squeaked when strong hands covered her eyes.

"Guess who."

Not only did she recognize his voice, but he had a distinctive scent she'd become familiar with, having visited his home on several occasions. "Master Anderson!"

"How did you know?"

"I smelled you," she answered.

He sniffed his armpits and shrugged. "Dang, and I even showered today."

Brie laughed, and her smile widened even more when she saw Mary. She walked over to her and joked, "Long time no see."

"Bet you didn't expect to see me here, did you?"

"Nope. Not at all, but I'm thrilled."

"The doctors said Faelan can't travel for a while, but he insisted I come, and wanted me to give you this…" Mary surprised Brie by hugging her.

It made Brie all teary—the love of both Mary and Faelan being conveyed in the embrace. She dabbed her eyes afterwards. "Please let Todd know I deeply appreciate his sacrifice letting you come…as well as the heartfelt hug."

"I'll be sure to tell him."

Mary seemed to be glowing with an inner satisfaction, so much so, that Brie felt compelled to say, "I have to admit, woman, you're looking especially good—all domesticated and docile."

"You know how to cut a woman down," Mary complained, but then she smiled. "However, you're right. I do find myself enjoying the collared life."

Brie nodded in understanding.

She rejoined Sir, soaking in the joy of the moment. "I don't think I could be any happier, Sir."

He kissed the top of her head. "Good. That's what I was going for, Miss Bennett. Do you know what this is?" he asked, gesturing to the group.

She shook her head, smiling.

"This is our wedding party. Rytsar is my best man, Lea your maiden of honor, Anderson and Nosaka my groomsmen, Mary and Autumn your bridesmaids, your parents, and my uncle and aunt acting as my parents for the ceremony."

Brie looked them over with a sense of awe. They were an incredible collection of people, and each had significantly influenced their journey.

All the sadness surrounding Ruth's death and the tension caused by the civil ceremony melted away that evening as Brie and Sir celebrated their upcoming nuptials with their closest friends and family.

I Do

Brie and Sir left Isola d'Elba early the next day. He insisted that she wear a blindfold for the trip. She found it romantic and adored the BDSM feel as he led her around in broad daylight.

Whenever strangers asked why, Sir explained that he was surprising his soon-to-be bride, and they gushed with congratulations. It seemed everyone loved a wedding, even when they didn't know the bride and groom.

Sir had her stand on the deck of the ferry so she could feel the ocean breeze on her face. "As you know, one of my loves is the ocean," Sir told her.

Brie nodded. "It has a life of its own. I feel like I'm breathing in its energy."

"That's an excellent way to describe it. The ocean does give off an energy all its own." He kissed her on the shoulder and asked, "Would you like to know where you're getting married tomorrow?"

She laughed. "No, Sir. I'm not curious in the least."

"Fine."

When he said nothing more, she begged, "Please, Sir, any little hint would be appreciated."

He chuckled, kissing her other shoulder. "My family has a long history here. Many generations, going back to the eleven-hundreds."

"I can't imagine having a family line with that kind of history," Brie confessed.

"It means I'm related to influential people who are honored to help out Alonzo's son."

"You have my curiosity piqued, Sir."

"Good—then I'll leave it at that."

Brie stuck out her bottom lip. "Such a cruel Master."

"I prefer to think of myself as a devoted fiancé."

Once the ferry had docked, Sir guided her down the long flight of stairs and off the boat, telling her the blindfold must remain.

"You're lucky I get off on this kind of thing, Sir."

He chuckled. "I do have method behind my madness, babygirl. I want to you to be fully aware of your surroundings. The smell, the temperature of the air, the sounds, even the feel of the ground beneath your feet—not only what you see. This land is a part of me, Brie, and I want you to be familiar with every aspect of it."

She did as he asked and took in everything, appreciating the language of the people as they walked by, the sound of the birds above her, the mechanical smell of the train station—everything. She was determined not to miss a single characteristic of his Italy.

After a lengthy train ride, Sir transferred Brie into a tiny convertible, which he drove way too fast once he got out of the metropolitan area. She could tell by his laughter that he was having fun as he whipped around the corners of the windy roads. She laughed along with him, loving the aromatic air and the quiet of the country roads once they left the bustling city behind.

When Sir finally pulled up to their destination he slammed on the brakes, causing a cloud of dust to swirl around them. "Do you have any idea where you are, Brie?"

She didn't answer him until she got out of the car, noting the freshness of the air after the dust had settled. It reminded her of the mountain air of Colorado, but there was an added sweetness to it. She listened to the chirping birds and the buzzing of bees nearby. She slipped off her shoes and felt ticklish grass between her toes and announced, "I think we're in hill country, but I don't know where exactly in Italy, Sir."

"Fair enough. Hold out your hand."

Sir walked her to a wall and placed her hand on it. "What do you think this is?"

She felt the rough surface. Believing they were in farming country, she guessed it was a simple building made of stone. "Is it an old barn?"

He laughed. "Definitely not a barn, but it's a reasonable guess."

Sir led her through an entryway and she felt the coolness of an enclosed room around her. There was a slight echo to it, hinting that it was large.

"You may take off your blindfold now."

Brie untied it and let the silk fall into her hands. She gasped when she saw the intricately painted scenes of rolling vineyards on the walls, with gold accents on the ceiling above. "What is this place?" she asked in awe.

"A castle owned by my great, great, great grandfather."

"We're getting married in a castle?"

"A castle in Tuscany," Sir answered, kissing her on the lips. "I wanted to wow you, babygirl."

"Consider me wowed…"

Sir pulled out two rings from his pocket. "Tomorrow, at the ceremony, we will be exchanging these rings. I wanted you to see yours before we do so."

Brie picked up the delicate ring, the entire band encrusted with diamonds. "It's beautiful, Sir."

"Look at the inscription inside."

She tilted the ring and saw an outline of a condor and the word *Mine* written on it. "It's perfect, Sir. Did you look at the engraving on yours?"

Sir shook his head, examining his wedding band closely. Brie had picked that particular ring because she liked the combination of black tungsten and white gold. It had a manly look befitting a Dom.

Sir read the inscription out loud, "Condors forever." He chuckled, charmed by the similarity. "Although we won't say vows for the civil ceremony, Brie, I want you to think what you would say to me. Tell me with your eyes when we exchange these symbols of our commitment."

"That's so romantic, Sir."

He leaned down to kiss her, and the two remained locked in the embrace—lost in their own little world.

After a morning of feminine pampering, Brie was met by Lea, Mary and Autumn who'd come to collect her. They led her through the labyrinth of halls in the castle to an isolated room, where her mother was waiting for her with the wedding gown.

It looked even more beautiful than Brie remembered. Her mom held it up proudly for her to see, but Brie noticed an odd expression on her mother's face as she stared at the back of the gown.

"Did something happen to the dress?" Brie cried.

Her mother smiled. "Something most definitely happened to the dress. I have to assume your fiancé had something to do with it." She turned it around to show Brie.

The beautiful lace gown now had three long strands of white pearls set at the shoulders, the loops draping down the back. The addition artfully complemented the shape of the scooped back and added an extra element of sophistication.

"I can't believe he did that," Brie said as she ran her fingers over the pearls. "They have a special meaning to us," she explained to her mother.

"I must say Thane has excellent taste, sweetheart. Shall we see how it looks on you with the new embellishment?"

"Yes please." Brie's heart skipped a beat as her mother lifted the dress over her head with Lea's assistance. The silk of the lining slid down over her body, caressing her with its soft embrace as the lace train pooled behind her.

Brie turned her head to admire the added loops of pearls caressing her back. Her mother was about to remove the cloth covering the full-length mirror, but Brie stopped her. "No, Mom! In Italy, the bride isn't allowed to see herself before the wedding."

"What fun is that?" Lea complained. "You should see how beautiful your ass looks in that dress. You're looking mighty fine, girlfriend."

"Actually, Brie, a bride *can* look in the mirror if she takes off one of her gloves," Mary informed her.

Brie rolled her eyes. "Ah…I'm not wearing any gloves, genius."

Mary had a superior look on her face when she fished out a long, thin box from her purse and handed it to Brie. "I happen to have a gift for you, although I am unsure now if you deserve it."

Brie smiled as she opened the box and took out two fingerless gloves made of delicate lace. "They're exquisite, Mary."

She shrugged. "I bought them just in case you wanted to play by the rules, but feel free to use them with Sir if you prefer."

Brie giggled as her mother turned a deep shade of red. Brie could only guess what she was imagining. The funny thing—whatever it was—she was probably right.

Lea slipped both gloves onto Brie's hands, stating, "Let's play by the rules, then. 'Cause you've got to see yourself in this dress."

She took off one glove and held it in her hand as her mother pulled away the cover from the mirror.

Brie was stunned by her own reflection. The princess neckline accentuated her full breasts, making a beautiful backdrop for the Italian lace that covered the entire dress. She turned to the side to admire the back of the gown. It was even more beautiful than she'd imagined. The strands of pearls accentuated her back and seemed to direct the eye downward to her shapely bottom, but Brie suspected it was really meant to draw the eye to the brand that barely showed. She knew with certainty that Sir's eyes would be riveted to that particular spot.

"Wait, the dress is too short," her mother lamented as she examined the hemline.

"Nope!" Lea announced, handing Brie a small silver box. "Your fiancé has something he wanted you to wear instead of heels."

Brie giggled with delight as she lifted the lid. Inside was a set of golden jewelry for her feet, accented with tiny pearls.

"He says he wants you barefoot for the wedding."

Barefoot and pregnant? Brie wondered, smiling to herself.

"What an odd request," her mother complained.

Lea helped Brie to take off her heels and stockings, replacing them with the jewelry that looped around her second toe and attached around her ankle. It made an enticing jingling sound when she moved her feet.

Brie knew it was slave jewelry and loved the symbolism behind his gift, even though she still wore her collar. On this most vanilla of ceremonies, Sir was reminding her that she was his beloved submissive.

"What girl gets married in bare feet?" her mother protested.

"I'm sure it's an ancient Italian custom, Mom."

Mary piped up, "No one will think it strange but us, and we're the only ones who know."

Her mother nodded. "I suppose you're right. The dress *will* cover her feet."

"It makes your feet look so darn adorable with your pink toenails, girlfriend," Lea squealed. "I could just kiss those cute little piggies."

"Probably what Sir plans to do tonight," Mary said, adding under her breath, "among other things."

Brie's mother blushed again and awkward silence ensued.

Luckily, there was a knock on the door and Sir's grandmother entered the dressing room. She took one look at Brie and tears came to her eyes.

Brie reached out to her. "*Nonna…*"

The old woman held a small silk pouch, which she handed to her. "*Qualcosa di blu.*"

Brie caught the word 'blue' and opened the pouch with excitement. Inside was a tiny antique stick-pin made of gold with a single blue crystal. Brie smiled at her, knowing it was meant as good luck. It seemed some traditions were universal.

Sir's grandmother took it from Brie with her frail hands to pin it on her wedding dress. To Brie's surprise, she let out a small gasp while she was pinning it. Sir's grandmother touched the lace of the gown with a look of wonder. She called out excitedly, and called out again when no one came.

Aunt Fortuna ran into the room, looking upset. "What, *Nonna?* Why the big fuss?"

Sir's grandmother pointed to Brie's dress, speaking excitedly.

Aunt Fortuna had the same look of amazement as she lovingly stroked the lace. She gazed up at Brie, shaking her head in disbelief. "Where did you get this?"

"I found the dress waiting for me at a little dress shop in Los Angeles."

Aunt Fortuna put her hand to her lips, looking like she was about to cry. "I made this lace, Brianna. The fact that this dress found you...that is *destino*."

Brie threw her arms around her. "Then I must thank you for helping to create my gown."

Sir's grandmother joined in on the hug. If there had been any misgivings before about the wedding, they all seemed to wash away in that moment.

Rytsar walked in on them, looking devastatingly handsome in his smoky gray suit with matching vest and light-gray tie. The refined Italian suit took Rytsar's rough, masculine charm to a higher level.

"Well, you certainly look handsome, Mr. Durov," Brie complimented.

A slow smile crept over his lips. "*Radost moya*, you are perfection."

Brie gave a little bow. "Thank you."

She noticed that all the women were staring at him, the younger ones in playful longing and the older ones in open admiration.

"Did you need something, Mr. Durov?" Brie's mother finally asked, breaking the spell he had created with his presence.

Rytsar snorted. "Your future husband wanted me to ask if you received his gift."

Brie lifted her gown to show off the slave jewelry gracing her feet. "Tell my future husband that I love his gift and will walk out to meet him wearing them proudly."

Rytsar looked down at her delicate feet decorated in gold and pearls, then gazed up at her. "I will inform him that they enhance the perfection that is you."

Brie blushed and looked away, embarrassed by his praise. Rytsar gave her a little bow and then did the same to the ladies in attendance before leaving the room.

"Such a fine Russian gentleman," Aunt Fortuna said, fanning herself. "He could teach me a thing or two in the bedroom..."

Mary smirked. "You have *no* idea."

Brie shook her head at Mary in warning. Aunt Fortuna did *not* need to know about Rytsar's uncommon tastes.

The sound of violins began, letting them know the ceremony was about to begin. Sir's grandmother and aunt gave Brie another hug before leaving the room.

Brie took the opportunity for one last look in the mirror, her stomach fluttering as she gazed at herself. The woman before her stood confident and proud in her gown of white lace. From her pink lips down to her pink toes hiding under the dress, she was the picture of femininity and elegance.

She knew Sir would be pleased when he saw his bride walking down the aisle. She touched the beautiful flowers Autumn had placed in her hair and thought of Tono. The love and confidence the Asian Dom had instilled were a permanent part of her now. She was the direct result of all of the Doms who had played a role in shaping her into who she was today.

Brie became teary-eyed at the thought, and hoped someday she would be able to properly thank all of them for this moment.

"Are you ready, Brianna?" her mother asked.

She smiled at her mother, dabbing her eyes, before putting her glove back on.

"For the best day of my life? Absolutely."

Her mother leaned in and whispered, "This may be the best day of your life for now, but I guarantee the day you bring new life into the world will top even this."

Brie's lip trembled and she had to fight back more tears, knowing her mother was referring to the day she'd been born. "I love you, Mom."

"You're so elegant and accomplished, Brianna. I couldn't be prouder."

Brie gave her a hug, bursting with overflowing love for her mother. She heard a click and saw that Autumn was taking a picture.

"You want to preserve moments like this," Autumn explained, sounding apologetic.

"Thank you," Brie told her, grateful to have these private moments recorded. "I don't want to forget anything about today."

"My pleasure, Brie. It's a joy to be part of such an important event."

There was a knock on the door and her father entered. He was dressed in the same stylish suit as Rytsar and looked like a completely different man because of it.

"Dad, you should wear suits more often."

He fussed with his tie. "I can't stand these monkey suits."

Her mother walked over and straightened his tie for him. "I wish you did, honey. You look absolutely dashing."

He grumbled, but gave her a kiss when she was done. "Thank you, dear."

Her father took a long look at Brie, shaking his head in gratified disbelief, looking every bit the proud papa.

"I've come here to collect the bride."

"Oh, my goodness, it's time!" Brie cried, throwing her arms around her father.

"Whoa, you're going to mess up your pretty hair," he cautioned.

"It's okay, Dad," Brie said, squeezing him tighter. She heard Autumn taking more pictures and was glad for it.

When her father let go, he looked at her mother and sighed deeply. "Are you ready for this, Marcy?"

She nodded, wiping away tears as she smiled at Brie.

Brie was anxious for the wedding to begin and asked Lea, "Where's the bouquet?"

Lea looked heart-stricken. "I don't have it, Brie! I've never seen it. Oh, heck, what does it even look like?"

"I don't know!" Brie whimpered. She scanned the dressing room while everyone else tore the room apart looking for the bridal bouquet.

"You wouldn't happen to be looking for a bouquet, would you?"

Brie knew that calming voice and looked up to see Tono. He looked swoon-worthy with his chocolate brown eyes, long bangs and sexy Italian suit.

"I was sent to inform you that a bouquet is waiting for you outside."

"That's highly unusual, isn't it? Do you want one of us to get it for you, honey?" her mom asked.

"That's not necessary," Tono assured Brie's mother. "It's being delivered personally."

"Thank you, Tono. That sounds lovely," Brie said, smiling at him.

Tono bowed his head slightly. "I must return to the groom and let him know the message has been delivered."

After he'd left, her father held out his arm. "I guess it's time, my little girl."

"Oh, man, I've got to get myself out there, girlfriend," Lea squeaked. She gave Brie a quick peck on the cheek before she left the room.

Mary came up next. "I always said you were a fool…"

Brie waited, ready for the worst.

"But you've done well, Brie."

Brie's jaw dropped.

Mary leaned in and whispered, "I really said that for your parents, Stinky Cheese. You're still an idiot in my book." She laughed as if she had shared a humorous joke with Brie as she followed behind Lea.

Brie loved Mary for it.

Her mother gave her one last kiss before leaving her to get in line.

Brie took a deep breath, looking at her dad. "This is really it."

"Want to run?"

She giggled. "Actually, I can't wait to tie the knot."

"Figuratively or literally?" he asked with a straight face.

Brie glanced at him. "Did you just make a joke?"

He looked ahead solemnly, refusing to answer.

"I can't believe you just made a joke," she said, smiling to herself.

They exited the room and followed the procession as they walked up a long flight of stone stairs. Brie noticed that every other step was decorated with lemons, greenery and baby's breath. She was so enchanted by the simple elegance that she didn't even notice who was waiting for her at the top.

"Hello."

Brie looked up to see Sir holding a bouquet in his hand.

The sight of him took her breath away. He wore a black suit, with a dark vest covered in a silvery vine pattern that matched the pattern of his bow tie. Sir was stylish perfection, all the way down to his polished Italian shoes. On his lapel he wore a single magenta flower that matched the ones in the bouquet he was holding out to her.

Sir smiled charmingly as he explained, "It's tradition in my family for the groom to present his bride with her flowers."

Brie took the stunning bouquet, admiring the white calla lilies and freesias with accents of greenery, baby's breath and the bright pink bougainvilleas she'd admired on Isola d'Elba.

She lifted the bouquet to her nose, taking in the sweet scent of freesias. "It's so beautiful."

"As are you, Brianna."

The sound of her full name rolling from Sir's lips was like a song. He walked away to take his position for the wedding, looking so unbelievably handsome that Brie wanted to cry.

The wedding party waited until the traditional wedding march began. Brie felt the tingling start. This had been fated from the moment she was born. Everything she'd experienced, everything that had transpired since— all of it had led to this point in time.

Brie held her head a little higher but kept it at a respectful angle, eager to walk down the aisle to meet her husband and Master.

"Ready, my little girl?"

"Yes, Daddy," she said with conviction as they took their first step to the rhythm of the song.

The courtyard was filled with people, far more than Brie would ever have imagined. She glanced around in surprise, recognizing many familiar faces she hadn't expected to see. It seemed Sir had invited most of the

Training Center to join them for this momentous day.

Brie's eyes traveled to the end of the aisle, where she spotted Sir waiting under a simple wooden trellis covered in the same flowers as those in her bouquet. Beside him stood Rytsar, Master Anderson and Tono, and on the left stood Lea, Mary and Autumn—the girls looking stunning in their sleek magenta gowns that harmonized with the bougainvilleas in her bouquet.

Brie was so mesmerized by Sir's smile as she came down the aisle that she could barely breathe.

Oh, Sir...

Her father released his hold and physically placed her hand in Sir's open palm, nodding to him before joining Brie's mother in the front row.

Brie looked up into Sir's eyes, stunned that she was actually standing beside him, about to take her wedding vows. Her smile faded as the importance of this moment suddenly hit her full-force.

Here, before all their family and even God himself, they were making the commitment of a lifetime. Although it had the same significance to her as the Collaring Ceremony, this union held more weight with the rest of the world.

The man who would marry them, the mayor of the local village, cleared his throat to get the attention of the crowd. He said something in Italian and half the guests sat down. Brie's American friends quickly followed.

Brie listened to the beautiful sound of the mayor's voice as he rolled off the legal requirements spelled out in a civil wedding. Although there was nothing romantic about what he was saying, everything sounded more romantic in Italian.

She knew the time was close when Sir looked into her eyes after the man paused. He smiled confidently at her and said loudly, "*Lo voglio.*"

Brie's heart fluttered.

The mayor then asked her the same question in Italian. With her heart racing, she said with passion, "*Lo voglio.*"

He then made a pronouncement, and the Italian guests smiled and clapped. Brie looked out at her friends and family, wishing they could understand what had been said.

Rytsar handed Sir her ring.

Sir took Brie's hand in his, slipping the wedding band onto her finger. As he did so, he looked into her eyes, expressing his love for her.

Rytsar placed Sir's ring in her hand and winked at her before taking his place behind Sir. Brie's hand shook so badly that she had trouble putting the band on his finger, and she had to laugh at herself. She looked up at him when she was done, forgetting the silent vow she had meant to say with her eyes and simply mouthing the words, "Condors forever."

Brie assumed the ceremony was over, until she saw Marquis Gray take the place of the mayor with Sir's cousin, Benito, joining him.

"Now that the civil wedding is complete, we will continue with the exchange of traditional vows."

Brie heard her Americans friends voice their approval while Benito translated Marquis' words into Italian for Sir's family. She looked at Sir in surprise, before turning her attention back to Marquis.

Marquis Gray met her gaze with those dark, intense eyes, but there was a spark of pride behind them she hadn't seen before.

"We are gathered here today in the sight of God, and the presence of friends and loved ones, to join in one of life's greatest moments. Thane and Brianna have invited us to share in this celebration of their marriage— their wedding. We are here not to mark the start of a relationship, but to recognize a bond that already exists.

"This marriage is one expression of the many varieties of love. It is fitting at this time to speak briefly about the power love can have in our lives. We live in a world of joy and fear, searching for meaning in the seeming chaos of life. Yet we discover the truest guidelines to our quest when we realize love in all its magnitudes. Love is the eternal force of life. Love allows us to face fear and uncertainty with courage."

Marquis turned to Brie first. "Brianna Renee Bennett, will you have this man to be your husband, to live together in the covenant of marriage? Will you love him, comfort him, honor and obey him, in sickness and in health, forsaking all others as long as you both shall live?"

Brie stared deep into Sir's eyes as she answered proudly, "I will."

Marquis turned to Sir. "Thane Lorenzo Davis, will you have this wom-an to be your wife, to live together in the covenant of marriage? Will you love her, comfort her, honor and protect her, in sickness and in health, forsaking all others as long as you both shall live?"

Sir raised his eyebrow charmingly when he answered. "I will."

"The couple will now exchange personal vows."

Sir smiled, lifting Brie's hand to his lips and kissing the ring on her finger before speaking. "Brie, from the moment we met, I was mesmerized by you. I've never known a woman more loving, kind or stubborn than you."

There were several knowing chuckles from the guests.

Sir glanced at them and grinned before returning his gaze to her. "I'm unsure whether these people know how truly extraordinary you are, but I do." He cupped her chin with his right hand. "This ring is a physical representation of my vow to you—my bride. With my body, I thee worship. With my heart, I thee cherish. All that I am, I give to thee. All that I have, I share with thee. From this day until forever done."

Brie had to fight the tears that threatened, and squeezed Sir's hand. She waited several moments before she spoke the words she'd wanted to tell him.

"Thane, you have shown me a whole new world I never knew existed. My love for you is boundless and my respect for you runs deep. Meeting you that fateful day in the shop altered the course of my life, *but* loving you has changed me. I look forward to growing old by your side as your lover, wife and best friend. Condors forever."

Sir's gaze held hers as Marquis spoke again.

"This is a moment of celebration, but let it also be a moment of dedication. The world does a fine job of reminding us of how fragile we are. People are fragile; relationships are fragile too. Every marriage needs the love and support of a network of friends and family.

"On this wedding day, I ask all of you to be friends of Thane and Brie as a couple. Be friends of their relationship and be there with them through the trials and triumphs ahead."

Marquis addressed Sir and Brie again. "May the flow of your love help brighten the fate of the Earth. May the strength of your love touch and bless us all, gracing our lives with its color and courage."

He looked out over the crowd and exclaimed proudly, "It is my pleasure to introduce to you...Mr. and Mrs. Thane Davis." Then he said to Sir, "You may kiss your bride."

Sir swept Brie into his arms, bending her backwards as he gave her a deep and passionate kiss, to the roaring applause of their family and friends.

It was a moment Brie would never forget.

The Dance

Brie couldn't take her eyes off her husband as they greeted their guests in the reception hall inside the castle. He seemed equally infatuated with Brie, and kept her close to him, his hand resting on the small of her back, lightly touching her brand.

Brie's mom was the first to come and congratulate them. "Such a touching ceremony, Brianna." She turned to Sir. "This has to be the most beautiful wedding I've ever seen."

Sir held out his left arm, still keeping hold of Brie as he gave her mother a hug. "Thank you, Mom."

Brie's mother looked proudly up at him. "It means so much that you call me that, Thane. Never stop."

Brie heard an undercurrent of emotion in Sir's voice when he told her, "It is an honor to be known as your son."

Brie's father held out his hand. "You know my thoughts on your extra-curricular activities, but as a husband to my little girl, I couldn't ask for a better man."

Sir shook his hand firmly. "That means a lot, sir."

Her father got an odd expression on his face. "Actually, I would prefer you called me Dad from now on."

Brie couldn't believe it.

Sir appeared equally shocked. "I did not expect such an honor. Thank you…Dad."

The word 'Dad' sounded so strange coming from Sir's lips, but it touched Brie greatly. Sir was part of her family now. A family with no other agenda than to see them happy together.

She threw her arms around her father. "You've made me so happy."

"I'm proud of you, my beautiful daughter."

Brie laid her head on his shoulder, soaking in the tenderness of the moment—making her feel like a child again.

Sir's grandmother was standing a distance away, but Brie could tell she was anxious to speak with them. She gave her father a kiss on the cheek before excusing herself.

Brie and Sir made their way over to his grandmother. Her eyes radiated youthful excitement as words tumbled from her mouth. Sir explained to Brie, "My *nonna* was very touched by the English version of the ceremony. She despised the civil ceremony, but was moved by what Marquis Gray shared, as well as our vows to each other."

Brie smiled at the old woman who was now her grandmother by marriage. "*Nonna*, it means the world to me that you were here to share in our happiness. I love your grandson very much."

She pinched Brie's cheeks hard in her zeal. "Joyful couple," she said in English, slapping Brie's cheeks afterwards. Although Brie's cheeks burned from the contact, she enjoyed the woman's enthusiasm.

"Yes, very joyful," she agreed, her smile widening.

Sir's grandfather walked up and gave her a quick kiss on the lips, his eyes twinkling mischievously. He spoke in Italian, letting Sir translate for him.

"*Nonno* says that I will make you happy."

The look in the old man's eye hinted at the fact that he meant more than simply as her spouse. Brie nodded, blushing as she answered, "Your grandson is a very generous man."

The old man nodded, then hugged Sir. Whatever his grandfather whispered in his ear left Sir teary-eyed. He quickly regained his composure, but gave his grandfather another hug.

"Mrs. Davis, may I be one of the first to congratulate you?"

Brie blushed, her heart thrilling at how her new name sounded when spoken with a Russian accent. She turned to him and nodded gracefully. "Thank you, Rytsar."

"I have been watching your husband closely, *radost moya*. The way he looks at you leads me to suspect I will be a *dyadya* very soon."

Brie let out a small gasp as she looked at Sir, imaging him taking her. The lust she felt was reflected in his eyes as they stared at each other.

"Possibly a *dyadya* to twins..." Rytsar stated, laughing as he walked away.

Sir pulled Brie to him. "It's true—I desire you, wife."

Brie felt butterflies on hearing Sir call her his wife. Such a simple thing, seemingly insignificant, but it thrilled her to the depths of her soul. She stood on tiptoes to kiss his cheek. "My husband..." she sighed contentedly. "I love calling you that."

"Soon you will be screaming it," he growled in her ear, grazing her brand with his finger before shaking the hand of the next person who approached them.

When Lea announced that dinner was being served, Sir escorted Brie to a long table where the entire wedding party already sat, waiting for them. The length of the table was decorated with simple white flowers and greenery lining the middle. It was simple in its elegance, like everything else.

As she sat down next to Sir, Brie took notice of the charming table setting. The linen napkins had been tied with sprigs of rosemary, and each person had their own tiny vial of olive oil and a small tulle bag with sugared almonds.

"Every single detail makes me smile, Sir."

Sir took her hand and kissed it tenderly. "I'm glad, wife."

Rytsar stood up, clinking his glass to get the attention of the guests. "Before we begin, I would like to propose a toast."

"Hear, hear," Lea said, smiling at Brie.

Rytsar turned to Sir. "This man has been my friend since college, but he is much more than just a comrade—he is my brother. There is no one in the world I trust more and no one else I would lay down my life for."

He looked at Brie. "I remember when he called me about a girl. *Moy droog* claimed she was something special and asked if I would come to America to meet her."

Brie blushed, remembering what had transpired during that first meeting...

"I had to agree with him. Brianna Bennett was indeed a rare find. I've never seen my comrade as content as he is now. The peasant has even been known to smile on occasion."

Several of the guests laughed.

Rytsar looked over the crowd, his tone and expression serious. "It is an honor to call Thane Davis my brother, and it is an honor to know his wife. I hope someday each of us will experience the kind of happiness these two share. It is tradition in my country for the first toast to be to the newlyweds' health, so I say with a full heart, *Dlya zdorov'ya molodozhenov*."

Everyone raised their glasses, and Brie heard Sir's family shout, "*Salute degli sposi*"

Lea stood up next, holding her glass out towards Brie.

"I met the lovely Miss Bennett over a joke about credit cards."

Brie giggled, remembering the lesson on obedience—one that Lea had failed miserably.

"This girl is like no one else I've met. Brie's fearless and strong, but she cares about people—I mean *really* cares about people—even those who are hard to love." Lea glanced over at Mary and winked. "She has the ability to bring people together. You just have to look around this room to see proof of that."

Lea looked at Brie with a wicked grin. "A little fact you may not know about my friend is that she's a sucker for a good joke. So in honor of that, I would like to tell one now."

"Oh, no…" Brie muttered under her breath.

"What do you call two spiders who just got married?" Lea giggled before she burst out, "Newlywebs!"

Loud groans erupted from the crowd.

"Okay, that was just the warm up—here's the real one. So a little girl was attending a wedding for the first time and whispered to her mother, 'Mommy, why is the bride dressed in white?' Her mother answered, 'Because white is the color of happiness, and today is the happiest day of her life.' The child thought about this for a moment and asked, 'So why is the groom wearing black?'"

This time her joke was met with chuckles from the men.

"But seriously, ladies, we know why Thane Davis is wearing black today. He's Italian and he knows the power of a good suit."

The women twittered in agreement.

"And just look at my girlfriend. Have you ever seen a more gorgeous bride? It's scary to think how good-looking their children will be. Am I right?"

Brie blushed as she glanced shyly at Sir.

"I can't wait to celebrate with them fifty years from now, when they're old and gray but still just as in love."

She held up her glass to them. "Here's to condor love, baby!"

Their friends shouted, "To condor love!" while the Italians answered with a hearty, "*Auguri!*"

Brie grinned as Sir intertwined his arm with hers so they could drink from each other's glasses.

Just before dinner began, Master Anderson stood up. "If you don't mind, I would like to add my own toast before the festivities begin. Like Rytsar, Thane and I became friends in college. You wouldn't know it to look at him now, but he was a real nerd back then."

The group laughed, with Sir shaking his head, a smirk on his face.

After the laughter died down, he continued. "Thane Davis is a rock, the person I count on. He's a leader among his friends, but still humble enough to take advice from them. In Brie, he's truly found his one and only—his counterpart. The strength of the love they share inspires even an old cynic like me."

He held his glass high. "May you two enjoy a long and fruitful life together."

Sir's family shouted in unison, "*Per Cent'anni.*"

The meal began with a small bowl of *ribollita*, followed by a course of fresh vegetables and white beans, both favorites of Sir's. The main course consisted of the most delicate and delicious *gnocchi* Brie had ever tasted, and she moaned in pure bliss.

"I hope to hear more of that shortly," Sir mentioned in a casual voice before he turned to talk to Rytsar.

Brie let out a little squeak, suddenly anxious for the meal to be over.

After the final course, Sir stood and held out his hand. "Shall we?"

Brie took his hand and proudly walked beside him, barefoot under her dress, each step making a delightful jingling sound. It was exhilarating to feel the smooth tile beneath her feet—their little secret.

Sir led Brie over to the wedding cake, a tall, simple, white, layered cake decorated with pink bougainvilleas and greenery. Rather than a traditional cake topper, Brie noticed the silver base that held the cake was etched with filigree that had both their names and an artful likeness of condors on either side.

Once again, Sir had charmed her with his taste and attention to detail.

Her heart skipped a beat when he moved behind her and took hold of the knife. His closeness had her senses reeling, and she blushed as they pushed down the knife and cut into the cake.

Brie took the piece to feed him, feeling a little silly about the ritual, but when she put the cake to his lips and he took a bite, she found it incredibly sexy. Brie licked her lips in sexual frustration as he took another bite, finishing it off.

She parted her lips, taking the bite he offered, her eyes locked on his. When he leaned down and licked the frosting from her lips, her knees almost buckled. Sir took hold of her arm to steady her and smiled, knowing the effect he was having on her.

"Are we okay, Mrs. Davis?"

She nodded, completely entranced by the man.

Lea announced, "Single ladies, it's that time! Get yourselves out there and get ready to catch that bouquet."

Brie moved where Lea directed her and turned around, facing the wall. When Lea said they were ready, she threw the bouquet into the air, then whipped around to see who caught it.

There was a frenzy of activity, but it was the girl who didn't move a muscle who ended up catching it. Autumn blushed as she held up the bouquet, to the applause of the crowd.

Rytsar brought out a chair and instructed Brie to sit down. He then covered Sir's eyes with a blindfold before he was allowed to remove the lacy garter she wore.

Sir looked sexy-hot as he knelt down before her and reached out his hands. Brie giggled nervously when he made contact with her knees. Just that simple touch alone had her quivering inside.

Once he got his bearings, Sir's hands found their way underneath her dress. He gently caressed her bare leg as his hand traveled slowly up. Goosebumps rose on her skin as he got closer to his target.

When he finally touched it, Brie let out a soft moan only Sir could hear. He shook his head and murmured, "Naughty girl." Sir pulled off the garter and held it up in triumph as he untied the blindfold.

Lea instructed the single men to line up, and had to push several reluctant bachelors standing on the sidelines to join before she would let Sir throw it. Unlike the women, the men seemed scared of it, moving out of the way as it came down. It was Master Anderson who ending up catching her garter, much to his chagrin.

Brie clapped, thinking he was the perfect man for the honor.

He held it up with a charming grin as a herd of eligible women descended on him.

Sir watched the pandemonium with amusement. "I'd say he doesn't have long."

"I agree, Sir," Brie giggled.

He turned to face her, a romantic look in his eyes. "Are you ready to dance with me as my wife?" he asked, holding out his hand to her.

The butterflies took over as she placed her hand in his. "I would be honored."

The area cleared as Sir guided her to the middle of the dance floor and waited. A solo violin began to play. Brie instantly recognized the sound of Alonzo's violin. Sir placed his hand on her waist and took her left hand in his, guiding her across the dance floor as his father joined them—the recording of his powerful performance filling the reception hall.

Tears came to Brie's eyes as they danced. "It's beautiful, Sir."

Sir twirled her around, then grasped her waist again, drawing her to him. "I knew he would want to be here with us today."

Brie lost herself in the moment, feeling as if she were floating on clouds as the sweet sound of his father's violin carried them along. When the melody ended, Sir led her over to Lea. Her friend slipped a delicate silk purse onto her wrist.

"What's this for?" Brie asked.

"Your gifts, silly" she replied. Lea held out a small envelope. "Although Ms. Clark couldn't attend, she wanted you to have this." Lea slipped it into Brie's pouch and gave her a quick kiss on the cheek before walking over to the crowd of ladies around Master Anderson and humbly requesting a dance.

Rytsar walked up to Brie with an envelope in his hand. "May I have the honor of this dance, Mrs. Davis?"

She looked at Sir, who explained, "It's tradition for the men to give a gift before they share a dance with the bride."

Brie nodded and turned back to Rytsar. "It would be a pleasure to dance with you, Rytsar Durov." She took his envelope and placed it in the pouch. "Thank you."

He whisked her away from Sir, grinning like the Cheshire Cat. "You make a beautiful bride, *radost moya.*"

"And you make a fetching best man. I've noticed quite a number of young ladies vying for your attention this evening."

"It is my Russian charm. No one can resist it."

He twirled her several times, the jewelry on her feet making a pleasant sound.

"Ah, I love the sound of slave jewelry. I appreciate the way your Master thinks." Rytsar twirled her several more times before he ended the dance in the middle of the song.

"Why so short?" she asked, surprised when he handed her over to Marquis Gray.

Rytsar leaned in and whispered, "We promised your husband not to take too long. He is anxious to make me a *dyadya.*"

Brie blushed as Marquis Gray presented her with a small silver envelope. "A gift for the bride," Marquis announced formally. She put it in her pouch, thanking him before taking his hand.

"The ceremony was exquisite, Marquis Gray," Brie gushed as they glided across the floor. "What you said at our wedding meant more to me than you'll ever know."

"It was a privilege to officiate the union of two people I deeply respect."

She smiled, touched by his praise. "I remember when you were not thrilled by my choice of Master."

"I never held it against you, Mrs. Davis. It was your Master I had issue with."

"Do you have issues with him now?" she asked, looking over at Sir, who was talking to her parents.

"He's proven himself worthy since then. I'm encouraged by the fact he dealt with his mother before you began this next part of your journey. It shows his level of commitment to this marriage—and you."

Brie's voice shook when she told him, "It was difficult, Marquis."

"I'm sure it was." He held her tight as he twirled her around so fast it left her breathless. Gazing deep into her eyes he told her, "You will be stronger for it. Hold on to that knowledge and enjoy your evening, Mrs. Davis. Many blessings to you and your husband."

Marquis led her over to Mr. Gallant, who was standing on the side waiting for her. Brie graciously accepted his gift before taking his hand to dance.

"Oh, Mr. Gallant, I can't tell you how pleased I am that you're here tonight."

"I'm grateful as well, Miss B—excuse me—Mrs. Davis. As a student you made an unusual choice on the night of the Collaring Ceremony, and you've continued to astound me with the direction your journey has taken. It is a joy and honor to know you."

She blushed. "The honor is mine. I still think back on my training days and wish I could attend class with you again."

"I recall those sessions with great fondness."

Before he let her go, Brie leaned in to tell him, "Mr. Gallant, I want to thank you for what you did for Candy. Mary, Mr. Wallace and I will forever be in your debt."

He was startled by her declaration and asked, "How did you—?"

Brie pressed her finger to her lips, gliding gracefully over to Baron, who was smiling at her.

"Kitten…"

"What a lovely surprise," she said, grateful that he had come.

"I would not miss such a happy occasion."

Baron handed her a red envelope with a devilish smile, then escorted her onto the dance floor. She stared up at him while they danced, captivated by his smile.

"Have you moved back to LA yet?"

"I have. Found a nice place in an established neighborhood. Good people, walking distance to most things, and best of all, I feel Adrianna's spirit there."

"That doesn't upset you?" she asked in surprise.

"No, kitten. It feels as if it's meant to be. That I have found my new home and do not have to lose her in the process."

"Then I'm glad for you, Baron, and even happier I'll be seeing more of you."

He hugged her before letting go. "I want you and Sir Davis to visit me when you get back. I have something I want to show you."

On that mysterious note, Baron handed her off to Master Coen, who was waiting for her next.

"This is an honor, Headmaster."

Master Coen placed his envelope into Brie's hand before holding out his beefy arm to her. "I had to pay my respects to the girl who tore the trainers apart."

"What?" she asked, stumbling over her own feet, unsure she'd heard him correctly.

Master Coen explained, "I'm headed off to Australia, Ms. Clark is stationed in Denver, and your Master is out of the program altogether. Three of the original four are no longer part of the Training Center. We were a stable group until you and your film came along."

She smiled shyly. "I guess you were right to be concerned after all."

"You're certainly a catalyst for change, Mrs. Davis. I never would have guessed Thane would marry. I'm still stunned by it, in fact, and yet here we are."

"Yes, here we are…"

"I have no doubt you will continue to shock and surprise me." He swatted her once soundly on the ass before letting her go. "But don't stir up too much trouble while I'm gone. I expect you to visit me Down Under—both you and your husband."

Brie looked over at Sir and found him staring intently at her. It seemed he couldn't take his eyes off her. It didn't matter where he was in the room or who he was with, his gaze kept returning to her. It was magnetic in its pull, and she longed to join him.

"Mrs. Davis, may I have this dance?"

Brie turned to see Captain looking quite distinguished in his military uniform. He was even more striking with the handsome leather patch over his eye. "I'd be honored, Captain," she replied, putting his gift into her pouch.

She gladly took the hand he offered. "You look quite dashing tonight."

His chuckle was low and deep. "My pet seems to agree with you."

"Where is she?"

Captain nodded to Candy, who was talking with Mary.

"You must be proud of her."

"Which one? Both are exceptional women."

Brie grinned, charmed by his answer. "I would agree with you, Captain."

His moves were exacting and flawless as he danced, guiding her effortlessly across the dancefloor. She felt graceful and beautiful in his skillful hands. Brie looked up at him in admiration.

"I never knew what a fine dancer you were."

He kept his serious expression, but the edge of his lip rose in a half-smile.

Brie felt proud to be his partner and was disappointed when the song came to an end. He took her hand and kissed it formally, thanking her before leaving to return to Candy.

Sir's cousin Benito came up to her holding out his envelope. *"Bella donna,* may I have the honor?" Brie graciously took his gift and continued to dance as she partnered with the men from the Italian side of her new family. They dazzled her with their beautiful language as they swept her along. Brie was acutely aware of Sir's eyes on her, and wondered if he could hear the jingle of her dancing feet whenever she twirled past him.

She was taking a much needed water break when Tono walked up to her, a tender look in his eye. "Mrs. Davis."

"Yes, Tono?"

"Master Anderson regrets that he cannot dance with you tonight, but he asked me to give you this." Tono handed her a thick envelope.

Brie took it and looked across the room at Master Anderson, who was surrounded by a harem of women. He shrugged with his hands up, an expression of "What can I do?" on his face.

She threw him a kiss and waved, happy to see the sexy Dom preoccupied.

Tono addressed her again. "Although the evening is still young, Sir Davis has asked me to retrieve you."

"Retrieve me?"

"Your husband wishes to speak with you—privately."

Brie's heartrate shot up. She looked around for Sir but didn't see him. "Where is he?"

"You'll find him down the spiral staircase through there," Tono said, pointing to an entrance on the other side of the reception hall. "I should warn you that the stairs are steep."

Tono handed Brie an envelope marked with his signature orchid. "I am forsaking my dance so that you may go to him sooner."

His kindness melted her heart, and she longed to return the favor. "Tono, I would love it if you would dance with Autumn in my stead."

He smiled but informed her, "She's not comfortable on the dance floor."

"Tell her it was my solemn request."

Tono bowed his head, a smile gracing his lips. "I will tell her."

When he turned to leave, Brie called out, "Tono."

"Yes?"

She threw her arms around him, laying her head against his chest to listen to his heart. Brie sighed softly when she let go. "I just needed to hear that."

Tono kissed her on the forehead. "May the years ahead be everything you wish for, toriko."

Exchange of Souls

B rie walked down the steep flight of narrow stairs, wondering where
they led. When she reached the bottom, she found a red carpet lined
with candles leading into the dark underground hallway.

She followed the trail and found Sir waiting for her at the end of it.

"Wife."

Her stomach fluttered pleasurably.

"What is this place, Sir?"

"It's a dungeon."

She gasped, looking at the iron gate behind him.

"It's real, used to protect the castle's inhabitants in the past."

She stared at the gate in fascination.

"Would you like to see it?"

When she nodded, Sir moved aside and opened the gate wide so she
could enter.

Inside was a single pole with iron cuffs attached. Two elaborate cande-
labras burned on either side, bringing warmth to the room. On the left side
of the room hung several tools used for punishment.

Sir came up behind her, caressing her shoulder with his fingers. "Do
you want to play?"

Goosebumps rose on her skin. "Yes."

With hungry hands, he caressed her body—touching skin, pearls and
lace...exploring her dress with all his senses.

"What's this?" Sir asked, when he came across the small blue pin.

"*Nonna* gave that to me."

He took it off carefully and examined it with a slight smile on his lips.

"When I was a boy, she told me this pin was her most cherished object
in the world." Sir looked at Brie with tenderness. "It was given to her by

her mother, an heirloom that has been passed down for countless generations. *Nonna* claimed it guaranteed the lucky bride who received it a strong and lasting marriage. This is fiercely coveted by the women of her family."

Sir shook his head as he stared at it. "The fact that she gave it to you, a foreigner, is almost scandalous, Brie."

She touched the small pin reverently. "I believe the gift was really meant for you, Sir. Your grandmother wanted to ensure you had a long-lasting marriage, even though we weren't married in church."

Sir stared at it, his expression unreadable.

Brie whispered his name, and when he turned his head towards her, she kissed him.

Sir slipped the pin into his pocket and went back to his task, caressing her skin as he removed each piece of clothing. When only the slave jewelry decorating her feet was left, Sir told her to kneel.

Sir placed a leather crop in her mouth. "Wait for me, wife."

He gathered her clothes and shut the iron gate behind him. The clank of the metal sent shivers through her as she watched him disappear into the darkness.

Brie could hear the muffled laughter and music from above, and smiled with the crop clamped in her mouth. Her thoughts drifted back to Sir, the thrill of the unknown enhancing her excitement. While she waited for his return, Brie watched the wax of the red tapered candles dripping seductively down their length. She was curious whether he would use the candles tonight.

Her heart started racing when she heard his footsteps returning. Sir opened the gate and stood before her, taking the crop from her mouth. "First I romance you with a wedding, and now I take what's mine. How does that make you feel, my bride?"

"Wanted, husband."

"Good."

Sir ordered her to stand next to the wooden pole, then cuffed her wrists in the hard, uneven shackles. There was no doubt the unforgiving metal had effectively held prisoners for centuries.

"We will play before I make love to you. I desire your body to ache as badly for me as I ache for you."

She moaned softly as he lifted her chin and kissed her, parting her lips with his tongue. His kisses were demanding, communicating the lust he'd conveyed all evening.

Brie's body responded eagerly to it, longing to sate that desire.

Sir pulled away, looking admiringly at her breasts. "You look cold, my dear. Shall I warm you up?" He took the crop and began warming up her skin with it. He started out light and progressively increased the licks of the instrument, pinkening her chest and torso.

"Now that the skin is warmed up, let's concentrate on the nipples," he said alluringly. Sir took one of the red candles from the candelabra and held it just above her left nipple, letting the wax drip onto it.

She sucked in her breath, the heat of the candle contrasting sharply with her cool flesh.

"Do you want more?"

"Please," she begged.

Sir covered both nipples in the hot wax, letting it fall at different heights to control the heat on her skin. When her breasts were completely covered, he put the candle back and slowly took off his jacket and vest, rolling up the sleeves of his shirt.

Sir took the flogger hanging on the wall and hit the tool against his hand so Brie could hear the distinctive sound of the leather.

"Chest out," he commanded.

Brie arched her shoulders back, thrusting out her chest. She held her breath as she watched Sir warm up in front of her. The first stroke released bits of the wax as it hit the side of her breast. He stroked the other breast and another cascade of candle wax fell to the floor as her breasts bounced alluringly from the impact of the flogger.

"How beautiful is that?" he murmured to himself.

With precise control, he released all the wax from her skin while stimulating her breasts with every swing. Brie threw back her head back, begging him to hit her harder.

"Very well."

Each stroke of his flogger resonated through Brie, the weeks of longing magnifying the effect of his attention on her body now.

"Are we wet?" he asked as he slapped the tails lightly against her pussy. Brie cried out in pleasure, the jolt of it making her clit pulse with need. He slapped the flogger between her legs again, a little harder, and she moaned with passion.

Sir hung up the flogger and returned to Brie, kissing her on the lips as he felt the wetness between her legs.

His groan was low and inviting. All she wanted was to be taken, pinned against the pole, defenseless to stop his claiming of her.

"Please," she begged.

With rough hands, he twisted Brie around so that she faced the pole and pushed her up against it, the chains on the cuffs tightening their hold as they twisted above her head.

"Would you let me do anything to you, wife?"

"Yes…" she breathed.

She heard the dangerous crack of a bullwhip beside her head and cried out.

He growled behind her. "This bullwhip may be smaller, but it still carries a nasty bite."

Her breaths came in gasps as he made her wait for his pleasure. Brie closed her eyes and consciously slowed her breathing, wanting her body to relax for his play.

"Good girl."

The first lick of the whip against her buttock was light, teasing her with its caress. The second was a little harder and stinging.

"I want your pretty ass pink for me."

Brie opened her eyes and looked up at the roughly cut roof above her as he began the rain of strokes. She grunted softly with each strike, afraid others might hear her.

"Cry out, woman."

Brie nodded, realizing her mistake. Her Master wanted her to vocalize.

With the next blow of the whip across her butt, Brie let out a scream. Nothing changed above, the party too loud for people to hear her.

"That's better…" he encouraged.

Brie cried out again as the whip left its stinging mark. "More, please."

Sir's chuckle was low as he granted her wish, some lashes light, some hard, with an occasional crack of the whip next to her ear. It kept her on her toes, trembling as she waited for the next stroke.

When he finally stopped, she heard the bullwhip fall to the floor. "I don't want you flying so high that you'll miss the moment of our union."

Sir took his time to unroll his sleeves and put on his vest and jacket, letting her wait expectantly as she hung in her iron bonds.

When he was finished redressing, Sir came up behind her. He undid the cuffs with care, rubbing her wrists, kissing the inside of each before kneeling down to kiss the warm skin of her tender ass. He stood up again, turning her to face him before he swept her naked body into his arms.

Sir kissed her deeply then, claiming her mouth with his tongue. Brie moaned, her whole body on fire for him.

"And now the lovemaking begins."

He carried her out of the dungeon and down the candlelit hallway, stopping midway. She heard the echoes of the party still going full-steam above.

Brie snuggled against his chest, sighing with contentment.

"Few know that this castle has a secret passage," Sir stated, as he pushed against a portion of the stone wall with his shoulder. It moved, revealing a narrow passageway.

Brie was intrigued as he walked through the opening, still carrying her in his arms. Sir took her up a new flight of stairs, these with steps decorated with the wedding embellishments she'd seen earlier, but with the added charm of burning candles.

"Today has been a fairy tale come true, Sir."

"I'm not done yet, wife."

Her stomach did a little flip. Brie didn't think she would *ever* tire of hearing him call her by that title.

Massive double doors greeted them at the top of the stairs. Sir pushed his back against them and the doors slowly swung open, revealing an opulent bedchamber fit for a king. An impressive canopy bed immediately drew Brie's attention.

"Are you ready to make love with nothing between us?" he asked huskily.

"I think I might combust from the pleasure of it."

"As long as you combust all over my cock, I'm fine with that."

Sir laid her on the massive bed and unfastened the slave jewelry from her feet, freeing her from it. "Listening to the jingle every time you took a step was a turn-on for me." He lifted her foot and kissed the tops of her painted toes as he looked ravenously into her eyes.

"It was alluring for me as well, Sir," she admitted.

He leaned forward, putting his finger to her lips. "Tonight we are simply husband and wife."

"Husband," she purred, loving the sound of it as it rolled off her tongue.

"I want you to put these on while I change," Sir said, gesturing to a set of white stockings and heels he'd laid out for her on the bed.

Brie begged, "Please don't change yet." She trailed her hands over the silver buttons of his vest and the chain of his grandfather's pocket watch. "You look so handsome; I just want to admire you a little longer."

"As you wish."

Instead of changing, Sir stood to watch as Brie put on the hose. She slipped them on sensually, smiling at him in an alluring manner as if she were doing a striptease. Then she stood and stepped into the six-inch heels.

"My favorite look for you, other than when you're bent over receiving my cock."

Brie had expected he would fling her onto the bed and ravish her, but he did not. Instead, Sir asked her to turn around. "Let me take in the beauty of my bride."

Brie slowly twirled for him, feeling the warmth of his gaze.

"Now come to me, wife. Let me touch you."

Brie walked to him, her steps long and graceful as she swayed her hips. She hoped the smile on her lips was equally irresistible.

When Sir touched her skin, she felt an electrical jolt, her body humming with a desperate need to connect. His hands, which had been rough with her before, were now gentle as he worshipped her with his caress.

Brie let out a long, impassioned moan as he stroked the brand on her back. "How is it that I find your body even more tempting than when I first took you? It's a mystery I plan to spend our lifetime exploring."

She cried out when she felt his warm lips on her neck and the light pressure of his teeth. Her body craved him like the air she breathed; it required satisfaction or she would die. "I'm burning with need, Thane."

"Undress me then."

Brie smiled as she started with his jacket, tiptoeing to slip it off his shoulders. She placed it on the back of a chair and went for his vest next, carefully unhooking his grandfather's pocket watch from the silver button before taking the vest off. She lovingly placed the timepiece on the desk and came back for the bowtie, grinning as she untied it and slipped it from his collar.

Brie held it in her teeth as she began unbuttoning the starched white shirt, each undone button exposing the handsome man underneath. She opened the shirt, tracing her finger over the brand on his chest.

Sir looked down at her, his gaze intense.

Brie smiled with the ribbon of the bowtie still in her mouth as she undid his cufflinks and pulled the shirt off his fine body. She put the items on the chair and returned to him, placing her hands on his toned chest. She slowly traveled downward, caressing his stomach muscles until she came into contact with his belt.

She looked up at him as she undid the belt buckle and slowly pulled it from the loops. She held it up and laughed sweetly. "And I remember when I used to be scared of your belts..."

Brie walked over to lay it on the chair and came back to him, walking with slow, graceful movements, knowing there was no reason to rush. She had waited too long not to savor this moment.

She sank to her knees and kissed each dress shoe before untying them. After slipping the shoes off, she removed his socks, purposely brushing his feet with her long hair and giggling when he wiggled them in response. She placed the socks inside the shoes and moved them to the side.

With trembling hands, she undid the button on Sir's pants and unzipped them, releasing his hard cock from its confines before sliding his clothing off.

Sir groaned in appreciation, causing Brie to gush with more wetness. "I'm on fire..." he whispered huskily when she took his shaft into her hand. It burned with the heat of needed release.

She placed her lips on the head of his shaft, but he groaned in protest. "Stop."

Brie looked up questioningly.

"I need to sink my cock into you. I have never wanted anything as badly as I want you now."

She purred, taking his hand as he helped her to her feet. Sir led her to the bed, picking her up and laying her on it.

Sir lay beside her in all his naked glory. Brie glanced down at his cock, framed by dark hair, and felt her loins contract. For the first time it was not just an instrument of pleasure. When he penetrated her this time, there was a chance his seed would find its mark.

She looked up at Sir, struggling to breathe. "Make love to me, husband."

He claimed her mouth as he moved between her legs, spreading her wide. She ached for the union, expecting he would thrust, but he stopped himself.

"No..." Sir said to himself, pulling back. "Just as I did when I took you as Master, I want you to remember this moment."

Sir moved down between her legs, licking her excitement. "God, you have never tasted so sweet..." His tongue began teasing her already sensitive clit.

She grabbed his head. "Please stop, I'll come too fast."

"I want you to come, wife. I want your body primed to receive my semen."

Brie threw her head back and moaned, her pussy already pulsing with an impending orgasm. Sir moved his head back and forth as his tongue danced over her clit, then the long licks began.

"Give in to it," he murmured passionately as he continued his slow, rhythmic licking.

Sir knew her body well, and soon her hips bucked as the climax took over. Sir tasted her watery come with obvious pleasure. Growling as he wiped his mouth, he crawled up from between her legs. "I can't get enough of you, woman."

He ran his fingers through her hair, looking deep into her eyes. "I love you, Brie. You are the breath of life to me."

"All I want is this moment—and you."

Sir positioned his cock against her wet opening, the head of his shaft almost scorching her with its heat. He looked her in the eyes as he slowly sank his hard shaft into her.

Brie wrapped her legs around him, wanting all of him, *needing* all of him.

Sir began slowly stroking her with his cock, rolling his hips to deepen the thrusts. She matched his rhythm, staring up at him with tears of joy. "Thane, I don't think there's anything sexier than making a baby."

Sir pressed his lips to hers, grabbing her ass cheeks as he forced himself deeper. "Two become one," he murmured as he came inside her, his cock throbbing with each release of his seed.

Brie cried out, the pleasure of it overwhelming on every level; the consummation of the marriage, the release of sexual tension, the intense connection and the primal act of procreation all rolled up into one monumental moment.

She held on to him fiercely, knowing his essence was inside her seeking to make new life. Brie closed her eyes in sheer ecstasy as her spirit melded with Sir's…

** Yes, my dear fans, I have heard your pleas and there is another Brie coming!

You can join Brie and the gang in 2016, when the NEXT Brie serial begins.

Love and hugs, ~*Red*

Red Phoenix is the author of:

Brie Learns the Art of Submission
* Available in eBook, paperback, and audio book

(Submissive Exploration—A young woman enters a world of new experiences when she enrolls in the Submissive Training Center)

Brie Embraces the Heart of Submission
* Available in eBook, paperback, and audio book

(Submission of the Heart—After being collared, Brie learns that submission is sexier and more challenging than she'd ever imagined)

Brie Masters Love in Submission
* Available in eBook, paperback, and audio book

(Submissive's Romance—Brie is on a journey around the world as she explores the many facets of love, sacrifice, and blissful romance)

Blissfully Undone
* Available in eBook and paperback

(Snowy Fun—Two people find themselves snowbound in a cabin where hidden love can flourish, taking one couple on a sensual journey into ménage à trois)

Sensual Erotica: The Erotic Love Story of Amy and Troy
* Available in eBook and paperback

(Sexual Adventures—True love reigns, but fate continually throws Troy and Amy into the arms of others)

His Scottish Pet: Dom of the Ages
* Available in eBook and paperback

(Scottish Dom—A sexy Dom escapes to Scotland in the late 1400s. He encounters a waif who has the potential to free him from his tragic curse)

Novellas and Novelettes available as eBooks

Novella

Varick: The Reckoning

(Savory Vampire—A dark, sexy vampire story. The hero navigates the dangerous world he has been thrust into with lusty passion and a pure heart)

Novelettes

Keeper of the Wolf Clan (Keeper of Wolves, #1)

(Sexual Secrets—A virginal werewolf must act as the clan's mysterious Keeper)

The Keeper Finds Her Mate (Keeper of Wolves, #2)

(Second Chances—A young she-wolf must choose between old ties or new beginnings)

Socrates Inspires Cherry to Blossom

(Satisfying Surrender—a mature and curvaceous woman becomes
fascinated by an online Dom who has much to teach her)

By the Light of the Scottish Moon

(Saving Love—Two lost souls, the Moon, a werewolf and a death wish…)

In 9 Days

(Sweet Romance—A young girl falls in love with the new student,
nicknamed 'the Freak')

---

9 Days and Counting

(Sacrificial Love—The sequel to In 9 Days delves into the emotional
reunion of two longtime lovers)

And Then He Saved Me

(Saving Tenderness—When a young girl tries to kill herself, a man of great
character intervenes with a love that heals)

Play With Me at Noon

(Seeking Fulfillment—A desperate wife lives out her fantasies by taking
five different men in five days)

Connect with Red on Substance B

Substance B is a new platform for independent authors to directly connect with their readers. Please visit Red's Substance B page (substance-b.com/RedPhoenix.html) where you can:

- Sign up for Red's newsletter
- Send a message to Red
- See all platforms where Red's books are sold

Visit Substance B today to learn more about your favorite independent authors.